Amanda is a two-time Scribe Award winner, a two-time Tin Duck Award winner, an Aurealis and Ditmar Awards finalist, and author of several novels and short stories. She is also a screenwriter.

Her original fiction includes the sci-fi crime thriller The Subjugate, which is being developed for TV. Her media tie-in fiction includes that written for Marvel (X-Men), Black Library (Warhammer 40k), and Z-Man Games (Pandemic).

# Also by Amanda Bridgeman

### Aurora Series

#1 Aurora: Darwin
#2 Aurora: Pegasus
#3 Aurora: Meridian
#4 Aurora: Centralis
#5 Aurora: Eden
#6 Aurora: Decima
#7 Aurora: Aurizun
#8 Aurora: Atlas

### Salvation Series

#1 The Subjugate
#2 The Sensation

The Time of the Stripes

### Marvel: School of X

Sound of Light

### Pandemic:

Patient Zero

### Short Stories & Novellas:

'Paragon of Faith' – Warhammer 40K:
Paragon of Faith And Other Stories Anthology
'Reconsecration' – Warhammer 40K:
The Emperor's Finest Anthology
'Rogue T.R.A.I.N.' – SNAFU Punk'd Anthology
'Resistance' – SNAFU Comms Anthology
'Eye of the Storm' – Marvel: School of X Anthology

# Aurora: Darwin

Amanda Bridgeman

# Copyright

First published in 2013
This edition published in 2025 by Amanda Bridgeman
Copyright © Amanda Bridgeman

The moral right of the author has been asserted.


A CIP record for this book is available at the National Library of Australia

Aurora: Darwin (Aurora 1)
EPUB format: 9780995425996
PRINT format: 9780995425910

Edited by Stephanie Smith
Cover design by Matt O'Keefe

To my mother, Joan, and my grandmothers
Lil and Iris—the strongest women I know.

*Life is like a game of cards. The hand that is dealt you represents determinism; the way you play it is free will...*

~Jawaharlal Nehru (1889–1964)

# Prologue

*Easy money. Yeah, right!* Lars had always been one for taking the easy road, but right now this didn't seem so easy. Right now, his bitch of a mother's words were ringing in his ears: *"If it sounds too good to be true, Lars, then it is! There's no such thing as an easy ride! You work long and hard, and then you die! That's just the way it is in this stinking life!"* Well, he'd taken the easy road, alright. Simple work on a cargo ship seemed honest enough. It looked good to his parole officer, and being stuck on a ship traveling around space for months on end was a good way of keeping you out of trouble. Except the gunrunning, that is.

His ship's captain, Quint, had been up front about it and the extra cash to look the other way didn't bother Lars at all. He wasn't stupid. He knew that was why Quint hired him in the first place. Quint didn't care about the long rap sheet against his name for burglary, assault, you name it. Quint, it turned out, was an ex-con too, although Lars guessed the "ex" part wasn't quite true. But to the authorities Quint looked clean, running a simple cargo operation between the Moon, the outstations, and Mars. So, yeah, Lars took the job, took the money and looked the other way. *Easy money.* That inescapable vice to a con like him. Like a bottle of booze to an alcoholic, or a hand job in a back alley to a sex addict. *Easy fuckin' money, alright!* And it was about to get him killed.

He heard footsteps approaching and held his breath. He wasn't sure whether he was the last one left alive. He hadn't seen anyone since it went down, but what went down exactly, he didn't know. One moment they were in the space station's mess hall eating dinner with the crew, the next...? He remembered the lights in the room went out. He remembered commotion, fighting, screaming, the smell of blood… He didn't stick around to notice anything else. Instead, instinct led him away, running back blindly toward the dock and their cargo ship. He had to get off that station and fast! Except the doors to the dock were locked; access overridden. He was trapped.

The screaming had ceased now. *So quick?* The lights were still out and panic shot through him like a spear. He clawed his way blindly to the cargo office, just inside the dock entrance, where he'd signed the datapane when they'd first arrived. He scuttled underneath the desk, smacking his head as he did, hissing quietly and curling up as tightly as his body would allow. *Just hide and ride it out!* he told himself. *Hide and ride it out! Just like you've done before from the cops, it's no different… Or was it? At least the cops were restrained by law. They weren't supposed to kill you without justifiable cause…*

Lars heard the footsteps stop at the doorway to the cargo office. He squeezed his eyes shut, hoping that somehow it would help make him more invisible. Heart racing, palms sweating, his throat had turned dry. The silence sat; he heard nothing. He slowly opened his eyes, wanting desperately to see what he could not hear. Then suddenly, he felt hot breath against his face.

He jumped a mile, smacking his head again, as the lights suddenly came on in the room. But he didn't have long to eye his attacker. He merely saw frenzied amber eyes, flashes of ginger hair, and gridiron shoulders that yanked him out from under the desk, lifted him and threw him against the wall like a rag doll. The beast (*it couldn't possibly be human, surely?*) then thrust itself upon him. His neck and throat were swiftly opened up in excruciating pain as whatever it was clawed viciously at him. He was sure he'd heard the flesh tearing. Then there was the blood, pouring down his neck, amidst the grunts and growls of some kind of wild animal. Tearing, shredding. The pain. The blood. Pools of it. Drowning.

*Easy money? Yeah, right!*

# 1

# The Call, the Run, and the Brief

Captain Saul Harris was standing in the middle of a vast field on Earth. It was not a field he remembered. It was dry and grassy and seemed to roll on forever over low undulating hills to the horizon. The sun was beating down on him, and he was so content in the warmth that he closed his eyes and stretched out his arms to capture it all upon his dark brown skin. He stood inhaling the fresh breeze and reveled in the feeling it brought his lungs. Earth air: there was nothing like it.

As he stood enjoying the sensation, he heard a faint sound in the distance. He opened his eyes and listened. He heard it again and realized it was someone calling his name.

"Saul..." It was a woman, and the voice was vaguely familiar. He turned around to find the source, but there was no-one there, just an empty, dry, grassy field. She called again, much louder this time, and he suddenly recognized the voice. It was his late grandma, Sibbie.

"Saul?" Her voice seemed tight.

His eyes scanned the field for her, but she was nowhere to be found. He suddenly noticed the wind pick up and the clouds began to swiftly overtake the sky as though in fast forward. Sibbie called his name again, and he began turning around in circles, searching for her.

"Where are you?" he called.

"I'm here!" she said.

He turned around once more and suddenly saw her standing there, just meters from him, with his great-grandma, Etta, by her side. They were dressed in their Sunday best: slender Sibbie in a lavender skirt and blouse, and plump Etta in a floral dress and pearls. He noticed Sibbie was clutching a phone to her bony chest.

"Something's wrong!" she said. Her dark brown eyes held a look of warning. Heart picking up pace, he began to approach her. Just as he was about to speak — he awoke abruptly to the sound of his phone ringing.

"Ugh..." he muttered, opening his eyes. He was in his bed, in his apartment in Fort Centralis, and it was still dark. He took a second to get his bearings, then fumbled his hand over to his bedside table and hit the speaker button on his phone.

He answered it croakily. "Yeah..."

"Captain Harris, this is Colonel Isaack. I understand you're on leave, but something's come up and we need you to report to Command at 0600."

"0600? What's the problem?" He managed with a dry mouth, still half asleep.

"0600, captain. You'll be fully briefed then."

He let out a sleepy sigh. "Yes, sir." With that the phone went dead and he hit the speaker off.

"Lights!" He called out into the darkness. The lighting in the room blinked on dimly, then slowly but surely brightened to allow his eyes to adjust to the light. He rolled over and stretched out his long body, then squinted through the light at the time on his watch. 04:49.

"Ugh..." he groaned again.

As a soldier he was used to rising at this time, but when he was on leave his body always managed to switch from soldier to civilian mode with no trouble at all. He'd been on leave now for only five days and couldn't think why, in peacetime, he was being called up at this godforsaken hour with a whole three weeks of leave left.

He threw the sheets back, swung his feet out onto the floor, and sat on the edge of the bed, rubbing his hands over his face and yawning. He suddenly pictured the faces of his crew and wondered whether any had gotten themselves into trouble on their leave. He pulled himself off the bed and strode naked to the bathroom. As he entered, the sensor lights came on automatically, and he walked over to the basin and washed his face.

He looked in the mirror at his tired brown eyes, the whites all pink, and remembered the whisky and the jazz club from the night before. The headache seemed to set in as he thought about it. He grabbed some painkillers and swallowed them with a scoop of water from the tap, then turned and eyed his shower longingly.

As he stood there under the warm water, he swore he could feel every single droplet crashing against his dark brown skin, as though it was slowly bringing him back to life, piece by piece. He washed off the dried sweat from his dancing the previous night and smiled to himself as he remembered the woman he'd met. She was cute, she was sassy, and boy could she move. They never really spoke much to each other, instead letting their bodies do the talking on the dance floor. He did get her number though, and a wink and a smile as she walked away. She never gave him her name. She simply wrote down 'Jazz Club Woman', so he'd remember. He'd call her tonight, he thought. Then suddenly dropped his smile. That is, if he was still on Earth tonight.

Years of service had taught him that there was nothing like a good breakfast to start the day. However, time was not permitting this morning. It would take him thirty minutes to cross the island and reach Command and he knew he couldn't risk being late. Besides, he was eager to know the reason for the early morning call from Colonel Isaack. Something was obviously going down, and it made him very curious indeed.

Corporal Carrie Welles was halfway through her morning run along the south-west coast of the island that was Fort Centralis. It was her ritual, the equivalent of someone else's morning cup of coffee. It brought her to life, got her blood pumping and gave her time to clear her mind, which kept her brain sharp throughout the day. Fitness was important to her. She knew that it had played a part in her success as a soldier to date. Although she'd been a late entrant into the forces, she'd easily made up for lost time: still relatively young at 28, she'd already been given more opportunities in her career than her training buddies, despite her physique, which was not that of a typical soldier. She was quite petite—only 5' 5" in height—but her fellow recruits only teased her about that for the first week or so. When they finally got on the shooting range, she very quickly earned their respect. She was faster and more accurate than anyone she knew. She had a natural talent but couldn't deny that the training her father had given her had helped to hone this skill. He'd made her an exceptional sharpshooter, and that had been her ticket to better things.

As she rounded the bend near the southernmost point of the island, she checked her watch. There was no time for taking it easy today. She could not afford to be late for her meeting at Command. She'd received their call only yesterday evening, notifying her that she was being called up for duty and to report to Command at 0700. She didn't know where she would be going or even what division she was being called up for, although she had recently applied for Space Duty. It was the thought of this that made her tingle with anticipation.

Curiosity had been eating away at her for weeks now. It was generally an invitation-only division, and there had been a lengthy screening process to be eligible for admission. She had endured a whole range of medical checks and skills testing to prove her worth and it had all been under a veil of classified secrecy. She was quietly confident that she would be accepted but still nervous by the long wait for answers. This was something she wanted more than anything, and she couldn't help but let herself wonder whether today would be the day she would finally become a Space Duty recruit.

As the thought sent a spike of adrenaline through her, she checked her watch again. 05:15. *Better head back...* She wanted plenty of time to get ready, plenty of time to make herself look soldier-smart. This posting was hers, she could feel it.

Harris arrived at Command at 0550. He had his identification at the ready and presented it to one of the heavily-armed guards at the entrance, who eyed it carefully and then nodded him to pass. The rank of captain in the UNF Space Division was held in much higher esteem than that of Earth-based military outfits. Although the SD had grown since its inception, it had started small with a limited amount of soldiers and a reduced ranking system. And so, in the SD, a captain was known as the captain of a spaceship, and it was held in much higher regard.

He entered the building and made his way to the screening area, as he'd done countless times before. He recognized the graying man at the security checkpoint and nodded a "hello" to him. The guard eyed him back and tightened his lips in acknowledgment. Harris placed his briefcase and hat on the table, and the guard placed them on the conveyor belt to pass through a screening device. As his items disappeared from sight, the guard waved him through to the main screening zone, which consisted of 'the Tube'; a cylindrical machine that would scan and x-ray his entire body.

The Tube was a phenomenal piece of technology. It ran scanners over the subject several times, reading the various layers of the human body, including an iris scan to confirm the subject's identity. It not only registered the usual metal objects or handmade weapons, but it also picked up chemicals and detected excessive heat or biofluids linked with viruses or any other biological weapons. The machine was impenetrable, and if one tried to get anything past it, the alarms would sound, the machine would lock in place, and a gas would be released to subdue the offender. Next thing they'd know, they'd be waking up inside a cell with a real bad headache and a potential death sentence hanging over their head.

The Tube was empty, so Harris stepped in and the doors closed behind him. He stood on the metal plate and looked straight ahead at the iris scanner and the second set of doors that would release him if he was cleared. It began to scan him. He took a deep breath and let out a long sigh. He hated this machine. He knew it served a purpose but hated the fact that nothing was private anymore. He knew that in a room, off to the side, sat some medical personnel checking out every inch of his body, and he didn't like that someone else could know more about him than he did.

After the green laser iris scan was completed, he closed his eyes and started thinking about why they'd called him in. He'd been working under Isaack's command for about eighteen months now, and although Isaack was old school, Harris respected him. He knew they wouldn't just pull him in like this without good reason.

He recalled the dream he'd had that morning of his grandma Sibbie and great-grandma Etta. He was intrigued by its strangeness, wondering if the whiskey from the night before had something to do with it. He thought it odd to all of a sudden dream of them like that, without any provocation. He couldn't actually remember having dreamed of them before. Every now and then he would recall memories from his childhood—their watchful eyes, their soft smiles—but they were fleeting moments that he never thought much of. He'd been fond of them, but he'd been nowhere near as close to them as his sister Holly had been. He could just picture Holly's face now if he told her that he'd dreamed of them. The analysis that would ensue! Harris smirked at the thought.

He heard the high-pitched beep and the light overhead turned green. The scan was complete. The second set of doors opened up and he stepped out. He collected his briefcase and hat, then approached the reception desk, where a uniformed woman awaited him with a smile.

"Good morning, sir. Welcome to the United National Forces. How may I help you?" Her big blue eyes and bright red lips were a welcoming sight for his tired eyes.

"Captain Harris to see Colonel Isaack, Space Force Division. He's expecting me," he smiled.

"Certainly, sir," she said, smiling in return. She turned slightly and began to announce his arrival into her headpiece.

Harris glanced around at the various soldiers and administration staff walking around. Everyone seemed normal, no-one was running around like a major drama was unfolding somewhere.

"Certainly, sir," she continued, before ending the communication and looking back at Harris. "Colonel Isaack will see you on the sixth floor, room 105." She hit a few keys on her console, then swiped a security pass over a scanner. "This pass will give you access to that particular floor and that particular room only, sir," she said, looking at him quite seductively through her eyelashes. She flicked her long, straight brown hair over her shoulder as she slid the security pass across the counter toward him. "Have a nice day, sir."

He took the pass and smiled back at her, curious to know whether she was this friendly with everyone or whether it was especially for him.

"Thank you," he said, checking her name badge, "Veronica." He walked over to the elevator, which opened as he approached, stepped inside and turned back to view her again. She was still looking at him, the seductive smile in place. They eyed each other for a second before the elevator doors shut.

He smiled to himself at the luck he'd had recently with women. He wasn't sure why exactly, although he'd always done alright. He considered himself a decent-looking African American man, taller than most at 6' 2" and he took care of himself physically, so he was in good shape for his age. *Strong body, strong mind* was his motto and, at the age of forty-two, it was even more important to him now. As captain of the *Aurora*, it was occasionally a job requirement to round up criminals and terrorists and bring them in, which meant there were often younger 'tough guys' thinking they could put him in his place. Thankfully, his years of service gave him the experience they lacked; it made him smarter and stronger than them. He liked to be several moves ahead, and he never wanted to let that lead go.

An automated voice announced that he'd reached the sixth floor. He swiped his security pass over the scanner and the doors opened to reveal an empty, white marble hallway. He made his way to room 105, knocked briefly, then swiped the card again and the door unlocked. As he entered, he saw Colonel Isaack sitting with two other men at a long table, involved in a deep discussion that, he noted, ended abruptly when they saw him.

Colonel Isaack, silver haired and medium built, stood and walked over to greet him. As he did, one of the other men, a tall strawberry-blond man with a pockmarked face, carrying the rank of a Major-General, left the room, avoiding eye contact with him.

"Captain Harris," Isaack said, then motioned to a refreshment table setup in the corner. "Care for coffee? Tea?"

Harris decided he'd better have a coffee to kill off the hunger pains, as he was starting to wish he'd eaten breakfast. "Thank you, colonel," he replied.

Isaack returned to his seat, whilst Harris made his way to the drinks table and poured himself a strong black coffee.

"Take a seat." Isaack motioned for him to sit opposite them.

Harris placed his mug and hat on the table and his briefcase on the floor, then took a seat, eyeing the man sitting next to Isaack.

"Captain Harris, this is Professor Derek Martin," Isaack offered. "He's providing us with background information and strategic advice on the matter at hand."

Harris and Martin acknowledged each other with a nod. Martin, he thought, although dressed in uniform, didn't look much like a typical soldier with his slight build and glasses. He turned back to Isaack. "So, what seems to be the problem, colonel?"

"Before I begin, captain, I must, of course, advise you that what we are about to discuss is extremely sensitive and therefore classified. No-one outside this room is fully aware of what I'm about to tell you."

"Yes, sir," Harris said, his curiosity piquing. He knew the drill, though. The type of missions his team undertook weren't exactly advertised to the general public. After all, with the UNF and governments around the world wanting to promote space living, the last thing they wanted Earth dwellers to hear about were such things as space pirates, mutinies or black market UNF weapons on the loose. On Earth, Space Duty teams were simply known to assist with things like colonization, ships in mechanical distress, or medical emergencies. *Space knights in shining armor*, he thought with some humor.

"Ok, well, I'll cut straight to it," Isaack began. "We picked up a distress beacon from one of our stations in an outer area of the UNF Space Zone. You won't find its location on any star maps available to the general public." As he spoke, Isaack hit a button that lit up a screen built into the table's surface between them. It showed a UNF map of the station's location.

"It's a small scientific station," Isaack continued, "set up for work on highly classified programs for the UNF. We have a team of nine personnel working up there, headed up by Professor Ray Sharley."

Isaack placed an e-file onto the table; a slim rectangular pane, about the size of a sheet of letter paper, and able to hold any number of data files. Harris eyed it curiously but continued to pay attention to the colonel as he continued: "So, yesterday, September 19th, at approximately 0817 Fort Centralis (FC) time, we picked up their emergency distress beacon. This occurred approximately six hours after we lost all comms with the station. Despite numerous attempts by our team on the ground we have not been able to restore contact."

Harris pulled the e-file toward him and began swiping his fingers across the screen to leaf through the information. There were profiles on the personnel and technical information about the station and its location.

"Captain Harris, we want you and your team to head to the site on a reconnaissance mission and let us know what's going on up there."

Harris looked up at Isaack. "You mean a rescue mission? You said there was a distress beacon enabled?"

"Well, yes, but we believe the distress beacon may be related to the issue we're having with the comms. A certain blackout period will trigger such an alarm. We've lost transmission with the station, but that does not necessarily mean something is wrong up there. At this stage we are treating it as a *technical* difficulty. You and your team are to go there, dock at the station and see if you can resolve the situation."

Harris looked from Isaack to the professor and back. "If this is a technical difficulty, then why do you want my men to go in? We do have technical skills, yes, but at the end of the day we're nothing more than good old-fashioned soldiers. We handle people problems, sometimes medical problems, even mechanical problems, but generally not problems of a comms-tech nature. What aren't you telling me?"

"Captain, this is purely a case of playing on the safe side. The station is located not far from the UNF orbital zone border between Mars and The Belt," Isaack told him. "To a certain degree it's uncharted territory out there. The world's focus is on our successful colonization of Mars. We want to keep it that way. We don't want people thinking we can't keep in contact with, or control, our own stations. Not good for business, you understand? This is under the radar. You go there, you fix what needs fixing, and you return home. Simple as that."

Harris scanned Isaack's face, noting the lines of experience creasing around his eyes. "Fix what needs fixing..." he repeated, thinking aloud.

"That is correct," Isaack nodded.

"Well, surely there must be other teams already out there, close by, who could go and check this out?"

"There are, but as I said, this station is highly classified. We're not prepared to send just anyone out there. If we honestly thought lives were in danger, we wouldn't risk it. Take it as a compliment, captain. The UNF obviously regards you highly to have selected your team for this," Isaack said plainly.

Harris thought about it for a moment, running his hand over his jaw. He eyed the two men again. "My men are going to want a little bonus for cutting short their R & R."

"Of course," Isaack said matter-of-factly. "They'll be duly compensated for their efforts."

Harris scanned through the file again, thinking. Something didn't feel quite right, but he guessed it was to be expected with a last-minute mission and limited facts. That was often the way of the UNF; everything was on a need to know basis.

He looked at Professor Martin. "Is there anything you would like to add, professor?"

"No, no, I think Colonel Isaack has covered it all off," he replied, adjusting his glasses as he spoke.

"Can you shed any light on what the scientists were doing up there?" Harris probed.

"Well, er... they were working on various technical programs, software and the like, and some items of a biological nature. The exact nature of which is, of course, classified. However, we do not feel this is of any cause for concern. The station is located in an outer area, which is vast but with few comms satellites, so there are bound to be issues from time to time of a comms-tech nature. There may simply have been a glitch in their software testing or a virus may have brought the system down," he offered, adjusting his glasses again.

"So how do you propose we fix that, then?" Harris arched his eyebrow at him.

"I've read through your crew files and I believe that our men on the ground can guide Private First Class Smith with any repairs if you run into difficulty. Otherwise, I've read his file and he seems more than qualified to handle it."

Harris eyed him carefully. "May I ask what your involvement with the station is?"

"Of course," Martin smiled. "I'm responsible for Station Darwin. I put the team together and effectively run the programs they're working on, and I report directly to senior UNF personnel on their progress. I know that station inside and out, so if you have any questions at any time during your mission, simply relay them to Command and I'll respond accordingly."

Harris eyed him again. Martin seemed pretty calm for someone who'd lost comms with his crew, located somewhere in that vast expanse of space.

"Your departure is set for 1900 this evening," Isaack informed him.

After a brief silence, Harris answered, "Yes, sir." He had never refused a mission before and was not about to start. Besides, this had him somewhat intrigued now. He stood, shook Isaack's proffered hand, then turned to Professor Martin who had his hand outstretched, beaming a smile of relief.

"Captain Harris, there's one more thing…" Isaack began, his face briefly flashing an uncomfortable look.

Harris gave him a solid stare in return. "One more thing? Aren't you meant to tell me that *before* we shake?"

"This comes from high above me, Harris. It's an order."

Harris eyed them both carefully, then slowly took his seat again. *Here it comes*, he thought, *the sting in the tail.*

"Your crew is being increased by three," Isaack informed him.

"My crew is just fine as it is, colonel."

"I'm sure it is, captain. However, it's been decided that for this particular mission it will be increased by three." He locked eyes with Harris. "Three women."

Harris stared at Isaack for a moment, then let out a chuckle. "You had me for a minute there."

Isaack just stared back. He appeared to have expected this reaction and was letting Harris have his moment.

"This will be done, Captain Harris," Isaack said firmly. "We're getting pressure to ensure we have female soldiers represented on all our ships. I know the *Aurora* has always had an all-male crew, but it's time for a change. They will join you for this mission as a test case to prove that we're giving female soldiers an equal opportunity to work with crews like yours, that sometimes undertake black ops missions."

Harris's mind ticked over for a moment. "A test case. Meaning one-off? They do this mission, then leave my ship?"

"Yes, Captain Harris, that's what a test case means."

Harris noticed he was starting to get a weird feeling in the pit of his stomach. Perhaps it was just his hunger creeping back in, but something was making him uneasy. He was starting to wish he hadn't drunk so much the night before.

"I thought we were under the radar, sir? If we're under the radar then why are we being asked to take part in what is effectively a PR exercise?"

"You *are* under the radar, captain. If your mission is a success, we'll include your data in our reports up the chain. If you and your men fuck it up, no-one will ever know it happened."

Harris clenched his jaw. He knew he wasn't going to get a say in the matter, an order was an order.

"Who are these women?" he asked irritably. "I take it they're experienced soldiers?"

"Yes," Isaack said, as he reached across to the e-file and tapped on three data folders, "they are all fine soldiers." Isaack brought up the first soldier's photo. She was Caucasian, with a thin face, short, bright red hair and pale pink lips. "We've got Sergeant Sarah Packham, a highly regarded space pilot —"

"I've already got two pilots," Harris interrupted.

"Well, now you've got another one," Isaack quickly retorted, tapping open the second folder. "This is Corporal Sabrina Colt, a fine solid soldier who, although her specialty is with explosives, also has good technical skills. She may be of assistance with the comms issues if it's a hard-wiring fault."

Harris looked down to see a dark skinned woman, well-built, with long braided hair, and a broad smile of straight white teeth.

"Lastly we've got Corporal Carrie Welles." Isaack opened the third file to show Harris another Caucasian woman with long brown hair, green eyes and a serious face. "She's a great markswoman, better than any we've seen in some time."

"I've already got a sharpshooter in my crew," Harris said, "why the double-ups?"

"I've already explained the reasons why, captain. This is a test case. They are not being assigned to your ship to replace anyone. They are supplementary." Isaack closed down the three files. "They will be here at 0700 for you to meet them. Read through their profiles. Your men are being called as we speak. They are being readied for 1600."

Harris let out a sigh. "Sir, don't you think it would be better to send these women on the *Aurora* after they've had time to train with my men first? Sending them out on a last-minute mission like this..."

"Your mission leaves at 1900, captain. I'm sure you will use your leadership skills to integrate them appropriately," Isaack said as he gathered his things together. "Oh, and one more thing."

Harris shot him an unimpressed look, wondering what else he was about to spring.

"The women are not to board the station until I give the order. Are we understood?"

Harris looked from the colonel to the professor and back again. "May I ask why?"

"PR exercise, Harris," Isaack reiterated.

"So, effectively…" Harris said slowly, "these women, these 'fine soldiers' as you call them, are merely coming along for the ride? They're to sit back while my men do all the work. Is that what you mean by a test case?"

Isaack looked at him sternly. "These women remain on your ship until I say otherwise. That's an order, Harris!" He stood abruptly. "I don't expect that your men are going to like this change, but you make damn sure you keep them in check. Do you understand me? Do not *fuck* this up!"

With that, Isaack and Martin swiftly departed the room, leaving Harris all alone, staring down at the e-file.

# 2

# New Recruits

Carrie arrived at the Command Center almost half an hour early. *Too eager*, she thought and decided to walk around the block to kill time and steady her nerves. She looked at the other soldiers and civilians walking past her, all in their own little worlds, completely oblivious to the significance of this day for her, oblivious to the major turn she was sure her life was about to take. She heard the sounds of spacecraft taking off from the UNF Space Dock close by and looked up at the sky to see a large mass of gray metal shooting skyward trailing a tail of fire and vapor in its wake. A smile spread across her face.

She walked calmly, noticing her reflection in the mirrored glass of a building she passed. She wanted to look perfect, smell perfect, *be* perfect. Whenever she interviewed, she couldn't help but feel that she was not only representing herself, but also her father, and therefore had a reputation to uphold. She never mentioned her father, of course, only acknowledging him if she was asked directly. She didn't want to invite the comparisons, or worse still, have people assuming she'd gotten as far as she had because of him. After all, he was an 'Original', one of the revered few who'd been on the frontier when both the Moon and Mars had been colonized, and that always carried a sense of legend with it.

Excitement prickled through her at the thought of being on the next frontier for the UNF. Space Duty was, after all, the pinnacle; the most sought-after division to enroll in as a soldier in today's world. But it was a step-by-step process to get there, and one that required patience. Everyone started out in their own country's national army, air force or navy. For the most part, however, they were confined to country-specific work, at least during peacetime.

Once a soldier had cut their teeth working in a local army, the next step was the United National Forces, which had two arms: Earth Duty and Space Duty. Earth Duty was the first step and enabled a soldier to travel and work in different parts of the world, with multicultural teams, and develop their skills with specialized training. Wherever there was a natural disaster, Earth Duty troops would assist. Wherever there were pockets of terrorist activity, they would help resolve it. If a soldier impressed their senior officers on Earth Duty, an invitation would be extended for them to apply for Space Duty. Invitations were strictly limited; only those considered the cream of the crop or those who showed future promise were taken, and so far very few females had been given the opportunity to go.

For most soldiers it was a personal choice. Some had no desire whatsoever to be working out in space. Others yearned for the opportunity. Carrie was one of the latter. When she'd been called in specifically for the Santos mission in Madrid, whilst on Earth Duty, she knew it was her chance to prove her worth and get noticed. She did prove herself, she did get noticed, and sure enough she soon had her ticket to apply.

Now she was ready for the next step in her career. She wanted to head out into space and help prepare unexplored sites for colonization. It would be challenging, she knew that. Spending months on end in desolate climates, facing the unknown, would not be an easy undertaking, but she thrived on the idea of being a pioneer and leading the way. Just like her father had done.

Besides, the human race had no choice but to expand its borders. Earth's capacity to sustain mankind had been reached long ago, despite the fact that science and technology had overcome most problems of living in previously uninhabitable regions on the planet. But as with all things, the technology that had helped man, had also become a hindrance. The prosperous Earth had become too prosperous. Populations grew, industries boomed, and environmentalists raced to revitalize the parts of the Earth that humanity had ravaged on its way through.

The great minds of the day were forced to find a solution. The Space Duty arm of the UNF was born, and exploration began into colonizing outer space. For the last thirty-five years, the UNF Space Duty Division, with international government and conglomerate assistance, had been setting up outposts and space stations off Earth; pockets of human existence, like small floating cities. Each had a scientific code name, such as "Z106", but had also been given a common name based on something historical or mythical, such as "Station Pegasus" or "Station Magellan". It had taken time to convince Earth dwellers to embrace the future and take to the stations, but eventually their popularity had grown.

As space living became a reality, the UNF decided to expand their realm and conquered the Earth's moon. Several colonies were established under the purification and gravitational domes, using convict labor. Over time this, too, proved so successful that they turned their gaze to Mars. On January 12th, 2059, the first spaceship arrived. A settlement was established, using convict labor, in the northern hemisphere of Mars. Once complete, the entire populations of Earth's maximum security prisons were transferred there into a state-of-the-art penitentiary which became known as 'Hell Town'. The UNF then set about using the convict labor to help run expeditions to the south, and began to develop the Mars Docking Station and the two civilian settlement colonies—Elon and Brahe — that now existed. So successful was the conquering of Mars, it was widely rumored that the UNF had begun planning a massive expansion of settlements there.

The adrenaline spiked through Carrie as she thought about the possibilities. She checked her watch, took a deep breath, and made her way back to Command.

*

Carrie waited patiently in the reception hall of Command. The receptionist had checked her in with a Lieutenant McEvoy, then told her to take a seat. She hadn't been seated long before she heard the Tube open and saw a Space Duty uniformed, dark-skinned woman, with long, braided hair make her way to the reception desk. Carrie heard McEvoy's name mentioned and figured she must be here for the same reason. She eyed the woman curiously. She looked fit and strong, maybe mid-to-late 20s. Carrie saw the receptionist motion over toward the seats and the soldier turned and headed her way.

They locked eyes and gave a polite nod. The new arrival sat down a couple of seats away, and the silence and minutes ticked by. Carrie busied herself looking around the grand reception area. It was wall to floor marble, white with gold flecks, shiny and cold. The large UNF shield insignias for Earth Duty and Space Duty were positioned on the wall behind the receptionist, beneath a glorious, protective Pegasus. The winged horse, the perfect choice of mascot for the UNF, representing both land and sky. To the right of the reception there was an elegant rocky waterfall, surrounded by lush greenery. The sound of its running water soothed her. She glanced up at the ceiling, which was shaped like a pyramid and had glass on one side for the natural light, then she looked over to the wall of elevators and wondered where each lead.

The Tube beeped again and a tall, slim, redhead appeared. Both seated women watched her approach the reception desk and heard McEvoy's name again. *Another one!* The redhead, also dressed in a Space Duty uniform, made her way over to the chairs and, as she did so, the dark-skinned woman stood and offered her hand to shake.

"Hi, how you doin'?" she said with an American accent. "I'm Corporal Sabrina Colt. I'm sorry, I overheard, but you're here to see First Lieutenant McEvoy?"

The redhead nodded, smiled, and shook her hand. "Sergeant Sarah Packham," she said with a crisp English accent.

The two women looked over at Carrie, sitting there in her Earth Duty uniform.

"Are you here to see McEvoy, too?" Colt asked.

Carrie gave a nod, stood from her chair and offered her hand. "Corporal Carrie Welles."

Colt shook Carrie's hand, and then Carrie shook Packham's.

"So..." Colt began as they all sat, "do we have any idea what's going to happen today?"

They shook their heads, but Carrie noticed the other women's eyes seemed to sparkle with just as much intrigue as she felt.

"So, you're obviously British." Colt said to Packham.

"Yes," she replied, "From Oxford. And you? I mean, you're obviously American..."

Colt smiled. "I was actually born in Barbados, but spent most of my life in Orlando, Florida." She turned to Carrie. "And you?"

"Australian. From Brisbane originally."

Colt chuckled. "Well, this really is the United National Forces, isn't it?"

A smile curled at their mouths.

Carrie thought the two women seemed alright, but until she knew why they were all here, she couldn't relax.

Harris sat in the empty room looking over the three women's profiles. Isaack was right, they all looked pretty good on paper. Sergeant Packham, 29, had a good clean flight record. She'd trained with both the British RAF and at NASA, scoring top marks during her training maneuvers and impressed her superiors while based in Russia during her time on Earth Duty. Since joining Space Duty she'd had successful stints on some of the space stations, then on Mars, and seemed to be doing well before she applied for a transfer a month ago. Now she was here.

Corporal Colt, 27, also had a good record. She'd trained with Special Forces in the US and then did time in East Africa and China on Earth Duty. She appeared to have a flair with electronics, and in particular with explosive devices. She entered into Space Duty only four months ago and had been based on a UNF cargo runner called *Andromeda*, taking supplies to all the outposts. She'd requested a transfer to a more "active" posting. So, now she was here.

The last of the women, Corporal Welles, 28, was the daughter of retired Australian UNF Space Duty colonel, Jeffrey Welles. Harris undertook a brief search on the UNF portal to ensure it was indeed the same Jeffrey Welles that he thought it was. And he was correct. Her father was *the* Col. Welles, one of the Originals; the first group of Space Duty soldiers there'd ever been. He'd been at the forefront of the space station migration, the Moon colonization, and the early days of the Mars colonization. All three waves. It made Harris wonder if this was why she'd been selected to take part in this PR exercise. The daughter of an Original continuing the tradition and flying the flag for the UNF. What a PR story that would make.

Regardless, she'd impressed her superiors with not only her excellent marksmanship, but also her determination and drive to succeed. Although she'd started out later than most, she was coming to Harris after several years on Earth Duty, mainly based in Indonesia, the South Pacific and Antarctica. Just recently she had been specifically called in on the Santos mission and according to her file, it had been her bullets that took down the rebel leader Jose Gardos and five other rebels, after a ten day standoff in Madrid. She had not yet been inducted into Space Duty, which was a concern, but she was about to get a quick initiation.

Harris was torn away from the e-file by a knock at the door. He heard the beep of the security card swipe and the door opened to reveal First Lieutenant McEvoy.

"Captain Harris, I have Sergeant Packham, and Corporals Colt and Welles for you," he announced.

"Show them through," Harris ordered, closing down the file and putting it to one side.

He stood and watched the women carefully as they entered. They marched straight ahead, single file, then turned to stand in front of him and saluted. They had passed their first test.

He stared at each woman for a moment as they stood in the lineup. He towered over them, which was not uncommon for him with most people, but compared to his soldiers on the *Aurora*, they looked minuscule. As well as visibly lacking in strength they didn't particularly look like the kind of hardened soldiers that would cause fear to the likes of space pirates, either. They were all quite feminine and attractive in the flesh, and could've just as easily replaced Veronica out on reception. That's what concerned him. He could just picture the reaction of some of his men.

Sergeant Packham was of reasonable height, at 5' 10", but she was too slim. Corporal Colt was shorter at 5' 7", but she did have the best build of the three. Corporal Welles was even shorter and had a petite build. Again, he pictured the reaction of his men, and it mostly involved laughter.

"At ease," he ordered, his voice devoid of any emotion. He wasn't happy about this late change to his team, but he had to accept it. Whether this was a babysitting job or not, he made a promise to himself to treat them no different than the rest of his men. If they wanted in, they would have to do it his way.

The women each took a seat on the opposite side of the table to him. He eyed the three of them again, studying their faces. They each made good eye contact. He liked that.

"My name is Captain Saul Harris," he began. "Today you will be joining my team on the UNF *Aurora*, as a test case, for a one-off mission. We leave this evening at 1900 hours. You will need to be at Dock 559 by no later than 1500 hours. You will be briefed and meet the rest of the crew then. Are there any questions?"

He noticed a spark of excitement light up their eyes.

"No, sir," Colt and Packham shook their heads.

"Sir," Welles began, her voice sounding a little unsure, "does this mean I've been accepted into Space Duty?"

"Well, you can't fly on my ship if not, so I guess that would be a yes," he said, in a slightly mocking tone.

The expression on her face showed regret for asking the question. "Yes, sir."

"Someone will be down shortly to take you to administration where you will complete the final authorities for your transfers," he told them. "They will then send you onto Stores where *you*, Corporal Welles, will collect your new uniform and any other items you may require for this mission," he continued. "After that, you will need to go home, pack your stuff and be down at Dock 559 by no later than 1500 hours. Are we clear, soldiers?"

"Yes, sir!" they chimed in unison.

"Good," Harris said flatly, then gathered up his things and exited the room. He was a matter-of-fact kind of man and felt there was nothing more to be said at this stage. He wasn't going to pretend to be thrilled that they were part of his team, but he would be professional nonetheless. He knew his men probably wouldn't take too kindly to the change in lineup. The team worked well as it was, and it could be a bad thing to mess with a winning formula.

Besides, three attractive women could prove a distraction. It had been well theorized that men instinctively felt the need to protect female soldiers more so than their male counterparts in a life and death situation, making the male soldiers that much more vulnerable. This *could not* and *would not* take place on the *Aurora*, he told himself. Test case or not, if they wanted to be part of his team, they were going to work as hard as the men, fight as hard as the men, and if it came to it, die as hard as the men.

Carrie smiled subtly to herself as that adrenaline spiked through her again. She stood in her apartment eyeing her new Space Duty uniforms. The first was an "official" service uniform that consisted of a smart-looking light gray blouse with matching skirt, which had the electric blue UNF Space Duty Division insignia over the left breast. Similar to that of Earth Duty, the insignia held an image of the Earth within a shield, but where the Earth Duty Division had the Earth surrounded by a laurel wreath, the Space Duty Division had the Earth surrounded by stars. The second uniform was the "general" combat uniform, consisting of gray cammo pants and a matching variety of gray tops: singlets, T-shirts and long-sleeved gray cammo shirts, all with electric blue stitching and the UNF insignia.

As if determined to thwart her eagerness, the time dragged. She'd packed within minutes, doing so lightly. Restless, she sat on the couch in her apartment and looked over at the photo displayed on the wall beside her LCD screen. It was a picture of her parents, laughing and fooling around, happiness splashed across their faces. It had been taken only days before her mother had passed away. She often stared at that photo and wondered: *if only they knew*? But there had been no way of knowing. Her father had left for a conference in Poland the day after that photo was taken, and her mother was dead two days later.

It was sad to think that no matter how advanced mankind had become, humans could still die in automobile accidents. Human error was something that no-one could ever erase. You couldn't control the fact that a man could turn off his vehicle's intelligent autocruise control system, take his eyes off the road and take a corner too fast, and drive head on into an innocent woman on her way home from dropping her daughter at school. And so, at fourteen, Carrie had lost her mother, and her father had lost his wife.

Deep down she knew that was the moment her father changed. The hero, the Original soldier, seemed to grow old almost overnight. After her mother's death, he sent her to live in a boarding school and she saw even less of him, if that were possible. She figured he was running away, trying to escape the pain by keeping himself busy. She understood it to a certain extent, but at the same time, part of her felt abandoned.

Her father grew to become a mystery, held together only by fond memories from her childhood of target practice, talking in secret codes, and inspiring transmissions sent from space. That spark he lit in her childhood, despite his absence, had not diminished. The lure of space was irresistible, and her father's success the cherry on top. He'd left his mark on this world as a respected space pioneer; now she felt compelled to do the same.

After working on Mars for a while after her mother's death, she guessed that her father finally realized he couldn't escape the pain or the loneliness. Tired and dejected and somewhat resentful of the military, he resigned and returned to Earth, just as his little girl was making plans to explore new worlds herself.

It was a surprise to her that, despite his years of service, despite raising her like he did, he'd initially discouraged her from joining the armed forces. When she'd wanted to enlist straight from school, he'd refused, arguing that he wanted her to experience life outside the military first. After much debate with the ex-colonel, she'd reluctantly agreed to work "normal" jobs in administration for the first couple of years, and she could barely manage that. The pull was too strong. It had never been far from her mind, and all it took to convince her in the end was an offhand comment from an old ex-soldier who'd seen her down at the local shooting range one day. He happened to witness her shoot, eyed the target she'd hit, then shook his head and said, *"Jeez, you're a bloody good shot, love. The army could do with someone like you!"* The very next day she applied to join the Australian Army.

Her father wasn't happy, but he'd managed to hold his tongue. She'd wanted to talk to him about it, why he was so against it, but that just wasn't the way they were. They never discussed the things that lurked beneath the surface. He was a soldier through and through, always on guard.

Her father knew she'd been promoted to Earth Duty a few years back, but she'd never told him about her application for Space Duty because she knew, deep down, the gap between them would widen with the news. After all, despite the distance between them, she was all he had left since her mother had passed away. But she knew the time had come. It had to be done.

And so Carrie sat there, planning the conversation with her father in her mind. She would do it the Army way, soldier to soldier. She'd just tell him like it is. There would be no questions. She had been accepted into Space Duty and she was going. He couldn't say or do anything about it. He had done it, and now so would she. It was that simple.

Spurred on by some imaginary courage, she picked up her Personal Data Port (PDP) and called him. At this time of year, he would be at his holiday villa in Florida. She tried the numbers she had for him, but they went through to a message service. *Where is he? I can't just leave him a message telling him I'm heading into space tonight!* She did leave a message, but only to ask him to call her. She looked down at her watch. 13:08. *There's still time. He'll call back. It's okay.*

She stood and walked around her apartment, one last time. She double-checked the windows and doors were locked, then surveyed how neat and tidy everything was. Everything was in its place. Everything was under control.

Now she just needed her father to return her call.

Harris felt somewhat better now that he had eaten, although there remained a strange feeling in the pit of his stomach. He was pinning it on the hangover, although his mind did wander briefly to thoughts of Sibbie and Etta and that strange dream again. He shook his head. *Damn that whiskey!*

He'd been reading over the e-file that Colonel Isaack had given him. The station itself, Z076—known as Darwin—was located, as the colonel had said, in the outer realm of the UNF Space Zone, which covered all the inhabited area of space to date, radiating out from Earth as far as the Mars orbit. The station was positioned not far off Mars, and given its close proximity to The Belt, it was an area generally avoided, as few recognized civilian flight paths ventured that far. *Nicely placed for something so classified*, he thought.

Although Darwin had one designated shuttle, the *Spector*, the crew replied heavily upon a regular rotation of specially assigned, UNF-cleared cargo ships for all their needs. Visitors were a rarity. He read the summary profiles on Darwin's crew. They'd all been officially inducted into UNF Space Duty and therefore had received the basic training, but their specialties lay within their particular scientific fields.

The man in charge, Professor Ray Sharley, had been on the station for approximately two years. Prior to that he'd been involved in the design and set-up of the high tech, state-of-the-art maximum security prison on Mars—MSP001 (aka "Hell Town") for the UNF, who were effectively in charge of Mars. After establishing the prison, he then went on to become Warden for several years, before taking up the post on Darwin. It seemed he was not only a man with vast scientific credentials, but also a PhD in psychology.

When Sharley started work on the Darwin, he had a small crew of two, and this had grown to eight rather quickly, due to the success of his programs, which were, of course, highly classified. Harris found it interesting that he could not access the crew's full staff profiles on the UNF HR portal, as they, too, were classified.

As Isaack advised, administration would be contacting his team with their call for duty. They would have been contacted by now and flying in on special UNF Super-Jets from wherever they'd escaped to on their leave. They would have received no more information other than where to be and when. Harris sat thinking about the mission ahead, and how he'd address his men. He stared at his phone sitting on the table, and decided to call Doc.

"Captain!" his first lieutenant answered. "No rest for the wicked, huh?"

Harris heard the sound of an SJ engine in the background and smiled. "No. We're clearly far too good at our jobs."

"Only the best will do, sir!" Doc retorted.

"So, were you sunning yourself in Hawaii?"

"Yeah, thanks for that. I was in a bar on the beach, about to drink some exotic cocktail served in a coconut when I got the call. I've just got back to the base."

"Coconut cocktails, Doc? You going soft on me?"

Doc laughed. "Hey, the cute barmaid recommended it."

"I see. In that case, I am truly sorry for the call-up."

He laughed again. "It's fine, captain. Her boyfriend was the rather large doorman. You probably actually saved me."

Harris chuckled.

"So, we still on for 1600?" Doc asked.

"The rest of the men will be there at 1600, but I need you to be there a little earlier."

"Sure thing. What's up?"

Harris paused momentarily, wanting to choose his words carefully. Doc obviously sensed something was different.

"Saul...?"

Doc was the only one in his team that could get away with calling him by his first name, but he only ever did it in private. In front of the men it was always "Captain". Doc was the longest serving member of the team. They'd worked together for about two years now, and they had a mutual respect for each other and the chain of command. Harris knew he could depend on Doc to help him with this situation. He knew Doc would be the conduit between the new recruits and the rest of the team, and his eyes and ears when he wasn't around. Doc was second-in-command on the *Aurora*. He was a good soldier, a great medic, and on top of that, they had become good friends.

"We've got three new recruits joining us on this mission," Harris informed him.

"*Three?* Jesus, where we going?"

"Not three ordinary recruits, Doc. Three women."

Doc took a second to respond. "Three women? That's... new."

Harris nodded to himself. "Yes, it is. I want you to give them their pre-flight physicals before the others arrive."

"Yes, sir." Curiosity was clearly jumping out of Doc's voice. "Do we know why they're joining us? Is there a particular reason?"

"Good old-fashioned PR. They tell me it's a test case."

"A test case? Okay..."

"Not buying it?"

"Well, there're hundreds of other ships out there I'd choose before us. We're not really a PR bunch of guys who do PR kinds of jobs, you know. We're not the kind of soldiers you see on the recruitment posters."

"Maybe that's why. Perhaps they're trying to give us a makeover?"

Doc laughed. "Are you kidding? I can't see McKinley, Brown or Bulk as the face of the UNF!"

Harris smirked to himself. "No."

"So, how do you think it's going to go down?" Doc's tone turned serious.

"I have no idea, but I'm relying on your assistance to get this over the line. I want you to help ease the transition."

"Yes, sir. No problems."

"It's just one mission, right? How hard can it be?"

"Sure." Doc's minimal response spoke a thousand words.

"I'll see you at 1500, lieutenant." With that, Harris hung up the phone. He felt better that Doc knew what was about to happen. He didn't want to spring it on his men all at once, and he knew Doc would be the one to jump on the other end of that seesaw and help him balance things out.

He checked his watch. 13:57. *Better call Tyson*, he thought. He grabbed the phone again and hit the speed-dial for his wife's number.

"Hello?"

"Taya, it's me," he greeted her.

"Saul, hi. What's up?"

He never realized how much he missed her voice until he heard it again. Sometimes it was easier not to talk to her. After all, they were separated and had been for some years, but neither of them had mustered the courage to finally divorce. The fact that they often fell back together didn't exactly help things either.

"I've been called up on an urgent mission," he told her. "I leave tonight, so I'm going to have to delay my visit. Is Ty there?"

"No, he's not home from school yet. He had basketball practice. What's going on?" She sounded concerned, and he hated worrying her.

"It's nothing, things are fine. I just need to postpone my visit, is all."

She sighed. "Saul, when are you going to give this all up for a desk job? Ty's getting older, you know. He's going to want a man around soon."

"Yeah? What happened to Larry?" he asked somewhat sarcastically.

She paused a moment. "Larry's Larry, but he's not you. Ty wants his father. And don't pretend like you're happy for another man to be raising your son, either. I know you, Saul Harris!"

"Well, tell Ty I'll see him in a week or so. Tell him I'm sorry and that I'll take him to another game as soon as I'm back, alright?"

"Yeah, okay," she sighed reluctantly.

"So…" He couldn't help the curiosity overflowing. "Is *Larry* going to be in town when I get back?"

"I don't know, Saul… I haven't seen much of Larry lately."

"Why not?" he asked, trying not to sound too pleased about it. She didn't answer him. "Don't be keeping him around if he's not treating you right, Taya. Ty deserves better than that."

"Yes, *he* does, Saul." Her voice was sweet and warm, but Harris still felt a hidden blow to the ribs with that one.

"So do *you*, Taya," his voice softening some. "You both do. Now, I gotta go. I'll speak to you when I get back."

She hesitated, then spoke softly. "Stay safe, Saul."

He paused, the sound of her voice sending a shot of regret through him. "I will. You too."

He hung up the phone and stared down at the finger where his wedding ring used to be. They'd known each other for sixteen years now. He'd met her while he was on Earth Duty and she was working on secondment for a legal firm contracting to the UNF. Instantly attracted to her, he'd asked her out within five minutes of meeting her at the local UNF bar. She agreed, and within seven months they were living together and he'd proposed. Something just felt right about her, he couldn't explain it.

Unfortunately, they'd had their difficulties over the years, adjusting to the amount of time he spent away from her, especially after Ty came into the world. They held it together for a while, but eventually succumbed and separated, although neither of them had wanted to take the final steps to divorce. Even thinking about it now, with the likes of the Jazz Club Woman and Veronica floating around in his head, he still couldn't bear the thought. Taya was his wife. It just was what it was.

He sighed again and shrugged the thoughts from his mind. He had to let that go and concentrate on what lay ahead. He grabbed his kitbag and headed for the door, focusing his mind sharply on Station Darwin.

# 3

# The Aurora

Carrie, dressed in her new service uniform, smoothed her hand over her ponytail, and glanced down at the UNF Space Duty insignia on her blouse. A sense of pride swirled within her to finally be able to wear this patch. Riding in the back of an air-taxi on her way to the Space Dock, she kept looking at her watch. She was a little edgy, not wanting to be late, and wanting her father to call.

She looked out the window at Fort Centralis, the gray buildings and the soldiers all whizzing past her as though she were in a time capsule that was swiftly taking her away from the life she knew. She smiled to herself at the thought, and looked up into the sky; her destination. She saw clouds gathering over the horizon and could almost feel the change of season in the air. Autumn was finally here. She would miss this, she thought, the chance to look up into the blue sky and sunshine. Soon it would be nothing but the darkness of space.

She'd called Fort Centralis home for just shy of a year now, in anticipation that one day she would be enrolled in Space Duty. Fort Centralis was an engineering masterpiece. Built on a man-made island, it was permanently fixed to the Mid-Atlantic Ridge in the Atlantic Ocean, approximately halfway between North America and the United Kingdom. Centralis was the administration hub for all UNF operations, covering both

Earth Duty and Space Duty. It was also the most secure city in the world, not just because of the elite forces that inhabited it but also because of the systems in place to protect it.

Advanced radar technology surrounded the island, picking up any craft approaching it, whether by sea, air or space. There was a constant rotation of the latest high-tech stealth submarines patrolling around the island, sweeping for possible attacks. An extensive port facility was located on the south side of the island for seafaring ships, and on the north side, the largest aerospace facility on the planet, which included a commercial airport, and of course, the Command Space Docks.

The entire city was designed to function as a massive military base, although a third of the island was classed as a civilian area for those companies supplying goods and services to the UNF. Soldiers, like Carrie, also had the option to live on-base or off-base in the civilian area if they chose. Regardless of which section one lived in, built in the middle of the ocean, with the best defense technology available, Centralis was an impenetrable fortress. It even had a weather shield to protect it from incoming oceanic storms. There really was no safer place in the world.

As the air-taxi hovered over the streets, she said her goodbyes to the city, trying to soak up her surrounds, and wanting to remember what her last day as an Earth Duty soldier felt like. She eyed the buildings again, like rectangular blocks of a barricade sprouting from the ground, and noted the soldiers on guard walking the pavement, a mixture of both Earth Duty "greens" and Space Duty "blues". She scanned the few civilians stopping at auto-coffee booths, distracted by their personal data ports. Then she watched the cargo-hummer trucks, big bulky carriers that still managed to fit on civilian width roads, bringing in supplies from the Sea Port. She studied the UNF troop vehicles (UTVs), like tanks crossed with small buses, and then, as she got closer to the Space Dock, the spacecraft zooming overhead.

When she arrived, the air-taxi hovered down to the ground, to its allotted parking station at the dock's entrance. She swiped her card for payment and the man at the controls gave her a nod. She stepped out and made her way to the security booth. She'd been here several times before but had always traveled through the commercial airport terminals to the west, not the UNF Space Dock, so she was keen to finally check it out. Her eyes eagerly scanned the perimeter. Although she couldn't see anything over the large security fencing surrounding the compound, she could hear a hub of activity going on behind it. Her pulse quickened and a subtle smile grew across her face.

Security checked her ID, then waved her through to the screening zone, where she would undergo a whole-body scan, similar to the Tube at Command. Passing through it successfully, she collected her kitbag, then stepped through the large steel doors and out onto the UNF Space Dock.

Pausing for a moment, she took in the scene before her. A mass of activity, the dock spread out as far as the eye could see. There were gray control towers, like mini-fortresses, surrounding the landscape, with runways and launch pads spread out before them like bumpy tentacles. Hundreds of spacecraft of all shapes and sizes were stationed in neat formations, while soldiers scurried among them, dodging the CargoBots— small robotic transport vehicles—that weaved swiftly in and out of the bays.

She saw a locator screen to her right and walked over to assess exactly where she needed to go. She typed in Dock 559 and the screen zoomed in on the destination, then traced a path from Dock 559 to her current location. The dock was located on an outer arm by the ocean to the west. Hitching her bag over her shoulder, she set off to find it.

She got such a thrill walking past the ships, watching the soldiers loading and unloading cargo, hearing the roar of engines firing up and the smell of smoke and vapor wafting in the air. Her body was awash with exhilaration. She was finally here, finally doing this.

Suddenly her PDP rang, making her heart stop. She quickly unclipped it from her belt. It was her father.

"Dad! Hi," she answered.

"Carrie, what's going on?" Her father's voice had a concerned edge to it.

"How're you going? Where've you been today?" She tried to buy time, suddenly unsure how to tell him.

"I was visiting a friend. What was it you wanted to tell me? It sounded urgent."

"Yeah, well, it is..." she said, looking around to make sure no-one was listening. She felt like a little girl fessing up to her father, as though asking his permission in a way. "I... applied for Space Duty," she told him.

There was silence down the phone. She swallowed and continued.

"I was accepted. They signed me up for my first mission already," she said with a "look on the bright side" feel to it.

He remained silent.

"Dad," she sighed. "I want this. I've worked hard for this. I know how you feel about it, but I'll be fine. It's what I want."

Still there was silence.

"Look... this is my time now. Just be happy for me. Please?"

He waited a few more seconds before responding. "If that's what you want," he said plainly. His voice was devoid of emotion, as though he was talking to a fellow soldier.

"I do, so don't lay a guilt trip on me, okay?" she said, rubbing her temple.

"I'm not doing anything, Ree. If this is what you really want, then I can't stop you. When do you leave?"

"I'm, er, at the dock now. Just found out this morning."

"This morning?" he blurted. "Urgent mission then." She could hear him rubbing his whiskers, could tell his mind was ticking over. "They're sending a p-star up there on an urgent mission?"

"Protostars have to start somewhere," she said a little defensively, taking offence to the Space Duty slang he used, basically calling her a greenhorn.

"Where you headed?"

"That's classified, Dad," she said, "you know that."

"Of course," he said, sounding a little hurt. She wondered whether she'd heard a twinge of regret? Did he miss life in the forces? Did he wish it was him going? Or was it because his only child was leaving the planet for some unknown destination?

"Who's the captain?" he recommenced in soldier mode.

"Captain Saul Harris."

"Harris? Never heard of him!" he said, dismissively.

"Dad," she laughed a little, "maybe that's because he's about twenty years younger than you."

He was silent again.

"Look, everything will be fine. I have to go."

"Well," he said, still in soldier mode, "you be safe. Don't take unnecessary risks. Make sure you sleep well and eat well. Space is different on the body, you know? And keep your gun close when you can." Then his voice softened again. "Just... make sure you come home, alright? And keep in touch. Time gets lost out there, when it's always night."

"I know it does, Dad," she said. "I grew up with you as my father, remember?"

He adopted his soldier tone again. "Alright... well, thanks for the call. Have a good journey." And with that he hung up.

She suddenly held an image in her mind of her father sitting alone in his apartment, no wife, no daughter. She was glad that he hadn't argued or made it hard for her, but at the same time this felt just as bad. His silence had been deafening.

Someone yelled in the distance, snapping her out of her thoughts. A CargoBot was reversing up to one of the ships and its bay was opening. She looked at her watch. 14:39. *Better move it*, she thought. Hiking her kitbag higher over her shoulder, she stepped up the pace in the direction of Dock 559.

Harris sat in his office on board the *Aurora* and began rereading the Darwin e-file. He did most of his work here in his office; it was his home away from home. Located just outside the main flight deck, it was a reasonable size, able to accommodate several soldiers should he ever need to address that many in private. The walls were a silvery blue and his desk, fixed to the floor, occupied a large section near the back wall, facing the door. On the wall to the left of his desk was a single large painting of a futuristic vision of life in space. Along the wall facing his desk, which was emblazoned with the UNF Space Duty insignia, he had his own coffee prep station. When he was working on reports, or having conference transmissions with Command, he needed to be shut off from the rest of the ship and work for hours uninterrupted, if necessary. He liked the solitude. It gave him focus.

Doc appeared in the doorway and rapped his knuckles on the frame. Harris waved his first lieutenant forward, then walked over to shake his hand.

"Doc. Looking tanned, I see," he nodded at him.

"Captain," Doc said, studying him. "You look... a little tired."

"Big night, Doc. I wasn't expecting a call at 0449." Harris returned to his desk and sat down.

"That our mission info?" Doc motioned to the e-file lying on his desk with multiple folders open on the pane.

"Yeah. Our new recruits," Harris said, as he took a blank e-file, laid it beside the other, then copied the information over from one to the other with a swish of his finger.

"When do they arrive?"

"Now. You better start reading." Harris handed the e-file pane over to Doc.

"Yes, sir," Doc turned and headed back toward the door flicking his fingers across the screen and scrolling the files as he went. A look of confusion suddenly crossed his face, and he stopped and turned back. "Saul, you've given me their whole file here?"

Harris stared back. "I want them back on my desk by 1800."

Doc, still looking a little confused, nodded anyway. "Yes, sir," he said, then left.

It wasn't normal procedure to hand over a soldier's entire personnel file to the ship's medic. Doc was usually only granted access to their medical file. However, Harris thought in this case it may just help things along. He figured that if Doc knew a bit more about the new recruits' profiles, he might find connections to help make their transition that bit smoother. After all, they would reach Darwin in just three days, so he didn't have much time for a suitable integration program.

He turned back to the mission file again and tried to read between the lines, wanting to guess what information Command had omitted in their classification. He called up his ultra-thin flat screen and keypad, which rose from a slot in his desk and began numerous searches on Professor Sharley and his crew. After searching for some time, he eventually came across one small piece of information that aroused his interest. It seemed there were certain human rights groups who disapproved of Sharley's rumored methods when it came to "treating" the prisoners in Hell Town. Although the information did not go into much detail, it did suggest his studies on human behavior had enabled him to perfect the manipulation and torture of people on both an emotional and physical scale.

Curious, Harris started looking further into Hell Town. It was the only structure built in the northern hemisphere of Mars, wedged on a plain between the mighty Olympus Mons and Ascraeus Mons. It was the most advanced prison in history for several reasons. Firstly, it was extremely isolated. Any prisoner who managed to escape the inescapable would not survive long on the outside without food or water, neither of which was readily available as the nearest colony was some 3,500 miles away. Of course no escapee could survive outside the purification domes without access to a spacesuit either.

Secondly, the prison itself was fully automated and fully monitored. The structure itself and surrounding areas, were under constant surveillance via a number of sensors and radars. No-one got in or out without iris and fingerprint scans. Prisoners even needed a scan to use the toilet in their cells. If their iris or fingerprints were picked up anywhere they weren't supposed to be, punishment ensued. You stepped a foot out of line, you paid the price. The prisoners learnt this very quickly.

Thirdly, human guards were still used in Hell Town. However, their uniforms were a synthetic sheath, impregnated with a special lightweight metal, making it impervious to both sharp *and* blunt objects. They were also armed with state-of-the-art taser weapons, which could only be activated by fingerprint recognition. The prisoners loathed the system but soon learnt that to fight against it meant they would be introduced to Warden Sharley's system of discipline and punishment. What exactly that was, Harris didn't know, but rumor or not, if human rights groups were against it, he could only imagine that it would not have been pleasant.

He sat there digesting this new information awhile before heading over to his coffee machine. He figured that he still had time for one more strong black coffee before he undertook his pre-flight physical and debriefed the men. He poured a cup and took a sip, feeling a little more alive now than he did this morning, but he had to admit he was looking forward to hitting the sack that evening.

He stood beside his coffee machine, circling his neck around and stretching out his back. He hadn't been this tense in a long time. He wondered if it was all that dancing in the jazz club the night before?

The dream he'd had of Sibbie and Etta flashed through his mind again, but he quickly shook it away with a chuckle. Growing up, he'd obviously listened to his sister, Holly, more than he'd thought he had. *Damn that woman!* He smiled to himself. He was sure he'd feel better tomorrow, once he'd slept the remnants of the hangover away.

He sipped his coffee and listened to how still the ship was. No voices, just the low hum of the ship as it idled, charging up its power stores. Soon enough the men would be arriving and that would all change. It only made him curious, then, as to how Doc was progressing with the new recruits?

Carrie, after clearing through yet another guard post, finally made her way onto Dock 559. It sprawled out in a doglegged fashion before her, angling off to the left behind a large electrical substation. As soon as she cleared the building, she suddenly saw before her the large, brown beast she assumed was the *Aurora*.

*So this is my ship, huh?* She smiled. She ran her eyes over the craft from tail to tip. A couple hundred meters long, and roughly oval-shaped, it had a rounded smooth core and underbelly, with sharp angular wings protruding here and there along its sides and spine. It looked sleek enough for speed, but bulky enough for sheer power, as it loomed large above her. From afar, its brown color looked like rust. As she neared, however, she took a closer look, running her hand along its side and realized that it was some sort of rough protective metal coating, no doubt playing its part when the ship's defensive shield was engaged.

It took her a minute or so to walk down to the boarding entrance. Although the ship was not as large as some docked there, it was certainly the biggest one she'd seen up this close. She wondered how many crew it carried.

After having her ID scanned by yet another guard at the ship's entrance, she stepped over the *Aurora*'s threshold, feeling goosebumps scatter along both her arms. Staring ahead at the Space Duty insignia on the wall opposite, and fighting hard to keep her smile in check, she turned left onto the main corridor as per the guard's instructions, and saw Packham up ahead, waiting outside what she assumed was the medic's rooms.

"Sergeant Packham," she nodded as she approached.

Packham returned the nod. "Corporal Colt's in there now," she motioned to the closed door.

Carrie nodded again and surveyed the long gray metal corridor either side of them. The place seemed deserted and she was jumping out of her skin to explore it all. Before too long Colt emerged from the medic's office. She gave Carrie a smile hello and told her to go through.

As Carrie stepped inside and closed the door behind her, she saw an empty office before her, and doorways to rooms either side of where she stood. The one to the left appeared to be a small hospital, as she saw a row of bed capsules through the doorway, with their pod covers and tubes hanging overhead from the ceiling. She looked through the doorway on her right and saw a line of cabinets against the wall, filled with medical supplies.

"Take a seat. I'll be with you in just a second," she heard a man's American accent call to her from inside the room.

She walked over to the desk, placed her bag on the floor and took a seat. The office in which she sat seemed a little unbalanced. The furniture was all crammed up the one end where the desk was, and it was bare at the other end by the entry door and adjacent doors to the other rooms. The busy end had a medium sized overflowing bookshelf, filled with various medical journals, UNF policy and procedure manuals, and strangely enough, travel guides. There was also an e-filing rack; long thin slots in the wall, like letterbox mouths, where the e-file panes were stored, under pin-code release. The medic's desk itself was covered with a few e-file panes, e-clipboards, and other equipment. She leaned forward a little in her chair, trying to get a better look at the panes, but heard him coming and quickly sat back in her chair.

He walked up to her and put his hand out. She looked up at him.

"How you doing? First Lieutenant Walker," he said in a firm but friendly voice.

She smiled and shook his hand. "Corporal Welles."

"Nice to meet you, Corporal. The guys on the ship call me Doc, so feel free to do the same." He walked around to sit on the opposite side of the desk, opening up what she assumed was her e-file, and began scanning it. "So you had your Space Duty medical just a few weeks ago," he said, reading her file, "and you've never been to space before. Not even on holiday?" he asked, looking up at her.

"No, sir."

"Never been to Station Atlantis?" He seemed quite surprised.

She shook her head again. Space travel was still considered a luxury and something she couldn't afford. And even if she could, she wouldn't be spending it somewhere like the funfair, tourist-park station of Atlantis.

"You're missing out," he smiled. "Great rides!"

She smiled back. He seemed pretty relaxed. As he kept reading through her file, she subtly studied him. He was a lot younger than she'd expected. When she was told to report to the medic she expected either some old guy with gray hair or some straitlaced middle aged man, but Doc looked only a few years older than her. He was good looking, too, with short brown hair, chocolate brown eyes, smooth features and a nice smile. His uniform sleeves were pushed up to his elbows and she noticed his forearms, and wondered how he kept a tan like that in space?

He looked back at her. "Okay, you passed your Space Duty medical with flying colors." He shut her folder and grabbed an e-clip sitting in a tray on his desk. "This physical is routine and fairly simple. We just need to ascertain your physical condition right now, today, before we take off. We check it regularly while we're away, and then we have a closing medical to say that we released you in fine condition," he explained.

Carrie nodded in understanding. "Yes, sir."

Doc grabbed an electronic pen and scrawled her name and the date at the top of the e-clip's electronic form. She guessed he would complete the details on the e-clip and when he was done, simply upload onto the UNF's network, where his handwriting would be deciphered into text, and the signature embedded into the final document. She used to process forms like that all the time in her old administration jobs.

The medic proceeded to ask a string of questions on her past medical history, and when the questions were done, he asked her to move into the examination room for the physical. She walked into the room opposite the hospital's entrance. Rectangular in shape and brightly lit, it was obviously the medic's main working area. There was an examination table against the wall, halfway down the room, and what looked like a small laboratory at the far end. There were various cabinets of medical supplies and equipment taking up the other wall space.

She made her way over to the table and sat up on it next to the blood pressure equipment. Doc came in shortly after with the e-clip. He placed it beside her on the table and pulled over a stool to sit down in front of her.

"Can you hold out your arm for me, please?" he asked, getting the BP equipment ready.

Carrie held out her right arm. He placed a flat, white monitor disc on the inside of her upper arm and began wrapping it tightly with the armband.

"So, I'm told you're quite the shooter?" he said, inflating the armband.

She smiled. "I'm alright."

"Alright? That's not what I hear."

Carrie shrugged. It wasn't her style to boast.

The armband was quite tight around her arm, and the machine beeped and started the deflation slowly.

"You must be looking forward to your first space trip?" he asked, watching her closely to gauge her response.

"Very much, sir. I've wanted this for a long time."

"Yeah, well, it's certainly different to Earth Duty," he said noting down her reading on the e-clip and unwrapping the armband. "Some newcomers get motion sickness, particularly on takeoff, so if you feel queasy just let me know and I'll give you an anti-nausea shot. Make sure you keep your fluids up, too. The air on the ship can dry you out. If you get any headaches or notice anything peculiar, just come and see me," he said, packing away the BP monitor.

"Yes, sir," she nodded.

"Now we've just got to check your vitals. If you can unbutton the top of your shirt," he motioned, "I'll place these suckers on." He held up a couple more of the white discs that he'd just placed on the inside of her arm, then turned and wheeled over a machine that was sitting to his right. Carrie undid the first couple of buttons of her blouse to just above her cleavage. Doc turned back to her.

"Ah, just a little bit more than that," he said, pointing to her stomach. "I need it down to here, soldier."

"Sorry, sir," she said, and undid the extra buttons, feeling a little embarrassed as Doc turned back to her again. She was starting to regret that she didn't wear the singlet underneath her shirt, not to mention the fact that she wore her best push-up bra that day. Underneath the uniform it made her look perky and great, but now it was exposed she was feeling more Playboy Bunny than serious soldier, offering Doc a great view. She made a mental note to pull out her boring bra from here on in.

Doc continued on as though he hadn't noticed, or at least, was pretending he hadn't noticed. He grabbed one disc and placed it halfway between her right shoulder and right breast, another over her heart, and the third he placed further down under her left breast. She immediately heard her heart beating on the monitor beside them, and wondered if maybe it was pumping a little quickly. She didn't want to seem nervous. She studied the machine's screen and saw it was broken up into three monitors, one for each disc. One was clearly registering her heartbeat, the other two she figured were her lungs, the chart's crest rising and falling in time with her breathing.

After recording the readings for a moment, and then testing her lung capacity, by having her blow into a long white tube, Doc looked back to the e-clip at the uploaded results, while she swiftly buttoned her blouse again.

"Right, that all looks fine. I just need to give you one last scan and we're done." He stood and walked to the opposite wall. "If you could just stand here and look straight ahead at the wall," he told her.

Carrie walked over to a marker on the floor, and did as requested, noticing him eyeing her carefully. He appeared to be judging her height. She heard a buzzing sound and saw a silver lever jutting out from the wall, which moved down in line with the top of her head. She glanced back at him, trying to judge his height and figured he was maybe just shy of six foot.

"This machine scans your brain," Doc told her. "It also reads your eye, ear and nose health."

She heard another noise and the lever extended out from the wall to become a metal arm. A series of metal fingers protruded from the arm and they began moving back and forth around her skull rapidly, scanning her.

"Some people have issues with their ears up there," Doc told her. "Again, if you have any problems, come and see me and I'll sort it out."

She nodded in reply, eyeing the silver fingers carefully as they finished scanning her and retracted back into the arm, and then the wall. The e-clip lit up again and Doc checked the results.

"Okay, we're done. If you just want to wait outside with the others, I'll be out in a moment to show you to your quarters."

Carrie joined the two women outside and Doc emerged soon after. He led them down the corridor to a T-junction, took a right, then a left, and continued on down. Carrie noticed that the corridors were all the same.

Gray metal flooring, with gray metal walls, occasionally emblazoned with the UN Space Forces insignia. It looked like any other military facility; formal and functional.

"These are the soldier's quarters," Doc said. "You'll need your pass to access many parts of this ship. Some areas are always open though, like the mess hall, the training facility, and generally the flight deck as it's always manned." He led them down to the furthermost door on the right. "We bunk up two to a room on this ship, but for this mission the three of you will be bunking together. Can I have one of your passes, please?"

Packham was closest, so she stepped up to the access panel and swiped the card whilst it was still attached to her waist. The door unlocked and slid open.

"There you go," Doc told them. "Unpack and settle in, soldiers. The beds have been assigned, so look for your name."

Carrie followed Packham into the room, but Colt stopped at the door.

"When do we get to meet the rest of the crew, sir?" she asked.

"There will be a briefing at 1700, but you're to remain here in your quarters until I come and get you."

"Yes, sir," Colt said entering the room, as Doc turned and walked away.

The door closed behind them, and the three women scanned their quarters. It was a little snug. There was a bunk bed against one wall and a single bed against the other. Off to the side, there was a door leading to an en suite bathroom, again a little on the small side but not bad considering some of the bathrooms Carrie had seen over the years. Colt walked over to the single bed and saw her name, threw her kitbag on it and sat down. Carrie saw she had the bottom bunk-bed, so she dumped her bag, and they each sat on their beds for a moment taking in the room.

"Well, this is it ladies," Colt said, nodding to herself as she looked around the room. "Looks like we'll be getting to know each other *real* well."

# 4

# The Crew

Harris was just getting his things together when Doc knocked on his door.

"The men have arrived and all pre-flight physicals have been completed," Doc told him. "They're waiting in the mess hall."

"And the new recruits?"

"Confined to quarters until further orders."

Harris nodded. "Good."

"Do you want me to go get them?" he asked.

"No," Harris said firmly, "I want to have a quick word to the men first."

"Yes, sir," Doc nodded.

Harris headed for the door. His lieutenant stood aside as he passed, then the two of them walked down the corridor side by side.

"So, what's your take on the new recruits?" Harris broke the silence.

Doc glanced at him. "They've got impressive files and they passed their physicals."

Harris looked straight ahead. "So what's your take on the new recruits?" he asked again.

Doc shot him another glance and shrugged. "They're alright."

Harris looked over at Doc, arching his eyebrow.

Doc elaborated. "There may be some teething issues," he shrugged. "Some of the guys might get a little territorial and based on the new recruits' personnel files, I'm sure they'll stand their ground."

"Mm-hmm," Harris said unenthusiastically in agreement, as they arrived at the mess hall. "Ever wanted to be a fireman?" he asked Doc.

As he entered, the seven men gathered in the room stood and saluted. Harris walked over to the mess hall counter in front of them, while Doc stopped by the door.

"At ease, gentlemen," he said firmly.

The men took their seats across the two rectangular tables and waited to be addressed. As Harris stood before them, he looked at each one, studying them as he always did, wondering what sort of leave they'd had, and whether they were ready for duty. He eyed Pete Smith, the young British guy, who was the comms tech and p-star of the ship. Jacob Hunter, the ship's New Zealander pilot. Farris Carter, the South African smart-ass, but a good solid soldier nonetheless. James McKinley, a fellow American who was a good, hard soldier, and one the others tended to follow, albeit probably out of fear. Marcus Louis, the strong, black Frenchman, who also happened to be an amazing cook. Alexander Bolkov, the Russian co-pilot, a man of few words, but whose huge size spoke volumes. And lastly, James-Jay Brown, a big, tough, African American tank, who not only knew his way around the *Aurora*'s engine, but also knew his way out of a fight.

For whatever reason, this team worked. Although Doc, Carter and McKinley had been on the *Aurora* the longest, Smith, the newest recruit, had still been aboard for a period of nine months. For nine whole months, he'd been building this team up to what it was, and there had been no change in this lineup. That was, until now.

"I take it you all enjoyed your leave?" Harris asked, making small talk.

"It was a little on the short side, captain," McKinley answered. Being third in rank behind Doc, he often spoke on behalf of the men.

"Don't I know it," Harris said flatly.

"So why the rush to get us back then, captain?" Carter piped up in that strong South African accent of his. "Couldn't the UNF survive without us?"

"Apparently not," Harris answered. "I'll brief you on our mission in just a moment. Firstly, I've got some news for you all."

The men quickly glanced at each other, before Carter quipped, "You getting married, captain?!"

Some of the men sniggered.

Harris gave Carter a deadpan look. "We have three new recruits joining us for this mission, gentlemen."

His soldiers looked at each other again, this time in surprise.

"New recruits, captain?" Hunter's Kiwi accent piped up this time, as he crossed his arms defensively.

"We don't need more men, captain," McKinley said with a sly smile. "We're already the best unit out there." Carter laughed and held out his hand, and McKinley slapped it.

Harris waited a second. The men settled down and looked at him.

"There are no men joining us on this mission, gentlemen, but there will be three *female* soldiers added to our crew."

"What?" Carter blurted out.

"Are you serious?" Louis's French accent piped up.

Brown's eyebrows rose, but he said nothing. Instead, he glanced over at Doc then back at Harris.

"You're pulling our leg, captain!" Carter continued.

Pete Smith laughed. "I guess I'm not the p-star anymore!"

Bolkov said nothing, but the look on his face was not impressed. McKinley just kept staring back at Harris, mirroring his captain's deadpan face, although his eyes shone with curiosity.

Harris gave them a moment, but that was all they were getting. "You done?" he asked firmly. They quietened down.

"We have three new *female* recruits," he spelled it out. "We are taking part in a test-case for the UNF. They are experienced soldiers. They will be joining us in just a moment and you *will* accept them into the team for this mission."

The men sat in near silence for a moment, soaking it in, before Louis decided to speak up again. "So, captain, three *women*. This must mean Smith and I are no longer on kitchen duty, no?"

Smith chuckled.

Carter looked around. "Command must have decided to give us a little mobile R & R, gents, to make up for our leave being cut short, eh? They going to pour us drinks, captain? Do they offer a topless service?" he laughed, some of the others joining in.

Harris kept his face deadpan. "Gentlemen, I do not need to remind you how the UNF feels about discrimination or harassment of any kind, do I?"

"C'mon, captain," McKinley began, "what the hell are they going to do around here?"

"I suggest you have a conversation with them and find that out," Harris retorted.

"So where are they sleeping?" Hunter piped up again.

"They can sleep in my room!" Carter answered. Laughter erupted.

"Yeah, right, Carter, 'cause you the man!" Brown said sarcastically, cocking his head to the side, eyeing him.

"Hey, I do alright, Brownie!" Carter hissed back.

"This is a joke, captain, no?" Louis seemed to be trying to find a reason for the shock announcement.

Doc finally decided to speak up. "Guys, just give them a chance. You might be surprised."

"You've met 'em?" McKinley's fiery blue eyes shot accusingly across the room.

"Yes, I have," Doc answered firmly.

"Well, Doc's the one to ask, then!" Carter smiled. "How were their physicals, man?"

"Ooh, yes!" Louis smiled. "'Ow about their lung tests, Doc? Hmmm?" He held his hands out in front of his chest as though he were holding a large pair of breasts. The men started laughing, and Doc shook his head at them.

"No, they're probably big beefy dykes!" Smith called out.

"Just 'ow you like them, Bulk, no?" Louis said, slapping the Russian on the back.

Bolkov snarled back at Louis.

Harris had had enough. He decided to end it.

"ENOUGH!" he bellowed. The men fell silent and paid him due attention. "These three soldiers will work alongside you, they will train with you, they will eat here in the mess with you, work out in the gym with you, stay down in the soldiers' quarters with you. This *is* real. This *is* happening, and you *will* accept this. This is my order to you. Do you understand?"

There was a slight hesitation but Brown, Hunter, Smith and Bolkov answered, "Yes, sir."

"DO YOU UNDERSTAND?" Harris shouted, looking directly at McKinley, Carter and Louis.

"Yes, sir," they finally answered.

Harris stared them all down for a moment, then he turned to Doc. "Bring them in."

Carrie, Packham and Colt had settled into their quarters, their gear unpacked into the small lockers standing against the wall outside their en suite. They each sat on their beds, while Packham began throwing a rubber ball into the air and catching it and Colt began sticking a few photos of her family up on the wall beside her bed. There was a photo of her parents, younger brother and sister, and a photo of her twin sister with her husband and their two little kids.

Carrie was staring at them. "I don't see any eligible young bachelors there, Colt. No boyfriend?"

"No," Colt replied with a tinge of sadness to her voice, "he didn't get into Space Duty, so he ended it."

"He ended it?" Carrie asked, curious.

"I don't know," Colt shrugged. "Guess he couldn't handle the fact that I was better than he was!" She flashed a grin at them.

Carrie and Packham laughed.

"Hey, I tell you what, that Doc is pretty fine for a white boy!" Colt said as she turned back around to them.

Packham gave a musical little laugh.

"You don't think he's cute?" Colt inquired, looking between the two of them.

Packham chuckled. "Yeah, he's cute. He's not my type though."

"Oh, yeah. And what's your type?" Colt asked her.

The sergeant shrugged. "I don't know. Older, I guess."

"Well, he's older than you," Colt replied.

"Ah, but not old enough." Packham winked at her.

"You like them gray, huh?" Colt eyed her strangely, then looked down at Carrie. "What about you? Doc's cute, right?"

"Me?" Carrie said, taken aback.

"Ooh, she's not saying anything! Silence speaks louder than words, girl."

Carrie shrugged. "He's alright," she said nonchalantly.

"Alright? No, he's pretty fine for a white boy," she repeated, then looked at Packham. "Although he's a little *too* white for me."

They cracked up laughing.

"So you got a man?" Colt asked Carrie.

"No." She shook her head.

"You?" she asked Packham.

Packham shook her head.

"Yeah, well, it's pretty damn hard trying to keep one when you're out in space, that's for sure," Colt continued as she put the last of her photos up. It was one of another young male, maybe early 20s.

"Who's that?" Carrie asked.

"That's my brother, Malik."

"The same one that's in the other photo you just put up?"

"No, I have two brothers. Malik's gone now, though. Stepped on a land mine in Africa on Earth Duty."

"I'm sorry to hear that," Carrie said softly. "You'd think they would've found them all by now."

"Yeah. I nearly quit when he died, but for some reason I hung in there. I guess it comes with the territory," she said softly, smoothing down the sides of the photo.

"How long ago?" Carrie asked curiously.

"Two years. February 14th, 2073. Can you believe it? Valentine's Day. My mama sure got her heart broken that day, let me tell you." Colt turned around and sat on the bed with her back against the wall. "Are you two putting up any pictures of your families?"

Carrie shook her head, "No. There's only me and my dad left, anyway. My mum died when I was 14. I don't have any siblings."

"Oh," Colt said sympathetically. It was probably hard for her to imagine life without a large bustling family around her. "What about you, Packham?"

The sergeant put the ball down and moved to the edge of the bunk. "I have an older sister and a younger brother. I speak to them occasionally. That's about it. We're not really that close."

Colt nodded, mind ticking over, before she decided to change the subject. "So I wonder why they're keeping us in here?"

Carrie nodded. "Strange, isn't it?"

Packham seemed to think about this for a second and then burst out laughing. "We've probably been thrown onto a whaling ship."

Carrie and Colt both looked at her puzzled.

"You know? A whaling ship. Full of sperm whales. Full of seamen? That's what they call an all-male crew. There's only about 40 percent of ships in Space Duty with female soldiers on them, and even then, they tend to place them on the cargo ships or docking stations, or they're pilots like me that don't really mix with the other crew. Hardcore mission work is still generally only handled by the guys on these whaling ships. Very few females get to do the really cool stuff. And this is a test case, right? My guess is that they've put us on a whaling ship and they're probably breaking it to the men as we speak." She laughed again.

Colt stared at Packham oddly.

"Can you imagine their faces?" Packham said. "They'll be so disappointed."

"Or excited?" Colt added.

"So, we can probably expect some grief then," Carrie said.

Just then they heard a knock at the door. It was 1655.

"Briefing time, soldiers," Doc called through door.

Colt opened the door and gave a nod to Doc, then turned and flashed the other two women a subtle, cheeky smile.

"Follow me, please," Doc said, taking off down the corridor.

As they made their way down the corridor, Carrie wondered what Captain Harris had told the men, preparing them for these three women who were about to walk in and break up their little group.

Arriving at the mess hall, Doc entered the room, followed by Packham, then Colt, and then Carrie who felt her heart racing a little. As she walked through the door, she heard Doc announce. "The new recruits, captain!"

As Packham and Colt moved in and to the left, they cleared a view for Carrie. She saw a group of soldiers sitting across two tables, sizing up each one of them as they walked in. Some were staring, some were glaring, and one or two cast a sleazy eye over them. Most did so with their arms folded across their chests.

Captain Harris also watched from over by the mess counter, but his face was hard to read. Doc moved to stand a few feet away from him, and the women lined up alongside. Carrie heard one of the men start laughing and mutter something, and she looked over to see a man with a strawberry blond crew cut cover his mouth, trying to stifle his amusement. This made a few of the other men smirk in response. Harris glared at the man and he jammed his lips together trying to stop. Carrie felt like the new student in school, forced to stand at the front of the class to be introduced as she had done many times as a child, as she and her mother moved about with her father's Earth Duty career.

Harris walked over to the women, then looked back to the men. "Gentlemen, meet our new recruits!" he said firmly. "We have Corporal Carrie Welles, Corporal Sabrina Colt and Sergeant Sarah Packham." He pointed to each of them in turn with his right hand. Then he raised his left arm and pointed toward the men. "New recruits," he continued, "meet the rest of the team. In order of seniority, you've already met Doc, aka, First Lieutenant Daniel Walker."

Doc gave them a nod.

"Then we have Second Lieutenant James McKinley..." Carrie noted he was a big guy with square shoulders and blond hair, who stared back at them with cold, blue, intimidating eyes.

"...and First Sergeant Farris Carter." He was the strawberry blond who'd been laughing at them.

Harris continued. "First Sergeant Jacob Hunter..." He was a good-looking guy, with light brown hair and chiseled cheekbones. He looked a little arrogant, though, eyeing them as though they'd just told a bad joke.

"...Staff Sergeant Alexander Bolkov..." He looked a lot older than the others, and big and bulky. He didn't bother looking at the women at all.

"...and Staff Sergeant James-Jay Brown." He was, she assumed, an African American, large in size, who simply gave them a blank stare.

"Sergeant Marcus Louis..." He had dark skin, almost black, and was built like a weightlifter. He sat there smirking at them.

"...and Private First-Class Pete Smith." He was the youngest of the group, with blond hair, dark blue eyes and a youthful grin upon his face.

Harris dropped his arm and looked back at the women. "Take a seat, soldiers."

The women fell out of line and took up seats at the tables, while Harris moved over to a keypad on the wall beside the mess counter and appeared to be logging into the ship's systems. Carrie used the opportunity to study him more closely. She'd noted how tall he was at their first meeting, but she hadn't quite realized how big his physique was until now. Judging by his arms alone, in the gray UNF T-shirt he wore, he looked strong and very fit. He had the right physical attributes for a soldier, now she was curious to see what his leadership was like.

A screen suddenly descended from the ceiling over the mess counter. Displayed upon it was a satellite picture of the Earth's solar system.

"Our mission, gentlemen… *and* ladies," the captain caught himself, "is to head out to space station Z076, aka Station Darwin. It's the most isolated space station we have, located off Mars and not far from The Belt." He hit a button on the keypad, and the satellite zoomed in, giving a closer picture of the station's location.

"Command lost comms with the station at approximately 0217 yesterday, September 19th," Harris continued. "Six hours later, the automatic distress beacon triggered. Command has been attempting to make contact with the station but has so far failed to get a response. So, it's our job to head out there and find out what's going on. Command are so far assuming this is simply a technical malfunction and that the crew are fine, but there could be something very wrong. Fact is, we won't know until we dock and board that station."

He pressed another button and a picture of a man who looked to be in his mid-to-late 50s appeared on the screen. He had longish gray hair, dark brown eyes and a large angular nose. "This is Professor Ray Sharley. He heads up a team of eight at the station. From the limited information I have, I can say that they were working on various items of a technical and biological nature for the UNF. I can't inform you about these items as they're all classified, so your guess is as good as mine. To sum up, I don't have a lot to tell you. We're flying fairly blind on this one. Until we get there, we've got no idea what to expect. Could be nothing, could be something. Now, I'm sure you have a lot of questions, but are there any I can actually answer for you?"

Carrie watched as the men moved around slightly, taking it in. Brown eventually broke the silence.

"Captain, you say it's a scientific station. Does this mean it's filled with nutty professors or are there soldiers up there?"

A couple of the men chuckled.

"They are all members of the UNF, so they've been through the basic training, but they have scientific backgrounds. Their focus has always been on developing programs for the UNF, not fighting, not personal defense. So

I guess my answer is, mainly nutty professors," Harris advised. "Which means, if they *are* in trouble, they could be needing our help."

"Captain, when you say biological," the one named Louis spoke in a thick French accent, "I assume you mean biological weapons?"

Harris shrugged, "Well, your guess is as good as mine, Louis, but if I was a betting man…"

"So we'll go in fully masked, no?" Louis continued.

"I will provide you with our plan of attack at another briefing when we are closer to docking, and when, hopefully, we'll know a bit more. Rest assured, Command would not knowingly send us to a station with this level of classification if there could be something detrimental to our health. Regardless, I'm going to do everything I can to find out more about this, and I'll have Smith and the flight deck continually searching the frequencies and trying to raise the station. So we'll see what comes up. Any other questions?"

"Yes, sir," McKinley spoke up. "I want to know why we were called in from leave to do this. If they're assuming it's just a technical difficulty, that is?"

"I guess they're sending us in, in case it's not," Harris said matter-of-factly.

"It must be serious, McKinley," Carter's Afrikaans voice sounded deathly serious. "They've sent three *big*, *strong* recruits to protect us!"

Most of the soldiers burst out laughing, and Louis gave the South African a high-five. Doc looked around at the men and then back at Harris, whose face was a mask. Carrie glanced at the other two women. Packham sat there smirking at the joke, while Colt looked directly Harris, not showing any emotion whatsoever.

"Are there any other questions?" Harris continued.

There was silence.

"Good, then let's move on, shall we? Hunter, Bolkov, stand up!" the captain ordered.

The two soldiers stood, and Bolkov looked even bigger now he was standing. He appeared to be early 40s, with slicked back dark hair and a five o'clock shadow. Hunter was younger, maybe early 30s, about 5' 11" or so, with a fit physique, but something about his body language screamed that he knew it.

"New recruits, First Sergeant Hunter is our chief pilot, and Staff Sergeant Bolkov is our co-pilot."

"Sergeant Packham, stand up!" Harris ordered.

She did so.

"Gentlemen," Harris continued, looking at Hunter and Bolkov, "Sergeant Packham here, is an SD-A class pilot..."

Everyone eyed her curiously and she glanced back at them, unaffected.

"Sergeant Packham will be shadowing you throughout this mission," Harris continued. "Whenever you are on the flight deck, she is to be present. You are responsible for her induction and ensuring she is up to speed with everything she needs to know as a pilot on this ship. Do you understand?"

Hunter and Bolkov exchanged a look. "Yes, sir," they said in unison, although it lacked enthusiasm.

"Take a seat," Harris ordered. They did. "First Sergeant Carter, Staff Sergeant Brown, stand up!"

They did so. Brown, like Bolkov, looked even bigger now he was standing. He appeared to be just shy of 6', with interesting black tattoos along his forearms. Carter, the South African, was about 5' 10" and stocky, his green eyes still finding humor in the situation.

"Corporal Colt, stand up!" Harris bellowed.

Colt did so, and the three standing soldiers eyed each other.

Harris looked at Colt. "First Sergeant Carter is in charge of the engine room. He, along with Staff Sergeant Brown, the ship's engineer, liaise with our pilots on any issues that arise and perform regular tests on all the equipment, including the onboard weaponry." He then turned to Brown and Carter. "Corporal Colt has strong technical skills and knows her way around electronics and hardwiring. She will work alongside your team. You two gentlemen will be in charge of Corporal Colt's induction onto this ship. Do you understand?"

"Yes, sir," came their reply. Brown said it well enough, but Carter had a stupid grin and was almost laughing when he answered.

"Sergeant Louis, Private First Class Smith, stand up," Harris called, while Colt, Brown and Carter sat down again.

Louis and Smith stood. Louis was about 5' 9", his torso bulging with those weight-lifter muscles. He had clean, dreadlocked hair to his shoulders, and bright white teeth that stood out against his midnight skin.

Smith was taller than Louis, at about 5' 10" or so, and although muscular, was quite small body-wise, in comparison with the other soldiers. Carrie picked him to be barely twenty. He must be good at what he does to be selected so young.

"New recruits, these two men work alongside Doc, who is in charge of the ship's medical and general stores. They take care of the meals here in the mess hall, and Private First Class Smith is also our comms–tech wiz. Sit down, gentlemen."

Carrie looked at the back of McKinley's head. They were the only two yet to be called.

"Second Lieutenant McKinley stand up," Harris called and he did, albeit slowly, reluctantly. McKinley was tall, around the same height as the captain, with a decent build to match, although not pure bulk like Brown or Bolkov, his physique was more defined. His longish blond hair was tied back in a small ponytail that trailed just past the nape of his neck, and he wore a silver band, together with one woven of brown leather on his right wrist.

"Corporal Welles, stand up," Harris ordered.

Carrie did so, aware that everyone was now looking at her. Everyone except McKinley, that is, who kept his back turned.

"Second Lieutenant McKinley is in charge of the weapons store on this ship." Harris eyed her firmly. "He is also our resident sharpshooter." He turned to McKinley. "Corporal Welles is also a sharpshooter. She will shadow you in the weapons store and you will be in charge of her induction onto this ship. Do you understand?"

McKinley hesitated and then answered, "Yes, sir." He didn't turn around to make eye contact with Carrie but instead took his seat.

"Good!" said Harris. "You know who everyone is and who you're working with. Go now, in your teams, and make your final checks. I want this ship ready for departure, soldiers. Dismissed." With that, Harris turned to the keypad, sent the screen back up into the cavity it came from, gathered his things, and left the room.

Everyone else slowly stood and started heading for the door to go to their posts. Not one of the men, Carrie noticed, looked in the direction of, or bothered to speak to, any of the women.

# 5

# Learning to Fly

Harris sat down at the desk in his office. It was only one mission, so he figured it was best to just throw them in the deep end and let them get on with it. Besides, the ship needed readying. He knew the Dock Officers would already have the ship's power cells charged, and have all the required cargo loaded, but the team had to double-check that all items were accounted for and undertake mechanical and electrical checks to ensure everything was in order. Their departure time was looming, and until they were on their way, he couldn't relax.

He began logging into the Command portal for his own last check with his superiors before departing. Within moments the screen beeped and revealed both Colonel Isaack and Professor Martin awaiting his transmission.

"Captain Harris, how did the introduction of the new recruits go?" Isaack launched into conversation.

"It went," Harris said plainly. "They're busy preparing the ship for departure now, sir."

"Good," Isaack said swishing his fingers about on an e-file pane that was lying on the table in front of him. "Your pilots are being sent the exact coordinates and docking codes as we speak. They've been given enough fuel for a hyperflight there and back, which means you should reach the station in approximately 53 hours from departure." Isaack looked up at Harris to see if he understood.

"Yes, sir," he acknowledged.

"When you arrive at the station standard protocols apply, and I reiterate that the female recruits are not to board the Darwin without my authorization. We're clear on that?" Isaack looked sternly down the screen at him.

"Yes, sir, I'm clear on the order," Harris said, staring back at Isaack, "but I must say that I'm still quite unclear as to *why* they can't board, sir. Their files looked decent."

"As I mentioned earlier, Captain Harris—" Isaack began.

"Colonel Isaack, if I may answer this query for Captain Harris?" Professor Martin interjected, leaning forward across the table.

"Of course." Isaack sat back in his seat.

"Captain, where possible we would like the female recruits to avoid any actual conflict. This improves our results for the test case, you understand?"

"So what exactly are you testing, then? That they can survive a flight out past Mars toward The Belt border?" Harris felt his tiredness starting to show through. "I've got news for you, Professor Martin, females can survive that, just as well as men can."

Martin gave a humoring laugh. "Yes, we know that, Captain Harris, but we would like our records to be spotless nonetheless. If they avoid conflict, *should* there be any, then they are unharmed and our trial is successful. This makes the diversity people happy and is good for business, you understand. It's what makes great PR."

"Okay. Can I ask why you've given me three solid soldiers, on file at least, if all they're going to do is just hang back? Why didn't you send me three p-stars?"

"Well, captain," Professor Martin pushed his glasses further up onto his nose, "Corporal Welles hasn't been into space before, so technically she's a, as you call it, a *p-star*, and Corporal Colt is still relatively inexperienced having only worked on cargo ships for four months."

"That's true," Harris agreed, "but both have several years' experience on Earth Duty. I would've thought that these women would be great examples to put through this test, particularly if there are unfriendlies awaiting us... *should* there be any conflict, of course," he mimicked Martin.

Isaack sat forward again. "Captain Harris, the order is clear."

"Colonel Isaack, I can't speak for the other two women, but this wouldn't have anything to do with the fact that Corporal Welles has an ex-colonel for a father, would it? A father who was not only a UNF Space Duty colonel, but an 'Original' to boot. Is she just here for the glory of her old man? For the UNF to leverage off?"

"Colonel Welles has been retired for some years now," Isaack responded. "He no longer has any pull here at Command whatsoever."

Martin nodded in agreement. "I can assure you that it is sheer coincidence that Colonel Welles's daughter is on your ship. She was placed there because she ticked all the boxes we needed. She was merely in the right place at the right time, captain."

Harris stared at the screen for a while mulling it over, but he bought what they said, despite his tiredness and irritability.

Isaack, sensing Harris was done, continued on. "You've got your flight plans and your ETA. We'll hook up again right before you dock. Do you have any more questions?"

Harris shook his head. "No, sir."

"Then have a good journey, captain." Isaack signed off.

"Yes, good luck, captain," Professor Martin joined in.

Harris gave a simple nod, logged out of the portal, and the screen slid back down into his desk. He stretched out in his chair, lengthening his back, and couldn't help but note that his stomach still had that strange feeling within it.

Carrie relented, staring at McKinley. "What would you like me to do, lieutenant?"

She'd followed him out of the mess hall and along the corridor to the weapons store. Not once had he looked around to see if she was following, whether she knew where she was going or whether she was lost. He didn't look at her and he certainly didn't speak to her. At first, she decided to play his game. She followed him, hanging back enough to be out of his sight, to check whether or not he was going to attempt to look around at her. He didn't. When they arrived at the store, he tapped a code into the panel, swiped his pass and the door opened. He went in, still not glancing behind him.

She'd followed him inside and looked around. The store was rectangular in shape and had metal cases lining one wall and smaller wooden crates the other, with racks in the middle to stack the weapons on once they were readied. Along the back wall were cabinets that looked to hold bullasers, top-line vests that offered protection against both bullet and laserfire, and she also saw oxygen backpacks. She watched as McKinley took a scanner gun from a hook on the wall and headed over to one of the metal cases. He flicked the metal catches open, examined the laser-fire rifle inside, then closed the lid again. He scanned the barcode on the case, checked the reading on the scanner, then hit a button on the scanner's keypad, which made it beep, then he moved onto the next crate. This was when Carrie decided enough was enough and asked him what he wanted her to do.

He looked over at her as if she'd just walked in and stared for a moment. His eyes were a piercing blue, and coupled with his messy longish, blond hair, it gave him quite a fierce look. Carrie stared firmly back, though. She wasn't going to let him intimidate her.

He chuckled to himself and shook his head. "I have to check that the weapons we have here are the ones Command told us they've packed," he said, speaking to her like she was an annoying little sister and continuing on with his work.

"So, what would you like me to do?" she asked again in a firmer voice.

He looked at her, then walked over to the wall, picked up another scanner and tossed it at her. She caught it.

"Start with those crates over there," he pointed to the wooden ones, "That's the ammunition for the non-laser weapons, and battery packs for laser guns. You open the crate, check the type and the count, then scan the crate and see if the reading is the same, then you click 'OK'. It feeds into a central computer that tallies it against what Command claim they've packed. I take it you know your ammo?" he asked condescendingly.

"I think I'll be right," she answered, then turned and walked over to one of the wooden crates. She noticed they were nailed shut and looked around for something to open them with. Spying a crowbar lying on top of one of the boxes, she collected it and moved back to the crate, jimmying it between the lid and the base. She pushed down on the crowbar and a small gap appeared. She pushed again with all her weight and bounced it, forcing it open wider, then moved the crowbar along a little to widen another spot. She could feel McKinley watching her, as her face flushed warm with the strain.

He overtly sighed and chuckled again, then dropped his scanner and walked over. "Move," he said, grabbing the crowbar from her hands, and bumping her out of the way with his elbow, as he took over. He gave one hard nudge and it popped open. He walked to the next crate, jimmied it, and popped it open. He walked onto the third and fourth and did the same. "That ought to start you off," he said, throwing the crowbar on the floor by her feet and returning to his side of the room.

"I had it covered, thank you!" she told him.

McKinley gave a short, sharp laugh. "We don't have all day, corporal."

Carrie swallowed what she wanted to say, turned to the crate and opened it. It was filled with boxes of clips for a standard UNF-issue handgun. She counted the boxes and scanned the crate, then checked the reading. It was correct. She hit the "OK" button, closed the lid, and went onto the next one.

She checked the next few boxes quickly, spurred on by the need to prove herself. As soon as she finished the fourth box, McKinley walked back over and opened another five. He did them in no time at all; a slight jimmy, a hard nudge and then a loud: *pop... pop... pop... pop*. She was sure he was doing it superfast just to prove he could. She let him, though. She wasn't going to react. When he was done he threw the crowbar on the ground and continued with his boxes. This went on until all the boxes were done. Not a word was spoken.

When he finished his cases, he keyed some data into the scanner, which beeped, and a touch screen panel on the wall near the door lit up. He walked over to it, and ran his eyes over it for a moment, then he made his way over to the bullasers and oxy tanks to begin a count on them. When he was done, he sat on a pile of crates and watched her, looking bored, while she finished the last of her boxes.

When she was done, she closed the last crate and stood up. McKinley approached and took the scanner from her, following the same sequence he'd done for his earlier items to make the screen by the door light up again. He then moved back over to the screen and studied it carefully. She was sure he was checking to see if she'd made any mistakes. She hadn't.

Giving nothing away, he raised his hand to the touch screen, ran his fingers over it for a moment, swirling and tapping here and there. The screen emitted a few more beeps, then seemed to shut itself down. As soon as the screen was off, he exited the store. Carrie shook her head and laughed to herself. She couldn't believe he was going to continue on like this, but she wasn't going to give up, so she followed him out the door.

They walked along the corridors and down into the bowel of the ship, which was crowded with cargo, a small escape pod emblazoned with the name *Borealis*, rows of electrical panels and the onboard weaponry. Eventually they came across the engine team. Carter was typing something into a wafer-thin screen panel, while Brown and Colt were standing by one of the electrical panels, checking things over. Carrie exchanged a look with Colt that indicated she was having an equally good time.

"Ah! Arizona!" Carter looked up from his screen.

McKinley walked up to him. "Weapons store checks are done. Results should be with you now."

Carter tapped at his screen for a moment. "Affirmative. Results received. Sending off with the onboard weaponry now."

"Have fun, ladies," McKinley smiled sarcastically as he turned and walked off. Carrie followed him, and when they arrived back up at the main corridors, she decided to break the silence.

"So, where are we headed, lieutenant?"

He turned around and gave her a look as if to say: *You still here?*

"Weapons are checked. We're done," he said plainly.

"So, what about the induction?" Carrie asked.

He stopped, turned and looked at her again, his blue eyes reflecting some kind of amusement.

"Captain Harris instructed you to provide me with an induction to this ship?" she reminded him firmly.

He chuckled. "I know what the captain said, corporal." He continued walking for a moment, then pointed off to the left at a set of double doors he was passing, "That's the ship's training facility. We've got a fully equipped gym and shooting range in there. You might want to check it out..." he glanced over his shoulder, "and practice," he smirked.

Carrie's eyes narrowed. *Suck it up*, she told herself. *Suck it up.*

The rest of her induction was much the same. He pointed her to the various doors of the places she needed to know, but never actually took her inside. When he was done, he swaggered back to the mess hall, walked up to the counter and started talking to Louis and Smith who had been checking the kitchen stocks. She couldn't hear what McKinley was saying, but the three men started laughing and looking over in her direction. She stood at the door for a moment, undecided as to what to do, but suddenly noticed an observation window on the wall opposite. She gravitated toward it and peered out. She couldn't see much other than the next ship to theirs, a little way off, but wondered just what kind of view it would provide when they were finally out in space.

She heard the soldiers laugh again, and turned back, just as Doc entered the mess hall. The medic glanced at the three men at the counter, saw them laughing in her direction, then he veered over toward her.

"Corporal Welles," he greeted her. "How'd it go? Looks like you got through your checks pretty quickly." He looked at his watch.

Carrie thought about her answer before she gave it, practicing some restraint. "Yeah, we did. We just got down to it and got straight through it, sir."

Doc looked as though he suspected she wasn't being completely honest. "And your induction? How did that go?"

She smiled sardonically, unable to hold back this time. "I saw a lot of doors that led into a lot of rooms that I didn't actually get to see."

"Oh..." Doc said, trailing off as he looked at the men then back at her. "Maybe he'll give you a full induction after we take off."

Carrie gave Doc a doubtful look. "Sure, sir."

The medic scratched the back of his head in thought. "Listen, Lieutenant McKinley takes a while to warm to people, but he's a good guy and a good soldier."

Carrie scoffed. "He's a prick!" she shot out but immediately regretted it.

Doc let out a laugh and nodded. "He can be. But he's also your senior officer, corporal. Hang in there, it's only been a couple of hours."

Just then Doc's name was heard being spoken in the conversation between the three men at the counter, and more laughter ensued. Doc turned and saw they were looking over at the two of them.

"Excuse me," he said, as he turned and walked toward them. They had a few brief words before Louis and Smith went back to checking their stocks, then Doc and McKinley seemed to have a private word for a moment.

Soon enough the engine room team entered the mess hall. A sense of relief settled over Carrie, and Colt must've felt the same way too, because she headed straight in her direction.

Harris made his way to the mess hall at 1840 where he knew the soldiers would be waiting after completing their final checks. When he entered he noticed the team sitting in two very distinct groups, with the women sitting on their own in the far corner of the second table. *To be expected,* he told himself.

He pulled his personal data port from his belt, and brought up the necessary screen to enter his authorization for takeoff.

"Engine room team," he called loudly, his voice booming. "Have your checks been completed?"

Carter stood up. "Sir, yes sir! All engine room equipment and onboard weapons are A-OK, sir!" he boomed back, and then sat down.

Harris tapped the screen of his PDP, locking in the authorization, then looked up again. "Flight deck team! Have your checks been completed?"

Hunter stood this time. "Yes, sir! All equipment on the flight deck has been checked and is A-OK, sir!"

Harris tapped the screen again, as Hunter took his seat. "Weapon store team! Have your checks been completed?"

McKinley stood. "Yes, sir! All weapon stores have been checked and are A-OK, sir!" He sat back down.

Again Harris tapped his PDP. "Stores team! Have your checks been completed?"

This time Doc stood. "Yes, sir! All medical and general stores have been checked and are A-OK, sir!"

Harris prodded his PDP a few more times, before clicking it back on his belt holster. "Alright, soldiers!" he bellowed, glancing down at his watch. "We have fifteen minutes and counting! Assume your departure positions on the flight deck!"

Carrie watched as Harris left the mess hall. The remaining soldiers followed protocol, staying seated until the pilots, Hunter and Bolkov, along with Packham, had risen and left the room. Carrie and Colt exchanged a glance, then followed the rest of the men out, as they walked quickly and silently toward the flight deck.

As they reached the deck, Carrie stood at the door, not really knowing where to go. This was one of the doors that McKinley had shown her, but of course they had not gone inside. The flight deck was set out in a tiered format, with stairs downward, just left of center. On the lower tier she saw Hunter and Bolkov seated at the control panel positioned in front of the ship's large observation window, hitting buttons and turning various dials. Packham sat off to the side, observing them. On the next tier, in a central seat at a long table, was Captain Harris. Seated to his left were his senior officers, Doc and McKinley, and to his right, Brown, the ship's engineer. The last tier, the level on which Carrie was standing, was where the other soldiers, Smith, Louis and Carter were seated, to the left of the aisle. Following Colt, she sat on the right-hand side.

They strapped themselves into their seats tightly, and Colt gave her an encouraging smile. Carrie figured it was her way of saying, *Good luck for your first flight.* Carrie sat there watching intently, soaking it all in. Hunter was talking into his headpiece. Bolkov seemed to be responding. Their hands darted here and there over the various controls. Harris was watching closely from his tier above them.

Carter and Louis shared a joke at the end of their row, looking at both her and Colt as they did. McKinley and Doc obviously heard what was said and looked back at them too. Doc looked curious and McKinley looked smug. Captain Harris did not turn his head at all. Carrie ignored them, trying hard to look cool, calm and collected. However, she realized that trying to look cool, calm and collected was probably making her look more nervous. She felt her palms sweating.

At that moment, an unidentified male voice came over a loudspeaker. *"UNF* Aurora *this is Ground Control. Do you receive? Over."*

Hunter responded. "Ground Control, this is UNF *Aurora*. We receive you. Over."

*"Aurora, your final checks have been received and confirmed. You have clearance for takeoff. Over."*

"Ground Control, roger that. We are ready for takeoff. You may start the countdown at your ready. Over."

*"Aurora, copy that,"* the voice said.

The loudspeaker went quiet. Hunter slowly pushed a stick forward on the control panel, causing the ship's low humming sound to increase dramatically. A loud beep sounded over the speaker and another male voice with a crisp English accent was heard.

*"T minus 30 seconds to takeoff..."* it said.

"We're ready to rock 'n' roll, captain!" Hunter called over his shoulder.

Harris pulled a small disc out of his pocket and tossed it to Bolkov, who caught it, then inserted it into a slot on the control panel.

*"T minus 20 seconds to takeoff..."* the voice called over the loudspeaker again.

Hunter looked at Bolkov and they nodded at each other. Bolkov adjusted his headpiece and Hunter grabbed hold of the large U-shaped control stick in front of him. He inhaled long and deep, then exhaled evenly.

*"T minus 10 seconds to takeoff,"* the voice called again, only this time it was followed by singular beeps, marking the final countdown.

*Beep.*

*Beep.*

*Beep.*

*Beep.*

*Beep.*

*Beep*

*Beep.*

*Beep.*

*Beep.*

*Beeeeeeeeeeeeeeeep.*

There was a loud thunderclap as the ship jolted forward violently, like a slingshot. Rushing through the air, the ship began to shake slightly, as though it were struggling and an intense pull was holding it back, but after another second or two it jerked again, and the soldiers were suddenly thrown back against their headrests as the *Aurora* surged skyward. Through the window ahead, the sky swiftly turned from the orange-pink of the setting sun, to gray, and then to an inky black, as the *Aurora* hurtled for space. A fine white mist lingered over the window, rather eerily, as a thousand tiny white lights seemed to dazzle their way onto the flight deck, luring them onwards. Hunter was holding the stick tightly, his jaw clenched in concentration. Under his rolled-up sleeves she could see the muscles in his forearms straining, veins bulging. Bolkov looked a little easier, reading measurements on the control panel.

The pull of the force was quite strong now. Carrie felt as though she was being pinned to her chair by a ton of invisible weight. She tried to move her hands but couldn't. This went on for about sixty seconds, until it seemed to even out a little and the pressure dropped slightly.

"Rock on, Bulk!" Hunter yelled.

Bolkov reached forward, hit a button, and suddenly the loud crunching sound of an electric guitar came over the loudspeaker. Carrie took a few seconds but soon identified it as Jimi Hendrix's version of Bob Dylan's "All Along the Watchtower", a song she remembered her grandmother playing to her. The volume was pumped loud, drowning out the noise coming from the ship. She saw a smile come over Hunter's face, despite the concentration and strain it still held.

*"There must be some kind of way out of here..."* Jimi began to sing.

Brown looked over at Captain Harris and smiled, his head nodding to the music, and the rest of the soldiers were in various states of smiling or laughter. Carter, too, was nodding his head to the music. She wasn't quite sure how they were doing it as the pull was still too strong for her. She glanced at Colt, who also had a big grin on her face, and despite herself Carrie was beginning to smile at the insanity. Here they were shooting through the Earth's atmosphere at a ridiculous speed, being thrown against their seats, heading toward a distress signal they knew very little about, with a team of strangers, cranking Jimi Hendrix over the PA, and they were loving every second of it.

The song eventually hit its lull and Jimi's guitar began to play a beautiful melody that seemed to slip and slide over the background beat. Carrie suddenly felt a bit emotional as she looked out at the starry space shooting through the window toward her. This was the first day of the rest of her life. She'd made it. She was on Space Duty. She was on her way to space...

*"Outside in the cold distance... A wildcat did growl... Two riders were approachin'... And the wind began to howl..."*

When the song finished, the men were whooping, hollering and clapping, and then more Jimi ensued. After about twenty minutes, the ship seemed to even out a little more, and the force pushing Carrie against her seat suddenly eased off considerably. As it did, however, she felt her stomach turn... She held herself still and tried to swallow the large bubble of air gathering in her throat. *No, no, no!* She pleaded with herself. *You CANNOT throw up! Not here, not now! Keep it down! Keep it down! Focus on something!*

She looked over at Hunter. He was still holding the control stick but only in one hand now. He reached over with his free hand and flicked a switch.

"Ladies and gentlemen," he called over the loudspeaker in a posh voice, "the seatbelt sign has been switched off. You may now leave your seats... and get the fuck off my flight deck!" he finished with a not-so-posh tone, smirking to himself.

Harris shot him a look, raising his eyebrows. "*Whose* flight deck?"

"Nice one, Hunter!" Carter called out as he stood.

"Yeah, fuck you very much!" Louis cascaded in his French accent. Hunter lifted his free hand and flipped him the bird. Bolkov laughed.

Colt turned to Carrie. "How cool was that?" Then she seemed to pause. "Y'alright?"

Carrie nodded but dared not open her mouth to speak. She pretended to busy herself with undoing her harness. The captain stood and headed for the exit, glancing at the women as he passed. First at Colt, then at Carrie, his eyes lingering a moment on her face, making her feel uncomfortable. The rest of the second tier then filed out: McKinley eyeing her and grinning to himself, Brown making eye contact but giving nothing away. Doc came next and he too looked at the women carefully, especially Carrie. She looked away, feeling as though she was sweating from every pore.

"You sure you're okay, Welles?" Colt said quietly under her breath, looking ahead, not wanting to draw attention. "You're looking pale even for a white girl."

"Fine," she managed, looking down to see Packham staring up at her too.

Carrie waited for the rest to leave, hoping they would be long gone down the corridor by the time she made her exit. When she eventually emerged from the flight deck behind Colt, she felt a little shaky on her feet. The ship was still at a slight angle and occasionally gave a shudder and a shake. Just outside the door, a voice startled her.

"You okay, corporal?" It was Doc, studying her face carefully.

Colt glanced back but kept on walking.

"I'm fine, sir," Carrie gave a nod.

"You look a little ill. You're not queasy?" he probed.

She shook her head.

"It's a very normal reaction to get queasy during takeoff. It happens to a lot of people. When the ship evens out and the pull eases off, it's like your stomach is doing a somersault or something. You get used to it after a while, but the first couple of times it can throw you... pardon the pun."

Carrie really didn't want to talk about her stomach right now. "I'm fine," she assured him, turning around to follow the others.

Doc walked alongside her. "Well, if you decide that you *are* feeling queasy, just come and see me and I'll give you a shot to take care of it. Alright?"

She could see out of the corner of her vision that his eyes were narrow, watching her closely. She nodded again, trying to walk normally, but desperately avoided stepping too hard on the ground. Her stomach needed a minimal amount of vibration right now.

"Where're we headed?" she asked, changing the conversation and trying to distract him from his analysis of her.

"Mess hall. You hungry?" He gave her a little smile, like he was challenging her to admit she was sick.

Carrie tried to keep a plain face, as a bead of sweat rolled down her cheek. The thought of food right now was not a good one.

"Sure," she said, managing a weak smile.

When they reached the mess hall, everyone lined up at the counter. Louis and Smith took up their positions and began pulling dishes out of the ovens. She tried to let Doc go ahead of her, but he stood back.

"After you," he said.

She reluctantly walked ahead of him but avoided looking down the counter at the men scooping the food onto their plates. She saw Carter sniggering, just waiting for her to falter. *Just hold it in... It's nothing. You can take this. You can do it. You cannot look weak. Even Colt looks fine. You can't be the only one!*

When it came to her turn in the line, she held out her plate but pretended to be looking around at where she was going to sit. Anything to avoid looking at the food.

"Tell me when?" Louis said to her, a big smile on his face as he mushed the spoon around in the dish, a little too long for what was necessary, she thought. He was enjoying this. Smith, also watching, was on the verge of laughter.

"When," she said quickly after the one scoop, whisking her plate away.

She turned around and automatically locked eyes with Harris, as she overheard Carter saying, "Oh, she is so going to hurl, man!" It felt like the whole crew were watching her, even Colt. Carrie made her way over toward the other corporal, and as she walked, the smell of the food, which appeared to be some kind of creamy chicken stew, wafted into her face. The smell automatically triggered her saliva glands into over-production, but not in a good way. As she reached Colt, she placed her plate on the table and stood there. She couldn't make herself sit down. She couldn't bend her stomach right now. Colt eyed her nervously.

Doc came and stood beside her, placing his plate on the table, "Would you like to come and get that shot now, corporal?" he asked quietly to avoid drawing attention.

Carrie felt terrible. She was positive that any second her stomach was going to explode. She had to get away from that smell. She glanced quickly at Doc and nodded.

"Follow me," he said, walking toward the door.

Carrie followed him and again felt all the eyes in the room upon her, particularly those of the captain. She tried to look as healthy as she could, but it was an extremely difficult task. As she exited, she heard the men burst out laughing and winced with embarrassment.

Doc turned around and looked at her. "You could've avoided that if you'd just come with me in the first place, you know."

"I get the feeling that it still would've happened regardless..." she managed quietly.

The walk to Doc's office seemed to take forever, although it was just down the corridor. As she entered the room, the clean antiseptic smell hit her and that air bubble appeared in her throat again. She felt the blood drain out of her face. Doc walked over to a cabinet, pulled out a ready-filled syringe and walked back over to her.

He gave her a funny look. "You want to throw up first?"

"Just do it," she managed, as she put her hand over her mouth and turned her shoulder to Doc.

He grabbed a paper bag from the countertop and shook it open. "Here," he said giving it to her, and within a spit second of handing her the bag, he'd pushed up her sleeve and jabbed her with the needle. The short sharp pain that shot through her arm as the needle pierced her skin was all it took to trigger her stomach to heave.

"Whoa… just in time!" Doc said quietly. He quickly disbursed the fluid into her arm, removed the needle and tossed it in a waste receptacle.

Carrie heaved again. Doc swabbed her arm with something cold and wet, then let go of her sleeve and walked across the room. Carrie looked down into her bag of vomit for a moment, waiting to see if she was done. She felt a warm fuzzy sensation come over her and assumed it was whatever Doc had just injected her with. She immediately felt better and decided it was safe to close the bag over.

"You done?' Doc said holding out a white plastic cup filled with water.

She nodded. "Where do you want it?"

"I got it." He took the bag off her and handed her the cup of water. "Sip it, don't skoal it down." He walked over to a window in the wall and pressed a few buttons on a keypad beside it. The window opened, he placed the bag inside, and after a whirring noise and a whoosh, the bag slid from sight.

Carrie sipped the water, it felt fantastic and her stomach felt no desire to heave it back up. Doc washed his hands and headed back to her.

"How're you feeling now, corporal?"

"Better. Thank you," she shot him a quick, embarrassed, smile.

"Don't be so stubborn next time," he told her. "I've had to give some of the guys shots from time to time. It happens."

He headed over to the door and motioned for her to follow. "C'mon, I'm starving."

She took her cup and followed him back to the mess hall. As they approached the door she straightened up, wanting to look the picture of health. She finished off the last of the water and crushed the cup in her hand, stuffing it into her pocket. Doc walked through first. He looked over at the table of men, which now included Louis and Smith, but kept on walking. Captain Harris was at the counter getting seconds. She saw the men look at Doc, then at her, but kept their sniggering to a minimum. She wondered whether the lieutenant had given them a "look" to leave her alone. As she walked by the table, however, she saw Carter lean over to McKinley.

"I wonder what Doc gave her to cheer her up so much?"

The table broke out in laughter and Doc looked around at them. Carrie made her way back to where she left her food, sitting down beside Colt, as Doc grabbed his plate and joined them.

"Now you look a normal white," Colt said to her.

Carrie smiled and let out an embarrassed laugh. Just then Bolkov and Packham walked into the room. They headed over to the counter and started serving themselves food. Carrie figured that Hunter must be manning the flight deck. Harris finished serving up his seconds and looked over at her table. He headed in her direction and took the seat opposite. The men at the other table grew quiet and watched him.

"Got your appetite back, Corporal Welles?" he asked frankly.

Carrie swallowed her mouthful and nodded through a slight blush, "Yes, sir."

"Good," he said taking a mouthful. "Be a shame for you to miss Louis's food. Not all our meals come from the Command kitchens."

Carrie was desperate to change the topic of conversation as she knew the other table was listening in. "Was that your song choice, captain? When we took off?" she asked.

He nodded, finishing his mouthful. Carrie smiled. She hadn't picked him for a rocker.

"Do you always play a song on takeoff, sir?" Colt inquired of the captain, as Packham joined them, sitting down beside the captain.

"We do."

"Is it always the same song or do you alternate? Does everyone pick a song?" Colt continued.

Harris shook his head. "Departure and arrival songs are always the captain's choice. *Occasionally* I let the men choose songs during our training runs, but it all depends on how much they've pissed me off that day." He shot the men at the other table a hard glance.

Doc chuckled, as he finished another mouthful on his plate.

"Speaking of training," Harris continued, looking back at Carrie, "I'm looking forward to seeing you on the shooting range."

Carrie swallowed her mouthful, noticing McKinley out of the corner of her eye as he looked over to their table.

"That Santos Siege was something special, corporal. You took out six men, that right?" Harris arched his eyebrow at her.

All eyes in the room were on her now.

"Wait," Packham interrupted. "That was that hostage situation in Madrid a few months ago, right? I saw that on the news. That was you?"

Carrie shrugged humbly. "Well, there was a team of us. I didn't get them all on my own."

"But you got *six* men, including Jose Gardos the rebel leader?" Harris appeared intrigued by her modesty.

Carrie nodded. "Once I took out Gardos, the rest of them were pretty easy. They panicked and started running around. It was like moving target practice." Carrie surprised even herself at the matter-of-fact way she'd said it, like she was talking about the stock market or something. She glanced around, noticing just how quiet the room was.

"You ever killed anyone before?" Harris asked, eyeing her carefully.

Carrie looked back at him for a moment. She tried not to think of her targets too often. She shook her head. "No. I've wounded plenty before, but my orders for the Santos mission were to shoot to kill. So, I did."

"Six men is a good haul, Welles, especially for your first time," Harris said. "Like I said, I'll be interested to see you on the range tomorrow."

"Yes, sir," Carrie nodded. It suddenly dawned upon her that Harris was trying to help her regain some face with the men. He'd been talking loudly enough for everyone to hear, asking the right questions. This was the first conversation he'd bothered to have with her since they met at 0700 that morning. It was short, it was sharp and his voice was completely devoid of any emotion, but she was grateful nonetheless.

*

Carrie yawned as she lay on her bed.

"So what were the guys like on the flight deck, anyway?" Colt asked Packham, as she stretched out in her own bed.

The sergeant gave a short laugh. "Typical flyboys. Hunter spoke to me as little as possible and I don't think Bolkov can speak at all."

"Hmph," Colt agreed. "Sounds like the two I was with. The only things Carter said were smart-ass, and Brown only spoke when he had to."

Carrie scoffed at both of them. "At least they spoke to you at some point. You should've seen McKinley!"

"You know they're just testing us out, right?" Packham said climbing into her bunk. "We've moved into their territory, and they're letting us know that. I've seen it again and again."

"Well, they better hurry up and accept my ass, 'cause I ain't putting up with that shit for very long," Colt said, jerking her neck to the side.

Carrie chuckled at her.

Packham rolled over in her bunk and looked down at the other two. "You've got to try, too, you know. Don't go sitting off to the side in mess hall or on the flight deck. You've got to get in the thick of it. You put your face in their face, they've got no option but to acknowledge and recognize you."

"Yeah, I know," Colt said quietly, mulling it over.

Packham looked over the edge at Carrie. "How's your gut?"

"Better now. Whatever Doc gave me did the trick."

"Yeah. The first time I went up I vommed so much…" Packham said, a glazed expression taking over her face.

"But you're a pilot!" Carrie laughed.

"I know," she shrugged, "go figure. My gut was used to fighter jets in the Earth's atmosphere, not spaceships floating around in space. I guess I just had to get used to it."

"Well, hopefully I got it all out of my system. Literally!" Carrie said, then she looked over at Colt. "Did you throw up your first time?"

Colt shook her head, as she stretched out again. "Not me. I got an iron gut. I grew up on all kinds of spicy food, nothing upsets it. I do remember it felt weird, mind you, but I didn't lose my lunch." She glanced between the two of them. "It's you skinny white girls who can't hold your gut." Her face broke into a cheeky grin.

Packham and Carrie smirked back at her, then one by one they touched their lamps, turning them off, and plunged the room into darkness. Carrie yawned again, as the long day weighed her body down with tiredness. To think this morning she'd merely been an Earth Duty soldier, and now hours later, here she was shooting through space. She smiled to herself, completely content, nestling the image she'd seen earlier into her mind.

At dinner, Packham had explained their flight process, telling her that as soon as the ship made it through the Earth's atmosphere and gravitational field, the hyperflight would be engaged. Therefore there was only a small window to view the Earth before it disappeared for good. Trying to contain her eagerness, Carrie had finished dinner, then calmly but curiously walked over to the mess hall's observation window, peering through. She recalled how her breath had caught at the sight. It was so beautiful. There, in its full awesome glory, was Earth; a massive orb of blues, greens, golds and whites. She swore she could've reached out and touched it; such a sight to behold.

Her eyes had then drifted to explore the dark space surrounding it, and the silvery pinpricks of starry light that twinkled at her. And as enticing and intriguing and as breathtaking as the stars were, her eyes were drawn helplessly back to the beautiful marbled sphere she called home.

# 6

# For and Against

Harris looked over at Doc after the women had left the dining hall.

"Take a walk?" He motioned toward the door.

"Sure."

The two of them dropped their plates at the counter, then headed for the door. As they passed the table where the rest of the crew sat, Harris gave them a stern look.

"Early start tomorrow, gentlemen," he warned.

The men groaned in response, and a satisfied smile crept onto Harris's face.

He started down the corridor with Doc, heading for their quarters.

"So how you think it went today?" he asked his lieutenant. "There didn't seem to be any major issues. Some joking going on, but that's about it."

Doc shrugged. "It's fine. There're clearly two distinct groups at the moment, but that's to be expected. It'll change."

"Yeah, that *will* change. I think we'll run through a few training exercises tomorrow and mix things up a little."

"Good idea," Doc nodded.

"And Welles?" Harris arched his eyebrow. "She throw up, or did the shot sort it out in time?"

"Nope. She threw up *as* I gave her the shot. She's got a stubborn streak, that one."

Harris shrugged. "Didn't want to look weak in front of the others. Understandable. She'll need to perform tomorrow, though."

"That was a good move at dinner. Your conversation. The guys took notice. Especially McKinley," Doc grinned.

"Mm-hmm. Like I said, she'd better perform tomorrow."

Doc nodded, crossing his arms as a serious look took hold of his face. "And on the Darwin, if needed."

Harris eyed him a moment, then nodded back. He wasn't ready to break the news about their confinement just yet.

He parted ways with Doc and entered his quarters, located in a separate section from the rest of the soldiers. As he showered, he ran over the day's events: his discussions with Isaack and Martin; his three new recruits and their supposed capabilities; the reactions of his men; and most of all, that distress signal from the far reaches of the UNF Space Zone that no-one seemed to know anything about.

He stepped out of the shower and eyed his tired self in the mirror, thinking yet again of the dream he'd had that morning. It seemed to be stuck there in the back of his mind, wedged alongside that file on the Darwin and the image of Professor Martin's face. Just like that feeling in the pit of his stomach, for some reason the dream would not shift.

The dream itself was reminiscent of a childhood incident that he remembered quite clearly. It had happened the day his father had died. He was nine years old, and for some reason Sibbie and Etta had come to visit his mother that morning. He remembered there was something very strange about their behavior. Their faces were serious, concerned, as they sat quietly drinking tea with his mother and casting subtle glances at him. He remembered looking at his mother and seeing her staring hard at Sibbie, like she was trying to work something out. Then the phone rang.

Sibbie and Etta stood quickly, moving in unison, like they often did.

"Bring Holly-Hope inside," Sibbie told Etta.

Etta went straight for the door to call his sister Holly inside from playing. Sibbie walked over to the phone and answered it, her thin bony hands clasping it tight. She listened, then turned to his mother.

"Something's wrong..." Her voice was grave and her eyes troubled, just like they'd been in his dream.

He'd looked over at his mother and saw her eyes well up immediately. She stood shakily, took the phone and stepped away from them, her eyes never leaving Sibbie's.

"This is Maeve Harris," she breathed, turning to stare blankly at the wall.

Silence filled the room, as Sibbie and Etta stared not at his mother, but at him. He heard a crash and looked back to see that his mother had dropped the phone, and her hand was on the wall to steady herself, gasping for breath.

"Mama," he said, moving toward her. "Mama, what's wrong?"

Etta caught him, while Sibbie took hold of her daughter and guided her back to a chair at the table. Then Etta followed.

"Honey?" Sibbie asked her softly, a pained look on her face.

His mother, dazed, looked up at Sibbie. "You knew…" She began to cry.

"No, honey…" Sibbie shook her head, saddened.

"You knew," his mother protested. "You knew and you didn't warn us!"

Saul saw Etta staring past him. He looked over his shoulder and saw Holly standing there, clutching her favorite doll, her big, innocent, six-year-old eyes unsure as to what was going on. He heard his mother moan like she was in pain. He turned back and saw her holding her stomach, the tears streaming down her face.

"You knew!" She shook her head, rocking back and forth.

"You felt it too, didn't you, child?" Etta asked, caressing her back.

"Mama, what's wrong?" he asked again, louder, to make himself heard.

Sibbie moved over to him then, placing her hands on his shoulders, and looked him deep in the eyes. "There has been an accident, Saul. Your father died today."

Harris remembered staring back at her. *What did she mean he was dead?* He'd just seen him that morning. They ate breakfast together. He left in his police vehicle. He waved goodbye.

"Saul," Etta called to him. "Don't fear now, son. He's gone to a good place."

"Why didn't you warn him?" his mother cried angrily. "Why didn't you warn *me*?"

Sibbie turned back to her daughter, wrapping her arms around Maeve's rocking body. "It doesn't work like that, honey… you know that. I don't know specifics, I just know it's comin'."

Harris stood there dazed; he didn't understand what they were talking about. Etta stood then and guided him and Holly to their rooms to pack a bag so they could stay with her that night. All the while his mother sobbed in Sibbie's arms, the horrible sound grating terribly on his ears.

"Do you know where Terence is?" Etta asked, referring to his older brother, as she handed him his toothbrush.

He shook his head. They often didn't know where Terence disappeared to.

"Alright," Etta said, her eyes firmly on his. "Sibbie will have to look out for him then."

"Great-gran Etta," he said, as she cuddled Holly and her doll. Etta's round face was old and soft, but her eyes were sharp and strong in contrast.

"Yes, Saul."

"Is he really gone?" he'd asked, feeling his own eyes begin to well; his lips trembling. "My dad's not coming home?"

Etta nodded slowly, closing her eyes as she did. She opened them again and looked deep into his eyes. "Y'all need to mourn him now. And after you mourn, your mama's going to need you to be strong, Saul. But I *know* you have that within." She reached out and laid her outstretched hand against his chest. "You have a good soul, child... you're going to step up and be the man of the house now. You were born to lead, Saul."

The next few days had been a blurry haze to him, but what he remembered most was that his mother was not the same with Sibbie and Etta after that, and right up until their deaths both Sibbie and Etta watched him like a hawk.

Of course, his sister had her theories about it all, about a family gift. She believed that Sibbie and Etta knew that his father was going to die, and she was always at him to believe in it, to believe in a shared family gift. She claimed it ran through the women but tried to tell him that he'd picked up the traits too. Apparently Sibbie and Etta had said it was so. Sometimes he'd humor her, but he never took it seriously. If his mother had believed in it once, whatever she'd believed died along with his father. And he trusted his mother. She was an honest woman, a good woman, so he followed her lead, unblinkingly. Besides, he was a realist. He accepted the fact that he had good gut instincts, but so did a lot of people. He believed in facts and what he could see in front of him. Not dreams, not hearsay. And certainly not any supposed family gift.

Staring into that mirror aboard the *Aurora*, Harris let out another sigh and ran his hands over his face. The night before had finally caught up with him. He stretched out his neck and his back, then made his way to bed. He was exhausted, and there was nothing more he wanted right now than to fall into bed and sleep a nice long sleep… and maybe dream about the Jazz Club Woman.

*

But dream of the Jazz Club Woman, he did not. Instead, he dreamt of Sibbie and Etta standing in the shadows at the foot of his bed, just staring at him. He awoke abruptly, sitting bolt upright, and for a moment he could've sworn they were really there, really standing at the foot of his bed. But he blinked a few times, wiped his eyes, and they were gone.

Carrie awoke with a start to a loud booming voice.

"RISE AND SHINE, SOLDIERS! YOU HAVE EXACTLY FIVE MINUTES TO BE OUT HERE, LINED UP IN FRONT OF ME, FOR YOUR MORNING RUN! DO YOU UNDERSTAND?"

She recognized it as Harris's. He seemed to be moving down the corridor and banging on each door.

"Jesus Christ!" Colt said groggily. "What's the time?"

Carrie touched her lamp and looked at her watch. "0425."

"Jesus Christ…" Colt said again, rubbing her eyes.

The women dragged themselves out of bed and quickly scurried around, bumping into each other as they got dressed.

"YOU'VE GOT 30 SECONDS!" Harris yelled down the hall.

Carrie raced out into the corridor. The men were already lined up, wearing their combat pants and singlets, some with their hair still standing on end. Colt, then Packham, quickly joined Carrie in the lineup.

"Okay, soldiers!" Harris boomed. "One lap of this ship is equal to half a mile. We are going to run eight laps this morning. Do I make myself clear?"

"Yes, sir!" they called in unison.

"WHAT ARE WE WAITING FOR?" Harris yelled.

He turned and began running, leading the team on a route that took them along the main corridor past Doc's office, then past the general store, the mess hall, the training facility and the weapons store, then curved around past the flight deck, came back along the main corridor past the captain's office, and comms room, before heading down into the bowel of the ship, past the cargo hold and engine room, then back up to the main corridor again, past the medical stores, Harris's quarters and down to the soldiers quarters, to start the loop again.

Carrie was glad for the chance to stretch her legs and clear her head. She'd had a weird dream last night that she could only remember in snatches this morning. The *Aurora* had been in trouble, the hull had been breached, and the air was trying to suck them all right out into space. She remembered telling herself to hold on, just hold on until they made it back to Earth. For some reason, something about the vast, dark space that had surrounded them, had scared her.

After the fourth lap, it was clear who the fittest runners were, as they had now fractured into three distinct groups. Harris still led the pack, barely raising a sweat. Doc was close behind him, neck and neck with Hunter. A few paces behind were the second group, comprising Carter, McKinley and Carrie. Brown then led the rest in a third, spread out, group. The only one missing from the run was Bolkov, who was obviously manning the flight deck.

As they turned each bend and the leaders ran past the stragglers, Harris seemed to make sure he locked eyes with each of his soldiers. Doc seemed to do the same, but more so in the line of duty, checking if everyone looked okay. Carrie noticed he seemed to be paying particular attention to the women. She smiled to herself. *Not today, Doc. I can handle this!*

She jogged along watching the bodies bobbing up and down. Somehow the men looked even bigger in their singlets, with their shoulders and biceps on display, highlighted by the slight sheen of sweat that was slowly building on their skin. Even Smith, who was the smallest of the men, looked somehow bigger. He still had enough muscle definition there to be highlighted by sweat. Of course he was no match for Louis, who was technically the most sculpted of the men.

Whenever the line passed her, she subtly sized them all up, but for some reason her eyes seemed to be drawn to both Doc and Hunter. They were both good looking, the best on the ship. Hunter had the looks of a male model; along with those chiseled cheekbones, he had turquoise eyes and nice smooth skin that he was proud to show off halfway through by taking off his singlet and tucking it into the back of his pants. He was almost too smooth and clean-cut, she thought.

There was something a little more rugged about Doc. He had a nice tan that made the sweat glisten twice as bright along his biceps. He clearly didn't wax his chest, as the evidence was poking out the neck of his singlet; not too much, just enough. He didn't seem too caught up in his looks. She liked that.

The run came to an end outside the soldiers' quarters where it had begun, forty-five minutes earlier. As she approached the end, where Harris, Doc and Hunter waited, panting and sweating, Carter and McKinley made a last dash for the finish. It was clear that they had to beat her. She let them. It wasn't worth fighting for. Besides, she was quite a way in front of the last group, so she was content with that. She didn't fail this test.

*

After breakfast, and a surprise room inspection, Carrie was glad to finally be heading for the training facility. When she arrived, she saw a large room with a well-equipped gym to the left, a digital shooting range straight ahead, and to the right, a matted area for hand-to-hand combat, and a climbing wall that went to the ceiling. Most of the men were gathered around the shooting range talking, except Louis and Smith who were over at the weight racks. Louis was lying on his back pumping what looked like a decent amount of weight and Smith was spotting him. When Harris called them to attention, though, they stopped and moved over to join the others.

"Listen up, soldiers!" Harris called, walking up to the shooting range. "We're going to begin today with a good old-fashioned shootout, and you will start by going head-to-head with your roommates!"

The men sniggered and laughed. Colt looked over at Carrie and shrugged.

"Second Lieutenant McKinley — as your roommate Hunter is on the flight deck with Sergeant Packham, you will be facing off against Sergeant Louis, as no doubt Bulk will be getting his beauty sleep right about now." Harris called out.

"He'll be sleeping a while, then," Carter quipped dryly.

Some of the men laughed, and Brown smirked. "Dare you to say that again when he's in the room."

"Alright!" Harris cut off any response. "McKinley, Louis, start us off, gentlemen!" He waved them forward.

McKinley and Louis walked up to the starting points of the two ranges, which stood side by side. Several meters away were the target screens showing a distant cammo-colored outline of a soldier's head and shoulders with three circles overlapping it. The circles were broken into an outer circle—number three; a middle circle—number two; and an inner circle—number one. Each circle was made up of thousands of tiny sensors able to pinpoint the exact placement of the shot.

The two soldiers picked up the training pistols lying on a ledge beside each range. They checked the laser aim was registering, flashing the red light on their hand, then practiced aiming at the target.

"Any time you're ready, gentlemen," Harris said, sounding a little bored.

McKinley turned to Louis, "Ladies first."

Louis scowled at him, then turned and glowered at Carrie and Colt. "No, *I* will go first, you buffoon!" he spat at McKinley. Louis turned back to the target and lined it up.

*Body is all wrong,* Carrie thought to herself. He pulled the trigger and there was a subsequent zipping noise, as the target on screen began to glow. Louis blew the top of his gun for a little dramatic effect. McKinley smiled smugly, then turned in his lane to line up his shot. He had good posture, weight evenly spread. He was right-handed and she watched the way he held the gun, the silver band around his wrist catching the light, as he gently squeezed the trigger, making his target glow.

Harris walked up to a console beside the ranges and turned on the screens overhead, showing a close-up of the targets and a placement score. As they appeared, it was clear to see that McKinley was the winner. He'd landed his shot inside the main target, although a little offside, but it was still a nice one. Louis was way off, with an outer number three.

"Pah! Fucking cowboy Americans," Louis spat, as he walked off.

McKinley just smiled and walked back over to the group.

"Next up, roommates Carter and Smith!" yelled Harris.

Carter and Smith walked up and chose a lane, while Harris worked the console to clear the previous targets. Smith took his shot first, then Carter. They both had fairly good posture, although Carter looked slightly more at ease. Carrie figured his experience over Smith would probably see him the victor. Although Carter was indeed the winner, it wasn't by much. They'd both landed a number two, but Carter's was visibly more central.

"Bollocks!" Smith hissed.

Carter laughed and reached over to pinch him on the ear.

Smith flung his arm up to knock him away. "Fuck off, Farris!"

"Doc and Brown. You're up!" Harris called, moving things along.

The two soldiers emerged from the team and picked a lane.

"You're going down, Doc," Brown told him.

Doc chuckled quietly to himself, and they lined up. Again, they both had fairly good posture. Doc went first, then Brown, who seemed to take just a little bit more time to line up his shot. It got him over the line. Again, they both had two's, but Brown's was right on the one border and Doc's was a middle two.

"What'd I tell you, Doc?" Brown said, holding his hands out in question.

"Yeah, yeah," Doc nodded. "Just don't get sick on this ship, okay, Brown?"

They all laughed.

"Colt and Welles!" Harris yelled.

The men grew quiet and watched as the two women made their way to the lanes. Carter murmured something and began laughing, but he stopped when Harris cleared his throat rather loudly and glared at him. Colt grabbed her gun and lined up fairly quickly, eyeing off the target at the end, taking a deep breath and firing.

Carrie took her time. This wasn't about beating Colt, it was about doing what she did best. She stood at the mark, legs apart, one slightly in front of the other, body on a slight angle, just like her father had taught her. She rolled her head to loosen her neck, then pulled the gun out in front of her and met it with her left hand. She steadied the aim, focused hard on her target and gently squeezed the trigger.

The men stood in silence as Harris brought the targets up on the screen. Carrie had a good, solid one. Colt had a three.

Colt pointed at the screen. "There goes your rebel leader!"

Carrie smiled at her joke and there was quiet talk amongst the men about the scores.

"Ok, round two," Harris called. "McKinley and Brown line up!"

"So are you going to take *me* down?" McKinley asked Brown sarcastically as they took their spot.

Brown eyed him up and down. "If I don't with my gun, I will with my fist."

"Ooh!" the men reacted.

"You can't hit me with your fist if you're already dead from my gun, Brownie," McKinley smirked.

"Just take your shot, white boy!" Brown scolded.

McKinley laughed to himself and then lined up again. Carrie could see concentration yet calm in his eyes and his body mirrored this. She had to admit, he held himself well, and it looked like another nice shot. Brown stepped up and took his turn. It looked alright too, but there was a certain stillness about McKinley's body she thought would be hard to beat. As she predicted, McKinley won. He hit another one, while Brown got another two–one border.

Brown stood there looking at his target, deflated. McKinley flashed him a smile, then swaggered back to the men.

"Carter and Welles!" Harris bellowed.

The team grew extra quiet with this one. Carter chuckled like he couldn't believe he was having to shoot against her.

"Ladies first," he said with a sarcastic smile.

She stared at him blankly then turned and walked to the line. She didn't take it slow this time around. She wanted to do it quick and put Carter in his place. She took her stance, focused sharply and fired. Carter lined up his, trying to make it look casual, but she saw the competition in his eyes. Harris brought up the results. Carrie, again, was a nice one, and Carter a middle two.

Smith burst out laughing, and Colt grinned.

"Ooh-ouch!" Brown called out.

"*So* close, Carter!" Doc said sarcastically.

"Lucky fucking shot!" Carter muttered sulkily, walking back to the men.

Carrie smiled inwardly.

"Ok, that leaves McKinley versus Welles!" Harris called.

McKinley stalked slowly out of the gathering again and took his place at the starting mark. It seemed he was still doing his best to ignore Carrie. He lined up and took his shot carefully, but a little more quickly than before. Perhaps he was trying to put Carrie in *her* place? When he was done he put the pistol down and continued to look directly at his target, with his arms folded like he had somewhere better to be.

Carrie smiled to herself. She wasn't going to let him get to her. She took up her stance carefully and spread her weight evenly. She looked hard at her target, pinpointing her focus as best she could. She held the gun tightly and squeezed the trigger, oh-so-gently.

Harris pulled the screens up and the team stepped closer. They were both ones, both positioned similarly, but on opposite sides of the center. Harris looked back and forth from one to the other for a few moments. He turned and glanced at McKinley, then at Carrie, and then around to the team.

"This one's a close call. I'm going to have to refer to the sensors for this." He turned back to the console and swirled his fingers about on the screen, eyed the result, then turned back to the group again, his eyebrows high upon his forehead. "The winner is... Corporal Welles!"

"What?" McKinley demanded. Harris hit a button and showed the sensor scores on the screen. There it was, for all to see. Carrie had beaten him. Narrowly, but beaten him nonetheless.

"The king 'as been toppled from his throne by a *girl*!" Louis called out teasingly.

The others laughed.

"C'mon," McKinley struggled to keep his voice light. "We're talking a millimeter here!"

Harris stared at McKinley with a deadpan face. "A millimeter of brain is a millimeter of brain, lieutenant."

McKinley laughed disbelievingly, shook his head and stalked off to the men. Carrie headed back toward Colt who had a huge smile on her face.

"Well, well, well..." Brown said, eyeing her as she passed. "It's Carrie the Kid."

"Nice job," Doc smiled, motioning to the target.

Carrie gave them a nod, trying to keep her emotions in check, but couldn't help the little smile of satisfaction that crept across her lips.

Harris called out to the team. "Over to the mats, people!"

He watched as his team gathered around him, then continued: "Alright, I'm dividing you into two teams." He held up his hand and cut an invisible line through the gathered soldiers. "Team one!" he pointed to Doc, McKinley, Smith and Colt, who stood on the left. "You're on the mats. I want you practicing your attack and defensive moves."

He pointed to Carrie, Carter, Brown and Louis, who stood on the right. "Team two! I want you on the climbing wall. You ascend, you touch the roof, you come back down, and the next person goes. When you are all done you will start running laps of the facility as a group. Do you understand?"

"Yes, sir!" they called.

"No time like the present!" Harris yelled.

With that, the first team walked over and grabbed a couple of cushions and began to square up against each other. McKinley vs Doc and Smith vs Colt. The latter in each pair were throwing punches and kicks, while the others were dodging them with the aid of the protective cushions. Harris watched them carefully. In particular, he paid attention to his two senior soldiers. They were a good match, he thought. McKinley was bigger and stronger, but Doc was faster. They each had what the other one lacked, so it did them good to sharpen their weaknesses.

Harris turned his eyes to Smith and Colt. Smith looked downright awkward, but Colt was not shying away, giving him what she could. Unfortunately, that's what concerned Harris. Colt looked to be the strongest of the women, yet as he darted his eyes between her effort and that of McKinley and Doc, he wasn't left feeling confident about any of the women's hand-to-hand combat abilities. Hardwiring skills, flying ships, and shooting well were good qualities to have, but at the end of the day, as a soldier, they meant nothing if you couldn't handle yourself in a fight.

He exhaled his disappointment, gritting his teeth as he watched on.

Carrie was not enjoying this part as much as the last. Fueled on by the laughter of Carter and Louis below, and despite her awkward movement, she finally reached the top of the climbing wall. She quickly reached out and touched the roof, wanting to end this, but as she did so her foot slipped.

Thankfully Brown had a good grip on her rope to stop her falling, and even though she quickly grabbed a handhold to steady herself, it was too late, they'd seen the slip. She glanced down over her shoulder and saw Carter and Louis curling over with laughter.

"Jeez, I'm out of here! We'll be here all day otherwise!" Carter called out as he took off to start doing laps of the facility.

Carrie saw Brown shake his head at Louis. "You heard the captain. We all gotta finish this before we do the laps. You know what he's like."

Louis waved him off like he was crazy and took off after Carter, as Brown glanced up at her again.

Carrie was glad Carter and Louis had gone. Her performance on the climb was clearly not quite as adept as her shooting, so the fewer witnesses the better. But it also made her dread moving over to the mats when they were done. She'd been watching the other team while she'd waited for her turn on the rock climb, and it wasn't pretty.

Carter had done his best to rib Smith, who'd been paired up with Colt. The private looked a little uncomfortable, not sure what he was allowed to do. Colt gave him what she could, but it was having little effect. On the other side of them, Doc and McKinley, provided a vast contrast. McKinley threw the cushion at Doc and started punching and kicking it straight away, but Doc's reflexes were pretty sharp, like he'd been expecting it. Regardless, she could hear the pounding sound of McKinley punching that cushion, and it was a far cry from the tapping Colt gave hers.

As soon as Carrie made it down from the climb, unhooked her harness and turned around, she saw Brown taking off. He'd waited for her, but the second her foot touched the ground, he was off. She started jogging after him, and as she did, she passed Carter who was on his way back to the rock climb.

"Made it down then, did you?" he smiled patronizingly, looking at his watch.

Before long, Harris called for the two teams to swap. Carter and Louis immediately paired up and faced off on the mats, leaving Brown to square off against Carrie. Brown grabbed the cushion reluctantly and waved her forward to start.

She hadn't really realized just how big Brown was until she was standing in front of him about to throw a punch. The cushion did little to hide him as he packed his body up against it. She moved forward and threw a few punches. He didn't budge an inch, not even his hands moved. It felt like a wall of concrete behind there. She tried a few kicks, same thing. This was going to be a futile exercise, that at best, would make her look quite pathetic. It didn't help things when she heard McKinley chuckling to himself. She looked over and saw him standing there, arms crossed, shaking his head, watching her.

She heard Louis exhaling heavily as he pummeled the cushion that Carter held. His muscles were bulging and the impact was moving Carter, yet Carter managed to contain the movement, simply jostling up and down on the spot. She tried to hit Brown harder, pummeling to the best of her ability, but knew she was making little impact. She was glad when Harris called for them to swap over.

*This is going to be interesting*, she thought. She tried to hold the cushion the way he had, tucking her body hard up against it, hoping that the cushion would be protection enough. Brown threw a punch. It was clearly not as hard as he could've done, but it moved her backward nonetheless. She tucked herself against the cushion tighter, trying to wedge her feet against the floor. He threw another, again not too hard, but she moved backward once more. She saw him glancing over at Harris, who nodded for him to continue. He threw another two in quick succession, again moving her backward. She figured as long as she didn't lose her balance she was doing fine.

She thought she heard more quiet laughter from somewhere. Brown came at her again, and this time she clenched her teeth and decided to ram herself and the cushion against the punch. She bounced up a little but didn't move backward this time. Brown gave an approving half-smile, as if to say, *Yeah, that's it.*

He threw more punches for a few minutes, then motioned for Carrie to return the cushion to him. She did.

"C'mon," he said, holding up the cushion, ready for her to take a swing.

She started up again, trying to mimic the body movements that Brown had just used; head down, shoulders hunched, arms in front of the ribcage, hands in front of the face. She threw a couple of lefts then jabbed with her right. She'd resigned herself to the fact that there was no way she was going to move Brown, but gave it her best anyway.

# 7

# Red Flags

Harris had seen enough. Watching Brown and Welles facing off on the mats made him cringe internally. Again, with Louis and Carter as a reference, giving each other everything they had, Welles wouldn't stand a chance. The smallest of the women, she was a mere fraction of Brown's size. If she met an opponent in the field of his caliber, she would be dead within minutes. Seconds, maybe.

Her only redeeming quality, he thought, was that she was an ace fucking shot. The fact that she beat McKinley was something. He hadn't seen *anyone* beat McKinley before. Regardless, it was a cold hard fact that if a soldier loses their weapon, they had better know how to fight. And watching her now, she did not.

He was starting to understand why Command didn't want the women to board the Darwin. They obviously excelled in their fields and they'd make great poster women for UNF Recruitment, but it *would* hurt their PR campaign if they got... damaged. And if the *Aurora* did have "unfriendlies" waiting for them on the Darwin, that is exactly what would happen to them, he had no doubt.

He sighed, decided to end Brown's boredom, and called everyone back over to the mats.

"Alright, soldiers," Harris bellowed. "You've got 45 minutes of gym time before we break for lunch. I will be coming around and watching each of you, so don't think about slacking off or I'll make your life even worse than it already is! Do you understand?"

"Yes, sir!"

"Alright," Harris continued, "Carter and Louis, before you do your gym time, you will give me ten laps of this facility for ignoring my orders on the climb. You did not wait for the rest of your team to complete the climb before you started your laps." He gave them a hard stare. "You did not wait for your team."

Carter and Louis exchanged a look. Harris stared hard at them, hands on hips, not budging.

"I told you," Brown shrugged at Carter and Louis.

Carter gave Brown a blank stare then turned and headed off for his laps. Louis followed sulkily.

Harris saw the other men watching him. He decided it was an opportune time to leave them alone for a while and see what took place.

He locked eyes with Doc, then left.

Carrie wasn't sure if she was happy with the punishment Carter and Louis received. The last thing she wanted was the captain to fight her battles for her; she could do just fine on her own.

She and Colt wandered over to the gym equipment, found some free weights and stood in front of the mirror that ran along the wall for a couple of meters.

"That was some great shooting earlier," Colt said.

Carrie smiled. "Yeah, I sucked on the climb, though. I should take some lessons from you. You worked it."

"Yeah? I missed that. You mean there's something you're not good at," Colt teased. "You can run and you can shoot."

Carrie was about to answer, but locked eyes with McKinley in the mirror. He was sitting at some equipment about to pull a heavy weight over his head, his blue eyes piercing as they sized her up.

"What've you got there, girls? One pound weights?" he asked patronizingly, his eyes twinkling at hers in amusement.

Colt eyed him in the mirror now, too, but they both chose to ignore him.

"That the best you can do?" he continued, chuckling.

Again they ignored him, but the rest of the team began glancing over at them now.

"Just make sure you don't overdo it now, you hear," he continued. "You don't want to go and wipe yourself out for the rest of the mission."

Carrie locked eyes with him again in the mirror. He stood and slowly walked over, watching them both lift their weights.

"Is there a problem, lieutenant?" Carrie couldn't resist the temptation to bite.

McKinley smiled smugly, folding his arms.

Colt looked over at her. "I believe his problem is that you *whooped* his ass on the firing range," she said dryly, shooting McKinley a challenging look.

This drew some *oohs* from the other men. McKinley looked over at Colt and then back at Carrie.

"You're an okay shot," he shrugged.

Carrie put down her free weights and turned around to face him. "No, I'm a fuckin' great shot!" she said defiantly. "Beat you, didn't I?"

Again, this drew some comments from the men, as Colt laughed, tucked a weight under her arm and held out her hand for Carrie to slap, which she did, happy for the support. Carter and Louis pulled up to join the throng and see what was going on, as the rest of the team had now stopped what they were doing and were watching.

"Is that so?" McKinley said smiling, stepping closer to her. "So what happens when you lose your gun, corporal?"

"I never lose my gun," Carrie told him.

"But what if you do?" He stepped closer.

"I told you I never lose my gun."

"What if I take it from you?" He continued to smile condescendingly. "What do you do then?"

"You'd have to take it from me first, and as you so eloquently told Brown earlier, your fist can't hurt me if my gun kills you first."

McKinley smiled and nodded. "Alright. But let's say that I *do* get to you and remove your gun. What then?"

Carrie looked at him and shrugged. "What answer are you looking for here, McKinley?"

"What answer? I want you to admit that you wouldn't have a clue what to do without your gun. That there's *nothing* you can do without your gun. That you're shit without it."

"Well, I disagree."

"But you are. So is she." He motioned to Colt. "So is Packham. Being a soldier is more than just shooting a gun, corporal. It requires *many* talents, not just one. I saw you on the mats. Pathetic. I think you're all a liability to the team and I don't care to put my life at risk when we go into the field, to save your ass because you can't cope without your gun."

"What makes you so sure we're a liability?" Carrie put her hands on her hips, trying to keep her cool, aware the rest of the team was watching. "You haven't seen us in the field yet."

"Then humor me, corporal. Let's say I take your gun and throw it away. What are you going to do about it?" He stepped closer again, now standing right in front of her, towering over her.

Colt slowly placed her free weights on the ground and moved closer to Carrie.

McKinley looked over at her, amused, then turned back to Carrie. "I can take on the two of you. Can you take on two, Welles? Huh? Tell me, what are *you* going to do to *me*, to save yourself and her? And don't think about the groin, I'm one step ahead of you. Although I must say, I wouldn't normally discourage a woman from thinking about my groin."

This drew sniggers from some of the men. Carrie noticed Doc get up from his equipment out of the corner of her eye.

"What do you want, lieutenant? You want me to fight you? Is that what you're saying?" Carrie's heart was beating fast, but she kept her cool. She didn't believe anything would happen with the rest of the team around, but she was nervous all the same. He was a big guy after all, and those piercing eyes of his scared her a little.

"No, I'm saying that you can't fight, period. We just saw proof of that when you squared off against Brown. One punch from him..." He shook his head, "You're weak, corporal. You're a liability. And the kind of work we do, you're only going to get in the way and slow us down."

"Enough, McKinley," Doc stepped up to them now.

"We're just having a conversation, Doc," McKinley said calmly, not taking his piercing stare off Carrie.

"You normally stand over people when you're just talking to them?" Doc asked.

McKinley stopped staring Carrie down for a moment and glanced over at Doc. "I can't help it if she's short, Doc." He shrugged. "I'm simply standing here making a *very* valid point." He looked her up and down, then back at Doc, motioning to her as he said, "*This* is supposed to cover my ass out there in the field? Give me a break!" He turned to eye Carrie again. "C'mon, Welles, give me your best shot. Prove me wrong. Show me how tough you can be." He pointed to his chin.

"Stand down, McKinley. That's an order." Doc said firmly, but coolly.

McKinley looked over at Doc, then stared back at her.

"As your senior officer, lieutenant, I'm ordering you to stand down, so stand down. *Now!*" Doc said with a harder edge to his voice.

McKinley's eyes darted over to Doc's, then he gave a short laugh, smiled and turned away, shaking his head. "Let's hope Doc's out there in the field next time you girls get into trouble," he said over his shoulder, as he walked back over to his weights.

"Back to your training, soldiers," Doc called firmly, then returned to the equipment he'd been working on, like nothing happened. The others started working out again, but they were stealing glances over at Carrie. She noticed that Carter and Louis were still standing there. When she locked eyes with them, they glanced at each other then took off jogging again.

"Forget about it," Colt said quietly, pumping her free weights again.

Carrie went back to her weights also, cheeks burning with anger. She started pumping the weights fast and hard. She refused to look in the mirrors in case she saw the others staring at her. She tried very hard to act like it didn't bother her but knew her cheeks were giving her away.

It felt like hours had passed by the time Harris returned to the facility, and now she was grateful for the intervention. The captain moved around and took a good look at everyone working out, studying them.

"Put your back into it, Carter!" he teased, as Carter struggled to lift a very heavy weight over his head.

He moved over to McKinley, then, who was resting between sets. "Have we tired you out already, lieutenant?"

"No, you don't have to worry about *me*, captain," McKinley answered, lifting his weights again. The comment was directed at her, she knew it. She refused to make eye contact or let it show on her face, though.

Over the next few excruciating minutes, Carrie pretended to be heavily involved in her free weights, all the while staring at her feet. Finally, Harris told the team to head for the mess hall. She took her time finishing up, wanting to make sure the others were gone before she turned around. Colt hung by and waited for her.

"Corporal Welles!" Harris called. "Are you hungry or not?"

"Yes, sir," she said quietly, stalking past Harris and Doc with a clenched jaw, looking dead ahead, avoiding eye contact.

Even so, she couldn't help but feel their eyes burning into her back.

Harris watched Welles and Colt walk out of the training room, then looked over at Doc. "What's that about? Why does Welles look so pissed?"

"It's nothing. We just had a little clash of wills between her and McKinley." They turned and started walking slowly after the rest of the group.

"What exactly were their wills clashing about?" Harris inquired.

"McKinley was just flexing his muscles. It's fine. I handled it." Doc was clearly not wanting to create a fuss about this, but it only made Harris more intrigued.

"What exactly was he flexing for?" he persisted.

Doc glanced at him. "He was trying to save face from losing the shootout is all."

Harris continued to look at Doc. "By doing what exactly?"

Doc sighed, stopped walking and turned to face him. He knew Harris wasn't going to drop it. "He was just trying to prove a point to the rest of the guys. He was arguing that the women were weak and therefore a liability to the rest of the team. He was pretending to challenge her to a fight to see how she'd react."

"And how did she react?" Harris arched his eyebrow.

Doc shrugged his shoulders. "She kept her cool and stood her ground, but it was pretty clear she wasn't happy about it. McKinley wasn't *actually* going to do anything, captain. He was just testing her, being a prick, trying to prove a point."

Harris thought about this momentarily, recalling watching the women on the mats. "He does have a point, though. Brown would only have to sneeze to knock Welles over. They're not the strongest female soldiers I've seen."

They exchanged a look, then Doc nodded. "Agreed, but he's just stating the obvious, captain. Of course the men are going to fight better than the women. It's genetics, we're bigger and stronger. But his same argument could be applied to other men in the team."

Harris waited for Doc to continue on, and he did. "Take Smith, for example. He's smaller than the other guys, younger, not as much experience. McKinley would beat his ass, too. So would the rest of us. Does that make him a liability on the team? The fact is that McKinley would probably beat everyone's ass... except for Brown and maybe Bulk," he shot Harris a look. "And maybe you, sir."

Harris arched his eyebrow and smirked at Doc. "I can hold my own, Doc."

"I know you can, captain," he smiled. "I'm just saying that if *that's* his argument, then we're all liabilities. I would never admit this to him, of course, but even me. He'd beat my ass."

Harris pressed his lips together and shook his head. "I disagree. McKinley would never beat your ass, Doc, 'cause you're not stupid enough to pick a fight with him."

Doc smiled back. "No, I'm not."

"Anyway, don't sell yourself short, Doc. McKinley's bigger, but you're faster. Don't ever discount speed in a fight. If you can land a hard punch quickly and get the hell out of there, then you got yourself a winner. And I've seen you do that before, you forget that."

Doc nodded, smiling. "Maybe."

"Anyway, this whole thing with McKinley, it's just the way he works, you know that. He uses fear and intimidation as a shield. Scare them enough, and they won't try it on. And if they do, then and only then, will he need to step up to the plate and deliver the goods. He would've learnt that the hard way, growing up the way he did."

Doc seemed to think about this a moment and nodded in agreement.

Harris shrugged at him. "McKinley can be an asshole at times, Doc, but I *like* having that asshole on my team."

Doc nodded. "Agreed."

*

When they arrived at the mess, Harris did his best to study the two sharpshooters without making it obvious. Welles was avoiding all eye contact with anyone but Colt. McKinley was making eye contact with everyone *except* Welles and Colt. It was no surprise when the two sharpshooters sat on different tables. The lieutenant positioned himself at the second table with Carter, Louis, Smith and Bulk, who'd joined them for lunch. Welles and Colt naturally joined Brown on the first table.

Harris and Doc got their meals, headed over to the first table and sat down. He struck up a conversation with Brown about the latest NBA scores, anything to keep himself occupied, ensuring he looked oblivious to what had just gone on. He didn't want to look like he knew what had happened, and certainly didn't want to look like he was overcompensating for the rest of the team's avoidance of the women.

It wasn't just for his sake, it was for Doc's too. It was important that the men didn't realize just how much information Harris managed to extract from him at times. But if Harris wanted to control a situation he needed to know every detail about it, and he often relied heavily on Doc flying under the radar to get it for him. Although, that said, Doc knew when to draw a line in the sand with Harris's demands.

Welles and Colt had been eating in silence. This was clearly killing Colt, who Harris had gathered loved to talk. She'd been looking around the room and listening in on Harris and Brown. As soon as their chat hit a lull, she looked over at Doc and started a conversation of her own.

"So where are you from, Doc?"

The medic finished his mouthful. "Colorado."

"Country boy?" Colt queried.

"Yes, ma'am," he nodded.

"Doc's quite the skier," Harris told her.

"Yeah?" She studied the medic curiously.

"State Junior Champion," Doc said proudly.

"Yeah? So what happened in your later years, then?" Colt joked.

Doc gave a laugh. "Studying for medical school and then joining the army, I suppose. Although, I *was* a ski instructor during my senior years in high school."

Brown laughed. "Ha! Is that where you honed your skills with the ladies, Doc? Taking all those rich women for skiing lessons."

Harris had a grin on his face as he watched Doc for his answer.

"Sergeant Brown, I've always been the consummate professional," Doc smiled, then seemed to want to move the conversation along. "What about you Colt? Where are you from?"

"Orlando."

"Florida? Nice," Doc said, then looked over at Welles, who was still quietly fuming. "So, Welles, whereabouts in Australia you from?"

She glanced up at Doc, then back at her food. "Brisbane. That's where I was born, but we moved around a lot."

"Yeah, why's that?" Doc wasn't going to let her go back to her lunch that easily. Harris knew Doc had seen her file, and knew very well why, but he was flying under the radar, as he did so well.

She looked up at him again. "My father's job meant we had to move from time to time."

"Yeah? What'd he do?" Doc asked, looking down at his plate and shoveling another mouthful.

Welles looked at him for a moment, glanced at the rest of the table and then back down at her food.

"He was a soldier."

Brown looked over at Welles, curious.

"Yeah? Anyone we'd know?" Doc continued.

"I don't think so, no," she said politely.

Harris found it intriguing that she wanted to hide the fact that her father had been a Space Duty colonel, and an Original at that. Most people he knew would brag about it.

"What about you, captain? Where are you from?" Welles, it seemed, wanted to move the conversation onto someone else now.

Harris finished his plate. "My family is from New Orleans, but after my father died, we moved to Detroit, Michigan."

Welles nodded at him. "'*De-troit* Rock City'?"

Harris smiled, amused. "You know your rock 'n' roll classics, corporal."

"Looks like you're at the wrong table, Welles," Colt laughed. "It would appear we're flying the flag for the USA at this one. The multicultural one is over there. Well, except McKinley, of course." She motioned over to the other table.

Welles glanced over at McKinley, then back at Colt. "I'm fine right here, thank you," she said dryly.

Doc flashed his eyes to Harris. He looked down at his watch and stood to take his plate to the counter, and then turned back around to the crew. *Time to throw them in the deep end again …*

"Soldiers," he called, "lunch is over. Break back into your main teams and do what you need to do. I want the stores unpacked, the engines checked, and the weapons locked and loaded. We'll meet back here in the mess hall at 1800."

Carrie sat there cringing. *Fuck!* An afternoon with McKinley in the weapons store was not something she was looking forward to.

"You have yourself a *fun* afternoon, now!" Colt said with sarcastic cheer, as she followed Brown out of the mess hall.

Doc stood from his seat at the table. "It'll be fine, Welles."

Carrie looked up at him. "So long as I don't go and shoot him," she said with a tinge of venom.

"Well, I'd prefer it if you didn't shoot him, 'cause that's just gonna make work for me," he said with a straight face.

Carrie didn't want to, but smiled in spite of herself. Doc seemed pleased with her reaction, smiling himself as he departed. She looked around for McKinley, but he'd left already. She sighed loudly as she got up from the table and headed for the weapons store.

When she arrived, he was already working, bending over inside one of the metal cases. She stood in the doorway for a moment, thinking about how best to tackle the situation.

"You going to get to work, corporal, or stare at my ass all day?" he said casually, pulling himself out of the crate and looking around at her with a smart-ass smile. "The UNF has rules about sexual harassment, you know."

Carrie gave him a blank look, as if the thought of staring at his ass bored her. She moved through the door and over to a box of crates, as McKinley gave a quiet, guttural laugh. She studied what he was doing. He appeared to be about to clean and load the weapon he'd pulled out of the crate.

"So we're checking and prepping the weapons, right?" she asked.

"That's what the captain said. You listen to orders?" he said looking down the sight of his gun.

She ignored him, biting her tongue.

He looked around at her and said in his best condescending voice, "I'm assuming you know how to check and prep all these types of guns, corporal."

She bit down harder on her tongue, feeling the steam build in her ears.

"Or do you only know how to shoot them?" he continued.

"Look, McKinley!" she fired, as the steam blew outwards. "You don't like me and I don't like you, that's a given, but unfortunately we've got to work together, so how about you drop the attitude?"

"Drop *my* attitude?"

"Yes, *your* attitude!"

McKinley stared at her like she was some kind of crazy woman.

Carrie seethed with anger but managed to reel it in and contain it. "Just tell me what you want me to do exactly, and I'll stay out of your way."

He stared at her again. "Boxes here," he pointed with his gun to the metal crates beside him. "These guns have to be polished, loaded and locked and on these racks ready to go. Can you manage that?" he said slowly as if she were stupid.

*Do I get to test them out on you?* she thought savagely, but went back to biting her tongue. She walked over to the crates he pointed to, opened one and took out the weapon inside. It was the latest, state-of-the-art, laser-fire assault rifle, just like the one he'd been prepping. It was sleek, black and huge, fitting between her shoulder and almost fully-extended arm. She grabbed a cloth from where McKinley stood and began to polish the weapon. She pulled it apart delicately and made sure it was clean throughout, then put it back together and double-checked the sight. She flicked the laser sight on and shone it against the wall, then turned and aimed it at McKinley to check the body heat reading on the top side of the gun. She saw his orange blob appear on the screen. It was perfect. She smiled to herself as she turned back and shone the laser against the wall again, picturing McKinley's head against it. *Bam!* She made the sound effects in her head, then smiled to herself.

She knew the laser-fire rifles were the way of the future, but personally she still had a soft spot for the weapons of old. Although some predicted they would soon become extinct, she believed otherwise. There were still many people who liked the idea of pumping lead into someone, leaving fragments of bullets that would need to be dug out and removed. But others liked the wounds the laser-fire rifles left on their victims: deep, penetrating cuts into the flesh with laser burns in and around the wound, which caused immense pain. Both weapons were deadly, both weapons could inflict serious injury. Some considered the laser wounds worse. After all, with a traditional bullet wound, you needed to dig out the bullet, stem the bleeding, and stitch the wounds back together again. With a laser wound, you had to stem any bleeding, control the burns by freezing the affected tissue until it could undergo Intense Tissue Rejuvenation, or ITR, therapy which was applied through a series of injected bio-organisms to eat the dead flesh, then light therapy to kill the bio-organisms, then skin grafts to rebuild what was once there. In Carrie's mind both wounds were terrible, but as a shooter her preference for a weapon was based simply on size and ease of use—the standard UNF handgun. At least, up close. From afar it was her sniper rifle.

McKinley watched her with a curious look on his face. He set the gun he'd finished onto the rack, closed the crate and moved to the next one.

"So, how'd someone like you get into guns anyway?" he asked as if it were a joke.

Carrie glanced over at him. "Oh, you're making conversation now?"

"Not a conversation, just a question." He kept his focus on what he was doing as though he wasn't particularly interested in her reply.

Her eyes narrowed and studied him.

"How'd *you* get into guns?" She turned the question back on him.

"I believe I asked you first, corporal," he said, still acting like he was uninterested.

Carrie studied him a while longer. He held his gun out in front of him, and she saw the silver band around his right wrist catch the light. His eyes looked back at hers, waiting for an answer.

"My dad was a soldier," she told him. "I grew up with guns, shooting targets and stuff. You?"

"Shooting targets," he said amused. "What'd you shoot back there in Australia? Kangaroos?"

"I've never shot an animal in my life. Only humans," she said with a calculated smile. "You?"

"What code?"

"What?"

"What code was he in? Army, navy, air force?"

"That's another question."

"I've let it slip until now, but I believe the correct way to address a senior officer is 'sir'," he said, still not looking up from what he was doing.

"That's another question, *lieutenant*?" she shot back, refusing to call him "sir".

McKinley looked over at her, smirking, waiting for an answer.

Carrie shook her head, relenting. "He started in the army and ended up in the UNF. You?"

"Space Duty or Earth Duty?"

Carrie pursed her lips and stared hard at McKinley. "*You*, lieutenant?" she asked again.

He gave a laugh and looked over at her. "Cop."

"Your dad was a cop?"

"Detective, to be specific." He looked down the sight of another gun.

"Yeah, what division?" she prodded him, the way he'd prodded her.

"DEA, undercover."

"So that's how you got into guns?" she asked, going back to the original question.

"Nope," he shook his head. "Daddy never took me shooting targets," he smiled condescendingly.

"Well, maybe that's why I beat you today," she retorted quickly. "You didn't get enough practice in with your daddy."

McKinley dropped his smile and gave her a cold blank stare with those blue eyes of his. "It's a little hard to fit in target practice when you father's *dead*, corporal."

Carrie lowered her smug smile a little. She wasn't sure whether to believe him or not. She wouldn't put it past him to lie just to win an argument. McKinley turned back to what he was doing.

"Yeah, well," she said, hoping to call his bluff, "we've all lost parents haven't we?"

He glanced over at her, then back to his crate, muttering quietly. "Not the way I have."

She looked at him, wondering what he meant by that, but it seemed he was going back to looking not interested, so she continued on with her work.

"You never answered my question, corporal," he asked after a little while. "Was he on Earth Duty or Space Duty?"

She looked at him again, confused. "Why are you so interested in my father?"

He shrugged; his face devoid of emotion. "I'm just trying to figure out how much of a military brat you really are. Did Daddy get you this job?"

Carrie felt a fire flicker in her chest. "No, my shooting got me this job, lieutenant. I thought I made that pretty clear on the range this morning."

McKinley gave a short, sharp grunt. "Well, like I pointed out earlier, corporal, a good soldier knows how to do more than just shoot. The day you can talk about something other than your gun, then we can have this conversation. Until then, I don't want to hear it. Until then you're a walking time bomb who, *I know*, will falter at the first fight you come across. 'Cause in *real* battles you don't get to hide behind sniper lines, corporal. You actually have to come face to face with other soldiers and get your hands dirty."

"Fuck you, McKinley!" she spat.

He shook his head. "I just hope that when you falter, you don't take anyone else down with you. Liability, Welles. Liability!" And with that he shut the crate he was working on and headed for the door. "I got more important shit to do than babysit your ass," he muttered as he left.

Carrie was fuming. She slammed the crate she'd been working on shut, and plonked herself down on top of it, running her hands over her face. She shut her eyes tightly, trying to calm down her anger. *Don't let him get to you. He'll see when we finally hit the field. He'll eat his words! Ignore him!*

"So, things are going well, then?"

She opened her eyes and saw Doc leaning in the doorway, an e-clip in hand.

"I just saw McKinley stomping down the corridor," he explained.

"I haven't shot him yet, sir, but I'm very, *very* close," she seethed.

Doc looked at her for a moment. "Welles, just let it go and he'll get bored. The more you bite the more he's going to bait you."

"Hmph!" she grunted. "He's not baiting. I know what baiting is."

Doc moved over and took a seat on the crate next to her. "Look, he's a hard-ass and he can be a prick, but at the end of the day he's a damn good soldier, and one worth following. He sets high standards for himself and for the team, and he pushes everyone to make sure they're pulling their weight. It's just what he does. Every team has the hard-ass that constantly tests them. Captain Harris usually fulfils this role and when he's not around McKinley kind of steps in for him. He's a hard man, but he helps to make the other men harder, too. Unfortunately, it's a prerequisite for this job."

Carrie looked skeptically at Doc, having a hard time buying the fact that McKinley was some kind of decent guy, doing a decent thing here.

"Look, Welles, every time we go into the field, that man covers my ass. They all do. I'm 2IC on this ship, but when we go into the field, I've got to hang back and let the other guys cover me. That's not an easy thing to do. I should be out front with the captain, but I'm the medic. I can't do that. If I die, they all die. So when we hit the heavy shit, those guys, McKinley especially, put their lives on the line, to ensure that I keep mine. I can't take that away from him. And I have to say, there's no another team on Earth I'd feel safer hitting the heavy shit with. Now, he is a hard-ass, and he's pushing you, trying to make you jump through some hoops to prove yourself, but you've got a choice here. You can resist the bite, take it on the chin, and get on with the job at hand. If you do, then eventually he'll realize he's not going to get a rise out of you, and he'll give you a break. *Or*, you keep waving that red flag of yours in his face and we keep moving backward until we hit a wall."

Carrie looked into Doc's calming brown eyes. "So, you think it's alright for him to call me and the other women liabilities, when he's never even been in the field with us to know what we're capable of?"

"No, I'm not saying that."

"Well, tell me this Doc," Carrie asked, searching his face for an answer. "If we're going to be on the same team, doesn't it make sense to try and work together? Shouldn't he be encouraging me to work *with* him? Not pushing me away."

"Yeah," Doc nodded.

"So, what's his problem, then?"

Doc tilted his head to the side in contemplation. "Well, I think the clash with McKinley comes down to your personalities. I think you'll find that you two might be a lot alike."

"Alike? Him?! He's nothing like me!" She waved him off.

"You're both competitive for one," he smiled, "and stubborn as hell."

Carrie balked at the idea. "He's *way* more stubborn than me."

Doc laughed. "Welles, this is your second day on the ship and so far you've put your health at risk several times already because you refuse to back down."

"When have I put my health at risk?"

Doc gave her an incredulous look. "You refused to admit that you needed the anti-nausea shot even though you made yourself sick. You let Carter's jibes get to you on the climbing wall and then overdid it and could've fallen and broken your neck. And *then*, you didn't back down with McKinley in the gym, even though you were clearly playing with fire there. Shall I go on?"

Carrie studied Doc. "You pay attention, don't you?"

He smiled confidently at her. "It's my job to pay attention, corporal. And that's why I know that if you just chill out with McKinley, treat him like your lieutenant, things'll settle down."

She chewed at her lip, watching him as he looked at her, waiting for her to give in. "I still think you should be telling him this."

Doc nodded. "I'll have a word. But you have to promise to put that red flag away." He raised his eyebrows and put out his hand. "Do we have a deal?"

Carrie looked at him for a moment, then relented. She was having a hard time saying no to his cute smile and friendly brown eyes. She looked down at the tanned forearm being held out to her, then reached out and shook his firm, warm hand.

"Good," he said standing up. "Now you'd better get back to work before the captain sees you and it's both our asses."

Carrie watched him walk back to the door. "Doc?" she called after him.

He stopped and turned around. "Yeah?"

"You owe me one."

"Yeah? What for?" He looked confused.

"I didn't shoot McKinley." She said it with a straight face, but her mouth soon curled into a wicked grin.

A smile crept across Doc's face, too. "Thank you for that."

"You're welcome."

Doc disappeared around the doorway. For some reason her anger at McKinley had dissipated. The medic seemed to have a calming influence about him. She sighed, stood back up from her crate and decided to get back into it.

# 8

# Records and Poker

Harris sat in his office staring at the star map in front of him. An uncomfortable feeling sat deep within. He'd just finished an unscheduled transmission with Command to check whether they had picked up the comms signal that the *Aurora* had just received. But they hadn't.

Just minutes before, Hunter had called him to the flight deck to advise that Smith's automated tracking scans had picked up the strange signal for about a minute. By the time Hunter realized what it was and began to home in on its location, the signal had been lost. He had managed, however, to narrow it down to the approximate vicinity of the Darwin — between Mars and The Belt.

Harris viewed the star map now, eyes fixated on the location of the comms signal origin. What intrigued him most was that not only did Command *not* pick up the comms signal, but several other UNF ships closer to the vicinity of the station didn't pick it up either. For some reason, the *Aurora* was the only one to do so.

So, what did that mean? Were they the only ones to pick it up because the *Aurora* was locked onto the station's specific coordinates that were unknown to others? Were Smith's tracking scans that good that they picked up something no-one else could? Or did someone on the Darwin know they were coming and was trying to send them a message?

He let out a sigh and sat back in his chair. Staring hard at the star map in front of him, he tried desperately to ignore that tight feeling in his gut.

*What the hell is going on up there?*

Carrie entered the mess hall for dinner and noticed the seating was similar to that at lunch; McKinley, Carter, Smith, Louis and Hunter, on one table, Brown on the other with Colt and Doc. It appeared that Brown was tolerating Colt. Carrie almost felt a pang of jealousy, wishing she'd been put on the engine room team. Somehow, putting up with Carter's smart-ass remarks seemed so much better than dealing with McKinley's confronting attitude.

She wondered where Packham was, but figured if Hunter was here, then she'd be manning the flight deck. Carrie took the seat beside Brown, opposite Doc. Brown glanced over as she sat, but didn't appear bothered. Doc nodded hello and Colt eyed her curiously.

"So, how was your afternoon?" Colt asked quietly, with a cheeky smile.

"How *was* your afternoon?" Doc reiterated.

She looked at them both. "Fabulous..." She smiled. "Solitude is a wonderful thing." She'd been glad that McKinley had stayed away until right at the end, but a look of disappointment shot across Doc's face. He must've been hoping McKinley returned to the weapons store.

Harris came over to their table with his plate and sat down beside Carrie.

"Captain," Doc immediately asked, "I heard we picked up a comms signal earlier?"

Harris nodded. "We lost it, but we think it came from the Darwin. I've got the flight deck poised to record and lock on it, if they pick it up again."

Doc nodded, as his mind seemed to tick over.

"So, anyway," Harris moved the conversation on, "you were discussing solitude?"

"Solitude?" Brown questioned. "No such thing as solitude on this ship. *Solitary confinement*, now, that's something else."

"Yeah," Smith chuckled from the other table. "It makes the solitary confinement I had at the institution seem like a dance party!"

"Institution?" Carter asked. "I didn't know you'd been institutionalized, Smith. What'd you do?"

Everyone looked at the young private.

"Nothing," he shrugged. "The *institution* is just what we called the 'home' I grew up in, you know, for kids without parents. When kids were bad, they were sent to this empty room. We called it solitary confinement."

"So you've never been to juvey? You don't have a record?" Carter inquired.

"Nope, but you could say the kinds of kids we got there made it seem a hell of a lot like a juvey."

"Shit, even *I* did a stint at juvey, Smith. And we all know that McKinley pretty much grew up there." Carter laughed.

McKinley looked up from his plate at Carter and smiled. "I might've spent a few years in and out, but at least I haven't done hard time like Brown."

Brown looked down his nose at McKinley and Carter.

"You've done hard time?" Colt exclaimed.

Brown turned his head to Colt, his almost black eyes studying her. "I've been to prison. I wouldn't say I've done hard time."

"He doesn't like to talk about it," Carter said, stirring. Brown shot him an unimpressed look and went back to his food.

"What did you do, Carter," Smith asked, "to get thrown into juvey?"

"He got done for stealing a porno mag," Hunter scoffed. "I don't think that counts!"

"It wasn't *one* porno mag," Carter rebuked. "It *started* with one porno mag. It ended up with just about anything they didn't nail down." He started laughing.

"Yeah, that's pretty hard-core, Carter," McKinley sniffed sarcastically.

"Just 'cause you lived your entire fucking life in detention, McKinley!"

"Not my *entire* life, Carter, just a few years in the middle."

"Anyway, Hunter," Carter chided, "we couldn't all afford to go to a preppy boys' school like you did, you fucking faggot!"

Hunter gave him a condescending once-over. "Well, that's pretty obvious."

"Now, guys," Doc intervened, "it's not a competition."

"Yeah," Carter snorted, "says Doc the fucking snowflake!"

"Snowflake?" Colt looked over at Doc. "This got something to do with your skiing?"

Carter snorted another laugh. "No, it's because Doc, here, is as pure as a fucking snowflake. No records, no institutions. I don't think he's even had a parking ticket. Little Mr Pure-as-snow."

The guys laughed. Doc looked over at Harris and shrugged his shoulders. "They say it like it's a bad thing?"

Harris smiled and shrugged back.

"I bet you even the captain's got a fucking record, eh?" Carter goaded.

Harris looked over at him. "I'll have you know I do *not* have a record, Carter."

"Ah, I don't believe you, captain. Surely you must?"

"Nope... I wasn't stupid enough to get caught like you did!" he said, going back to his meal. Everyone broke out in laughter, McKinley being the loudest, clapping his hands in appreciation, as Carter sat there without a comeback.

"So what'd you go to prison for, Brown?" Colt asked, breaking their laughter, clearly itching to know.

Brown's big, round face looked at her, knitting his eyebrows together in curiosity.

"I told you, he doesn't talk about it," Carter told her.

Brown hardened his face and turned it toward Carter. "You've never asked me about it."

"Carter's too scared to ask you about it," McKinley quipped.

Carter shot McKinley a seething look and flipped him the bird.

"Well, I'm asking you," Colt said matter-of-factly. "What'd you do?"

Brown glanced at Colt then looked around at everyone staring at him. He laughed quietly to himself like everyone was crazy. His eyes came back to Colt, whose expression told him she was still waiting for an answer.

He relented and shrugged. "Grievous bodily harm. They tried to get me for attempted murder, but I got a lesser charge."

The room fell silent.

"You tried to kill someone?" Colt was the only one game enough to ask. "What'd he do?"

Brown gave her the knitted-brow look again, the mess hall lights shining off his dark brown skin. "What makes you so sure it was a man?"

Although the room was silent, Carrie could almost hear the curiosity ticking over inside everyone's head. Everyone's except maybe Harris and Doc, that is. They didn't look surprised like the others. She figured that Harris probably already knew because it would've been in Brown's file. And Doc probably knew because he was, well, Doc. He was also Brown's roommate, and they appeared to be pretty close.

"Well, now, I know you ain't fool enough to raise your hand to a woman," Colt said matter-of-factly again, eyeing him up and down.

Brown looked over at Doc and they exchanged an amused smile, while a couple of the other men sniggered.

"So who was it? What'd he do?" Colt prodded again.

Brown gave up and shook his head. Clearly he was not going to get to eat in peace. He sighed, eyes focused on his plate and began speaking slowly between mouthfuls of food.

"My sister's ex-boyfriend. She was dating this junkie fuck. They had a kid, but he couldn't keep it together, so she broke it off. One night, he came back and broke into her house, all junkied up, trying to rob her... She tried to stop him, but he beat the shit out of her in front of their kid. Left her lying in a pool of blood with the kid standing there in his cot, screaming his lungs out for hours until someone found her..." He looked back up at Colt. "So, I found the junkie fuck... and I fucked him up back."

The mess had fallen so silent, the only sound was Brown's fork hitting his plate. Harris and McKinley were still eating, but they'd been careful not to disturb the silence around them.

"Did you mean to kill him?" Colt asked, a little softer now.

"I don't know. Probably. I'm glad I didn't though. 'Cause every time that junkie fuck looks in the mirror, he's gonna see what I did to his face, and remember not to go anywhere near my sister or nephew again."

Colt stared at Brown for a moment, then slowly held out her hand in front of him. He looked down at it and she motioned for him to give her five. He looked at her, then dropped his fork, reached out and hit it.

"So, your sister's alright, then?" Carrie broke the silence.

Brown looked at her, eyes still dark, brows still knotted.

"You said he left her in a pool of blood," Carrie elaborated. "She made it out alright?"

Brown nodded. "Just. She walks with a limp now. He busted her back from kicking it so hard... and her face will never be the same again neither."

Brown pushed his plate out in front of him and threw the fork onto it. "That's enough of my bullshit."

It was clear that Brown was done talking now. As Carrie's eyes left his face, they fell onto McKinley's. He gave her his blank stare, not quite as cold as it had been before, but a blank stare nonetheless. She wondered whether he was trying to make another point.

"So, what about you ladies then?" Carter picked up the slack in conversation, a sarcastic tone to his Afrikaans voice. "Done any time? Got any records?" he laughed like he already knew the answer.

"None here," Colt offered. "I tended to *date* them, not earn them myself."

Harris chuckled.

Carter looked over at Carrie. "What about you, Carrie the Kid?"

She gave him an unimpressed look and shook her head. "Sorry to disappoint you, Carter. Good student, good grades, no records and I never dated them either."

"Hmph! Carrie the Princess," Carter laughed. "Fuck, you and Doc should get together. Mr and Mrs fucking Snowflake!"

The men laughed. Doc gave Carrie a quick glance to intimate that Carter was an idiot. The captain appeared to be the only one not finding it amusing. Instead, he was looking down at his plate focusing on scooping another mouthful of food.

The rest of the dinner conversation was sporadic, as the tables seemed to revert back into their little groups of chatter. Carrie's table was fairly quiet. Brown remained silent. Harris, too, was being introverted. Colt had started telling Doc about a skiing trip she'd done to Colorado, going into great detail about her every fall down the slopes and Doc seemed amused.

Carrie looked over at Harris. "Why so quiet, captain?" she asked.

He looked up from his finished plate. "Just thinking, corporal."

"About the Darwin?"

He nodded. "Among other things."

"Twenty-four hours, huh? And we'll be there."

"Yes, we will."

She noticed his answers were short and sharp, making it difficult to get a conversation flowing. "Do you think everything's alright up there, sir? Do you think it's just a technical difficulty, or something else?"

"I have no idea, Welles. I guess we'll find out when we get there."

She gave a short, sharp, nod. "I'm looking forward to it, captain," she said firmly. "I can't wait to board her."

Harris gave her a strange look, then stood with his plate. "Good to know," he said, then walked over, put his plate on the counter, and left.

Carrie eyed the empty mess doorway, wondering if it was something she'd said.

"Hey, Welles?" Colt grabbed her attention.

"Yeah?" she looked up.

"You play cards?" Colt motioned over to the other table. "They're playing poker."

Carrie looked over and saw Carter was dealing out cards to the guys sitting around him. Doc moved to stand by McKinley and watch. Brown got up, too, but headed for the door.

"Brownie, you not playing?" Smith called after him, hands out in question.

"Nah," he replied. "I'm going to read."

"You can read?!" Carter exclaimed, flashing Brown a shocked expression.

Brown didn't bother turning around as he walked for the door. He simply stuck his hand in the air and flipped Carter the bird, to the amusement of the rest of the troops.

"Hell, I'll have a go!" Colt said, taking the seat next to Louis, opposite Smith, as Carrie moved over to stand beside Doc.

"C'mon, deal me in," Colt insisted.

"We've already dealt this round. You have to wait until we're done," Carter waved her off, as they all studied the cards in their hands.

Colt stared at them for a moment. "Yeah, something tells me you ain't going to deal me into the next round either, huh." She started getting up from the table again.

"Sit the fuck down, Colt," McKinley ordered.

The corporal stared back at him unimpressed.

He looked up from his cards. "Keep your panties on, corporal. We'll deal you into the next round. I'll be quite happy to take your chips off you."

Some of the men sniggered. Doc glanced at Carrie, his eyebrows raised as if to say: *Did you see that? McKinley said she could stay!* Colt stared at McKinley a little longer, but then slowly sat down at the table.

They began to play the round and before too long, Smith and Louis had folded, leaving Hunter, McKinley and Carter in the game. Hunter seemed to have the most chips, or in this case, toothpicks, obviously left over from previous games. McKinley and Carter were eyeing each other carefully. Shortly after, Carter folded, leaving McKinley and Hunter trying to stare each other out, which was difficult as they sat side by side. Eventually, they laid their cards down, and Hunter was declared the winner.

He laughed wickedly as he scooped the toothpicks up.

"You preppy fucker!" McKinley spat.

Hunter laughed again. "Yeah, well, this preppy fucker just beat your juvey ass, McKinley, so suck on that!"

"Fuckin' goddamn Kiwis, Saffers, Aussies! Get a fuckin' accent," McKinley continued to sneer, while the group gathered enjoyed the banter.

"Hey, the South African accent is the best fucking accent on the planet, mate. Don't you fucking worry about that, eh!" Carter boasted confidently.

McKinley stared at Carter. "I'm sorry, what? What did you just say? You sound like you got something stuck in your mouth."

Carrie couldn't help it but she actually broke a smile on McKinley's comment. Doc noticed. She jammed her lips together hard, quickly trying to bury the smile, much to Doc's amusement.

"I hate to love you and leave you, gentlemen," Hunter said gathering up his toothpicks, "but I'd better relieve the flight deck."

"Doc, you up?" Louis asked, dealing out again.

"Thought you'd never ask," he beamed, taking Hunter's spot beside McKinley, and pulling a load of toothpicks out of his shirt pocket.

"I thought I fucking banned you from this game, Doc," Carter said, seemingly displeased with the new player.

"You still bitter about that?" Doc asked, gathering the cards on the table in front of him.

"He's still bitter," McKinley said.

"I fucking had it in the bag, Doc! And then you come along and in one fell swoop take the fucking lot!"

"That'll teach you to bet your entire stack on the one hit. It was an accident waiting to happen," Doc shrugged.

"Yeah, bullshit, eh! Someone cheated. Someone told you my hand," Carter spat, looking down at his cards.

"Whatever," Doc said nonchalantly, studying his cards and moving a few around.

"You playing Welles?" Smith asked her.

Carrie shook her head. "No thanks."

"C'mon, why not?" he asked, giving her a friendly smile.

"Not my thing," she shrugged.

McKinley looked up from his cards at her, then over to Smith smiling. "That means she's no good at it, so in order to save face she's not going to play."

"Think what you want, McKinley," she said with a bored tone.

"Ain't no thinking. I know it," he smiled smugly.

Carrie went to say something back, but saw Doc looking at her, so she bit her tongue. She watched the round in silence. Smith folded early again. Carter wasn't far behind and clearly not pleased about it. Colt held her own against the guys, staying in the game longer than Louis and McKinley who eventually folded. So it came down to Colt versus Doc. The toothpicks kept going in. They kept staring over their cards at each other. Eventually, they laid their cards out on the table and Doc was the winner.

"Sorry 'bout that Colt!" he said, with a satisfied smile.

"Damn!" Colt whispered.

"You son of a bitch, Doc!" Carter complained again. "You're not playing cards with us. Fuck off!"

The medic laughed, enjoying the fact that Carter was pissed. McKinley, too, had a smile on his face.

"Nobody told me about the poker game, gentlemen!" Harris's booming voice came over Carrie's shoulder.

"Captain, we were just coming to get you!" Louis lied.

"You still losing, Carter?" Harris asked, walking up to the table.

"Don't you mean is Doc still fucking cheating?" he replied.

"Give it up, man," Doc said, shaking his head and shuffling the cards.

"Move over." Harris ordered Carter, Louis and Colt to move up one, then took a seat opposite McKinley.

Carrie decided she'd watched enough cards for one evening.

"I'm outta here," she told the gathering, crossing paths with Packham who entered for dinner. "Kick some ass, Colt!"

"I'll certainly try!" Colt replied, eyes staring intently at her cards.

*

Harris watched Welles leave the mess hall, but not before she'd smiled a goodbye at Doc. There was something about Carter's snowflake comment earlier that had stuck in Harris's mind. He wanted to shut down any linkage between a male and female soldier immediately, regardless of whether it was a joke or not. Luckily, the conversation at the time had moved on, so it wasn't a big deal, and he noticed now that although Doc smiled back at Welles, he went straight back to his cards. *There's nothing to worry about,* he told himself.

Packham took a seat at the table beside theirs, scoffing down her meal. The rest started playing the round of cards, and one by one they folded, until only Carter and Doc remained.

"Right, Doc, you fuck," Carter blurted out. "Game on!"

Doc shot his goofy poker smile at Carter and winked. They stared each other out for a while, upping the ante, then finally showed their hands. Doc was again the victor.

"FUCK!" Carter hissed, beating his hand on the table, while the others laughed.

Colt looked at Carter like he was psychotic, "Yeah… okay," she said. "I've had enough fun for one night. I'll leave you guys to it." And with that, she left, and Packham followed, dropping her empty plate on the counter.

Louis leaned back in his chair and watched them walk away.

"What are you looking at?" Smith laughed quietly at him.

"Colt 'as a juicy ass," Louis breathed in a husky voice.

Harris immediately turned and glared at him. "I did not just hear that!" He looked around at the other men and saw they were all looking over at the door watching her walk out. Doc quickly darted his eyes back to Harris's, and then down to the cards he was shuffling.

"DID I?" Harris said again loudly to the rest of them.

They all looked back at him.

Louis held his hands out in innocence. "C'mon captain, it's just looking! You put them on this ship."

"No, *Command* put them on this ship, sergeant!"

"Still, captain," Smith shrugged, leaning in as though he were telling him a secret, "they're not the ugliest soldiers they could've given us, are they?"

Harris gave the private a stern look.

"Smith 'as a crush on the princess," Louis grinned, white teeth glowing against his dark skin.

They all looked over at Smith, while Carter laughed. "Who? Carrie the Kid?!"

"I do not!" Smith objected.

"I've seen you looking at herrrrrr!" Louis teased.

"I have not!"

"Well, she *is* good with pistols, Smith!" Carter said dryly, then both he and Louis broke into laughter. Despite their best efforts, McKinley and Doc broke smiles as well.

Harris sat back in his seat, glaring at them. "What the fuck is wrong with you people?"

"Captain, you can't bring women onto a ship full of men and think we're not going to check them out?" Carter debated.

"I think they're your fellow soldiers and should be thought of only in that regard," he replied firmly.

"Please!" Carter said in a disbelieving tone.

"I'd definitely take Colt," Louis said nodding, then nudged Carter with his elbow. "Which one for you?"

Harris turned his glare back to Louis.

"Fuck, I don't know. I prefer blonds," Carter answered. "I'd probably go the English bird with her long legs. What say you, McKinley?"

McKinley scoffed as though they were all beneath him.

"I reckon he'd go Packham, too," Smith said, eyes narrowed in study.

McKinley gave Smith a look of displeasure.

Carter smirked. "Nah, I reckon he'd like to show the princess a thing or two with *his* pistol!"

McKinley turned his look of displeasure to Carter.

"Are you deaf? Am I not fuckin' sitting here?" Harris continued.

"Doc, what is your selection?" Louis continued.

The lieutenant looked up from the cards he was shuffling. "My *selection*?" he chuckled, shaking his head at Louis's choice of words.

"I know which one he'd prefer," Carter said smugly, eyeing him. "Then again, lover boy here would probably fuck all three of them!" Carter and Louis started howling with laughter as Smith tried to stifle his and McKinley grinned.

Doc glanced over at Harris, registered the look on his face and gave a half-smile. "I think our game of poker is over, gentlemen," he announced.

"I think you're right!" Harris said, as he stood up and snatched the pack of cards from Doc's hands.

"Oh, c'mon man!" Carter moaned.

"I suggest you change your topic of conversation, gentlemen," Harris said as he turned and headed for the door.

"Which one do you think the captain prefers?" Louis asked quietly, drawing a giggle from Carter.

Harris stopped in his tracks and turned around slowly to glare at Louis. The table was silent. Louis pulled an innocent face, putting his hands in the air as if to say, *What?* Harris saw Doc shake his head at the sergeant's stupidity.

Harris glared at Louis a while longer, who slowly but surely shrank into his seat, before he turned and continued for the door. As he walked off he heard McKinley warn, "Oh, you are going to pay for that one, Louis."

And he was right. Harris would let him stew tonight, then make him pay for that in the morning.

Carrie was in bed attempting to read a book but struggling. Her mind kept wandering off, rehashing the day's events, and thinking about what would happen on the Darwin when they got there. She felt as though some progress had been made with the team today, but only a little. She'd had the chance to show them what she was good at, but she'd also been forced to show them her weaknesses. She closed down her bookpane and put it beside her pillow. *Tomorrow is a new day,* she thought, *and it will be the day I board the Darwin. That'll be my chance —*

"Hey," Packham greeted her softly, entering the room. She plopped herself on Colt's bed, waiting for Colt to finish in the bathroom.

"How was your day on the flight deck, sergeant?" Carrie asked.

"Interesting," she nodded, shooting her a look of intrigue.

"Oh, yeah! So, what was with that mysterious comms signal?" Carrie suddenly felt a little more alert.

Packham shook her head. "We don't know. It looks like it was from them, but we lost it and there's been no other trace of it. The UNF still can't get a hold of the station, so we're continuing as planned."

Carrie nodded, thinking it over, then proceeded to get the lowdown from Packham of her day on the flight deck. They still wouldn't let her touch anything, but apparently Hunter had opened up a little, so she managed to get a conversation out of him.

"He's not so bad," Packham shrugged.

Colt emerged from the bathroom. "Sergeant Packham," she exclaimed. "You survived flight deck, I see."

Packham smiled, then turned back to Carrie. "How'd you go with McKinley today?"

"Oh, you wouldn't have heard about the confrontation in the gym!" Colt jumped in excitedly.

"Yeah, I did." She nodded, smiling.

"Who told you?" Colt and Carrie asked at the same time.

"McKinley came up to the flight deck, and he and Hunter sat up the back talking about what went on. I think they're buddies. They were talking low, but I could still hear."

"So what'd McKinley say?" Carrie's interest sparked.

"He said something about you and him having words, but that Doc stepped in, and that you girls were useless on the mats."

"Oh, yeah?" Carrie started to seethe. "Did he tell Hunter about me outshooting him on the range?"

"He said you were *alright* on the range."

"Hmph. Half the story then," Carrie muttered.

"It's okay, though, 'cause later Smith came in and he gave a different version of you on the range. I believe he used the word, *smokin'*," Packham grinned.

"Ha!" Carrie laughed, feeling a little vindicated. "What'd Hunter say to that?"

"He just said, 'That's not what Arizona told me'. Apparently that's McKinley's nickname. Anyway, Smith just said, 'Yeah, that's 'cause Arizona got his ass whipped!'. Hunter just blew it off and said, 'No-one beats Arizona. I'll believe it when I see it.'"

Carrie rolled her eyes as Packham chuckled and disappeared into the bathroom.

"McKinley's such an asshole," Carrie said still seething over his comments. "I would love to smack him in the mouth."

Colt glanced at her as she pulled back the sheets on her bed. "Yeah, good luck with that."

Carrie lay there staring at the bunk overhead, literally fantasizing about punching him. Colt obviously noticed this.

"Welles, just let it go," she said, climbing into bed. "There's nothing you can do about it."

"Yeah, there is. I will prove to him that I'm *every* bit as good as he is."

"But you're not going to be as good as he is in some things. It's called *life*," Colt said staring at her. "Just be good at what you're good at and let him be good at what he's good at. It's not a merry-go-round, it's a seesaw."

Carrie looked over at her, confused.

Colt rolled herself over and hiked herself up on her elbow. "He's a guy, Welles, and a big one at that. So he can fight better than you; so he can lift heavier shit than you. So what? Let him. There are certain things that they are always going to do better than us. You just need to sit back and when the time comes, step up and do what you can do better than him. Like with your shooting. That's what I did," she shrugged, "when I was stationed in East Africa, and they got wind of some major terrorist plan to bomb the UNF HQ there. They looked into it, discovered the threat was a reality, and my team got sent to defuse the bomb. It was a massive job. The terrorists had rigged up this big fucker across four city blocks. The only problem was that the receiver for this whole thing was planted down a tiny drain. My team couldn't tear the drain open in case it set it off, and none of the men could fit their hands down there. So, they looked to me.

"Now up until then, they didn't let me do shit, but because I had smaller hands than them, they had no choice. So, I put my hands in the hole and I defused the son of a bitch. It wasn't easy, it took several hours, but I did it. I did it, and *they* sat there wiping *my* brow for once! I defused that bitch and saved their asses and they knew it. So, do I care that they're bigger and stronger? Hell, no! Let them lift the heavy shit, let them fight the big guys, I ain't trying to match them. 'Cause I know that there's always going to be a time when there is something that they can't do, and they will look to me to do it for them. What goes around comes around, Welles. There'll be a day when they call on you to do what they can't do. Just like on your Santos mission. Ain't no-one denying that you kicked ass on that one."

Carrie lay there thinking over Colt's words.

Colt, sensing no rebuttal, snuggled down into her bed, rubbed her face and yawned. "I'm going to sleep. Goodnight."

"'Night," Carrie said softly as she reached up and touched her lamp off too. Deep down she knew Colt was right, but she also knew she had a stubbornness within that was going to be hard to shift. She wanted to be as good as the men, in everything they did. It was like some kind of mental block that prevented her from seeing sense. And the truth was, she didn't like to admit defeat either.

She let out a sigh and closed her eyes. *Just focus on the Darwin. Tomorrow will be the day. You will board that station, and you will show them what you can do.*

# 9

# War Games

Harris was leading the team on the morning run. It was no surprise that after a few laps, Doc and Hunter were right behind him. They were the fittest of his soldiers; all-rounders who generally did well at everything. McKinley and Carter were not far behind them, which was also par for the course. Their fitness was pretty good, but what really kept them up there was their basic all-round toughness, their sheer resilience and never-give-in attitude. What Harris was still getting used to, however, was that Welles was sticking with them. She was fit and determined, he had to give her that.

The rest of the team were bunched in a group just off the pace. As he passed each member he eyed them as he did with every run. Doc and Hunter ran side by side, almost step for step, a mirror image of the other. McKinley always looked focused, serious, as though he were running toward the enemy, while Carter looked a little bored, like he was simply carrying out a chore that had to be done. Brown's scowl indicated he would rip someone's head off for the chance to stop running. Louis, on the other hand, ran like he was dancing to some music in his head, pumping his arms and blowing out rhythmic breaths. Smith always looked to be on the same wavelength as Brown, like he was begging to hit that finish line.

Looking at the other women now, Harris noted that Colt looked as if she was pushing herself to get through the pain, to squeeze as much fitness into her body as it would allow. Packham was clearly in Brown and Smith's court, wanting the run to be over. She held a tortured look as though someone had just killed her beloved pet. To her credit, though, she wasn't giving up.

When the run finally came to an end, he waited for them to gather, then addressed them, eager to start this very important day.

"Breakfast is at 0630, soldiers. We have a very big day ahead of us. Our ETA for the Darwin, if I'm not mistaken, First Sergeant Hunter, is 2330, is it not?"

"Yes, sir! That's our ETA!" Hunter responded.

"Alright," he nodded at the team, "so we've got a lot to do before then, to have this ship and crew ready to board that station. We need to brief on our plan of attack and prepare for all contingencies!" He looked around at them, sweaty and puffing. "Now, Sergeant Louis, as per our discussion last night you will give me another fifteen laps—"

"What?" Louis exclaimed.

"—and First Sergeant Carter, seeing how Sergeant Louis is unable to attend to his mess duty, *you* will take his place. Do you understand?" he said firmly.

Harris watched as Carter hung his head back and gave a deep sigh. He looked over at Louis who was clearly pissed off.

"DO YOU UNDERSTAND?" Harris yelled, not standing for any bullshit this morning. It was obviously pretty loud, as he noticed both Packham and Welles flinch.

"Yes, sir," Carter and Louis chimed reluctantly.

"Dismissed!"

Louis took off running and Carter made his way to his room. Harris, satisfied, turned and headed for his quarters, but as he did, he heard Hunter ask McKinley, "What was that about?"

Harris paused and turned around. He saw the rest of the troops looking at McKinley, waiting to hear his answer. Harris gave the lieutenant his best *Do not say a word!* look, which McKinley seemed to register because he disappeared into his room.

Harris went back to his quarters and showered. As the water flowed over him, he found himself mulling over yet another strange dream he'd had last night, involving Sibbie and Etta. They just stood there and stared at him, Sibbie clutching onto that phone for dear life. He figured his recent thoughts of Holly and family gifts must've manifested this dream from his subconscious. It niggled at him, but he cleared it from his mind. He had other things to focus on here.

He began planning what training he would put the troops through today, and what needed to be done before they docked at the Darwin that evening. All the information from the files ran through his head. The station's setup, its crew, the scant information he had on the programs they were running, and of course, Professor Sharley and his controversial background. He thought about his own crew, their strengths and their weaknesses. He thought about the female recruits and his orders to have them remain on the ship. He pictured Welles's eager face again, saying "I can't wait to board her." Unfortunately, she was not going to get that chance.

After his shower, he headed straight for the mess, and noticed that his soldiers were quiet, treading carefully after his explosion at Louis and Carter earlier. When breakfast was announced, he headed up the queue, Colt joining his side.

"Morning, captain." She gave him a friendly smile as Carter filled his plate.

He looked down his shoulder at her. He admired her courage, for going where the others feared to tread.

"Morning, corporal. Sleep well?" he replied.

"Yes, sir. Like a baby. Although Welles did wake me up, talking in her sleep, but I just went back out again. I'm good like that."

Harris looked down the line at Welles. He noticed she was standing next to Doc, who was talking about something, then they both laughed.

"What was she talking about... in her sleep?" Harris asked curiously.

Colt shrugged. "I don't know." She chuckled and waved it off. "She's been dreaming aloud every night since we got on here. I just roll over and go back to sleep."

Harris focused his eyes on Welles again in study, then headed for the tables.

Breakfast went quickly and quietly. He thought the troops seemed a bit tense this morning. He wasn't sure whether he'd brought that on, but knew it was to be expected when soldiers faced a boarding with potential unfriendlies. There was bound to be anticipation and edginess in the air.

He hoped their morning training session would help get some of that out of their system.

"Soldiers!" he called out, once the eating was done. "Yesterday I gave you some target practice and we found out those of you who can shoot straight. Today we will see who can shoot in the field, under pressure, and work as a team to accomplish their mission." He eyed them all. "I'm breaking you into two teams. One will start from the cargo hold and make their way in attack mode to reach the flight deck and rescue our pilots, Hunter and Packham. The other team will have the mission of defending their prisoners on the flight deck and intercepting the attack. Whichever team's left standing at the end, wins. We'll be using the laser-fire rifles on training mode for this one. Each of you is to wear a target vest. For you new recruits, so you know, if you get hit that vest will light up like a star and then you will sit the rest of the exercise out. Understand?"

"Yes, sir!"

"Ok, First Lieutenant Walker, and Second Lieutenant McKinley, step forward."

Doc and McKinley moved to stand either side of him.

"These are your two team leaders," Harris announced. "Doc, you will be on attack, and McKinley will be on defense. Do you understand?"

"Yes, sir!" they answered.

"On McKinley's team defending the prisoners will be: Staff Sergeant Brown, Sergeant Louis and Corporal Colt. On Doc's team attacking the flight deck will be First Sergeant Carter, Corporal Welles and Private First Class Smith. Are we clear?"

"Yes, sir!" they replied.

"I will be in my office watching the exercise over our surveillance cameras, so that will be the only room out of bounds. All other rooms will be accessible for the exercise. Weapons store crew, collect the laser-fire guns and vests and bring them back here to the mess hall. The rest assemble in your teams!"

Carrie's heart began to pump with excitement. She and McKinley collected the vests and laser-fire rifles from the store, locked them into training mode, then headed back to the mess. McKinley was silent. She could see his mind ticking over, planning his defense already. She watched him carefully, trying to sharpen her own mind. They made it back to the mess and divided up the guns and vests amongst the crew. McKinley took his team to the flight deck to discuss battle plans, while Doc called his to the cargo hold.

"Alright," Doc began, as they gathered around him, "if I know McKinley, he'll send some of his crew out to intercept us and stop us from getting anywhere near the prisoners. So, we will make our way up to the flight deck, in a two-by-two formation. Carter, you and I lead. Welles, you and Smith take the rear. We check every room between here and the flight deck, and try to take out McKinley's men, so they don't come up behind us." He turned to Carrie. "Welles, I hope you've got your sharpshooting eyes in today!"

"Yes, sir," she nodded firmly.

"Okay, let's not give them too much time to get in position!" With that Doc turned around, raised his gun and began to ascend the stairs, with Carter close at his side; Carrie and Smith headed followed a few paces behind. When they made it to the top of the cargo hold stairwell, Doc and Carter got into position. They exchanged a nod, then opened the door and sprang out. Doc aimed his gun north, whilst Carter aimed south.

Satisfied the corridor was clear, Doc disappeared from the doorway, and a few moments later Carter followed. Carrie and Smith quickly moved to take up their positions in the doorway, mimicking their north–south coverage. She saw Doc and Carter taking cover in the nearest doorway, which was Doc's medical rooms. As soon as Carter saw them, he turned his gun to face north with Doc.

Carrie and Smith moved over and lined up against the wall behind them. Doc motioned for them to stay put and continue their coverage of the corridor, while he and Carter prepared to check out the rooms. They opened the door, swiftly took their positions and entered, whilst Carrie and Smith moved up to take cover in the doorway and control the corridor. A few minutes of nervous silence passed, but soon the two soldiers emerged; the rooms were clear.

Doc motioned for them to stay put, whilst he and Carter moved on to the next room, the general store, down a short corridor off to their left. The room wasn't large, so they cleared it quickly. They then crossed the main corridor, under Carrie and Smith's cover, and cleared the medical store in the same manner. Continuing the two-by-two cross-cover, they took it in turns to move up the corridor, and while Carrie and Smith sheltered in the doorway of the general store, Doc and Carter crossed back over the corridor yet again, and stopped outside the next room up, the mess hall. Doc turned, motioned for Carrie to come forward, so she swiftly ran over to them, under Smith's cover.

"I think if they're going to have someone waiting for us it's going to be here," he whispered. "When I open the door I'll go north, and I want you to go low and south to the counter, Welles. They'll be hiding there somewhere. Okay?"

"Yes, sir," she whispered.

Carter moved forward out of the doorway, so Carrie could get into position. Doc had his hand over the door lever, gun at the ready to face north. He hit the button and the door slid open. She suddenly heard the whizzing of laser-fire and ducked. Recovering quickly, she raised her gun in the direction it had come from, fired three blasts back, then took cover back behind the wall. There was silence for a moment, then she saw the screen on her gun light up red with the register reading, 01. She saw the corresponding red glow from behind the counter.

"Fucking bitch!" came Louis's French mutter.

Doc continued scanning the room. He entered carefully and she followed. They cleared the rest of the room, mess hall kitchen and stores included. All they found was Louis giving them his dirtiest glare.

"Good work," Doc said quietly to her, as they headed back for the door.

While Smith quickly crossed the corridor to nestle in the doorway of the medical store, Carrie stayed at the mess entrance, and they both provided cover for Doc and Carter as they prepared to clear the next room diagonally up the corridor, the comms room. As soon as Doc and Carter had entered the room, Brown suddenly dived out of the next door up ahead — the training facility — shooting wildly. Carrie and Smith immediately took cover in their doorways, while the firing soldier ducked back inside the training facility.

Doc slowly opened the door of the comms room and made eye contact with Carrie across the corridor. She indicated there was one unfriendly in the door diagonally opposite him. He whispered something to Carter, then motioned to her indicating that Smith should move up and join her. She quickly turned and conveyed this message to the private. As Smith began to move up, Brown swiftly jumped out again and shot at him. Carrie returned fire, as did Carter through the doorway. The corridor suddenly seemed to be glowing red. She looked around at Smith and saw he was part of it. Brown had got him. She looked over at Brown, who came out of the doorway glowing as well. She looked at the reading on her gun, but it wasn't her. Then she noticed Carter's gun glowing 01.

Once Brown and Smith removed themselves from the scene, Doc motioned for Carrie to cover the south corridor, while Carter covered north and he moved up to the training facility door where Brown had been. They then took it in turns to provide cover, while Carter joined Doc at the training facility and Carrie moved to the comms room doorway. They proceeded to then carefully check out the training facility and the weapons store in the same manner, in quick succession, but they were empty. The only room left unchecked was the captain's office, but they knew that was out of bounds for the exercise. That meant there was only the flight deck left to check.

Doc motioned for Carrie to join them, crouching outside the flight deck door.

"This is the tricky part," he said, breathing a little heavily from the excitement, a slight sheen of sweat on his brow. "The other two must be inside with the prisoners. We'll open the door and stand back while they fire at us, then Carter and I will go in, cross-cover, and I want you to go in low through the middle, Welles. Knowing McKinley, he'll probably be keeping the prisoners close, so make sure you *don't* hit the prisoners. Make sure you aim for Colt and McKinley."

They nodded, and moved to stand at the door, Carrie checking the corridor behind them again just in case. Doc looked them both in the eye, and mouthed, *"One, Two, Three!"*. He hit the door lever and they threw themselves back flat against the walls. The doors opened and laser fire whizzed through the air for a few seconds. The moment it stopped, Doc nodded to Carter and they both entered the room with a drop and roll, under heavy crisscross fire with their enemy. Doc slid behind the chairs on the upper level to the left-hand side of the aisle, and Carter stopped on the right-hand side. As they did, Carrie snuck in low, and took up a position beside Doc. She looked down to the bottom tier and saw McKinley holding Packham well and truly in front of him, crouched behind the bottom row of chairs. Colt was crouched too, but over to the left-hand side, while Hunter sat in the pilot's chair behind her, casually watching the action.

Doc motioned for both her and Carter to provide cover while he made a move down to the second tier to the captain's table. He counted to three and moved forward shooting. McKinley and Colt fired back and Carter, shooting while he moved, followed Doc. He stopped suddenly, however, and looked down at his vest which was now glowing red. Everyone saw McKinley's gun glowing.

"Fuck it!" Carter muttered, pulling himself up. Doc looked over at him, his eyes flashing disappointment, then anger. Carter slowly turned and disappeared from the room.

Doc looked up at Carrie. He indicated that he would cover her as she moved to where Carter had been. He quickly jumped up shooting and then dropped back out of sight, whilst Carrie rolled over to her designated spot. She caught her breath a moment, while Doc looked around trying to figure out their next move. She noticed McKinley motioning for Colt to move around to the left side of Doc, but the medic saw this too. He watched her make her move, then quickly flung his body out around the row of chairs and shot at her. She tried to pull back, but the room swiftly glowed red again, and Doc's gun lit up. Colt sighed, looked sheepishly over at McKinley, then pulled herself to her feet and left the room.

Carrie kept her gun trained on McKinley through the seats as she maneuvered slowly down to the edge of the second tier to join Doc, at his order. She noticed that although McKinley's vest was covered by holding Packham hostage, he was also at a disadvantage for movement.

"We need to corner him," Doc whispered. "You go down and around to the left, and I'll run across to the right-hand side and down. He won't know which one of us to target. If you get a shot, go for it, or he'll take one of us out."

She nodded. Doc counted to three, then bolted. Carrie moved quickly down the stairs, hiding by the front corner of the captain's table, near where Hunter sat. She could see McKinley moving about not knowing which one to shoot at, with Doc on one side and Carrie on the other. McKinley stood and began backing himself slowly into the corner, while holding Packham in front.

"Stop or I'll shoot the prisoner!" he said from behind Packham's head.

Doc slowly stood with his gun trained on McKinley. Carrie did, too, positioning herself in front of Hunter, protecting the hostage. Three red dots danced across Packham, two near her shoulders trying to find McKinley's vest, and one that McKinley had trained on her temple.

"You're supposed to save the prisoners, people," McKinley sang teasingly.

Doc didn't say a word. He was a ball of focus, waiting for that shot. It was a Mexican standoff and no-one was giving in. The red laser-lights continued to dance across Packham as the tension built along with the sweat that gleamed upon their foreheads.

"Release the prisoner and we won't shoot!" Doc ordered after realizing he couldn't get a shot in.

"Yes, you will," McKinley said.

"Let her go, McKinley! Game's over," Doc ordered. "It's two against one."

"Maybe I'll shoot her anyway and take someone else down with me. Maybe one of you, maybe Hunter," McKinley said.

Carrie focused her eyes sharply on McKinley's gun. She traced it down, found his fingers and followed his arm, looking to find his vest, but he'd covered it very well. Doc glanced over at her and seemed to understand what she was trying to do. He carefully jumped down to the bottom tier, and moved further to McKinley's side, trying to draw him around to expose part of his body for her to aim at. It was working. McKinley was trying to resist the movement, but knew he had no choice. He gave in. With a swift movement he pushed Packham in Doc's direction with one hand and brought his gun up to shoot Carrie with the other.

She saw it coming, however. She shot at him, then quickly spun around and launched herself at Hunter, knocking him off his chair to the floor. She landed on top of him with a thud, forcing the air out of his lungs.

"Ugh! Jesus!" he cried out.

Carrie looked down and saw a glowing red light.

"Fuck! Is that you or me?" she said, peeling her torso off the pilot to take a look.

"It's not me," he said looking down at himself.

Carrie saw that it was her own vest glowing. She quickly turned around to see McKinley looking down at his glowing vest, too, with Doc and Packham standing in the corner staring at them both. She looked back at her glowing vest and sighed.

"You want to get off me now?" Hunter said, looking at her body straddling him.

She quickly pulled herself to her feet and turned around to McKinley again. She was glad that she'd taken him out, but disappointed that he'd managed to get her too. She wondered who got who first? They stared at each other for a moment, his piercing blue eyes shining, obviously intrigued, no doubt wondering the same thing.

Harris's voice suddenly boomed over the public address system in the room: *"Make your way to the mess, people."* He spoke in an even tone, not giving his thoughts away as to whether or not he was satisfied with the exercise. The soldiers on the flight deck looked around at each other, then began to make their way up the stairs.

"Jesus, you fuckin' winded me, Welles," Hunter said, rubbing his chest and pulling himself back into his pilot's chair.

"Yeah, but you're alive, Hunter," Doc told him, then looked at Carrie. "You did a good job."

They entered the mess and removed their glowing vests and took a seat. Harris stood out front by the counter, waiting for them to come to order.

"Well," he eventually began, "was the exercise a success? Did we accomplish our mission?" He paused and looked at each of them. "The UNF, on paper, would say yes. Doc's team accomplished their mission to rescue the prisoners. Doc was the only one to make it out alive, but the prisoners were unharmed. So, *yes*, they succeeded."

He looked over at Louis.

"Sergeant Louis, your death was foolish. You're not a bad shot, but you're not as good as Welles or Doc who came in at you. You were hidden behind the counter, and if you were smart, you would've waited, drawn them nearer and then tried to take one if not both of them out. But you didn't. As soon as that door opened, you fired and tried to get in first, but you missed and then Welles took you out. Downright stupid. It's not necessarily about getting in with the *first* shot, Louis. Sometimes you have to wait until you have the *right* shot."

Louis gave Harris a short, sharp nod, but sat with his arms folded like a petulant child. Harris turned to Smith.

"Private First Class Smith, your death was a little unfortunate. You had three of your crew up ahead, but that didn't stop Brown from getting you. Based on the angle that Brown was on, you should've crossed the corridor first and then made your way up behind Welles's cover, instead of running up the middle of the corridor to her. That cost you. *Always* pay attention to where your enemy is, and where their line of sight may be."

"Yes, sir," Smith nodded.

Harris looked at Brown. "Sergeant Brown, you took out Smith. That was good shooting. You saw a weakness and you went for it. I do feel, however, that it was a little risky taking on *four* armed soldiers on your own. *Courage* is taking a risk to do what is right, *not* just taking a risk. Don't mistake that."

Brown nodded very slightly, acknowledging what he said. Harris then turned to Carter.

"First Sergeant Carter, you took out Brown. It was a quick, clean shot and you nailed it. But then you got cocky. Your death was sheer stupidity. McKinley didn't kill you, you killed yourself. Doc's order was for you to cover him while *he* moved down. Instead, you covered him whilst moving to a new position yourself. You ignored your team leader's orders. You tried to do too much at the same time; you took your mind off the game and it got you killed. You gave McKinley easy pickings. First Sergeant Carter, I highly recommend that you don't *ever* ignore any of my orders in the field. Do you understand me?"

"Yes, sir," Carter answered. He wasn't happy about it, but it was obvious he knew the captain was right. Harris then turned to Colt.

"Corporal Colt. *You* on the other hand, followed your team leader's orders, but you were too slow and too obvious. Doc knew what you were doing the second you went to do it and he took you out. *Stealth* is highly recommended in the field, corporal. Do not advertise what you are about to do to your enemy or it will be more than your vest that turns red. Do you understand?"

"Yes, captain," she said, taking it on board.

Harris looked over at McKinley.

"Second Lieutenant McKinley. It was a good idea to send Brown and Louis out to cut off Doc's team. However, as they failed you, it would've been much more productive to leave them in that room with you. You would've had four soldiers down there and it would've been a very difficult task for Doc to make his way down to where you were. Nice move using Packham as a shield, though. I also find it interesting that you chose death over surrender? I would have said in these circumstances, that surrender would've been the better option. It is not in the UNF's policy to torture captives, only to imprison them. Had Doc's team been rebels or terrorists, then perhaps death would've been the better option. *Know* your enemy, and *know* your options."

"Yes, sir," McKinley replied.

Harris looked at Carrie. Her heart fluttered nervously, wondering what critique he was about to unleash.

"Corporal Welles, you took out two soldiers. You also put your life on the line to not only take out McKinley, but also to save that of one of the hostages. You did a good job. Next time, however, it might serve you better to release Hunter a little earlier and get him out of harm's way, so that when the time came, you could throw yourself *out* of the way of the enemy's fire, instead of throwing yourself *between* it and the hostage."

"Yes, captain," she said, relieved.

Finally Harris turned to Doc.

"First Lieutenant Walker. You achieved your mission. You got the prisoners out alive. You showed good leadership, and you thought ahead about what your enemy was planning. Your team died, but that was generally due to mistakes on their part, not yours. Well done."

Doc gave a nod and a half-smile.

Harris looked around at the team again. "So, I want everyone to think long and hard about today's exercise. I want you to think about where you went wrong, where everyone, on both sides, went wrong. Learn from *your* mistakes *and* theirs… and make damn sure you do not repeat them. In this line of work there are no second chances. Do you understand me?"

"Yes, sir," they replied.

"Right," Harris said looking at his watch, "Weapons store team, take the equipment back then return here to the mess hall. Smith, prep the comms room for the soldiers' final transmissions home. After the transmissions, we will break for lunch. Are we clear?"

"Yes, sir!"

With that McKinley and Carrie stood and began gathering the equipment, while Smith exited the room.

Upon returning to the mess hall, Carrie took a seat next to Colt, who was chatting with Brown and Doc at one of the tables. Louis and Carter sat at the other table and McKinley joined them there. Harris, she noted, had disappeared.

"Nice going, girl." Colt held out her hand for a high-five.

Carrie slapped it halfheartedly. "I don't know what you're high-fiving me for," she said, "I died."

"We all did," Colt shrugged. "Doc, here, is the only one who made it!"

"Hey, if Welles hadn't taken out McKinley, I may not be here," he replied.

"You did alright, Carrie the Kid," Brown offered, his dark eyes friendly.

She looked back at him and smiled warmly. "Thanks, Brown."

"Ooh, I can't wait to talk to my family!" Colt said excitedly, clasping her hands in front of her chest. She looked at Carrie. "You calling your dad, huh?"

Carrie nodded, smiling at her enthusiasm.

"What about you Brown? Who you calling?" Colt asked.

"All of 'em. My sister and my nephew live with my mother now," he answered.

"What about your dad? He still alive?" Colt's excitement mellowed.

"Could be," Brown shrugged. "Got no idea where that fool is. Don't care neither."

Colt smiled sadly at him, then turned to Doc. "What about you, Doc?"

"My folks," he nodded.

"What, no *special* ladies," Colt teased, jumping her eyebrows at them both. "You ain't got any tucked away somewhere?"

Brown looked down his nose at her. "Please. Women ain't nothing but trouble."

Doc laughed.

"Oh, and men ain't?" Colt said with attitude.

Brown grunted, shaking his head, as Colt turned back to Doc.

"You're being quiet, lieutenant?" she asked, eyeing him suspiciously.

"Am I?" he smiled.

"Yeah. So, you got a girlfriend? I don't see a wedding ring."

Doc smiled again. "It's not exactly the best line of work for maintaining relationships. In fact, it brings a whole new meaning to the term 'long distance relationship'."

"Ain't that the truth!" Colt nodded in agreement.

Just then Smith entered the mess hall and called out, "Okay, who's first up?"

Carrie, Doc and Brown looked over at Colt, whose eyes went wide with excitement, but Carter stood and walked over to him.

Colt's shoulders slumped a little.

"So, what about you ladies, then?" Brown asked. "I take it from your comments you ain't calling no '*special man*'," he said, imitating Colt.

Colt waved him off. "I thought I had one but he didn't make it into Space Duty, so therefore we couldn't date anymore. *His* words, not mine!"

"Ouch!" said Brown. "So he a player then?"

Colt eyed Brown like he was crazy. "What makes you say that?!"

"Well, yo' ass gonna be floating around up here. He clearly ain't waiting for you down there. Guess you should be grateful he broke it off with you first."

"Ouch!" Carrie laughed.

Colt looked over at Carrie and then back at Brown. "I guess so, brother. You really know how to make a woman feel special, don't you?" she said sarcastically.

"You a soldier, not a woman. On this ship, anyway."

The three of them chuckled at Brown.

"So, what about you, Welles? You didn't answer, either," Doc asked, his eyes curious.

Carrie shook her head. "Nope. None for me."

"What? You like women?" Brown teased.

"No," Carrie said, "I mean there's no '*special guy*' for me." She made the inverted commas with her hands.

Colt and Doc smirked at her reaction.

Brown looked around at them all and shook his head. "Well, aren't we a sorry bunch of soldiers. Wearing a uniform like *this*, and we all calling our parents!"

They burst out laughing, much to the curiosity of McKinley and Louis at the other table.

After a few minutes Carter came back in. As soon as he did, Colt jumped up. "I'm next!" she called out and raced over to the door.

"Jeez, maybe I should give her my timeslot. I think she's going to need it," Carrie said.

Doc gave her a curious look, "You don't want to talk to your old man?"

"No, I just think Colt would..." she thought about her choice of words, "... benefit more from the time."

Doc's curious look now became a confused one. Just then she heard her name being mentioned at the other table, and Carter and Louis started laughing. She looked over at them. McKinley's eyes were amused, and there was a slight smile on his lips. Carrie continued to eye them for a moment.

"Something you want to tell me?" she asked them.

Louis shot her an arrogant glance, "We're talking *'bout* you, not to you."

Carter laughed. "Oh, go on. Tell her."

Louis ignored him.

Carter looked over at her. "We were just discussing how you threw yourself at Hunter, before."

Carrie looked hard at Louis, then back at Carter, who continued on.

"*Very* enthusiastic, Welles. I mean, you had him on the ground and everything."

Louis started laughing, while Carter grinned.

"You seem to know a lot for someone who wasn't in the room at the time," she said, throwing McKinley an accusing stare.

McKinley stared back with his piercing blue eyes. "And you're looking at me because...?"

She didn't say anything, she just returned his stare with her own sharp eyes.

He gave a quiet laugh. "I didn't say shit."

"No, actually," Carter offered, "Smith piped the surveillance through to the monitor in here, so we had front row seats for the, er, action," Carter began to laugh again. "You know you could've just asked Hunter for a fuck, Welles. I'm sure he would've obliged. He does the occasional bit of charity work."

Louis burst out laughing and Carter looked pleased with himself, as Carrie's face turned steely.

"Alright, that's enough," Doc spoke up.

"In fact, if you're going to be *that* enthusiastic, Welles, I know a few others here who'd be happy to help out, too," Carter continued looking at Louis who was laughing hysterically. "Smith for one! Although, *you'd* probably be doing him the favor."

"I said enough!" Doc fired his voice firmly at them. "Clearly you didn't learn from your extra laps and mess duty this morning, gentlemen. Would you like some more?"

They steadied their laughter and looked at him. McKinley, amusement shining in his eyes, slowly sat back in his chair, folding his arms as he moved out of the firing line between Doc and the two men.

"Captain's not here now, Doc, so how would he hear such a thing?" Louis asked, his voice light enough, but there was accusatory edge to it.

Doc stared at him hard. "Louis, you seem to forget my place in the food chain on this ship. You also seem to forget that it's within my rights to hand out punishments as I see fit. I think the captain would support my decision when I conveyed my reasoning to him. So, you goin' to move on or you want to keep this up?"

Carter sat back loudly in his chair. "It's just a fucking laugh, Doc. Calm down."

"Find something else to laugh about!" he shot back.

Carter and Louis looked at each other. Louis was pissed, but Carter seemed indifferent, letting it roll off his shoulders. McKinley sat there looking down at the table in front of him, a slight smile playing on his lips. Carrie looked down into her lap. She was angry, but her mind was more consumed with Doc standing up to them like that. Again, like with Harris, she wanted to fight her own battles. But at the same time, she was intrigued. It was the hardest she'd seen him be with the men so far and clearly they weren't prepared to push it with him. She somehow felt that it wasn't just his rank that made them stop.

She glanced over at Brown. He was rubbing his hand along his jaw and looking over at the other table. He almost had a smile on his face, like he was amused they'd been put in their place. She made brief eye contact with Doc, before he looked away. No-one spoke after that, and the silence hung heavily around them.

Harris was walking down the corridor from his quarters, when Bolkov's voice rang out over the ship's PA.

*"Captain! Report to flight deck immediately!"*

Harris broke into a jog and headed for the deck. *Had they picked up the signal again?*

He burst through the doors and hurried down the steps to where Bolkov sat, listening intently to his earpiece. Harris picked up Hunter's headset lying on the console beside him and put it on. He stared hard at Bolkov, listening, but heard nothing.

Bolkov shook his head. "Is gone again."

"Fuck!" Harris hissed. "What was it?"

The Russian looked at him. "I heard something, but didn't quite capture. Was not distress signal, was comms again. Let me listen again." He reached forward to replay the recording.

"It definitely came from that location?" Harris asked.

Bolkov nodded. "I traced it right to Darwin, sir." He motioned for Harris to get ready, then hit play.

They listened carefully, sitting absolutely still. It went for approximately fifteen seconds, but whatever it was, was garbled. They listened to it again, and then for a third time. It sounded, at a stretch, like it could be voices, but there was a lot of static distorting it.

Harris removed the headset and stared at the console for a moment, thinking.

"Alright, Smith should be just about done with the comms home. As soon as he is, get him up here. See if he can clear it up and decipher what the hell it is."

"Yes, sir." Bolkov gave a single nod.

"And check in with Command," he ordered. "Let me know if they picked that one up."

Bolkov nodded again, then turned back to the console and immediately began logging into his portal to contact Command.

Harris stood, resting his hands on his hips, as he stared out the flight deck window. With their hyperflight now over, the ship was traveling at normal speed. Mars was visible, a pebble of orange rock in the far distance that would grow in size by the second. His eyes scanned the vast expanse of space surrounding it, and felt an edginess rise within. Soon enough, the Darwin would appear. Soon enough, they would find out what was going on there.

He felt a sudden need for more research, feeling hamstrung by the lack of information to hand. He clenched his jaw, and swiftly left the flight deck, as that strange sensation in his gut rose up once again.

# 10

# Final Countdown

Carrie volunteered to go last for the transmission home. Even though they were restricted to just five minutes, she wasn't really sure what to say to her father.

"Hey, it's Carrie the Kid," Smith greeted her with a smile, as she arrived at the comms room.

She smiled back, almost blushing, thinking about Carter's comments earlier. Smith stood there with an e-clip, clicking through the pages, trying to find her details. She watched him closely. He seemed so much younger than the other guys. He still had a bit of a baby face, almost cherubic. His eyes were a deep glassy blue, his lips a shiny, dark maroon and his blond hair was cropped short.

"Oh, there it is." He half smiled, half laughed, showing his slightly crooked teeth.

He looked up at her. "You just go and sit in the booth. I'll punch in your transmission code and you'll see a screen come up. When you see it connect, you fire away. Yeah? There shouldn't be any delay between comms. We'll be bouncing our signal via the Mars colonies which are linked with Earth."

Carrie nodded and Smith waved her toward the door ahead. She entered the booth and sat down. It was very bare inside with plain, silver-metal walls, floor and ceiling. A camera sat in front of her with a screen just below it and lights overhead. It seemed a little snug. She wondered how some of the men got on in such a tight space.

The screen lit up, and she saw a code appear across the screen. She figured that must've been what Smith was entering. It gave her a sudden thought. She called out to him. "Smith, can you hear me from out there?"

He didn't reply. The screen flashed again and a message blinked: *One moment while we connect you.*

She waited a few moments, then the screen flashed again and she saw her father. He was standing in the living room of his villa in Florida, the TV was on in the background.

"Carrie," he answered, an expectant look upon his face.

"Dad," she smiled hello.

"So, how's it going?"

"Good," she smiled confidently. "And you? How're things back there?"

"Fine," he answered abruptly, furrowing his brow in concentration. "You must be about to hit your target if they're letting you phone home, huh?"

"Yeah."

"Do you know where you're going yet?"

She heard a jingling noise, as he lifted a scotch on the rocks to his mouth and took a sip.

"Dad, you know I can't talk about it."

"You can tell your old man, Ree. I'm quite familiar with the UNF, you know. Planet, star or station?" he asked, taking another sip.

She sighed and gave him a passive look. "Dad."

"Well, what's your team like then?" He changed tack.

She shrugged. "They're okay."

"Okay?" He studied her a moment. "You're a bad liar, Ree. You need to work on that."

"Some are nice, and some are..." she hesitated.

"Assholes." He managed to finish her sentence before she thought of an appropriate word.

She smiled.

"Yeah, I've worked with a few of them in my time. Listen, Ree, don't you take any shit," he pointed firmly at her, "unless of course it's your captain... or any superior officer for that matter. Unfortunately, sometimes you've just got to put up with it. Unless it's completely un-job related, then you have to stand your ground! You shot any of them yet?" A slight smile curled the corner of his mouth, as he took another sip of his scotch.

She smiled at him again, eyeing the scotch in his hands. He was more relaxed than normal. "Not yet, but I've thought about it," she answered, then changed the subject. "So what are you up to tonight? You sound like you've had a few drinks. Have you got company there?"

He glanced over his shoulder. "Yeah, I've got an old friend here at the moment." He looked back at Carrie, and the serious look took hold of his face again. "So, do we know how serious the job is yet?"

"Not yet. It's probably nothing, knowing my luck."

Her father paused a moment. "'Nothing' is not so bad, Ree. 'Nothing' will get you home again. Remember that." The look on his face held a tinge of concern. She felt a sudden pang of guilt hit her in the chest.

She nodded.

"So, how's this Captain Harris?" He continued his line of questioning.

"He seems alright. Hard, but fair."

"Well, that's what you want in a leader," he nodded, "hard but fair. There isn't any room in the UNF for a spineless man, that's for sure. The team giving you any stick about having a retired colonel for a dad?"

Carrie hesitated for a moment. "No, not yet."

He eyed her down the camera. "You didn't tell them, did you?"

"Need to know basis, Dad," she replied.

He grunted. "Probably Ree, probably. Although, it can earn you respect too. Don't forget about that."

"I'd like to earn my own first."

He looked down the camera at her, then nodded. A 60 second warning flashed across the screen.

"Time's run out already," she noted. "Well, hopefully, I'll have something more interesting to report next time."

"Maybe, maybe. I'm happy with dull, though, like I told you. 'Nothing' is good, Ree."

She nodded. "I'll see what I can do, colonel."

Her father stared at her a moment. "Okay, corporal," he said, then raised his glass. "Good journey."

"Thanks, colonel. Have another scotch for me," she smiled.

His eyes glanced to the clock counting down, and his face seemed to drop suddenly. "Ree?" he said quickly, darting his eyes back to hers.

"Yeah?"

"Just..." Her father's mind seemed to tick over for a nervous moment. "Just remember everything I ever taught you..." His eyes stared hard at hers. "And don't trust anyone. I mean it. You trust no-one and nothing except you and your gun. You hear me? Remember everything I taught you! *Everything!*"

Carrie's mouth seemed frozen, unsure of what to say. They stared at each other, but only for a brief moment before the screen finally went dead.

She sat there for a moment, a little shocked, as his words rolled around in her mind. She'd never seen him so intense. Was he trying to throw her off? Scare her? She exhaled with frustration and rubbed her hands over her face. *I will do this, whether he likes it or not. I can handle this. He won't scare me off.*

Exiting the booth, she saw Smith sitting there at his console, looking at her strangely. She stopped suddenly in her tracks.

"You couldn't hear what was said in there, could you?"

Smith shook his head. "No... I just didn't know your dad was a colonel. An Original."

She looked back at the booth, stumped as to how he'd found out if he couldn't hear her conversation. He must've seen the confused look on her face, because he angled the screen in front of him around toward her. "His full name and credentials came up when I punched in the transmission code."

Carrie looked at the screen, and there it was, in big bold letters.

**900–569–742-A; COLONEL JEFFREY WELLES, UNF-SD Orig.**

"Oh," Carrie said slowly, trying to think of what to say. She eyed him nervously.

"That's pretty cool," he shrugged.

She gave him a friendly smile. "Thanks."

He smiled back then looked down and started flicking through the screens on his e-clip again. "That's it! The captain's the only one left," he said to himself. He got up from his console and went to leave, but Carrie caught his arm.

"Smith?"

He turned around and looked at her with his youthful eyes.

"I, er, I'd appreciate it," Carrie stuttered, "if you didn't mention this to any of the guys... *or* girls... if you don't mind?"

"Mention what? That your father's an Original? Or a colonel?"

"*Retired* colonel, and yeah, both. I've worked hard to get to where I am and I don't want anyone thinking this had anything to do with him."

He eyed her for a second, then nodded. "Fine. I don't know why you're hiding it though. I think it's cool."

"Carter doesn't need more ammunition to fire at me," she said. "Or McKinley."

Smith laughed. "Yeah, I guess you're right. It's okay. Your secret's safe with me."

Carrie smiled, relieved. There was something about his eyes that made her believe him.

"Thanks, Smi—, what's your first name again? Pete?"

"Pete," he nodded.

"Thanks, Pete. It means a lot." She smiled warmly.

He smiled back at her a little awkwardly, then looked back down at his e-clip and scratched his head. "I, er, have to go," he said, then quickly turned and left.

*

Lunch was a fairly subdued affair. Packham joined them for a bit, updating Carrie on the very standard and uneventful flight path they'd been taking. The ship was just approaching Mars, on its final leg toward the Darwin. They'd seen an asteroid shower, and passed a few other ships but that was about it. She also mentioned that Harris had been called to the flight deck earlier when Bolkov was on duty, as he'd picked up another signal from the Darwin. When pressed as to what the signal was, she simply shrugged and said "They're still trying to figure it out."

Carrie felt a spike of tension travel up her spine. She was so close now. So close to being able to seize this opportunity and prove to her father, and the team, what she could do. She eagerly headed to the flight deck wanting to lay her eyes on Mars. Again, her breath caught at the sight. The massive orb floated silently in front of them, almost ominously. She studied it fixedly, noting that the color wasn't quite as vibrant as she'd pictured it to be. It was a mingling of orange and brown hues, interrupted by the occasional marbling of black. Although it was nowhere near as beautiful as

Earth, it was still a magnificent sight to behold. *Mars!* After years of dreaming of seeing it this close, it was now a reality. She stared at it for what seemed an age, completely fascinated, hoping that one day she would get the chance to explore it at ground level.

It only made the excitement and tension rise even higher within her. It seemed to echo the pressure she sensed building among the crew, especially since they'd spoken with their families back home. It meant they were a step closer to boarding, a step closer to facing whatever might be waiting for them on the Darwin. She wondered where Harris was and what he was doing. Was he planning their attack and contingencies if something went wrong? Most of all, she wondered where he was going to play her in all of this.

Harris stood on the flight deck and stared at Smith.

"It says what?"

"Take a listen, sir." He hit play on the transmission recording he'd managed to clean up a little in the comms room.

Harris listened as the static came over the deck's PA. There was some warbling, then the static faded to the background and a voice came over loudly, albeit very briefly.

*[static] "... its way. The test is ready..."*

*"Good. We're set to g—" [static]*

"And that's it?" Harris asked, a mixture of disappointment and frustration washing over him.

Smith nodded. "It's only a short recording, sir. That's all I could unscramble in the clean-up."

Harris looked over at Hunter. "And Bolkov was right: this *definitely* came from the Darwin?"

"Yes, sir," Hunter nodded, pointing to the radar screen. "He locked it right onto the station, sir."

"And neither Command nor any other UNF ship have any record of this?" Harris continued.

Hunter shook his head. "Bulk said they got nothing. It's just us."

"Well, how is that possible?" Harris looked back at Smith. "Surely if they were transmitting, then they were transmitting to someone?"

Smith shrugged. "I don't know, sir, maybe that was them trying to fix the comms. Maybe something happened in the scrambling process while they were trying to transmit, and we accidentally picked it up because we have a lock on their coordinates. The scanning program I devised is pretty top-notch, sir. If I do say so myself."

"Play it again," he ordered Smith, as Doc walked onto the flight deck. Harris had sent for him.

"What's up, captain?" Doc asked curiously, as he made his way down the steps.

"Listen to this," Harris said, motioning to the console.

The four of them stood in silence and listened again to the garbled voices.

*[static] "... its way. The test is ready."*

*"Good. We're set to g—" [static]*

Harris looked at Doc. "It came from the Darwin. Sounds to me like there's someone still alive and well up there."

Doc nodded, eyes narrowed in thought. "Someone who's testing something."

"Must just be a technical issue up there, huh?" Hunter shrugged.

Harris and Doc exchanged a look, then Harris turned back to Hunter. "Send a copy of that through to my private portal and keep your ears open. I want to know if you pick up anything else. Anything at all, understand?"

"Yes, sir," he nodded.

With that, Harris locked eyes with Doc again, then turned and left the flight deck.

*

Harris sat alone in the mess hall scoffing down his lunch. He'd sent the team off to do their final checks in readiness for boarding the Darwin, instructing them that they would meet back in the mess hall at 1700 for an early meal, then they would get some sleep before their mission kicked off in the evening.

He cleared his plate quickly. He'd been hungry as he'd lost time sitting in his office searching for any information on Sharley, stopping only when Smith had called him to the flight deck. His search had been somewhat fruitless, although he had managed to locate a bunch of obscure science papers that had been published on some of Sharley's behavioral studies, prior to his time at Hell Town.

The papers were scientific in nature and very technical, but Harris got the basic gist of them. Sharley had studied in detail the great hunters of the animal kingdom. Animals such as wolves, lions and other big cats, and seafaring creatures such as the great white shark and the killer whale. Sharley then compared these findings with a study he had done on serial killers. In particular, he studied their methods of stalking and killing their prey. He had discovered traits in some of the animals where a quick kill wasn't always made, and instead a slow torturous one took its place.

Sharley compared the survival instincts between the two groups, and their methods of perfecting the kill. He had come to the conclusion that, all in all, the desire to hunt and kill was the same regardless of species. Some were just better at it than others, and if it were not for the complex social boundaries that humans imposed upon themselves, we would be just like the lion on the savanna, or the tiger in the jungle, or the shark in the ocean.

It was interesting enough to read, but Sharley seemed a little obsessed with the dark, deep-seated issues of the human mind; fixated on death and torture and control. It was a little unnerving. It made Harris wonder what sort of programs Sharley was running on the Darwin, and exactly how much control he had over them?

Harris took his plate back to the counter, where Louis had been clearing the dishes away. He thought briefly about making a transmission home, which, in itself, was strange. Smith, of course, knew better than to ask him, as he didn't believe in the "last" call. Besides, there was no-one really to make that call to. His mother was in a nursing home and probably wouldn't remember who he was, depending on what kind of day she was having with her Alzheimer's. His sister, Holly, would be busy with her job and her kids, and he didn't speak with his brother, Terence.

He always made the most important call to Tyson and Taya *before* he left Earth, and years in the UNF had taught them not to expect one while he was out in space. He just didn't like it. It wasn't natural. If things were to go bad, he preferred them to remember his last visit with them in the flesh, not some five minute goodbye from miles out in space. Although, that said, he never got to see either of them this time around...

To distract himself from his thoughts, he decided to undertake his last in-person checks and pay a visit to the engine room. He made his way down into the bowel of the ship and found the crew over by the onboard weaponry, next to the ship's tiny secondary escape pod, the *Borealis*, aptly named to suit the ship. The *Borealis* was only a two-man pod, generally just a backup if the flight deck could not disengage as their real escape pod.

"How's it coming along, Sergeant Brown?" he asked, as he approached the team.

Brown looked up at him. "All's well, captain. The guns are in tiptop shape, the engine's running like a dream, and the *Borealis* is ready to go."

Harris nodded, looking over the equipment. "Good. And you've tested the arming of the ship's guns with the flight deck's controls?" He glanced at Carter for an answer.

"Yes, sir," Carter answered. "We did initial checks yesterday and will be doing a full exercise this afternoon."

Harris turned to Colt who was standing beside the men. "Are you familiar with these weapons, Corporal Colt?"

"Not these particular ones, sir, but I have worked with similar."

"And are these soldiers giving you the opportunity to become familiar with these weapons, corporal?"

Colt glanced over at Brown and Carter, then back at Harris. "Yes, sir."

"*Hands-on* opportunity?" he asked directly.

Colt hesitated before giving an answer and that told him everything.

"Carter," Harris ordered. "Step aside and let Colt take over."

Carter glanced at Harris, then slowly stepped aside. Harris looked both men in the eye.

"What happens if this thing misfires and you two get blown to pieces? Who's going to try and fix the damn thing? Who's going to make sure it doesn't blow up the whole goddamned ship? What about the rest of these electrical panels?" He waved his arm around the cargo hold. "Corporal Colt *must* be up to scratch on all this equipment. I will be back later this afternoon and I'd better be convinced that she knows what she's doing. Do you understand?"

"Yes, sir," they answered.

"Good. I'll see you in a few hours."

Harris turned and headed up to the main deck. He wasn't surprised that they hadn't let Colt near the equipment. He knew that Brown didn't have an aversion to her, as he'd seen them talking at mealtimes. It was simply the fact that Brown was very particular with his work and never let anyone get too close to it. Even Carter, technically Brown's senior officer and team leader, was always his assistant in the engine room. Brown knew the equipment like the back of his hand and he didn't like anyone messing with it; which was good in that Harris had the utmost faith that Brown knew what he was doing and kept the ship running tiptop, but it was also a concern that if anything ever happened to Brown, they'd potentially be in a spot of trouble. Carter worked closely with Brown, but sometimes watching things being done and actually doing them, were two very different things.

Harris headed to check on the flight deck, to make his final checks there. As he entered, he saw Bolkov sitting in the pilot's chair looking out the window, sipping a cup of steaming hot coffee.

"Staff Sergeant Bolkov," he greeted him.

Bolkov glanced over his shoulder. "Captain," he acknowledged in his slow, deep voice.

"How are we doing up here? We on track?" He asked, taking a seat in the chair next to him.

Bolkov nodded, closing his eyes briefly as he did. "Yes, sir."

"No more traces of that signal?"

"No, sir."

"What time are Hunter and Packham back on deck?"

"2100, captain."

"So you'll be running the weapons exercise with the engine room team this afternoon?"

Bolkov nodded his head slowly again. "Yes, sir."

"Good. I want a full report, sergeant. Make sure you note down whether Corporal Colt takes part in this exercise too."

Bolkov gave him an inquisitive glance. Harris ignored it, instead paying attention to the steam rising from the mug Bolkov was nursing close to his chest.

"That coffee hot enough for you, Bulk?"

Bolkov looked down at his coffee and back at Harris. "Coffee can never be too hot, captain."

Harris smiled. "Bet it got pretty cold in Russia, huh."

Bolkov gave his slow nod again. "You wouldn't believe."

Harris eyed his soldier, amused. Bulk was quite a character. He wasn't necessarily a laid-back guy; just a big, slow guy. He talked slow, he moved slow, he even seemed to think slow, as if considering everything carefully before speaking. But the Russian knew what he was doing on the flight deck and, when it was needed, he could emerge from that slow shell and he could run, he could fight and he was strong. Harris liked that about him. He had the element of surprise.

Harris sat back in the chair for a moment and looked out the window. Mars had faded off to their starboard side, and now all that sat in front of them was an enormous black expanse of nothing. Nothing but a handful of scattered stars. He searched far into the distance with his eyes, wondering when the Darwin would appear. Would it be banged up from a pirate attack? Or would it be floating there, shiny and new, just needing a little technical know-how?

He looked over at Bolkov, who was also staring out into the nothingness. Harris wondered what he saw out there, staring at it all day like he did. Bulk looked as though he were watching a football match or something; eyes fixed in the distance, waiting for someone to kick a goal. The truth of it was, though, that he was more like an old sea captain, standing on the ship's deck watching the horizon and waiting for land to appear.

Harris chuckled to himself. Bolkov turned his head slowly, glancing curiously, then turned back to the window again sipping his coffee.

"I'll see you later, Bulk," Harris said, patting him on the shoulder.

Bolkov gave another slow nod and Harris chuckled again.

After leaving the flight deck, he decided to head for the weapons store and see how his two competitive sharpshooters were getting on. The door was left ajar and as he walked in he saw McKinley on one side of the room, Welles on the other, backs to each other, working in silence. *At least they're tolerating each other.* They'd clearly been hard at work, having lined up each type of weapon in sets of fifteen: one for each team member, if need be, with spares as well. There were the laser-fire rifles, the simple UNF-issue handguns and a few of the smaller ankle-strap pistols. They'd also set out clips of ammo for the handguns and battery packs for the laser-fire rifles for quick and easy access.

McKinley noticed him standing at the door. "Captain," he nodded.

Welles turned around and nodded too. "Sir."

"Looks like you've made good progress here," Harris noted, looking around the store.

"Yes, sir," McKinley responded.

"You're familiar with these weapons, Corporal Welles?" Harris asked her.

"Yes, sir," she answered confidently.

"And Lieutenant McKinley has run you through our logging process?"

She glanced over at McKinley and stuttered a response. "Er, yeah, I think so. Do you mean when we scanned the weapons when we first came on the ship?"

McKinley looked down at the crate he was clearing away, like he'd just been caught doing something he shouldn't.

"Part of it," Harris said firmly. "You also need to check the count in the system, log what weapons you've readied here and, when we go onto the station, you'll need to log who's taken what and log what comes back in. You, and the system, must account for every weapon on this ship and know where it is at any given moment. I'm sure Lieutenant McKinley has explained that to you."

Welles shot McKinley another glance. He ignored her and looked directly at Harris.

"I was just getting to that part, captain," he said. "We were just clearing these crates away."

Harris stared at him for a moment. "I'm sure you were, lieutenant. I know you realize the importance of Corporal Welles learning everything about the weapons store, should you not be here to run it for us. Who knows, McKinley. You may decide to trade in your armory for a science lab and jump ship at the Darwin."

McKinley gave him a mischievous smile. "Unlikely, sir."

Harris looked around the room again. "Well, I guess I'll leave you to it. You've clearly got a lot to talk about."

As he left the room he saw Welles flash McKinley a challenging look and McKinley standing there waiting, ready to take the barrage he was about to receive — and then give it back in equal doses. Harris smiled to himself. He didn't sense there was any real issue between them. They were just both competitive and stubborn. He knew how McKinley liked to push people's buttons, and clearly Welles was fiery and prepared to stand her ground. He liked that.

He made his way to Doc's office for one final check and found the medic sitting at his desk typing into his console.

"Hey, captain," the medic greeted him, as he entered.

"You got everything in order here? You all stocked?" Harris glanced into the rooms off to the side.

"Yes, sir."

"And you're set for the pre-board physicals?"

"Yes, sir. Just getting set to load the e-clips now." Doc motioned to his console. "I'll probably start calling them up around 1530 and have them done before dinner. I can do yours now, if you like?"

Harris briefly thought about it, scratching his head. "Alright, let's go."

Doc took a blank e-clip, ejected Harris's e-file from its slot in the racks and they walked toward his examination room. Harris headed straight for the trolley with the BP equipment on it as Doc scribbled details at the top of the e-clip, then moved over to put the armband on Harris.

"So," Doc began, "any thoughts on the Darwin? What do you think we're in for?"

Harris shook his head. "I honestly don't know, Doc. The information I was given is very limited, which concerns me. I'm not too sure about the guy in charge up there, either. He's into some pretty weird shit."

Doc looked up from the BP monitor to Harris. "Define weird?"

"He seems to have a keen interest in the darker side of human behavior. I think he spent too much time with the prisoners when he was warden of Hell Town." The BP machine beeped and began to deflate. Harris looked down at his arm. "I managed to find some scientific papers that he released. I think you should read them, give me your take on them," he said.

Doc nodded. "Sure thing."

Harris gave a short, sharp laugh. "Hell, you're bound to actually understand the mumbo jumbo in it. It'll be some nice light reading for you."

Doc flashed him a grin as he unraveled the band from around Harris's arm and scribbled something on his e-clip. He then turned to wheel over the heart-lung machine.

"The team exercise this morning was interesting, wasn't it?" Harris started unbuttoning his shirt.

Doc nodded in agreement as he put the three discs on Harris's chest. "Yes, it was." He began to ready the machine. "It would appear that Welles is as good a shot as her file suggests, moving *or* still."

"Yeah. It was a shame that Colt didn't get a chance to do too much, but I guess that was the circumstances of the game. Even Packham, too. I have no idea what her real capabilities are, other than what's in her file, of course. If I'd had the time I'd like to run the exercise again, get Packham involved, and maybe put you guys on the prisoners this time, see how that would play out. Better still, put Welles and McKinley on the *same* team. *That* would be interesting, to see who got past them."

"Mm-hmm. They'd be pretty hard to beat," Doc nodded, then handed the tube to Harris for him to blow into. Harris had done this so many times he could probably run the tests himself. He took the tube, waited for Doc's okay and then blew into it. When he was done, he handed the tube back, and waited for him to do his thing. The e-clip lit up.

"So, anything interesting to report in terms of how the troops are getting along?" Harris asked, eyeing Doc carefully.

"No," he answered, not looking up from his e-clip. "McKinley's been behaving himself."

Harris gave a laugh. "I stopped by the weapons store and saw them standing there on opposite sides of the room, working in complete silence. At least they're not at each other's throats, I suppose."

Doc gave Harris another grin.

"You had a word with him?" He arched an eyebrow at his lieutenant.

Doc shrugged modestly. "I might've had just a little one. I told him to ease off. I told him that the other guys watch him for their lead and he was setting a bad example."

"So, what about the others then? Most of them seem to be tolerating the women, but Louis and Carter aren't really branching out, are they?"

"They will soon enough. When they see everyone else accepting them, it'll happen. Besides, you know what Carter's like. He's even worse than McKinley when it comes to stirring people. He's just having a bit of fun with them at the moment. He'll get bored with it soon enough."

"After I left the mess hall last night, did they continue their conversation?" Harris narrowed his eyes, studying Doc closely.

A mischievous smiled crawled onto the medic's face. "You want to know which one they thought you preferred?"

"Hell no!" Harris said loudly. "And if you try and tell me, I'll break your goddamned neck!"

"Yes, sir," Doc laughed, getting up and moving over to the cranium scanner. Harris followed, buttoning his shirt and watching Doc, still unimpressed.

Doc noticed. "What?" he asked, the mischievous smile still on his face.

"I catch *any* of you pairing my name with one of theirs," he pointed firmly at Doc, "you'll be in pain, I promise you that."

"I didn't say shit, captain. I'm not that stupid." Doc was trying to swallow his laughter. "Now, will you please stand in line and face the wall."

Harris glared at him, then stood in position. When the scanning was done Doc checked the results with those from his pre-flight physical.

"You're cleared, captain!" he announced.

"Good! Now I got shit to do. I'll bring you those papers to read on Sharley."

# 11

# Docking

Carrie was too wired to sleep. She just couldn't get her brain to switch off. It was 1930 and she knew they'd be up again soon to prepare for the station boarding. She kept thinking back over the day: the team exercise that morning, what she did right and what she did wrong; the afternoon prepping the weapons with McKinley. All things considered, it had gone relatively smoothly. He spoke to her only when it was work related, but at least he wasn't arguing with her anymore. Although she'd been tempted to take a verbal swipe at him after Harris's visit, she chose to bite her tongue instead. It seemed to work, as he didn't take a swipe at her either.

Her mind rehashed the pre-board physical with Doc. The visit had been fairly brief and there hadn't been much time for chatter; a quick rehash of the morning's exercise, an inquiry about McKinley's behavior, more tips for keeping healthy on the ship and that was it. Although she recalled feeling a little strange during her visit. She'd worn the boring bra which she should've been pleased about, but found herself wishing she'd opted for the push-up instead. She felt like she had a reputation to uphold now. She recalled the close proximity between them when he ran the tests. She knew it would've been the same for everyone, but couldn't help thinking about it nonetheless. She recalled how warm his hands were as they brushed her skin; placing and removing the armband and discs. She thought about his brown eyes, the way they smiled at hers, along with his pearly teeth.

Then she recalled the crew's mealtime during which she noticed the edginess had increased among them again. Colt had made a good effort to keep conversation going, questioning the guys about some of the other missions the *Aurora* had been on. Brown told of their last mission to disband a group of rebels who'd staged a mutiny onboard a cargo ship just off Earth. There'd been five men involved and three were taken alive. McKinley had killed one of them, wounding another two, and Carter had taken out the other. They were young guys looking to make a quick buck by hijacking a cargo ship and actually thought they would get away with it.

Smith had talked of some of their other missions. One where they went to the rescue of a small tourist ship that had been attacked by pirates, lost all power, and was floating toward The Belt. Another where an ex-UNF pilot was caught smuggling people from Earth to colonies on both the Moon and Mars. Louis told of an encounter where an exporter was using slave labor to work his cargo dock on Station Magellan. The guy had strong underworld connections and was also running illegal UNF weapons to the various colonies. The *Aurora* had shut him down.

All in all, it appeared that controlling mutinies and space pirates were their main source of employment. Carrie wondered whether pirates had taken over the Darwin.

She rolled over in her bed and watched Colt. The corporal seemed to be fast asleep and Packham's even breathing indicated that she was too. Carrie decided to go for a walk, thinking it might help her relax knowing that everyone else was asleep. She pulled herself out of bed quietly, not wanting to disturb the other women, then dressed but left her hair hanging loose, and exited the room.

She figured she'd head toward the mess hall or flight deck. If anyone was awake, they'd surely be there. As she turned the corner into the main corridor, she noticed Doc's office door was open. She meandered in that direction and stuck her head around the doorway. Doc was sitting back in his chair with his feet crossed over up on the desk, nibbling at the e-pen in his mouth, completely engrossed in something he was reading on an e-file pane. She decided not to disturb him, but as she turned to leave, he saw her.

"Corporal Welles... can't sleep?"

She shook her head, leaning against the doorway. "Looks like you can't either."

He removed the pen from his mouth and looked at his watch "Yeah, but I'd better try and get some soon. Time's run away from me." He rested the pane in his lap and looked up at her again. "You know I can't give you anything for it now or you'll still be asleep when we're trying to board."

"That's okay. I was hoping a little walk might help."

He nodded.

"Sorry to disturb your reading." She motioned to the e-file in his lap. "You seemed pretty enthralled."

He ran his fingers down the screen of the pane, closing it. "Just some science papers."

"You reading them to put you to sleep?" she smiled.

"Give me nightmares more like," he muttered.

Carrie shot him a confused look. "So, how'd your transmission go?" she asked curiously.

"Good. My folks are all good. Yours?"

"Alright. My father was trying to squeeze me for information." She laughed to herself. "How do your folks feel about your line of work? I suppose they must be used to the 'final' transmission by now."

"Yeah, they're used to it. I've been doing this for a while and so far I've always made it home," he said.

"Are you the first one in your family to do this kind of stuff?"

He nodded. "Technically. My dad did some training when he was younger, but he never went on any missions."

Carrie allowed her curiosity to get the better of her and continued to probe. "Any brothers or sisters?"

Doc nodded again. "Two brothers. One older, one younger."

"Oh, middle child, Doc?" Carrie teased.

Doc gave a sharp laugh. "This coming from an *only* child!"

Carrie felt herself blush. "You got me there." She quickly tried to take the spotlight off herself. "So, what do your brothers do for a living?"

He tapped the pen on the file in his lap, eyeing her curiously, "The older one, John, is a lawyer and the younger one, Ben is a pro ice hockey player."

"Are you serious? A lawyer, a doctor and a pro ice hockey player in the one family? Your parents did something right."

Doc smiled to himself. "Yeah. We were pretty lucky. We had a good home, and good genes."

Carrie smiled and wondered whether Doc's brothers had his good looks as well. "So, does medicine run in the family at all?" she continued, trying to shake off the feeling that she was turning into Colt with all the questions.

"My mum was a GP, then she stopped and had us kids, and my parents opened up a bed and breakfast lodge in Colorado. They've been doing that ever since."

"She doesn't practice anymore?"

"She's continued doing a little temp work here and there to keep up her license. My dad's an accountant. He does that from the lodge."

Carrie thought about this and laughed to herself, tucking her long hair behind her ear.

Doc smiled and shot her another curious look. "What?"

"I was just thinking about Carter's 'snowflake' comment."

Doc's mouth quirked a little. "Alright, and what about you, then? Tell me about *your* dad."

Carrie looked at him suspiciously. There was something about the way he asked her, like he knew already.

"What about my father?" she eyed him carefully.

"Well, he's a soldier, right?" He tapped the pen on his thigh.

"He's retired."

Doc nodded. "And what about his career before that?"

Carrie eyed him again for a moment, then narrowed her eyes. "You know, don't you? Smith told you, didn't he?"

Doc shot her a confused look. "Told me what?"

"About my father."

"Told me what about your father?"

"Why haven't you asked about my mother?" she asked, leaning off the doorway.

Doc paused for a moment. She could see his mind was ticking over. "Okay, what does your mother do?"

Carrie paused a moment, her own mind ticking over. He was playing dumb. Suddenly she clicked. "Right. Smith doesn't know about my mother, so if he didn't tell you, you must've read it? How did you know that I was an only child? You read it in my file, didn't you?"

"Read what, corporal?" he smiled.

"You know what I'm talking about," she smiled back.

Doc laughed and held his hands out, questioning. "Know what?"

They looked at each other, a standoff to see who would fold first. *Damn!* She thought. *I forgot he was a good poker player!*

She relented and sighed. "You know that my mother's dead, that's why you didn't ask about her. And you know that my father's a... *was*... a colonel, an 'Original', because you wanted to rub it in, didn't you?" she challenged.

He looked at her, keeping his poker face.

"Didn't you... lieutenant," she repeated.

He paused for another moment, then gave in, nodding. "I might've read it in your file."

"I knew it!"

"So, Smith knows, huh?" he grinned.

"He saw the name come up when he punched in the transmission code. He's been sworn to secrecy, though, as are you," she pointed at him.

"Have I said a word so far, corporal?"

Carrie folded her arms. "Not that I know of."

"Look, I understand about you not wanting to tell the guys. My lips are sealed." He held up the e-pen and mimicked pulling a zip across his lips. They stared at each other for a moment, then he put the end of the pen back to his mouth and simply said, "*Miss* Snowflake."

She tried to hold it in, but a smile broke out on her face, bringing laughter with it. She brought her hand to her mouth to cover it. Doc smiled back at her, then glanced over her shoulder and suddenly straightened his face, cleared his throat and removed his feet from the table, sitting upright.

"Captain," he said.

Carrie looked over her shoulder at Captain Harris standing in the doorway. She quickly stood aside for him.

"Am I interrupting something?" Harris asked.

Doc shook his head, putting the file that had been on his lap onto the table.

"Shouldn't you be sleeping, Corporal Welles?" Harris stared down at her.

"I tried captain, but I couldn't," she said.

"Well, I suggest you try harder," he said flatly.

"Yes, sir," she nodded. She shot Doc a glance, then headed for the door.

Harris stared Doc in the eye as he walked into the room. "You finished with those papers yet?"

"Yes, sir." Doc handed back the e-file pane.

"And?"

"And… you're right. He does seem a little obsessed with all things dark and torturous, but I guess that's why Hell Town's as successful as it is. He knows how to fuck with people and push their buttons. Break their will, as the case may be."

Harris nodded. "Keep this," he held up the e-file, "in mind when we board tonight. If it's not a technical difficulty, there might be something useful here. God knows what study he's working on now."

"Yes, sir."

Harris turned and headed for the door. When he reached it he looked back at Doc. "Your office isn't for social calls, Doc. You wanna have a conversation, you save it for the mess hall. Understood?"

Doc looked up at him and nodded. "No problem."

As Harris left he called out over his shoulder. "Clock's ticking on your sleep time, Doc!"

"Yours too, Saul!" he called back.

Harris smiled at the comment, heading toward his quarters. As he walked along, he thought about what he'd just seen in Doc's office. He told himself they were just talking and there was no need to be concerned. But he'd heard the sound of her laughter and saw the smile on Doc's face as he looked at her, and it did concern him. It was only friendly banter at the time, but Harris knew if he didn't control the situation, it could spiral.

Doc was never shy of female attention, Harris knew that. But he also knew that Doc wasn't the kind of guy to be an asshole about it, either. Sometimes he was just too friendly for his own good. Unfortunately, Harris also knew the type of woman who attracted Doc's attention, and if he wasn't mistaken Welles could fit the profile. She was cute, and she had a certain strength of spirit about her that might just spark his interest.

Harris sighed. That was always a risk with co-ed teams; it was human nature. But if his team was to run efficiently, there had to be strict boundaries. He made a mental note to watch them both closely from here on in. He couldn't allow this to be anything other than friendship.

*

At 2120 Harris made his way to his office.

He'd managed to get about an hour of shut-eye, albeit with more confusing dreams of Sibbie and Etta, their eyes boring holes into him as Sibbie clutched that phone, telling him *"something's wrong!"*. It ended with him waking abruptly again, sitting bolt upright in bed and calling out *"Holly-Hope!"* It was the name Sibbie used to call his sister. Her birth name was Holly, but for whatever reason, Sibbie added on the "Hope". He hadn't heard the name since Sibbie had passed, and thought it odd to have resurfaced all these years later.

He shook their faces from his mind, because right now they were crowding it and he had to get moving. He was due to have his final briefing with Command at 2130. He entered his office, walked straight to his coffee station and poured himself a long black. He took a sip, then moved over behind his desk and logged into the Command portal.

Sitting back in his chair, he waited for the system to connect. It beeped and the screen revealed Colonel Isaack and Professor Martin.

"Captain Harris," Isaack greeted him.

"Colonel Isaack, Professor Martin," he returned.

"So I believe you're on target to board at 2330. Is that correct?" Isaack asked authoritatively.

"Yes, sir, we are on target for that time. Have you managed to make any contact with the Darwin as yet?"

"Negative, Captain Harris. We are still in blackout with the station."

"You've found no-one else who picked up the comms, as we did?"

"That's a negative, captain."

"And you have no other information to give me?"

"Not at this time," Isaack said firmly.

Harris looked over at Professor Martin. "And you still can't advise me as to just what sort of programs the Darwin is running?"

Professor Martin pushed his glasses higher on his nose, shaking his head. "Unfortunately not, Captain Harris. That still remains classified."

"I read some papers that Professor Sharley released, his studies on human and animal behavior involving the great predators of the animal kingdom and serial killers. He has a keen interest in some pretty dark stuff."

Professor Martin thought about this for a moment. "Well, er, yes, I guess he does, albeit in a scientific capacity. He's a psychologist by trade, an expert in human behavior. So that would be a fair statement, Captain Harris."

"So, the UNF put a psychologist in charge up there, in charge of biological weaponry?"

"That's correct," Martin gave a single nod. "When dealing with biological weaponry, one must ensure the right people are involved, and no-one knows this better than a psychologist."

Harris thought for a moment. "So, you'd suggest we take all possible precautions for the boarding?"

Professor Martin nodded. "That would be a wise move, yes. Definitely masks and breathing apparatus to be on the safe side."

"Captain Harris, what *is* your plan for the boarding party?" Colonel Isaack interjected.

"I'll be taking the full team aboard, colonel, except my pilots, of course."

"And except the female recruits," Isaack stated firmly.

"Yes, colonel, *and* except the female recruits. Although I ran a training exercise today and Welles, in particular, did very well. I would like the opportunity to test her out in a live situation, sir."

"And perhaps one day that opportunity will come, Captain Harris, but for now, she is to remain on the ship. Once we're sure the Darwin is stable, I will issue the order to let them board. Until then, your order remains the same. I hope we're clear on this, Captain, because I do not want to have this conversation for a *fourth* time. Are we clear?"

Harris was disappointed by the order but nodded. "Yes, sir."

"Captain Harris," Martin began, "when you dock at the Darwin, there is a receiver port that your ship can plug into to access the Darwin's power and transmit back to Command. It's rigged separately from the main station's power, so we're hoping that you might be able to use it and save your ship's power stores. If it is working, though, we would've presumed that Professor Sharley would have attempted to use it. Regardless, it's worth a try."

"I did see that on the plans, professor. My engineer, Staff Sergeant Brown and my comms-tech PFC Smith, will look into that for us."

Professor Martin nodded. "One more thing, captain. I'd like you to use extreme caution with your weapons. Darwin is a state-of-the-art facility and we'd like to avoid any damage whatsoever."

Harris stared at the screen for a few moments. "Professor Martin, I will use extreme caution with our weapons, providing my soldiers' lives aren't in any danger. If we are at risk, then we'll do what is necessary."

"I'm sure it won't be a problem, captain. You're a good leader with a great team. Weapons shouldn't be necessary."

Harris stared at him. *Like hell*, he thought.

"Yes, sir," was what he said, however.

"Well, good luck, Captain," Isaack said, rounding up the conversation. "Hopefully, this is only a technical difficulty and we can have you back on your leave in no time."

"Yes," Martin added, "good luck, Captain Harris. We'll speak to you again after you board."

"Will do." Harris ended the transmission and sat there staring at the blank screen for a moment, fist to chin, thinking. All the while he tried to ignore that strange feeling swirling in the pit of his stomach again.

Carrie made her way with the team to the flight deck at 2215. They were all fairly quiet, except Carter. He was rehashing to Smith a previous boarding the *Aurora* team did where they came under heavy fire; talking animatedly about explosions and gunfire, laughing about how freaked out they'd been. Carrie met eyes with Doc, who flashed her a smile of hello. She wondered what the captain had said to him after she'd left?

They reached the flight deck and saw Hunter and Packham at the controls. Packham looked concentrated, yet calm. The sergeant was finally going to get to do something other than just observe. Carrie gave her a smile of encouragement. Packham acknowledged it with a subtle nod.

They took their same seats as the launch, Colt and Carrie on the third tier again. Bolkov sat off to the side at the console, observing Packham closely, looking as though he was ready to intervene if she did something wrong. Carter was still talking animatedly with Smith and Louis, while Doc and McKinley were engrossed in a deep discussion about something, which Brown listened to also.

"Almost there, girl," Colt flashed a confident grin.

Carrie smiled back. *Yes!*

After a few minutes the captain entered and the team hushed down. He moved to the flight deck console, standing beside Hunter as he looked through the observation window.

"How are we tracking, sergeant?" he asked.

"The target has appeared on our radar and we're on time for an ETA of 2327." Hunter pointed to a radar screen located between him and his co-pilot. From where Carrie sat, she could just see the target blinking at the top of the screen.

*So that's the Darwin...* Goosebumps erupted over her arms.

"Good," Harris said, then abruptly turned to face the crew. "Okay, listen up. In less than one hour we will be docking at Station Darwin." He looked around at everyone, making sure they were paying attention, then turned back to Hunter. "Bring up the station's floor plan," he ordered.

Hunter went to work and the observation window in front of them glazed over with Darwin's floor plan. The station was more or less hexagonally shaped and divided into three sections. A main corridor circled the station, splitting each of those sections into two halves.

"There is only one entrance into the station, which is here." The captain pointed to a doorway to the right of the U-shaped docking bay. "These doors, here and here..." he pointed to a door on the left-hand side of the docking bay and one in a central position "... are emergency exits only. Hunter, I want you and Bulk to keep an eye on them as we go through. You see anybody try to run out, you detain them. I'd be surprised if they'd come out with the *Aurora* in dock, though."

"Yes, sir," Hunter replied, while Bolkov gave a firm nod.

Harris looked back at the rest of his soldiers. "So, we make our way to the entrance and then move through the three sections, clearing and securing them one by one. The first section is made up of the offices and general store; the second section is labs and a bio cell for containment; and the third is the mess hall, rec area, and crew quarters. We will board in a two-team formation. I will lead the first team with McKinley, Carter and Brown. Doc will head up the rear team with Louis and Smith."

Carrie and Colt glanced at each other.

"We will be boarding in full bio gear," Harris continued, "which will remain on until Doc confirms it's safe to remove. We've been ordered to exercise extreme caution and only use our weapons as an absolute last resort. This *could* simply be a technical difficulty, gentlemen. The people on board the station may not be in any danger. *However,* if this *is* more than a technical difficulty and they are under threat, I need you to be alert, and not wounding the wrong people or causing any serious damage that could destabilize the station. Do you understand?"

"Yes, sir!"

"Now, remember our training exercise. Remember where you went wrong, and make sure you don't do it again."

"Yes, sir," the men called out.

Harris turned to Hunter again and motioned for him to bring up a different screen, which began scrolling images of the Darwin's crew. "Familiarize yourself with these faces, gentlemen. They are the Darwin crew and we are to assume they are all friendlies. *Do not* injure any of these people, unless they try to attack you. Are we clear?"

"Yes, sir," the men replied.

"Excuse me, captain," Colt called out. "What about us?" she pointed to Carrie and herself.

"What about you?" Harris said with a stone cold look on his face, unimpressed with the interruption.

Colt glanced at Carrie, confused, then back at Harris. "Which team are we in, sir?" she asked.

"Did I call your name out, corporal?"

"No, sir."

"Then you're not on a team."

The rest of the unit flicked their eyes between the two women and Harris.

"You mean we're not going in?" Carrie blurted, her brow furrowed.

"Very intuitive, Corporal Welles," Harris said flatly.

Her heart started racing and her mouth went dry. "But, sir, we've trained for this. We want to go in. We want to help," she protested.

"You want to help, Corporal Welles? Stay here and guard the ship," he said bluntly, then turned his focus back to the men and boomed. "Let's move out!"

Harris strode up the stairs and off the flight deck looking straight ahead. Carrie watched him, somewhat stunned. She looked back at the men. Carter seemed amused and Louis was smirking. Smith, Hunter, Bolkov and Brown's faces were noncommittal, but Doc and McKinley looked as confused as Carrie and Colt were. McKinley, in particular, stood out to her. She half expected him to be smirking like Louis, but he wasn't. He exchanged a look with Doc, but neither said a word, as they began to fall out and follow the captain.

"Good luck, gentlemen!" Hunter called out.

"Yeah, you have fun in the henhouse, Hunter," Carter called back and then laughed. "We'll go out and do the real work, eh?"

Hunter flashed him a sarcastic smile and flipped him the bird. "I hope you don't get left behind, Carter," then he turned back to the control panel and put on his headset. Packham's eyes flicked to both Colt and Carrie, but she too turned back to the console and did the same.

As the men departed, Carrie and Colt looked straight ahead. The only one who tried to make eye contact with the women was Doc, but Carrie avoided it. She looked dead ahead out the window, her face completely expressionless, except her eyes, which she knew were colder than ice.

Once they were gone, she glanced at Colt, who sat there jaw clenched, equally unimpressed.

Colt took a deep breath in and exhaled loudly. "I know what you're thinking Welles," she said with a hard voice.

"I can't believe this," Carrie said.

"I know."

"What's the fucking point of being on this ship if we're not allowed to board?" Carrie said, her voice rising in volume.

"I know!" Colt said again, her voice strained.

Carrie saw Hunter exchange a look with Bolkov, who shrugged back at him.

"I *fucking* outshoot all of them!" Carrie spat, venomously.

"Welles, just drop it," Colt said firmly. "There's nothing we can do about it. Ain't no point going on."

Carrie sat back in her chair and folded her arms tightly. "So what are we supposed to do, then?"

Colt looked over at her, eyes as cold as Carrie's felt.

"Guard the ship," she said flatly.

Harris watched the weapons store become a hive of activity as the men prepped for boarding. McKinley was passing out guns and ammo, scanning each of them as he did. Smith was handing out the comms headsets, and Doc was issuing gas masks with lightweight oxy tanks. As Harris passed out the bullaser vests, he could see Doc trying to catch his eye, but he expertly avoided it. He did not have time to answer his lieutenant's questions right now.

Carrie sat there looking out the window, still seething. *Why wouldn't he let us board? Why would he just leave us out like that?*

Suddenly, she saw something twinkle in the distance.

Hunter leaned forward, hit a switch, then spoke into the mouthpiece of his headset. "Captain, we have a visual on the Darwin. Over."

*"Copy that, Hunter."* Harris's voice boomed over the ship's speakers. *"Can you see any visible signs of damage? Over."*

"Too far out to tell at this stage, captain. I'll report back in a few minutes. Over."

*"Copy that."*

Carrie unfolded her arms and placed them on the armrests of her chair. As the seconds turned into minutes, the ship flew closer and closer, and the cold gray mass that was the Darwin grew larger and larger.

Hunter hit the switch and once again spoke into his headset. "Captain, we have a clear visual on the Darwin now. There appears to be no structural damage. Over."

Harris walked to the wall and hit the PA button.

"Copy that, Hunter," he replied, then released the button and turned to stare at each one of his soldiers. "That doesn't mean shit, gentlemen!"

*"Captain, we're set to begin comms with the Darwin to announce our arrival. Over,"* Hunter's voice rang out over the PA.

"Copy that, Hunter. We're switching to the headsets. Over."

*"Yes, sir,"* Hunter answered.

Harris looked around at his men and motioned for them to switch on their comms. They snapped the headset device around their left ears, adjusting the mouthpiece which protruded out from underneath the ear, a small compact camera that sat perched on top of the ear, and the audio earpiece which plugged inside the ear itself.

Carrie watched the *Aurora*'s pilots intently.

"Switch over to headsets," Hunter ordered Packham, who began flicking a series of switches on the console.

"Headsets are now on," she replied.

Hunter's hands danced around the console for a moment. "Starting comms."

Carrie looked out the window and saw the Darwin continuing to draw nearer, and continuing to grow larger and larger. It almost looked like a large steel shark swimming toward its much smaller prey, the *Aurora*.

"Space Station Z076, this is UNF *Aurora*. Do you copy? Over," Hunter announced.

Static blared back over the speakers, cutting through the stone cold silence.

"I repeat, Space Station Z076, this is UNF *Aurora*. We are about to dock and board you. Do you copy? Over."

The static blared again for a few moments. Hunter tried for a third time. Still no response. Nothing, but static.

"Captain, we're getting no response," Hunter said into his mouthpiece. "Permission to send our authority codes to dock. Over."

*"Copy that, Hunter. Go ahead. Over,"* Harris replied.

Harris noted there was silence for a few moments following his instruction. The men shuffled around him, tightening their gear and checking their weapons. Finally Hunter's voice sounded through their earpieces again.

*"Authority codes sent and beacon transmitting a response, Captain. Over."*

"Copy that," Harris replied into his mouthpiece. He started to pace, looking each of his men over, checking their suits and weapons with his eyes, all the while still managing to expertly avoid any eye contact with Doc.

"Remember gentlemen, extreme caution with your weapons. Be alert and be smart about what you do. Know what your target is before you hit it."

They nodded in response as Hunter's voice came back over their headsets.

*"Captain Harris, our authority codes have been accepted and we are heading in. Over."*

"Copy that, Hunter." Harris took his gun, held the sight up to his eye and aimed the red laser point on the door ahead. Then he lowered his gun and turned to the men.

"Let's move out, gentlemen!"

Everyone grabbed their oxygen backpacks in their hands, as Harris led them toward the *Aurora*'s exit.

*

Carrie watched, absolutely glued to the flight deck.

"Reducing speed. Release the docking lock," Hunter said into his mouthpiece.

Packham pushed a console lever upward. "Docking lock released."

"How's our approach angle?" he asked.

She checked one of the screens on the console. "Approach angle on target."

"Kill power cells four, five and six," Hunter ordered.

"Power cells four, five and six are gone," Packham responded, quickly twisting three dials.

The ship's drone cut to a medium-level hum.

"Extend the docking lock," Hunter ordered.

"Docking lock extending."

Carrie heard a loud mechanical noise and could feel a slight tremor move through the ship.

Harris watched keenly as the men stood by the exit door in their teams, still shuffling, adjusting, stretching.

Carrie noticed how large the Darwin was now as it loomed up in front of them.

"Okay, we're at three klicks," Hunter's voice broke the silence. "Kill power cells two and three."

"Power cells two and three gone," Packham replied, twisting another two knobs.

The ship's murmur disappeared, leaving only the slightest of vibrations. A blue ribbon of light shimmered over the Darwin then disappeared, then a large metal door slid open slowly, revealing the inner dock of the station. It was empty.

"The Darwin's shield is down and we're at 1500 meters," Hunter advised. "Is the docking lock lined up to intercept the Darwin's anchor?"

"Yes, sir," Packham responded looking at one of the screens in front of her, "Docking lock on target."

"Kill power cell one."

"Power cell one is gone." She twisted the last dial.

The ship felt utterly motionless now, as it floated into the open mouth of the Darwin.

Harris noted it was dead quiet. The men eyed each other expectantly. He shook his legs, anxiously waiting for the word. Ready to begin.

Carrie saw the docking lock extending out in front of the *Aurora*, its big claw-like anchor heading for a large metal ring on the wall of the station ahead. She heard an alarm sounding, and noticed the dock's red warning light flashing overhead, alerting the station to an incoming ship and of the atmospheric danger to the station's occupants. There was a loud bang and a crunching, scraping sound of metal on metal as the *Aurora's* anchor hit its target and locked on with computerized beeps. The arm began to retract as it slowly, delicately, pulled the ship up to the dock's edge. About fifteen meters from the ring, it came to a complete stop.

Both pilots' eyes and hands were busy, sweeping across the flight deck console in front of them. They flicked switches, hit buttons, turned dials, and read monitors. Carrie heard a loud vibrating noise. She looked at one of the monitors on the flight deck console and saw the Darwin's mouth closing behind them. It clunked loudly, echoing around the empty dock. There was the sound of a heavy, rushing wind, like a hurricane. The red warning light ceased, so too did the alarm. All fell incredibly silent.

And Carrie couldn't help but feel a sudden sweeping sensation of being trapped.

Harris spoke into his headpiece. "Report, Hunter."

*"Captain, we've successfully docked on Darwin,"* Hunter's voice replied. *"Initializing decompression now. Over."*

"Copy that, Hunter. Is the station's ship, the *Spector*, in dock? Over."

*"Negative, sir. Dock is deserted. Over."*

Harris nodded to himself, then turned and stared hard at his team. "Seconds now, gentlemen!"

He moved closer to the door, gripping his gun tightly in his hands, then he looked over his shoulder for the reassuring sight of McKinley, his right-hand man in the field. They locked eyes and exchanged a subtle nod. They were ready.

Carrie sat forward in her seat, watching Hunter and Packham carefully. They were both carefully focused, reading monitors on the console. Hunter then looked at Packham and gave a nod. Packham began to pull a lever down, as Hunter simultaneously pushed another lever upward. There was another loud sound of air rushing, but Carrie felt none on her face. A series of shrill beeps sounded, followed by a long loud one, and the *Aurora's* observation window suddenly misted over. The pilots checked their monitors again.

"Internal reading is correct," Hunter announced, then looked over at Packham.

"External reading is correct," she replied.

Carrie watched as the covering mist slowly evaporated.

"Captain, the ship has decompressed and is in line with the Darwin. Over," Hunter announced.

*"Copy that, Hunter. Power up the visual comms. Over."*

"Yes, sir," Hunter said, as Packham reached forward and flicked another series of switches.

The window in front of the two pilots clouded over again and a series of monitors appeared. Some were screening the visuals from the ship's external cameras, but there was also a screen for each soldier's headset.

Carrie watched as Harris looked around into McKinley's camera. *"Visual comms are on. Do you receive flight deck? Over,"* he said.

"Copy that, captain. Visuals and audio are A-OK," Hunter replied.

Harris turned to the rest of his men.

*"Masks on, soldiers!"* he called.

A flurry of movement appeared across the screens as the men pulled the oxygen packs onto their backs and masks over their faces. A spike of tension travelled up Carrie's spine as she watched them all standing there, masks on and weapons ready. Her eyes then fell to Smith's camera, as he stood behind Doc. Suddenly, her breathing became shallow.

Harris moved over to the *Aurora*'s door.

"Five, four, three, two, one!" he called, punching the lever hard and swinging his gun up to his face. The door quickly slid open, and he moved to stand on one side, while McKinley took the other. They both scanned the dock with their guns.

Carrie, on the edge of her seat, carefully eyed the screens of Harris and McKinley, but it all looked clear. Heart thumping, she watched as Harris ran out under McKinley's cover, and the rest followed suit.

# 12

# The Bio Cell

Harris led his men slowly onto the Darwin's dock, under a two-by-two cross-cover. He'd memorized the floor plan and knew the route they had to take as they swept the station. His team made their way across the dock to the formal entrance of the facility, while Doc's team held back alongside the *Aurora* providing cover, keeping their eyes on the two emergency exits and high walls surrounding the Darwin's dock. Harris slid up to the edge of the entry doors and hit the button to open them, but they didn't. They were locked. He motioned for Smith to advance and resolve it.

The private ran across the dock to Harris and quickly removed the cover from the door's control panel. He took a small, square digital decoder from his backpack, plugged it into the control panel, and began hitting a sequence of buttons. The light on the control panel flashed, beeped, and the door began to slide open. Smith fell back, as Harris and McKinley took a stance either side of the door.

They were greeted by a darkened, wide corridor with several doorways off each side. Harris flicked on his weapon's light and checked the body heat sensor on the top of his gun. It showed nothing other than McKinley's mass who occasionally stepped into its 180 degree range. The first room to clear was the cargo office on the left. He and McKinley entered and cleared it alone, lights flashing around in the silence, while Brown and

Carter controlled the corridor. The cargo office was a fairly small room with one desk and several e-filing racks. Other than that, it was empty. Everything looked in order.

They crossed over the corridor to the right-hand side and the next set of doors: the general store. This room was much larger, so Harris's whole team entered to sweep it, whilst Doc's team moved up to the station entrance and guarded the corridor. The store had long shelves running through the middle, stacked with general and mechanical supplies. They slowly moved through, checking it carefully, an aisle at a time, weapon lights bouncing here and there, dancing amongst the red target lasers, but it too was clear.

Around the first bend of the corridor, still in Section One, were four offices, two on each side, belonging to the resident scientists. Although the corridor lights were off, the office lights were on, throwing a bright whiteness through their glass walls onto the gray corridor floor. Harris again checked the body heat sensor on the top of his gun. It read nothing. He approached and peered through the glass wall of the first office, confirmed it was empty. Regardless, he and McKinley entered and took a look around, while Brown and Carter took the second; then they moved on to the third and the fourth in succession, while Doc's team kept watch, down the corridor a little. All offices were empty; all neat and tidy as if no-one had been using them.

Section One had now been cleared, so they made their way along the corridor to a set of metal doors which led into Section Two, containing the control room, the laboratories and bio cell. Harris hit the button and the doors slowly began to open, while his team stood back weapons ready. They saw another darkened corridor ahead, that again, lay empty.

Harris motioned for Doc's team to move up and wait at the doors, while his went on through alone.

Carrie's heart was still thumping as her eyes darted from one screen to the next, trying to cover all angles, see what they were seeing, and maybe pick up something they couldn't. She could hear them breathing through their mouthpieces and saw a sheen of sweat beginning to build on faces as the soldiers passed another team member's camera. She tried hard to focus on Harris's and McKinley's visuals as they were front of line, but her eyes kept falling back to the others, searching for Doc.

Harris led his men slowly into Section Two. As they moved forward, he and McKinley flanked either side of the corridor, with Brown and Carter positioned behind them, aiming their weapons through the middle. As far as they could see it was empty. After a few seconds, Harris checked the body heat sensor again. Still nothing. He motioned for Doc's team to start moving up.

They began to make their way down to the series of micro-labs, which, like the offices, had their lights on brightly. Each micro-lab was filled with varied pieces of equipment and cabinets containing assorted chemicals, compounds and fluids. There were four labs, two either side of the corridor. Again, like the offices, the walls were made of floor to ceiling glass, and with the lights shining so brightly within them, he decided there was no need to enter. There was no-one inside, and nothing looked disturbed on the benches. They were all clean and tidy, sparkling new, like they were part of some kind of display or something.

"This is a surprise party for my birthday, isn't it, gentlemen," Carter joked quietly. "When we hit the end all these strippers are going to jump out, eh?"

"Shut the fuck up," McKinley whispered, a ball of concentration.

The next room in line was the control room. Again, they went in and searched it, and it was empty. The room had several pieces of computer equipment against the walls, and two desks with two monitors lined up next to a PA system. All the equipment was on, lights flashing, but nothing disturbed.

They walked toward another bend in the corridor around which would be the bio cell, a large room with another floor to ceiling glass frontage; its function, to contain any suspected hosts of biological outbreaks, and when required, it could be used as a holding cell. McKinley was slightly in front as they approached, and his gun suddenly lit up. He stopped, holding his fist up for the others to halt also, and looked down at the reading.

"I'm picking up heat," he said quietly into his mouthpiece.

"Where?" Harris whispered back, darting his eyes down to his own sensor.

McKinley motioned around the bend to the left. "Looks like four of them."

"Bio cell," Harris said quietly. He quickly motioned for Doc's team to hold back, while his team inched forward. They reached the corner and peered around. Four men stood still under the bright white lights of the bio cell, heads turned toward them, as though they'd been waiting for them.

"Don't move!" Harris yelled, as soon as he realized they were the only targets present. Both he and McKinley held their weapons firm against their shoulders, eyes focused on their sight-line, while Brown and Carter ducked low between, sweeping the area around them. All they saw beyond the bio cell was another metal door, leading into Section Three.

"We are UNF soldiers! I repeat, do not move!"

The four men did not move, nor did they say a word. They stood perfectly still, heads turned toward them, hands by their sides, no weapons. Their faces stared expressionless. Harris and McKinley moved forward under Brown's and Carter's cover, to stand in front of the bio cell. The four men's eyes followed them. Harris kept his weapon aimed despite the wall of thickened glass between them. McKinley kept sweeping off to the side, checking around them. Harris stepped forward and pulled on the glass door that led into a small, square, glass chamber, that then led onto a second door and into the cell itself. It was locked. He nodded back at Brown and Carter to move forward, which they did.

Harris looked closely at the men in the cell and recognized their faces from the file he'd studied. They were part of the Darwin's crew, although they looked a little paler than their photos had shown. He wondered how long it had been since they'd seen some real sunshine.

"Where are the others?" Harris asked tightly.

No response. They just looked at him.

"Where's the rest of your team?" Harris asked again.

One of the scientists standing in the middle of the group, a tall man with closely shaved white-blond hair, answered in a calm, clear, English accent.

"We do not know." His voice sounded a little distant as it came over the speakers of the sealed cell.

Harris stared at him for a moment. "Doc," he said into his mouthpiece.

Doc's team crept around the corner then, weapons out front, eyes to sightlines.

"Guard these men," Harris ordered.

Doc nodded.

Harris motioned for his team to follow, and they moved along to the next set of doors and prepared to enter Section Three.

Carrie, Colt and the three pilots watched the screens of Doc, Smith and Louis, eyeing the men in the bio cell. All four of them were standing just centimeters apart. Three of them were tall and all were very broad, but with faces that were a deathly pale, despite a tiny flush of crimson across their cheeks. One had very short peroxide-white hair, one jet black and long down his back, one dark brown and curly, and the other one short gray hair.

"Well, they look a little weird," Colt noted aloud.

"They're some of the crew, aren't they?" Packham inquired.

"Yeah," Hunter said pulling up another screen with the staff profiles on it.

Carrie looked at the screen. The blond was Bradford Chet, an Englishman who was second-in-command at the station. The one with long black hair was Mattieus Logan, an Armenian-American. The one with curly hair was Tynek Grolsh, a Czech. The gray haired one was Karl Fairmont, a Canadian.

The four men remained standing completely still, staring directly at Doc, Smith and Louis, who stood in front of their cell.

"Are any of you hurt?" Doc asked, keeping his gun trained on them.

They shook their heads in unison.

"You do not need those masks," the blond one, Chet said.

"I'll take my chances for now, thank you," Doc responded.

Carrie's eyes flicked over to Harris and McKinley's cameras. They were moving down the corridor, their two-by-two coverage continuing. From their cameras, Carrie figured that the station's mess hall was to their right and the rec area to the left. The rec area was a large room that had screens dotted around, a pool table in the middle, and a seated area on the side, with bookshelves, and a substantial amount of gym equipment. The whole area was of course tidy, lifeless. *Just like the rest of this place…*

The mess hall was a little larger than that on the *Aurora*, and of a sterile white with shiny plastic red seats. It was also empty. Clean. Unused.

Her eyes darted back to Doc's monitor. He was crouching on the floor, looking down at a piece of equipment he was holding. He twisted some dials, keyed some data in and then checked the reading.

"You register that, Hunter?" he spoke through his mouthpiece.

Hunter looked hard at a screen on the flight desk. Carrie saw information scrolling. Hunter grabbed his mouthpiece.

"Copy that, Doc," he replied.

"You concur that the readings are correct?" Doc asked him.

"Just running an air sample now." Hunter leaned forward and pressed a couple of buttons on the control panel. There was another whirring sound and a few beeps. Hunter checked another monitor on the flight desk and flicked his head back and forth between that and the one showing the information that Doc had sent through.

"Copy that, Doc. The samples match those inside the *Aurora*. Over."

"Copy that, Hunter," Doc placed the equipment in his backpack and stood again.

Carrie watched as his hands came up to his face and he began to remove his mask.

Her breath caught.

The mask came off and Doc stood there and inhaled deeply. Louis and Smith were watching him, picking up his profile on each of their cameras. He stood there for a moment, eyeing the four men in the cell, then bent down and picked up his gun to resume cover.

"It's okay," he told Louis and Smith. "You can take them off. The air is good."

Harris and his team continued down the corridor to the staff quarters. They'd heard the conversation between Doc and Hunter and had removed their masks as well. They did their two-by-two checks of each of the rooms, all of which were empty, clean, and seemingly unlived in. They were now at the end of the line with only the emergency exit door facing them, which would lead back out to the dock and the *Aurora*.

Harris clenched his jaw a moment, thinking, then turned around to his team. "Let's head back."

"What, no strippers?" Carter held his hands out.

Harris gave him an unimpressed stare as he walked past. They made their way back to the middle section where the "survivors" were, and he walked straight up to the glass wall.

"Where are the others? Where's the station's ship, the *Spector*?"

The Englishman eyed him. "You have not formally introduced yourself, sir. I would like to know with whom I am speaking. I take it you're the leader here?"

Harris gave a nod. "I apologize, gentlemen. Captain Harris of the UNF *Aurora*."

The man gave a nod in acknowledgment.

"So, the rest of your crew? The *Spector*? Where are they?" Harris asked.

"I told you I do not know," he answered.

"How can you not know? How do five people just vanish without a trace?"

The man eyed him again. "There was a blackout."

"What do you mean a blackout?" Harris asked with a furrowed brow.

"The power went out. The lights went out. We went out," he said rhythmically.

"*You* went out?" Doc interjected curiously.

"Yes," the man turned his head to Doc. "We don't remember anything. We woke up in here." He turned his head back to Harris. "And we'd like to get out now, thank you."

Harris exchanged a look with Doc, then turned back to the four men.

"Your name is Chet, right? You're second-in-command?" Harris asked the spokesman.

"Yes."

"And you're Logan?" he said to the one on the left with long dark hair and unusual emerald-green eyes.

He nodded.

"Grolsh?" he said, to the one with short, dark curly hair and dark eyes.

A nod in reply.

"Fairmont?" motioning to the large gray haired one with blue eyes.

Another nod.

"Do you know how long you've been in there?" Doc asked them.

They all shook their heads.

"And you're not hurt? You're not in any pain?" Doc probed.

They shook their heads again.

"We're hungry," Logan spoke up in a deep, gravelly voice.

"I bet," Doc eyed him, nodding.

Harris exchanged another look with Doc, then studied the four men for a moment. "Until further notice, you will remain in that cell."

The four stared back at him, expressionless.

"I know you were running biological experiments up here," Harris explained. "If Doc gives you the all-clear, I will then give the order and you will be released. Until then you stay put. Do you understand?" Harris said.

The four continued to stare, their faces completely devoid of any emotion.

"Do you understand?" Harris said again, a little firmer.

Chet motioned to Doc. "And what exactly will he have to do to give us the all-clear?"

Doc went to speak but Harris cut him off.

"He will ensure that you are not infected with anything that may harm my men."

"And what does that involve?" Chet asked, his voice even and smooth, looking over at Doc this time.

"I'll need to check your blood, scan for foreign micro-organisms and such," he answered.

Chet eyed him for a moment, then gave a nod. "Very well."

Harris turned to the rest of the men. "Brown and Carter, guard these men. Louis, Smith, you assist Doc. McKinley, you come with me."

Harris took McKinley and made his way back down to the offices in the first section. Doc, Louis and Smith followed as they made their way back to the ship to get what they needed for the physicals on the four men. As Harris and McKinley made the offices, he motioned for McKinley to take one side of the corridor.

"Search through and see if you can find anything that may tell us where the rest of the crew are or what happened here," he ordered.

"Yes, sir," McKinley responded, as he disappeared into the first room.

Carrie, still watching from the *Aurora*'s flight deck, saw Doc, Smith and Louis heading back to the dock from the station. She glanced at Colt, then stood and made her way to meet them. As they entered the ship, the three men glanced over at her but kept heading toward Doc's office, so she followed.

Doc swiped his pass and entered, then headed straight into the examination room and started collecting the equipment he needed: syringes, swabs, rubber gloves. "Get that cart, disconnect it from the power source and switch it to battery," he said to Smith, motioning for him to get the cart containing the vital signs monitoring equipment.

Smith moved quickly, flicked a few switches and wheeled the cart back to Doc, who started putting the gear he'd been gathering onto it.

"Louis, in that cupboard is the portable scanner," Doc pointed.

Carrie stepped forward. "What can I do?"

Doc glanced at her. "We got it, thanks."

Carrie stared at him for a second, then looked over at the other two men. Smith gave her a friendly half-smile, and Louis a blank stare.

"Can I help carry something, at least?" she offered.

Doc was scanning the glass cabinet which contained many small vials of fluid. He came across what he was looking for and pulled out four of the vials, adding them to the cart. He looked over at her again. "Captain's orders. You guard the ship, corporal." He went to another cabinet and pulled some more items out, then grabbed the BP tester and added them to the cart. He looked around the room. "That's it for now. Bring the cart, Smith."

As Doc walked toward the door again, he passed Carrie, and they locked eyes briefly. He went into his office and picked up four blank e-clips from his desk.

"Let's move out!" Doc ordered.

Smith and Louis left the room, and Doc followed. As he reached the door he stopped and looked back at her; one hand on the lever ready to close it, e-clips tucked under the other. She flashed him a disappointed look, and as she passed one of the e-clips he had tucked under his arm, fell. She quickly bent to retrieve it at the same time as he did, and they connected, bumping shoulders.

"Sorry," she said, putting her hand on his shoulder to steady them both. She bent down picked up the e-clip, and tucked it back under his arm, then turned and headed back to the flight deck.

She re-entered the room, slumped back in her chair, and looked up at the screens. Colt eyed her curiously, but she ignored it. Carrie noted the four survivors hadn't moved. They were still standing in a row, centimeters apart, staring at Brown and Carter, looking somewhat intrigued. Carter walked up to the glass and rapped his knuckles on it. He turned to Brown and said: "It's thick, but it's not bulletproof or laserproof." Then he turned back to the survivors and eyed them again with a slight smile, before stepping back.

Her eyes darted over to Harris's and McKinley's screens. They were still looking through desk drawers, scrolling through e-filing panels, and flipping through the minimal paperwork present. She moved her eyes back to Doc's monitor. He was making his way down the corridor to where the survivors were. As he turned the corner to where the bio cell was, the four men stood impassively, watching as he walked toward them.

"How do you want to do this, Doc?" Brown asked, stepping forward.

Doc looked at the survivors.

"I need to check you out, one at a time." He spoke to Chet: "I'll start with you. You other three stand back."

Doc moved over to the door, snapped on some gloves, and pulled his breathing apparatus on. "Smith, get this thing open."

Smith walked over to the door and pulled out the equipment he'd used to get them into the station. It worked its magic, and the cell door unlocked. Brown, Carter and Louis trained their guns on the four men. Smith fell back and did the same.

Doc stepped into the first square glass chamber and closed the door behind him. A series of beeps sounded, like a countdown, and suddenly a rush of white mist washed over him, making him vanish for a second. It suddenly cleared, they heard another set of beeps, and the door leading into the cell proper, opened.

Doc stood at the door, unmoving. "Logan, Grolsh, Fairmont, stand back!" he ordered.

They looked at him, then glanced over at Chet who gave a slight nod. The three of them looked back at the *Aurora*'s soldiers, then moved slowly and silently back against the wall. Doc quickly glanced around at his team, checking their guns had him covered, then he stepped into the cell. As he did, Chet took a step toward him.

"Don't move!" Carter yelled.

Chet turned his head slowly toward him. "He can't examine me from over there, can he?" Chet spoke calmly enough, but there seemed a slight edge to his voice.

"Put your hands up and turn around," Doc ordered him. "You too," he ordered the other three men. "Turn around, face the wall and put your hands in the air."

Chet looked at him.

"I'm going to frisk you," Doc explained.

Chet nodded, then slowly turned around with his hands in the air. The other three followed suit. Doc patted him down thoroughly, then moved over and patted the other three down. As soon as he confirmed they were unarmed, he pulled out his equipment to test the air quality in the cell, confirming with Hunter that it matched the readings outside. Doc removed his breathing apparatus, holding his breath while he exchanged it for a simple surgical mask.

"Okay, Smith, bring the cart in," he ordered. Smith, wearing a surgical mask as well, wheeled the cart into the square chamber, then stepped back out and closed the door, as the "cleansing" process occurred. The second door unlocked and opened. "Get me a couple of chairs too," Doc ordered as he took the cart and wheeled it into the cell.

Carrie's eyes flicked over to Harris's and McKinley's monitors. Harris was still searching through one of the offices but didn't appear to be having any luck.

"I got nothing," McKinley said, leaning through the doorway of the office Harris was searching.

"They were Chet's and another guy—Ravearez's—offices you had, right?" Harris asked him.

McKinley nodded. "Nothing."

"Go down to the cargo office, see if you can find anything there," Harris ordered. McKinley nodded and left.

"Hunter?" Harris said taking hold of his mouthpiece.

"Yes, sir," Hunter answered from the flight deck.

"The office I'm in is supposed to be Professor Sharley's. Am I right?"

Hunter hit a button and another screen appeared alongside the others. "Just double-checking now, sir," he answered, hitting a few more buttons on his console. The plan of the station appeared on the screen, then zoomed in on the location of the offices. "Yes, sir. According to the plan, you're in Sharley's office."

"Hmph. Bullshit!" Harris muttered, as he slammed a drawer shut on the desk he'd been looking though.

Carrie's eyes flicked back to Smith's camera as he fed the two chairs into the bio cell through the square chamber one by one. Doc took them and placed them down opposite each other, motioning for Chet to take a seat, which he did.

The lieutenant pulled out his BP equipment and began to unravel it. "Place your left arm out," he ordered.

Chet rolled his arm toward Doc, who began to tighten the band around his upper arm. The lieutenant glanced down and his camera picked up the bulging veins in Chet's forearm, along with that of a tattoo on the inside of his left wrist. The tattoo looked similar to that of a barcode, except with fewer lines; there looked to be six in all. Doc looked back up at Chet who was staring blankly at him.

"Put this in your mouth." The medic held out a thermometer.

Chet leaned slightly toward Doc as he placed the thermometer in his mouth, then seemed to hesitate a moment. Carrie wasn't sure what he was doing exactly, but it looked as though he was inhaling.

Doc pulled back, giving him a weird look. "Something wrong, Chet?"

"No," he smiled, "on the contrary."

Doc stared at him, waiting for an explanation.

Chet seemed amused by this. "I'm just very glad you're here."

"He gives me the creeps," Colt said, eyeing Doc's monitor, which showed a close-up of Chet staring directly into the camera.

"Who's watching us, lieutenant?" Chet asked, the thermometer dancing around in his mouth as he did.

"Some people," Doc answered, as the BP monitor beeped. He looked at the reading. "Blood pressure is pretty high," he said, shooting Chet a glance, then noting the result on the e-clip. He removed the thermometer, checked the reading, and a concerned furrow grew across his brow. He placed his free hand on Chet's forehead. "You're burning up."

"I feel fine," Chet replied, his voice still devoid of emotion.

Doc's hand moved down to Chet's eyes and placed his thumb across the survivor's eyebrow, lifting his eyelid open for a closer look, then checked the other. He turned back to his e-clip and wrote the figure from the thermometer down.

Chet, still staring into the camera over Doc's ear, asked slowly, calmly. "How many people?"

Doc didn't answer.

"How many people are watching? With Hunter? He must be your pilot, yes?" Chet asked again.

From the angle of Smith's camera it seemed as if Doc glanced at the *Aurora* team, then looked back at Chet before saying, "I see you've been paying attention."

"I am a scientist. That's what I do."

"Take off your shirt," Doc ordered, ignoring Chet's initial question.

Chet looked down at his white T-shirt, then began to pull it up over his head, revealing a muscular torso covered with several scars and a large, black tattoo of a dragon over the right half of his chest.

The *Aurora* crew watching from the flight deck reacted. "Whoa!" Colt said, "he's pretty buff for a scientist!"

"They all are," Packham agreed.

"What's with those scars?" Hunter said.

"Those are some pretty nasty scars..." Bolkov nodded in agreement.

"You've got a few scars there," they heard Doc say, as though reading their minds.

Chet gave a single nod.

"How'd you get them?" Doc asked casually, pulling the cart a bit closer.

Chet shrugged. "Here and there."

Doc picked up the three discs. "I've got to put these on you."

Chet nodded. Doc leaned over, watching Chet's eyes, as he placed one disc on his upper chest, one over his heart and one below his chest. The machine immediately began beeping rather quickly. Doc glanced over at it. From what Carrie could tell, it sounded like Chet's heart was racing, although his breathing seemed steady.

Doc looked back at Chet. "Are you sure you're okay? You're not lightheaded? Any pain in your shoulder? Your arm?"

Chet shook his head. "I'm fine."

Doc looked between the machine and Chet. "According to this you're on the verge of a mild heart attack."

Chet shrugged. "I feel fine."

"So why is your heart racing, then?"

Chet looked over at the *Aurora* team on guard, then back at Doc. "There are four soldiers aiming their weapons at me. Perhaps that is why?" he said calmly.

The machine beeped, Doc hit a series of buttons and the e-clip lit up. Chet was staring back down the camera again. Carrie could see a sheen of sweat gathering on his brow.

Doc held up the white tube. "Blow long and hard into this when I tell you."

Chet took it and held it to his mouth.

"Go," Doc said.

Chet blew into the tube, all the while staring into the camera.

"Stop," Doc ordered. He hit another series of buttons on the machine and again the e-clip lit up.

"You never answered my question, lieutenant?" Chet asked calmly, looking from the camera to Doc. "Who else is on the ship with your pilots?"

"No, I didn't answer your question, Chet, but you don't need to worry about who or what is on our ship," Doc replied firmly, writing down the figures on the e-clip, then glancing back up at Chet. "Alright? Now, I've just got to scan you and take some blood samples, then we'll be done."

Doc took a syringe, along with a rubber cord, off the cart.

"You won't need that," Chet said, rolling his arm over to expose the bulging veins again.

Doc looked down at his arm. "No, I guess I won't." He took the needle and held it up to Chet's inner elbow; glanced up to make eye contact with him, then proceeded to insert the needle and begin to withdraw blood.

"Ugh! I can't watch that," Packham said, averting her eyes from the screen on the flight deck.

Hunter gave her a crazy look. "You can't look at blood? Then what the hell are you doing in the UNF?"

"Flying ships!" she shot back, then returned her eyes to the screens.

After two vials were taken, Doc fed them back through the glass chamber to Smith. "Head back to the examination room and switch the autoanalyzer on," he ordered the private.

Smith nodded and departed, seemingly understanding what he was talking about.

Doc grabbed another device off the cart, pulling it out of its black pouch. It was shaped like a silver paddle. He turned it on and held it in front of Chet's face. "I'm just going to scan your head and neck."

Chet nodded, and Doc began to run the paddle over him. Carrie, watching Louis's screen, noted that Doc seemed to pause when he scanned the back of Chet's head, but said nothing. Once he was done, he processed the information as normal and the e-clip lit up again.

Doc grabbed one of the vials he'd collected from the cabinet on the *Aurora*, then taking another needle, filled the syringe with the liquid. "You're a little dehydrated. This will help hydrate you," he said, holding up the needle to Chet.

Chet nodded and Doc injected the fluid into his vein. When he was done he threw the syringe into a waste box that was sitting on the bottom shelf of the cart.

"Okay, we're done," Doc announced.

Chet nodded, then stood and walked, shirt in hand, over to the wall with the others.

"Who's next?" Doc asked.

Logan moved forward silently. His face was expressionless, but his strange emerald-green eyes focused sharply on Doc.

# 13

# Quarantine

Harris sat at Sharley's desk, trying to get his head around what had happened. There was nothing of substance in the offices. Certainly nothing classified. It looked like the station was ready for a handover, like one team was moving out and another moving in. There were no signs of a struggle. Nothing. *Where was the Spector? The other five must have left, abandoned the station. Maybe there was a falling out with the four 'survivors'?*

There was only one way to get answers and that was by speaking to the four men. He left the office and approached the holding cell, watching as Doc tested Logan's lungs.

"Brown," Harris called. "Get the corridor lights on, then get the *Aurora* locked into the Darwin's external power source on the dock. Then go to the station's control room and see what's going on with the comms. I'll send Smith to help you when he gets back."

"Yes, sir," he replied, then left.

Louis moved over beside Carter to take up his spot.

"How's it going, Doc?" Harris asked, scanning his eyes around the cell. It was an extremely minimalist, sterile room. There looked to be only four beds for sleeping, pulled in and out from slots in the wall, and a toilet inside a small cubicle. Everything looked as though it were made from a glossy white fiberglass material.

"We're getting there," Doc answered, not taking his eyes off Logan.

McKinley walked back in to join the group. "Nothing in the cargo office, captain," he said. "Last ship to dock was a cargo runner called the *Belgo,* and that was about four weeks ago."

Harris turned around to look at the survivors, then walked up to the glass wall of the cell. "What is the last thing you remember before the blackout?"

They all looked to Chet.

"What was going on right before it happened?" Harris asked firmly. "What were you doing?"

"I was in the gym, working out," Chet answered.

Harris studied his build, and nodded, then turned to Logan. "And you?"

"Eating."

"You two?" Harris turned to Grolsh and Fairmont.

"Sleeping," Fairmont answered.

Harris looked over at Grolsh, who was smirking.

"Taking a shower and… jerking off."

Everyone stared at Grolsh. Harris gave him an unaffected look. Fairmont started smirking too, but when Chet gave Grolsh a cold look they both instantly dropped their smiles.

"What was everyone else doing?" Harris asked.

"It was a staggered shift change," Chet answered for them. "Some had just come off shift and were eating, some were still getting out of bed, some were on duty already."

Harris looked at him hard. "So, the lights went out and you woke up in this bio cell?"

"Yes. That is correct."

"Can we have some food now?" Logan asked in his low gravelly voice, as Doc took blood from his arm.

Harris eyed Logan for a moment, then called out over his shoulder. "Louis, fetch these guys something to eat."

Louis nodded and headed for the ship, just as Smith came back.

"Smith, head to the comms room and help Brown figure out what's wrong," Harris ordered.

"Yes, sir," Smith said, turning around and heading back down the corridor.

Harris turned his attention back to the survivors. "And Professor Sharley was on the station when this happened?" he asked.

"Yes," Chet answered.

"We're done," Doc told Logan. "Fairmont, you're next."

Logan walked slowly over to the other men, as Fairmont quietly stepped forward.

Carrie studied the survivors though Harris's camera. Logan was a bit shorter than the others, and seemed to stalk like a panther, his long, shiny raven hair slinking down his back.

Fairmont was the tallest and broadest, and looked younger than Chet and Logan in the face, despite his gray hair. Grolsh was the leanest of the four, but he was still muscular, like a greyhound. He seemed to be the youngest, watching the others constantly for his lead.

Carrie focused back on the captain as he continued with his questions.

"Where was Sharley when this happened?"

Chet shrugged.

"What programs were you developing here?" Harris continued.

Chet smiled. "You know that's classified, otherwise your superiors would've told you." His voice distantly echoed through the speakers.

"Let me rephrase the question," Harris said, his voice a little tighter. "Could one of your programs have caused this blackout?"

Chet eyed him, face expressionless, the sweat still building on his brow. "Anything's possible, Captain Harris."

The two men stared at each other for a few moments.

"What I'm looking for here, Chet, is a 'yes' or 'no' response," Harris said firmly, as though it were an order.

Chet smiled again, cocking his head to the side, in contemplation. After a moment he gave his response. "No."

Harris nodded at him. "Then do you have any idea what could've caused this blackout?"

Chet shook his head.

"You're a scientist and you're second-in-command on this station. You have no theories whatsoever?" Harris asked in a flat tone, suggesting disbelief.

Again, Chet shook his head.

"Nothing suspicious has taken place here and no person has behaved suspiciously?" Harris asked. "No visitor or visitors to the station have behaved strangely? No unidentified comms were received? Nothing out of the ordinary with any of your equipment? No strange cargo? Nothing?"

"No, captain." Chet spoke slowly and deliberately, as though he were talking to a child, whose game he was beginning to tire of. "I have not identified anything out of the ordinary that could have possibly caused this blackout or the loss of comms with Command."

"So, you weren't the one sending out those comms signals we picked up en route?"

"I'm sorry, captain?" A look of confusion swept across Chet's face.

"We picked up some scrambled comms that came from this station. That wasn't you?"

Chet shook his head, then motioned around the bio cell. "We have no transmission facilities in here as you can see. We were working, then we were in here. There was no in-between."

"Someone sent them from this station. You're all that's left."

Chet shrugged casually. "We've obviously had technical difficulties, that's why you're here. Perhaps some pre-recorded transmissions were released into the ether when the comms went down?"

Harris eyed him for another moment, as the silence sat around them. Eventually he turned to McKinley. "Guard these men. When Louis comes back, he and Carter are on first watch."

Carrie watched as the captain turned and stalked off down the corridor.

Harris stared at the screen in front of him, waiting for it to connect with Colonel Isaack and Professor Martin back on Earth.

"Captain Harris," Isaack greeted him. "We weren't expecting to speak to you so soon. Talk to me."

"Well, sir, the Darwin is fine—" Harris began, but Isaack cut him off.

"What's the story with the comms?"

"Are you on the Darwin's power supply?" Martin added.

"Not yet. We're still on the *Aurora*'s, but I've got Brown working on it."

"So the team are safe?" Martin asked anxiously.

"We found four of your crew locked up in the bio cell. Chet, Logan, Fairmont and Grolsh. There are no other people on board and the *Spector* is missing. There are no other ships docked here and there are no signs of any struggle. The whole station is clean as a whistle, like there's been no-one here at all."

"Only four team members?" Martin asked, his brow furrowed. "The rest must've left on the *Spector*. That's odd. We've had absolutely no communication from them."

"What explanation did the four remaining crew provide for their absence?" Isaack asked.

"None. They said there was a blackout and they woke up in the bio cell," Harris said, leaning back in his chair.

"And the remaining four. Do they seem okay?" Martin asked, the furrow in his brow still prominent. "Are they injured in any way?"

"No, no obvious injuries. Doc is checking them out now, though. We'll know more in a few hours."

"And the station is stable?" Isaack focused his eyes in concentration.

Harris nodded. "The station is structurally A-OK. Looks like it's just the comms, sir."

"So, what's your plan moving forward?" Isaack asked.

"Doc's going to run some tests to find out if there's any health risk to my men, in case the survivors have been exposed to something. Until I'm satisfied, they will remain in the bio cell. In the meantime, we'll work on the comms and keep searching through this place until we find out what happened here."

"And the women?" Martin asked.

Harris's eyes darted to Martin's and eyed him for a moment. "They remain here on the *Aurora* as instructed." Then he looked back at Isaack. "Although as there appears to be no obvious danger, sir, I would like your permission to put them to work."

Isaack considered his request for a moment, then shook his head. "No. They'll remain on the *Aurora* until further notice. Let's see what Lieutenant Walker comes up with first."

Harris bit his tongue, subtly exhaling any comments through his nose.

"If there's nothing else to report, captain, then we'd better let you get back to it," Isaack said firmly. "We'll put a trace out on the missing ship and contact you when we locate it. You get in touch when you have any further information."

"Yes, sir," Harris replied.

Isaack nodded back, then turned to Professor Martin, as the screen went black.

Harris stood up from his desk and put his headpiece back on.

"Captain Harris back on comms," he announced into his mouthpiece, as he made his way out of his office.

*"Captain, this is Brown. We've locked the Aurora into the external power source, and it appears to be A-OK. Await permission to switch over, sir."*

"Good," Harris responded. "Hunter, do you copy? Over."

*"Yes, sir!"* Hunter's voice now came over his earpiece.

"Switch the *Aurora* over to the external power supply effective immediately. Over," Harris ordered.

*"Yes, sir. Switching from onboard power cells to external source. Over."*

The lights on the *Aurora* flickered and blinked for a moment, then came on brightly again. Harris studied them carefully as he made his way off the ship and back onto the Darwin's dock. As he headed for the station's entrance, Doc and McKinley came walking out.

"You done?" Harris asked Doc, motioning to the vials in the cart he was pushing along.

"Yeah. I'll start the lab work now. I would like to speak with you, though."

Harris nodded. "I'll come and see you in a bit." He turned to his second lieutenant. "McKinley, you might as well get some sleep and tell Bulk he can head off too. We'll need some fresh heads in the morning."

"Yes, sir."

Harris continued on, making his way toward the Darwin's control room. When he arrived, Smith was at the main control desk and Brown was off to the side checking some wiring in an opened panel.

"What's the story, gentlemen?" Harris asked, entering the room.

Brown looked over at him. "Well, we've confirmed the comms are down, sir, but we can't find out why. Nothing appears to be blown out or damaged. We're investigating the possibilities now."

Harris took a close look around the room again. It looked like the rest of the ship. Everything seemed in order. Nothing out of place.

"Have you been able to check the logs?" he asked Smith.

Smith leaned forward, grabbed a bound document and handed it to Harris. "The manual log stops on July 19th. We've not been able to access the mainframe as yet to get to the electronic logs," he told him.

"Okay," Harris said, "forget the comms for now. Get into that mainframe and get me those electronic logs. I want to know every single transmission that went in and out of here leading up to this blackout, as well as any information on the ships, cargo or otherwise that were incoming and outgoing from this station. We're flying blind here. We need some information, *any* information. Do you understand? We've got five missing people to find."

"Yes, sir," they replied.

Harris nodded at him. "Call me as soon as you have something."

"Yes, sir."

Harris left the control room and decided to make his way around to Section Three and have a closer look at the staff quarters. All the while he ignored the muscles tensing in his neck and back, and the swirling in his gut. Something didn't feel right. *What the fuck happened here?*

Carrie watched Colt yawn. Seconds later she was stifling a yawn herself. She'd been watching the monitors, but not a hell of a lot was happening. Louis and Carter were guarding the cell in silence, following standard UNF protocol.

Brown and Smith were trying to break into the Darwin's mainframe with help from Hunter and Packham. Their conversations were somewhat geek-speak, but she listened regardless, through boredom mainly; her basic IT knowledge allowing her to grasp the general gist.

Harris was still looking through the staff quarters and not having too much luck, while both McKinley and Doc had switched their headsets off altogether.

Carrie gave in to a yawn. "I need to do something, or I'm going to fall asleep."

"Me, too," Colt agreed, stretching out.

"Shall we at least see if Doc needs a hand with something?"

Colt nodded and together they left the flight deck. They found Doc in his examination room, sitting on a stool alongside the far bench, reading an e-clip and scrolling through an e-file pane with his other hand.

"Hey, Doc," Colt announced their arrival.

"Corporals," he replied, looking up at them.

"You need a hand with anything, sir?" Colt asked.

"No, I'm all good." Doc said. "The blood work is being tested as we speak." He motioned to a white cylindrical piece of equipment sitting on the bench which emitted a low whirring sound. "And I'm about to take care of the data upload now." He pointed to the e-clips in front of him.

Carrie nodded and Colt shuffled around on the spot.

"Those guys look normal to you, Doc?" Colt asked, stuffing her hands in her pockets.

"I guess that depends on how long they've been without food and water," he said, turning back to the e-clips.

"They were acting pretty weird, though, huh?" Colt continued.

"Well, you deprive the body of food and water and your faculties become affected, especially your brain..." Doc's voice trailed off as he became absorbed in the e-clips again.

Carrie and Colt stood there for a few moments in silence, before Carrie decided to break it.

"Doc, do you know why the captain wouldn't let us take part in the boarding?"

He looked up and shook his head. "No, I don't, corporal. Perhaps that's something you should be asking him?"

"Based on the response we got earlier..." she shrugged, turning to Colt. "So much for this being a test case?"

"Why do you say that?" Doc asked.

Carrie looked back at him. "Well, if we're not actually allowed to do anything when it counts, what's the point? If this is a test case, shouldn't we be tested?"

"Packham helped dock the ship."

Carrie looked at Doc for a second and then glanced at Colt. "Yeah, well, we can't fly ships so I guess that means we're out of luck."

"Be patient, Welles. I'm sure there'll be work soon enough."

"We'll leave you to it, Doc." Colt tapped Carrie on the arm and they headed over to the door, just as Harris entered.

"Soldiers," he nodded.

"Captain," they responded. Carrie did her best to avoid eye contact, though, still angry.

"You two might as well hit the sack. I need you to replace Louis and Smith on mess hall duty tomorrow morn— er..." Harris looked at his watch. "Make that *this* morning. 0630 sharp, breakfast is to be served. Understand?"

Carrie and Colt exchanged looks.

"Yes, sir," they responded and left.

Harris watched Colt and Welles leave, hit the button by the door to shut it behind them, then walked over to Doc.

"What have you got for me?" he asked.

Doc turned on his stool to face him. "Well, on the face of it they look okay. They're dehydrated but they generally look fine. *However*, they all have high temperatures, they're sweating, they've got elevated heartbeats—and I'm talking on the verge of a mild heart attack. Their lung and brain scans seem alright, but when I was doing the brain scan, I noticed they all have these scars that trace along the backs of their ears?"

"What does that mean?" Harris asked him.

"It means they've had some sort of surgery on their ears, but nothing out of the ordinary showed up on the scan."

"Did you ask them what it was from?"

"They said they had an implant when they first arrived on the station to combat space sickness, but after six months it was removed."

"That's possible."

Doc shrugged. "Well, it's possible, I guess, but *all four* of them suffering from space sickness?"

"And the scars look old?"

Doc nodded. "Yeah. They're not recent. Not blackout recent, anyway."

"So how long until the blood work is ready?"

"A couple of hours."

Harris nodded.

"One other thing," Doc said. "They've each got a barcode-like tattoo above their left wrists. There are six bars on each, alternating between thick and thin. Each has an individual number. And they've got several scars across their bodies, different on each of them."

"And?"

"And, I don't know… it's just weird. They're built like soldiers. They're scarred like soldiers. They even seem to think like soldiers. Chet kept trying to find out how many more of us there were on this ship, like he was trying to figure out what they were up against. And they were fully checking every one of us out, eyeing us head to toe, sizing us up."

"Well, if they were attacked, they're probably a little edgy around strangers," Harris shrugged.

"Yeah, I don't know. It just feels a little weird; something's not sitting right for me."

Harris thought about this for a moment. "Did you tell them how many we had on the ship?"

Doc shook his head. "Chet figured our pilots, but that's about it. I let his imagination run wild. He knows we have more soldiers on board, I just didn't let on how many."

"Good, let's keep it that way. Let me know the results of their blood work, and we'll take it from there. Something isn't sitting right for me, either. I've found nothing on the station to tell me what happened here. This place is too clean, too controlled."

Doc nodded, and Harris turned to leave.

"Captain, one more thing?" Doc called after him.

Harris turned back and saw his lieutenant had a slight look of confusion across his face. "How come you didn't let Welles and Colt join the boarding party?"

Harris stared at him for a moment. "You got a problem with my orders, Doc?"

"No, you always have a good reason. I'm just curious as to why?"

Harris stared at Doc again. The lieutenant noted his silence and continued on. "I thought this was a test case?"

Harris put his hands on his hips and sighed. Normally he wouldn't respond if a solider questioned his orders or his motives, but his relationship with Doc was different, so he let it slide. Doc was his sounding board, a support mechanism to bounce ideas off, gain feedback from and sometimes, on those rare occasions, even a critique.

"You ever stop and think about the orders I get, Doc?" he asked, staring him squarely in the eye.

Doc looked puzzled for a moment. "That was an order from Command, not to let them take part? But they put them on here?"

Harris continued to stare at Doc but didn't respond.

"Why?" came Doc's next question.

Harris shrugged. "Fuckin' PR exercise, Doc."

"Was it just for the boarding or indefinitely?"

"Until further notice, they are to remain on the ship."

Doc nodded slowly, his mind clearly ticking over. "Interesting."

"Isn't it," Harris said, leaving the room. He didn't wish to go any further with the conversation right now. He didn't understand it himself, so he certainly couldn't explain it to Doc.

*

Harris, sitting in his office on the *Aurora*, looked up to see Doc at his door. It was 0321. Harris waited for him to speak.

"Blood work is fine. There are no antibodies present, the white blood cells are normal. There appears to be no known virus or bacteria present." He shrugged. "Their blood count is fine."

"So does that mean we have to release them?" Harris asked.

"Not necessarily. I'm not willing to accept responsibility for letting them go just yet, not while they're still displaying the symptoms they are. For all we know they're infected with some virus they themselves have created, that could maybe take several hours, even days, to fully display symptoms. I can't risk it yet."

"So what do you recommend?"

"I think we should hold them a while longer. I'll do some more blood work in another 12 hours and make sure nothing has changed."

Harris thought about this for a moment. "Agreed. I'd like some more time to get into those electronic logs and try to find out exactly what happened here before I let them go."

Doc nodded.

"Okay, then, we'll tell them the good news in the morning," Harris concluded. "Right now, we should probably try and get a few hours' sleep."

"Agreed," Doc replied, giving a wave as he left.

Harris let out a tired sigh, then stood from his desk and powered down the e-files he'd been reading. A few hours sleep was just what he needed to refresh and clear his mind. Something just wasn't sitting right and it was bugging him and his gut no end.

Carrie looked at her watch. 0627. Any minute now, she was expecting the hungry hordes to fill the mess hall. It was her first time on *Aurora* mess hall duty and it was pretty straightforward. There was actually a detailed manual on how much food to serve, so she and Colt got to work preparing a heap of boiled and poached eggs, grilled ham, mushrooms, tomatoes, toast and a couple of jugs of juice, along with large pots of tea and coffee. It wasn't what she thought she'd be doing on a mission like this, but at least she was finally being of some use.

Harris and McKinley were the first to enter. Harris didn't look like he'd had much sleep, but McKinley looked fresh. Doc, Brown, Smith and Bolkov followed. They too looked a little weary, except Bolkov, that is. They lined up and began scooping food onto their plates, then sat down, managing to fit around the one table.

"So what's the plan today, captain?" McKinley asked, between mouthfuls.

"You and Bulk are going to relieve Louis and Carter on that cell," Harris responded, not looking up from his plate.

"They didn't pass their physical?" McKinley looked over at Doc.

Doc exchanged a glance with Harris. "They did, but I want to wait another 12 hours to be sure."

McKinley nodded and went back to his food.

Harris turned to Brown. "Now you and Smith have had some sleep, you're going to get back to that mainframe, aren't you?" he asked firmly.

"Yes, sir, we're close," Brown answered.

"Good. Make that a priority."

Carrie watched the men chow down their food, then studied Harris sitting opposite her. She waited a moment to see if he was going to issue her with any orders. He didn't.

"So, what would you like us to do today, captain?" Carrie prompted him.

Harris glanced up at her. "You're on mess hall duty. You keep the rest of us fed and watered."

"Yes, sir. And after that?" Carrie continued, looking him in the eye.

"You clean up and get ready for the next meal."

She paused, feeling her face beginning to harden, "Yes, sir. And after that?"

Harris stared at her. "After that, you got some free time, until I otherwise allocate it."

"Free time?"

"Yeah, you know, you do some target practice, work out in the gym, go for a run —"

"Can we go for a run on the Darwin?" Carrie interrupted.

"No, you cannot. The station is not for running. You want to run, you do it on the *Aurora*."

"Sir, can we at least help you look for information on the Darwin?" Carrie was determined not to give up. "Surely a fresh set of eyes —"

Harris dropped his fork to his plate, eyes firmly fixed on hers. "Welles, you are on mess hall duty. *That* is your job. *That* is my order to you. You finish your job early, you do what you want, but you will do it on the *Aurora*. Do you understand me?"

The mess hall had fallen silent. Carrie felt her cheeks begin to burn. She didn't understand why he was being like this. Why was he trying to block her efforts?

"I want in on the action, sir," she said firmly. "I want to help."

"Good to know," he said sharply, as he continued to eat. "But right now, I don't need you."

"So, I can just go lie on my bunk and read a book then, sir?" she asked smartly.

Harris glared at her. "The order is clear. Do you, or do you not understand my order, Corporal Welles?" The volume of his voice had risen.

She glared back.

"We do, sir," Colt answered for her.

"I'm not talking to you," he snapped at Colt.

"Corporal," Doc interjected. "I've got plenty of work you can do. You can help me out in the lab."

Carrie glanced over at Doc. His eyes were wary, warning her to stop pushing Harris. She looked back at the captain, whose eyes were bulging a fierce glare in her direction, still waiting for an answer.

"Yes, sir," she said with a tight jaw.

Harris continued to glare at her a moment then stood up sharply, grabbed his plate and stormed off, leaving the room.

The table sat quiet for a few seconds, before Smith looked over at her wide-eyed. "Jesus, Welles, you've either got a set of balls on ya or you're — "

"— completely fuckin' stupid," McKinley muttered, shaking his head.

"Why?" she shot at McKinley. "Because I want to do my job? Because I want to do what I'm paid to do?"

"An order is an order! *That's* what you're paid to do," he replied pointing his finger across the table at her. "To take fucking orders!"

"So if he ordered you to sit here on the ship and do nothing, you'd be fine with that?"

McKinley shrugged. "Well, you see, Harris would *never* order *me* to sit on the ship and do nothing."

"Look, corporal," Doc interjected again, "the captain's order is final. Whether you like it or not, that's it. End of story. Now drop it."

Doc was clearly pulling rank to control the situation. She was fuming, but she relented. She had to. It was futile, as clearly their allegiance was to the captain. She fully understood the chain of command and the power of an order, but she was frustrated at being held back and it was her gut instinct to fight against it.

Packham and Hunter entered the mess then and headed for the food. McKinley looked over at them, then started to get up.

"Come on, Bulk. Let's go relieve the Saffer and the Frenchie," he said.

Bolkov grunted and stood up as well. He glanced at Carrie, shook his head, and they left the room.

Colt let out a big sigh, stood and headed over to the counter. Carrie looked at Brown who was eating quietly. He made eye contact with her but then looked back down at his plate. He clearly wasn't getting involved. She turned her eyes to Doc, who gave her a disappointed look.

She sighed and made her way over to the counter and began to clean up. Colt gave her a frustrated look and kept on working.

"We've got to stand up for ourselves!" Carrie protested.

Colt just put her hands up in the air, shook her head and walked over to the other side of the kitchen.

# 14

# Logs

Harris sat in his office, where he'd finished eating his breakfast. He was pissed. He could understand Welles's frustration, but she was way out of line questioning his order like that. Despite that, he was actually more pissed at Doc for intervening. He knew his lieutenant was just trying to calm the situation, but he should've kept his mouth shut. It hadn't happened before. Even when Doc thought he was being harsh on a soldier, he normally refrained from passing judgment until they were alone. Intervening like that in front of the other soldiers belittled Harris's authority and he could not have that on his ship.

He pushed his plate away angrily and slumped back in his chair. He took a deep breath and closed his eyes. *Forget it. Deal with it later. Focus on the issue at hand. Find out what happened here. Find out what is going on with those survivors. Find out the truth. As soon as you get to the bottom of this, you can get back home and finish that leave.* Thoughts of his son Ty and the basketball game he owed him filled his mind, and he remembered the disappointment in Taya's voice. He sighed again and swallowed his anger, as the dream he'd had last night resurfaced. He'd been lost in a dark place, breathing heavily in fear, moving his weapon's light about in the nothingness. He remembered being afraid of that darkness, and praying to find a way out of the trouble he was in. Then suddenly, his light shone on the faces of Sibbie and Etta, who reached out and latched onto him, saying: "Something's wrong". Panicked, he pushed them away, and awoke abruptly again in a pool of sweat.

And as he thought about it now, they were right. Something was wrong, here on the Darwin. He just didn't know what it was.

Leaving his office and shaking the dream from his mind, he made his way into the station and headed for the bio cell in Section Two. As he approached, he saw McKinley and Bolkov standing there, guns by their sides, and Doc standing at the glass wall talking to the four men inside. Harris decided to stay back and observe, not making his presence known to the others.

"Your initial tests were fine, but I'm not satisfied that you're in perfect health yet," Doc was telling them.

"That's because we've been locked up in here!" Logan argued. "Let us out. Give us more food, water, proper beds to sleep in and then we'll be fine!"

"I just need you to wait another 12 hours to be sure, then if there's no change I can let you out," Doc said calmly, trying to reason with them.

"Fuck you," Grolsh spat. "You sit in here for days. See if you're fine."

"I understand where you're coming from," Doc continued, holding his hand out in a placating way.

"You don't understand shit!" Logan rushed up to the glass wall in front of Doc's face and thumped it with the heel of his hand.

Doc flinched in reflex and McKinley snapped his gun up.

Logan glared at McKinley. "You going to shoot a man in a glass cage?" he asked, in his deep gravelly voice.

McKinley didn't answer, but kept the gun trained on Logan.

Logan began walking up and down the cell wall, like a tiger in a zoo, staring demonically at McKinley.

"Look, you've all got high temperatures, high blood pressure and you're sweating profusely," Doc said, trying to use his most calming voice but Harris could hear it tightening. "They're common signs of a virus."

Chet spoke up calmly. "Our blood work was fine, you said it yourself."

"Yes, it was, and if it's still fine at 1800, we'll have no reason to hold you any longer."

"Our symptoms are also that of stress, are they not?" Chet asked. "Wouldn't you agree that's more likely the cause? We've been in this cell for who knows how long. We've got soldiers aiming their weapons at us, we don't know where our colleagues are and, to be quite frank, we have no idea who you are, or whether your qualifications are adequate enough to keep us in here. You can't possibly expect us to be calm about this situation?"

"No, but I ask that you *do* remain calm, or we'll be forced to consider other measures," Doc said.

"What measures?" Logan hissed through gritted teeth.

"Logan, if you're fine at 1800, you've got no reason to be concerned. We'll let you out of that cell. But if you show any aggression toward me or any of our soldiers, things won't be fine. Do you understand? We're here to help you, don't forget that."

Logan snarled to himself and continued to pace the cell.

Doc looked over at Chet. "Do you understand?"

Chet hesitated a moment, then nodded. "We do. Now, can you help us? We're thirsty."

Doc eyed them all for a second, then looked over his shoulder at Bolkov. "Get some water sent up."

Bolkov nodded, then spoke into his mouthpiece. "Hunter, we need water at bio cell."

Doc pulled out a syringe and a bottle of fluid from his pocket. "I'll give you another shot of this. Your bodies should be almost fully hydrated again by now."

"Thank you," Chet said calmly, looking eagerly at the fluid.

Harris's lieutenant studied Logan, who was still stalking along the cell wall glaring at them. Doc slipped on his surgical mask, then walked over to the control panel near the door. He hesitated, then pulled a lever which opened two windows in the glass wall with a loud echoing sound. One small window was at face height, the other larger window was at waist height, to pass things through. Harris noticed a continual fine mist spraying down over the openings, killing anything that had means of escape. Doc turned back to Chet. "Stick your arms out through the gap. I'll do it from here."

"What?" Logan's gravelly voice held a hint of sarcasm. "Come on in, Doc. I won't bite."

Chet put his arm through the larger window, and Doc gave him the injection. Chet held his face close to the smaller window near Doc's face and seemed to be inhaling deeply. The medic eyed him strangely, a puzzled look upon his face. When he was done, Chet stepped back quietly, and Doc reached in his pocket for more syringes and bottles. Fairmont and Grolsh both stepped forward and received their injections. Doc eyed them closely. When they were done, Logan stopped stalking and approached, holding his arm out in readiness.

Doc and Logan stared at each other, as he threaded his arm through the window. The medic filled another syringe with the fluid, tested the needle, then inserted it into Logan's arm. He injected the fluid, and just as he finished up, Logan swiftly latched onto Doc's arm and yanked him hard against the glass wall. Thankfully, Doc's reflexes were sharp and he shot out his hand just in time to stop his face from hitting it.

"Let him go!" McKinley called out, aiming his gun at Logan, Bolkov doing the same.

Logan and Doc stared at each other through the window, their faces millimeters apart. The survivor seemed to whisper something to him. Whatever it was, it didn't pick up on the headsets and was too low to be audible from where Harris was standing.

"Is that right?" Doc said, eyeing Logan squarely.

"What'd he say?" McKinley asked, gun still trained.

Doc and Logan continued to stare at each other, millimeters apart.

"Boyfriend's talking to you," Logan smiled.

Doc gave a steely smile in return and snapped his arm from Logan's grasp. He turned around and walked away from the cell. "Nothing important," he told McKinley.

At this point Harris stepped forward and made his presence known. His soldiers glanced over at him, but he noticed that the men in the cage didn't seem as surprised by his appearance.

"Is there a problem here?" he asked, in his best authoritative voice.

Doc looked at the men in the cell and then back to Harris. "No, sir."

Just then Hunter came walking in with a fresh supply of water.

"Ah, yet another new face. This must be Hunter," Chet said smoothly, eyeing the *Aurora* pilot over. "How many more are there to meet, captain?"

Hunter gave Chet a blank look. Doc took the water and passed it through the misted window to the men, who eagerly grabbed the bottles and began draining them.

"Hmm," Chet said wiping his mouth, waiting for an answer from Harris. "How many more?"

"There's enough," Harris said bluntly, then turned to Hunter. "Follow me to the control room."

*

"Captain! I was just about to call you," Smith greeted him, as Harris and Hunter entered the Darwin's control room. "We're in the mainframe and we're downloading the info."

"Good," Harris said, then turned to Hunter. "Once that's downloaded, I want you to go through it and let me know if anything stands out."

"Yes, sir," Hunter said, taking a seat at the console beside Smith.

"Brown, I want you to get working on the comms situation now. We need to know why Command lost connection with this station."

"Yes, sir," Brown said, making his way to the wiring in the corner of the room.

"Smith, you head back to the *Aurora* and make sure all this info is being downloaded onto our systems. I want a full record on our files."

"Yes, sir." Smith nodded and left the room.

Harris leaned over the back of Hunter's chair, scanning the information that was scrolling across the monitor in front of him.

"There has got to be something in there that tells us what the hell happened here."

Carrie looked around the mess hall. Everything was clean and the lunch was under control. That was the wonder of Command's stores. A lot of the meals were pre-prepared and only had to be heated up. Colt had left a few minutes ago. She'd followed Smith back to the flight deck when he'd come in for some coffee. Clearly, Carrie was someone she needed some space from for a while. She felt guilty for the trouble over breakfast, but she'd wanted this for so long that to be here now, have it in her grasp, and not be able to do anything, was frustrating.

With nothing else to do, she decided to head to the training room. When she got there she found Packham on the gym equipment.

"Hey," Carrie greeted her.

"Hey," she puffed back.

Carrie sat down on the equipment next to Packham. "What time did you finish up? I didn't hear you come in."

"About 0230 Harris came and told us to get some sleep."

"Hey, good job on the docking, by the way," Carrie smiled.

Packham stopped what she was doing and nodded. "Thanks. Space docking's the easy part, it's all about the timing. Launching and landing in different atmospheres, now there's where you work!"

Carrie smiled. "Oh, to be able to work!"

Packham gave her a sympathetic smile. "Hey, technically it's a good thing if they don't need you to shoot somebody, right?"

"Yeah, I guess."

"You want to do some weights? I'll spot you."

Carrie nodded. "Sure."

They moved over to one of the weight racks and worked through a few sets, then moved over to the treadmills when their arms couldn't take it anymore. Carrie listened as Packham talked about some of her previous assignments on transport routes, flying between Earth, the Moon and Mars. She talked about the different ships she'd flown and what the docks and landing areas were like on each planet.

"So which one is better?" Carrie asked her.

"Which *planet* is better? To live?" the sergeant asked her. "Oh, that's easy. Earth. Definitely. I mean, in terms of landscape, the others are barren and bare. There's a reason why we've flourished on Earth. Although, I do kinda like the Moon. There's something very peaceful about sitting there and looking out into the sky and seeing the Earth floating where the moon should be."

"Did you like Mars?"

"Mars is very much a frontier right now. It's like a modern version of the old Wild West. The two colonies are up and running, but it's still a little rough around the edges, if you know what I mean. It's filled with geologists, engineers, miners, and tradesmen. There're no families out there yet, no children allowed. There are females around, but only at about seven to one. And the red dust! It's like you're stuck in the desert. You half expect to see a cowboy come riding down the main streets," she chuckled. "One publican had a sense of humor and named his bar the Red Dust Saloon. There's a piano in the corner and whores upstairs. It's hilarious."

"You weren't based there very long?"

"Er, no…" Packham shook her head and shot her a strange look.

Carrie waited for the rest of what she thought she was going to say, but nothing came. "Oh… not a good experience?" she asked slowly.

"No, no, the work was fine. It was just, um, more of a… a personal issue."

Carrie continued to look at her, waiting to see if she was going to elaborate. Packham noticed.

"I was, um… seeing somebody. We were in the same unit." She shot Carrie a glance. "It didn't work out. I had to leave."

"Oh," Carrie said, looking back at her treadmill.

"Yes. Oh, indeed."

Carrie flashed her a sympathetic look. "Hey, their loss, our gain. Right?"

"So, tell me about Antarctica?" Packham smiled, changing the subject.

"You ever been there?" Carrie asked her.

"No, but I imagine it's fairly similar to some of the places I've been to in Russia!"

Carrie laughed.

"Sorry to interrupt, soldiers." Doc's voice sounded behind them. They turned to see him making his way toward them. "Welles, when you're done, if you come to my office, I've got that work for you."

Carrie slowed her treadmill to a stop. "Sure." She wiped the sweat from her brow and stepped off the machine.

"Finish up here and I'll see you there in a few minutes," Doc said, holding his hand up for her to stop.

"Yes, sir."

Doc departed as she grabbed her towel and wiped her face. Packham gave her a questioning look.

Carrie shrugged at her. "Well, I guess I did ask for work!"

Packham grinned back, as Carrie threw the towel over her shoulder and made her way to her room to quickly change.

Harris, seated at the console beside Hunter, listened intently.

"The last entry is August 24th. A cargo ship called the *Belgo* left the station —" Hunter told him, as he stared at the screen in front of him.

"Wait a minute," Harris interrupted. "McKinley said that the *Belgo* docked about four weeks ago, which would make that around August 10th. Why the hell did the ship stay here for two weeks before departing? Did it break down or something?"

"It just says here that it was delivering laboratory supplies. It doesn't mention anything about any repairs or problems."

Harris stood and moved over behind Hunter's chair. "Smith, do you copy? Over."

*"Yes, sir. Over,"* Smith's reply came.

"Get me the crew details for the cargo ship, the *Belgo*. Over."

*"Yes, sir. On it. Over."*

Harris bent down over Hunter's chair again, reading over his shoulder. "What kind of supplies were they delivering?"

Hunter swirled and tapped his fingers over the screen and another window popped up. He began reading it aloud to Harris. "Okay. Various chemicals... the names don't mean anything to me. Um... vitamins, all sorts of medical supplies. Some equipment, I don't know what the hell that is used for... and er... er... cats!"

"Cats?" Harris asked in disbelief, sure Hunter had read it wrong.

"Cats, 12 cats. Looks like they came from a company called EnviroWire."

"Why the fuck did they order a load of cats?"

"Maybe they were lonely," Hunter shrugged.

"Well, they're not here now," Harris said, not sharing the joke.

"Perhaps they got hungry," Brown teased from the corner of the room.

Harris shot him a look, as he straightened up. "Get me a data transfer for that manifest," he ordered.

"Yes, sir," Hunter said, reaching over to a stack of blank e-files. He grabbed one, hooked it into the side of the monitor, swiping his fingers from the screen to the e-file, transferring a copy of the data.

Harris took the e-file pane. "I'll get Doc to look at this for me and see if he can identify any of this stuff."

"Now," he said, leaning over Hunter's chair again, "can you get me details on their cargo orders for, let's say, the past 12 months?"

"Yes, sir, I should be able to do that. They have a cargo history here..." Hunter got to work and various screens flashed up on the monitor in front of him. "Right, I think this should do it." He took the pane back off Harris and began copying the data over.

Just then, Smith's voice came over their earpieces.

*"Captain, this is Smith. Over."*

"Go ahead. Over."

*"Captain, I can't access the crew files for the Belgo. They're all classified. Over."*

"Classified?" Harris asked surprised.

*"Yes, sir. All access is denied. Over."*

"But they're UNF approved cargo crew? We should be able to access that."

*"Sorry, sir."*

"Is the *Aurora* picking up the information we're looking at here?"

*"Yes, sir. The information download to the Aurora is in place. Over."*

"Alright, well, how about you get your ass back here to the control room. Over."

*"Yes, sir."*

Harris let out a long sigh and put his hands on his hips. *Why the fuck would their files be classified?*

Hunter read through the data he transferred onto the pane, then handed it back to Harris, "Sir... it appears cats weren't the only animal on their menu. They've ordered owls, a heap of bats..."

Harris scanned the list. "Animal parts, too... Polar bear, greyhound noses, pig snouts. Jesus! What the hell kind of programs were they running here?"

He closed the e-file down. "Keep looking through and let me know anything else you come across that seems strange. When Smith gets here, I want him working on the transmissions right up until the power cut out. I'm going to take this stuff to Doc and see what he can make of it."

*

Carrie entered Doc's office. "So, what have you got for me, lieutenant?"

"Corporal Welles," Doc said, looking up from the computer screen at his desk, "take a seat." He motioned to the chair in front of his desk.

Carrie moved over to the chair, eyeing Doc carefully while she did. She had a sudden sensation of entering the Principal's office.

"Before we start, I just wanted to have a word with you about your conversation with Captain Harris earlier—" he began.

She interrupted him. "Doc, I know what you're going to say—"

"He's the captain, Welles," he shot back at her.

"I know it was wrong to speak to him like that. I just really wanted to sink my teeth into this mission, you know?" She ran a hand over her face. "But... I know I need to learn when to shut up and deal with it. An order is an order, I know that. It won't happen again, sir."

Doc sat back in his chair, eyeing her.

She gave him a sheepish look. "Thanks for stepping in before I said something really stupid."

He ran a hand across his chin. "You know the best thing to do is to get in first and apologize to him. Knowing the captain as well as I do, he's going to want to have a word with you about it at some point."

Carrie nodded. "Yes, sir, I will."

Doc looked at her, his eyes searching hers.

"I will," she added.

"Okay. Just make sure you keep your head down, corporal. Captain Harris does not respond well to those who give him any grief. You want to get on his good side, then do *as* he says, *when* he says it, and do it well... and don't complain."

Carrie smiled and nodded. "Yes, sir."

Doc sat forward in his seat again and looked at his monitor. She studied his face. He looked a little tired, but there was something else about him that seemed different. His eyes looked a little heavy, as though he had a lot going on behind them. He reached his hand out to the touchpad beside his console. He started moving his fingers around on the pad, while his eyes focused on the monitor. She watched his hand, circling here and there, his fingers tapping every now and then. Her eyes moved from his hand to his wrist and along to his forearm, where the tendons were jumping about with each movement. She noticed some fresh bruising just above his elbow, wondering where it came from. Then her eyes traced over his upper arm and shoulder, right up to his neck. He glanced over at her and she snapped her eyes to his.

"I'll just be a second," he said.

She nodded awkwardly, embarrassed that he might have noticed her looking at him.

"What happened to your arm?" She asked as a means of distraction.

He glanced down at the bruising, then dismissed it. "It's nothing."

"So, are we any closer to knowing what happened here?"

"No," his eyes darted to hers and then back to the screen, "not yet. There's not a hell of a lot of information available."

He moved his hands over to the console, hitting a few keys, then grabbed an e-clip and ran it over the scanner attached to his monitor. There was a beep, Doc glanced at the screen, tapped away at the console again, then handed it to her.

"Alright, so I actually lied before when I said I had plenty of work for you to do, but you can get this stuff together for me, if you like."

"Oh," she gave him a quizzical look, then smiled. "You lied, sir?"

He smiled back, his eyes moving away from hers, briefly. "I was, ah, trying to defuse a situation between you and Captain Harris, remember?" he said, looking back at her.

"Ah, yes," she nodded. She looked down at the e-clip he'd given her. It appeared to be a form for a physical, with a list down the side of the items required to carry out the tests. Obviously she had to get the stuff ready for the next round with the survivors.

"Well, thanks for giving me something," she said.

"I'll show you where the stuff is," he stood from his desk.

He ushered her into the examination room and showed her where everything was, then told her to restock the shelves from the medical store across the corridor when she was done. She gave him a nod and set about going through the drawers in the cabinet, pulling out the items he needed and placing them on the cart. She double-checked the labels with what was written on the e-clip. It took her a while to find the fluids he needed but eventually located them. They were up high in the glass cabinet and she just reached them on tiptoe. She double-checked the list and the quantities on the cart to make sure they were all correct. Syringes, fluids, swabs, gloves, thermometers, BP gear, vitals cart, antiseptic wipes, and scanner.

She flipped over to the last screen and looked at the list of items he'd already used that needed restocking from the medical store. She walked back into Doc's office. He was at his desk again staring at the monitor, hand moving about on the touchpad.

"Is the store open?" she asked him.

He looked up. "Done already?"

"Yes, sir," she smiled.

He led her across the corridor to the store and punched in a code to unlock it.

"Everything is labeled so you should be fine," he said, as Carrie stepped inside. "The door will lock automatically behind you when you're done. Oh, and don't think of stealing anything. Every single item is accounted for." He flashed her a grin.

"Damn, I really wanted a sick bag as a memento!" she joked.

"I could probably dig your used one out of the trash if you like?" he said with a straight face.

She looked at him in mock horror and he flashed another grin as he walked out of the room.

She turned around and surveyed the small room. It was white and bright and smelt like a hospital, with a few rows of shelves stocked with goods. She began to search the rows for the items used. It only took her a few minutes to locate them all. When she was done, she double-checked the count on the tray. Satisfied she had them correct, she made her way back across the hall to Doc's office, making sure the storeroom door closed behind her. She entered the office, nodding at Doc as he looked up from his screen. She didn't want to disturb him so she headed straight back into the examination room to start putting the items away.

"Wait a second," Doc said following her into the room. "I need to double-check those."

"Sorry."

"That's alright. Normally Louis and Smith do this. It's standard practice that all items are checked by a second party. Can I have the list, please?"

She handed over the e-clip and he began scanning. He looked up from the list to the items on the counter a few times, counting them. He looked back down at the list again and winced.

"What's wrong?" she asked, moving to stand slightly behind him, so she could read the list too.

He shook his head and looked down his shoulder at her, still wincing.

"What?" she asked.

Then he dropped the wince and smiled. "I'm just kidding, it's fine. You can put it away now."

She snatched the e-clip out of his hand, narrowing her eyes playfully, then began to grab the items off the counter. Doc grinned and began to walk out of the room, but she called out to him.

"Doc?"

He stopped in the doorway.

"Thanks for giving me something to do. I appreciate it."

He glanced down at his watch and nodded. "Even if it was only twenty minutes."

"Hey, twenty minutes is twenty minutes, I'll take it," she smiled.

"Good. Now get back to work!" he smiled back. Doc turned and took a step into the office but pulled up short. "Captain? What's up?"

Carrie turned around and saw Harris standing there studying her from the other room. Doc looked between them both. "Er, I've got some stuff to do. I'll leave you to it?" he said, checking for Harris's approval.

Harris looked over at Doc, then at Carrie again, watching her put the items away. "No, I would like Corporal Welles to leave," he said, with a dry emotionless voice.

Carrie shot Harris a glance, then nodded. "Yes, sir. This is the last of it," she threw the syringes into the draw and began to leave, but then hesitated, stopping in front of him. "Captain, I would like a word with you about our conversation earli—"

"Would you?" he cut her off.

"Yes, sir. Perha—"

"Perhaps another time." He cut her off again, staring down at her.

Carrie hesitated a moment, then nodded. "Yes, sir," she said, flashing Doc a quick glance as she left.

Harris held the e-file pane at Doc's chest, before he had a chance to question him about Welles.

"What's this?" Doc asked, taking it.

"I want you to look at those lists and tell me what the items on there are, and what they're used for. You've got fifteen minutes and then I want to see you in my office." He looked Doc in the eye, then turned and left.

He could feel Doc's eyes staring after him. Harris could've easily discussed the list in Doc's office, but after seeing Welles there, *yet again*, he felt it was time to have a different discussion with Doc. The kind of discussion that was best held in the captain's office. It was as it had to be.

He'd had many a serious discussion with Doc over the time they'd worked together, but generally Doc was sitting on the other side of the desk on a somewhat equal footing. Today, however, his lieutenant would be standing. Harris would address the issues quickly and to the point. He didn't believe that Doc would argue or disagree, but they needed to be said regardless. Harris had bigger fish to fry and this was one little thing to be nipped in the bud, asap.

Entering his office, he went straight over to the coffee machine and poured himself a strong, black coffee. He took a sip and then stretched out his back and neck, trying to relieve the tension within. He tried not to think about the dream of Sibbie and Etta. It seemed to have become a recurring one; the two of them appearing like they did. He gave a deep sigh and then went and sat at his desk. He stared blankly at his bookshelf, running through in his mind the conversation he was about to have with Doc.

His mind began to wander back to the four men in the bio cell, however. He thought about how they'd been angry with Doc that morning. He thought about the Belgo. *Why had it been here for two weeks? And why were they bringing animals and animal parts onto the station? Why was any information hard to come by? Was everything surrounding the programs classified, too? What the hell happened to the other five workers? What are the four survivors not telling me? And was Doc right about them trying to work out how many were on the Aurora? Were they just scared of strangers, or was it something else?* He recalled Chet asking him about Aurora's crew this morning, as both Hunter and Bolkov had been new faces to them. *Why were they so interested in who was here on the station with them?*

Harris's thoughts were disturbed by a knock at the door.

"Come in, Doc," he said, before taking another mouthful of his coffee.

Doc entered the room, manifest e-file in hand, and stood on the other side of his desk. His lieutenant obviously sensed something was up, as he didn't take a seat. Harris didn't offer him one either.

"So what can you tell me about the list?" Harris asked.

"Well, I'm not 100 percent on all the items, but there's definitely growth hormones, certain amino acids and steroids on here, along with other vitamins and proteins used for strengthening muscle and bones and promotion of general good health."

"Growth hormones?"

"Yes, sir."

"For animals or humans?"

Doc shrugged. "They can be used on both."

"Did you see the list with the animals on it?"

"Yes, sir."

"What do you make of that?"

Doc looked down at the manifest, scanning over it. "Well," he began, "Sharley studied hunters of the animal kingdom, so maybe this is some extension of that. I mean, owls and bats, they're great nocturnal hunters. Dogs and cats—good hunters too. I don't know, it's definitely weird. They're running classified biological programs here. Who the hell knows what they were doing with them. It's a list and it's a start, but it's only a piece of the puzzle. For all we know, it has nothing to do with what happened here. Or maybe the crew didn't agree with what they were doing? Maybe they believed in animal rights or something? Maybe they got a conscience and took off in the *Spector*? Maybe these four guys left were the only ones who wanted to go ahead with the experiments?"

Harris nodded. "Could be... I'm still not satisfied, though."

Doc shrugged. "All we can do is check those labs this afternoon and hope there's no change, which at least will mean there's no virus."

Harris nodded and sat back in his chair. He took another mouthful of his coffee, placed the cup down and looked Doc in the eye. "I want to talk to you about what happened this morning."

Doc nodded. "I spoke to Welles. She knows she was out of line and I don't think you'll have any further problems with her."

Harris placed his hands into his lap and interlocked his fingers. "Welles was not who I was referring to, Doc. Although, believe me I will be speaking with her at some point. I was referring to you."

Doc looked a little surprised, but it didn't last long. "Yes, sir?"

Harris sat forward in his chair again. "You jumping in like that undermined my authority in front of the other men."

Doc thought about this for a second, then nodded. "I apologize, captain. That was not my intent."

"No, your intent was to protect Welles from my wrath, I believe."

Doc shook his head. "Everyone was a little short on sleep, captain. I was just trying to defuse the situation before it got out of hand unnecessarily for both parti—"

"Before *Welles* got herself into a world of trouble. I certainly didn't need your protection, Doc."

His lieutenant looked like he was about to say something, but he hesitated, then answered. "Captain, I apologize if I undermined your authority in front of the other men. That was not my intent, nor was it my intent to appear to be taking any sides. I assure you I was just trying to jump in the middle, sir. I'll stay out of it and keep my mouth shut in future."

Harris eyed him for a moment. Doc was a good soldier who generally knew when to keep his mouth shut. Every good soldier makes mistakes and he knew his lieutenant never meant any offense to him when he'd spoken up. It was simply a mistake in judgment.

"Alright," Harris told him.

"Was that all?"

"No, one more thing," Harris said, taking another sip of his coffee.

Doc waited expectantly.

"I want you to take a step back from the new recruits."

Doc looked at him, seemingly a bit lost. "I'm sorry?"

"The new recruits. I want you to back off."

Doc's brow furrowed. "Is something wrong, captain?"

"No, Doc. I just think it's time to take a step back... from Welles at least. Packham and Colt are fine." Harris reached forward, grabbed his coffee and took another sip, eyeing Doc carefully.

Doc's brow furrowed even further in confusion. "Wait a minute, I haven't done anything wrong, but you've singled out *one* soldier that I'm to back off from."

Harris let out a big sigh and rubbed his hand over his face. "Okay, Doc, I'm going to level with you."

"Please do!" Doc said quickly.

Harris eyed him again for a moment. "I want you to take a step back from Corporal Welles, because I think she's attaching herself to you and I can't have that on my ship."

"Attaching herself?" Doc seemed to be having trouble understanding exactly what Harris was trying to say. Either that, or he was playing dumb. Harris couldn't decide.

"Doc, let me be very blunt... I think Welles is attracted to you. She's come on this ship where the other men haven't exactly been welcoming, and you've been the friendly face for her, and I think she's attaching herself to you because of it."

Doc stared at Harris. "Wait a second, you asked me to help assimilate the women onto this ship because you knew the guys would give them a hard time. That's what I've done. And now I'm getting shot down for it?"

"I'm not shooting you down, Doc. I *did* ask you to help assimilate them and you've done that for me, thank you. As I said, Packham and Colt are fine. I just didn't account for Welles having a thing for you, but now I know that's where we're at, I'm asking you to take a step back. I'm just looking further down the road on this thing than you are. I'd prefer to stop things now, before something *does* happen."

Doc gave a laugh of disbelief and shook his head slightly. "Are you questioning my integrity, Saul?"

Doc was using his first name. That meant the conversation was no longer between a captain and his soldier, but between two friends. He could see Doc was starting to get angry, his jaw clenching up. Harris sat back in his chair, eyeing him. He'd never seen him direct any anger or intensity at him before, though he was doing his best to control it. This was new. He was curious as to why Doc was being so touchy about this.

Harris softened his voice a little. "Doc, she's an attractive woman. It would be… understandable, if you slipped."

"Slipped?" He raised his eyebrows.

"Are you trying to tell me that you're not attracted to her? 'Cause I know you, Doc, and I know your type!"

Doc kept looking at Harris but didn't answer. *There was that line in the sand of his.*

"Hmm?" Harris pushed it a little further. "You don't find her attractive at all?"

"Are you going to ask me the same question about Packham and Colt? They're attractive?" Doc deflected.

Harris kept his voice calm and steady, but firm. "No, I'm asking you about Corporal Welles. Welles, who always seems to find her way into your office, or sit near you in the mess hall, and who you seem to feel the need to protect on occasion. I'm not attacking you, Doc, I'm just pointing out what I see. She's attracted to you and because of that, I want to put as much distance as possible between you two, so that this thing can be quashed. Now, I'm not going to discuss this any further. My order to you is, take a step back from Corporal Welles and keep her at arm's length. Do I make myself clear? She is not to hang out in your office and maybe once in a while you could sit at different tables in the mess hall. She's not going to get to know the other soldiers if she's following you around, is she? Understand?"

Doc clenched his jaw as he looked down at his feet, exhaling deeply through his nose. He knew very well that Harris was having the last say on this. "Yes, sir," he said, looking back up at Harris.

Harris looked him in the eye for a moment.

"Doc, I'm not just saying this to you as your captain, alright. I'm saying this to you as a friend. I just want to make sure we don't let Welles make a huge mistake that could affect you, too."

Doc's jaw unclenched slightly. "I understand, sir. It's not a problem."

"Fine." Harris nodded.

"Is that all, captain?" Doc asked quickly. Clearly he was keen to leave.

"No, one more thing."

Doc shot him a "*What now?*" kind of look.

"What did Logan say to you at the cell this morning?" Harris asked, eyeing the fresh bruises on his lieutenant's arm.

Doc's face softened a little, obviously happy this wasn't directed at him, personally. "He said it would be a huge mistake if I didn't release them at 1800."

"A huge mistake? Why?"

"He didn't elaborate."

Harris eyed the bruises again. "They from him?"

Doc glanced down at his arm and nodded. "He's got a strong grip on him."

Harris looked at Doc, rolling Logan's comment around in his mind. "Very well," he nodded. "Dismissed."

Doc immediately turned and left the room.

# 15

# Cargo Ships

Carrie and Colt were busy heating up the food for lunch. Colt appeared to have enjoyed the time away and seemed more relaxed now.

"So what was Smith doing on the flight deck?" Carrie inquired.

"Downloading some files from the Darwin onto our systems here."

"Yeah, what files?"

"I don't know. I didn't get a good look."

"There has to be something going on. How do people just disappear?" she thought aloud.

"Well, the station's ship is missing. I say they just left and didn't tell anybody. Went AWOL," Colt said, placing a stack of plates on the counter.

"Yeah, but what's with the whole blackout story? Something weird's going on with those survivors."

"Yeah, definitely something not right about those dudes."

Carrie grabbed a heap of knives and forks and put them out near the plates. "Hey, I'm sorry for getting you in trouble earlier," she said softly to Colt.

Colt looked at her and nodded. "I guess I got myself into trouble for speaking up. Like *you*, I gotta learn when to keep my mouth shut too."

"Well, I promise I'm going to keep my mouth shut from here on in." Carrie picked up a white napkin, unfolded it and waved it about in the air at Colt in surrender.

Colt smiled, flashing a mouthful of white teeth, and grabbed it off her. "Stop wasting the napkins, Corporal Welles!" she said in her best Harris voice.

Carrie laughed, but they both stopped abruptly when Brown, Hunter, Carter and Louis entered the mess hall.

"Where the hell's my food, woman?" Brown asked Colt with a straight face.

She gave a sassy look back. "Sit the hell down before I open up a can of grievous bodily harm on yo' ass!"

Brown gave a short sharp laugh, and Hunter smirked.

Louis turned to Carter. "If I was behind there, the food would be ready by now."

"Feel free to take over any time," Carrie smiled sarcastically at him.

"Sorry, ladies, we've been busy working on the Darwin," Carter said, folding his arms. "You should've been there for the boarding, it was great. Oh, that's right, you didn't quite make the cut, did you?"

Carrie narrowed her eyes slightly and gave him a big smile. "I'm sure they'll call me in when there's some real work to be done."

"Ouch!" Hunter said quietly.

"Jesus, it's too hot in the kitchen today. I'm going to sit back over here," Brown said moving toward the tables.

"Keep your pants on, it's here," Colt said carrying a tray of food over to the warmers. "Start on that."

The men began grabbing plates and lining up, as Harris, Smith and Packham entered.

Carrie brought out a second tray of food and placed it in the warmer beside the other dish. She made eye contact with Harris as he took a place in the queue, but she quickly looked away, as he seemed to look straight through her.

When everyone was served, they sat down and started eating.

"How's things on the Darwin, captain?" Colt got the conversation started. "Are we any closer to locating the missing crew?" she asked.

"Nope," he said simply, scooping food onto his fork.

"Oh," Colt said, a little disappointed with his sharp reply.

Harris appeared to feel a little bad and offered something more. "We're working on a few things. As soon as we have something concrete you'll be briefed."

"Pass me the salt," Brown said, leaning across Carrie toward Hunter, who passed it over. As he did, Carrie got a close look at the tattoo along Brown's right forearm. It was a pattern in black ink, the core of which sat on the inside of his forearm, and long tentacle-like stands wrapped around to the front.

"Brown, what is that?" she asked.

He saw she was looking at his tattoo and glanced down at it. He turned his arm over and held it out to show her. "That there's the sun," he said pointing to the swirling core on the inside, "and these are solar flares." He pointed to the tentacles curling around to the front.

Carrie took a good look. "So does it have some significance? What does it mean?"

Brown looked from his arm to Carrie. "It means... you see these solar flares coming your way? You better get the hell out of there!"

The table broke into laughter, just as Doc entered the mess hall. He walked over to the counter, grabbed a plate of food then walked back out, without so much as a glance at any of them. It was a bit strange, Carrie thought. She glanced over at Harris, whose eyes were on the door as Doc exited. He looked back down at his plate and continued eating, not skipping a beat.

They continued to eat in silence for a time. Carrie furtively glancing at Harris, trying to gauge his mood. She thought she'd try to have that "word" with him after lunch, but wanted to check it was safe to do so. He didn't look too bad. *It might be worth a try.* They continued to eat in silence, the only sounds were their knives and forks hitting their plates.

Carter, however, now seemingly more awake with a bellyful of food, piped up. "So captain, did I miss anything while I was sleeping?"

Harris shook his head and placed his cutlery together across his plate. "No. We've just got bits and pieces that don't add up yet."

"And we're waiting until 1800 before we let those guys out?" Carter continued.

"If they pass their blood tests," Harris confirmed.

Louis piped up. "There's *got* to be something wrong with them. They were definitely acting strange."

"What do you mean?" Harris looked over at him.

"They did not speak a word to each other, the whole time. Dead silence. And they didn't sleep much on our watch, did they?" Louis turned to Carter.

"No," Carter confirmed. "Just for short amounts of time and one of them was always awake, looking at us."

"They were sweating a lot too, despite the controlled temperatures of the station. And they seemed... agitated," Louis continued.

"And the slightest noise, they would sit upright and look off in the direction it came from," Carter said.

"Sometimes they did that when there was *no* noise," Louis added, "and I *swear* Logan and Chet were watching us in the dark. But whenever I turned to look at them, their eyes were closed. It was weird."

"Maybe they fancied you, Louis!" Carter said, and most of the table laughed.

"Well, with *you* as my only competition, can you blame them?" Louis retorted, holding his arms out in demonstration.

Harris smiled, and then looked over at Brown. "Brown, you and Hunter take the afternoon shift on the cell, and relieve McKinley and Bolkov. I'll get those guys to work with Smith in the control room."

"Yes, sir."

"And pay close attention to them," Harris said firmly, looking between Hunter and Brown. "I want you to tell me if any of their behavior is out of the ordinary."

"Yes, sir," they said, as they got up from the table and left.

"Do you need us to do anything, captain?" Carter asked, "Or can we get a couple more hours of shut-eye?"

"Nothing right now, but I want you back on deck by 1430."

"Yes, sir," Carter said, as both he and Louis got up from the table and left.

Harris turned to Packham. "I want you on the flight deck, in case we need anything. Smith will give you a quick rundown of our data systems."

"Yes, sir." She gave a nod, then turned to Smith, who stood and motioned for her to follow.

Carrie picked up her plate and started to head over to the counter. She wanted to show Harris that she was going to do her duty and not complain.

"Corporal Welles?" Harris called after her.

She turned around.

"When you and Colt are done here, head up to the flight deck too and see what you can learn about our data systems."

She nodded, "Yes, sir," content that he was giving her something other than mess duty. Had she gotten her point across, after all?

Harris stood from the table, walked over to her and handed her his plate.

*Perhaps now is the time?* she thought.

"Captain, do you have a moment to speak with me?" she asked.

"Not now, corporal," he said in a flat voice, then walked away.

Harris sat in Darwin's control room, looking over the items that Hunter had pointed out to him earlier. The Darwin had had regular shipments for the past 12 months. Approximately four ships serviced the station in rotation. Every six weeks one arrived to deliver supplies and take waste away. Smith, from the flight deck, had accessed the crew files for two of the ships, but the other two, the final two to service the station before the loss of comms—the *Stella Maris* and the *Belgo*—were classified. They had, however, managed to dig up some general information on the two ships.

The *Stella Maris* was a stock standard private enterprise cargo ship that ran general supplies between Earth and the outstations. The *Belgo* was a little more interesting in that it was a cargo ship that ran mainly chemicals and medical supplies, and was owned by an ex-convict named Gray Quint, who it turned out had done time in Hell Town. Whether he was on the ship at the time of docking was unknown as the files were classified, but it certainly sparked Harris's interest. He'd asked Smith to try and dig up some more information about him, but all they could find was his prison record. Quint was an ex-soldier, who'd done time for his part in a crime ring as the muscle who "cleaned up problems". He had several counts of murder against him and had been sentenced to 77 years in Hell Town. For some reason, however, he was released for good behavior after six. That sent a red flag rather swiftly to the top of Harris's warning pole.

Brown had confirmed to Harris that any comms issue had to be something on the internal network system. He could find no wiring or hardware fault that could explain the lost connection. This was something the captain hoped to get Bolkov working on as soon as he'd had a bite to eat.

Just then Smith entered the room.

"Smith," Harris greeted him. "Get me those transmission logs!"

"I'm on it, captain. They're not far away," he said, taking the seat next to Harris at the console.

Smith starting working the system, while Harris continued to read through the information they did have. He reread the manifests, looking carefully at the items they had delivered. He turned to the console in front of him and started researching the steroids and growth hormones they'd had delivered. He then began researching the animals they'd had delivered. Nothing made any particular sense and the frustration continued to rise within him. Not knowing what programs they'd been running on the station meant he couldn't determine whether they could have somehow been implicated in the lost connection with Command or the disappearance of the crew. More to the point, so far he couldn't find evidence of any technical programs, only biological ones.

"Captain, we're in!" Smith said excitedly.

"Talk to me, private," he said, leaning over to his console, hopeful.

"Last transmission out was on September 16th."

"What was it?" Harris asked impatiently.

"It was a transmission to Command. It was brief, barely five minutes. It looks like it was under Sharley's log-in, and it was made to a Professor Martin."

"Can you tell me what was said?"

Smith tapped the screen, but it beeped in a way that Harris knew was not good. His private shook his head. "It's classified."

"Fuck!" Harris hissed. "Was that the very last transmission?"

Smith hit a few more buttons. "Just the last one from the Darwin. There was an incoming transmission from Command on September 19th."

"That was the day they lost comms. Who was it from?"

"Professor Martin."

"Let me guess. It's classified." Harris asked flatly.

Smith tried to open the file but the screen beeped again. "Yes, sir. Although... it looks as though they lost comms during that transmission. There's an error code."

Harris rubbed his hand along his jaw, staring at the screen, deep in thought. "Pull up a list of the transmissions from, let's say, a couple of days before the *Belgo* docked, to the day it left."

"Yes, sir," Smith said, already on it.

McKinley and Bolkov entered the room.

"Captain," McKinley greeted them.

Harris looked up. "You eaten?"

"Yeah."

"Good," Harris said, standing up. "Bolkov, I want you to get on here and figure out what the hell is wrong with the comms. Brown assures me it's not a hardware or wiring issue. It's got to be something in the software."

"Yes, sir," Bolkov made his way over to the chair Harris vacated and sat down.

Harris moved to stand behind Smith's chair. McKinley flanked him, curious as to what they were looking at.

"We're into the transmission logs," Harris informed him.

Smith tapped away for a moment. "Okay," he said, pointing to the screen as he read. "It looks like there were a few around the time of the *Belgo*'s docking… one the day before, one the day of docking, and one the day after. The first two were made from Command to the station… and the third was from the station to Command. There was another one five days later, from the station to Command… then there's nothing until a day before the ship left."

"Let me guess. Classified?" Harris asked.

Smith swirled his fingers around the screen. "No! Not all of them."

Harris leaned closer, as Smith accessed the files.

"The first two we can access," he said, tapping away. "So, that's the day before docking, and the day of docking. The others have been classified, though."

"Tell me what they say."

"Okay. The first one, which is the day before docking, was made from Professor Martin to Sharley," Smith said, scanning the transcript that was scrolling up his screen "Professor Martin is talking about a special shipment that is coming into the station… blah, blah, blah… it's apparently the most important shipment to date… He's asking whether Sharley is sure he's ready for this shipment… Sharley's saying he's confident they can handle the shipment... Professor Martin is saying okay, they'll go ahead with sending it in... that's about it."

"What about the other one?" Harris asked.

"The other one was made the day of the docking. Again, from Professor Martin to Sharley... he's confirming the ETA of the *Belgo*... he's asked that they receive the goods as per normal... then once the general cargo has been received in, they perhaps invite the crew to stay for dinner... Sharley confirms they will proceed with docking the *Belgo* as suggested... he says he'll be in touch when all the cargo has been attended to. That's it."

"That make sense to anyone?" McKinley asked. "It sounds aboveboard, but—"

"That's a hell of lot of transmission time to talk about a standard cargo delivery they've had for the past twelve months or so," Harris agreed. He straightened up and placed his hands on his hips. He glanced over at McKinley, then back down at Smith. "Find me the transmissions around the time of the *Stella Maris*'s docking."

Carrie and Colt sat at the flight deck console with Packham, who was going over the data systems that Smith had shown her. As they spoke, information seemed to be scrolling up the screen.

"What's that?" Carrie asked.

"Whatever they're looking at on the station. It uploads onto our systems here," Packham said, leaning forward to take a careful look at the screen. "It looks as though they're transmission logs. Something about a cargo delivery on a ship called the *Stella Maris*."

Carrie leaned in, eyeing the screen carefully. "June," she read aloud. "I wonder what that's about? Can we take a look at what they've downloaded already?"

"If there's something important in there, the captain will brief us soon enough," Packham said.

Carrie nodded and sat back in her chair, but kept her eyes on the screen, scanning the transcripts. It was a conversation between a Professor Martin and Professor Sharley, the man in charge of the Darwin. They were discussing a shipment of cargo coming into the station. Professor Martin was requesting Professor Sharley let Command know how much waste the ship would be taking away.

"Cargo and waste," Colt had been reading the screen too. "What's so important about that?"

Carrie shrugged.

"We're supposed to organize a data dump to an e-file every five minutes," Packham continued with her tutorial. "In case of any power failures, they'll still be able to access information, if need be. The system does an autosave every 60 seconds."

"Where are the panes you've loaded so far?" Carrie asked.

Packham motioned to a drawer beside her. "Some of it's in there, but Smith said the captain has the rest."

Carrie moved over to the cabinet and opened it. There was a stack of blank files and two or three that were glowing, which indicated they contained data. She picked one up and started scrolling through it.

"You sure you oughta be nosing in that?" Colt's voice had a motherly tone to it.

Carrie shrugged and glanced over at the other two. "An extra set of eyes can't hurt, can it?"

Colt and Packham exchanged a wary look.

"It's just more stuff about another cargo ship called the *Belgo*," Packham told her.

Carrie looked up at the sergeant.

"Who do you think did the data dump?" Packham said.

Carrie flicked through it quickly, scanning the transcripts. It was much the same as those of the *Stella Maris*; conversations about cargo deliveries. She shut down the file and placed it back in the drawer.

"Did you see the other stuff? The stuff that the captain's already got?" Carrie asked Packham.

She shook her head. "Smith was on duty, then."

Carrie sat back in her chair and stared at the monitor. *What's the captain trying to find? Why is he so interested in these cargo deliveries?* Her mind suddenly went back to the mess hall at lunch. She remembered that Doc came in late and didn't stay. She remembered Harris watching after him as he'd left. *He must've been busy working on something for the captain.*

She stood up. "I'm going to see if Doc needs a hand with anything."

The other two exchanged another glance.

"I thought Harris said for you to stay here," Colt reminded her.

"He said to learn the data systems and I have." She looked at her watch. "Doc might need a hand getting ready for the next lot of physicals on the survivors." Of course, she was lying as she'd already gathered the stuff together for him, but she was curious to find out more about what was going on with the Darwin.

"Corporal, you should stay here," Packham said somewhat firmly, as though pulling rank.

"I'll be back in a minute, sergeant," Carrie assured her.

Packham shot her a warning look as she turned and left the flight deck. Carrie wasn't sure what it was about, but it stayed in her mind for the entire journey to Doc's office.

*

"Hey, Doc," she said, knocking and entering his office. He was at his desk, head in hand, looking intently at some files he had in front of him. He glanced up at her and an uncomfortable look shot across his face. He looked down at his files.

"What is it, corporal?"

"I just thought I'd see whether you needed a hand with anything?"

"No, I'm fine, thanks." He glanced up at her then back down at his files.

"You seem to be up to your ears in something there?" Carrie approached and came to a stop on the opposite side of his desk. "You sure I can't help you with any research or anything? I know my way around search engines." She smiled. "Used them a bit in my previous life."

Doc let out a quiet sigh but continued looking at the files in front of him. "What orders did the captain give you?"

"He said to learn the data systems on the flight deck and I've done that. I just thought maybe you could use my help. They seem to be downloading a lot of information from the Darwin."

"Well, like I said, I'm fine. You should go back to the flight deck until Captain Harris orders you otherwise." He looked up at her briefly and then returned to his work.

Carrie eyed him. *Something wasn't right. What was that uncomfortable look for, earlier?*

"Is everything okay, Doc?" she asked. "You look a little on edge."

"I'm fine, Welles. I'm just busy," he said, not looking up from the files.

He was avoiding eye contact with her now.

"I'm sorry, have I... done something wrong, Doc?" she asked slowly, scrutinizing him.

He glanced up at her, shook his head. "No," he said, then looked at his monitor and started typing something.

"I tried to have a word with the captain but he's avoiding me," she said, wondering whether it had anything to do that.

Doc didn't answer and kept looking at the screen.

"I've tried a few times now, but he won't talk to me. He's not exactly open to people, is he?" Carrie added.

Doc looked at her. "Corporal, don't mistake the captain being good at his job for him being an asshole," he said tersely.

She looked at him, a little surprised. "I don't... I just mean he's a little hard to speak to. He's not exactly approachable, like you are."

"Well, you shouldn't mistake me being good at my job for anything else either!"

Carrie was taken aback by the cutting way Doc spoke. She stared at him, a little stunned, as he quickly turned back to the screen in front of him, clenching his jaw as he did so.

"Er, I... don't," she said quietly. She felt a strange sensation in her chest, as though his words had somehow winded her. "I'm sorry, Doc, you said I haven't done anything wrong?"

He sighed again, frustrated. "Welles, I'm busy and you should be on the flight deck where Captain Harris ordered you to be." He didn't look up from the screen.

She stood there quietly for a moment, then nodded. Clearly, he was angry at her for something, she just didn't know what it was. All she knew was that she had to leave him alone, and fast, making her exit as formal as she could.

She straightened her posture and spoke in her best soldier's voice, albeit still somewhat taken aback. "I apologize, Lieutenant Walker. I won't disturb you again." She saw Doc's face soften and his body slump slightly as she turned and headed for the door.

"Welles," he called.

She didn't look back, but kept walking toward the door, wanting to leave immediately.

"Welles!" He scooted around her and placed his arm between her and the door, hitting the lever to close it.

She eyed him and saw he was staring at the floor, rubbing his hand over his forehead, mind ticking over.

"It's okay, Lieutenant Walker, I understand. I shouldn't have disturbed you." She kept her formal manner.

"Welles," he began, his eyes a little defeated, "I'm sorry… I didn't mean for what I said to come out like it did. I just mean… you can't just keep dropping by here like this."

She gave him a confused look.

He looked down at the floor again for a moment, then took a deep breath, and looked her in the eye. "I can't be seen to be spending too much time with you," he said slowly and carefully. "At least, not more than the others. It doesn't look good."

Carrie felt her brow furrow. "Why?"

Doc gave her a look as if to say: "you know what I mean."

"Oh," she said, suddenly understanding. She gave a slight nod. "And if I was a male soldier? Would it be a problem, then?"

He looked at her and gave a slight shake of his head. She nodded again, staring at the door in front of her, suddenly feeling utterly stupid. She took a deep breath and turned to him. "Well, I apologize if I got you into trouble or caused you any embarrassment, Lieutenant Walker. It won't happen again."

Doc's face looked even more defeated. "It doesn't have to be like that, Welles. We just need to… watch the time spent alone."

Carrie looked him in the eyes for a moment but felt uncomfortable and turned back to the door. For some reason his words made her nervous. She suddenly became aware of how close he was standing to her, his arm still outstretched to the lever, blocking her pathway to the door.

"Can I go now, lieutenant?" she asked, staring at the arm that blocked her path.

Doc let out another sigh and slowly removed his arm. Carrie immediately hit the lever, and as soon as she could, vanished.

Harris stood in the control room, thinking. McKinley was watching him, trying to read his thoughts. Smith had moved his chair closer to Bolkov's as they tried to determine the reason for the comms issue.

"So, the last two cargo ships' crew files are classified. As are most of the transmissions once the ships have docked. We can access their incoming manifests, however. So, there's something that's happened once they've docked that's made their voyages all of a sudden classified. It's not what they've brought *to* the station. It must be something they've taken away," Harris said, thinking aloud.

McKinley nodded. "Let's see if we can bring up the manifests of what the ships have taken with them," he suggested.

Harris nodded back at him. "Smith?"

Smith moved his chair back to the other console. "On it!" He started tapping and swirling about on the screen. "Alright," he said scanning the data. "On the *Stella Maris*... it looks just to be waste... and some data files. On the *Belgo*... it's the same. Waste and data files."

"And I suppose there's no information on those data files?" Harris asked unenthusiastically. He already knew the answer.

"No, sir," Smith confirmed.

"Alright. Well, how does the outgoing manifest of these ships compare with the outgoing manifests of the other ships over the past twelve months?" Harris asked.

"Just give me a second," Smith said, as he once more turned to his screen.

Harris and McKinley stared at each other while they waited, as though trying to find the answer on the other one's face.

"It would appear... anywhere between 80 and 100 containers of waste are collected every six weeks," Smith said.

"And on the *Stella Maris* and the *Belgo*?" Harris asked.

"The *Stella Maris* had... 115 drums of waste. Oh, wait... it says here 95 are general waste and 20 are labeled as *classified* waste."

"*Classified* waste?" Harris felt his brow furrow. "And the *Belgo*?"

"The *Belgo* had 118 drums of waste... 99 general and 19 classified."

"Were there data files on the other manifests?" McKinley asked.

"Just a second," Smith said scanning the monitor as he flicked between screens. "Yes, there was. Not quite as much data as what the *Stella Maris* and *Belgo* took away, though."

Harris rubbed his jaw again, deep in thought. "So these two ships have become classified, and they've taken extra waste and extra data files away. Something has happened on the Darwin while they were here. Something classified, that has therefore made these ships and their crews now classified. Smith? Can you find out where these ships docked after they left here?"

"Yes, sir. It might take a few minutes."

Bolkov looked over at Harris and McKinley. "Maybe the crew were smuggling something? Or perhaps they were jumping ship? Stowing away in drums as classified waste?" he offered.

Harris cast an implausible look in Bolkov's direction, but Bulk stared back in all seriousness.

"Some people do some crazy things to get out of some places," the Russian offered in his slow deep voice.

"Some people just put in for transfers, too, Bulk," Harris replied, flatly.

"Alright!" Smith piped up. "The *Stella Maris* went straight back to Earth and docked at... *Command!* So did the *Belgo.*"

Harris paused, staring at the screen, his mind ticking over at a fast pace.

"Why are standard cargo ships docking at Command?" McKinley asked, "Don't they just pick up the UNF supplies from the commercial docks?"

Smith shrugged. "Classified waste from a classified station?"

"Where are they now?" Harris asked Smith.

"They're both still at Command. Looks like they've been listed for decommissioning and sale."

"They're both still at Command," Harris repeated, rubbing his jaw more animatedly now. "So, the *Belgo* departs the station with its classified waste and docks at Command. Two weeks later they lose comms with the station, and then we're sent here to find out why."

Harris and McKinley looked at each other again.

"I think I need to have another discussion with Command," Harris said flatly.

# 16

# Bloods

Carrie sat on the flight deck with Colt, Packham, Carter and Louis. They were watching the monitors displayed on the flight deck window. Brown and Hunter were still on duty, guarding the bio cell. Carrie found herself studying the four men held within it. The one with long, dark hair, Logan, was walking up and down behind the glass frontage, eyeing Brown and Hunter carefully. Grolsh was pacing also, but he remained toward the back in the shadows. Fairmont was sitting on the edge of one of the pulled out beds, rocking, while Chet was standing completely still, arms by his sides, silently watching everyone.

"They're still acting weird," Louis commented.

"Are you kidding?" Colt asked. "Look at them, they're acting weirder!"

"Well, Doc's just about to get their next lot of bloods, so this'll be interesting," Packham said.

Carrie kept looking at Brown's monitor. She really wanted to avoid all mention of Doc's name right now. She'd been left somewhat mortified by their conversation. Never before had she needed to be pulled up on her interaction with another soldier. Here she was living her ultimate dream on Space Duty and, four days in, she was on the verge of potentially screwing everything up. She didn't want to talk about Doc and she certainly didn't want to think about him. She just wanted to focus on the

Darwin and the solid soldier she knew she could be. She cringed internally at the realization of what a fool she'd been: spending too much time with one soldier, and talking back to her captain. *What the fuck was I thinking?*

The four men in the cell all of a sudden stopped what they were doing and, in unison, looked over to their left. Brown and Hunter turned to look down the corridor in that direction. No-one was there. Hunter glanced at Brown, who shrugged, and they looked back at the survivors. They were still staring off to the bend in the corridor. Hunter looked back to where they were staring and then saw Doc and McKinley come walking around the corner with the cart. The *Aurora*'s chief pilot glanced back around at Brown, and they seemed to stare at each other for a moment. Doc gave them both a quizzical look as he wheeled the cart over to the cell, obviously wondering what the glance between them was for. He reached up and clicked on his headpiece, and his monitor lit up on the screen on the flight deck. McKinley did the same.

"Dead on time," Chet said, looking at his watch.

Doc eyed the men in the cell, then glanced over at McKinley, who moved forward and unlocked the cell door, then stepped aside, holding his gun ready.

"You've brought extra protection, Doc?" Logan said, his voice sounding even more gravelly than before.

Doc ignored him, pulling on his surgical mask and squeezing the cart into the entrance chamber with him. The door sealed behind him, the mist washed down, and Doc vanished briefly, then reappeared again. He opened the second door and entered the cell.

Logan stared at him. "What do you think we're going to do? Kill you? Kill you and then be showered in laser fire from your friends?" He motioned to McKinley, Hunter and Brown outside the cell.

Again, Doc ignored him. He looked up at Chet and waved him forward to sit on one of the chairs that remained in the cell and begin the tests. Chet moved slowly over to the cart, removed his shirt and took a seat. Logan began pacing again, while Grolsh shuffled about uncomfortably.

"Why don't you pull out one of those beds and relax, Logan?" Doc told him.

The survivor's emerald eyes fixed on the medic, a slight smile playing on his lips. "I'd prefer to stretch my legs..."

Carrie watched as Doc did the tests. She tried to look elsewhere around the room, at the other monitors, but all the action was happening with him. Chet was still sweating, his heartbeat was still racing and from what Doc said over his mouthpiece, his temperature was still high. He took out the empty vials and started collecting the blood.

Chet sat there staring into Doc's camera for a while, then leaned in close, and appeared to be inhaling him again.

"What the fuck?" Doc asked pulling away from him. "Why do you keep doing that?"

"I like your aftershave," he smiled.

The other survivors sniggered quietly. Doc eyed them all carefully, then turned back to Chet.

"Yeah? That's funny, 'cause I'm not wearing any," Doc said with a slight hardness to his voice.

Chet shrugged and smirked. "Perhaps it's just your deodorant then. It smells... good, whatever it is."

Doc stared hard at Chet.

"I'm just paying you a compliment, Doc, that's all," Chet said holding his hands in the air in surrender.

"Well, I recommend you don't do it again," Doc said firmly.

"Pay you a compliment?"

"*Smell* me!" Doc's voice seemed to match the hardness in his eyes, captured on McKinley's camera.

Chet smiled silently, as the other survivors smirked.

"Lunch was very tasty," Chet changed the subject. "My compliments to the chef."

Doc looked from Chet's arm to his face. "I'll be sure to let Command know."

"What? Pre-packed food? No live-in cook onboard? Is Command cutting costs?"

Doc didn't answer him.

Chet looked around at the *Aurora*'s soldiers. "No new faces this afternoon, Doc? Is this all you brought with you? Hmm."

Again, he didn't answer. He marked the vials and put them in a thermo container on the cart.

"Next," Doc said, staring at Chet blankly.

Fairmont stepped forward.

There was little conversation during the rest of Doc's testing, just the odd comment here and there. The four men were still carefully eyeing the three soldiers outside the cell, looking them up and down, sizing them up almost. The *Aurora* team, in turn, appeared to be sizing the survivors up. Carrie wasn't sure whether it was just a male dominance thing, but there seemed to be tension in the air, although for the most part, they were polite to each other. It was all very weird.

The only other thing that stood out to her, was Logan's comment to Doc at the very end. As the lieutenant was placing his vials on the cart, Logan leaned over to him and said in a low voice, which would've been inaudible to the others had it not been picked up on Doc's headpiece: "Remember what I said earlier, Doc."

Logan sat back slowly in his seat, smiling oddly at the medic. "I'm sorry about the bruises," he motioned casually to Doc's arm. "No hard feelings, huh."

Doc didn't seem to react. He just stared back with a cool poker face.

"Doc?" Chet interrupted their staring contest. "Can we have one last shot of the hydration fluid? For good luck."

"You've had plenty already. You shouldn't need any more."

"But I'm still thirsty," Grolsh piped up, his voice was almost begging. "I don't feel like the water is making any difference."

"We're sweating it all out!" Fairmont added, his voice almost pleading, too.

Doc studied each of the four men.

"What can it hurt, Doc? One more?" Chet asked calmly. "The air is so drying on this station."

"I'll see how you are when I come back with your results," he told them.

Grolsh went to say something, but Chet cut him off, holding up his hand to stop him.

"Very well, Doc."

Harris was staring at the crew files for the Darwin. He still couldn't find anything that jumped out at him and his conversation with Command had been brief.

"That's classified" was the answer he'd been given regarding the two cargo ships and their waste. Professor Martin had assured him there was no reason for concern with regards to the contents of those waste containers. He said he knew what the contents were and he was certain they had nothing to do with the loss of comms or loss of crew onboard the Darwin.

They had also, so far, been unable to locate the Darwin's missing ship, the *Spector*. "We'll advise you as soon as we know something," he'd been told. So that left him with absolutely nothing.

All he could do now was wait and see what the blood tests revealed, as that would dictate what happened next. Command confirmed that if they did reveal some sort of virus, then a special team would be deployed to the station to quarantine everyone, including the *Aurora* crew. If the tests were fine, they were to release the survivors and eventually hand them over to a team of Professor Martin's men who would be deployed to take over the investigation into the whereabouts of the missing Darwin crew. So, for now, it was merely a babysitting job. They just had to wait for those results, then advise Command which team they needed to deploy.

Harris looked at his watch. 16:00. He rubbed his hands over his face. He was starting to get tired, worn out. He looked over at his coffee station. It was in need of some replenishment. He thought about Welles and her requests to speak with him. He sighed. *It has to be done sometime...* He reached forward and hit the intercom button that connected him with the flight deck.

"Flight deck, this is the captain. Over."

*"Captain, this is the flight deck, go ahead. Over."* Packham's voice came back over the speaker.

"Send Corporal Welles to my office with a fresh pot of coffee. Over."

*"Copy that, captain. She's on her way."*

Carrie walked along the corridor with the pot of coffee toward Harris's office. She was a little nervous. She knew he had asked for her because he'd decided now was the time to speak about the morning's incident. She was hoping to hell he wasn't going to mention Doc. She pictured her father's face, determined not to let thoughts of dishonoring his name cloud her mind. *Strong and steady*, she spurred herself on. *You're a good soldier, and you mean business. Let Harris know that.*

She reached his office and knocked on the door. It slid open, she stepped inside, and the door closed behind her. She suddenly realized that she hadn't actually been inside his office until now. She quickly looked around. It wasn't much unlike Doc's, except perhaps a little more furnished and homely, less hospital-like, more neat and tidy.

Harris was seated at his desk on the other side of the room. He looked up at her from reading a file that was lying on his desk.

"Coffee's over there." He motioned to her right.

She looked over her shoulder and saw the drink station. She moved over and took the old pot out and put in the fresh one.

She looked back at the captain. "Did you want one now, sir?"

"Yes, please," he said, picking up his cup and placing it on the edge of his desk, not looking up from the file he was reading. "Straight black."

She took the cup and filled it up. Then, taking the empty pot with her, placed his cup back on his desk in front of him. He reached forward, picked it up and took a sip, still not looking up from the file he was reading.

"Is that all, sir?" she asked firmly.

He finally looked up from his file, then sat back in his chair and studied her carefully. "You tell me, corporal. Have you not been wanting to speak with me all day about something? I would've thought now would be an opportune time."

She glanced down at the empty coffee pot in her hands, then looked back up at Harris and nodded. "Yes, sir. I wanted to apologize for talking back to you this morning at breakfast. It was out of line and I was wrong to do it."

He stared back at her. "Yes, you were, Corporal Welles."

"Please accept my apologies, sir. It won't happen again."

He seemed to study her. His eyes searching hers as though he was trying to gauge whether she was genuinely sorry, or just going through the motions.

"We all have a part to play on this ship, corporal. Big *or* small. You don't always get to do the top line stuff. That's life. You're a new recruit on this ship and you need to earn my respect first. I don't just hand it out. Do you understand me?"

She nodded firmly. "Yes, sir."

"You'd better think twice before you speak to me like that again. Understood? I will *not* take attitude from anyone, *especially* a corporal."

"Yes, sir." Carrie nodded, Harris's hard face making her heart pound against her ribcage.

A moment of silence passed as Harris stared at her.

"Good. Is that all you wish to speak about?" he said, sitting forward in his chair.

She looked at him nervously and swallowed. "I believe so, sir."

"Alright. Dismissed."

Just then there was a knock at the door. Harris opened it, and Carrie turned around to see Doc. He was about to enter, but paused when he saw her there. He eyed the empty coffee pot in her hands.

"I'm sorry, captain. Is this a bad time?" he asked.

"Nope. Welles was just leaving. Come on in," Harris said.

Carrie headed for the door, as Doc stepped inside. She saw him trying to make eye contact as she passed, but she kept her eyes front and focused on her exit.

Harris watched Doc as he walked over to his desk. He seemed quite businesslike and not his normal relaxed self.

"Take a seat, Doc," he said. "How long before the results are in?"

"Just under 90 minutes," he said, looking at his watch and taking the seat.

"What about the rest of their tests?"

"Their temperatures are still high. They're still sweating profusely. Their heartbeats are still accelerated, on the verge of mild cardiac arrest, and they're still acting edgy. More edgy, if anything. But I won't know until I see the blood work."

Harris looked at him. Doc looked a little tired and edgy himself.

"What are you thinking?" Harris asked him.

"I don't know. I've still got an uneasy feeling about them. They're hiding something," Doc sighed. "Did you find anything out?"

"Bits and pieces. The last two cargo ships that docked here are suddenly classified. They both became classified after they docked and took away with them classified waste and classified data files, on top of their normal load of unclassified cargo. Both ships have been docked at Command ever since, and are being decommissioned as we speak, being sold for scrap like they never existed. The last ship, the *Belgo*, is owned by an ex-con named Gray Quint, who just so happens to be an ex-resident of Hell Town."

"Yeah, what for?" Doc's curiosity was piqued.

"Murder. Several counts of it. He was in for 77, but got sprung after six for good behavior."

"That's some deal." Doc sounded surprised.

"Yes, it is. And I can't find much information on him either. Although he was at Hell Town while Sharley was resident there." Harris took another sip of his coffee.

Doc scratched his head, thinking for a moment. "You think this guy, Quint, whacked Sharley for revenge, for all the mind-fucking he got in Hell Town? Maybe ran off with his top-secret programs?"

Harris pursed his lips together. "Not a bad theory. Either that, or Sharley let him out early in return for some favors. Perhaps he worked the mind-fucking to his advantage? Made Quint his bitch in return for an early release?"

Doc nodded, thinking about that theory.

"You dig up anything else?" Harris asked, gulping his coffee this time.

"Not really. Nothing concrete. A lot of the items on the manifest are used in bodybuilding." Doc narrowed his eyes at Harris. "Those scientists are well built?"

"Yes, they are."

"And the machine on the list," Doc continued, "it's used to test hearing levels... on humans."

Harris and Doc stared at each other for a moment, as the hair seemed to prickle across the back of Harris's neck.

"You think there's a connection between this machine and the scars behind their ears?" Harris's voice had dropped an octave or two now.

Doc nodded slowly, "Could be. It's interesting... the animals they ordered... they're all renowned for particular senses. Cats, for their hearing; dogs, pigs, polar bears, for their sense of smell; owls for their night vision. Cats, too, in that regard."

Harris kept staring at Doc, his face deadpan. "What are you suggesting, Doc?"

"I'm not suggesting anything, captain. I have no idea what they were doing here. I'm just noting a few things that could perhaps tie together."

Harris sat back in his chair, eyeing him carefully.

Doc shrugged. "Maybe the scientists like to work out. Maybe they were just taking steroids to make themselves buff, and that's all it is."

"But they wouldn't order the steroids on the UNF's tab, surely?"

Doc shrugged again. "Unless they were doing a dodgy deal. Passing it off as work?"

Harris narrowed his eyes in thought. "And the ear thing?"

Doc shrugged again. "That I can't explain. Maybe they're working on an improved hearing device for soldiers or something. Maybe that *is* one of their programs?"

Harris took another gulp of his coffee, his brain ticking over. "You know, Louis said something at lunch… about how he was sure Chet and Logan were watching them in the dark."

It was Doc's turn to stare at Harris.

"You did say something about owls, cats, and night vision?" Harris asked, his voice sounding a little unsure.

Doc nodded slowly. "When I was doing the tests… Chet kept smelling me."

Harris nodded back slowly. "Louis also said that they seemed to be quite attuned to noises in the distance. That could definitely explain those scars, but you said the scanner picked up nothing unusual?"

"Nothing unusual with regards to a man-made device. I wasn't looking for something biological, something not human. I just check for obvious blockages."

Harris felt a pang of uneasiness shoot through his body.

Doc leaned forward in his chair and ran his hands over his face. "This can't be right, can it?" he said eyeing him with disbelief. "They couldn't be doing that shit, surely?"

Harris didn't answer.

"We can't be talking about…" Doc continued, "biologically engineering UNF soldiers? Improving them? Making them better—"

"… hunters?" Harris finished his sentence.

Doc looked as though a pang of uneasiness had just shot through him as well.

Harris shrugged. "That is what he studied, isn't it? Perfect hunters, perfect killers?"

Doc nodded.

"It makes sense," Harris continued. "This is a UNF facility. They are working on biological programs for the benefit of the UNF. The UNF is in the business of supplying soldiers for complicated missions like conquering other planets. It's not unrealistic to think that they're trying to upgrade their current stock."

Doc rubbed his face again and let out a deep sigh. "So how does this tie into the loss of comms and the missing team members?"

Harris shook his head. "I don't know. Maybe it doesn't. Maybe we've just stumbled upon one of their programs, and that's it. It may not have anything to do with it."

Doc sat back in his chair. "Okay. Let's say we're right. These guys are not just scientists, but scientists trained like soldiers, with heightened senses, beefed up on steroids and who knows what else. What do we do if their blood tests are fine? I have no reason to hold them medically."

"And I have no reason to hold them under UNF law, if I can't link them to the missing crew."

"Which we can't and it's unlikely that we'll be able to in less than 90 minutes. So where does that leave us?"

"I don't know, Doc." Harris paused, his mind working. "There's a chance they may not have had anything to do with the disappearances. It could've been Quint, like you said. Maybe Quint took care of the missing crew and shipped their bodies home. Maybe Bulk wasn't nuts when he said there were bodies in those barrels of waste. The survivors may not be a threat to us."

"But they know something."

"Yeah, they know something... and Logan did threaten you."

"And he reminded me of that threat again this afternoon."

Harris glanced at the bruises on Doc's arm, and began to rub his hand along his jaw. "So, they're edgy, they've been locked up a while now."

"Making threats is not a way to get yourself released."

"No. But I would probably have a thing or two to say to my rescuers if they didn't release me either."

Doc sighed again. "Yeah."

They sat in silence for a few moments, thinking.

"If those tests are fine, we've got no choice but to release them, Doc. We're just going to have to watch them like hawks, pardon the pun, until the next UNF team gets here to take over the investigation."

"And how long is that? Two and a half, three days?"

Harris nodded. "Doc, until we know for sure, we can't say anything to the others. I don't want a bunch of freaked out soldiers with itchy trigger fingers running around."

"Yeah. Agreed."

"We'll just tell them to be vigilant… especially McKinley."

Doc looked at Harris and nodded, rubbing his face again.

Harris sighed. "Why don't you try and get an hour's shut-eye, Doc."

His medic looked at him and gave a laugh. "Are you kidding? How the hell am I going to switch my brain off this now?"

"It's easy. You just close your eyes and think about something else."

Harris looked at his watch. 16:31. "I might take my own advice. If we end up releasing them, I want my brain to be alert."

Doc stood from his chair and began to head for the door.

"I'm serious, Doc. Give it a try," Harris called after him, getting out of his chair and following.

Doc glanced around and gave him a halfhearted smile. "Yes, sir." As he walked toward the door, Harris saw Doc catch sight of the coffee machine and stop, the smile disappearing from his face.

"You want a coffee, Doc?" Harris asked. "That's not going to help you sleep."

Doc looked back at him, face serious. "You think our theory might be the reason why Command ordered you to keep the new recruits on the ship?"

Harris looked back at the coffee machine and remembered that Welles had just changed the pot over. He shrugged. "Could be, Doc. That would definitely hurt their PR exercise if something went wrong."

They exchanged a concerned look.

"Doc, on that, our conversation earlier, I didn't mean t—"

"It's fine," Doc cut him off. "The situation's been handled."

Harris eyed him for a second. "That why she ran out of the room just now?"

Doc shot him a blank look, then turned and left the room.

Carrie looked around the mess hall. It was all set for the crew's dinner. When she'd brought back Harris's empty coffee pot, she figured she might as well get everything done while she was there. Besides, it wasn't like she had anything else pressing to do. Colt was still on the flight deck and Carrie actually enjoyed the time alone. Although, being left to her own devices meant her mind had time to run away with far too many thoughts.

She was paranoid about Doc meeting Harris after she left, but realized it was probably to do with the tests. Harris hadn't mentioned anything about Doc to her, so it wasn't a big deal. She thought of her father again and what he would think of her behavior. It had honestly caught her by surprise. She ran over all the events since she'd been on the *Aurora*, racking her brain to think of when and where she might've overstepped the mark with Doc, but she struggled to find any of serious concern. She'd had one-on-one conversations with him, but they'd been no different to her one-on-one conversations with Colt or Packham. So, where had she gone wrong? Why had Doc suddenly raised it with her?

She conceded to herself that she was attracted to him. Regardless, she didn't think she'd made the attraction obvious. Perhaps she had. Perhaps Doc saw something; a look that she didn't even know she'd given. Had she been oblivious to it up until now? Why had she suddenly felt so uncomfortable when he'd said they needed to watch their time spent alone? Why had she suddenly become so aware of how close he was standing? And why couldn't she look him in the eye now? Was it just professional embarrassment? Or was it because the truth was out there between them now?

She sighed again and shook her head. *Jesus Christ. Here you are on Space Duty, pursuing your ultimate goal, and this is what you're thinking about? Some guy. And a fellow soldier at that! Focus!*

She looked at her watch and headed for the exit. As she reached the door to the mess, she nearly slammed right into Doc, who was walking in.

"Whoa!" he said, grabbing her upper arms and holding her back to avoid a collision.

"Lieutenant Walker," she said formally, stepping back out of his grasp.

He frowned a little at her. "I told you it didn't have to be like that."

She looked through the doorway and nodded, avoiding eye contact again. He stared at her for a moment, then took a step to the right, into her line of sight, forcing her to look at him.

"Calling me 'Doc' is fine, and you *are* allowed to talk to me," he said, making sure she locked eyes with him. She stared back into his warm, brown, friendly pools.

"Except when we're alone like this, right? I'm trying to keep you out of trouble, lieutenant," she said, then looked away again.

"No, the mess hall is fine. It's a communal place," he told her.

"Well, I was on my way out anyway." She glanced back at him.

He looked at her, his eyes disappointed. "Is there some coffee going?" he asked, placing his hands on his hips.

"Over on the counter, sir," she said, pointing.

They looked at each other for another moment, then Doc conceded and moved aside, and as he did she swiftly left the room.

Harris was worried that he might not be able to switch his mind off for a while there. What Doc said had well and truly lodged itself in his brain. Why did Command insist on the new recruits not leaving the ship? Was it because of their inexperience? Were they a possible liability if things got out of hand with these... *men*? And why had he been given three new recruits for this mission, if that was the case? What could be gained from this? Sending three women up here on a dangerous mission they couldn't actually take part in?

He took a deep breath, stretched out his entire body, and purposely cleared his mind. It took some concentration, but years of practice had taught him that a soldier needed to be able to sleep whenever and wherever it was able to be taken. He focused on nothing. He pictured the view he saw out of the flight deck window when he'd been chatting with Bulk; the big, black, nothingness. Before too long he was back in the Jazz Club, dancing with that woman. And not too much longer after that, he was fast asleep.

Some 30-odd minutes later, however, he awoke with an uneasy feeling in the pit of his stomach. He'd had that dream again. He was back on Earth, in that field, and his grandmother Sibbie and great-grandmother Etta were there. Sibbie was holding that phone, trying to pass it to him, and telling him something was wrong, while Etta stood beside her and simply nodded encouragingly for him to take it. He refused, however.

He knew it related to that repressed childhood memory from when his father died. Sibbie had answered the phone that day and passed it to his mother, who then received that awful news; his father, a cop, had been killed in an armed hold-up gone wrong. A tragic accident, but according to his sister Holly, somehow Sibbie and Etta had known it was going to happen. At least, they'd known something bad, in general, was going to happen. It only made him wonder whether these dreams meant something bad was going to happen to him now? He knew, deep down, that was why he didn't want to take that phone.

He remembered hearing his sister Holly ask Sibbie about it, not long after it had happened. Sibbie had told her that she'd had a strange dream the morning their father had died and she knew it had been a warning. Holly always believed that Sibbie and Etta hailed from a long line of female New Orleans ancestors blessed with a gift for sensing things. Some called it ESP, some said it ran deeper than that; from strong gut feelings to dreams of the future.

Although he sometimes humored Holly and entertained the thought that his grandmother may have had it, he'd told himself that if she did, it had ended with her. Holly attested to having no such dreams, nor any particularly strong gut feelings. The only gift Holly seemed to have inherited was her belief. She and Sibbie would spend hours talking about it, but Harris always took it to be a "girl" thing; something the women in his family liked to believe in. Except his mother, of course. And although Holly had pestered him about it over the years, even she had started giving up trying to convince him. He'd conceded to her that he had good instinctive gut feelings, but that he did not believe this came from some family legend. He believed it came from his own intuition, his education and his years of service. Besides, Holly's argument was flawed. He was male. Even if the legend were true, there's no way it could possibly run through him. Despite her trying to convince him otherwise.

He lay there on his bed, staring at the ceiling, thinking about it all. He chuckled tiredly and sighed. *You didn't get your leave, Saul*, he told himself. *Here you are, out in the middle of space near the goddamned Belt, trying to find some missing crew, and all you can think about is your damn family folklore. You need a rest. You're burning out, going crazy. You need to focus!*

He looked at his watch, 17:18, and sighed loudly again, feeling his shoulders slump a little. Any minute now, Doc would have the results of the blood tests.

Any minute now, he just knew that he was going to have to release the survivors.

*

Harris found Doc in his examination room, at the far counter by the autoanalyzer, which tested the blood. Doc looked up at him.

"You get some sleep?" Harris asked.

Doc glanced over at an empty cup of coffee on the bench.

Harris shook his head and moved over to stand by him. "Okay, lay it on me, Doc."

The medic brought up the results on the monitor attached to the apparatus. Information started scrolling across the screen. Doc read it in silence for a few minutes, every now and then sliding his fingers along to bring up a new page of results. He had his poker face on, giving nothing away. He hit another button, then a print copy spooled out. He tore it off, looked at it again, then sighed and handed it to Harris.

"We're going to have to release the survivors."

Harris grabbed the printout and scanned it, but couldn't make any sense of the readings. "There's absolutely nothing here that we can use to hold them any longer?" he asked.

Doc shook his head. "The readings are fine. I can't explain it. I don't feel good about it, but I've got nothing to work with. We can't hold them on my hunch."

"And you've done every single test you can think of?"

"Saul, I've run a full search. Every virus and every suspect bacteria known to man is loaded into this system. Their blood is clean." Doc ran his hands through his hair. "Their agitated states, the sweating and the accelerated heartbeats could be due to the steroids they've possibly been taking, but I can't even find traces of that in their blood. I've even searched for known masking agents, just in case, but I can't find them either. Unless, of course, they've developed a new masking agent, in which case, I wouldn't know how to detect it. I'm relying solely on the standard searches this machine can do. I'm a medic, not a scientist!"

Harris sighed and leaned back against the bench. The silence sat between them for a few moments. He rubbed his jaw, "Well, we tighten security on the ship. The flight deck and the cargo hold will now remain locked at all times while they're here. We'll keep the weapons store and soldiers' quarters locked as they have been. The only room that will remain open will be the mess hall. That's it. I'll have at least two men on guard around the clock."

"Maybe we should leave them on the station? Guard them there."

Harris shook his head. "No. Too big. The *Aurora* is smaller, more confined. There's not many places to hide and we know it well. The station is a different story."

"And what are you going to do about Command's orders regarding the new recruits?"

Harris eyed Doc. "My orders are for them not to leave the ship. Command said nothing about bringing people aboard."

Doc stared back and Harris noted his look of concern.

"The *Aurora* is the safest place for all of us, Doc. We stick together, there shouldn't be any problems. We outnumber them, don't forget. Besides, we *could* actually be wrong about everything. Let's not allow lack of sleep to color our judgment here."

Doc conceded with a nod. "Are you going to tell the team to carry weapons onboard?"

"No. Like I said, I don't want a heap of itchy trigger fingers. We'll leave it at just you, me and McKinley. That ought to cover us."

Doc pursed his lips, thinking. "Maybe one more for good measure? Carter? Brown? That's four of us watching four of them."

"Good point. I'll arm Brown too. He's less trigger happy than Carter. But we'll just tell them it's a precautionary measure. We say we don't fully trust these guys and that's it. I don't want people jumping at shadows. We have no proof that they're a threat to us yet."

"Yes, sir."

Harris exhaled loudly, placing his hands on his hips. "I'll send for McKinley to load us up. Then I guess we better tell our survivors the good news. Looks like we're having guests for dinner!"

# 17

# Juice

Carrie stood at the end of the firing range. She felt a calmness wash over her, as though radiating from her eyes, down to her heart and out through her fingertips, which were curled around the gun. There was something about hitting her targets that felt so right to her. She was in control, in her element. This was her domain. The one true place she felt comfortable and in control.

She spent time on target practice every day, where possible. She was almost afraid that if she didn't give it attention then she might lose the skill, and as it was the one thing she had, she couldn't afford to let that happen. She closed her left eye, held the gun out front, steadied her weight and took an even breath in. She squeezed the trigger gently, and *zip*, the laser hit its target. She walked over to the other range and fired another one quickly, then brought the results up on the screen. More 1's, just like the rest of her session. She smiled.

She looked at her watch. 17:55. *Shit! They'll be giving the results to the survivors.* She hung up the gun and rushed back to the flight deck. When she arrived, she saw Packham and Colt at the console, and Carter and Bolkov sitting at the captain's desk watching casually.

She looked at the screens and saw Harris, Doc and McKinley making their way to the holding cell.

"Where's Louis and Smith?" she asked.

"They're in the mess hall getting some food together," Colt told her.

"I already did that," Carrie said confused.

"They went to put more on. We're letting these guys out. They're joining us for dinner."

They all looked to see her reaction.

"They are?" she said taking a seat.

"Yes, ma'am," Carter said, eyes fixed back on the screen. "Blood work was fine."

Carrie found herself glued to the cameras. The four men were in the cell, waiting. Logan was no longer pacing but shuffling around. Fairmont, too. Chet remained still, while Grolsh sat on one of the beds, shaking his leg continuously. They all suddenly looked to their left. Carrie's eyes jumped to Harris's monitor. They were walking around the bend and as the cell came in sight, there were four pairs of eyes eagerly awaiting them. She noticed Harris and Doc exchange a glance.

"Right on time," Chet said calmly.

Doc walked up to the glass wall.

"Tell me you have good news, Doc?" Logan tilted his head to the side, as though a bird eyeing its prey.

Doc put his hands on his hips and carefully watched them. "How are you all feeling?"

"Thirsty," Fairmont offered.

"Hungry," came Logan's gravelly reply.

"Dying to get out of here," Grolsh said, in a desperate voice.

Doc looked over his shoulder to Brown and Hunter. "How much water did they drink?"

"About four bottles each," Hunter answered.

"Four bottles," Doc said, turning back around to the men, "and you're still thirsty?"

"Well, you didn't give us that shot, lieutenant," Fairmont said calmly.

Doc eyed him carefully.

"Doocc," Chet began, his voice low and eerie, "don't leave us in suspense. How was our blood work?"

Doc exhaled loudly. "Your bloods were—"

"Yes?" Logan stepped toward the glass wall that separated them.

"Your bloods were fine. We're releasing you."

"Excellent!" Chet smiled, his shoulders visibly easing off the tension.

"Wait a second," Doc held up his hand, stopping him. "We're releasing you from this bio cell into our custody."

The four men looked at him blankly.

Harris stepped forward then. "You will be in our custody until Professor Martin's team arrives. I've just spoken with Command. They're departing Earth today and will be here in approximately two and a half days to take over the investigation into your missing crew. So, you will be out of that cell, but you will remain unarmed and under our supervision. Are we clear on the conditions, gentlemen?"

The four men looked at each other, then Chet turned and gave a big smile. "We are happy with those conditions, captain."

"Good," Harris said firmly. He turned to Doc and nodded.

Doc reached into his pocket and pulled out a few vials of the hydrating fluid he'd been injecting them with. Their eyes seemed to light up.

"This will be your last shot. Do we understand each other?" Doc told them firmly, pulling the lever to open the window again.

They nodded. Doc eyed them suspiciously, as they each took a turn to poke their arms through the window and have their injection.

Harris stepped forward again. "Well, gentlemen, as captain of the *Aurora*, I invite you to dine with us this evening."

The four of them smiled broadly.

"We'd be delighted, captain," Chet said, in his most cultured English accent.

Harris looked over at Brown. "Let them out."

Brown nodded, stepped forward and unlocked the cell door. The four men inside glanced at each other, then slowly and calmly exited through the small chamber just inside the door, each disappearing briefly in the mist before reappearing. The survivors then lined up just outside the cell.

Chet held out his hand for Harris to shake, and he did so.

"Thank you, captain," Chet said, bowing his head.

"And thank you for your patience with our protocol." Harris gave a nod.

Logan moved over to Doc, and he too extended his hand to shake. "You made the right decision, Doc," he smiled.

They shook, but Doc didn't say anything, nor did his face give anything away.

"This way, gentlemen," Harris announced, ushering them in the direction of the *Aurora*.

Harris, Doc and Hunter, moved off down the corridor with the four men. Carrie noticed, however, that McKinley held back and motioned for Brown to do the same.

"I need a word," he said, reaching up to turn off his headset.

Carrie's eyes darted to Brown's camera and watched as McKinley reached up and turned the sergeant's headset off too. Her brow furrowed. *What was that about?*

She looked away from the screens and saw that Carter and Bolkov were halfway out the door, on their way to the mess.

"Well, ladies, looks like grub's up and we don't have to serve it tonight," Colt smiled.

"Excellent," Carrie smiled back and stretched out in her seat.

"I've just got to shut down these comms," Packham said.

"We might as well wait for you," Carrie shrugged. "It's not like we're going to beat that lot to the food queue, anyway!"

Colt chuckled.

Carrie watched as Packham carried out the fight deck shut down procedures. The sergeant finalized a download to an e-file pane, which she then stored in the cabinet. The screens then went blank and disappeared from the main window, all except the external cameras for the ship.

Hunter entered the flight deck. He'd already removed his headwear and weapon.

"Move it, soldiers!" he ordered. "Captain wants the flight deck locked up."

The three women nodded, and headed up the stairs.

"Let's go meet our guests," Colt said.

Harris sat at the far table with Doc, Carter, Smith and the four survivors. McKinley, Brown, Bulk and Louis were on the other table, and all were beginning to tuck into their meals. Harris noted the four survivors were eating like they hadn't eaten in days. Ravenous. He glanced at Doc, who seemed to have noticed as well.

"So, we have the pleasure of your company for two and a half days then, captain?" Chet asked.

"Yes, you do."

"How wonderful," Chet smiled, then began scanning the room.

"I don't see Hunter? Is he not eating with us?"

"He'll be here soon."

Just as Harris said that, Grolsh stiffened at the end of the table and snapped his head around to look at the door. The other three survivors followed suit, stopping mid-mouthful, straightening up and eyeing the door carefully.

Harris glanced at Doc, and then back to the four men. "Something wrong, gentlemen?" he asked them, eyeing the door and seeing no-one.

Brown and McKinley were paying attention, too, from the other table. Within a second of Harris saying that, Hunter walked through the door, closely followed by Packham, Colt and Welles. Harris and Doc exchanged another look. Carter and Smith shot each other puzzled glances, then went back to eating. Logan turned back around in his seat and stared at Chet. The two looked at each other as though they were communicating with their eyes.

"Is there a problem?" Harris made his voice more commanding.

Chet turned and smiled at him. "We didn't expect to see female soldiers on your crew, captain."

Fairmont turned his attention back to the conversation as well.

"This is a test case," Harris told them.

"I see." Chet nodded. He glanced over at Grolsh, who had not yet taken his eyes off the women.

There was thud under the table, Grolsh jumped and snapped his head back around to glare at Chet. Chet held a big smile on his face as he turned back to Harris and Doc.

"I apologize, gentlemen. It has been a while since we've had the company of females. Grolsh forgot his manners."

Harris didn't respond, but gave Grolsh a blank stare, then went back to eating.

"Have they been with you long, captain? This test case, how new is it?" Chet probed.

"Fairly new," Harris said plainly.

"Fairly new?" Carter piped up. "That's one way to describe it, captain. Four days here and they think they fuckin' own the place!"

Doc shot Carter a stern glance. Smith saw it, too, and they both dropped their eyes to their plates. Logan looked back over to Chet with a tiny smile on his face. Both he and Chet seemed to have another conversation with their eyes. Grolsh glanced back over at the women who had now taken seats at the other table. Fairmont was watching them as well.

"Is there only three of them, captain?" Chet continued his line of questioning.

"Why the interest?" Harris asked impatiently, dropping his fork to his plate.

Chet almost bowed his head in submission. "I'm just curious, captain. I never thought I'd see them on a crew like yours, that's all."

"Well, there's a first time for everything," Harris told him.

"So, tell me about what you guys did on the Darwin?" Doc said, changing the conversation and doing what he did best, pretending he hadn't already read their files, what little of them that wasn't classified, that is.

Chet gave Doc a smirk. "You know we can't tell you that, Doc."

"I'm not asking you to tell me about your classified programs. I'm just asking what you did? What you do? What's your background? Physics? Chemistry?"

Chet nodded patiently at Doc. "Very well. My background is in biochemistry. Believe it or not, I started my career in sports science, working with athletes, then I joined the UNF and they helped develop my career further. I guess you can say that I've always been interested in the human body and how to get the most out of it."

"Biochemistry, huh?" Doc nodded, then turned to the others. "And you guys?"

Logan went to answer, but Chet answered for him. "They are studying under me in biochemistry and biology, the UNF way," Chet said, then let a smile creep onto his face. "But I'm sure you've already read that in our files, Doc. Hmm?"

Doc shook his head. "I only get access to medical files, and unfortunately yours were classified, you see."

"Ah, yes. Of course," Chet replied.

"Had you worked with Professor Sharley long?" Doc asked, keeping the conversation focused on them.

"For some time. He's a great scientist," Chet answered.

"Yeah, I read some papers of his once. His comparison of animal hunters and serial killers was quite interesting," Doc smiled, finishing his plate.

Carter furrowed his brow and looked at Doc. "What do animals and serial killers have to do with the UNF?"

"Serial killers are incredibly smart specimens," Chet answered him. "Most of them have extremely high IQ's and study their prey in order to defeat them, the way true hunters do."

"He did a lot of interesting work building Hell Town, too." Harris entered the conversation, watching the men for their reactions.

Chet nodded at Harris. "Yes, he did. I did not work with him then, but Logan here did."

Harris and Doc looked over at Logan. Up close, Harris noticed his thin dark lips looked blood red against his pale skin.

"And what did you do there?" Harris asked him.

Logan's strange green eyes, flecked with yellow, flashed to his. "I assisted him with some of his programs," his gravelly voice replied.

"Yeah. Doing what?" Doc asked in a casual voice.

"I helped him with his behavioral programs. *Disciplinary* programs, mainly." Logan stared down at his hand as he ran his fingers along a scratch in the table's surface. Harris noted that his dirty fingernails were slightly long, and filed in such a way that they came to a point, instead of a blunt edge or natural curve.

"Ah," Doc said sitting back in his chair. "Are we talking about the controversial techniques Sharley used to keep the prisoners in line?"

Logan looked up from his finger to Doc. "Some of," he nodded.

Just then they heard Colt's laughter over at the other table. Harris watched as the four survivors turned and stared at her. The three women glanced over at the staring men, then back at each other. Colt said something that made Packham smirk and Welles chuckle, although she tried to stifle it.

"How did your men take to your new recruits, captain?" Chet asked curiously.

"Fine," Harris answered sharply, "like any other recruits."

"Mm," Chet murmured, eyeing the other table, absorbed in his own thoughts.

"So, what do you guys do for fun on the Darwin?" Harris said, pushing his plate out in front. He felt it was time to change the subject and lighten the mood a little.

The men looked at each other.

"I'm a fairly mean pool player," Fairmont suggested.

Harris shook his head. "Unfortunately, the UNF doesn't supply us with a pool table."

"We've got one back on the station?" Grolsh offered eagerly.

"We're settled in here now," Harris told him, "and although we don't have a pool table, we do have cards."

"Cards?" Logan smiled, "Now that's my language."

"We'll let's clear these plates and get a game going, shall we?" Harris said.

Carrie watched as Smith cleared the plates and Harris, Doc and Carter began playing cards with the four survivors. The rest of the team gathered around the table to watch, but for some reason she stood back a little, off to the side with Colt and Packham. She was finding the survivors and their stares a little strange, so right now she preferred to keep her distance.

The first game was long and played mostly in silence. Everyone seemed cautious, studying how the others played their hand, and strategizing their own moves. Carrie could still feel the tension in the air. She wondered if a game of poker, a competition of sorts, was the right answer for a bunch of testosterone-filled males.

Chet folded first, smiling. "Unfortunately, cards aren't my forte."

Carter and Grolsh soon followed suit. Harris, Doc, Logan and Fairmont went on a while longer, but then Fairmont and Doc folded simultaneously. So it was left to Harris versus Logan. She noted the survivor's card face consisted of a sly smile, while the captain's was the opposite—completely deadpan. They held out as long as they could, then both laid their cards on the table. Logan was the winner.

"There's a new king in town!" Harris acknowledged his win.

Logan shrugged modestly. "Perhaps."

Carrie noted that McKinley was standing back, leaning against the wall beside the women. She recognized the hardness in his face as he watched the survivors. *So, that was the look he gave every stranger. It wasn't just us.* Although, studying him now, she noted the stare he gave the survivors was a little harder than the looks she was used to. Suddenly, McKinley's piercing blue eyes shifted to hers. He'd noticed her watching him. She held his stare for a moment with her best poker face, then looked away.

She watched several more games as the players interchanged. Doc won a couple, as did Logan. Hunter managed one win, and Harris came close several times, but was always pipped at the post by another. Carter continued to get frustrated every time he lost. He always seemed so sure that he was going to win. Carrie figured he should be used to it by now.

As Hunter gathered the cards to reshuffle them for the next game, Chet looked over at the women.

"Would the ladies like to play?" he asked with a debonair tone.

Carrie and the women exchanged a glance.

"Are they allowed to play, captain?" Chet asked.

Harris nodded. "Of course they're allowed to play."

Chet turned back to the women and smiled, raising his eyebrows in question.

Packham gave a half-smile. "No thanks."

Chet moved his eyes to Carrie.

"I'm no good," she blurted, then flashed McKinley a quick glance, as a smile curled the corner of his mouth.

Chet looked over at Colt with raised eyebrows.

"Maybe later. I'm happy watching for now." She waved him off.

"Alright, so who's up?" Harris called.

Louis, Smith, Brown and Bolkov all squeezed in around the table.

"Whoa! We better crack out the second deck," Carter noted.

"Ready to go!" Smith pulled one out of his shirt pocket and placed it on the table.

Hunter passed the cards down for Harris to deal out, and the next game started. Carrie noted that the atmosphere seemed a little more relaxed now. Despite her earlier reservations, it would appear that the cards were a good idea after all. They seemed to have enabled a little male bonding of sorts.

She decided poker-watching was making her thirsty, so she walked behind the mess counter, took some juice from the cool room and put it out on the bench. She looked over at the group playing cards. *Maybe I should get a round of drinks happening...* she noticed Grolsh watching her, his head turned as far as it would go. She looked at him for a moment, then turned back to the cool room and took out some more juice. She bent down, grabbed a tray from a cupboard, and slid it up over her head onto the counter, then started pulling glasses out as well. When she was done, she stood back up and was startled to see Grolsh standing on the opposite side of the counter, staring at her.

"I'll help," he said. His accented voice was devoid of emotion, but his eyes stared at her in a way that made her feel uncomfortable.

"Er, sure," she said, pushing the tray of empty glasses his way. As she did, her eyes fell over Grolsh's shoulder and saw McKinley watching them from against the far wall. It didn't look like a casual glance. McKinley was paying attention to them. *What was going on with him?* She wondered. *What did he say to Brown before when he'd turned their comms off?*

She walked over with the juice to the empty table beside the group, Grolsh walking silently by her side. She motioned for him to put the tray down, which he did. She started pouring the juice, looking up occasionally at the group. They were enthralled in the game, although she did notice the other three survivors glance over at both her and Grolsh. Doc did, too.

She took the tray of juice over to the playing table and everyone started reaching for a glass. Louis reached over Smith to get one, while focusing on his current hand, but as he brought the glass back toward him, he knocked over the remaining glasses, tipping the heavy tray and sending juice flying into Smith's lap and down Carrie's arm.

"*Fuck*, Louis!" Smith cried out.

Louis saw Smith's lap covered in orange juice and started laughing. "Oh shit!"

Carter joined in laughing and some of the others smiled, amused. Harris shook his head. Carrie stood there for a second and looked at her wet arm, wishing she hadn't been wearing her long-sleeved shirt. She turned around and put the tray of tipped-over glasses on the spare table.

"Oh, man!" Smith sat there looking at his lap and shaking the juice off his arms.

"I'll get some napkins!" Carrie offered. She ran over to the counter, grabbed the half empty tray of serviettes and handed them to Smith. She saw the puddle on the table and on his chair and figured there wasn't going to be enough to wipe up all that was spilled.

"I'll get some more from the store," she offered.

She headed for the door, looking at her wet arm again. Remembering she had her UNF singlet underneath, she removed the wet overshirt and hung it over the back of the chair to dry, then left the mess hall.

Harris and Doc watched on, slightly amused, at the commotion at the table. Smith and Louis were abusing each other, albeit mostly in jest. Carter was laughing so hard, Harris thought he was going to have a coronary. Packham and Colt were giggling to themselves where they stood beside the table, and McKinley was shaking his head, smiling at the abuse Smith and Louis were throwing at each other. Brown and Hunter were looking at Brown's sleeve, as he was convinced he got some spilt over him, too, while Bulk sat there quietly looking at his cards and thinking about his next move.

"Oh, dry up, you little English girl," Louis laughed teasingly at Smith.

"Fuck this, you French fuck. Take your *fucking* snails and shove them up your *fucking* ass," Smith said, standing up, trying to dry himself with a handful of saturated napkins that were quickly disintegrating over his clothes. "I'm going to change." He looked over at McKinley. "Play my hand for me, and make sure this French fuck doesn't cheat," he spat at Louis, who was still laughing at him.

McKinley grinned as he picked up Smith's hand and studied it. Carter and Louis were still laughing, mimicking Smith, while Brown and Hunter were debating whether he had any juice on him.

"I can feel it, man!" Brown told him.

"I'm telling you there's nothing on there, Brownie! Look!"

McKinley glanced around the room as he took a seat at the table. As soon as he sat down, he suddenly paused, dropped his grin and looked at Harris.

"Bad hand?" Harris asked him, amid the ruckus.

McKinley looked around the room again, as though he was searching for someone.

Harris looked around the faces at the table. *Smith went to get changed*, he thought, then looked over and saw Welles's shirt hanging over a chair. *That's fine, she's gone to get some more napkins.* Then he, too, stopped suddenly. He looked back at McKinley, who was staring at him.

*Grolsh was missing.*

Harris's eyes darted over to Doc, who had obviously realized the same thing, and was sitting back in his chair, eyeing the doorway.

"I'm going to fold," McKinley said calmly, placing his cards face down and getting up from the table.

"Fuck, was his hand that bad?" Carter asked. "He probably tipped the bloody juice on himself to get out of it!"

Carter and Louis started howling again.

Without drawing attention, Harris and Doc watched quietly as McKinley headed calmly toward the mess hall door. In between glances at his second lieutenant, Harris noted the three other survivors weren't smiling anymore. Their eyes were directed at their cards, but he could tell they weren't looking at them. Their minds were somewhere else.

"WHOSE *FUCKING* TURN IS IT?" Bolkov growled loudly.

Everyone abruptly quietened down and looked at him.

Then someone yelled in the distance.

They looked over in the direction it came from. Just as McKinley made the doorway, they heard it again.

*"DOC! DOC!"* It was Smith, and he was panicked.

Doc shot up from the table lightning quick, jumping over the empty chairs at the other table, racing for the door, as McKinley started running down the corridor. Harris stood and turned around to Brown.

"Stay here. Watch them," he ordered, pointing at the other three survivors. He started walking quickly but calmly for the door. He didn't want to cause panic and he knew that McKinley and Doc were ahead of him. As he turned into the corridor, he saw McKinley up ahead at the intersection. He had his pistol out, sweeping around for something or someone. The look on his face struck Harris. It was anxious, maybe a little rattled, but he also saw a tinge of guilt in his eyes. Smith stepped backward into the corridor intersection then, staring off to the side at something on the floor. Harris quickened his pace to a jog. *Where was Doc?* he thought.

As he approached them, he heard a hideous gasping sound from around the corner. He turned and saw Welles on her knees on the floor. Doc was crouched in front of her. He held her head in his hands, in front of his face, her somewhat limp body falling against him.

"Fuck, Welles! LOOK AT ME," Doc yelled at her. "BREATHE!"

Welles looked like she was only semiconscious, struggling to keep her eyes open. Her face had a bluish tinge to it and her neck was bright red.

"Welles!" Doc shook her slightly, a touch of panic in his voice. "CARRIE! Carrie, look at me," he demanded.

She seemed to register her name and looked at him, still fighting for breath, a long line of drool now hanging from the corner of her mouth.

"Carrie, *breathe*. Relax and *breathe*," he told her firmly but calmly, his eyes boring into hers, trying to hold her attention.

There was another hideous sound as she took a big gasp of air and started coughing and choking, grabbing onto Doc's shirt for dear life.

"Good! That's good," Doc told her, rubbing his thumb across her mouth, wiping the line of drool away.

Harris spun around to Smith. "What the fuck happened?" he barked.

"I... I don't know! I was just going to change, a— and I saw Grolsh running off and then I found her there on the floor," Smith said.

"You didn't see what happened?" Harris glared at him.

"No, he just... just gave me this pissed off look and ran away, and th— then I saw her."

Harris glanced at McKinley, whose face was hard and serious now. Smith looked over at him, too.

"How come you're armed, man?" he asked quietly.

McKinley didn't answer, he just kept his eyes on his captain.

Harris scanned the empty corridors around them, then looked back at Welles. Doc was holding her head with one hand now, resting it against his shoulder and rubbing her back firmly with the heel of his other hand, as she continued to cough and splutter and choke. She was still gripping hard onto Doc's shirt, using him as an anchor, as her lungs struggled to get air into them.

"Doc?" Harris almost shouted, finding it difficult to contain his anger.

His medic pulled the corporal from his shoulder to sit in front of him. He angled her chin up slightly and examined her neck. The red looked darker, as though it were beginning to settle into a purple color.

"LIEUTENANT!" Harris insisted.

Doc looked at Harris, his face even harder than McKinley's had been. "She's been asphyxiated. He strangled her," he said, clenching his jaw.

"What?" Colt and Packham came running up beside Harris, looking at Welles.

"What are you doing here?" he barked at them.

"Welles was missing. I was worried, sir," Colt said, moving straight over to Doc. Packham just stood there looking wide-eyed at them.

Harris looked over at McKinley. "Get a team, go find him and bring him back here to me!"

McKinley nodded and headed back to the mess.

"Smith, lock this ship down, NOW!" Harris barked at him.

Smith nodded and headed off after one final worried glance down at the corporal.

"Can you stand up?" Doc asked Welles.

She nodded, seemingly a little more with it now, but still quite groggy. She burst into another coughing fit.

"Colt, help me get her up," Doc ordered. "We have to get some oxygen into her."

Doc and Colt took an arm each and lifted her weight off the floor. Welles put her feet on the ground, but they buckled immediately. They quickly caught her.

"Here!" Doc said, bending down to pick her up. "I'll take her. It's quicker."

Welles looked like she was trying to protest as the lieutenant lifted her up off the ground, but no words came from her mouth. Doc shot Harris a concerned look as he carried her past him, heading down the corridor to his hospital, with Colt following closely behind.

Harris turned around to Packham. "Get back to the mess!"

She turned and quickly started walking, but Harris soon overtook her as he strode angrily down the corridor. As they approached the door, McKinley, Hunter, Carter and Louis were heading off to search for Grolsh. They all looked down the corridor past Harris, no doubt watching Doc carrying Welles away.

Harris stormed back into the mess hall. Brown stood with his gun pointed at the three remaining survivors, who were still seated at the table, cards in front of them. Bolkov was by Brown's side. Packham stayed by the door, not sure what to do.

"What the fuck, gentlemen?" Harris yelled at the three survivors, as he approached.

"What the fuck, indeed, captain?" Chet said calmly, albeit a little concerned. "What's going on? Where's Grolsh?"

"You tell me?" Harris stared at them.

Chet stared blankly back at Harris. He wasn't offering any smiles now.

Harris glared at him. "Less than two hours. Less than two hours out of that cell, and one of your men attack one of my crew," he bellowed at them.

"Attacked? What do you mean?" Chet asked.

"Like you didn't know?"

"Captain, I've been sitting in here playing cards. Tell me, what should I know?"

"You didn't hear it?" Harris stared hard at Chet.

"Hear what?"

"You didn't hear your man Grolsh strangling Corporal Welles down the hall?"

Brown and Bolkov glanced at Harris a little surprised, then looked back at the men.

"Strangling her?" Chet sounded concerned, but Harris wasn't buying it.

"She okay, captain?" Brown asked with flat voice, gun firmly on the survivors.

"She's with Doc," Harris said quickly, not taking his eyes off the three men. "Give me one good reason I don't throw you back in that cell?"

"One good reason?" Logan piped up through gritted teeth. "We were sitting here playing cards. That's not a jailable offense."

Chet sat forward. "I'm sure there's been a misunderstanding, captain. Grolsh is young, hotheaded. I'm sure he didn't mean any harm to Corporal Welles."

Harris put his hands on his hips and looked down at Chet. "Didn't mean any harm. Didn't mean to grab her by the throat and nearly kill her?"

"He doesn't know his own strength. I'm sure he didn't mean any harm. There's just been some misunderstanding," Chet said confidently. "What did she say to him, anyway? She must've set him off somehow?"

"You sound angry at yourself, captain," Logan suggested. "Were you expecting this? Is that why you had some of your men armed? Were you supposed to be looking for something and you missed it?"

Harris gave the three men a cold stare. "I made the mistake of trusting you. I won't make that mistake again." He turned and headed for the door. As he approached it he glared over at Packham. "You come with me."

# 18

# Oxygen

Carrie let go of Doc as he placed her on one of the pod-beds in the ship's small hospital. He moved away and started doing something to a machine beside the bed. She groggily looked at Colt who was watching her carefully, her eyes wide with concern. Carrie's throat hurt. It was dry and coarse, like she'd swallowed fire. She brought her hand up to her neck. It felt tight, as though Grolsh's hands were still on it. She coughed again, and her lungs burned as they tried hard to suck more air into them. Doc came back and placed an oxygen mask on her face. The air was cold and wet, and it made her flinch.

"Lay down," Doc told her, pushing her gently back.

She tried to resist but couldn't. She felt weak. She closed her eyes for a moment as her head hit the pillow. She didn't want this to be happening. This wasn't how things were supposed to go... *Harris was furious. How did this happen?*

Doc walked away for a second, then came back and placed his thumb along her brow ridge. He flashed a light in her right eye, then did the same with her other.

"What's wrong with her eye, Doc?" Colt asked, as he shone the light into the left one. "Why is it red like that?"

"Burst blood vessel," he said, turning the light off and putting it back in his pocket. "How's the oxygen? You feeling better?" he asked her.

Carrie nodded, her brain was beginning to feel less cloudy. He turned and walked out of the room.

"What happened?" Colt asked in a motherly tone.

Doc came back with a cup of water. "Sip this," he said handing it to her and disappearing again.

Colt leaned forward and lifted her mask. Carrie sipped the water, then Colt took it from her and repositioned the mask on her face. Doc came back carrying a strange glove and a tube of gel or cream. The glove was covered in a thin metal sheeting, with wires protruding that connected to a small screen. He pulled the glove over his right hand, twitched his fingers and eyed the screen for a response.

He sat on the side of the bed. "Look up for me," he said, as he tilted her head back.

Carrie stared at the ceiling, trying to stifle a cough that was wanting to escape from her throat. She felt something cold on her neck and saw Doc put the tube on the bedside table. He took his gloved hand and ran the metal-plated fingers gently over her throat and neck, spreading the cold gel around. He looked down at the screen again, now resting on the bed in front of him.

"Ok, this'll be uncomfortable for a second," he said as he pressed his fingers harder into her neck and throat.

Her head jerked forward in reflex and her hand shot out to pull his wrist away, as she coughed into her face mask.

"I'm sorry, Welles, I'm just trying to see if there's any damage. I'll be as quick as I can." Doc held her neck still with his ungloved hand, locking her chin upward with his thumb. He placed his gloved hand firmly against her throat and massaged it over her skin. She started to cough again, but didn't move as Doc's firm grip held her neck and chin in place. It was uncomfortable, but after a couple of minutes he was done.

"It looks okay. There's no serious damage," he told her, wiping the gel from her neck. He got off the bed, wiped the glove down and put it aside.

"Welles, what happened?" Colt asked again.

Carrie's eyes drifted to the corporal.

"I don't know if she can talk yet," Doc answered for her.

Carrie went to speak, but her throat was dry and her words caught and stumbled out in another cough. Doc took the water off Colt and moved back over to Carrie, sliding her mask down to her neck. "Have some more of this."

She took another sip. The cold water felt good running down her throat, putting out the fire within, if only briefly. She went to speak again, but her throat felt cluttered with debris and she launched into another coughing fit.

"Just give it a few minutes, Welles. There's no hurry," Doc told her, with a concerned edge to his voice.

She took another sip of the water and cleared her throat. "I— I'm okay," she managed to croak, her husky voice sounding as painful as it felt.

Doc looked down at her, skeptically. "How long did you black out for?"

Carrie looked away from him. She didn't know. She vaguely remembered being on the floor, and how her knees and her cheek hurt. She half remembered hearing Smith calling for Doc. She assumed it was Smith. It was faint, almost dreamlike, but she recalled seeing his face. She didn't know how long it was before she was suddenly upright and Doc was in front of her. Although, at first, that was almost dreamlike too. Until she started coughing and choking, that is.

She looked up at Doc. He was watching her closely, waiting for an answer. "You don't know, huh?" he said putting her mask back on.

"What the *fuck* happened?" Colt pleaded impatiently with her for an answer.

Carrie looked at her and went to speak, just as Harris came marching through the door with Packham in tow.

"Colt! Out," he barked, motioning back into Doc's office, where Packham had stopped.

Colt nodded and left the room. Harris followed and closed off the hospital from Doc's office.

Carrie sat herself up a little in the bed as Harris walked back over to her.

"What's the story?" he asked Doc.

"She'll be alright. I don't think there's any permanent dama—"

"Good." Harris cut him off, turning to Carrie. "Now tell me what the fuck happened?"

Carrie looked nervously at Harris. He seemed angry and she wasn't entirely sure whether it was directed at her or not. She went to remove her mask to speak.

"Leave it on," Doc told her. "We can hear you."

"I've got Smith working on the surveillance footage," Harris said, his voice still angry, "but until I see that, someone needs to tell me what the fuck happened here?"

"I— I don't know," she began, her voice dry and husky.

"What do you mean, you don't know?"

"It happened so fast…" She shook her head.

"What happened fast?"

"He just grabbed me by the throat… and slammed me against the wall," she croaked.

"Grolsh?"

She nodded.

"Why? What did he say to you? Did you say anything to him? He couldn't have just snapped like that for no reason. Something must've lead up to this."

"Captain," Doc said firmly, as a way of asking him to go lightly.

Harris shot Doc an angry look. Carrie felt an anger within her begin to rise too. She didn't ask for this. This wasn't supposed to happen. She hadn't done anything wrong.

"Well?" Harris said impatiently.

"I was walking down the hall and I heard him following me," she began speaking quickly, in a defensive tone, her eyes staring down at the bed trying to recall what had just happened. "He said, 'I'll help you.' I told him I was fine, but he kept walking. He started saying, 'I know why you're here—' and then he started saying things…" Her throat started closing up on her.

"What things?" Harris pushed.

She eyed Harris nervously then looked down at the bed again. "He said that it had been a long time since he'd seen a woman…" She started coughing.

Doc held out the cup of water. She refused it.

"Then what?" Harris continued probing.

"We get to the store, I get the napkins and he said it had been a long time since he'd… smelled a woman." She continued to cough. "I came out of the store and he was in my face and he said… it'd been a long time since he'd… touched a…" Carrie started coughing more now, almost choking. Her eyes began to water, and saliva flooded her mouth.

"Welles, drink this!" Doc ordered, removing her mask and shoving the water in her face. She took a few sips and coughed some more, then cleared her throat.

"Then what happened?" Harris asked, a little calmer now, finally appreciating the fact that she was struggling.

"I tried to push past him and… as I did, he grabbed me by the throat and slammed me against the wall." She held her hand up mimicking Grolsh's grip on her throat and saw that the fingernails on her right hand were bloodied. She twisted her hand around eyeing them, both intrigued and revolted.

"That his blood or yours?" Harris asked, his eyes quickly scanning her over.

Carrie noticed her hand was shaking. She quickly put it back down in her lap to make it stop, but kept her eyes focused on the dried blood. "His…" she said remembering, her voice very croaky now. "I dug them into his face…"

"Good," Doc said, folding his arms.

"So then Smith came along and disturbed him?" Harris asked.

"I don't know… I dug my nails in and he lifted me off the ground by my throat… I started to pass out… he must've heard Smith coming. Next thing I know, I was lying on the ground… and someone was yelling."

Harris nodded, rubbing his jaw, thinking.

Doc turned to Harris. "I'm pulling her off duty for a while for observation."

"I thought you said she was going to be okay?"

"Yeah, she is."

"So why does she need observation, then?"

"It doesn't have to be *me*, captain!" Doc said tersely with his hands in the air. "Colt can watch her! Packham? I don't care. But she blacked out and we don't know how long for. That means her brain was starved of oxygen for a certain period of time. So someone needs to watch her to make sure she continues to be okay. 24 hours is the standard observation!"

Carrie wanted to stop them arguing. She didn't want to be the cause of any trouble between them. She quickly sat up in bed and removed her mask.

Doc looked over at her. "Welles, what are you doing?"

"Stop arguing," she croaked at them, as she quickly got up off the bed. "I'm fine." She turned to Harris. "Sir, it's okay, I'm ffffiii—" She took a step toward him, but suddenly felt lightheaded. Her brain seemed to briefly buzz out and she face-planted into Harris's hard stomach. He caught her by the arms and a slight zap of static electricity shot between them. Doc stepped forward to assist and they both sat her back on the bed. She looked up at the two of them staring down at her.

"I— I just got up too quick," she said groggily, rubbing her forehead.

Doc put the mask back on her and pushed her back to lie on the pillow. "Stay there, Welles. That's an order!"

She saw Doc look over at Harris with a self-assured look.

"Okay, Doc, that's fine. But I need you." Harris pointed at him, then walked to the door and opened it. He motioned for Colt and Packham to enter, which they did.

"Doc is going to finish up here with Welles, then he is going to escort you three back to your quarters, where you two will keep an eye on her until I send someone for you. Do you understand?"

"Yes, sir." They nodded.

Harris headed for the door.

"Captain?" Packham said, stopping him.

"What, sergeant?"

"Shouldn't we be armed? Like the others."

"Doc's carrying." He nodded in Doc's direction, then turned and left.

Carrie and the other women looked at Doc. He eyed them all back for a moment, then sighed. He reached behind his back, pulled out a UNF handgun and showed them, then put it back in place.

"You've had that the whole time?" Carrie croaked.

"Not the whole time," he said quietly, then quickly looked away as he walked over to a cabinet and fished something out of a drawer. He walked back holding a camera and tossed it to Colt, who caught it.

"I need a record." He motioned toward Carrie. "Get a shot of her face, her neck and her hand."

Doc disappeared again, as Carrie sat up a little and tried to stretch out her back and winced.

"Is your back hurt, too?" Colt asked, pulling her forward to take a look.

Doc walked back in and saw Colt studying her back.

"Doc, should I get a shot of her back, too?" the corporal asked him.

He walked over and leaned behind Carrie, pulling her singlet out, and pressing along her shoulders and upper back. "Yeah. He's a strong bastard…"

Colt took a couple of photos, then showed Carrie the image on the screen. She had a purple bruise from shoulder blade to shoulder blade, from where she was slammed into the wall.

"Your neck and eye are worse," Colt told her.

Carrie lay back down for a minute, placing her oxygen mask on again. She looked over at Packham and asked as clearly as her bruised throat would allow, "What's going on out there?"

"McKinley took off with Hunter, Carter and Louis to find him. Smith's locked the ship down, and Brown and Bulk are guarding the other three survivors in the mess hall. Harris and I armed Bulk and Smith, but Brown already had one, like Doc."

Carrie nodded to herself. *That must have been what McKinley had a word to Brown about…* She remembered glancing up from the floor and seeing McKinley looking around with a gun in his hand. She hadn't clicked at the time that he shouldn't have had one on him. *So, McKinley, Brown and Doc were all armed.* She bet Harris had been, too.

Her mind began to churn over as rapidly as it could in her recovering state. This was not how she'd planned her Space Duty debut to be. This simple mission had just taken a serious turn, and she suddenly felt very uncomfortable with being smack, bang in the middle of it.

Harris waited outside the mess for McKinley to return, trying to remove the images of Sibbie and Etta that had suddenly appeared, like splintered little fragments of mirror stuck deep within the flesh of his brain.

He refused to wait inside with the three remaining survivors. What Logan had said had struck a chord with him. He did feel responsible. He should've been watching Grolsh. If he had been, he would have seen him leave after Welles. He would have followed him and stopped anything from happening, and they would still be playing cards right now.

*Yeah, but for how long, Saul? Until the next time he was alone with her or one of the others?*

He sighed, disappointed. He'd dropped his guard and Welles had paid the price for it. He knew it and it unnerved him that Logan knew it, too. The last place he wanted to be was in that room with Chet and Logan trying to get inside his head, like he was some prisoner in Hell Town. He pictured Welles lying in the ship's hospital again; her bloodshot eye, bruised neck, bloodied hand.

He dreaded his next conversation with Command, having to explain to them that he'd fucked up the one thing that Isaack had been drilling into him: keep the female recruits from harm. *There goes their fuckin' PR exercise.* He stood there wishing that this was just a bad dream. He wanted to wake from his sleep, go release the survivors and start the evening over again and do things differently.

He'd let Smith go to change his clothes and left Brown and Bulk, now both armed, watching the men. Thirty-two minutes had passed since McKinley left and still there was no sign of him.

Harris started pacing along the corridor, his mind ticking over. Something that Welles said had stuck in his mind. She'd stated that Grolsh said he knew why they were here, as though the survivors had been expecting them. *But what did that mean? Expecting the* Aurora *or expecting the new recruits? Expecting to be saved? Or expecting something else?*

He heard footsteps and spun around. It was Doc.

"Are they secure?" he asked.

"Yeah," Doc said, reaching him.

"Welles make it without falling over?" he arched an eyebrow.

Doc nodded. "She just needs a few hours to get herself back together. You saw that big handprint across her throat, Saul. He nearly killed her. I think she's in shock to be honest."

"Yeah, well, I think we all are. We were expecting something, but not this and not this quick." Harris put his hands on his hips and shook his head. "Four armed men and we all missed it, because of some spilt juice and wisecracks."

"Yeah, we did," Doc nodded. "But Saul, I don't think any of us thought they'd be so bold as to attack one of our soldiers less than two hours out of that cell. Why do you think he did it?"

"Well, from what he allegedly said to her," Harris answered, shrugging, "the motive appears to be pretty clear."

"I don't know, Saul. I don't think the motive was sexual assault. Her clothes weren't torn in any way and from what she said he didn't try anything else. It seems like he was just literally trying to strangle her or subdue her and that's it."

"But he was interrupted, Doc."

They looked at each other for a moment.

Harris shook his head again. "I don't know, but did you hear Welles say that he said he knew why they were here? Or why *we* were here? Like it's not just a rescue."

Doc nodded. "But what does that mean?"

Harris shrugged. "Means something."

Just then McKinley and the three other men came walking down the corridor toward them. Grolsh was not with them. Harris stared hard at McKinley waiting for an answer.

"He must've got off the ship before Smith locked it down. We've searched this place top to bottom and he's not here, captain," McKinley told him as he approached.

"Fuck!" Harris hissed.

"Is Welles okay, Doc?" Hunter asked.

"She's a little bruised, but she'll be alright."

"Where is she?" McKinley asked. "And where're the other two?"

"Secure," Harris said, his voice tight.

Just then Smith's voice came over the ship's PA. "Captain! That footage is ready when you are, sir."

"Right, I want to see this shit," Harris said, turning and heading for the flight deck, as the others followed.

When they reached the flight deck, Smith looked around at him.

"He definitely got off the ship. I saw it on the footage," Smith told him. "He hid somewhere for a bit, then just slunk out when no-one was looking."

Harris nodded. "Show me, Welles. I want to see exactly what happened." He moved to stand behind Smith's chair while Doc, McKinley, Hunter,

Carter and Louis gathered around them. They looked at the large screen across the window in front of them.

Harris watched the footage carefully. It was as she had described it to him. They were walking along, Welles slightly in front, and Grolsh close behind, staring at her. She got the napkins, came back to the door and turned to close it. As she turned back around, Grolsh was blocking her path, standing right in her face. She eyed him for a moment, then went to step around him, but he moved in her way, blocking her. She tried the other side and he blocked her again. He said something to her and she eyed him strangely. She then went to push past him, but his reflexes were lightning fast and he had her by the throat and slammed hard against the wall in an instant. Her feet briefly left the ground and she dropped the napkins.

He held both hands on her throat, as Welles struggled to free herself. Quickly realizing that she wasn't going to be able to remove his hands, she began punching him hard in the face. In response, he used his right hand to pin one of her wrists against the wall, and used his left elbow to pin her other arm back. As he squeezed his left hand around her throat, he moved his face in very close to hers, his nose touching her cheek, saying something to her that Harris couldn't make out. To her credit, she continued to attempt to fight him off with everything she had. Harris watched as the corporal managed to free the arm pinned by the elbow and punched at the arm holding her throat. She kicked at his legs and brought her knees up for his groin, but he pressed his weight against her limiting her movement. Finally, she clawed his face, viciously grabbing hold of his cheek and digging her nails in hard. He reeled his face away, tearing the flesh as he did, and the blood spilt down his cheek.

"Oof, jeez," Hunter muttered, wincing.

"Go, Welles," Smith smiled.

"She's feisty, I'll give her that!" Carter added, crossing his arms.

They continued to watch as Grolsh's torn face only seemed to make him angrier. His eyes turned wild and he lifted her off the ground by her throat, as high as his arm could hold her. Welles looked alarmed now, her legs flailing about in midair.

"And he's stronger than he fucking looks," Carter noted, dropping his folded arms and placing his hands on his hips.

Grolsh only had her in the air for a matter of seconds, but they watched as Welles began to black out, her eyes rolling back in her head, fighting to stay open. Then Grolsh suddenly turned and looked over his shoulder. He snapped his head back around to Welles, somewhat panicked, then dropped her and ran off. She fell like a rag doll to her knees and then onto her torso and face. Within seconds Smith was there leaning over her shaking her shoulder trying to wake her, before he turned and yelled for help, then bolted off screen yelling some more.

Harris stared at the screen, mind ticking over, while the men shuffled restlessly, throwing each other looks.

Louis shook his head. "She turned her back on him. Stupid!"

"Would've made no difference, Louis," McKinley said, staring at the screen.

Carter agreed. "He lifted her up with one fucking hand, man," he told Louis.

"You do *not* turn your back on the enemy," Louis continued defiantly.

"She didn't know he was the enemy!" Doc said bluntly, shutting down the discussion.

The footage continued to roll. Smith ran back onto the screen and knelt by her side, trying to lift her up, as she slowly began to respond. McKinley came onto the screen then, gun in hand, glancing down at Welles, and then scanning the perimeter. Doc came running in next and took her off Smith's hands, pulling her up to her knees.

"Stop it," Harris ordered Smith. "Fire up the visual comms. We're going in. Doc you stay here and be my eyes and ears. Let's move out!"

*

Harris and McKinley made their way onto the Darwin, using their two-by-two cross-cover, with the other three men following close behind. They began to go over the path they'd taken when they first boarded the station. Moving from room to room, checking carefully any spots that Grolsh could hide. Everything seemed somehow quieter and cleaner than when they'd first come aboard. They took their time and checked everything thoroughly, but they cleared the three sections and found no sign of him. The station was empty. Quiet. Completely deserted.

"Fuck!" Harris hissed, dropping his weapon to his side. He took hold of his mouthpiece. "Doc? You pick up anything? Over?"

*"Negative, captain. Over,"* came his reply.

He looked at McKinley. "You sure you checked every spot on the *Aurora*?"

"Captain, I assure you we did," he replied firmly.

Carter backed him up. "Captain, we checked everything. There was no way that little fucker could've been hiding on our ship."

"How the fuck can he just disappear like that?" Hunter asked, brow scrunched. "We've missed something."

Harris looked at him, thinking. "Head back to the ship," he ordered, then turned and led the way.

He strode ahead, thinking hard as to where Grolsh could be. His gun was by his side, but he gripped it tight, ready for anything. As he made his way through Section One, back toward the dock, he heard Louis whisper loudly behind him.

"What the fuck is it?"

Harris turned and saw that McKinley had paused and was aiming his gun at something. Louis was close by his side, and Carter not far behind them.

"What?" Harris asked, sidling up beside him, gun at the ready.

McKinley's eyes were focused as he inched slowly toward one of the offices. "I don't know, sir," he said quietly. "I saw something move. I think it was a..."

A cat leaped out at them, narrowly missing Louis's face. McKinley went to fire but dropped his gun when he saw what it was.

"You fuck!" Louis spat, firing his gun at it as it ran away. He missed.

"Louis! Louis, HOLD YOUR FIRE," Harris yelled.

Louis dropped his gun, as Carter gave a throaty laugh.

"Fuck you!" Louis spat at Carter.

"Where was that fucker hiding before when we came in?" McKinley asked, not sharing the amusement of the others. "We didn't pick it up on our heat sensors."

"They're cats, McKinley," Louis said. "They fucking sneak up on people. That's what they do."

"Move out," Harris said, as he strode ahead again, making his way back to the *Aurora*. He didn't speak, but his mind was racing furiously. McKinley had just raised a very good point indeed.

*

As they entered the *Aurora*, Harris spoke to Smith over his mouthpiece, ordering him to lock the ship down behind them. He made his way to the mess hall with McKinley, Louis and Carter in tow. Hunter broke off and headed for the flight deck, telling Harris he wanted to check something out.

They entered the mess hall and saw the three survivors playing cards, while Brown and Bolkov stood and watched.

"Where is he?" Harris glared down at the three survivors.

They looked up from their card game, innocently.

"Where is he?" he continued. "He's disappeared. He has to be somewhere. Is there some sort of panic room or something on the Darwin that's not on the plans?" Harris stared at them.

"Captain, your men have just missed him," Chet said calmly. "He's scared and he's hiding. Maybe if you back off with your guns, he'll come out."

"Are you even allowed to use those weapons in our facility?" Logan challenged.

"Yes, I am," Harris said firmly, "and if this is just a misunderstanding as you say, then why is he hiding?"

"I just told you why, captain. The guns," Chet's tone, although civil, had an acidic edge to it. "Put them away, face him man to man, and he'll come out. Now, are you going to insist on keeping us prisoner? I thought we had an arrangement?"

"The arrangement didn't include you attacking one of my soldiers," he said, placing his hands on his hips.

"I *didn't* attack one of your soldiers, captain, neither did these two men."

"So, help me find Grolsh, then?"

"So you can do what, exactly?" Logan's eyes narrowed in accusation.

"Eye for an eye..." Brown's voice was low and threatening as he gave Logan a cold empty stare.

Harris flashed Brown a glare, then turned back to the survivors. "So I can lock him up and have him charged with assault on a UNF soldier."

Logan continued eyeing Harris as though he was trying to get inside his head. Harris did his best to ignore it.

"Will you assist us, gentlemen? Or will I have to throw you back in the bio cell for withholding information and obstruction?"

Fairmont looked over at Logan and Chet, who continued to stare, unblinking at Harris. The silence sat thickly around them for a few moments.

"How can we assist you, captain?" Chet said slowly, in a deep voice. "If you can't find him, how are we supposed to?"

"You can start by telling me whether you have some sort of hidden room on the station that he could be hiding in?"

"If we have a hidden room on the Darwin, then I don't know about it." Logan's gravelly voice offered, sounding quite uninterested.

Chet shrugged, and Fairmont mirrored him.

*They're lying. All of them.*

Just then, Doc's voice came over his earpiece.

*"Captain, I think you should come up to the flight deck for a moment. There's something you should see."*

"Copy that. Over," he said into his mouthpiece, then turned to the others. "McKinley, with me. The rest, stay here."

Carrie had fallen asleep on her bed. She'd wanted desperately to stay awake, but the attack had taken its toll. She'd told the other two women what had happened, and they were concerned. It was fairly obvious that it could have been any one of them. It was just Carrie who'd drawn the short straw and walked off by herself.

After she'd told them, Colt urged her to roll over and rest, so she did. She faced the wall and closed her eyes. She thought about Grolsh but didn't want to. She was angry. She should've seen it coming, but she hadn't. She went through the incident in her head and wondered whether she could've done anything to avoid Grolsh's attack, but she thought of nothing. He was too quick. She kept seeing his face as he strangled her. She thought of the words he'd spoken to her; his face had been so close. His eyes were dead, yet somehow alive with the excitement of it all. When she dug her nails into his face, the excitement had turned to sheer fury as he reeled back, then lifted her off the ground. The strength he possessed had scared her.

She knew she had to get her mind off Grolsh or she would never sleep. Without even thinking about it, her thoughts traveled to Doc. She remembered seeing those brown eyes staring into hers and his voice telling her to breathe. She remembered grabbing onto him, as she choked and coughed, struggling for air. She remembered him carrying her to the hospital, although she hadn't wanted him to. She knew Harris and the others were watching, so she'd wanted to walk herself, but she remembered how groggy she'd been, and how nice it felt to rest her head against Doc's shoulder and neck.

She recalled the last time she'd spoken to him that day, when he'd walked into the mess hall to get some coffee. She felt a little bad that she had been cold to him, but what did he expect? She ran their earlier conversation through in her mind. She remembered him saying that they needed to watch the time spent alone. She remembered the look on his face and his hand on the door, blocking her exit. Just like in the mess hall when he stood in front of her. *It was as though he didn't want to have to do it*, she thought. *He was doing it because he had to.* Did he want her to understand it wasn't coming from him, but he couldn't tell her? And what was the cause of that heated discussion he had with Harris in the hospital?

*The captain was behind it. Of course. He was the one who wanted to control their time spent alone.*

And that was the last thing she'd remembered when the tiredness finally overcame her and she'd fallen asleep.

*

When she awoke again, Packham was reading on her bunk and Colt was dozing. Packham heard her stir and tipped her head over the bunk to look at her.

"Hey, that wasn't long?" she whispered, looking at her watch.

"What's the time?" Carrie croaked, in desperate need of some more water.

"Almost 2130. You've been out for about 45 minutes," she whispered again, but Colt stirred anyway.

Carrie was feeling weird. Not just because of what had happened, but because of the dream she had just had. She got up slowly, making sure she didn't fall over again, and headed for the bathroom. Turning on the light, she looked at herself in the mirror. She was taken aback, at first. She hadn't seen herself since the incident. Half of her left eye was no longer white, but dark red in color. Bloodshot. The cheek underneath was a light purple from where she'd hit the floor. She looked down at her neck and saw a clear handprint across it. There was a distinct bruise from a thumbprint under the left side of her jaw and four small bruises along the right side of her neck. In between these darker bruises, the rest of her neck had turned a faint purple color.

She bent down to the basin, cupped some water in her hands and drank it. She cupped some more and drank and drank until her belly felt full. She turned away, undressed and stepped into the shower. She had to wash the past couple of hours away and refresh herself. She closed her eyes, held her face under the water, and tried to clear her mind, but she couldn't shake the vision of Grolsh's face, nor the dream she'd had, from her mind.

In her dream, she'd been standing against a wall with her eyes closed and felt she couldn't breathe. She opened her eyes and saw Grolsh strangling her again. He was sweating and shaking, squeezing the life out of her. She looked over his shoulder and saw Harris standing there. He gave her an unimpressed look. She turned back to Grolsh, but suddenly realized it wasn't him strangling her, it was Doc. He was staring at her, sweating and shaking, one hand around her throat, and one on the wall beside her. She panicked and grabbed onto his arm and tried to pull it away from her throat. She looked back at Harris, who was now standing there with his hands on his hips, shaking his head. She looked at Doc and suddenly realized that he wasn't actually strangling her. His hand was on her throat, but he wasn't hurting her. He was trying to push himself away, sweating and shaking as he did. Her eyes flew back to Harris and saw he was walking away. She looked at Doc again. He was closer now, failing to hold himself back, shaking, sweating and wincing, one arm against the wall. Her hands slid onto his shoulders. She tried to help him, pushing and pushing, but nothing was happening. His arms slowly began to fold, bringing him closer and closer, until his body was on hers. Her heart was racing and she could feel his was, too. Still fighting to hold himself back, still straining, somehow he moved closer and closer. She felt his breath on her face, his nose touched hers, then brushed her cheek. Then, with her heart racing and breathing rapid, his lips touched hers. Just. That's when she suddenly woke up.

She stood in the shower, trying to shake the dream from her head, despite her body wanting to be back in it. She took a deep breath and put her arms out against the wall and dipped her head down so that the water ran freely over it. *It's just a stupid dream. Like all the other stupid dreams you've been having since coming on this ship. Your subconscious is running wild. Just because Harris wants you to keep your distance, does not mean Doc has feelings for you. Doc is just friendly. He's a medic and it's his job to care for people. He said it himself, don't read anything into him being good at his job.*

*So why did he block your path both times? Why did he care about what you thought? Why didn't he just let you go and get over it?*

*Oh man, the shit you're in, and this is what you're thinking about? Grolsh nearly killed you and he's still on the loose. You're stuck in the far reaches of the UNF Space Zone, out by The Belt, with a team that barely acknowledges your existence. There are bigger things to think about here!*

She sighed and rubbed her hands over her face, resting her forehead against the wall of the shower. *Pull yourself together, Welles! You're screwing this whole thing up. You have to go out there and get back to it. You can't sit around while they deal with this. You need to step up. You need to be the soldier you know you can be. This shouldn't have happened, so don't let it continue to happen. Take responsibility. Go out there and show them your resilience. Show them you can take anything they throw at you.*

She pictured her father's wary, concerned eyes, but it only spurred her on. *Don't fail this! Don't let your father be right.* She climbed out of the shower, dried and dressed herself and when she came back out Packham and Colt were sitting on their beds waiting expectantly for her.

"You okay?" Colt asked her.

Carrie nodded a sharp soldier's nod and moved to sit on her bed. "How long do you think we'll be stuck here for?" she croaked.

Colt shrugged.

"I think we should head out and find the others," Carrie suggested.

"Are you kidding?" Colt looked at her wide-eyed. "Have you not learnt one thing about the captain yet? He's quite particular about his orders, you know."

Carrie sighed and slumped back on her bed. "Just tell me where Grolsh is, give me my gun, and I'll shoot the bastard!" she said.

Packham and Colt grinned at her, then started laughing softly, but it grew, and within seconds they were howling with laughter.

# 19

# The Vanishing

Harris and McKinley reached the flight deck to find Doc and Hunter at the console, with Smith looking over their shoulder.

"What is it?" Harris asked.

Doc motioned for Hunter to speak.

"Captain, I kept thinking about how Grolsh could just disappear like that," Hunter began, "and I remembered thinking when you guys first boarded the Darwin that it seemed smaller internally than it had looked externally as we approached it."

Harris stared blankly at Hunter.

Hunter glanced at Doc, then turned around to the console and brought up footage captured from the *Aurora's* forward cameras, as they approached the station. Harris studied it closely. It did appear substantially larger than the floor plan suggested.

"Could the extra space just be insulation and purification vents?" he asked Hunter.

"Possibly, but that's a lot of insulation and shaft space, sir."

McKinley nodded to himself as he studied the screen. "It would explain where the cat came from. We scanned every inch of that station when we boarded, and other than the four survivors, we didn't pick up any body heat, human or otherwise."

Harris looked back at Hunter. "We need to look at this footage and compare it to the floor plans. We need to figure out whether or not it's possible for there to be a hidden area on the station. I'll send for Brown and Bolkov to help."

"Yes, sir," Hunter nodded.

"Smith, you go watch the other three with Louis and Carter and send the other two up here."

"Yes, sir," he said as he turned and left.

*

Harris was looking over the Darwin's floor plans with Brown, Bolkov, Hunter, McKinley and Doc. Due to the classified nature of the station, they were unable to obtain a satellite image from overhead, but Hunter used the ship's cameras to estimate the width, using the *Aurora* and its distance to the station as a comparison. They then compared the width with the floor plans on the screen.

"Width looks fine," Brown said. "It's gotta be in the height."

"Okay, so what's the height of the Darwin?" Harris asked. "Can we work it out by using the *Aurora* as a comparison again?"

"Yes, sir," Bolkov offered, as he began tapping away on the console. Another screen appeared on the flight deck window. It displayed the image from the *Aurora*'s forward camera of the Darwin again. As Bolkov's big hands whisked around the console, the onboard computer took measurements of the distance to the station and the height of it.

"I'll get the Darwin's exact floor measurement off one of our comms sets," Hunter said, bringing up Harris's headcam on another screen, showing footage from their earlier foray to find Grolsh. Another measurement appeared on Hunter's screen. Bolkov took note of it and compared it to the measurement on his screen.

"Make sure you allow for the pressurized hull," Brown told him. "And the insulation, pipework, air purification vents and crawlspace."

The room waited in silence while Bolkov studied both figures, looking between the screens.

"According to my calculations, captain," Bolkov began, turning around to lock eyes with him, "there's plenty room for whole other floor."

Harris nodded slowly, staring at the floor plan on the screen in front of him.

"That has to be where he is," Doc said.

"If there's a whole other floor," Hunter said thinking aloud, "then what the hell else is up there?"

"And *who* else is up there?" McKinley added.

Bolkov looked over at him. "You think maybe missing crew up there?"

"Why would they be hiding from us?" Brown asked. "The *Spector*'s gone, man."

Harris and Doc exchanged a glance.

"The problem right now," Harris mused, bringing their focus back and steering them away from speculation, "is finding out how to get to this other floor."

"Is it worth a transmission to Command?" Doc asked.

Harris nodded. "You'd better join me for this one."

Doc nodded back.

Harris stood and looked around at his crew. "Keep working on these plans. If you were going to build a hidden floor on a station, where the fuck would you put the door?"

*

"Captain Harris. What is it?" Isaack asked as the transmission connected.

"Colonel Isaack, Professor Martin, as I'm sure you're aware this is First Lieutenant Walker," Harris motioned to Doc, who was sitting beside him, "the *Aurora's* medic, and my 2IC."

"Yes, we're familiar with your crew, captain," Isaack said nodding at Doc. "What's this all about?"

"I have reason to believe the floor plans for the Darwin are not complete, sir. I just wanted to ascertain whether there were some, let's say, more updated versions, or perhaps more *classified* versions, that you would like to give me?"

Professor Martin interjected. "What do you mean, captain? You have the only set of floor plans there are."

"The only *issued* floor plans, professor. I believe there to be secure, hidden rooms on the Darwin that could possibly account for the whereabouts of the missing crew."

"I'm sorry, captain. What?" Isaack asked, eyebrows raised.

"The station is approximately two stories in height, yet we have access to only one story, sir. It could account for the whereabouts of the missing crew."

"Captain, are you telling me you think the missing crew are *hiding* from you on the Darwin?" Colonel Isaack asked in disbelief.

"No, sir, I don't think it. I'm quite certain of it," Harris responded. "They're in hiding, hostage or dead."

"Why on Earth would they hide, captain," Isaack asked incredulously, "and why on Earth would you think they were hostage or dead? You found four survivors locked up."

Harris went to answer, but Martin spoke first. "Captain Harris, we found the missing ship, the *Spector*. Its homing device had been disabled, but it was spotted docked on Station Babylon approximately two hours ago."

Harris stared down the screen at them. "Alright, and you were going to tell me this, when?"

"As soon as we had the sighting confirmed and the crew located," Martin responded.

"So, have you located the crew?"

"Er, well, no. Not yet." Martin stumbled over his words, as he pushed his glasses up his nose.

"So they're still missing then?" Harris asked.

"They can't be too far away," Martin said.

"And was the *Spector*'s autopilot engaged?" Harris asked.

"Harris, the *Spector* is on Babylon, as will be the missing crew. Have you resolved the comms issue yet?" Isaack asked, changing tack.

"Not yet, no."

"Well, may I ask what you've been doing? I believe that was your mission was it not? To resolve the comms issue?"

"Yes, it was, but then we had a case of some missing crew to resolve and a virus watch on our survivors, which, although it turned out to be a false alarm and we released them, has now created another issue. One of the survivors attacked one of my soldiers and the survivor in question is now also missing."

"Attacked?" Professor Martin's curiosity was piqued.

"Yes. Tynek Grolsh attacked Corporal Welles." Harris cringed internally, waiting for the barrage.

"What?" Isaack asked. "I thought I ordered you to leave the women on the ship."

"I did, colonel. The surviving crew were released according to UNF law, and under our watch, we brought them onto the *Aurora*. You did not issue me with orders to avoid contact between the new recruits and the Darwin's crew, sir."

Isaack shook his head. "So, under your watch, Tynek Grolsh managed to attack one of your *12* soldiers? May I ask what the other *11* soldiers were doing at the time?"

Harris stared at him.

"And her condition, Lieutenant Walker?" Martin asked Doc.

"She's bruised and battered but she'll be okay," he answered.

"And the... *nature* of the attack?" Martin sounded apprehensive. His eyes stared fixedly at them.

"Asphyxiation. He strangled her," Doc said.

"I see." Martin nodded. "And do we know what led to the attack? Did she provoke him in any way?"

"No, sir. He invaded her space, she asked him to move away, then he attacked her," Doc said firmly.

"And you say that Grolsh is now missing?" Isaack entered back into the conversation.

"Yes, he is," Harris answered, "and I believe he may be hiding in some secret space on the station, that I was hoping, classification aside, you may be able to point me to."

"Well, I would love to captain, but I'm afraid that such an area does not exist," Martin said, almost mockingly.

Harris gave him a flat stare. "Well, do you have any ideas as to how this man could just vanish into thin air?"

Isaack glanced over at Martin, curious for his response.

Professor Martin shrugged and shook his head. "I'm sure you've just overlooked him somewhere."

"I assure you I did not overlook him, professor," Harris said firmly.

Isaack leaned forward over the table. "Captain Harris, I suggest you stick to your mission and focus on fixing those comms. As you're aware, when you released the survivors, Professor Martin dispatched a ship to take over the investigation. They will be there in just over two days. They'll deal with Grolsh then. If he shows his face, you throw him back in that cell, but in the meantime you stick to the plan. Do you understand?" Isaack ordered.

"The missing crew will turn up on Station Babylon, captain. I am sure of it," Martin added.

"Colonel Isaack," Doc said, "will Grolsh be formally charged with assault on a UNF soldier?"

"He will be dealt with," Professor Martin answered for Isaack.

"Good. I've kept a detailed record of the incident. I'll make sure you both get a copy," Doc told him. His voice was light enough, but Harris could still hear a sharp edge to it.

Martin gave him a slight nod in acknowledgment.

"Are we clear on your orders, captain?" Isaack piped up again. "Fix those comms."

"Yes, sir," Harris said, then leaned forward and ended the communication.

Doc looked at him. "So, did I understand that right? They said forget about trying to find the man who attacked one of our soldiers. And forget about chasing up any lead with regards to hidden chambers on the station, or the missing crew. Just, fix those comms?"

"You understood correctly."

They both sat there in silence briefly, thinking.

"So, what's the plan then, Saul?" Doc finally said.

Harris sighed, rubbing his jaw. "Plan is, we put the other three back in the bio cell until Grolsh gives himself up, or until Brown and the guys figure out how to get to where he's hiding. Meantime, we keep working on the comms to keep Command happy."

Doc nodded.

"Alright," Harris said standing up, "we're going to need all hands on deck. Go get Packham or Colt, or both if possible and bring them back to the flight deck."

"Yes, sir."

Carrie sat upright when she heard a knock at the door.

"It's Doc. Open up," he called.

She felt a flutter of nervousness rush through her at the sound of his voice. Colt opened the door.

"I need a volunteer to come help out on the flight deck," he told her.

Carrie stood and walked over to the door. "We can all go," she offered.

Doc eyed her warily. "How are you feeling?"

"I'm fine. I'm good. But I'm going stir-crazy sitting here and so are the others. Let us help." Her voice was still a little husky, her throat still dry and sore.

"No more dizziness? Did you rest?" he asked, taking hold of her chin and angling it up to view her neck.

"No more dizziness and I did sleep for a bit. I'm all good. I promise."

"Doc, she's been fine." Colt backed her up.

He dropped his hand, eyed the other two women for a second, then looked back at Carrie. "Okay, but I'll be watching you closely. Light duties only."

Carrie nodded, tied her hair back in a ponytail, then exited the room with the others.

*

As they entered the flight deck, she saw Harris pause and look up at her.

"Shouldn't you be resting, corporal?" he asked firmly.

The others in the room, McKinley, Hunter, Brown and Bulk, turned and stared at her. She suddenly felt self-conscious, especially under McKinley's piercing stare.

"She assures me she's up to it, captain," Doc answered for her, walking down the tiers of the flight deck.

"I am, sir," she said confidently. "And I don't want to sit back while everyone else is working hard to find him."

Harris studied her for a moment, eyes wary. "Alright, Welles, but you so much as *look* like you're about to pass out, I'm banning your ass until we get home," he told her. "Do you understand me?"

"Yes, sir," she said firmly, clearing the croak from her throat as she reached the console. She glanced over at Brown and saw him looking between her neck and her eye, Hunter and Bolkov doing the same. "I'm fine. Trust me," she told them.

"Welles." Harris narrowed his eyes at her. "A question."

"Yes, sir?"

"What was Grolsh saying to you when he had you up against the wall? Can you remember?"

Carrie thought for a moment, recalling Grolsh's hot breath on her face. She looked back at the captain as an uncomfortable feeling prickled her skin. "He said, 'You're ours now. You belong to us.'"

The silence sat in the room for a moment, as they all stared at her.

Harris stood and turned to McKinley. "I want you to get the others and take the survivors back to the bio cell. If they argue, tell them I'm locking them up for withholding information and obstructing justice. Wear your comms. I want evidence if they decide to speak."

"Yes, sir," McKinley gave a nod. As he walked past Carrie, his piercing eyes locked with hers. She wondered whether he was quietly reveling in the fact that he'd been right about her self-defense capabilities. Although, if he was, his face wasn't showing it.

"Bulk," Harris continued, "when Smith comes back, I want you two to fix the Darwin's comms issues once and for all. Understand?"

"Yes, sir." Bolkov gave him a slow nod.

"And I want the rest of you to keep searching for ways to get to the Darwin's hidden floor."

Colt stepped forward to look over Brown's shoulder. "There's a hidden floor?"

*

Carrie looked at Harris. "You say you saw the cat in one of the offices?"

"Yes, but that doesn't mean it came from there," he answered.

"Is there an air vent in that office?" Packham asked.

"Yeah," Brown replied, "but we checked the headcam footage. Gap's not big enough for a cat to squeeze through."

"Can you merge the current floor plan with a satellite picture to see where there are gaps big enough for an elevator or stairwell?" the sergeant continued.

Brown shook his head. "Station's classified, so there's no satellite picture, but we did figure out the approximate measurements of the station. Kiwi, bring that back up on the screen."

Hunter turned back to the console and brought up the floor plan, merged on top of a rough hexagonal background with the Darwin's approximate measurements, as worked out by Bolkov. Just then four monitors appeared beside it; McKinley's, Carter's, Smith's and Louis's.

The captain focused his attention on them. "I want to watch this."

Everyone looked at the monitors and saw Chet, Logan and Fairmont eyeing the cameras with expressionless faces.

"Taking us somewhere?" Chet asked in a low voice.

"Stand up," McKinley ordered them.

They remained seated. Fairmont looked over at Logan and Chet for his lead.

"I said stand up!" McKinley said again, more forcefully.

"I would like to know where you plan to take us?" Chet said, his voice now an octave or two higher.

"They're taking us back to the bio cell," Logan said, staring at McKinley.

"As the captain warned you earlier, due to your lack of cooperation, you are now being held for withholding information and obstructing justice," McKinley advised.

The three stared back in silence for a moment.

"Get... *up!*" McKinley ordered, his voice tight.

They continued to sit silently at the table, staring back. The seconds ticked past.

Fairmont suddenly jumped up, roaring as he did, and flipped the table over at McKinley. The lieutenant quickly dodged out of the way and snapped his gun up. Louis, Carter and Smith did the same as cards rained down over them.

"Do that again and I'll blow your FUCKIN' HEAD OFF," McKinley yelled.

Logan and Chet stood up slowly, calmly, as Fairmont breathed heavily with anger, shoulders broad and pulsing for a fight.

"You didn't say please," Chet said menacingly, his dead eyes staring at McKinley.

"C'mon Fairmont," Logan said, walking around the upturned table.

Carrie saw Harris and Doc exchange concerned looks, then turn back to the screens.

Harris watched carefully, as the three survivors walked ahead of McKinley's team. His lieutenant had motioned for his men to tag a survivor each, so Carter and Louis moved to walk slightly behind Fairmont and Chet, and Smith walked just behind Logan. McKinley stood back a little further watching all of them.

They walked in silence as they left the *Aurora* and cleared Section One of the Darwin.

As they entered Section Two, Chet turned to Fairmont. "Wouldn't it be great if Grolsh were here right now?"

"Yeah!" he laughed.

As soon as he'd spoken, there was a thud, McKinley's monitor went haywire and was suddenly viewing the floor. All at once there was yelling, gunfire and chaos, while Harris quickly eyed the monitors trying to figure out what was going on. He saw Fairmont standing over Carter, tossing his gun down the corridor. Louis and Chet appeared to be fighting, his camera moving about everywhere, and Smith's camera appeared to be falling to the floor.

He quickly eyed McKinley's monitor again and saw him getting up off the ground and shooting in the direction of what appeared to be Grolsh.

"FUCK! MCKINLEY!" Carter yelled.

McKinley snapped his head back around to see Carter's bloodied face leaning over Smith and the other three survivors darting around the corner of the corridor. He raised his gun to fire, but it was too late. They were gone. He quickly snapped back around to see that Grolsh was gone too.

"*Fuck!*" he hissed, as he swiftly moved over to Carter and looked down to see him pressing his hand on Smith's neck, which was bleeding profusely, as he choked and gargled up blood.

Doc shot forward to the console and yelled into the microphone. "Get him back to the ship, McKinley. NOW!"

Carrie watched in disbelief as McKinley swiftly removed his gun, tore off his shirt, shoved it against Smith's neck, then swung his gun back on.

"Help me grab him," McKinley barked at Carter.

The two of them lifted Smith, Carter grabbing his legs and McKinley lifting him under his arms and around his neck, holding the shirt in place.

"Louis, cover us! Stay sharp!" McKinley yelled.

"Brown, let's go get them!" Harris yelled, as he raced up the flight deck stairs.

"Meet you in the hospital!" Doc said, as he flew up the stairs behind them.

Carrie began to run up the stairs too, and Colt followed. She wasn't sure what to do, but she knew she had to go. Packham, Hunter and Bolkov stayed behind, eyes glued to the screens, their faces showing alarm.

Carrie reached the hospital and found Doc frantically running around with bags of blood in his hands.

"What can we do?" Carrie asked.

"Over there." He pointed to a cabinet. "Get out bandages and swabs. Lots of them."

Carrie and Colt started pulling out armfuls of the stuff and ran it all over to Doc, who threw them on one of the beds. He snapped on some gloves, then grabbed swabs, ripping open the sterilized bags they were in. Then they heard yelling in the distance.

"Out of the way," Doc ordered as he rushed for the door.

Carrie stepped aside and Colt cleared out into the office. Within seconds, Doc came running back through with McKinley and Harris who were holding Smith, as he continued to cough and gargle blood. They put him on one of the pod-beds, and McKinley stepped away, as Doc immediately removed McKinley's sodden shirt from Smith's neck and started applying it with fresh swabs.

"Hold them tight!" he ordered Harris, who moved into position.

Carrie eyed McKinley. His was face pale and tight. He stood there for a moment, watching, then backed off and left the room. Doc grabbed the IV he'd connected up to one of the blood bags and quickly inserted it into Smith's arm.

"Smith, you stay with me, you hear!" Harris said urgently.

Doc ripped Smith's bloodied shirt open, then quickly wiped the blood away so he could stick some monitors on him. She heard his faint heartbeat as the corresponding monitor lit up.

"D— Do— oc..." Smith gasped, as he snatched tightly onto Doc's shirt.

"I've got you, Pete. You save your breath," he told him, squeezing Smith's fist as it scrunched his shirt.

"Private, you look at me!" Harris almost bellowed at him. "We've got you, you hear? We've got you."

Doc moved the swabs slightly, trying to figure out what the damage was. Carrie saw blood pooling over his hands.

"Fuck," he said worriedly, "he's losing a lot of blood."

"Capta—" Smith gargled as he struggled to get out the words he wanted to say. Within seconds his body began to calm, and his grip loosened around Doc's shirt.

"Smith! SMITH?" Harris yelled.

The heart monitor suddenly fell to a single long beep. Doc looked over at it, then snapped his eyes back to the young private.

"PETE!" Doc yelled, as he started pumping his chest. "Stay with me, Pete!"

"Doc, his eyes aren't looking at me," Harris said worriedly.

"Just keep holding his neck!" Doc furiously pumped Smith's chest as his body fell completely limp, his hand falling from Doc's shirt; Carrie could see it bounce with every compression Doc made.

She turned and walked slowly to the doorway of Doc's office. She saw Carter standing there, holding a bandage to his bleeding nose, which was clearly broken. Colt stood by Louis, holding a bandage to his shoulder, and Brown stood on his own, staring at the wall.

"C'mon, Pete. *C'mon...*" she heard Doc's voice pleading.

She looked out the doorway into the corridor and saw Smith's blood on the floor, smeared by their footprints. She listened as Doc continued to pump Smith's chest, exhaling loudly, rhythmically, stopping only to breathe his breath into the young man.

"Doc," Harris said quietly, "his eyes aren't coming back to me. They're staring at nothing."

"He's lost... a lot... of blood... too much," Doc managed as he continued to pump breathlessly.

"Doc?" Harris said.

"I'm not giving up! A few more minutes," Doc panted.

Carrie looked around at the pod-bed. Doc was sweating now and he had Smith's blood halfway up to his elbows, breathing desperately into soldier's mouth. The silence on the *Aurora* was deafening, broken only by the sounds of Doc's panting as he continued with the chest compressions, and the long flat beep of the heart monitor.

Harris's brown face looked pale as he reached up with one of his bloodied hands and closed Smith's eyes.

"Doc, call it," he said. "His eyes are lost. He's gone."

Doc glanced up at him, then back down to Smith's face.

Harris eyed the private as well. "You said it yourself. He's lost too much blood." The captain looked Doc firmly in the eye. "Call it," he ordered.

Doc started slowing the pumps to Smith's chest.

"What's the time, Doc?" Harris asked softly, but firmly.

Doc stopped and stepped back from Smith's body, holding his bloodied hands out slightly to the side. He wiped his mouth on his shoulder, staring at Harris, then back at Smith's lifeless body. Doc reluctantly lifted his arm to read his watch. He looked at it but couldn't see as it was covered in blood. He pulled his shirt up and wiped the face of it.

"2209," Doc said.

Harris nodded at him slowly, then let go of Smith's neck.

Carrie turned and moved slowly out into the corridor, feeling as though she were floating. The only sound now was the single flat beep of the heart monitor. She heard Doc yell *FUCK!* and there was a simultaneous loud bang that made her flinch. She stood in the corridor looking down at Smith's blood smeared along the floor and felt her whole body begin to rattle with shock.

Something moved to her right, and she looked over to see McKinley standing there, shirtless, and covered in Smith's blood. His hands were by his sides, and he was looking down at his feet, his face ashen, his jaw clenched.

"A— are you okay?" she managed to croak. "Are you hurt?"

He looked at her out of the corner of his eye and shook his head very slightly.

The heart monitor stopped, then. Doc must've turned it off. It was so quiet now. Colt made her way out into the hall. She had some towels in her hand and walked over to the line of blood and began to clean it up. She looked numb, like she was on autopilot. Carrie walked over and took one of the towels and began to help her.

She could hear slight movement coming from the rooms, but no-one was speaking. She wiped at the blood, amazed at how much there seemed to be. Her heart raced, mirroring the shaking of her hands. Colt's vigorous wiping movements sent a whiff of the blood straight to Carrie's nostrils. She suddenly felt woozy. *Oh, shit! I can't pass out. Not now.* She plonked down on her backside and slid her way backward to lean up against the wall and started taking deep breaths.

"Put your head between your knees," McKinley said in a quiet, tight voice.

She glanced up at him, and those piercing blue eyes stared back. She put her head down and began taking deep breaths again. She started feeling better.

"What do we do now, captain?" she heard Carter ask, his voice strained.

"You get your nose looked at," Harris said, somewhat softly.

"Fuck that, captain," Louis shouted angrily. "We have to get them and *get* them now!"

"No, Louis," Harris told him.

"What do you mean, no?"

"We need to regroup, Louis." Harris told him. "They'll be long gone into their hiding place. If we go after them now, it will be futile. You're injured, Carter's injured. We need to regroup! Hunter will have the ship locked down, so they can't get on here. We have to deal with Smith, and we need to figure out where the fuck they're hiding, so we know what we're dealing with," Harris said in tense, angry voice.

"And we need to fully brief the team, captain," Doc said firmly.

Carrie looked over her shoulder through the doorway and saw Doc and Harris staring at each other. Just then, Hunter, Bolkov and Packham came walking down the corridor. They saw the bloodied towels.

"Smith..." Colt shook her head at them.

"We saw over the comms," Hunter said, clenching his jaw.

Carrie looked back into the hospital and saw that Smith still had his headpiece on.

"Ok, listen up!" Harris called from the doorway to Doc's office. He looked around to make sure everyone was paying attention. "Everyone just take a few minutes to absorb this, alright? Smith is dead. Do what you have to do, but I want you all in the mess hall in 20 minutes. That's all I can give you. We need to move on this. Do you understand?" Harris voice was authoritative, but not harsh. She heard the compassion that he was trying to convey.

He turned and walked off in the direction of his quarters. Brown exited the room and headed down the corridor toward the mess and the pilots followed. Colt stood up and took her bloodied towels back into the rooms.

"Where shall I put this, Doc?" she asked softly.

Carrie stood and turned to see Doc looking down at the towel as he took it from her. He looked over at Louis. "Laser fire?"

Louis shook his head. "He ripped into me with his hands and teeth!"

Doc shot him a confused look, then turned and studied Carter's face.

"I'll be with you in a second," he said, and headed back into the hospital where Smith lay.

McKinley turned abruptly then, and walked off in the direction of his room, and Colt followed behind, to hers. Carrie stood there for a moment not sure what to do. She looked through into the hospital and saw Doc placing a sheet over the young private.

*How did this happen …?* A couple of hours ago they were all playing cards, and now this. All because of the incident between her and Grolsh. Did she cause this? Was this her fault? If she hadn't left the mess hall on her own, would this have happened? *Would Smith still be alive?*

She moved to stand in the doorway, "C— can I do anything?" she asked, although her voice did not come easy.

Doc looked at her, and his eyes held a quiet devastation to them. He shook his head slightly, then walked over to a basin, snapped off his gloves, and started scrubbing his hands.

She watched him for a moment, then looked down at her own hands, and noticed they were surprisingly clean.

Harris sat on the edge of his bed and rubbed his face in his hands. Two years he'd been on the *Aurora* and he'd never lost a man. Some had been injured, but never before had he lost one, despite all the battles they'd had with pirates and thugs. Never before had he lost a team member on his watch, under his command. *Smith was just a kid. A kid with a bright future ahead of him and now it was gone in the blink of an eye… the blink of an eye… Twenty-one was just too young. Did I do this? Could I have stopped this?*

*Should I have warned them? Told them of my suspicions? What the fuck have I done ...?*

An image of Sibbie and Etta seemed to gently settle in his mind, and something about their presence was almost calming, reassuring, nurturing. He gave a saddened chuckle and shook his head. *You're going crazy, Saul... you're going crazy...* He inhaled deeply, trying to shift the lump in his throat. He hardened his face, clenched his teeth and violently shook the two old women from his mind. He had to pull it together. He had to be the person with strength and leadership for his crew. He had to pull the rest of them together so they could move forward and do what they had to do. He stood from the bed and eyed his clean shirt in the mirror, then looked down at his watch. He'd had to clean it just like Doc had had to do with his. He eyed the time and noted that the 20 minutes were almost up. It wasn't long, but that was all the time he could afford.

When he arrived at the mess, he saw that half the team had already gathered, with the exception of Carter, Louis, Doc and McKinley. Those that were there displayed a mixture of emotions: concern, anger and shock, primary among them.

"We'll give the others a few minutes to get here," Harris told them.

McKinley walked in then and took a seat. He'd used his 20 minutes to clean up and change. Everyone sat in silence for a few more minutes, before Louis and Carter walked in. Louis had a bandage over his neck and shoulder, and Carter still held a bandage of ice to his nose, which was now looking rather fat and purple. Clearly, Doc had run out of time to see to him. Harris gave Carter a subtle nod. He was Smith's roommate, and he was going to feel it later. If they ever got to sleep, that is.

Doc came in then. He'd also found time to change. He'd had to. Walking around covered in Smith's blood, was not what the team needed to see right now.

"Ok, listen up," Harris said, trying his hardest to sound strong and firm. "Here's where we are at. We have four men on the loose. Four *dangerous* men, who we now want for murder, not to mention several counts of assault." He swiftly looked in the eyes of each team member. "We have good reason to believe there is a second, hidden floor on the station. We believe this is where Grolsh went into hiding, and where all four of them are hiding now. Although we still don't really know what happened on this station, it would seem obvious that these four men had something to do with it.

"Now, we know the station's ship, the *Spector*, was missing when we arrived. Last I spoke to Command, they informed me it had shown up on Station Babylon, but they'd been unable to locate the missing crew. The way I see it, this could mean one of two things." Harris held out his fist, then unfurled his thumb: "*One*, the rest of the crew took off to escape these four men and have vanished for their own safety." He unfurled his index finger: "Or *two*, the missing crew are here and are being held hostage on the second floor, or they're dead, and the *Spector* was sent off so that we would assume they'd left, and the survivors then locked themselves in that cell so we'd believe they were victims in all of this. It's not crazy to think that these four men killed the other five... because we do not believe that these men are entirely normal."

"What do you mean, not entirely normal?" Carter asked, his brow furrowed in confusion.

Harris eyed him and took a deep breath, "Doc and I have come to believe—now we have no proof of this, this is just a theory—but we believe these guys aren't just UNF scientists. We think they may have been put through full UNF training, like real soldiers... and when I say real soldiers, I don't mean just any soldiers. We think they've been engineered to a certain extent to improve their capabilities."

"What the fuck does that mean?" Louis asked, struggling to control his anger.

Harris went to answer, but Doc stood and turned to the men.

"We're fairly certain they've had their senses heightened, for one," he told them. "It would appear that Sharley and the crew were studying animal hunters, that's why all those animals were on the manifests. We think he was studying their senses and how their particular senses enabled them to be great hunters. We're almost positive the four men's hearing is advanced. They all had scars behind their ears and it seemed that they heard people coming long before they saw them. Now, we're not 100 percent sure, but there's a good chance their eyesight and sense of smell are also advanced. And clearly, they're very strong and they can fight."

"I *knew* Logan was watching me," Louis seethed, eyes as dark as his skin.

"Why didn't you tell us about this before?" Carter was clearly trying to restrain his anger.

"We weren't sure of anything before," Harris answered his question. "We're still not exactly sure—

"You must've known something," Louis accused, shaking his dreadlocked head. "Why were Brown and McKinley armed earlier?"

Harris noticed both McKinley and Brown flash each other uncomfortable looks.

"They were armed because I did not trust those men. I had no proof against them, only theories, so I took my chances and *yes*, I armed some of my men." Harris tried hard to control his voice. He wouldn't normally stand for such attitude from a soldier, but Louis had spent a lot of time working with Smith in the stores and on mess duty, so he was going to cut him some slack.

Harris looked around at everyone. "These men are cunning. They've studied great hunters, animal and human alike. They clearly know how to stalk their prey. Grolsh proved that when he snuck up on McKinley. They also know how to escape unnoticed, hence the reason Grolsh got out of that mess hall in the first place. Now you connect all of that with the possibility of them using Sharley's mind-fucking techniques from Hell Town and you got yourself one hell of an enemy. We need to be extremely careful with these guys. We cannot take any further chances. Do you understand me?" Harris looked around at them. "Anybody got any questions?"

Brown piped up. "Yeah. If what you say is true, how the hell are we going to get these guys, seeing as they've got these extra senses and shit? They're going know we're coming way before we get anywhere near 'em."

"Well, that's something I need to figure out, but before we deal with that we have to figure out where they are exactly and how to get to them," Harris answered.

"You think they're some kind of experiment gone wrong?" Hunter asked.

"I think the experiment was planned. Whether it has gone wrong, I don't know. I guess we'll find out if we find the bodies of the other five men. I think the UNF was trying to create the perfect soldier. Let's hope, for our sake, they haven't accomplished that."

Harris looked around the room to see if there were more questions.

"Captain?" Welles spoke up.

He looked over at her.

"Permission to carry a gun, sir. Like the others," she asked.

"Permission granted, corporal. You too, Colt and Packham. I want everyone armed at all times." He eyed them all again. "I will not take any more chances, I can assure you. Now, we've got some work to do. Colt, Welles, get some coffee and food going. We need to fuel up the team. I want everyone else on the flight deck looking at those plans... except you, Doc. You... go do what you need to do. Alright, let's get to it."

Harris clapped his hands together and the team went into action.

# 20

# The Key to the Door

Carrie and Colt made up pots of coffee and tea and plates of sandwiches, doing so in complete silence. Both their minds utterly consumed with what had just happened. Colt's face was paler than usual and there seemed to be gray clouds where her sunny eyes had once been. Carrie could not erase the image of Smith's dying face from her mind. It seemed to be stuck there, as though it were a broken-down slide show. She focused hard on the sandwiches trying desperately to expunge it, but her shaking hands and jittery heart were a constant reminder.

Colt spoke into the intercom and notified the flight deck that the food was ready. Harris responded, telling them he'd send the crew down, one by one, to fuel up. Carrie's mind wandered to thoughts of Doc and how he was doing. She'd watched his face closely during the briefing. He had a haunted look about him as he sat there listening to Harris. When he got up to speak, his face and eyes were hard. The quiet devastation from before was now coupled with anger. She wanted to tell him it wasn't his fault and that things would be okay, but she knew they wouldn't be. Smith was dead. And there was nothing anyone could do to bring him back.

Her thoughts pressed uncomfortably inside and a need to check on the lieutenant overwhelmed her. She felt as responsible for his pain as she did for Smith's death. She poured a mug of coffee and grabbed a plate of sandwiches to take to him. As she made her way down the corridor, she met Carter, who now had some tape across his bulging purple nose.

"Broken?" she asked him.

"Well and fuckin' truly," he seethed, as he continued past her down the corridor. "I'll break more than Fairmont's nose when I see that fuck again!"

When she made Doc's office, he was coming out of the examination room.

"Hey," she said, throwing him a sympathetic smile. "I thought you could do with some fuel."

"Thanks," he said quietly, taking the coffee from her. "I need this." He had a sip, then took the plate from her and walked over and placed it on his desk.

Carrie glanced into the hospital and saw Smith's body still lying there under the sheet. Doc saw her looking at it.

"I'm going to take care of him now," he told her, taking another sip of his coffee, then placing it down on the desk as well.

"Do you want a… a hand?" she asked him.

He shook his head. "No, I'm fine." He walked past her into the hospital.

"I'm sure Captain Harris won't have a problem with me helping you in these circumstances."

He stopped and looked around at her for a moment, his eyes searching hers, perhaps curious as to where the comment about Harris had come from. "I'm sure he wouldn't either, but you don't need to see this stuff." He continued over to Smith's bed and looked down to where he lay. "This is my job, Welles. I'll deal with it."

"Doc, we're soldiers. Unfortunately, people die in our line of work. That's a given. But it doesn't mean we have to deal with it on our own."

He looked at her for another moment. "Welles, this stuff stays with you. You don't forget it once you've seen it."

"It's too late, Doc. I already did." She stepped into the room. "Besides, with my, er, *specialty*, I've seen dead bodies before."

Doc nodded. "You've seen enemies die… from afar. This is different."

"So, I won't look at him. I'll look somewhere else. I'll look at you."

Doc stared at her again briefly, then looked back down at the sheet covering Smith.

She walked over and stood on the other side of the bed. "I'm still here because Smith came along when he did. I owe him this much. Now, what do you want me to do?"

"Jesus, you're stubborn," he said, shaking his head.

"Yes, I am. So what do you want me to do?"

He sighed. "Alright. Bottom drawer over there," he pointed, "body bag."

For some reason the words "body bag" struck her like an ice pick to the spine. So final, so horrible. Regardless, she kept any expression from her face, nodded, and moved to the drawer. She heard Doc flick on some gloves and start doing something behind her but didn't look around in case she saw Smith's face. When she had one of the body bags in her hand, she made her movements obvious, so Doc would know she was coming back his way.

He was standing at the foot of the bed. He'd removed the sheet altogether and was now removing Smith's boots.

She took a deep breath. "Okay, so how do you want to do this?" she asked.

"Lay it out on that bed," he pointed to the bed adjacent, "and I'll lift him over onto it."

She nodded and laid out the bag. Once in place, she unzipped it, then she moved around to the opposite side of the bed facing Doc. She kept her eyes on the empty body bag in front of her but could see Doc in her peripheral vision removing the heart monitor discs and dragging the IV and blood bag away from Smith's bed. He kicked a lever and wheeled the private's bed alongside hers, keeping it away from the wall slightly. She focused hard on the medic's face, trying to keep her eyes away from Smith. Unfortunately, she could still easily make out the dark red color that seemed to be all over him.

Doc looked at her. "Can you kick your lever and move the bed out a bit?"

She looked down, found the lever and kicked it, the wheels unlocked, and she moved the bed down to line up with his.

"You ready?" he asked her.

She nodded.

"Hold the bag open as wide as you can," he told her, "and just... look somewhere else."

She nodded again, still focusing hard on Doc's brown eyes, and trying to ignore her peripheral vision.

"Have you had to do this often?" she asked, trying to keep her mind busy.

"Yeah, a few times," he said, "but I never really knew them before their death. It's never easy, but at least when they're strangers you have a better chance of letting it go."

"Yeah," she nodded vaguely. "I mean, I've killed people, right. I've watched people die, but I never knew them, and they were bad people so it was easy not to care. I still think about them from time to time, but the only dead person I've seen that I cared about was my mum."

Doc paused and looked up at her for a brief moment, but then continued on. He grabbed Smith's feet and moved them across to her bed, tucking them inside the end of the body bag. Carrie moved her eyes to focus hard on the far wall.

"We had a viewing of her body before the funeral," she continued. "I was glad I saw her one last time but... at the same time, I wished I hadn't seen her like that. *Dead*. You're right, you know. It doesn't leave you."

Doc looked up at her again, and their eyes connected.

"Are you sure you're up for this?" he asked her.

"Yeah," she nodded and gave a half-smile. "I'm just trying to distract myself."

His eyes scanned hers skeptically, but he let his gaze go and continued on. He then moved to the head of the bed, slid his arms under Smith's body, hooked his hands up around his shoulders, and lifted his torso over to the other bed. As he did, she felt Smith's arm fall against her hand and she recoiled slightly. Doc quickly grabbed it and tucked it alongside the torso, glancing briefly at her again. He moved the other bed away and stood alongside Smith's body, straightening it in line with the bag, then he reached down and started zipping it up. He paused for a moment as the zip reached Smith's chin, then zipped it closed.

He looked up at her. "You okay?"

She nodded, swallowing. "What next?"

"I've got to move him into the cool room."

He walked over to a door in the far corner of the room, which she had assumed was another storeroom. He punched in a code, the door unlocked and he wheeled Smith's bed inside.

"Do you need a hand?" she called out.

"No, I got it," he said.

She heard the sound of the body bag ruffling as Doc moved it, then she thought she heard the zip again. *Was Doc saying a last goodbye? Maybe this was something he'd wanted to do alone?* She looked over at Smith's empty boots lying on the floor and felt a pang of sadness squeeze her chest.

After minute or two, Doc came back out of the room, wheeling the empty bed. Somehow the image of the empty bed turned her pang of sadness into a deeper pain, like a tearing of flesh right down to her gut. Doc closed the door, locking it. She looked from the empty bed to the locked door. Again, so final.

Doc began lining up the bed underneath its pod cover and locked the lever to hold it in place. She walked over to the other one and did the same, then looked down at the bloodied sheets.

"What do we do with these?" she asked, forcing the words past the lump in her throat.

Doc grabbed the sheets and pulled them off. She saw the mattress underneath was covered in plastic, and more blood sat pooled on top of it. Doc walked into the examination room, to the window in the wall, and sent the sheets through it. She heard the snap of gloves and the sound of water running.

She stood looking at the bits of blood that had splattered onto the cupboards. "What should I clean this up with?"

He saw the stains on the cupboard and the mattress cover. "There's some hospital grade disinfectant over there," he pointed. "Make sure you put some gloves on first, though."

She found the disinfectant, grabbed some gloves and paper towels and headed back to the cupboards. She eyed the pool of blood gathered on top of the mattress and paused. Smith's body had been removed, but he was still here. She glanced down at his empty boots and pictured him in her mind, standing in the comms room giving her his awkward smile and flashing his slightly crooked teeth. Her eyes began to sting and she felt them begin to well along with the lump in her throat. She quickly pressed her eye with the back of her hand to remove the excess water.

"Is your eye hurting?" Doc asked, walking over to her. He placed his hand on the side of her face, his thumb lifting her eyelid open slightly, so he could examine it.

She quickly realized it was her bloodshot eye that she'd pressed. She grabbed hold of his hand and removed it from her face. "No, it's fine. I'm just... it's fine, really." She gave him a reassuring smile.

He studied her for a moment, his brown eyes searching hers, then he looked down at his hand, which she was still holding. She released it, awkwardly, then turned to the wall and began cleaning it. Doc stood there for a moment looking at her, then cleared his throat and bent down to pick up Smith's boots.

She cleaned the cupboards and mattress cover in silence, while Doc packaged up Smith's shoes and locked them in the cool room with his body. He then began to pack up the IV and blood bag.

"I'm done," Carrie finally said, looking at the clean cupboards and mattress cover. She scrunched up the bloodied paper towels and dumped them in the small clinical waste bin in the corner of the room then removed her gloves. She then scrubbed her hands and arms. She looked around the room. "Is that it? Shall I remake the bed?"

Doc glanced around. "It's just the report work now. I'll do the bed later."

Carrie nodded. "I guess I better get back then."

"Yeah," Doc gave her a half-smile. "Thanks. I appreciate it."

"No worries," she smiled gently back. "And don't forget your coffee, Doc."

He glanced at the doorway to his office, where he'd left his 'fuel'. "Ah, yes," he said, then returned his eyes to hers. He put on his best Australian accent, albeit softly. "No worries."

Carrie gave him a warm smile and left. As she walked down the corridor she thought about how Doc seemed to be handling things okay. It should've made her feel better, but it didn't. Her chest hurt a little, and there was a strange empty feeling in the pit of her stomach.

Smith was still dead.

She felt her jaw tighten. *Where was Grolsh? Where the hell were the survivors?*

Harris eyed Bolkov intently, awaiting an answer.

"Captain, I see four possible points of entry for hidden access."

"Where?" Harris moved to look over his shoulder at the floor plan superimposed over the basic hexagonal shape of the station they had measured.

"There's gap here behind Sharley's office." Bolkov pointed with his thick, rough, fingers. "Also here, behind labs. One here by mess hall, and one by rec area."

Brown looked over his other shoulder. "Nah, the mess hall and the labs will be pipework space. The rec room space is probably air vents, as the main shaft is located here." He pointed to an area close by.

"Well, that leaves us with only one area then?" Harris arched his eyebrow at Brown.

"It's that easy?" Hunter queried skeptically.

"Wait, what about this space here?" Packham said, pointing to a small gap near to where one of the emergency exit doors lead onto the dock.

"That looks small," Harris said.

"Well, what if it's not a stairwell, but a ladder?" Colt offered. "Manhole size?" "I guess secret rooms need their emergency exits, too?"

"Hunter, bring up some camera footage of that area from when we first boarded," Harris ordered.

"Yes, sir," Hunter started scanning over the footage.

Harris looked back over at the plan. "What about these? Too small?" he asked Brown, pointing to some gaps behind the store and some of the other labs."

"Nah, I think that's pipework. The store will be an air vent or air well. But we can check it out," he shrugged. "Without the structural drawings, I'm just guessing here."

"Okay, got it," Hunter announced.

Everyone looked up at the screen and saw Harris's monitor as they approached the emergency exit.

"Alright, pause there," Harris ordered. The image on the screen clearly showed the exit door and the wall beside it, which jutted out a couple of foot.

Harris looked at Brown. "That wouldn't be pipework behind there?"

"Well, it could be," he shrugged again, "but there's no real reason for it to go there when it's only corridor and dock. It's worth a look."

"Good work." Harris gave Packham and Colt a nod. "Alright, so our guess is that the main access is behind Sharley's office, with another exit by the dock. Hunter, get me footage of when we cleared Sharley's office. We need to figure out how to access that space."

*

Carrie walked out to the firing range. She kept picturing Smith lying in the body bag, kept seeing Doc take off Smith's shoes, kept seeing the blood. She felt strange. Numb. It had been Smith who'd ultimately saved her from Grolsh, yet he was the one who was now dead. *How did that come to be?*

She picked up the laser pistol beside the range and fired. She barely aimed, she just shot. Then she closed her eyes, took a deep breath, aimed again and fired. It felt somewhat therapeutic, as though she was breaking the ice shell of numbness around her with each shot. She ran over to the next range and snapped off a quick shot, she spun around and ran back to the first one and fired again. She walked a few paces backward, then swiftly stepped to the left and fired at that target, then she stepped to the right and fired at the other one.

Then she heard a noise behind her.

She spun around to the gym equipment and saw McKinley sitting there on a weight bench, sipping a cup of coffee, watching her. They stared at each other for a moment, before he put his cup down, stood, and strode in her direction. His cold stare and quick pace made her nervous. He looked as though he was charging straight for her, but as he reached her he skimmed past to the range console and brought up the targets on the screen. He turned and stared at her for the seconds it took to bring up the results. She stared back, trying to control her nerves, wondering what he was doing exactly.

When the targets came up, he examined them carefully. All 1s. He looked back at her curiously for a moment, then moved right up close, towering over her.

"If you ever get the chance to get off this fuckin' ship, you make damn sure you do *that*, out there!" he ordered in a low, tight voice.

She stared into his piercing blue eyes. They didn't seem quite so cold now. Instead, they burned with a fiery anger, but she knew it wasn't directed at her.

"I'd love to," she told him firmly, although her throat was still tight.

"Good," he breathed, then turned to walk back to the gym and his coffee.

"McKinley?" she called after him.

He stopped and turned around.

"I need you to officially issue me with my gun. I can't shoot anyone without it."

He looked at her, nodded, then waved her to follow.

*

When they got to the weapons store, Colt, who'd joined them, looked around like a kid in a toy shop.

"Which one can we have?" she asked eagerly.

"On the *Aurora* you have standard issue," McKinley said, walking over to the UNF pistols. "When you go off the ship, they get bigger." He picked up a pistol and checked that it was loaded. He handed it to Colt, along with a box of clips, then did the same with Carrie. He turned, got one more set and handed it to her. "For Packham," he said. "Now I've officially issued you with your gun. We're done here."

McKinley headed back to his coffee, while Colt and Carrie headed back to the flight deck. As they entered, they saw the team watching an enhanced version of Harris's headcam footage. It appeared to be Sharley's office. Harris glanced over at them and then back at the screen. Carrie handed Packham her gun and clips. The sergeant checked the gun was loaded, then stood up, tucked the pistol down the back of her pants and left the clips on the console.

"What about the picture frame?" Brown asked.

"Perhaps underneath desk," Bolkov offered.

"Noticeboard," Hunter suggested.

"What are we looking for?" Colt asked.

Packham leaned over and filled them in quietly, whilst Harris continued to stare at the screen.

"We're not going to know until we go back in there and try, captain!" Louis said impatiently.

"Time is money, Louis," Harris said, not taking his eyes off the screen. "We need to know what to try before we get there, in case we come under attack."

"What if the access requires some sort of security code?" Carrie asked.

"We've got equipment for that," Harris told her, eyes focused on the screen. "Smi— *Brown*... will get us in."

The room fell silent.

Harris walked into Doc's office. The medic sat at his desk in front of some e-files. He looked up at Harris, but nothing was said. Harris glanced into the hospital and saw that Smith's body was gone.

"I've just finished the report," Doc told him. "You want to sign it off while you're here?"

Harris walked over and sat down at the desk. Doc handed him the e-file and he scanned it. His eyes jumped to the "Cause Of Death". It read:

Massive blood loss due to ruptured int. jugular vein. Cause of rupture unknown.

He quickly scanned the rest of the report.

"I've also done the reports for Welles, Carter and Louis," Doc told him.

"What was Louis's injury?"

"It certainly wasn't a gun or a knife. He said Chet just ripped at him with his hands and teeth."

"His hands and teeth?"

Doc nodded. "His wounds looked like an animal attack; teeth marks, scratches, bruising."

"And that's what happened to Smith?" Harris furrowed his brow.

"I guess so." Doc sat back in his chair. "They appear to like going for the jugular... not unlike a lot of hunters in the animal kingdom."

"Do you think that's possible?"

Doc shrugged. "Given their strength? You've seen what desperate and psychotic people will do in battle situations, Saul. Anything goes."

"But Chet failed with Louis?"

"Louis's stronger than Smith. Maybe he just put up a better fight? Then again, Logan did seem a lot more aggressive than Chet."

"Yeah, or maybe Chet just hides his aggression better?" Harris said skeptically.

Doc shrugged again and sat forward, leaning his elbows on the table. "Why didn't Grolsh kill Welles? She's weaker than Smith. It would've been easy for him."

"I don't know. Maybe he's not as adept as the others. Maybe Smith coming along spooked him."

"It doesn't make sense," Doc said, shaking his head. "Smith was taken down in an instant. I think if Grolsh wanted to kill Welles, he would've done it. He very clearly choked her. There was no tearing at her neck, and in the end, he let her go. I don't think he was trying to kill her."

Harris shrugged. "I don't know, Doc, but I think we've found out how to get to them."

"Yeah?"

"We found two spots. One we think is a main entrance, the other a smaller, secondary route."

"What's the plan?"

"We go, figure out how to get in, then we try and smoke them out."

"What if the missing crew are up there being held prisoner?"

"Then they're all incapacitated for a while, but they'll live. We'll have two teams. The main one on the entrance, and a smaller one on the secondary access route." He looked at his watch. "It's 00:16. Let's go and end this shit."

Carrie stared hard at the floor plan. If she ever got the chance to go on the Darwin, she wanted to know it like the back of her hand. She wanted to know every possible place someone could hide and attack from. Of course, the floor plan was only for the ground floor. What the second floor held was anybody's guess.

Harris, Doc and McKinley entered the flight deck.

"Listen up, people. We're going to do this, and we're going to do it now. We'll move out in two teams. Team one will focus on breaking through from Sharley's office and that team will be myself, Doc, Brown and Louis. Team two will be at the secondary route and that team is McKinley, Carter, and Bulk? I'm calling you up!"

Bolkov nodded. "Sir!"

Carrie looked at Harris, who registered her look of disappointment.

"Welles, you are injured."

"So are Carter and Louis, sir?"

Harris shot her a stern look.

"Yes, sir," she said, looking him in the eye, controlling any emotion she felt. She glanced over at Doc, wondering whether he'd said anything to Harris. He looked back at her, but she couldn't read his face. She glanced at McKinley too, but he, like Doc, was unreadable.

"Let's move out," Harris yelled.

She watched as they all left the flight deck. She didn't say anything; didn't complain or sigh. She was going to handle this differently. She moved to stand behind Hunter and Packham, who both glanced at her as she did. She avoided their eyes and stared hard at the screen as the headcams began to click on, one by one.

She watched as the teams re-armed themselves with laser-fire rifles and bullasers, and headed for the exit.

They did their two-by-two cross-cover as one group. Slowly and without incident, they reached Sharley's office, then McKinley's group broke off and continued on around to Section Three and the emergency exit. Carrie and the team on the flight deck watched the monitors carefully, but the Darwin was empty. Deathly quiet. Eerie.

"Well, both groups have made their targets easy," Hunter noted. "That's either a good sign or a bad sign..."

Carrie, Packham and Colt exchanged glances.

Together, they watched both groups as they got to work trying to find a way to enter the hidden spaces. McKinley stood guard as Bolkov and Carter searched for theirs. In Harris's team, Louis stood at the door while Harris, Doc and Brown tried to find a way into their space. Brown was inspecting the picture frame on the wall, Doc was feeling his way around the desk and Harris was running his hands along the noticeboard. Suddenly they heard a clicking noise.

"I've got something," Harris said quietly, and he began rotating the noticeboard around from a landscape to a portrait position. They heard another noise and the wall which Brown had been inspecting started to rise up. Doc, Brown and Harris stepped back and snapped up their guns.

Suddenly a loud, high-pitched squeal pierced their ears.

The comms went dead, and the power blacked out on the *Aurora*.

"Fuck!" Hunter called out into the blackness.

———— ★ ★ ★ ————

Harris yelled in pain at the squealing in his ears. "Aargh, jeez!"

He glanced around and saw the other men were holding their earpieces away too. As soon as the high-pitched squeal stopped, static filled their ears.

"What the fuck was that?" Louis winced.

"Flight deck, do you copy? Over." Harris spoke into his headpiece as he put the earpiece back in. Static continued. He looked over at Doc.

"Maybe it's got something to do with the wall?" Doc suggested, eyeing it.

Harris looked over to where the wall had risen. Behind it, the closed doors of an elevator.

"Brown, get over here and help me open this fucker," Harris ordered. "Doc, keep trying to raise the flight deck!"

Carrie, Hunter, Colt and Packham sat on the flight deck in darkness, until the emergency lighting slowly blinked on. At first it bathed them in a dim red hue, but it slowly blanched out into a bright white again.

"Okay, where are the screens?" Hunter asked anxiously. "Where are our comms?"

Packham's hands flew around the console hitting buttons and flicking switches. "I'm not getting anything. It's dead!"

"Fuck, we're blind here. We gotta get the comms up and we gotta get them up now!" Hunter yelled. "What else is down?"

"I can't re-connect to the external power source," Packham told him. "We're on the *Aurora*'s power cells right now."

"Colt, you know where the comms panel is, down below in the cargo hold?" Hunter called over his shoulder.

"Yes, sir," she answered.

"Check it out! Welles go with her."

"Yes, sir."

Carrie and Colt ran for the cargo hold. They knew the ship was locked down, but they moved swiftly, arms out in front with handguns ready, doing a cross-cover past each doorway. When they made it to the hold, Colt ran to a structure in the corner, swiped her pass and opened the glass paneling that covered a board of buttons, switches and cords. She started running her fingers over every item, checking them and mumbling to herself, while Carrie kept her eye and gun on the door.

"There's nothing wrong here. It looks fine," Colt said with a sense of urgency. "We better head back."

As they reached the top of the stairs, Colt stopped at the intercom and tested to see if it worked. It didn't.

"Shit! The entire system is down," she said. "Even the internals."

They made their way back to the flight deck assuming the same cross-cover, Colt facing forward and Carrie watching behind them, gun in hand, heart racing. As they reached the flight deck, Hunter called out to them.

"Talk to me, Colt!"

"The panel, it's not burned out and everything's still connected."

"*Fuck*," Hunter hissed, looking over the console again, thinking.

Packham, Colt and Carrie eyed each other nervously in the silence. Hunter ran his hand over his mouth, his mind struggling to find an answer. He looked up to the ship's dead security monitors and stared at them. After a moment, he seemed to surrender himself to a resolution, exhaling measuredly and standing up.

"I gotta go out to the external power source and take a look," he said. "I can't leave the guys blind out there."

"But what if *they* did this?" Packham asked worriedly. "What if they're out there? It could be a trap."

"I'll cover you," Carrie offered quickly, as though a knee-jerk reaction, her heart beginning to race even faster.

Hunter looked over at her.

"I'll go, too," Colt nodded.

Hunter looked at Packham. "Lock the flight deck when we leave. Lock the ship down, too. I've got the access codes."

Hunter grabbed his gun from beside his chair and double-checked it was loaded. He turned to Carrie and Colt. "Are you sure you're up for this?" he asked firmly.

"Yes, sir," Carrie said with conviction.

"Let's get the comms back on," Colt said, equally assured.

He nodded, then started up the flight deck stairs.

They stopped briefly at the weapons store to grab three bullaser vests, then continued on to the *Aurora*'s exit. As they reached it, Hunter stopped and turned around to them.

"Welles, you and I go first, and we cross-cover. Colt, you follow and watch our back. Stay close to the ship. Do *not* go out in the open!"

They both nodded in return.

"Okay... one, two, three!" Hunter hit the lever and both he and Carrie aimed their weapons out the door.

Harris looked over at Brown.

"It's not working, captain. It won't read it for some reason," he said, looking down at his equipment, as static continued to filled their ears.

"Don't stop. Keep working on it!" Harris barked.

"Flight deck, do you copy? Over," Doc called again into his mouthpiece, as he paced the room, eyeing Harris with concern.

Harris could feel himself mirroring the concern, while that funny feeling settled into his stomach again.

"It might not just be us, captain," Doc told him. "McKinley's team could be running blind too."

Carrie, Hunter and Colt slowly made their way onto the dock. Carrie's eyes darted about everywhere, searching for a target. Then she paused and held very still, focusing on one spot, waiting for something to move around in her peripheral vision. Nothing. She made eye contact with Hunter and he nodded at Colt to hit the lever and close the door behind them.

They made their way along the dock slowly, around to the front of the ship, sticking close to it as Hunter ordered. There were no signs of any of the survivors. Everything was quiet, the dock deserted. They reached the front of the ship and looked over at the external power source on the wall of the Darwin. It seemed okay from a distance, the lights flashing normally. Hunter then followed the power source cable to where it was connected to the ship, beside the anchor. It looked as though it was still coupled, but Carrie only glanced at it, quickly turning around to scan their perimeter again.

"Cover me," Hunter said, as he tucked his weapon down the back of his pants and knelt down to get a closer look. Carrie and Colt watched either side of the ship. Carrie's eyes darted about looking for a target, then she paused again, focusing on the one spot. Still no movement in her periphery.

"External power source is fine, so it has got to be something in here," Hunter said quietly, as though to himself, poking and prodding around the anchor. After a minute or so he hissed, then stood and turned around to them. "Fucking connector chip's gone. They've ripped it out!"

Just then, something heavy collided with Hunter in a sickening thud, knocking him down to the ground. It was Fairmont. He'd come from on top of the ship. Carrie flashed her gun up to see if there were more, but saw no-one. She spun back around and tried to take aim as the two rolled about wrestling on the ground. Her eyes shot up to Colt, who was trying to take aim herself, and saw Grolsh quickly moving up behind her. For a nanosecond Carrie froze at the sight of his scratched face, a shiver shooting down her spine.

"LOOK OUT," she yelled at Colt, then quickly spun around to check whether someone was creeping up behind her as well. No-one. She turned back to Colt and saw her struggling with Grolsh over her gun. A hail of bullets fired, ricocheting off the ship's protective coating, sending Carrie scrambling for cover. She saw Fairmont throw a hard punch at Hunter's already bloodied face, knocking him onto his back, barely three meters in front of her. In one swift movement, he grabbed Hunter's arm and twisted it, snapping it like a twig. Hunter screamed in pain and looked down at the bone protruding slightly from his arm. As Fairmont knelt over him, Carrie saw a clean shot and fired. It caught him in the shoulder. He grunted in pain and reeled back. Fairmont looked down at his wound, flashed her a ferocious look, then growled as he swiftly got to his feet and lunged for her. Heart racing, she quickly took aim again and fired. She saw part of his head blow away, then his body swirled and fell limp to the ground with a thud.

Hunter glanced at Fairmont's body, then shot Carrie a surprised yet grateful look. With teeth clenched, he grabbed the gun out of his pants with his good arm, groaning in pain as he did. Carrie turned back to Grolsh and Colt. Grolsh was behind her, his arm around her neck, her nose bloodied, and he was pointing her gun at Carrie. He started shooting and she ducked back for cover. She saw Hunter scrambling for cover too, pulling himself along with one arm, trying to get to his feet. She stepped out to cover him, but Grolsh fired again sending her back. Then she heard more gunfire and saw Hunter's body bounce in unison.

"NO!" she screamed.

She watched in horror as his body slumped to the ground and pools of blood quickly formed over the back of his good arm and the side of his thigh.

Harris saw Louis straighten and look carefully down the corridor.

"What the fuck was that?" Louis blurted.

Harris stared hard at him. "What?"

"It sounded like gunfire," Louis said.

"Where?"

They all stopped and listened. They heard it again.

"It's coming from the dock!" Louis exclaimed.

"The dock?!" Harris asked. "Fuck! Fall out! FALL OUT."

Carrie watched as Grolsh started to back away, dragging Colt with him. She couldn't let him take her. Panicking, she stepped out and started firing around him to try and scare him.

"DROP HER," she yelled.

Grolsh held Colt tight in front of him and started shooting back, and again Carrie was forced to duck for cover. Colt continued struggling with him, as he tried to drag her away. She started flailing her elbows at his ribs and scratching at his face. Whilst Grolsh was distracted, Carrie slowly stepped out and tried to take aim again. He saw her making her move, though. He went to raise the gun back up to her, but Colt knocked it out of the way and they began to struggle with it again. As they did, more shots fired and ricocheted off the *Aurora*. Suddenly she saw Colt's body bounce and swing back. Grolsh looked down at her, wide-eyed and pulled her body back up to face him. Blood quickly oozed across Colt's neck and down her arm.

"NO! COLT," she screamed.

"FREEZE!" she heard another voice shout, and turned to see McKinley at the open exit door with his gun on Grolsh. Bolkov and Carter were behind him.

Grolsh looked a little panicked now, his eyes darting between Carrie and McKinley. He kept moving back slowly toward the second emergency exit on the dock, keeping Colt's limp body close to his. Carrie saw him suddenly look up high, as a rain of laser fire hailed down upon them. McKinley was forced to retreat back into the first emergency exit and shut the door. Carrie took cover alongside the ship and when she looked back at Grolsh, saw him dump Colt's body to the ground and disappear through the second door, which had somehow opened for him.

"COLT," Carrie yelled, as Harris's team appeared at the main entrance of the Darwin. They were looking around the dock, guns in the air, then over at Carrie and the three bodies lying on the dock with her. Doc immediately ran over to Colt and knelt down beside her.

Carrie heard Hunter gargle in pain, where he lay on the floor. She dropped her eyes from Colt and rushed forward to him. She rolled him over and he opened his eyes, groaning, his face bloody, bruised and swollen. She saw McKinley was back out and both his and Harris's teams were providing cover, so she tucked her weapon away and placed her hands over Hunter's arm and leg to stop the bleeding. She looked over at Doc, who lifted Colt's body off the ground and handed her to Brown, who began running toward the *Aurora* with Louis in tow providing cover. Doc turned and ran low toward Carrie, glancing over at Fairmont's body as he did. He dropped down by Hunter's side and saw the bone protruding from his arm and Carrie's hands on his bloodied bullet wounds.

"We have to get him inside," he told her hurriedly.

Bolkov ran over to them, from McKinley's exit door.

"Help me get him inside, Bulk," Doc called out, then he turned to Carrie. "Try and keep your hands there."

Bolkov grabbed Hunter's torso and Doc grabbed his legs and they lifted him up, as he groaned loudly in pain.

Harris watched as Doc, Bulk and Welles rushed Hunter onto the *Aurora*. He heard Hunter groaning in pain. That was a good sign. That meant he was still alive. He looked over at McKinley who was scouring the walls of the dock, looking for someone, as he slowly made his way over to him.

"What the fuck happened?" Harris asked, standing next to Fairmont's dead body, as his own eyes and weapon still searched the walls for a target.

"I don't know. We heard gunfire, got the door open and saw Grolsh and Colt struggling, then him trying to take off using her as a shield," McKinley said looking down curiously at Fairmont's body. "I think he went through that exit." He pointed to the opposite door from which he'd come.

"We need to get to that fuckin' hiding space!" Harris hissed. "Did you have any luck?"

McKinley shook his head, just as Bolkov came running back off the ship.

"Captain! You come quick!" he yelled.

# 21

# Shards of Glass

Carrie watched as *Aurora*'s hospital became a flurry of activity. Everyone was apprehensive after discovering Doc's examination room had been ransacked. At least, the fluids had been. Chet and Logan must've boarded the ship somehow while they'd been checking the external power source. The glass cabinet had been smashed and many of the bottles stolen. The medical store across the corridor had been raided as well, its sliding door left ajar.

Hunter was placed on one of the beds and Carrie was told to keep applying pressure to his wounds, while Doc quickly gave him a shot of morphine. He then tended to Colt, who was moaning in pain. The blood had soaked down the entire arm of her shirt and over her chest.

"Is she going to be okay?" Carrie asked.

"She's been hit in the side of her neck. She's damn lucky it missed her artery," he said, as he gave her a shot of morphine too. "Brown, keep holding the wound and keep her torso elevated. I gotta fix Hunter first. He's bleeding from three wounds."

Harris and Bolkov came striding into the hospital. Bolkov showed him the smashed glass and Harris examined the area closely.

"How the hell did they get in?" he asked no-one in particular, then turned to Doc. "You locked the rooms, right?"

Doc nodded hurriedly, not looking up from his patient.

A sudden thought struck Carrie. "Where's Packham?" she asked, worriedly. "Is she still on the flight deck?"

"Bulk, check it out," Harris ordered, and Bolkov left the room. "Doc, what was taken?"

"I don't know yet. I'm a little busy here," The medic answered tightly, gathering together some tools to dig out Hunter's bullets.

"Welles, what happened?" Harris strode toward her. "Why did you leave the ship?"

"They blacked us out."

"The ship?" he asked.

"The power went out and the comms wouldn't come back up. Colt checked down below, but everything was fine. Hunter had to check the external power source, so Colt and I covered him. We didn't want to leave you guys blind out there."

"So what happened?"

"They were hiding on the nose of the ship. Fairmont jumped Hunter and Grolsh got Colt."

"You kill Fairmont?"

Carrie nodded. "Yeah. I tried to just wound him first, but he came at me. I had no choice."

"That's fine, corporal," Harris dismissed it quickly. "You did what you had to. Did Hunter figure out what was wrong with the comms?"

"He said they'd ripped out the connector chip."

The captain nodded, glanced at the cabinet again briefly, then left the room.

Harris quickly caught up with Bolkov as he approached the door to the flight deck. They both paused when they noticed the door looked slightly dented, although it still appeared to be locked. He exchanged a look with Bulk, as they raised their weapons in readiness. Harris banged on the door.

"Open up! This is Captain Harris," he bellowed. He had the entry code but he wanted to see what the response was.

After a few moments they heard the door unlock and it opened. Packham stood there with her gun pointed at them, albeit shakily. Harris held out his hand to her. "Relax, sergeant. It's alright."

She dropped her gun. "Where're the others?"

"Hunter and Colt are down," he said, walking onto the flight deck and looking around. "Welles is in the hospital helping out. You know what happened?" He turned back around to face her. She looked nervous. *Or was that shaken?*

"We had a power blackout and the comms died. They went to check the external power source and that's the last I saw of them."

"Did you know the survivors were on the ship?" Harris asked her.

She nodded, her face looking paler than normal. "They were at the flight deck door. They were ramming it, trying to get in... but they went away."

Harris continued eyeing her for a moment, thinking.

"Bulk," he turned to the Russian, "get over to the console and do a scan on the heat sensors, and make sure there's no-one else still on the ship, then I want you to see if you can fix the blackout problem. I'll get Brown and Carter out on the external power source. Apparently the connector chip's gone."

"Yes, sir." He nodded, then moved over to the console and began tapping away.

"Captain, are they going to be okay?" Packham asked.

"I don't know, but go to the hospital and relieve Brown. I need him out here," he said.

"Scan is clear, captain," Bolkov announced. "Hospital is only room picking up heat."

"Good," Harris answered, leaving the flight deck.

He walked off the ship and back to where McKinley, Carter and Louis were, keeping their eyes peeled for the survivors.

"Carter, I need you and Brown to try and fix this external power source. Apparently the connector chip's missing. McKinley, you and Louis cover them. Keep your eyes sharp!"

"Yes, sir."

Harris made his way back onto the ship, noticing that the *Aurora's* entrance looked untouched. There were no signs of a forced entry. After studying the dented flight deck door again and thinking to himself that Packham was lucky to be alive, he made his way back down to the hospital.

He wanted to take another look at Doc's examination room. It would seem the survivors got on the ship specifically for one thing and as far as Harris could tell, it was something in Doc's cabinet. As he approached the medic's rooms, he stopped to study the medical store across the corridor. The door was ajar and the shelves the vials of fluids had been on were empty, with one or two of the bottles smashed on the floor.

He walked into Doc's office, glancing into the hospital to see Packham holding a bloodied bandage over Colt's neck and Doc and Welles attending to Hunter, whose leg was bandaged and hanging out of his cut up clothing. Harris turned into the examination room and took a good look around. His feet crunched over the broken glass as he made his way to the cabinet. There appeared to be only one type of fluid taken. He guessed it was the same fluid that Doc had been injecting them with. *Why on Earth would they want that? Did this have something to do with the experiment? Or was it something else?*

He turned and walked back into the hospital. "How they doing, Doc?"

His lieutenant looked up at him, face somewhat strained. "I've got them both high on morphine. I've just fished a bullet out of Hunter's leg, but it hadn't gone too deep. The one in his arm went right through, so I'm just trying to patch it up now. Next, I'll try and fish the one out of Colt's neck, but it looks tricky. Then I'm going to try and set Hunter's arm."

"So they'll be okay?"

"Well, we're going to need to get them to a fully functional hospital. Hunter's broken arm is fucked and if I can't get that bullet out of Colt... I'm going to lock them both in a pod to keep them stable until we can get them to one."

Harris nodded grimly, just as Brown's voice came over the PA.

*"Captain, this is Brown on the flight deck. Internal comms have been restored, but we got bigger problems. Over."*

Harris and Doc exchanged a look, then Harris moved over to the intercom. "What is it, Brown?"

*"Well, firstly, there must have been some sort of surge during the blackout and it's sucked a lot of power out of the Aurora's cells. We're currently sitting on only 9%. We've inserted a spare connector chip, but still can't reconnect to the external power supply which means we're running down those power cells as we speak. Bulk seems to think that they've put a block on us, to prevent us hooking back up. The block also excludes any external comms."*

"So what does that mean?" Harris stared at the intercom on the wall, trying to ignore the crawling feeling along his spine.

*"Well, for one, it means that we can't contact Command for help. It also means that if we can't reconnect to the external power supply, we'll run down the Aurora's power cells and the ship won't be able to take off, let alone make it home. Basically, as it stands, we're grounded and we're going to run out of power well before the other team arrives."*

Harris shot Doc another look. "How long?" He spoke into the intercom, trying to keep his voice strong and steady.

*"I'd say we've got approximately seven hours left before we run out, and about another 40 hours on top of that before the other team arrives."*

Harris exchanged a look with Doc.

"The pods need power," the medic said. "They can run on battery only so long."

*Fuck!* Harris hissed inside his mind.

"So how do we fix it?" Harris spoke into the intercom.

Bolkov's voice came over the PA then. *"Captain, we'll need to go to Darwin's control room and try and remove block, but it's not simple task. We'll need to decipher their security codes to access the system. This could take hours, captain."*

Harris stared at the intercom speaker for another moment. He turned around and saw Doc, Welles and Packham staring at him. He didn't have a good feeling about this, but there was no other choice.

"Packham, get your ass to the flight deck. Welles, take over on Colt. We have to go in and find those fuckers and get our access back," he said, walking for the door.

"Captain," Doc called. "Wait and I'll join you."

"No. You take care of Hunter and Colt. You're in charge of the ship."

"Watch your back," his lieutenant called.

"Always do, Doc."

Harris made his way down the corridor toward the flight deck. His mind was in a weird state; numb but racing. *What the fuck is going on? How did this turn to shit so quickly? They're smart. They know they've trapped us. They've sucked our ship's power, it's days until the other team arrives and we can't call for help.*

*Why are they playing with us like this? What the hell do they want?*

*

Within minutes Harris had reconvened his two teams, albeit without Doc.

"Right, I'm changing our tactics. Myself, Brown and McKinley will go to the main entrance and we'll make our way toward them. Carter, you and Louis wait at the secondary point and get whoever we flush out.

"When you say 'get them', captain..." Carter narrowed his eyes carefully.

"I mean do whatever it is you have to do to get them to stop," Harris said in a low, flat voice. "If they resist you, then I'll leave that judgment up to you, but just know that you'll only have seconds to make that choice."

Carter and Louis nodded.

"Captain, I come too, no?" Bolkov queried.

"No, with Hunter down, Bulk, you keep your ass on the flight deck, or we're not going anywhere."

Bolkov gave a nod.

They grabbed their gear and headed back out. There was a certain edginess in the men's eyes, but it didn't worry Harris, because he also saw a fire within them. Smith was dead. Hunter and Colt were down. They knew this shit was serious. They knew this wasn't a test. This was real, and they were ready to do whatever was necessary to fix it.

*

They made it to their targets again without any problems. He didn't like that it was so easy for them. The Darwin was too quiet. Although he trusted his men, he still had that feeling in the pit of his stomach. And an image of Sibbie and Etta flashed inside his mind again, like shards of a mirror stabbing into his brain. It worried him that they still didn't really know what the survivors' full capabilities were. But he couldn't think of any way around it right now. They had to find them and they had to get their access back.

When they entered Sharley's office, he noticed the wall was still up. Now they just needed to figure out a way to open up the elevator. Brown got back to work with the digital decoder, while McKinley kept his sharp eyes on the corridor.

Carrie stepped away as Doc began to work on Colt who, like Hunter, was knocked out from the morphine. He removed Colt's riddled bullaser vest with Carrie's help, then grabbed some scissors and cut along the sleeve of her shirt and bra strap, peeling them back. There was one wound clearly visible, right where her shoulder joined her neck, a small pool of blood sat in the groove above her clavicle.

"I'll need you to swab the blood like you did with Hunter," Doc told her.

She nodded and fetched some more swabs. It was surprising just how used to all the blood she was becoming. Not that she had a choice, though. Doc took a fresh scalpel and pair of tweezers and began to fish around for the bullet in the side of Colt's neck. Carrie turned her head away. The blood she could handle, but the fishing she could not. They continued on in silence for a while, Doc hunting for the bullet, and Carrie swabbing her neck whenever he pulled away.

He was a mass of concentration as he carefully picked and pulled at her flesh, searching for the bullet, commenting that her clavicle had also been damaged. It seemed like hours had passed before he finally said, "There it is!" He fished around some more and after a couple of false starts, he eventually got it. Carrie tried to block out the squelching sound, as he pulled it out of Colt's flesh and dropped it with a clunk into a dish he had waiting. He looked around the wound, making sure he had it all.

"Alright, that's it. I can stitch her up now."

Carrie stepped away, removed her gloves and went to wash her hands, as Doc began to sew the corporal up.

"I'll clean up the glass in the other room," Carrie offered.

Doc looked over through the doorway at the glass on the floor. "Don't touch the cabinet. I want a close look at that."

She nodded, fetched a broom from the mess hall and raced back, knowing that time was of the essence. She starting sweeping up the glass and listened to the silence coming from the hospital as Doc continued stitching. After a while, though, he called out to her.

"Welles, did Grolsh shoot Colt?"

"No. He was shooting at me, but his aim was poor… Colt struggled with him, the gun fired, and it ricocheted off the ship."

"Right." Doc was quiet for a moment. "What was Grolsh doing with her? Was he trying to kill her?"

"He was using her as a shield, dragging her off with him."

Doc was quiet again for a moment.

"Why?" she paused, staring at the pile of glass she'd swept up on the floor.

"Just curious," he said.

Carrie shrugged to herself, scooped up the glass and emptied it into the nearest bin. She walked back into the hospital and saw Doc threading a stitch through Colt's skin, tugging it. She looked away again. "Is, er, there anything else you need?"

"No. I'll give them one last check over, then seal them in their pods. Go to the flight deck and see if the others need your help."

"Yes, sir." She turned around to leave.

"Welles," Doc called out, stopping her.

She turned back to him.

"Good job on Fairmont," he said, his brown eyes warm as they looked at hers. "You saved Hunter's life."

She gave him a halfhearted smile. "I had a shot at Grolsh and I didn't take it. I looked around to check whether anyone was coming up behind me instead. I should've just shot him first, then turned. If I did then Colt wouldn't be lying here now and Hunter wouldn't have a couple of bullet holes in him."

"No, you did the right thing," Doc said firmly. "You've always got to check your own safety first. You can't save anyone else, if your own life's in danger."

She gave him another halfhearted smile. "I still should've shot him while I had the chance."

"They'll be okay," he said. "You did well. We've got one less to worry about. That's a good thing." There was something about his voice and the way he looked at her that made Carrie pause. It was like he had more to say, but wasn't saying it. He held her gaze for a moment then turned back to work on Colt's shoulder.

Harris eyed Brown eagerly.

"Captain, we're in!" he smiled, as the lights on the elevator's console began to flicker.

They quickly got into position, and McKinley did the same. Harris held his gun in tight and close to his sight-line. They heard a delicate, high-pitched chime and the elevator doors opened slowly. It was empty.

"Carter, Louis, we're going in," he said quietly into his mouthpiece. "Be ready when we flush them out."

"*Copy that. Over,*" Carter replied.

Carrie sat on the flight deck with Bolkov and Packham watching the screens anxiously. Harris, Brown and McKinley stood in the elevator, gas masks on. The doors closed and they started to rise. Locked in an attack stance, bodies rigid and guns out front, the three solid soldiers filled the space easily. The elevator came to a stop. A second passed, then they heard the chime and a set of doors opened behind them. It was a two-way elevator.

They quickly spun around, bumping into each other, as they readjusted their stance. Within seconds Harris threw out three canisters of tear gas. The room at first glance appeared to be empty, but it was hard to tell once the smoke filled the air. She saw them looking down at their guns, trying to pick up any body heat, but they registered nothing. One by one, they slowly edged out onto the floor.

From what Carrie could see through the smoke, it was one large room with a corridor at the end. The large room was another lab of sorts, although this looked like a working one, unlike those on the floor below. As they moved about through the wafts of smoke, she could see e-files and paper manuals strewn across tabletops, and consoles alight with information. Watching Harris's monitor, she saw him pause at a series of screens showing security footage of the Darwin's ground floor.

"They've been watching us the whole time," McKinley whispered, stopping briefly at the captain's side.

The three men made their way carefully around the room, through the thinning mist, checking under every desk and around every corner. They picked up no heat. Nothing. They began to move down the corridor, which had the occasional door coming off it. Every door they passed was locked.

They saw no-one through the glass walls and nothing registered on their heat sensors.

"Carter? Anything?" Harris whispered into his mouthpiece.

"No, captain," he replied.

Carrie looked over to Louis's monitor and watched as Carter held his gun tight and focused on the built-out wall beside the emergency door. Her eyes moved back to Harris's camera.

"They sure as shit ain't here," McKinley seethed softly.

"How the *fuck* did they get out?" Harris spat quietly into his mouthpiece.

"Must've been another exit we missed," Brown answered in a hushed tone. "One of the spots I took for pipework, maybe?"

"Wait!" Louis yelled.

They heard the sound of zipping laserfire.

Carrie's eyes jumped to Louis's screen. She saw Grolsh run off in the distance.

"Carter! Quick!" Louis called, trying to take aim as he chased after him.

"Louis! What is it?" Harris asked anxiously.

"Grolsh," Carter replied. "We're going after him!"

"Which way? I'll cut him off," McKinley said, quickly moving back toward the elevator.

"He's running toward Section Two!" Louis yelled back, panting as he ran.

"McKinley, watch your back!" Harris warned, before turning to Brown. "Quick! Look around. See if you can find any information we can use!" he ordered.

They began scouring the main room again, and Harris moved over to a desk that was clear except for a portable touch screen device. As he neared, a small piece of paper could be seen lying on top of it. He reached out and picked it up, and saw the following word scrawled across it: *Harris.*

Carrie's heart picked up pace as she watched Louis and Carter run after Grolsh.

"STOP OR I'LL SHOOT, YOU FUCK," Carter yelled at him.

Grolsh kept running. Carter took aim and fired, but he missed; the golden laser-fire bouncing off a doorway. They cleared Section Three and entered Section Two, on approach to the labs. Carter fired again and grazed Grolsh's upper arm. He skidded off-course, but straightened up and continued running, trying to pat out the laser burn.

Louis and Carter started gaining ground on him. Just as they passed the labs, Logan and Chet suddenly charged out, smashing into them; one from each side. Logan rammed Louis into the glass wall of the lab opposite, cracking it. Carter saw Chet coming at the last moment and swung his gun around but he wasn't quick enough. Chet knocked him off his feet to the floor.

Carrie watched as Bolkov's hand flashed out and hit his comms switch.

"Captain! Louis and Carter are under attack. They've been ambushed. I repeat, they're under attack!"

Harris quickly straightened as though a jolt of panic had shot through him.

"Fuck! Move out," he called to Brown, quickly snatching the device labelled with his name and tucking it inside his shirt. "McKinley, you hear that? Watch your back," he yelled into his mouthpiece as he and Brown ran back toward the elevator.

"Copy that," McKinley replied quietly.

Carrie's eyes darted from Carter's to Louis's monitors. Logan was all over Louis. They were now wrestling on the floor and Logan was growling like a wild animal. On Carter's monitor she saw Chet throwing Carter's gun down the corridor. Carter scrambled to his feet and charged at him, knocking him to the floor and they too began wrestling. She looked back over at Louis's monitor. She could see his hands around Logan's neck trying in vain to hold him away, the veins bulging in his dark, weight-lifter arms as they gleamed with sweat.

Back on Carter's monitor, Chet threw a hard punch knocking Carter off him. She saw Carter reach up to his face, groaning, and then pull his hand away bloodied. Chet had targeted his broken nose. Carter moved to get to his feet, as Chet nimbly sprang up off the ground toward him. He landed a swift kick to Carter's upper arm, causing it to buckle. The survivor grabbed at Carter's vest and tore it off, then swiftly kicked him several times in the ribs. Carrie swore she heard them crack and crunch, as Carter yelled out in pain.

Carrie looked at Louis's monitor, as Logan raised his fist and punched Louis's arm, snapping it. Louis roared desperately, in agony, releasing his hands from around Logan's neck.

She looked anxiously over to McKinley's camera in the hope he was close by. He was at the door of Sharley's office and peered out. He seemed to have heard something though and quickly curled back around the door. He readied his gun and waited, motionless and quiet.

"Oh, Jesus!" she heard Packham gasp.

"FUCK! FUCK! FUCK!" Bolkov yelled.

Carrie darted her eyes over to Louis's monitor, where they were staring. She saw Logan's face had blood smeared around his mouth and across his cheeks. His strange, emerald eyes stared down Louis's camera like someone possessed, then he turned slightly and spat out a chunk of meat. She heard Louis gurgling deep in his throat, just like Smith had.

"Oh, fuck..." Carrie whispered in pure dread.

Heart racing now, she quickly looked back to Carter's camera. Chet appeared to be having fun with him. He was walking slowly around the first sergeant, stepping forward every now and then, and kicking him. Once again in the ribs, another crack. Carrie heard the awful pain in Carter's groan. Chet circled him again, then landed one in the head, right near his camera.

"FUCK! FUCK! FUCKING FUCK!" Bolkov shouted, slamming his fists on the flight deck console, shaking it.

"We gotta get Doc!" Carrie shouted, panicked.

"There's *nothing* he can do," Bolkov snarled, his eyes glued to Carter's screen.

Carrie saw a flurry of movement on McKinley's camera, as he sprung out from around the doorway and fired at Grolsh. The survivor dropped to the ground suddenly and skidded along the corridor. Carrie saw the front of his shirt singe with the laser-fire and the blood begin to rapidly stain him. McKinley hit him squarely in the chest.

She looked over to Harris's and Brown's cameras as they moved out of the elevator and into the corridor behind McKinley, who was now stalking off quickly ahead, gun at the ready. Harris briefly stood over Grolsh, who was coughing and spluttering and gasping for air. His entire torso was now saturated in blood, the place of impact revealing the melted flesh beneath. It was a good shot and Carrie knew that in moments, it would prove fatal. Harris seemed to wait until he took his last breath, wanting to be sure perhaps, before moving on and leaving his lifeless body behind.

Her eyes darted back to Carter's camera. She could still hear him groaning in pain, but there was no sound at all coming from Louis's now.

Carter's hands were covered in blood and slipping on the floor, as he tried to drag himself away. She saw Chet still circling him.

"Louis is dead, Carter," Chet taunted him. "You're all alone…"

"FFFFUCK YOU!" Carter managed, spitting blood everywhere.

Logan moved up beside Chet. "Finish him, or I will," his gravelly voice snarled, then he quickly turned his head to stare down the hall toward Section One. "They're coming… *quickly*."

Chet smiled and walked forward slowly. He crouched down and took Carter's head in his hands. Carter's bloodied hands tried to remove them, slipping still, but Chet's grip didn't release.

"You're a fighter, Farris Carter," he said eerily. "I like that. I wanted to keep you, you know. Oh, well…"

He held Carter's face in front of his, dropping his smile, as a glazed expression came over his face. Then his eyes drifted to look directly into Carter's camera and he very quickly and very sharply, made a twisting movement with his hands. There was a loud crack and Carter's hands fell limp. Chet released his grip and Carter's body hit the floor with a thud.

"Oh, Jesus!" Carrie said, shaking, her eyes wide-eyed with panic. "Fuuuck!"

Bolkov hit the comms switch. "Captain. Louis and Carter are dead. They're *fucking* dead! Logan and Chet are still in Section Two. I repeat, they're still in Section Two."

Carrie snapped her eyes to McKinley, Harris and Brown. They'd been stuck at the door to Section Two, which had been locked, but Brown had just reopened it using the digital decoder. Upon hearing Bolkov's news, they shot each other a shocked glance, then carefully hastened their pace forward.

Carrie shot up from her seat and ran for the door of the flight deck. Not knowing what else to do, she just had to get Doc.

Harris moved swiftly but carefully, with McKinley and Brown, into Section Two. His heart was racing, his breathing shallow and his palms sweating around his gun. As they entered, they saw Carter's and Louis's bodies up ahead. A sharp pain shot through him, from his head down to his feet. *Jesus fucking Christ!*

There was no sign of Chet or Logan.

They carefully checked each lab as they passed, until they reached the bodies.

Harris scanned the corridor up ahead, glancing down briefly at his two dead soldiers. Louis was lying in a pool of blood, the side of his neck torn open. Carter's face was bloodied, bruised and swollen, and from the angle his head sat on his shoulders, Harris knew that his neck had been broken.

*FUCK! Two more men... two more fucking men!* He struggled to breathe for a moment.

"Their weapons are gone," McKinley noted.

Harris's eyes shot over to McKinley and Brown. McKinley was staring down at Carter's body, his jaw clenched tight and his eyes burning with anger. Brown was bending over Louis, closing the dead soldier's eyes. Brown's cheeks were flushed pale, and his face held a look that was a frightening kind of numb.

"What do you want us to do, captain?" McKinley asked through gritted teeth.

Harris stared down the corridor ahead. He suddenly felt calm and cold and numb himself.

"We keep going," he said in a low voice. "We find these fucks and we end this!"

"I was hoping you'd say that," McKinley said moving off down the hall.

# 22

# Revelation

Carrie raced into Doc's examination room. He was sitting by the autoanalyzer at the end of the room, a vial of fluid in his hand, reading an e-file intently.

"Doc! Quick!" she called frantically.

He looked up at her, startled.

"Louis and Carter are dead!" she panted.

"What?" He shot up from his seat and ran toward her. "What the fuck happened?"

"They were chasing after Grolsh. Chet and Logan ambushed them," she said as they headed for the door.

"Fuck! Where are the others?"

"They're going after them. McKinley took out Grolsh."

As they stepped into the corridor, on approach to the flight deck, they suddenly saw Bolkov wrestling with someone up ahead.

Someone they didn't recognize.

They both pulled up quickly and took out their guns.

"DON'T MOVE!" Doc yelled.

The man looked over at them, rammed Bolkov into the wall and then pulled him in front as cover. They saw Bolkov's side was covered in blood and his gun was on the floor meters away from him. Carrie tried to take aim, but it was too difficult as Bolkov was too big. Both she and Doc moved in a careful but quickened pace toward them, guns out front.

"I SAID DON'T MOVE," Doc yelled again.

As they passed the mess hall door, something grabbed Carrie's ankle and she tripped over. She fell flat on her stomach, forcing the air from her lungs, and her pistol went flying. She didn't get the chance to see what it was, but something or someone quickly grabbed her feet and pulled her backward toward the doorway. Doc turned suddenly, let off three quick shots, and Carrie felt a heavy weight collapse upon her. She rolled over and saw it was yet another man she didn't recognize. She tried to heave the heavy body off her, and Doc quickly kicked out his leg to help, keeping his gun on Bolkov's attacker. She flashed the lieutenant a startled look, then scrambled forward to get her gun.

As they looked back toward Bolkov and the other man, she saw that they had each other by the throat. Bolkov, roaring as he did, suddenly smashed his fists down heavily on his opponent's arms, releasing them from his neck. He swiftly stepped aside and the second he did, several shots rang out, forcing both Carrie and Doc flat back against the walls. The attacker's chest exploded, and he slowly fell forward to reveal Packham standing there, gun fixed firmly on the man.

Carrie quickly turned around to check the corridor behind them. No-one. They continued forward as Bolkov suddenly collapsed to his knees. Doc ran up and caught him, and sat him back against the wall between the captain's office and the flight deck. Bolkov looked down at his side. He was bleeding profusely from his wound, a river of blood flowing onto the floor.

"Jesus, we gotta get you to the hospital, Bulk," Doc said nervously, placing his hand over it.

"Is not good, Doc." Bolkov winced, as the color drained from his face. "Is too deep."

Carrie saw a large, gaping slash all the way down his side, exposing the red flesh beneath. For a moment she saw something protruding from the wound, before Doc quickly pushed whatever it was back inside and tried to close the gap. The lieutenant glanced over at the other man on the floor.

"Who did this? I don't see a knife?" he asked quickly.

Bolkov motioned into the flight deck. Carrie looked past Packham and saw yet another man lying dead on the floor.

"Fuck," she said, "how many more are there?"

"How the hell did they get on board?" Doc asked.

Packham stepped forward, her voice trembling. "They just opened the door! Bulk saw a warning light up on the console, alerting us that someone was entering the ship. We knew it wasn't the team. But they knew the code to get on! Bulk went to check it out and they were there… at the flight deck door!"

Bolkov grabbed at Doc's hands that were holding his wound together. "Is not good, Doc… is okay… let go," Bolkov said, nodding his head at Doc, the sweat shining across his pale face.

"No, Bulk. I need to stop the bleeding." Doc stared firmly at him.

"I tell you, is no good. You're prolonging inevitable… is no good… please."

Doc shook his head. "I can't do that, sergeant. I *won't* do that!"

Bolkov grabbed hard at the medic's hands, face clenched, as he mustered all his strength and tore them away. His eyes rested on Doc's as he panted. "Even in death… I am strong."

Doc stuck his hand on Bolkov's shoulder and squeezed it, his eyes staring firmly into his. "Bulk, don't do this. Let me try and help. Please, let me try…"

"I took one of them out… I am happy." Bolkov's eyes began to blink slowly, heavily.

Carrie looked down at the blood spilling across the floor from Bolkov's side. Trying hard to steady the vigorous shaking that was taking over her body, the three of them remained silent, as Bolkov, slowly, quietly, died.

Doc exhaled loudly, bowing his head to the floor, eyes squeezed shut, still holding Bulk's shoulder tightly.

"What the fuck are we going do?" Packham sounded panicked. "Even if we get the access back, who's going to co-pilot the ship?"

Doc stood up slowly but continued to eye Bolkov's body. He looked devastated, disheartened, distraught.

"We're fucked! We're all fucked," Packham said, shaking her head.

Doc looked at her. Somehow, he seemed to push the pain to one side. His face hardened and his jaw clenched. "Brown can do it," he told her. "He knows this ship and how it works."

"But he's out *there* somewhere," Packham continued, verging on hysterical. "What if he doesn't make it back? We're *fucked*!"

Doc walked over to her, grabbed her by the shoulders and shook her slightly. "He will, sergeant. We'll call him back now. We'll override and change the ship's access codes, so they can't get back on. The ship will be safe," he said firmly, then quickly entered the flight deck.

Carrie stood at the door with her gun ready, her eyes darting between the corridor and the flight deck, trying to ignore Bulk's dead body that sat a few feet from her. Packham followed Doc to the console. He ordered her to check the ship's cameras and heat sensors to see if there was anyone else on the ship. Thankfully, there wasn't. They looked at the screens and saw Harris, Brown and McKinley making their way to the end of Section Three. It looked as though Chet and Logan had disappeared again. *Why?*

Doc hit the comms button, taking a second to steady himself.

"Captain, this is Doc. You need to return to the ship immediately... Bolkov's dead."

Harris stopped walking. "What?"

*"And we've killed three more of those guys onboard the* Aurora.*"*

"Three more!" Harris looked around at McKinley and Brown. "What do you mean three more? Two are dead and we only had four to begin with?"

*"Well, three new ones turned up on the ship and they had our access code. We need Brown back here. He's now Packham's co-pilot!"*

"Fuck..." Harris seemed to whisper in disbelief. He exchanged shocked looks with McKinley and Brown, then his voice quickly hardened again. "Copy that. We're heading back."

*

Harris, McKinley and Brown moved swiftly back toward the dock. As they approached Carter's and Louis's bodies, Harris grabbed Carter by the arm and Brown grabbed Louis. They were not going to leave any of their men behind, so they dragged their bodies back to the *Aurora*, under McKinley's watchful cover.

They made it back without incident. Chet and Logan were in hiding again. But why, he didn't know. He found it odd that they'd strike then go into hiding, when they could have potentially had a good shot at the rest of them. *Why are they playing with us like this?*

When they got back to the ship, the three of them quickly surveyed the scene outside the flight deck. Harris looked at the three strangers' bodies. He recognized their faces from the Darwin's crew files. *So they were here all along...* And they clearly weren't victims like he'd thought. *Those fuckers have been sitting up on that secret floor watching us this whole goddamn time ...*

He crouched down beside Bolkov. The Russian sat there against the wall, his head hunched over as though he were asleep, a large pool of blood beside him. It was as though Bulk was giving a final slow nod to his captain. Harris reached out and squeezed his shoulder, and gave him a slow nod back, trying to fight the crushing feeling he felt inside.

He quickly pulled himself together and ordered Welles to guard the entrance while Packham and Brown got to work overriding the entry codes. He then proceeded to help McKinley and Doc move the three bodies of the Darwin crew out onto the dock, and then Carter, Louis and Bolkov's bodies up to the hospital. When they were finished, the three of them stood there in complete silence. Shocked.

He stared at his dead soldiers. Louis's and Carter's bodies lay on the two free beds, and Bolkov's on the floor, all covered with sheets. His eyes drifted to Hunter and Colt who were in their pods, out to it. Then he thought of Smith, lying in the cool room, already on ice. He closed his eyes briefly.

*Decimation*, he thought. It was the only word that came to mind.

Doc was the first to move among them. He turned abruptly, left the room and returned a moment later holding a vial of the fluid.

"Command has seriously fucked us in the ass on this one," he said angrily.

Harris eyed him and the vial of fluid he held up.

"The fluid they stole," Doc continued, "the same fluid I was injecting them with when we first got here? I ran some tests on a few bottles I had left in the store, tucked away in another spot. They're laced with growth hormones; all the stuff on the manifests that I couldn't find in their blood. I had to break it down to specific amino acids to find it, but they're in there. They've obviously created a new masking agent to cover it in their blood, and it must be a strong fuckin' one to have lasted this long. These growth hormones gave them their strength and their aggression, and I've been feeding it to them the whole *fuckin'* time!" He exhaled angrily. "Command stocked this ship, captain. They planted it. They knew I'd give it to them because they seemed dehydrated."

Harris stared at Doc for a moment. He saw McKinley watching for his reaction out of the corner of his eye.

"You weren't to know, Doc. It's not your fault," Harris assured him.

"There's something else," Doc began, his voice a little calmer, but not in a way that made Harris feel at all comfortable. "Welles said that Grolsh was trying to drag Colt away, and that her getting shot was an accident."

"It was. I saw it," McKinley said.

"Well, isn't that a bit strange when they're not hesitating to kill the rest of us?" Doc asked them.

"What's your point?" Harris asked him back.

"Chet and his boys don't seem to want to kill the women for some reason. At first, I figured that maybe they were, you know, just going for the obvious." Doc shot him a look and Harris gave a nod, understanding. "But I decided to take another look through the women's files," Doc continued, "and I remembered noticing when you first gave them to me, that there'd been some extra testing done on them. I didn't realize why, until now. I just assumed the UNF was getting a little more detailed with its enrollment procedures."

"What testing, Doc?" Harris looked hard at his lieutenant. He knew he was about to tell him something he wasn't going to like.

Doc stared hard back. "Fertility."

McKinley looked back and forth between the two for a second.

"Fertility?" Harris repeated in disbelief.

Doc nodded. "There's a brief section in their files on the health of their reproductive systems, and it clearly notes that none of them are on birth control. They're very healthy and strangely enough, all three are due to ovulate within a few days. Their files have rough dates and everything."

"What the fuck are you saying?" Harris asked him.

"I'm saying that Command suddenly put three women on your ship, for *this* particular mission, for a reason. And that's why they wouldn't allow you to mix the women with the survivors until they were ready. Ready to start a new phase in their experiment."

"Wait a minute," McKinley interrupted. "Command ordered you to keep them away from the Darwin team?"

Harris nodded at him, almost ashamed. "They were not allowed off the *Aurora*."

McKinley nodded to himself, as though suddenly the pieces fell into place.

Harris turned back to Doc. "Packham said before, when the fluid was stolen, that they were at the flight deck door trying to get to her. But they didn't know I had Hunter change the access code for the flight deck, just to be sure."

Doc nodded. "Command had access to our codes before we left. That's how they stocked the ship."

McKinley agreed. "It explains how they got aboard and into Doc's rooms, but not the flight deck."

Doc looked at Harris and clenched his jaw. "They're trying to create the perfect soldiers," he continued, "so why not start from scratch? Get the DNA right from day one. Imagine what good soldiers they'd be after a lifetime of mind-fucking, growth hormones, animal senses and UNF training."

The three of them stood in silence for a few moments, soaking it in.

"You think the women knew what they signed up for?" McKinley asked. "Maybe they volunteered for those tests."

Doc shook his head. "No. I think they just thought they were joining Space Duty, and I think it was our job to deliver them to the survivors. We were expendable. We were just the delivery boys."

Harris stared hard at Doc for a moment. He felt a blaze of anger lick up inside him more swiftly than he'd ever felt before. He exhaled forcefully and brought his hand to his jaw and began rubbing it. He moved to rub the back of his neck, as he stared at the floor, trying hard to remove the image of Sibbie and Etta that had suddenly thrust itself inside his mind, like the blade of sharpened knife. A stab of realization, perhaps? He swore he could see their reflection in that blade, clear as day, staring at him. *Had they tried to warn him of this?*

"So what does this mean, then?" McKinley broke the silence.

Harris looked at him. "It means that we're alone. We're down five men, plus Colt, of course… and they'll stop at nothing until they get their hands on the women."

McKinley put his hands on his hips. "Why didn't the UNF just bring them here themselves and do their experiments straight away? Why bring us into it? Why risk their current stock of soldiers? It doesn't make sense."

Harris ground his teeth. "Who the fuck knows what the UNF was thinking. I *knew* there was something about Martin..."

The three of them stood in silence again for a moment longer.

"Unless we were a test..." Doc suddenly offered, his eyes narrowing in thought.

"A test?" McKinley asked, furrowing his brow.

Harris looked over at Doc.

"Yeah..." Doc nodded. "Maybe it was a test to see how the new breed of soldier went against the current breed?"

Harris, hit by another realization, nodded slowly. "The third test. The first test was the *Stella Maris*, just a stock standard cargo crew. The second test was the *Belgo*, a crew of hardened ex-cons, and we're the third. UNF soldiers. UNF soldiers flying under the radar, that not too many people will miss."

"And the women are just the next phase of their experiment," Doc added. "They kill us to get to them."

Harris, McKinley and Doc all looked at each other for a moment.

"Captain, we have to tell them," Doc said. "Welles and Packham need to know."

Harris nodded, albeit reluctantly. "Call everyone into my office." He went to leave, then suddenly stopped as the device he'd picked up on the Darwin moved inside his shirt. "I forgot this," he said, pulling it out and showing it to Doc.

Doc looked at him confused.

"I took it off the Darwin just now," Harris told him. "They left it for me. Let's find out what they have to say."

Carrie stood guard by the *Aurora*'s main entrance, trying hard not to think about the world of shit they were in. *Three more dead in a matter of minutes... Jesus fucking Christ!*

She heard Doc call her name and turned to see him standing just down the corridor.

"Captain wants everyone in his office," he told her.

She motioned toward the entrance and went to speak, but he cut her off.

"Packham and Brown have overridden the access code. It's safe."

She nodded and they started down the corridor. Doc was slightly in front, but she quickened her pace to walk alongside him. He seemed anxious.

"What's going on?" she asked, searching his face.

He glanced briefly at her, his eyes burdened, but all he said was, "Captain's going to brief everyone."

The tone of his voice concerned her, but she nodded again. "Thanks for... before, outside the mess. You saved me. I owe you one."

"You don't owe me anything, Welles. You would've done the same thing. Except maybe you would've got him in one shot." He gave her a weak smile, then looked ahead and kept walking. She could tell he was avoiding her eyes now, and it disturbed her.

"Doc, what is it?" She reached out and grabbed his arm, stopping him. "What's wrong?"

"The captain will speak to you in a moment." He tried to keep walking, but she stopped him again and her eyes searched his for an answer.

He stared back. "Welles, we have to go." He broke off her gaze and started walking again.

She stood there watching him. *Something's wrong... what isn't he telling me?*

He stopped and turned around. "Corporal!" he called in a firmer voice, as though it were an order. She started walking again and they went the rest of the way in silence.

When they reached the office, she saw Harris at his desk scrolling through an electronic device, with McKinley standing beside him, reading over his shoulder. The two of them stopped what they were doing and looked up at her. Doc moved to stand beside the captain's desk, and McKinley moved to the back wall by the door, giving her a strange look as he passed. Her eyes followed him, wondering what it was for.

Brown and Packham came in then. Carrie turned around as they entered, and saw McKinley motion for Brown to stand beside him, which he did. She locked eyes with McKinley again for a moment, then turned back around to Harris. *What's going on? Why are they all acting strange?*

Packham moved forward to stand beside her, which, Carrie noticed, left just the two of them standing in front of Harris's desk.

"Ok, listen up," Harris began. "We need to make sure we're all on the same page, here." He glanced at Carrie, Packham and Brown.

"It's obvious now that the missing crew have been here all along. You guys killed three of them. That's good. Unless they've snuck extras on board, then I calculate that leaves three, possibly four, but I'm still not sure where Professor Sharley fits into all of this. We certainly haven't seen him, so we don't know if they've killed him, or whether he's a part of all of this.

"Now, Brown's overridden the access to the ship, which means we're locked down and safe. But the question is, what do we do now?" He looked around at everyone. "As soon as we released the survivors, Command deployed another ship to this station. Now, we can wait until that team arrives, locked up here on the ship, but we'll have to do so for a lengthy amount of time without power, temperature control, etc., and we need to be mindful that we've got two soldiers in pods. Having said that, Doc seems to think that Hunter and Colt *will* survive outside those pods once the battery dies, they just won't be as comfortable as they are now and we'll have to watch them carefully, 'round the clock.

"An alternative, Brown tells me, is that we could go to the Darwin's control room, disable the bar on the power so we can regain access, fire up and fly out of here much sooner, and get Hunter and Colt to further medical aid. Of course, if we go for the control room we risk further casualties. These men are extremely dangerous," he told them, holding up the device he and McKinley had been looking at. "I grabbed this when we were on the secret floor. They left it for me. It goes through in some detail the experiment that are these... men. The experiment is called the UNF Advanced Soldier Program, UNFASP for short. These guys, these specimens, have been nicknamed 'Jumbos', basically for the fact that they're a culmination of several advanced features.

"According to this report, so far they've created eighteen of them. Over time, ten of them have died. Some were due to heart problems because of the high concentration of growth hormones they injected them with. Some were killed by other Jumbos. They had eight left and so far we've killed five of them. That leaves..." he looked down at the device, "Oxer, aka Jumbo 16, whom we've not yet had the pleasure of meeting, but according to this file he has the eyes. Logan aka Jumbo 17, and Chet, Jumbo 18." He looked back up at them all. "From what I can gather, they've improved with each one, which would make Chet their best one yet. Not only is he their best yet, but both he and Logan were the two main guys working alongside Sharley on this experiment. It's as much their brainchild as it is his. They were obviously pretty confident with this experiment to volunteer themselves as guinea pigs.

"Now, the Jumbos are extremely strong and fit and they are well trained in how to kill and kill quickly, as we've seen already. The four survivors we initially found all had increased hearing capabilities on top of this. Logan and Chet, their two latest models, have also got improved vision, particularly in the dark. Chet, their very latest, also has an acute sense of smell."

Harris seemed to pause in consideration for a moment. "The UNF sent us here to test them. They've sent two other unsuspecting ships here prior to us. We're the third and final test. My guess is, they were to gain our trust, get out of their cell, get amongst us... and kill us. A real life UNF war game." Harris paused a moment, then looked at Carrie and Packham. "Sergeant Packham, Corporal Welles... when I say their plan is to kill us, I don't mean all of us. There's something else you should know."

Carrie stiffened slightly and shot Doc a glance. His eyes looked back at hers, almost apologetic. Packham shuffled where she stood and the women exchanged a nervous glance. Carrie looked back at Harris, waiting for him to speak. She saw him glancing down at three e-files lying side-by-side on his desk.

"Yes, captain?" she prompted him, suddenly feeling very nervous.

He looked up at them both with a deadpan, expressionless face. "You were put on the *Aurora* for a reason. The UNF wanted you women to take part in their programs up here on the Darwin."

Carrie and Packham shot each other a glance.

"Take part? How?" Packham asked.

"It seems the UNF is looking to expand their perfect soldier experiment by branching out into genetic engineering. You were being put forward as the guinea pigs."

Carrie looked at Doc again. He was staring down at Harris's desk. She looked back at Harris and shook her head. "I don't understand?"

Harris eyed the two women for a moment. "We believe they want to use you as, um… incubators for some sort of genetic… biological experiment with the survivors."

Carrie froze, eyes glued to Harris.

Packham gave him an incredulous look. "What do you mean? They were going to… are we talking… some sort of… *baby* thing here? Is that what you mean?"

Harris nodded. The room was silent.

Packham laughed strangely. "Er… excuse me, sir?"

Again, the room was silent.

Carrie glanced over at Doc again. His eyes were still on Harris's desk. She followed his line of sight to the three files that Harris had been looking at before. She figured they must be their personnel files. Doc looked up and met her stare. His eyes were still apologetic, albeit with a painful edge to them now. Her heart began to pound. *Why are they telling us this? Why now? Why here? What's going on?* Carrie looked back at Harris again, his face still expressionless.

Packham glanced down at her hands, her face suddenly pale and somber. "Is that why… why they were trying to get to me on the flight deck before, when the power went out?"

Harris nodded. "That's why they haven't attempted to kill any of you," he answered, then looked at Carrie. "That's why Grolsh didn't kill you, Welles."

Carrie locked eyes with Harris. Her frozen exterior was quickly melting with an angry molten fire.

"But," Packham continued, "I don't understand. Why me? Why *us?*"

Doc shrugged. "You're fit, you're healthy—"

"And you've all excelled in your fields," Harris added. "You have good, solid track records and you're determined, you're career driven. You must be the sort of breeding stock they're after."

*Breeding stock?* Carrie felt the molten fire scorching her chest now. She looked around at the four men in the room.

"So, you're telling me," she began, trying to steady the angry waver in her voice, "that we weren't actually sent on this mission because we're good soldiers, to *work* like good soldiers. We were sent here because… because we're *women*, basically. That's it. Just women?" She shrugged.

Harris looked at her but didn't answer. Her burning chest was now accompanied by shaking, sweating hands and shallow breathing.

"S— So how long have you known about this, captain?" Carrie asked, her eyes flicking between his and Doc's, as her cheeks began to burn red. "Did they tell you this when they added us to your team? Was it your job to make sure we behaved? That's it, right? That's why you wouldn't let us off the ship, isn't it? It's all in those files, isn't it?" Carrie pointed to the files on his desk they'd been eyeing.

"Look, Welles—" Harris began.

"No!" she fired back at him. "This was in our *FUCKING* FILES, WASN'T IT?" she yelled.

"Welles!" Doc stepped out in front of the desk. "Calm down."

Harris sat back in his chair, stunned by her outburst.

"NO!" she shouted, pointing at Doc. "*Don't* tell me to calm down!" Her mind was racing now, confused with a thousand thoughts. She started moving backward away from Doc, trying to corral a confused Packham behind her and darting her eyes between the men. She wasn't sure what was going on, but suddenly felt very uneasy about the fact that it was the women the survivors were after all this time. Her mind continued to race. *Why did Harris call us here? Why are they telling us this? What are they planning to do? Why did Doc look apologetic? What was that strange look from McKinley before? What are they going to do to us?*

She very quickly became even more uneasy about the fact that she and Packham were outnumbered, particularly with the likes of McKinley and Brown by the door.

She eyed them both carefully, then locked eyes with McKinley. "Why are you guarding the fuckin' door?" she accused in a low, tight voice.

McKinley and Brown shot each other a puzzled glance, as something seemed to click inside Carrie's mind. Something she didn't want to believe, but something that made complete and utter sense.

She spun back around to Harris. "You're going to hand us over to them, aren't you? To save your own necks? Our lives for yours?"

"What?" Packham exclaimed, looking around the room, panicked.

Carrie swiftly slid her hand behind to the gun tucked into her pants. McKinley immediately stiffened and reached for his gun too.

"Welles... *don't*," he warned.

"Welles, take it easy." Doc moved slowly toward her with his hands out in a peaceful gesture. "It's not what you think."

"No?" she hissed, slapping one of his arms away, hard, making him wince. "Then what is it? Did you know about this?" She tried to make her voice hard, but it faltered on the last part, as her brow furrowed in disappointment.

"Just calm down a second... take your hand off the gun," he said, moving another step closer.

"You did, didn't you?" she continued, as her throat tightened. "You and your fucking physicals! Always *so concerned* about our health!"

She swung a punch at his arm, but he blocked it, grabbing her at the wrist. She was angry and unfocused, so her effort was poor. She let go of her gun and tried to throw one with her other arm, but he quickly grabbed that too and twisted her around, crossing her arms over. She tried to rip herself free, but he held her wrists tightly, pinning her arms across her chest.

"FUCK YOU!" Carrie yelled, as she struggled against him.

"No! Let her go!" Packham cried out, as she leaped forward and threw her arm around Doc's neck trying to pull him away. McKinley instantly stepped forward and removed her, forcing her back against the wall. He stood between her and Doc with his hand in the air motioning for her to stay back.

"Welles, calm down!" Doc yelled. "We're not going to hurt you."

Carrie struggled hard, but he brought her in tight against him, curling his body over hers, and tucking his head firmly alongside, to restrict her movement.

"Welles!"

"No! *Let me go*," she yelled, still trying to struggle free.

"I'll let you go when you calm down. I will not hurt you, alright? I am *NOT* going to hurt you!" Doc squeezed her very tight now. Her movement was completely restricted, even her breathing, as her arms were pinned so tightly across her chest.

"It's okay, alright," he said with a firm, but gentle voice. "Just calm... down."

She stood there trapped, breathing heavily in panic.

"Welles!" Harris barked, now seeking to take charge again. "Do we look like we knew about this?"

Carrie tried to look at him, but Doc's head was blocking her line of sight. He turned their bodies slightly and lifted his head back, so she could see Harris.

"Huh?" Harris continued. "Four of my men are dead because I didn't know what the fuck we were up against. You think if I knew it was you they were after, I would've let them out of that cell? That I would've risked my team? *Four* men, Welles. Four *fucking* men! And I have to live with that."

Carrie tried to control her anger, the burning in her cheeks and the large lump gathering in her throat. Silence sat in the room for a few painful seconds.

"We all got fucked over on this, Welles," Doc said quietly. "*All* of us."

Carrie didn't say anything. The room was so quiet, all she could hear was her heavy breathing. She felt the lump in her throat increase dramatically and her eyes began to sting with tears. She pressed her lips together and swallowed hard, trying to keep her composure.

"I'm going to let you go now," Doc told her with a steady voice, "but I need you to stay calm. Alright?"

She gave a very slight nod, fighting the lump in her throat and the welling in her eyes. Doc watched her for a moment, then slowly loosened his grip on her wrists. He moved his arms away from her cautiously, as though she were a bomb that could go off any second. When he seemed sure that she wasn't going to freak out and attack him, he stepped away from her.

She kept her back to him but saw him look over at Harris out of the corner of her eye. As soon as he looked away, she swiftly headed for the door, rushing past McKinley and Brown, who thankfully made no attempt to stop her.

Harris watched as Welles quickly vacated the room. He sighed heavily with frustration. It wasn't the fact that she'd exploded the way she had. That was actually understandable to a certain extent. What got him was the fact that she thought he'd hand her over to the survivors. His *own soldier* thinking that he would trade her life for his own. She really didn't know him at all. Then again, what did he expect? He hardly knew her either. He had to admit the circumstances may have looked suspicious. There was little reason to trust anyone right now.

Doc looked over at the empty doorway, disappointed, then turned back to him, placing his hands on his hips, defeated. Harris eyed him for a moment, then motioned for him to go after her. Doc nodded and left.

"That went well," McKinley said flatly.

"What the *fuck*, captain?" Brown asked, his face somewhat bewildered by everything that had just happened.

Harris sighed again. "What the fuck, indeed!" He ran his hand over his face, then looked at Packham, who still stood in the corner of the room, looking pale and nervous. "Y'alright, sergeant?" he asked her.

She eyed the three men, then shook her head. "Not particularly, no."

"Maybe you should take a seat, you look pale. Everyone just take a second, until Doc comes back with Welles."

McKinley looked at Packham, then walked over and pulled out the chair in front of Harris's desk. He motioned for her to take it; his way of calling a truce. She eyed him nervously for a moment then she walked over to it, sat down and collapsed forward, placing her head in her hands.

Harris, McKinley and Brown watched her, then exchanged a look with each other that seemed to scream aloud the same thought: *What the fuck are we going to do?*

Carrie walked quickly down the corridor, turned the first corner she came across and stood there. She was shaking like a leaf, still fighting the lump in her throat, as the tears threatened to burst their banks. She couldn't believe this was happening. All her dreams of Space Duty had been shattered in one fell swoop. She was a good soldier, a great shooter, and here she was being offered up by the UNF as a host for a biological experiment, like she was worth nothing. She placed her hands on top of her head, then slid them down to the back of her neck and took a deep breath, trying to control her emotions. *How could this be?* Was this what her father was trying to warn her about? Telling her not to trust anyone?

"Welles..." Doc's voice came softly behind her, but it gave her a scare regardless.

She turned around and saw him at the corner of the corridor. "I swear we didn't know about any of this." His apologetic eyes pleaded with her. "We've only just figured it out."

She looked at him a moment, searching his eyes for the truth, and she found it. She believed him. She gave a slight nod, and as she did the banks burst and tears started falling down her cheeks. She quickly wiped them away, but they kept coming. She turned her back to him and shoved her palms against her eyes to try to plug them. She gasped for breath, begging herself: *Don't cry! Don't cry! Don't cry!*

She stood there for a few moments, picturing her father's stern colonel stare. She focused on the image and used it to pull herself together. *Don't fail,* she told herself. *You can't fail.* She took another deep breath and removed the hands from her eyes, drying them. She turned back around and flinched when she saw Doc standing right in front of her now. She looked at him for a second, saw the concern in his eyes and the painful edge to them, then more tears started streaming down.

"Fuck…" she whispered, trying to wipe them away again.

Doc reached out and put his hand on her shoulder, squeezing it gently. She didn't look at him. She knew it would only make things worse. She hated feeling this weak. He moved his other hand up to her chin and brought her face and eyes back to his.

"Welles, we're not going to let anything happen to you, or Packham, or Colt," he said. "If we stick together, we can make it through this. But we *have* to stick together."

More tears came rushing down, as she gasped for breath again. Doc seemed to wince at her tears and clenched his jaw. He brought his other hand up, cupped her face firmly, and ran his thumbs across her cheeks wiping the tears away. She tried to calm her breathing, grabbing hold of his wrists.

"We can do this, but we need you," he told her firmly. "We have to stick together, alright? We're on the same side here."

Carrie nodded at him. She had to pull herself together. *They need you.* She pictured her father again, his firm face, his challenging eyes. It started working. She took a few seconds, then took another deep breath, exhaled her release, and looked at Doc again. This time no tears fell.

He stared at her for a brief moment, his eyes searching hers to make sure she was alright, then he slowly dropped his hands from her face. She let go of his wrists, but he caught her hand and squeezed it, shooting her another look.

"You ready to go back in?" he asked her.

She nodded, sniffing. They dropped hands then headed back toward Harris's office. As she approached the door, she wiped her eyes one last time and took another deep breath, exhaling loudly.

# 23

# Control

Harris watched Doc walk back in with Welles following behind. Her eyes were red. It was clear she'd been crying, but her face now held a stony resolve.

"Coffee?" he asked, staring at them both.

Doc turned and headed for the machine and Welles followed, avoiding eye contact with McKinley and Brown. They poured themselves coffee, then Doc walked back to stand near Harris's desk.

"Okay," Harris announced, "this is where we're at. Let me first reiterate that we did *not* know about any of this until now. *Nor* do we have any plans to hand anyone over to the survivors. We are a team. That's the way we came here, and that's the way we're going to leave this place. Do you understand me, Sergeant Packham, Corporal Welles?"

They both nodded to him, Welles doing so awkwardly.

"Good," he said firmly. "Now, make no mistake, we are caught up in a game, here. We saw the monitors on the secret floor. They've been watching us the whole time, attacking us one minute, then hiding the next. They had the whole crew hidden up there. They've been playing with us.

"The way I see it, we have three choices. Our escape pods are useless to us, because like the *Aurora*, they don't have enough power. So, option *one*, we lock down the *Aurora* and sit tight until the other team gets here. But as I said, that will mean just under two days in the dark with no air temperature control and hoping to hell that Hunter and Colt cope without their pods. Option *two*, we wait on the Darwin until the other team gets here. If we all stick together in one of the smaller areas, with a *lot* of guns, hopefully they won't come at us, although again we have the issue of Hunter and Colt and their pods. Or, option *three*, we go to the control room, regain our access, and sit tight until the *Aurora* has enough power to get us out of here. Either way, with three or possibly four of them still out there that we know of, it's too risky for us to try and find them and take them down. In my eyes, the strategy is no longer one of *offense*, but one of *defense*. That is now our game-play. So, what is it going to be? I want everyone's vote on this." He sat back in his chair and looked around at them.

Packham spoke up first. "Maybe we should just sit tight, here. We'll have food and water, and we can look out for Hunter and Colt, and they can't get to us."

Brown shook his head in disagreement. "I say we go to the control room, get our power back and fuck the hell off this place."

Harris looked at McKinley, raising his eyebrows in question. His second lieutenant stared back with determined eyes.

"I say we go to the control room and get our power, and you put me on guard so I can kill those fucks, like I did Grolsh."

Harris turned to Welles. She was eyeing McKinley, who was now staring back at her in return.

"And you?" Harris prompted her.

She looked at Harris for a moment, then down at her coffee. "Who's to say that the other team aren't coming here to feed us to them?"

Packham shot her a look of surprise.

"They sent us here to be slaughtered, or... whatever," Welles continued. "Why would they rescue us, now? The mission hasn't been completed and we know too much."

"So what's your vote?" Harris asked her.

She thought for a moment. "I'm with Brown and McKinley. We get our power and fly out of here."

"And go where?" Harris asked. "You don't think they'll be looking for us?"

She seemed to think for a moment, then shrugged. "We go straight back to Earth, to the UNF. I'm sure there will be people interested in what we have to say."

"She's got a point," Doc piped up. "This was a classified mission. We were under the radar, here. There are a lot of people who wouldn't have known about this, nor approved of it."

Harris nodded. "This was a classified mission, that's true. But a classified mission signed off by Colonel Isaack."

Welles shuffled uncomfortably. "My... my father might know some friendly faces we could talk to," she offered.

"Your father?" Harris arched his eyebrow at her. "The *retired* colonel?" He noticed McKinley, Brown and Packham look at Welles curiously.

"He may be retired but he's an Original, sir. He's been around Space Duty since day one, he knows the UNF inside and out." Welles stared back at him and gave a sad laugh. "He warned me, you know, not to trust anyone. But I think if there's someone left to trust in the UNF, he'll know about them. He'll help us, if he can."

Harris gave her a nod. "First we have to make it out of here." He turned to look at Doc. "Your vote?"

Doc seemed to think things through for a moment. "I'm not comfortable waiting for the other team to get here. If Professor Martin sent them, then I don't trust them."

"So you want to try the control room?"

Doc nodded. "It's the only option we've got that doesn't involve the other team."

Harris looked around at everyone. "You all know that we risk further casualties?"

They nodded.

"What's your vote, captain?" McKinley asked.

"I don't trust the other team, either," he said. "The control room is our only option as far as I'm concerned, but I needed to know that you guys would back me on that."

He saw Packham look down guiltily to her lap. He moved his eyes to Welles, whose face was a ball of concentration. She seemed to be mulling something over.

"Captain, I'll go," she spoke up suddenly.

Doc looked at her, as did the others.

She stared firmly back at Harris. "Think about it, it's our only option. They won't kill me. I'm the only one who can survive it. Packham has to fly the ship. Colt's injured. I'm the only one left."

Harris eyed her for a moment, noting her steely resolve, admiring her courage.

"And if they catch you?" he asked.

Doc spoke up. "Welles, if they catch you… it could be a lot worse than death."

"So, I don't let them catch me."

Doc shook his head. "You can't go on your own. You need someone to watch your back while you log into the systems. I'll go with you."

"No," Harris said firmly, glancing at Doc. "You need to stay here and take care of Hunter and Colt. I'll go. It's my ship, my responsibility."

"But Captain, they'll ki—" Welles went to protest.

"No, Welles," he said firmly. "Doc's right. You can't break into the system and watch the corridor at the same time. You need back up. I'll go with you."

"I'm with you, captain," McKinley said.

Harris gave him a nod.

"Hell, sign me up!" Brown offered.

"No, sergeant," Harris said. "You need to help Packham get the *Aurora* back to Earth, and we might not make it back to the ship. Even if we don't succeed in getting power back to the *Aurora*, there *is* always a chance the other team may be genuine. If they are, I would like to see five members of my team make it out alive."

Packham looked nervously over at Welles. Harris sat forward in his chair and studied her too. Welles's neck was still purple, her eye partially bloodshot.

"You sure you're up for this?" he asked her.

Carrie felt the adrenaline spiking through her body. She felt determined and strong, as though her anger had melded her flesh into steel. She nodded firmly at Harris. "The UNF may not think so, captain, but I assure you I am."

Harris nodded. "And you have enough IT skills for Packham and Brown to coach you over the comms?"

"Yes, sir. If they tell me what to do, I'll be fine."

Harris nodded back in acceptance. "Brown, Packham? You know what you're doing to get into their system?"

Packham nodded. "Smith showed me how to do it. All we need to do is connect the Darwin's systems to the *Aurora* like we did before, then we should be able to work it out from the flight deck."

Brown nodded in agreement.

Harris eyed them both. "Alright, then it's done. Let's get our shit together, people! Welles, I want a word with you. The rest of you, dismissed."

Welles nodded at him, as McKinley, Brown and Packham left the room. Doc walked slowly to the door, eyeing the corporal. He stopped by her as though he was going to say something but changed his mind and kept walking. After he left and closed the door, Harris looked down at his desk, thinking about what he wanted to say to her. She obviously thought it was about her earlier outburst because she started apologizing.

"I'm sorry about before, captain. I just... it was a shock. For all I knew you were in on it. But I believe you when you say that you didn't know."

He studied her. The steely resolve was still intact, her eye contact good.

"I'm glad about that Welles, because I don't want to go out there with someone who doesn't trust me and who I can't trust in return. I need to know that you'll do everything within your power... I need to know that I can rely on you to do what you need to do, when the time is right. See, I know McKinley will. We've been on the same team for a while now. We work well together and I know I can trust him with my life. Can I trust *you* with my life?"

Welles looked offended. "Of course you can, captain. You just haven't given me the chance to prove it yet."

Harris slumped back in his chair, sighing. "Yeah, well, I had my orders too..."

She gave him a strange look.

He stood and walked around the desk toward her. Placing his hands on his hips, he looked down at her, towering over her small frame.

"Do *not* lose your gun, Welles," he told her.

"I won't, captain," she said.

"If you lose your gun, you're as good as dead. You hear me?"

"I hear you, sir, but you don't need to worry."

"Welles, you are a *great* fuckin' shot, but without a weapon you're an easy target. You're weak. You *cannot* lose your gun or turn your back for a second. It's reality. You don't stand a chance otherwise."

He saw the corporal's eyes flash stubbornly with anger.

"Welles, I could knock you through that fuckin' door right now!" he said pointing to the door several feet behind her. "Hell, Smith would've knocked you through that door and he was half my size. These guys, these Jumbos, are *twice* as strong as I am. So, if you lose your gun, you better run, you hear me? I'm certainly not planning on losing mine. I want to make sure we're real clear about that. I'm not picking on you, Welles, I'm trying to help you!"

She took a deep breath and nodded, the anger dissipating. "I understand, captain, but they have to take my gun first, and in order to do that they have to come within range."

Harris couldn't help but break a smile. He shook his head. "You got fire, Welles. I'll give you that. You just make sure you channel that shit into your gun, and aim it at their heads."

"I will, sir."

He eyed her one last time, then gave a nod. "Go get ready."

He watched as she left the room, all the while noticing that Sibbie and Etta had suddenly floated into his mind again, like feathers floating on a gentle breeze.

Carrie headed for the weapons store, her heart racing, her throat tight. She felt that surge of adrenaline flushing around in her veins, as the nerves danced in her belly. This was it. This was major. This was life or fucking death and the whole team was relying on her. She had to succeed. There was no other option.

When she reached the weapons store, she saw Doc and McKinley standing close, talking, but they stopped abruptly as soon as she entered. She eyed them both quizzically. McKinley stared back at her while Doc took a headset from him and handed it to her. She took it as he gave her a soft smile and left the room.

McKinley walked up and handed her a laser-fire rifle.

"I'm keeping my handgun, too," she told him.

"Good idea." He walked over to a crate and pulled out a smaller pistol. He checked that it was loaded, grabbed its holster, then walked back to her.

"Take this, too. For the ankle," he told her.

She took it from him and put it on. "What about one more for good luck?"

"No," McKinley said standing in front of her. "Three's enough. You wanna weigh yourself down, then do it with ammo. Besides… you don't lose your gun, remember?"

She stared firmly into those piercing blue eyes of his. "Not yet, McKinley."

"Good. So, just make sure you shoot straight."

"And *you* make sure you shoot straighter and keep up," she retorted.

He looked down at her for a moment, then smirked.

"So, you're dad's a colonel, huh? A fucking Original. Figures." His smirk slowly turned into a smile. It was a friendly smile, a teasing smile, not like the smug ones she'd grown used to.

"So, your dad was a cop? That figures, too." She smiled back.

He stared at her for a moment, trying to keep his smile to a minimum. "Grab some more ammo and you're all set," he said, breaking their stare.

"Yes, sir!" She smiled to herself, noting McKinley's face as he registered the "sir".

Harris, Doc, Brown and Packham entered the weapons store then. Harris moved over to collect some more ammo, while Doc handed out small pouches of a red liquid.

"It's a concentrated sugar solution," he told her. "It's packed with vitamins and minerals, so if you start getting tired, suck one of these down. It'll keep you going."

There were six of them in all, and she slid them into her shirt pocket. Doc moved back and stood in the doorway, glancing over at her occasionally. He looked concerned and maybe a little disappointed that he wasn't going with them. She wanted to talk to him. She wanted to put him at ease. Most importantly, she wondered whether he could be of help to her in some way.

"Doc, can I have a word?" she asked.

He nodded, and she walked out of the weapons store and started down the corridor.

"Where are we going?" he asked, following.

"Your office."

When she arrived, she found it open and paused at the doorway to the hospital. She saw five of their team lying there. Three of them covered in sheets. She felt a sudden stab of realization of what she was about to do.

Doc saw what she was looking at, then moved to stand in the doorway, blocking her vision. "What's up?"

She looked down at the headset in her hands. "I was just wondering whether you had anything I could maybe use... if I should lose my gun? Which I shouldn't, because I have three of them... but, you never know."

"What do you mean, that you could use?"

"I don't know, some drug, some chemical that I could maybe inject..."

"No. I'm not giving you something like that." He walked past her and headed back for the main office door.

She grabbed his arm. "I don't mean for me. I mean to stab *them* with, you know, if... if they get me. Although, if it came to it... I *could* use it on myself..." Her voice began to trail off.

He stared at her, his mind ticking over.

"Do you?" she asked.

"I have something," he said looking into her eyes, "but I would need you to promise that you wouldn't use it on yourself."

Carrie glanced down at the floor, then back up at Doc. "I'm not sure I can promise that. You said it yourself, if they catch me... Doc, I hope to god that I don't need to use it on myself, it would be a last resort. I'd try and use it on them first, but I can't promise."

He stared at her, mind ticking over. "Can you promise me that when you're ready to use it, you'll wait? Just wait another ten minutes. In case we're coming to get you."

She studied him for a moment. His eyes were intense.

"I could promise that, but I wouldn't want you taking the risk to come and get me. I don't want you to get hurt."

"Funny that, 'cause I don't want to see you get hurt either," he said firmly, eyes still pinning hers.

They stared at each other, as a slight air of awkwardness swirled about.

"We've... lost enough of our team already," Doc said, glancing around the room avoiding eye contact for a moment.

Carrie nodded, feeling that lump trying to return to her throat. "Okay. I'll promise. If it comes to that, then I'll hold on, in case... in case you're crazy enough to do that."

"Crazy like you volunteering to do this? Or being crazy enough to hang around and wait for the other team? It's crazy either way."

She stared at his face and fought the urge to touch his cheek. His brown eyes were looking into hers, still trying to say something she couldn't figure out. She could feel the lump in her throat growing, and her chest felt tight. *God, what is it about him?*

"I'll go and get it," he said, disappearing into the examination room.

She followed and watched as he took three syringes and filled them up with a pink fluid from his cabinet. She placed her headset down on the bench, as he put the safety covers on each of the needles, then turned to her.

"There are three of them left, and there are three syringes," he said, handing them to her.

*And there are three of us going out there, she thought.*

"Stab it anywhere, preferably the thigh muscle and pump it all in," he continued. "You'll have a couple of minutes to hold out before you should be able to get away."

"Thank you," she said softly.

He looked back at her, clenching his jaw. The urge to touch his face swept over her again. She wished he wouldn't look at her like that.

She took the three syringes and separated them, placing them in different pockets.

"Well, they'll be waiting for you," he said, rubbing the back of his neck.

She nodded and headed for the door but noticed that he wasn't following her. She turned and saw him standing there, his jaw still clenched, looking at her with those eyes, like he desperately wanted to say something but couldn't.

She felt a sudden urge wash over her to say: "*Why not?*" She was going out there to face the unknown and there was a good chance she could die, so what did it matter right? This could be her only chance. And for once in her life, Carrie threw caution to the wind.

She hit the lever, closing the door between his examination room and office. He threw her a confused look.

"Doc," she said walking back up to him, "if I don't make it back…"

"You will, Welles. You *will*, and you have to keep telling yourself that," he said firmly.

"But if I don't…" her voice was soft and husky with nerves as she stood in front of him, "I just want to…"

"What?" he rested his hands on his hips and a strange look came across his face.

She took a moment, looking into his warm brown eyes, then down at his mouth. She quickly reached up, slid her hand over his cheek and kissed him. She closed her eyes, moved her mouth and kissed him again.

Then she suddenly realized he wasn't kissing her back.

Her heart stopped, her eyes flashed open and she slowly pulled away. His face was expressionless. Her heart kick-started again and was almost belting out of her chest now. *Oh, shit… What have I done?*

"Sorry, Doc," she mumbled, moving back from him. "I shouldn't have done that. I'm sorry." She turned to walk away, but his hand shot out and caught her arm. She glanced at his grasp, then back to his face.

He was looking down at the floor in front of him. "Welles… I can't," he said quietly.

"I know. I understand. I shouldn't have. It's okay, really…" she said, trying to free her arm from his grasp. She turned to walk off again, wanting to get out of there as soon as possible, but his arm caught her around her waist and didn't let go.

She looked back at him. "It's okay, Doc. Don't feel bad. It's my fault, really. I shouldn't have. It was just a stupid last minute thing… Heading off to die and all that…" The words continued to dribble from her mouth, like a verbal diarrhea.

He started reeling her in toward him. She was confused now. He was still looking at the ground, his brow furrowed but his arm brought her in very close, so that her body was almost against his.

"I really shouldn't be doing this," he said finally, his eyes showing signs of some internal struggle.

"Doing what?" she asked breathlessly, his face just centimeters from hers.

He pulled her tightly against him and kissed her back.

Carrie was stunned. It was firm but gentle, and took her breath away. He raised his free hand to her cheek and slowly pulled his face back. Their eyes connected, before she moved back in, and they kissed again. It was like a chain reaction, as if they had started something that couldn't be stopped. Her hands traveled up his arms, over his shoulders, and around his neck, as he moved her up against the bench behind them. The soft kiss was now deep, heavy, breathy.

But as quickly as the wave had formed, it rolled away. Doc placed his hands on her hips and moved himself back from her. They looked into each other's eyes, as her hands fell back down to his arms.

"We'll continue this conversation when you get back," he said quietly.

She nodded. She couldn't speak. She could've sworn Doc had stolen all the air from her lungs. He took another step back, their arms falling to their sides and he glanced over at the door.

"They'll be waiting for you. You'd better go."

She stood up straight, took a deep breath and nodded. She slowly headed over to where she had left her headset, brushing her body past Doc's as she did, taking his hand in hers briefly. Then she walked out the door and didn't look back.

*

"Welles, where the fuck have you been? We gotta go!" Harris barked upon her return.

"I got these off Doc," she said holding up one of the syringes. "Just in case."

"For you or for them?" McKinley asked, eyes narrowed in study.

"For them, I hope."

"Test your comms," Harris ordered.

She snapped the headset on around her left ear, plugging the earpiece within. "Flight deck, this is Corporal Welles. Do you copy? Over." She spoke firmly into her mouthpiece.

*"We copy you. Visuals are fine too. Over,"* Packham's voice answered.

Harris stared at the syringe, then locked eyes with her again. "Alright, let's move out!"

She nodded, then followed Harris and McKinley to the exit of the *Aurora*.

Harris and his lieutenant sprang out of the doors, weapons held tightly in a cross-cover. Sensing it was clear, they quickly advanced to the Darwin's entrance, as Welles followed closely behind, surveying the dock and its walls for shooters. Harris was hoping she was going to be able to handle this but couldn't stop to think about it right now. He had to trust that she would, and focus his mind on the Jumbos that awaited them.

Once inside the Darwin, they continued their formation slowly through Section One without incident. They noticed that Grolsh's body was gone. All that remained was a trail of blood smeared along the floor, running parallel to that of Louis's. They crept into Section Two and made their way slowly, but surely to the control room. It was a little too easy, he thought. He wondered whether a trap was being set but pushed it from his mind. They had to get their power back and fast.

"We'll guard the door, you get in there," he told Welles. She gave a firm nod and quickly made her way to one of the consoles and took a seat.

"Okay, flight deck," she said quietly over their headsets, "lay it on me."

Packham and Brown coached Welles on how to get into the Darwin's mainframe and its security files, and then how to enable a remote access link from the *Aurora*. She seemed to understand their instructions, which made the tension around Harris's neck ease up just that little bit. It took about 20 minutes but she did it, and they now had access to try and crack the code from the flight deck.

Harris motioned for Welles to swap and take up his position on the door. He wanted to get a good look at what they were up against in terms of cracking that code, and figure out just how long they were going to have to guard the control room for. He took a seat at the console and eyed his soldiers standing watch at the door for a moment. McKinley and his gun faced west down the corridor, and Welles faced east. Although it looked somewhat like David and Goliath, it was actually a reassuring sight to have his two best shooters on guard. *Nobody will make it past that line of defense!*

Now it was just a waiting game, for Brown and Packham to crack the access. He looked at his watch. 04:53. It would be hours yet. They were in for a very long night and he was glad Doc had given them the sugar concentrate. They were going to need it.

*

An hour passed without incident. Harris watched the monitor while Brown had the system going, cracking the code. It was made up of 12 characters, which could consist of a mixture of letters—English or foreign—numbers, and symbols. So far they had three locked in. At this rate it was going to be another three hours. He pulled out the pouches that Doc had given him, tore one off and downed it. It was sickly sweet and hurt his teeth. He winced, then stood and walked to the door.

"McKinley, take a break," he ordered.

McKinley relaxed his gun and moved into the control room. He took a seat, put his feet up on the desk, and began to stretch out his neck and shoulders.

"How are you holding up?" Harris asked Welles.

She quickly glanced at him and nodded, then returned her eyes to the east corridor.

"You've been standing here an hour," he said. "Take your sugar solution."

"I'll wait until I'm in there, sir," she motioned to the control room. "I don't want to drop my gun."

"I got it. Take it," he ordered her.

She lowered her gun for a moment and poured one of the pouches into her mouth. She, too, winced. Harris noted that his heart was beating faster now, the solution already working. He felt alive, he felt awake, he felt ready for anything. After a few minutes, he saw Welles glance over at him with wide eyes, nodding to herself. The solution had obviously begun working on her too.

"Good stuff, huh," he said quietly.

"I feel like running a marathon," she whispered back.

He gave a short, sharp laugh. "That's the point of it." He thought for a second, then dropped his smile and looked down at her small frame. "You probably should've only had half a pouch, if we're having whole ones."

Welles looked back at him and nodded. "Possibly. How long do they last?"

"A couple hours."

Welles nodded again, staring down the corridor, eyes wide.

"Just watch your trigger finger," Harris whispered.

*

Another hour passed without incident. He heard Brown say over the headsets that they now had seven characters, which meant there were only five to go. McKinley sucked down his first pouch and came over to relieve Welles on the door.

She went into the control room, sat down and eyed the monitor, but after a few minutes, Harris saw her get up and start looking around the room.

"Welles, sit the fuck down and rest your feet!" he said quietly, but firmly, into his mouthpiece.

She moved back over to the table and sat down.

"Put your feet up on the desk like McKinley did," he ordered.

She did, but he could tell she wasn't exactly relaxing, too wired from the solution still.

*"That's another one,"* Brown announced over their headsets. *"Four left."*

*

About 40 minutes passed. Brown had announced yet another two characters. Two left. Once Packham got the *Aurora* in, all Brown had to do was enable access for the *Aurora* to hook onto the external power source again and start charging, then reset the access code so the survivors couldn't change it. At least, not for as long as it had taken their team to get their access back.

Harris estimated about another hour; then it was simply a matter of waiting until the *Aurora* had charged its power cells enough to get them back to Earth, or a nearby station, depending on how Hunter and Colt were holding up.

He looked back down the corridor. His body was starting to feel the sugar concentrate wearing off. He looked at his watch. 07:42. He was curious as to why the Jumbos had not tried to attack them yet. *Perhaps they were waiting... giving us false hope. Letting us get near the end, then making their move when our guard is down thinking we're home safe? This is a game, remember. They like to mind-fuck people.*

He reached in his pocket and took out another pouch. He wanted to be ready for anything. He glanced down at the pouch and went to tear the top off, when he saw something dart across the corridor up ahead.

"Fuck! What was that?" he said, dropping it and swinging his gun up.

"What?" McKinley asked, eyes focused sharply down the east side of the corridor.

"I saw something. One of *them*… dart across the hall up ahead."

McKinley brought his gun up tighter to his sightline. It was deathly quiet for a few moments as they both scanned their sides of the corridor. Out of the corner of his eye, he saw Welles sit up straight and look attentively at them.

McKinley suddenly fired down his side of the corridor.

"Fuck," he whispered, obviously missing his target. "One just ran past my side."

"Which one?" Harris asked.

"Didn't recognize him. Ginger hair."

"Oxer?"

One raced past Harris's side again. He fired, and he too missed.

"That was Logan," he said.

"What are they doing?" Welles asked, directly behind them now.

"Playing with us," McKinley answered quietly, eyes fixed on the east corridor.

"Captain, I'll relieve you now," Welles said eagerly.

"I'm not going anywhere," he told her, focusing on his sightline.

She picked his pouch up off the floor and tucked it back in his pocket. A few minutes passed in complete silence.

*"Just got another one! Can't be much longer, captain,"* Brown reassured him over the headsets.

Just then, Logan came running back across the hall, a laser-fire rifle in his hands, firing aimlessly in their direction. Harris and McKinley quickly pulled back into the room, knocking Welles out of the way in the process.

"Stay back!" Harris barked at her.

He ducked back around the doorway and aimed, but Logan was gone. Then from the opposite direction, Oxer ran past and shot at him. He ducked back into the room as laser fire hit the doorway.

"Jesus!" Harris said.

"Captain, I'll go! I'll lead them away!" Welles's voice was edgy.

"No, Welles. Just sit tight!"

"But we're so close! We can't let them stop us. Let me lead them away."

"Stand back, Welles, *that's* an order."

Brown's voice came over their headsets then. *"Captain, we just got the last number. We're in. Packham's just gotta grant us access and remove theirs. Hold 'em off,"* he said anxiously over the headsets.

Harris reached in his pocket for his solution. He tore the top open and began to pour it in his mouth. More laser fire.

"They're getting closer," McKinley said. He quickly stepped out of the doorway and fired, then ducked back in.

Things went quiet again. Minutes passed and nothing. Harris and his lieutenant stood in the doorway, again. Watching. Waiting. Ready.

"Where'd they go?" Harris said, thinking aloud.

Another fifteen minutes passed. Welles was pacing right behind them in the control room.

"Is it just me or is it fuckin' hot in here?" McKinley asked, wiping sweat from his brow.

Harris suddenly realized just how hot he was, and wiped his saturated brow as well.

"They've turned up the heat," he said, as he ducked back into the room. He quickly removed his bullaser vest and long-sleeved shirt, then placed the vest back on over his singlet. When he was done, McKinley followed suit.

Just then they heard smashing glass. Short bursts of it. Harris looked as far down the corridor as he could, before it curved off into Section One. It suddenly looked darker down there.

"Some lights go out down your way?" he asked McKinley.

"Mm-hmm."

Harris nodded to himself. "They don't need the lights to see like we do," he said quietly.

*"Captain, we've got access!"* Brown announced. *"We're connecting the Aurora now!"*

"As soon as he disables their access, we move back to the ship and fast!" Harris told his David and Goliath soldiers.

"Their aim was for shit," McKinley said, thinking aloud as he stared down the hall. "It was way off…"

"They couldn't risk hitting Welles, or they'd have a repeat of Colt," Harris said. "Like you said, they're just playing with us, trying to mind-fuck us. When we make a move back to the ship, they're going to come for you and me. We have to be ready."

"I was born ready, captain," McKinley replied.

# 24

# Darkness and Light

Carrie was pacing the control room floor now. They were so close. Brown was in, and the *Aurora* was powering up. As soon as he disabled the Jumbo's access, they were to make for the ship, but it wasn't going to be easy. They had one and a half sections to clear, plus the dock. They were so close, but still so far. She pictured the *Aurora*, sitting docked and focused on it. That was their safe haven. That was where the others waited for them. That was where Doc waited.

*"Okay, captain. Access has been disabled. The Aurora is locked in. We're done!"* Brown announced excitedly.

"Okay, Brown. We're heading back," Harris said, then motioned for Carrie to move over toward them, which she quickly did. "Alright," he said, "we head back to the dock, slowly. We be real careful about each room we pass. I need you to be on the lookout, Welles, because when they come, they're going to come at me and McKinley. When they do, I want you to try and get a shot in. They're quick, they're strong, and they'll know we're coming way before we know they are. Understand?"

"Yes, sir," Carrie nodded firmly.

"Let's do this. Welles, get in back," he said, quickly wiping away more sweat that had gathered on his forehead.

Carrie took over McKinley's coverage of the east corridor, while he turned and covered west with Harris. They began to move back along the corridor, with Harris walking slightly in front on the left-hand side and McKinley on the right. Carrie walked sideways, keeping her eye on the rear, as well as trying to ready herself for a frontal attack. Her hands were moist. It was so hot, she was pouring with sweat. She wished she'd taken off her long-sleeved shirt when Harris and McKinley had, but she'd wanted the extra pockets for the syringes and sugar solution.

They cleared Section Two and slowly entered back into Section One. It was dark. Very dark.

Harris flicked on his weapon's spotlight, and Carrie and McKinley followed suit, scoping things out. She quickly glanced around to the front and saw that the office lights were out, as were the corridor lights; glass crunched beneath their feet. The only light she could see was coming through from the dock, as it distantly rimmed the entry doors in white.

She'd never been afraid of the dark before, but now, in this pitch blackness, knowing what was out there, she was.

One of them darted across the corridor behind her. She swiftly turned and fired, the golden beam of laser fire hitting the wall and sparking off.

She'd missed.

*Fuck!*

Harris listened for the aftermath.

"You hit him?" he asked, not taking his eyes off the corridor in front.

"No," she whispered.

"Captain, what's your gun reading in terms of body heat?" McKinley asked quietly.

Harris looked down at the screen atop his weapon. It was one big orange blur. He nodded to himself. "That's why they turned up the heat. So we can't see where they are. Be ready."

Carrie saw a silhouetted figure dart across the corridor again. She flashed her gun's light in its direction and fired off another shot. She'd been closer this time, but still missed. They heard laughter. It was Chet.

"Keep it steady," Harris said in a low voice, walking slowly.

They approached Sharley's office on the right. Harris passed it, then McKinley. Slowly, quietly, they flashed their lights inside the darkened room, but saw nothing. They moved on, focusing their lights back on the corridor in front of them. Carrie followed, keeping her eyes fixed on the corridor behind them. As she passed Sharley's office, two large shapes suddenly launched out at them. She swung her gun around, but her assailant was too fast. He knocked the weapon away with one hand and punched her face with the other, knocking her to the ground. She heard McKinley fire, but he missed, as the Jumbo ducked then lunged, sending the lieutenant thudding back into the glass wall behind.

*"Fuck!"* Brown's voice hissed over the headset.

Carrie took a second, dazed, her cheek throbbing from the hard punch. She looked around the darkened corridor at the dancing weapon lights, red target beams, and occasional golden laser firing off the walls or floor. Her eyes made out Logan wrestling with Harris and his gun, and the other Jumbo—she assumed it was Oxer—wrestling with McKinley and his. Her eyes fixed on her gun, which had slid down the corridor, its light like a beacon of hope. She scampered for it in the darkness, but Chet swiftly appeared and kicked it out of reach. She instinctively grabbed the handgun tucked down the back of her pants, took aim and fired. He ducked around the bend in the corridor, but she was sure she caught him with the shot, as he grunted in pain. She spun back around and tried to find a shot at the others. They were moving about rapidly, and she panicked that she might hit the wrong person in the shadows of the erratic light.

She edged toward them, trying to take aim, keeping her back to the wall, ready if Chet returned. McKinley rammed Oxer into the wall, but swiftly got smashed back into the opposite wall, all the while refusing to let go of his gun. Oxer looked strong, his long ginger hair stuck to his sweating face. They continued to struggle, moving about, neither giving an inch.

Harris and Logan wrestled their way into Sharley's darkened office. Carrie fired high through the glass wall, shattering it, trying to get a better view and scare Logan, but other than a minor flinch, it had little impact. Both Logan and Harris, still wrestling, went flying over the desk and fell off the other side, disappearing. She squinted through the blackness but couldn't see anything to take aim.

She swung her gun back to McKinley. Oxer had him pinned against the wall, pressing his gun across his throat, the weapon's light illuminating off the splintered glass beside them. Oxer suddenly stomped violently on McKinley's lower leg. He yelled out in pain, as it buckled beneath him, dropping his body lower toward the floor. She saw her opportunity for a clear shot, and fired. Oxer's head sprayed over the glass wall behind him, his long ginger hair blending into the flesh and blood of the explosion. His body flopped, almost in slow motion, to the ground.

Exhausted, McKinley let his body collapse to the floor beside Oxer, his upper body shining wet with the Jumbo's blood. Suddenly she heard footsteps running off down the corridor behind her. She swept her gun around, but it was too late. Chet was gone. She turned back to Sharley's office and saw that Logan and Harris had vanished. All was quiet. She squinted through the darkness and saw the lights on the elevator were blinking. *Did they go up*?

She quickly spun back around to McKinley, who sat on the floor holding his leg. It was clearly broken and he was gritting his teeth, trying to fight the pain. She moved over to stand in front of him, scanning the corridor in cover. Her mind was racing. *What do I do? Where's Chet? Where's Logan? Where's Harris? Where the* fuck *is Harris?*

*"Good shot, Welles!"* Doc's voice came steadily over the headset, startling her. He'd obviously been waiting until it was clear before he'd spoken.

"They've got Harris. What do I do?" she asked, unable to hide the panic in her voice.

*"Logan turned his headset off, but Harris was still alive when he did it,"* he told her.

"Do I get him? Or do I get McKinley back to the ship?" Carrie asked.

"No," McKinley said, his voice tight with pain. "Hand me my gun. Go find Harris!"

"I can't leave you here, McKi—"

"Yes, you can!" he said, cutting her off. "But you *can't* leave Harris with them. Just hand me my gun."

Carrie didn't answer, she stood in front of him, flicking her head back and forth, eyeing either side of the corridor.

McKinley groaned in pain. "Welles, my back's to the wall, they can't surprise me. They have to come face on, in my sight-line. So just fuckin' go. Now!" He breathed heavily to control the pain. "That's an order!"

"Doc, are you sure he's still alive?" she asked.

*"Yes... but I don't know how long for."*

She looked at McKinley.

He stared back hard. "I'll guard the corridor. Just get him and bring him back," he said.

She nodded, picked up his gun and handed it to him, then swiftly removed her bullaser and long-sleeved shirt. She felt instantly better. She'd been sweating hard, and her singlet underneath was saturated. She decided to leave the vest behind. They weren't going to kill her, right? She quickly grabbed the syringes from her shirt pocket on the floor, placed two in her pants pockets and handed one to McKinley.

"Just in case," she told him.

He took it, eyeing her apprehensively. She then took her sugar concentrate out of her pocket, ripped one open and gave it to him. He swallowed it in a single gulp. Then she downed one herself and slowly moved into Sharley's office.

"Welles!" McKinley whispered loudly into his mouthpiece.

She turned around.

"*Don't* lose your gun!" His fierce blue eyes pierced through the shadowy light at hers.

She gave him a nod, then stalked into the office, over to the elevator. She hit the button, took a sharp stance with her gun out in front, and it opened. She looked in and saw Harris's vest on the floor and a small amount of blood smeared across the wall.

Harris wasn't sure why, but Logan hadn't killed him. They'd fought their way through Sharley's office, and into the open elevator. Somehow in the struggle, Logan managed to take Harris's gun and ordered him to remove his vest. As soon as he had, Logan dug the butt of the rifle into his ribs a couple of times and Harris heard them crack. Some were broken, he could feel the sharp, burning pain, and his breathing grew tight. But instead of finishing him off, Logan simply aimed the gun in his face and ordered him to turn off his headset.

When the elevator opened on the secret floor, Logan backed out slowly, sticking his leg in the door and keeping the gun on Harris. Chet was waiting for them, his left arm covered in blood. *Welles must've caught him. Good. He's injured.*

Chet smiled at him. "Captain Harris. Welcome," he said, in a most pleasant English manner, which he then dropped for a darker, more serious tone. "Come. Join us."

Chet waved his hand and motioned for Harris to step out of the elevator. He figured he had no choice. He got up slowly, trying not to let them see he was in pain and walked out onto the floor. His mind briefly ventured to thoughts of Welles and McKinley. He'd heard McKinley yell in pain, and he'd heard a gunshot, but he was confident that Oxer was down. He had to be. Welles was there with her gun. It was two against one.

"Please, sit," Chet said, holding out a chair for him.

Harris eyed them both as he took it. "What do you want?" he asked them. "Why haven't you killed me?"

Chet gave a low guttural laugh. "Why kill you when I can use you as ransom… or bait. I have the King of the *Aurora*. Long live the king!"

"They will not hand over the women. I guarantee you that," Harris said, with a cold hard stare.

"Looks like she's coming to us," Logan said, looking at a screen above the elevator.

Harris darted his eyes to it. There was Welles rising in the elevator with her gun out. *Fuck! Why didn't she head back with McKinley to the ship?*

"WELLES, NO! GO BACK DOWN!" he yelled.

Logan stepped to and hit him across the head with the gun. The crack knocked him off his chair and landed him on the floor with a thud.

"Get him out of here," Chet ordered. "I'll take care of this. The *bitch* shot me!"

Harris, dazed, felt Logan pull him to his feet, then suddenly he was being shoved down a darkened corridor, with a gun to the back of his head.

*

Carrie was taking deep breaths, trying to steady her racing heart and sweating, jittery hands. *Where's Harris? Is he still alive? Is it safe to leave McKinley below?* She felt uneasy that they were now all separated. She tried to focus, her father's face flashing briefly in her mind. She needed to be steady if she was going to shoot straight. She gripped her pistol tight, ready for whatever was going to be on the other side of the door. Finally it opened, and she saw Chet standing there, hands up in surrender. Her arms instantly jerked, ready to shoot, but there was no sign of Harris.

"You got me!" Chet smirked, wiggling his hands in the air like some cabaret performer.

Carrie's eyes darted around the room. He appeared to be alone.

"Where's Harris?" she asked, stomping her foot against the elevator door.

"Around," he answered, dropping his arms by his side. "Do come in."

"Tell me where he is, or I'll blow your fucking head off," she hissed. She knew there was no time for games.

"Oh, I do believe that, Corporal Welles. You're a *very* good shot. Poor Fairmont was not expecting that from you. Nor Oxer, for that matter. You've taken out two of our boys, corporal. And you're going to have to pay for that."

"WHERE'S HARRIS?" she yelled.

"Come out of there and I'll show you."

"I don't trust you!"

"Then shoot me and find him yourself," he said in an uninterested tone, "but if you shoot me, Harris will certainly die."

Carrie stared at him for a moment. "How do I know he's even still alive?"

"Logan?" Chet spoke as though the other survivor was standing right next to him. "Corporal Welles needs to know that Harris is still alive. Can you show her?"

In the distance she heard a thud and a groan, then Harris yelled: "WELLES, GET BACK TO THE SHIP!" Then she heard another louder thud, and things went quiet.

"See," Chet said calmly. "Now, how about you step off that elevator and we'll go say hello?"

"No, you bring him to me!" she fired back.

Chet laughed to himself, shaking his head, "So stubborn..."

"NOW!" Carrie yelled, breathing heavily in anger.

Chet dropped his laugh, and his eyes turned cold. "You want him, then you come and get him."

Carrie's mind raced, and the seconds ticked by.

*"Be careful, Welles."* Doc's voice came over her headset. *"Make him walk in front of you and keep your back to the wall."* It was somewhat reassuring to know she had Doc, Packham, Brown and McKinley with her over her headset. She didn't feel alone, even though she knew she really was.

She nudged herself slowly out of the elevator. "After you," she said, motioning with her gun for him to move.

"Very well." He bowed to her.

He turned and started walking down the corridor at the far end of the open office space. It was dark, like the corridor below. She walked behind him, ensuring she was out of his reach, but close enough that she could still see his outline, to have a good clear shot at his head. He turned around occasionally and smiled at her. It was very quiet, so much so that her heavy breathing sounded almost like a roar. She kept her back to the wall like Doc said, and kept darting her head around either side to check it was clear.

"How far?" she eventually asked. "His voice wasn't this far."

"He's just down here," Chet said pointing further down the corridor. "Can't you see?"

She squinted her eyes, trying to get a better look at where he was pointing, then heard a flurry of movement beside her. She snapped her head around as a dark shape descended. She instantly swung her weapon and fired, as she felt a heavy blow to the side of the head.

Then everything went black.

Harris heard Logan and Chet talking heatedly in the distance.

"Fuck, Logan! You've probably fractured her fucking skull!"

"She nearly blew my fucking head off," Logan growled. "I heard the goddamned bullet zip past my ear. Look, it's bleeding. We can't risk her getting off another shot. This way she's out good!"

While they argued, Harris crept away as deathly quiet as he could. He knew they might hear him otherwise. He took out the pistol he'd had strapped to his ankle, glad that Logan had been too sloppy to frisk him for it, then flicked his headset back on. His ribs hurt and he could feel blood running down the back of his neck from where Logan had hit him. He'd blacked out for a second, but continued to play unconscious to fool Logan into walking away from him. He did. And now Harris was trying, ever so silently, to escape.

# 25

# Survival of the Fittest

Carrie was having a dream. She felt like she was floating in space. Floating in complete blackness, as her body moved about in the wind. It was cold against her skin: her belly, her arms, her cheek. And the wind was strong, pushing her cheek upward and forcing one leg backward in the air. She heard a voice. A man's voice. At first she couldn't make out what he was saying, then it slowly became clearer, as though marching its way through a dense, gray fog.

*"Welles! Welles, can you hear me?"*

She wondered who it was, then pictured Doc's face in her mind. It sounded a lot like him.

She felt a heavy weight begin to press against her head, over her left eye, cheekbone and ear.

*"Carrie?"* Doc's voice called again. *"Carrie, it's Doc. Can you hear me?"*

And the pain grew heavier, and the wind grew thick and hard against her belly and cheek. And she felt something tight around her ankle, the one blown back in the air. She slowly opened her eyes. Her vision was blurry and red. *Red?* She blinked heavily. She saw something go past her vision. Something black. Something rectangular. She blinked heavily again. She felt tired. She opened her eyes slowly once more, then she saw another black rectangle. *A doorway?* She tried to straighten her head, but she couldn't. Something was in her way. She looked down at it. It was white, smooth and felt icy cold, but it was too blurry to make out.

*"Fuck! Carrie, can you hear me?! Are you okay?"* Doc was sounding panicked now.

She moved her eyes slowly over to look at her outstretched arms, and saw a line of red by her left arm. She followed the line, down to her hands and stared at them a moment. Something wasn't right, but she couldn't think what. She blinked heavily again... then suddenly she clicked. Her hands were empty. *My gun!* Her eyes widened with terror as she suddenly realized where she was. That was not wind, cold against her belly and pushing her cheek upward. It was the floor. She was being dragged by her ankle, along the floor!

Her head pounded and throbbed. *Fuck! What do I do?* She wanted to ask Doc but couldn't put the words to her mouth. She focused for a moment, trying to tell if her headset was still on. *Of course it was.* That was why she'd heard Doc's voice. She looked back at her hands and wiggled them slightly, then very subtly made an "okay" sign with her thumb, holding it in the direction of her camera. She had to let the flight deck know she was alright.

*"She moved! She's okay,"* she heard Doc say, sounding relieved but still anxious.

The dragging began to slow now. She shut her eyes and pretended to still be unconscious.

*"Logan,"* a strange voice hissed angrily.

"I told him," Chet said.

"She's still alive," Logan growled at them both in his gravelly voice.

"Yes, but you've damaged her! Look," the voice said.

Carrie felt someone touch her face along the bone of her left brow. It hurt, as though they'd pressed into her with the edge of a knife, and not the soft, cold fingers they had.

"Let's take this headset off," he said.

*No!* A wave of panic shot through her, but she couldn't do anything as she was paralyzed with fear.

"There," she heard the voice say calmly. "I'll put the headset here, so her friends can watch."

Logan gave a deep, throaty laugh.

"Chet, I'll need you to look after her for me. We need to persuade the *Aurora*'s soldiers to comply."

"What do you want me to do?" Logan asked the voice.

"Bring me Harris. He'll help us get Sergeant Packham off that ship."

"What about McKinley?" Logan asked.

"He's still in the corridor. Oxer broke his leg, so he's not going anywhere. I wouldn't approach him while he's got a gun in his hands. You've read his file. He's a *very* sharp shooter. He'll surrender to us later," the voice said. "At his captain's request."

She heard footsteps that stopped beside her.

"Save some for me," Logan said, then she heard the footsteps leave the room.

"Check her pulse," the voice ordered Chet.

She felt him kneel over her and put his hand on her neck. He was quiet for a moment. "We have a strong pulse. And eye movement," Chet told the voice.

"Hmm. Pretending to be unconscious, perhaps?"

"Shall we see?" Chet said, his voice very close to her ear, his breath brushing across it.

"Roll her over," the voice ordered.

Carrie felt Chet's hands slide underneath her arms and slowly turn her over onto her back. She kept her eyes closed, trying to ignore the dizzy feeling in her head as it moved. She focused on visualizing where her two remaining syringes were and suddenly realized that her leg was wet where one of them had been. *Fuck!* Then she remembered that she still had the small pistol strapped to her other ankle.

Chet was right over her now. "Oh, Weeelles," he sang eerily. "Let's see if I can't awaken you, hmm."

She felt his fingers touch her bare stomach, exposed from being dragged along the floor. He traced his fingers slowly upward until he hit her singlet bunched beneath her chest, then he flattened his hand and went underneath.

"Make sure you don't block the camera, now," the voice said quietly, but excitedly. "I wouldn't want the flight deck to miss this."

Chet gave a quiet, throaty laugh. "How's your heartbeat, sweetheart?" he asked in a low voice. She felt his hand outstretched over her heart. It was warm and seemed to amplify the beating in her chest. "Heartbeat's fine. What about the rest of you..." His voice trailed off as he moved his hand, sliding his fingertips underneath the cup of her bra.

She opened her eyes slightly and saw he was kneeling over her, legs either side of hers.

"Ah, sleeping beauty awakes," he smiled as he clasped her breast firmly in his hand. "My hands have the gift of life!"

Repulsed by his touch, she quickly mustered all her strength and brought her knee up hard into his groin and punched his face. Neither were as strong as she'd hoped for. She felt her wrist jar on impact, causing them both to grunt in pain, as he clutched his crotch. Spying the doorway, she quickly rolled over and tried to scuttle away.

She didn't move as fast as she'd hoped for, though. Her head felt too heavy for her body to carry and her vision blurred. She heard the voice laughing as Chet lunged after her, grabbing hold of her belt and dragging her swiftly back. She tried to fight against him, but her wrist hurt and her head throbbed badly. He flipped her over while she tried to kick at him weakly, but he grabbed her legs and split them either side of his body, as he leaned over her again, grabbing her by the throat and squeezing tight.

He held her firmly, not losing control like Grolsh had. This was how Grolsh had been supposed to do it, hold her firm and make her submit, but Grolsh had lost his temper and nearly killed her. She had to make sure Chet didn't do the same.

"I'm sorry." She strained to get her voice out.

Chet stared down at her with cold, pale blue eyes.

The voice laughed quietly, almost purring. "You will be if you try that again, my dear, Carrie. I can only hold Chet off for so long."

She tried to look over Chet's shoulder in the direction it came from, but Chet saw and squeezed her tighter.

"Please! I'm sorry," she said again.

"You shot me, you *bitch*. I'm going to make you pay for that," Chet hissed, then leaned in even closer so that his lips brushed her cheek. "Tell me, Welles, what's your pain threshold like?"

She patted his arms, his chest, his sides, as though she was trying to calm him. What she was doing, however, was making her way down to the pocket on her pants where her last syringe was tucked. She started thinking about how she was going to do this. She decided she needed to make sure he kept his hands on her throat, to give her an extra second or two with the syringe, so she changed her tactic.

"Let me go, you fuck," she hissed at him, angrily.

He stared back at her, eyebrows slightly raised.

"Carrie, my dear, that is not going to help you," the voice said. "You can't win this."

"Fuck you," she said, then spat blood in Chet's face.

He growled and squeezed her tighter. She felt woozy as her head began to throb even harder. She brought her knees up high as though trying to buck him off, but it only brought her hand to her pocket. She slipped it inside and felt the syringe between her fingers.

"*You*... can't... win... this," she managed.

The voice laughed at her.

"I think Logan hit her harder than we thought." Chet smiled.

"I told you she had a fighting spirit," the voice said, as though in admiration.

"Spirits are meant to be broken," Chet said, his expression turning to a deadly stare as he leaned down and licked the side of her face.

Logan came back into the room then, walking quickly, heavily, over to the voice. "Harris is fucking gone!" he said angrily.

"What?" asked the voice.

"He's gone! I left him unconscious and now he's gone. I can't find him."

"Logan!" the voice said. "Couldn't you hear him?"

"No. I told you we can only hear things in the distance when there is silence around us. We need to work on strengthening the senses," Logan argued.

Chet started to loosen his grip as he absorbed himself in the argument between the two men. Carrie flipped the lid off the syringe and held it tight in her palm. She saw her opportunity to strike. She quickly pulled the syringe out and stabbed it into Chet's thigh.

His head shot around, lightning fast, wincing in pain. He growled and quickly smacked her hand away from the needle before she could inject the fluid. His fiery eyes locked with hers and he raised his muscular arm in the air. She squeezed her eyes shut as he unleashed a hard backhand across her face, knocking her head to the side. She opened her eyes and through blurred vision, made out Harris hiding in the doorway with his gun. She looked back at Chet who was pulling the syringe out of his thigh. She saw his nose suddenly twitch as he quickly looked up in Harris's direction. She heard the crack of Harris's gun as he fired and Chet's body flew back, his upper left chest area spraying red.

Logan and the man behind the voice quickly fled through another door as Harris fired after them but missed. She blinked to clear her vision. The man behind the voice had white-gray hair. He was side on, but she recognized him from the pictures Harris had shown them during their mission briefing.

"Sharley!" she exclaimed.

Harris was suddenly beside her, aiming his gun at the doorway through which they'd disappeared and motioning for her to get up.

"Let's get the fuck out of here," he said urgently. "You got a gun?"

She stumbled groggily to her feet, then bent down, scrambling to get the one on her ankle. She stood up with it and staggered as a wave of dizziness overcame her. She grabbed onto Harris's shirt to steady herself, and he latched onto her arm in support, as a slight zap of static electricity passed between them. He glanced at her arm, noticing it, too, then at her bloodied head.

"Welles, I can't carry you. You need to walk. You hear me?"

She nodded absently, studying him. He had blood down the back of his neck, bruises and swelling across his face, and as he moved to the doorway and peered around it to see if it was clear, she saw him hold his ribs for a moment, wincing in pain. She took a deep breath. She had to hold it together. They could make it out, but she was going to have to focus and walk herself out.

He motioned for her to do a cross-cover with him. She did, but her hands were only half-mast with the gun. They felt so heavy she could barely raise them, and that worried her. She tried desperately to attune her hearing to make up for her eyes as they blinked heavily. But it was useless, her hearing was no better than her eyesight. Her brain was caught up in heavy, painful fog.

They made their way down the corridor to the elevator quickly, taking as much care as they could in passing each closed doorway. Her head continued throbbing and she was still unsteady on her feet, but she tried her hardest to ignore it. She could just make out Harris's tall silhouette in front of her and stuck closely to it. She kept checking the hallway behind them, but it was clear. Empty. Quiet.

It felt like an eternity but they eventually made it to the elevator, stepped in, and sealed the doors behind them. As soon as they shut, they both dropped their arms to their sides, exhausted, and leaned back against the walls. Carrie wanted desperately to slide down and sit on the floor, but she fought the urge with all her might.

She knew if she did, she would not be able to get up again.

Harris eyed Welles carefully. The left side of her face and neck was covered in blood, and her eye and cheekbone were so bruised and swollen, her eye was half closed over. He could just imagine what her head felt like.

"Hang in there, Welles," he told her. "We're nearly there."

She moved her eyes slowly over to his and gave a slight nod.

The elevator came to a stop and they raised their guns, although Welles's arms weren't quite as firm as he would've liked. He knew that it was going to be up to him to get them safely back to the ship. The doors opened and they slowly moved out into Sharley's office. As they approached the doorway to the darkened corridor, they saw a weapon's spotlight suddenly shine in their direction.

"McKinley, it's us!" Harris spoke quietly into his mouthpiece.

He peered out the door of the office and saw McKinley sitting on the floor, against the wall diagonally opposite, gun firmly in their direction. In the shadowy light of his weapon, his lieutenant looked a little pale. He was sweating and Harris saw his left lower leg looked bent out of shape.

*Fuck! I can't carry Welles, and I sure as shit can't carry him either.*

They moved over to him, carefully covering each side of the corridor. McKinley glanced hopefully at Harris as they did, then shone his light on Welles's face for a moment and the hope on his face seemed to fade.

"Give me your hand," Harris said to McKinley. He had to try.

McKinley held out his hand. Harris gripped it and tried to pull him up. His lieutenant got halfway, but Harris's ribs couldn't take it and he dropped him. McKinley groaned loudly as he fell back down. Harris steadied himself on the wall, bringing his hand up to his ribs and wincing.

"Fuck!" he wheezed in pain.

"Dddrrrraagg him," Welles slurred, moving over to them.

They each took one of McKinley's hands and tried to drag him down the corridor. Welles got a couple of steps, but then dropped his hand, grabbed her head, staggered and fell to her hands and knees. Harris tried, but his ribs wouldn't let him move an inch. They felt worse now and it was hurting him to breathe. Welles stumbled slowly back up to her feet. They stood there in the corridor for a moment, catching their breath, trying to think of a way out of this situation. Then they heard a voice.

"Don't shoot," it said calmly.

They both spun round raising their guns in the direction of Section Two. The light from McKinley's weapon spotlighted Professor Sharley and Logan walking toward them out of the shadows, hands in the air.

"We are unarmed," Sharley said, his large, angular, nose casting shadows across his face.

Harris watched as Welles, positioned in the middle of the corridor between him and McKinley, turned around to check the corridor leading to the dock. Her defensive tactics were still working. That was something.

"You are safe," Sharley told them in calm voice, reminiscent of Chet's, albeit with a European accent of some kind. "We are the only two left." He and Logan walked slowly around to stand in front of them, cutting off their path to the *Aurora*.

"Stop right there, Sharley!" Harris said, holding his gun firmly on them. "What do you want?"

"I would like you and Lieutenant McKinley to turn off your headsets, please."

"You want my headset off, then you come and get it," McKinley challenged him through gritted teeth.

"Not with that gun in your hands, lieutenant," Sharley smiled.

McKinley looked confidently back at him.

Sharley turned his eyes to Harris. "Your team has done well, captain. You should be proud."

"What do you want?" Harris barked again.

"To talk, captain. To negotiate."

"Negotiate what?" he spat.

"Your lives." Sharley's voice was calm, but his words cut through Harris like a knife.

He stared hard at the professor.

"This was a test, Captain Harris. I know you figured that out," Sharley told him. "You were sent here by the UNF to test my Jumbos. And your team has done well. You have lost only four men and I have learnt a lot about my Jumbos' strengths and weaknesses."

"*Only* four men," Harris said incredulously.

Sharley smiled. "Consider it a cleansing of your team, captain. Your strongest have survived.

Harris continued to stare at him. He could feel his eyes burning a hatred that seemed to match the fire lashing at his ribs with each breath he took.

"So, here we are," Sharley continued, shrugging. "I am content with the results of the test that your men have provided, and I am willing to allow you to take what's left of your team and go, *but*... you will leave this one behind." He pointed to Welles. "She is part of another phase of my experiment."

Welles look nervously over at him. *She still didn't really know me...*

"Corporal Welles is a part of my team and she is coming with me," he told Sharley firmly.

Sharley smiled again. "I admire your bravado, Captain Harris, but it's not needed. I have UNF backing. You are allowed to walk away from this. No questions asked. You see, I told them that when I was ready I would send them a sign. They knew that when they got this sign, they were to send the selected *hosts*, here to me. We didn't accidentally lose the comms with Command. We purposely disabled them so that a team would be sent here to rescue us. Of course, Private Smith was clever and his systems managed to track some of our scrambled messages, after the fact." He smiled. "Still, that worked in our favor. We were sent a team that was alert and on guard. Wary. A team that would test us well. A team that would have something we wanted from them.

"Although, at first, we were unsure as to whether any women had been sent. Our survivors, as you called them, had not seen them. But Chet knew... he could smell them on Lieutenant Walker as he ran his tests. He knew, and so instead of attacking you outright, they won your trust, you released them and you brought them together. This was a test against your soldiers, a test to get the women into our custody. You have proven yourself, Harris. So you and your team may go. But I still want the women. They were sent here for my program. They belong to *me*."

"Like I said," Harris stared menacingly at him, "Corporal Welles is a part of my team, and I will not leave without her."

"Neither will I," McKinley raised his gun a little higher in Sharley's direction.

Harris saw Welles glance at McKinley, then back at Sharley. Obviously feeling reassured, she, too, raised her gun a little higher.

"Captain Harris," Sharley began, a little more of an edge to his voice now, "I am allowing you to leave and take the rest of your team home, *alive*. I can tell you that was not a part of my original plan. And that's including the other two women, who technically belong to *me...* but I know Corporal Colt is injured and you need Sergeant Packham to get you home. So I am willing to make a sacrifice, but *you, too,* will sacrifice and leave Corporal Welles here with me."

"What's she to you, Harris?" Logan growled.

"Corporal Welles is a part of my team and I will *not* leave her behind," Harris hissed through gritted teeth. "Now you better accept that, because my opinion will not change. The way I see it, you've got three guns on you. Disagree with me too long, and we will shoot you, regardless. It's as simple as that. So, it is *I* who am allowing *you* and your last Jumbo to live, but the choice is yours."

Sharley laughed a long, guttural laugh. "Very nice, Captain Harris, turning it around like that. But you're ignoring the fact that the UNF sent her here knowing full well what would happen. Look at her." His eyes scanned over Welles. "She needs medical attention and we can provide that for her. We mean her no harm. In fact, we wish for her to be as healthy as she can be."

Welles pulled her gun up higher and steadied it. "Get the fuck out of my way, or I'll blow your FUCKING BRAINS OUT," she yelled at him, spitting blood and saliva in the process.

Harris glanced at her. She was breathing fast, clearly starting to freak out, and although she was still unsteady on her feet, she managed to aim her gun alright. He looked back at Sharley and Logan. "Sharley, you know as well as I do that she will not miss. She *will* kill you. Now you'd better decide what your fate is going to be, because *'I'm not sure how long I can hold her off*. Sound familiar?" Harris asked, pointing to his headset, indicating that he'd heard Sharley's words to her before.

Logan stepped forward, squaring his shoulders. "Why don't you drop your gun and let's see who gets out of here alive?"

"Logaaan!" Sharley warned, his voice low and drawn out.

"You shouldn't have kept me at bay," Logan spat back. "They need to be taught a hard fuckin' lesson!"

"Logan, trust me." Sharley turned back to Harris, his eyes holding an unnerving sense of evil in them. "They will be taught."

Sharley and Harris stared each other down for a moment.

"Captain Harris, would you like me to get your superiors at the UNF on the line to see what their orders will be?" Sharley said calmly, but tauntingly.

"You do what you want, Sharley, but my decision is final, and for the last time I will fuckin' repeat it," Harris began, as Logan suddenly turned and eyed the corridor behind him. "Corporal Welles is a part of the *Aurora* team, and we will *not*... leave... without her!"

"FUCKIN' A, CAPTAIN!" Brown's voice boomed down the corridor.

Harris looked over Logan's shoulder to see Brown and Doc creeping toward them, their red target lasers dancing over Sharley and Logan, weapon spotlights beaming down the corridor.

*What the fuck are they doing here? They should be on the ship.*

Harris hid his anger and pointed at Sharley. "That's five guns now, Sharley! The way I see it you don't have a choice."

Logan growled, hunching his shoulders, crouching for a fight.

"You're making a *big* mistake, Captain Harris!" Sharley's face twisted into a snarl. "Tell your men to stand down, or I will make you pay for this!"

Harris fought the urge to pull the trigger with all his might. Part of him wanted the man dead, but part of him wanted to see him locked up, to see him pay for the rest of his life for what he did to his soldiers.

"Start walking to the bio cell," he said through gritted teeth.

Sharley looked around at each member of Harris's team for a moment. "Are there none of you who will hand her over to me? You're all going to defy the UNF, hmm?"

Neither Brown, Doc, nor McKinley answered, they simply held their guns firm on their targets. Sharley turned back and glared at Harris for a moment, then dropped his snarl and replaced it with a smile, regaining his composure.

"Very well, Captain Harris. You've made your choice. You've *all* made your choice." He glanced around at the team again.

"Start walking," Harris said flatly.

Logan glared over at Sharley, who turned and locked eyes with him. Sharley's face was serene, but his eyes firm, as though he were communicating with him. Logan's anger seemed to ease off. Sharley smiled again, put his hands in the air and slowly began to walk toward the bio cell.

Carrie watched as Sharley and Logan came toward her, then veered away slightly, skimming past her outstretched arm and handgun. Sharley's smile and eyes chilled her to the bone with his haunting stare.

"I'll see you soon, Carrie Ann Welles," he purred.

"You're mine," Logan pointed at her, snarling viciously, his emerald eyes psychotic, "and I'm gonna fuckin' make you pay!"

Carrie felt a spike of fear shoot through her, as Harris forced him away from her and barked "MOVE!" Brown followed his lead.

Doc locked concerned eyes with her briefly, then quickly crouched down beside McKinley and looked at his leg. He pulled out a needle and jabbed him with it.

Carrie, not sure what to do, turned and followed Brown and Harris down the corridor. She had to see Sharley and Logan locked up for herself. They didn't seem to be putting up a fight, for which part of her was grateful, but it made the other part of her feel somewhat uneasy. She would have preferred to see them dead.

Harris locked the glass chamber on them, then pulled the lever to close the exchange windows with a loud bang that seemed to echo through the station. Sharley stood up close to the glass, near Harris, and gave him a big beaming smile.

"This is not the end, Captain Harris." His distant voice sounded over the speakers. "I might be submitting to you now, but the next time I see you, it will be *you* who submits to *me*."

"I submit to no-one, you fuck," Harris replied with a deadpan face, seemingly not in the least bit threatened.

Sharley laughed as he turned and walked over to one of the chairs left inside the cell. He sat down, crossing his legs, "I hope you don't get into trouble for this, captain. I'm very valuable to the UNF, you know."

Carrie watched as Harris pulled on the door to ensure it was locked, took one last careful look around the cell, then slowly backed away, still targeting his gun. Sharley sat there smiling, bouncing his crossed leg, while

Logan stalked up and down the glass frontage like a trapped panther, snarling at them.

"Y'alright, Welles?" Brown asked, grabbing her arm.

She managed a slight nod. The bright lights of the bio cell were hurting her head, and her eyes were refusing to adjust. Now that Sharley and Logan were locked up, she felt a wave of relief sweep over her that made her head feel heavier by the second. It was as though her neck were made of straw and her skull filled with concrete.

They made their way back to Doc and McKinley, who was looking slightly better as the morphine had kicked in. Doc was just tying off a makeshift splint on his leg. He looked up at them. "They locked up?"

Harris nodded. "I thought I told you to stay on the ship?"

"Yeah," Doc said, "and how were you going to carry McKinley back with those ribs, or Welles was with that head injury?" he replied firmly. "You left me in charge of the ship, captain, and I made a decision."

Harris merely grunted at him. From the look of his bruised and swollen face he was too exhausted to argue. Doc moved over to Carrie and placed his hand near her swollen eye, examining it. She pulled away at his touch, the pain excruciating.

"Can you make it back to the ship?" he asked. She nodded, stealing a quick glance into his eyes. He turned back to Harris. "You right with those ribs?"

Harris nodded. "Welles and I will cover you… just in case."

Doc, with the help of Brown, slowly lifted McKinley and began to head for the ship. Harris led the group and she tailed behind as they slowly made their way through the darkness of Section One. Carrie's heart was still racing slightly from the sugar concentrate, but her whole body was starting to feel heavy with exhaustion, pain and throbbing. She felt as though she'd been in a car wreck, the muscles in her back and neck beginning to ache and burn.

When they hit the dock, she squinted her eyes as they struggled to adjust to the brightness again. Each beam of light felt like a laser slicing through her retinas and piercing her brain. She moaned in pain and brought her hand up to shade her eyes. No longer able to provide coverage of any sort, she somehow managed to stumble her way back to the entrance of the ship, where Packham awaited them.

Harris watched as Doc and Brown took McKinley straight through to the hospital, and Packham slung Welles's arm around her shoulder and followed them. Harris remained at the *Aurora*'s entrance, wanting to be sure the ship was sealed and safe. He even manually changed the entrance code again, just to be sure.

As the door slid closed and locked in place, he exhaled in relief and rested his tired forehead against it.

*Thank god*, he whispered in his mind. *Thank fuckin' god …*

# 26

# Morphine

Carrie heard McKinley groaning as they put him on a bed. She noticed the bodies of their fallen soldiers were gone. Doc had been busy during the hours it had taken to decode their access. He'd prepped the hospital for the worst, and it was just as well he had. She opted to wait in his office, where Harris joined her, announcing that the ship was locked down. They both sat on opposite sides of Doc's desk, staring tiredly at each other.

Trying to get a grip on their injuries, Doc, with the help of Packham, scanned Harris's chest, then Carrie's head, although she had to make a slight detour to vomit first. The ice pack Doc had given her when they first got back, burned cold against her swollen face, and the throbbing in her head became so bad it had made her empty stomach feel sick. Thankfully, he'd steered her over to a sink in time, where she offloaded a small amount of red liquid. At first she worried it was blood, but Doc assured her it was the syrup from the sugar concentrate. He'd wet some paper towels and gently patted the good side of her face and the back of her neck, cooling the sickness away, then gave her a small dose of morphine to take the edge off the pain.

Feeling marginally better, she had her scan, then Packham led her back to the chair opposite Harris at the desk, and she and the captain stared at each other again: eyes tired, faces swollen. Despite the hazy state of her mind, she thought she noticed a curiosity in her captain's eyes as he stared at her.

"Ok, now the hard part." Doc walked back into the office reading their results. "Prioritizing the casualties."

Brown appeared in the doorway between Doc's office and the hospital, where he'd been with McKinley.

"Welles, you've got a fractured cheek, the top left of your zygomatic bone. You'll have a mild concussion, but there's no further sign of any major swelling or bleed to the brain. Captain, you've got two fractured ribs, one of which is pressing close to your right lung, and McKinley's got a badly broken leg." He looked up at them both. "You're first, captain."

"I'm fine. See to the others," Harris waved him off.

"Your lungs take priority, captain. You stop breathing, you die."

Harris looked over at Carrie. "She doesn't look so good."

"No, she doesn't, and the longer you keep me talking, the longer it takes for me to see to her. Now move!"

Harris looked over at Doc and tiredly arched his eyebrow at him.

"Sir…" Doc added with a smile.

Harris held out his hand and Doc assisted him out of the chair. He gave a grunt and groan of pain as he stood.

Doc looked at Packham. "I'll bring out some oxygen. Keep her talking. She has to stay awake."

"Brown?" Harris called as he followed Doc. "I manually reset the ship's access codes. Just in case. I want them changed every 30 minutes."

"Yes, sir."

*

Carrie sat on the chair for what seemed like an age. The oxygen mask was soothing across her face, but that combined with the morphine was making her want to fall asleep. Packham tried to keep her talking, but she found it hard to pay attention. Brown came back and positioned himself in the doorway, occasionally glancing at her in between checking the security feed he'd patched through from the flight deck, which showed the ship's external cameras.

Eventually, Harris came back out with Doc. She'd heard their voices in the other room, but only now really listened to them talk.

"Doc, I'll cope. I need to make sure this ship takes off and I can't do that if I'm doped up to the eyeballs. As soon as we've taken flight, you can give me something, but I'm not going to lay down right now."

"You need to stay still or that rib will puncture your lung," Doc said heatedly.

"My pilots will escort me to the flight deck, where I will sit still until we leave, I promise."

Doc turned to Packham. "Go with him and do what you need to do, but make sure he sits still and rests!"

"Yes, sir," she said, moving over to Harris.

Brown went to go with them, but Doc stopped him. "I'm going to need your help later when I try and straighten out McKinley's leg."

Brown shot him a look of revulsion, but nodded, then turned and left with the others.

Doc turned to Carrie. "Okay, let's take a look at this head of yours."

*

Carrie sat on the last empty bed, looking down the line at the others. McKinley lay on the far bed against the wall, eyes closed from the heavy dose of morphine he'd been given, and Hunter and Colt lay asleep in their pods in between.

Doc shone a light into her eyes, and she winced in pain as he tried to open her left eye more. "Sorry. But your pupils are reacting, that's good."

"How long until the ship takes off?" Carrie asked wearily.

"It will be a couple of hours yet until the full re-gen is complete," he replied.

"Jesus! Shouldn't we be on guard or something?!"

"They're locked up in the bio cell and the ship is sealed. We're fine. We're safe."

"Are we?" she eyed him tiredly. "Never thought I'd want to be back on Earth so much."

He gave her a soft smile in understanding. "Let's clean up this face of yours." He gathered some supplies and came back. He took a bowl of warm water and a cloth, and began cleaning up the dried blood down her face and neck. Despite the dose of morphine her head still hurt when he touched it.

She groaned.

"I know you want more morphine, but I just need you to wait a little longer. I need to monitor you for a bit and make sure you're going to be okay first. Same with any fluids or food. It's nil by mouth for a couple of hours."

She sat in silence while Doc cleaned up the rest of the blood. When he was done, he took a good look at the cut that seemed to mark the spot of the fracture Logan had given her.

"That's going to need stitches. It'll scar, too."

Carrie looked at him, tiredly. "You mean I'm finally going to look like a real soldier?"

Doc smiled. "If that's what you want. I can stitch it real messy and make it real ugly."

She smiled back. "Nah... I like it when other soldiers don't take me seriously."

Doc shot her another smile, then started tipping a strong smelling solution onto a swab and held it up to her face. "Alright, this is going to sting."

He started cleaning the cut with the solution, making Carrie reel backward.

"Ah, Jesus!"

"I know, I know, but it has to be done." He took his free hand and held the other side of her face to keep it still. He continued cleaning the cut and she grabbed onto his arm as a reflex, quickly sucking in air to combat the pain, as it burned like acid.

They suddenly heard the ship begin to murmur. Doc stopped for a second and listened. "We've got enough power to idle her. God, that's a beautiful sound."

"I'll be happier when it's louder and we're moving," Carrie said.

He stared into her eyes for a moment, then looked back at the cut. He finished cleaning it, and threw the swabs away, all the while leaving his free hand on the side of her face to keep it still. She felt another wave of exhaustion and relief wash over her. She was so glad to be on the ship, so glad they'd made it back alive, so glad to have Doc standing there right in front of her. She felt safe now. So safe that she was ready to relax and shut down her body for some much needed sleep.

She turned her head in toward his hand that still cradled her face. She pulled it down gently until it brought his palm to her mouth, closed her eyes and gently kissed it. He quickly moved his hand away, however, and she looked at him a little surprised.

"Did I ever tell you the hospital has a surveillance camera?" he said quietly, pretending to mess with the items in the tray beside her, then he very subtly glanced around at McKinley's bed.

"Oh," her eyes fell to where McKinley lay, but noted his eyes were closed. She quickly scanned the room for a camera.

"Yeah." Doc's eyes flicked up to hers briefly, then subtly motioned to a spot behind her. "Command might choose to access the footage, given what's happened up here."

Carrie looked at him, her eyes hurting along with her head now. "And the examination room?"

Doc shook his head. "No. That... conversation, wouldn't have happened otherwise." He spoke quietly, subtly looking around at McKinley again.

Carrie nodded and they stared at each other for a moment.

"I have to do these stitches," he said gently, breaking the silence.

She nodded, her tiredness growing, and the solution making her head throb even more.

"I'll put in a little local for the stitches," he said, walking away. She closed her eyes for a moment and thought about how good it would be to lie down and go to sleep.

"Welles!"

She snapped her eyes open.

"You have to stay awake!" he said walking back over to her.

"Are you sure, 'cause I *really* could do with some sleep right now."

"I'm positive. Just a little while longer, then you can sleep. I promise."

He injected the local anesthetic, then pressed beside her left eye. "You feel that?"

She shook her head.

"Okay. This shouldn't take too long."

She nodded again and looked over at Colt's face in the pod beside her. She looked somewhat peaceful, despite the large bandage across her neck and shoulder, soaked with blood. Carrie would give anything to be her right now, sleeping soundly.

She felt Doc tugging on the cut. It didn't hurt, but she could tell when he was doing each stitch. She looked at McKinley and saw him blinking his eyes slowly, then close them again. *Did he just wake up? Or has he been awake the whole time?* She brushed it off, too tired to care.

Doc continued threading the stitches and eyeing her occasionally.

"Jesusss, Doc, you're killing me here." She slurred her words slightly, in utter exhaustion.

"You're doing good. Just a few more minutes."

Eventually those few minutes passed and he was done. "Nine stitches, Corporal. Not a bad effort."

She gave him another weary smile, as he put more solution over the top. He then sealed it with a thick bandage that resulted in her left eye being almost fully covered. He moved over to the sink with his tray of implements, removed his gloves and washed his hands.

He returned to her bed shortly after and took another look at her. "Alright, besides the head, is there any other pain? Does anything else hurt?"

"My whole body hurts," she said.

He nodded. "Well, having the likes of Logan hit you in the head and then slam you into a wall is bound to do that."

She looked down at her right arm, at the large bruise that had grown from her shoulder to her elbow. "So that's where that came from, then?"

"Yeah." Doc grabbed her arm and gently prodded and squeezed it. "Nothing's broken though or you'd know about it."

She lifted her singlet slightly and peered down the side of her combat pants, eyeing the bruises that seemed to travel down over her hip.

"May I?" Doc said, moving his hands over to her side. She shrugged her permission, and Doc began to gently prod her ribs, her back, her abdomen and her hip, checking them. "You'll be black and blue, but there doesn't appear to be any serious injury. You were very lucky to get out with only this," he said, pointing between her head and side.

"Thanks to you guys."

Doc gave a brief half-smile, scratching the back of his head. "Well, I'd better get Brown here and try and set McKinley's leg."

Carrie looked back over to the far bed. McKinley was virtually asleep again from the morphine.

"When can I have some more of that?" she asked, motioning toward the sleeping soldier, referring to the morphine and sleep.

"Soon," he said, as he swung her legs up onto the bed, making her wince. "In the meantime, I want you to *sit up* on this bed and relax." He removed her boots, dropped them on the floor and kicked them underneath her bed, then walked over to the intercom and paged Brown. She watched him move over to McKinley and start examining his leg.

Carrie couldn't even muster the energy to speak now. She looked at her watch. 09:52. *Jesus, no wonder,* she thought. *It's been a hell of a long night.* She thought about the previous 28 hours, and all that had happened. Most importantly, she thought about the four soldiers the *Aurora* had lost: Smith, Louis, Carter and Bolkov. Gone.

She thought about those who were left. Thought about Grolsh and the napkins. Chet's hands on her, feeling her heartbeat. She thought about the discovery of the UNF's betrayal. At least, the small "classified" section of the UNF that had betrayed them. And after everything that had happened, she had the bittersweet sensation of finally feeling a part of the *Aurora* team. Harris and McKinley had been hard to break, but she felt as though she'd finally gained their respect. And of course, there was Doc ...

"Welles!"

She flicked her eyes open. She hadn't even realized they were closed. She looked over to McKinley's bed and saw both Doc and Brown staring at her.

"Doc, I'm fine... I jusss really need sssomesssleeeep," she slurred.

Doc moved to her bed. He flicked his light across her pupils again. He hesitated for a moment, then sighed. "Alright, you can sleep, but I'm wiring you up to monitor your breathing and your heartbeat. Alright?"

Carrie nodded. "Anything for sleep."

"Lay down."

Carrie moved her aching body further down onto the bed with Doc's help. He kept a few pillows behind her to keep her elevated, but at least she was lying back now. He brought over the white discs attached to the monitor, slid his hands beneath her singlet and put the three in place, then turned the machine on. It started beeping away, steady and clear. He then grabbed an oxygen mask and placed it on her face.

"I want you to keep this on," he ordered.

Carrie barely managed a smile, she was so exhausted. But a last thought sent a shot of fear through her. They were still on the Darwin, after all. She flicked her eyes open wide and latched onto his shirt.

"Are we really safe now?" she blurted.

Doc nodded. "It's okay. Sleep."

His reassuring words sent a flood of tiredness washing over her, and she let go of his shirt.

"Just call out if you need anything," he told her, although his voice sounded cloudy.

She tried to smile but her face quickly numbed with sleep.

Harris sat in his chair watching Packham give Brown a rundown of the procedure for takeoff in space. She went through, step by step, each part of the process, and what levels and readings she needed him to check for her. She did three dry runs just to be sure that he was familiar with the sequence and the timing. Brown seemed relatively comfortable. Being the ship's engineer he had a good working knowledge of the instrument panels and their functions. He focused hard on learning the sequence, as though etching it into his memory for a lifetime. When Packham was done with the training, Harris watched as Brown sat there and looked over the console, again and again, running through things in his mind. He knew everyone was counting on him. He was particular in his work, a perfectionist, and Harris knew he wouldn't let them down now.

Packham looked a little anxious, but only in terms of whether Brown was going to do his part. Of course, she didn't know him like Harris did. Packham herself looked comfortable in the pilot's chair. The most comfortable he'd seen her look on the ship since this whole fiasco began. He was confident in her abilities. She did well on the docking and she'd been flying cargo ships for some time now. Besides, Hunter had always told him that taking off from a station in space was a walk in the park. But how Packham and Brown would go re-entering the Earth's atmosphere was another thing. That is, if they got that far before Command intercepted them.

All the while Packham and Brown studied the flight deck console, Harris kept an eye on the *Aurora*'s external cameras. The dock was clear. There had been no sign of Sharley or Logan. He had faith in the bio cell that he'd left them in. He'd checked it himself. It was securely locked, and when he'd scrutinized their surroundings, he couldn't see any means of escape, especially given that the *Spector* was gone. He knew the other ship would be there soon enough to take them into UNF custody. So as far as he was concerned, they were locked up and no longer his problem. His priority now, was to get his wounded to a fully-functioning hospital.

He checked his watch. Thirty minutes, give or take, until they could fire up and fly out of there. He moved uncomfortably in his chair, trying to find a way of sitting that didn't make his ribs hurt, but he found it impossible. He'd give it an hour. He had to last just one more hour and lend moral support to Packham and Brown to get this ship on its way home. Then and only then, could he even think about resting.

Carrie awoke to her head throbbing and her body sweating. She groaned as she opened her eyes. The oxygen mask was still on, and the monitor was still beeping. A few seconds later, Doc was there beside her, leaning over the bed, his eyes looking tired, the stubble showing clearly across his face.

"You okay?" he asked, moving his hand to the damaged side of her face.

"My headssthrobbing... baaad..." she managed groggily.

He took out his light and flicked it across her eyes again.

"I'll give you a heavier dose of the morphine now," he said, reaching over and wheeling a drip closer to the bed. He'd obviously prepared it while she'd been sleeping. He took her hand, which she noticed already had a cannula inserted, and quickly connected her to the drip.

"You need sleep, Doc," she said, rolling over stiffly onto the bruised side of her body, but the good side of her head.

"Yes, I do," he said, as he injected the contents of a syringe into a tube that fed into her drip bag.

"Issseveryone okay?" she asked.

"They're stable," he nodded. He pulled a chair over and took a seat, placing his elbow on the side of her bed, and resting his head in his hand.

She stared into his beautiful brown eyes for a moment. "Are we flying yet?" she asked, beginning to blink heavily as the pain relief began to envelop her.

Doc nodded.

She gave a half-smile, "Get some sle—"

That was all she managed, before she was out like a light.

Harris sat awkwardly in his chair. His ribs were aching pretty bad, and he was starting to think it was time to take Doc up on his offer of drugs. After a successful departure from the Darwin, he was satisfied that the *Aurora* was on course. Packham had done a good job of coaching Brown through every step, and Brown assisted well, remembering the sequence, and keeping cool under the immense pressure he must've felt. As soon as they'd departed the Darwin, Harris felt a large portion of his anxiety fall by the wayside. Packham looked at Brown and smiled: "Good job, staff sergeant." Brown, relieved, had smiled and nodded back: "You too, sergeant."

It was the first thing that had gone smoothly since they'd landed on the station. It was also a far cry from the scene in his office when the women thought the *Aurora*'s men were going to hand them over to Sharley's crew. They'd torn down that mistrust, they'd pulled together and they'd made it out.

He'd watched the Darwin as it disappeared from sight on the rear camera, hoping with every fiber of his being that he would never see it again. Deep down in the pit of his stomach, though, he knew that place would haunt him for years to come. After all, four of his men were now dead, and the rest of them were headed back to a UNF they didn't know whether they could trust. And as terrifying as the Jumbos had been, facing the massive beast that was the UNF actually worried him more.

He sighed, deciding it was time. Groaning in pain, he attempted to get out of his chair.

"Captain!" Brown said, rushing over to help him up.

"Thanks, Brown. You did a good job."

Brown nodded in appreciation, and Harris looked over at Packham, still sitting in the pilot's chair eyeing them.

"You too, Packham. Well done."

She nodded back at him.

He looked at Brown. "You two take it in shifts now, to keep watch up here. I'll come back and check up on you. You run into any problems, call me, you understand?"

"Yes, sir," they answered.

"No matter what," he emphasized. "And stay off the comms. We fly silent until I say so."

They both nodded, and satisfied, he left the flight deck.

As the door closed behind him, leaving him alone in the corridor, he couldn't help but stare at the bloodied spot where Bulk had fallen. He suddenly pictured the quiet Russian sitting at the flight deck console, sipping his piping hot coffee and staring out into the nothingness. *All that serenity*, he thought. *And then all the chaos that ensued.* He sighed again and shook his head as a heavy feeling settled into his chest that he knew had nothing to with his ribs.

When he arrived at Doc's office, he looked into the hospital and saw Doc bent over asleep on the side of Welles's bed. He walked over for a closer look, eyeing the other three patients as he did, listening to make sure everything sounded alright. He reached the foot of Welles's bed and looked at Doc again. He had both arms folded on the bed, his head resting on them. Welles was on her side facing him. Their arms were parallel, resting against each other. There was something about it that seemed a little too comfortable, a little too familiar.

He glanced around again, then back at them. *Doc was exhausted, Welles was injured and they were both sleeping. That's all it is*, he told himself. Besides, he was in too much pain to care right now. His own brain was shot to pieces with exhaustion, and his body brutally ached for some pain relief. He made his way into Doc's examination room and began to search through the cabinet. As he fished around, his fingers accidentally clinked the bottles noisily against each other, knocking them over. After a few seconds, Doc walked into the room rubbing his face.

"Saul. What you looking for?" he asked groggily.

Harris looked at him. "I'm ready for the drugs now."

Doc nodded, yawning, and set about prepping a shot for him.

"Not too much, Doc. I need to be able to wake up if needed."

His medic gave another nod, swabbed his arm, then inserted the needle. "You need to lie down and rest, Saul."

"I'm going to do that right now, Doc. You know, you look like you could use a bed, too. Your *own* bed," Harris said, motioning back into the hospital. He wanted to let Doc know that he'd seen them.

Doc glanced over his shoulder and nodded. "Unfortunately somebody has to stay here and we're a little down on numbers *and* beds."

"Give me a couple of hours and I'll relieve you," Harris said, beginning to feel relaxed as the drugs kicked in, making his ribs feel a bit lighter, too. He started making his way to the door.

Doc called after him. "When are you going to tell Command what's happened, and report that we're on our way home?"

Harris turned around. "When I've had some sleep and my head is clearer."

"They'll be tracking us."

Harris nodded. "I know. But I can't speak to them like this."

Doc nodded, his face a little apprehensive. He ripped the top off a sugar concentrate pack and downed it.

Harris was pleased to finally make it back to his room. He went straight to the bathroom and washed his face and neck before moving over to his bed and easing himself down onto his back. He looked at his watch. 12:26. He lay there for a moment, trying to think about what he'd say to Command, but he couldn't think. He was in a mixed state of total relaxation, with a tight chest and shallow breathing.

Exhaustion swept over him rapidly and there was little time to think about Command, or even the Jazz Club Woman. He did manage, however, to briefly picture Taya and Ty in his mind, which seemed to lighten his chest that little bit more. *I'm coming home...* he whispered to them in his mind. The sleep came swiftly then, grabbing a firm hold and dragging him under into its blackened depths.

*

Harris woke abruptly. It took him a few seconds, but he realized that he was still on the *Aurora*, in his quarters. He looked at his watch. 16:30. *Shit! Doc!* He went to get out of bed and a sharp pain across his chest reminded him to take it slow. He sat on the edge of his bed for a moment and focused on his breathing, noticing that he was drenched in sweat.

His mind felt a little hazy. He wasn't sure whether it was the remnants of the pain relief or the bizarre dream he'd just had. He'd been flopping about in a lifeboat in the middle of the ocean. Set adrift and waiting to be rescued. At first Taya and Ty were sitting there with him, but they soon morphed into Sibbie and Etta. Their faces startled him again, like they always did. It suddenly made him wonder where the rest of his team were, which, of course, had violently jolted him awake.

He made his way to Doc's office, having just checked the flight deck, where Brown was at the controls and Packham asleep on the floor in the corner. They'd been taking it in turns and had recently swapped over, but Packham thought it best to be on hand in case something happened, which Harris had to admit he was actually relieved about.

He entered Doc's office and saw he was looking a little ragged.

"How you doin'?" he asked the lieutenant.

Doc sat back in his chair and looked at him wearily. "I've been better."

"Well, go get some rest. Take as long as you need. I'm good." Harris walked over and stood on the other side of Doc's desk and put his hands on his hips, although somewhat gingerly.

"Need another shot?"

Harris nodded. "A little. Not as much as you gave me last time."

Doc fetched what he needed and gave Harris the shot.

"Okay," Doc said throwing the syringe and swab away, "they should all be fine. I just topped up McKinley's morphine and you don't need to worry about Hunter and Colt. I've got their pods programmed to give them what they need. They should just sleep, except maybe Welles. If she wakes up and she needs another shot, then just grab me and I'll come and give it to her. Just get me if anything happens, no matter how minor. Okay?" Doc said, rubbing the back of his neck.

"Go get some sleep, Doc. I got this," Harris ordered.

The lieutenant nodded and headed for the door, stopping briefly to glance into the hospital one last time before he left.

Harris decided to check on the four patients in the hospital and see for himself how they were doing. They were all asleep, and their monitors sounded good. McKinley's leg didn't look great, but it was splinted tightly. There wasn't much Doc could do until he got to a real hospital. Hunter's broken arm was heavily bandaged, so it was hard to tell what state it was in. His bullet wounds were bandaged, too, but easily spotted by the blood that had seeped through to the surface.

Colt looked a little sicker than the two men. While they looked like they were asleep, she looked like she was in pain. She had a large bandage over her neck and shoulder, and a fair amount of blood had soaked through. Harris watched her heart monitor for a moment, but it seemed okay. He walked over to Welles's bed and studied her. She was still on her side. From what he could see outside of the bandage, her eye and cheekbone were purple and very swollen, and she still had the bruises on her neck from the strangulation. She'd been through a lot, but she'd hung in there. She was tough, he had to give her that.

For some reason, as he stared at Welles, Sibbie and Etta stepped delicately into his mind again. Just like they'd done when he'd been searching for her on that hidden floor, like they were guiding him to her or something. It was odd, he thought, that they were coming to him just as much outside of his dreams, as they were inside them. This hadn't happened before. He'd physically thought of them before, recalling memories, but they'd never just appeared in his mind without his own doing. It made him curious, but more so, it made him concerned.

He couldn't help but wonder whether this mission had gotten to him, whether his mind was starting to fray. He knew this could happen to soldiers. Sometimes they saw things that stuck with them, things they could not erase; things that haunted them. Things that made their minds begin to unravel... Harris had seen a lot in his time, but he'd always prided himself on his strong mind and his ability to leave the shit behind and switch off the soldier, and back into civilian mode. But this mission had been different. Very different. Had this mission been the one to finally make him crack? Was this mission the one that would be his undoing? Then again, he'd had that first dream of Sibbie and Etta *before* he got the call...

*So what did that mean? What if this wasn't a soldier's mind fraying with some kind of PTSD? What if this was purely a medical thing? Purely genetic? What if these strange nuances were the start of him following his mother down into the murky depths of her Alzheimer's? What if...?*

He shook the image of Sibbie and Etta from his mind, exhaling in a controlled manner, as he continued to stare at Welles. *Pull it together, Saul. Focus!*

He walked back out to Doc's office, sat down, and tried to clear his mind. It was critical that he was thinking sharp when he made that transmission to Command.

# 27

# Sparkie

Carrie opened her eyes slowly. She was groggy, like she had just woken from the deepest of deep sleeps. For a moment she thought she was back on Earth, in the spare bedroom at her father's holiday villa in Florida. She looked up at the lights on the ceiling, but they looked different. She blinked heavily, wondering what the beeping noises were. Then she focused her eyes on Colt's sleeping face. She was still on the *Aurora*.

She went to roll onto her back, and suddenly felt the weight of her head, although it hadn't seemed to be throbbing until she turned. She tried to push herself over with her arm, but it hurt, as did her back. She groaned aloud in pain, fell onto her back, then closed her eyes again. After a few seconds she heard a noise and opened her eyes again. Harris stood in the doorway, and he started toward her.

"Y'alright?" he asked quietly.

"I just..." she said with a little difficulty, then swallowed to clear her throat. "I couldn't turn over."

She saw him eyeing the bruised side of her body.

"But you're okay, now?"

"Yes, sir," she whispered.

"Alright. Well, you need anything, just call out." He turned to walk away.

"Captain," she called, although it was not as loud as she planned.

He paused.

"Thank you," she said. "For coming back... for saving me."

Harris eyed her for a moment, as a humble expression washed over him. She studied the bruises on his face and wondered how his ribs were.

"No problem, corporal," he said. "Thank you for coming to get me, too."

She managed a half-smile. "I didn't save you though."

Harris pursed his lips and shook his head. "No, but you distracted them so I could get away. If you hadn't come back, I'd still be there. So, I guess we saved each other."

She blinked heavily and gave him another half-smile. She noticed he wasn't using his captain's voice. He'd put away the formalities and was showing her a piece of himself unconstrained by his uniform. She recalled seeing Harris with his gun, and the relief she'd felt. She hadn't recognized the room they'd held her in from any of the footage she'd seen, but somehow Harris had found her.

"How did you find me?" she asked.

He eyed her again for a moment, then glanced over at McKinley's bed. "Doc and McKinley armed a tracking device on your headset in case you got caught. So, I guess technically they saved you," he shrugged. "Doc just guided me where to go."

"Where is he?" she asked.

"Doc? Getting some much needed sleep," he said, his captain's voice returning. "And you should get some more, too, corporal," he ordered.

She nodded, closed her eyes, and heard him walk away.

Harris walked back into Doc's office with a plate of food. Doc had just come back on shift and was in the hospital checking on his patients, but soon joined him to eat, sitting down at his desk.

"You going to call them soon?" Doc asked. "Command?"

Harris nodded. "Right after this. Packham said they've been trying to make contact. I can't hold off any longer."

"You think they'll send Martin's ship to intercept us? Or send another one?"

"Hopefully another. I think Martin will be keen to check on the station. If they send another one for us, they'll send the nearest ship, which means it could be at any moment. That's why I've been stalling, but I know our window of goodwill is closing fast. They'll be tracking us and wondering why we're not responding to their contact."

"Should I start waking them up, in there," Doc motioned to the hospital, "so they know what's going on?"

Harris shook his head. "Hunter and Colt have been out for half of it. There's not much information they can provide. But I want to talk with Welles and McKinley. Once the UNF get a hold of us, we'll be separated and quarantined. If they put us through the correct channels, we'll be locked in a debriefing room for god knows how long after that, under guard. That is, if they handle us legit."

He exchanged a concerned look with his lieutenant.

"How classified do you think this mission was?" Doc asked, eyes narrowing slightly. "You think Welles was right? Do you think there'll be some friendly faces when we get back?"

Harris shrugged at him. "I really don't know. I can't see them advertising the fact that they used their own men as bait for an experiment. I think this was probably on a need-to-know basis, and not many people needed to know. But until we know who we can trust, we need to toe the line like good, obedient little soldiers. If we do, then they won't see us as a threat and we'll be safe. Hopefully it's only a few who fucked us over, Doc. Not the whole of the UNF."

Doc nodded in agreement, although his face still showed concern.

Harris let out a big sigh and stood. "What I want to know most, is where Colonel Isaack stands in all of this. It's time I call Command."

*

Harris waited for the screen to connect.

"Captain Harris. Finally!" Isaack greeted him sternly. "You're aware we've been tracking you for the past ten hours? Do you care to explain why your ship has left the Darwin *without* orders to do so, nor any request from yourself? And why haven't you responded to our comms?"

"Where's Professor Martin?" Harris asked, clenching his jaw.

"Answer my question, captain. And what happened to your face? I've got a lot of important people here wanting an explanation, so you'd better start giving me the fuckin' answers."

Harris tried to control the anger bubbling inside him. "I'll explain myself, colonel, but first I would like you to explain why you sent us there to be slaughtered. Or why you sent three female recruits there to take part in an experiment they had not given their consent to."

Isaack looked confused but quickly regained his composure. "Captain, I have no idea what the hell you're talking about, nor do I like your tone. Your team were sent there to resolve a comms issue, which I might remind you, you have failed to do. Your ship has also been off the contact radar for almost twenty-four hours and on top of that you've left your post without authorization and I need a damn good explanation as to why."

*Good soldier, Saul. Be a good soldier. Hold it in.*

"Colonel Isaack, four of my men are dead. First Sergeant Carter, Staff Sergeant Bolkov, Sergeant Louis and Private First Class Smith. The crew of the Darwin are responsible for this. I also have four injured soldiers: Second Lieutenant McKinley, First Sergeant Hunter, and Corporals Colt and Welles. The crew of the Darwin are also responsible for this."

"What? Four men did all of this to your team of soldiers?" Isaack interrupted, his face showing signs of either confusion or anger. Harris couldn't decide which.

"No, colonel. The rest of the Darwin crew were, in fact, still on the station, as I suggested."

Isaack stared at Harris for a moment. The seconds passed. "How many casualties in the Darwin crew?"

"Seven."

"Injured or dead?"

"Dead."

Isaack stared at him again. There was something about his face that piqued Harris's interest. Isaack was trying to keep a poker face, but Harris could tell from his eyes that this was all news to him.

"And what started this? The incident with Welles?" he asked, the harsh tone gone from his voice.

"No. The incident was a by-product of why we were really sent there." Harris stared down the screen waiting to see what Isaack had to say to that.

A few seconds passed as Isaack's mind ticked over. "Captain Harris, a UNF ship will reach you in approximately eight hours. You will let them board, and they will assume control of your ship and bring you back to base. You are to talk to no-one about this until we debrief. This is classified. You understand?"

"This UNF team you're sending, is it their mission to silence us?"

Isaack's face hardened. "The UNF team will bring you back to base *alive*, Harris. Now, I don't know what the fuck happened up there, but I want a full debrief on this. Do you understand?"

"Where's Martin?"

"On his way to the Darwin. Now, do you understand my order?"

Harris studied him, trying to judge his sincerity. "Yes, sir," he said, trying to keep any emotion from his face, but struggling with the accusatory look in his eyes. "Answer me one thing, though, colonel?"

"What's that?" Isaack eyed him sternly back.

"Why did you order me to keep the women on the ship?"

Isaack stared at him for what seemed like an age. Finally he answered. "We'll discuss that upon your return, Harris."

Isaack leaned forward, and the screen went dead.

Carrie heard the sounds of faint murmuring.

"Welles? Welles, it's okay!"

She woke with a start and panicked when she saw someone standing over her. Instinctively, her hand shot up and held them at bay.

"It's okay. It's me." Doc held his hands out, peacefully.

She looked down from his face to her hand, which was clenched in a fist, tightly grasping his shirt within it. She let it go.

"Sorry," she said groggily, raising her hand to her head.

"You alright?"

She nodded and the tension eased off her shoulders.

"Some dream, huh?" he said, eyeing her carefully.

She blinked her eyes, trying to remember it, then decided she didn't want to, as she pictured the terrifying faces of Chet and Logan. She looked back at Doc. "How long have I been asleep? Are we back on Earth yet?"

"No. We're still a way off Earth. You've been sleeping on and off for about eighteen hours."

"Jesus!"

"How's your head?" he asked, flashing his light into her eyes again, making her shy away.

She lay there for a moment and concentrated. Her head was still sore, but not quite as heavy as it had been before, nor did it seem to throb as much.

"It's okay. It feels more like a migraine now."

Doc put the light back into his pocket. "Good."

Just then she heard McKinley groan. Doc glanced over at him, then back to her. "I had to wake you both up," he told her. "Command knows we've left the Darwin and another ship will intercept us in a few hours. Captain wants to talk to you before they do."

Carrie nodded, then Doc walked over to McKinley. Harris entered the room with Brown by his side, and stood, hands on his hips, eyeing them all.

"How long?" Harris asked Doc impatiently.

"Just give them a few minutes to wake up," he told him.

Harris hit the intercom button. "Packham? You hearing this?"

*"Yes, sir,"* her voice sounded over the PA.

Carrie watched as Harris turned back, bringing his hands up to hold his ribs.

"Fuuuuuck, Doc..." McKinley said groggily.

"How's the pain? Alright?"

McKinley groaned a little. "Yeah... we at Command?"

"Not yet," Harris interjected, "but Command is coming to us. They'll be here in approximately," he looked at his watch, "two hours."

McKinley rubbed his face, glanced at Carrie, then back to Harris. Doc fetched some water for his two awakened patients.

"When the UNF ship gets here," Harris continued, "they'll be assuming command of the *Aurora*, and we'll all be under armed guard. They will probably separate us, and we won't see each other again until after we're back on Earth, quarantined and debriefed."

"Do we trust the team that's coming?" McKinley asked.

Harris pursed his lips and nodded. "I think maybe we can. Colonel Isaack seemed surprised by what I told him. It could be a ruse though. So, I just want to give you all a heads-up about what's going to happen. If they process us legit, you can bet your asses on a major debrief when we get back and a possible court-martial. Seven UNF scientists have been killed by our crew. That's seven deaths we have to answer for, and on paper it'll look like a clear-cut case of soldiers versus scientists. And you know who'll be left looking bad in this situation. This was a classified mission. We don't know who we can trust or how much our debriefers will know. And if this thing goes against us, charges could be laid. And don't think for a second that they're going to focus their grilling on me and Doc, as the senior officers. They will grill the fuck out of all of you. Especially you, Welles, and you, too, Packham, you hear me?"

Carrie nodded, and Packham's voice came over the PA. *"Yes, sir."*

"You're both fairly new to Space Duty, so they're going to assume that you're the weakest link and try and push that. You'll get special attention, Welles. I know you've had a serious debrief before with the Santos mission, but with that head injury, the fact that you killed two of their Jumbos, wounded another, not to mention the incident with Grolsh, or the fact that the Jumbos actually caught you. They will be squeezing you, corporal, you can guarantee that."

Carrie nodded firmly at him.

"So, assuming our debriefers are privy to the classification, all you have to do is tell the truth," Harris told them. "I've been over every casualty in my head and there wasn't one that wasn't deserved on their side. They were killed when one of our own was at risk. The UNF cannot deny that. But we still don't know how things will play out when they get their hands on us. We don't know whether we can trust them, so I will leave it up to you as to what you do and do not tell them. All I ask is that you be smart about what you say and how you say it. These guys, these JAGernauts," he said using the slang term for UNF JAG officers, "the ones that will handle the debriefing, are worse than lawyers. They'll go for the jugular if they feel it's necessary, they'll get real personal, and they can twist the shit out of anything. So you all need to be strong and hold firm. We did what was right, in a mission that was completely wrong, and you need to remember that. Questions?"

The room was silent, but Carrie decided to speak up.

"Captain, should I see if my father can help?"

Harris eyed her for a moment, mulling it over. "What exactly do you think he can do for us?"

"He's an Original," she shrugged. "He's bound to know some friendly faces at Command. He can try and make sure the *right* people get involved in our case. Make sure that we're not burned at the stake." Carrie touched her hand to the side of her face, trying to caress away her aching head, and thought for a moment. "If I make a transmission to him, will they be able to track it?"

"Probably," he answered. "Packham, can you somehow censure what is said on the transmission?"

Packham's voice sounded nervously over the PA. *"I don't know. That was really Smith's forte, scrambling. I can try, but I can't guarantee a result."*

"I... I can probably do it in code, sir," Carrie told them.

Harris arched his eyebrow at her.

"When my father came home from a mission, he would talk in code with my mother about it. It was his way of letting her know what went on, without actually telling her and breaking UNF protocol. I'm the only other person who knows it."

Harris and Doc exchanged a look, then he turned back to Carrie. "Give it a try, Welles. We might need a friendly face. Packham, set up the transmission."

"Yes, sir."

*

Carrie felt a little dizzy as she sat there staring at the transmission screen. Until now, her head had distracted her from the pain down her neck and back from Logan's wall crunch, but now it was becoming more and more evident. She tried to stretch out her muscles as the message blinked across the screen: *One moment while we connect you...*

She waited a few moments, the screen flashed, then she saw her father. He was in his living room, in his dressing gown. It looked to be the early hours of the morning there.

"Ree! You scared the *shit* out of me. I thought I was getting 'the call' about you. What happened to your face? Are you alright?" he asked, a little frazzled. He'd obviously just awoken.

"Dad, hi," she began slowly, calmly.

"Ree, what happened?" he asked, angrily.

"It's fine. I'm fine. I just wanted to speak with you." She squeezed her eyes tight for a moment trying to force her brain to think back to the conversations she'd heard between her parents, and the games they'd played in her childhood. It had been a while. "I— I'm going to be home soon, and I wondered whether you could… could get me a gift? For when I return."

He looked confused. "What the hell are you talking about? Is your head okay? Has someone checked you out?"

"The head is fine, Dad. I just, er… I missed you and… I missed mum, and I started thinking about those conversations you used to have with her. You know? About Sparkie and Uncle David? I was reminiscing…"

He stared down the screen a moment, then rubbed his face as though he were trying to wake himself up. She could tell he'd cottoned on to what she was trying to do. "Yeah, sure, Ree. You said you wanted a gift?" He stared rather fixedly into the camera, not wanting to miss anything.

She smiled. "Yes. We're going to have a party when we get back to town, and I thought you might want to invite your friend along? You know, the one with the friendly face? The good listener. I can't remember his name… he's always good to have around. The life of the party. I've told my team all about him. They'd like to meet him at the party. We'll need some entertainment."

He stared at her a moment. "Yeah, he's a good guy, that one. I know a couple. I could invite a few along," he said, as he rubbed his gray whiskers.

"That'd be great, Dad. We would all really love to see them."

"Your head, your neck? Doesn't look like blast wounds. Looks like you did several rounds with a heavyweight boxer." His voice was softer, but still firm. She could tell his mind was racing, his eyes searching hers for answers.

She gave a slight nod.

"You got band-aids?" he asked her, referring to the wounded.

"Er, yeah. There're less than six."

He nodded. "And you mentioned Sparkie and Uncle David?" Sparkie had been her great-uncle David's dog that had been hit by a car and died. So fond of the dog was her terminally ill great-uncle David, that he'd passed away, just days later, quite poetically in remorse. They had always taken Sparkie and Uncle David to mean death.

She felt her eyes tear up as a sudden rush of emotion swept over her. Her father was so close to her on the screen, yet he was still days away. The thought that she nearly died, the thought of the unknown future ahead, made her realize just how much she'd missed him. How much she needed him in her life. Why had they let the distance come between them? Why had they been so selfish and stubborn? Why do people not realize what they have until it's too late?

This emotion was alien to her. She wasn't one to weep at the drop of a hat. She usually kept a tough facade, but right now, she couldn't. Right now, more than anything, she needed her father and his strength.

"Yeah," she nodded. "I know Sparkie and Uncle David were around for 12 months all up… but a third of those were bad," she said, as a tear rolled down her cheek.

Her father nodded, his face darkly serious. "Don't you worry about a thing, Ree. I'll buy you a gift and we'll have that party when you get back. It'll be like you were never gone and nothing's changed."

Another tear rolled down her cheek. "Thank you," she whispered. She wanted to be the strong soldier in front of him, but she was tired and drained. Right now, she could only be his daughter.

"You get some sleep, Ree. I'll see you safe at home." His voice was firm, his eyes shining with determination. She knew he would take care of things. That's why he'd been an Original, that's why he'd been a colonel. He was as tough as they come, and he didn't back down without a fight. That's where she got it from.

She hesitated, but then reached out to touch the screen, just as it went black. He was gone.

She took a few moments to pull herself together, wiping her cheeks. She felt better knowing that her father was going to do what he could, but at the same time, suddenly wondered what she was dragging him into?

Harris made his way to the flight deck with Doc. Brown had called them over the PA. A UNF ship was approaching and requesting permission to board. They entered the flight deck and Brown and Packham looked anxiously at them.

"The UNF *Vortex*, has made contact, and its captain would like to speak with you, sir," Packham advised him.

Harris bent down awkwardly to the console, holding his ribs and spoke into the mouthpiece.

"UNF *Vortex*, this is Captain Harris of the UNF *Aurora*. Do you copy? Over."

*"Captain Harris, this is Captain Lee of the UNF Vortex,"* a man with an American accent responded. *"Request permission to board."*

"Permission granted. You may proceed." Harris stood up from the console. "Packham, you done one of these before? Can you guide them on this?" he asked her.

Packham nodded. "I've only done one mid-space boarding, as co-pilot, but I know what we have to do."

Harris stared at her firmly. "You make that clear to them."

"Yes, sir."

He turned to Doc. "Let's go and welcome our new guests."

*

Harris and Doc stood by the door in silence. Several minutes passed. Packham had transferred the comms between the two ships over the PA, so they could hear what was going on. The ship was alongside and the transfer chute engaged. There was a loud humming, then a whooshing sound as the ship transfer chute was pressurized. A long, high-pitched beep followed, then after a few minutes Packham's voice came over the speakers.

*"Captain Harris. The chute is pressurized and the boarding party are outside. Over."*

Harris hit the PA button. "Copy that, Packham. Preparing to disengage the entry doors of the *Aurora*."

*"Roger that."*

Harris released the intercom and stepped back from the door. He exchanged one last look with his lieutenant, then reached out and hit the release button for the door. It slid open to reveal seven men standing there. All but one were armed and aiming their weapons at them. The unarmed one, a tall man with dark hair streaked silver, and closely-cropped peppery beard, stepped forward.

"Captain Harris? Captain Lee." He gave a nod.

Harris nodded back.

"I've spoken with Colonel Isaack," Lee began, "and he informs me that you are aware, that as of this moment, the *Aurora* is now under my control. Yes?"

Harris nodded again, despite his reluctance. The *Aurora* was *his* ship.

"You are also aware that, until all investigations and the court-martial are complete, you will be in UNF custody?"

Harris nodded again. *So a court-martial had already been decided upon.*

"Good," Lee said. "Put your hands on your heads and turn around."

Harris and Doc glanced at each other, but did so. As soon as they turned their backs some of the *Vortex* soldiers barged onto the *Aurora*, pushed them against the wall and began to frisk them. Harris winced and grunted as a sharp pain shot across his side from his injured ribs. The rest of the soldiers split off; two headed for the flight deck and two headed down the opposite corridor toward the hospital.

"Is this necessary, Captain Lee?" Harris said through gritted teeth. "We're not resisting."

"My apologies, captain, but I do not wish to take any chances. I've been informed that your team are responsible for the deaths of seven scientists."

Again, Harris exchanged a look with Doc. The soldiers finished frisking them, then pulled their hands behind their backs and cuffed them.

Doc looked over his shoulder at Lee. "I'm the medic on this ship and I've got patients. Uncuff me."

"I know who you are, First Lieutenant Walker. Our medic will assume care of your patients from this point forward," Lee advised.

The soldiers holding Harris and Doc turned them around to face Lee. Harris looked them over carefully. They were fit, but rather young. Kids, almost. After a few moments, Packham and Brown were marched under armed guard down alongside them. They, too, were shoved against the wall and frisked.

"Hey!" Packham called out, bringing her arm in to cover her chest, and shooting her guard a filthy glare.

Harris, Doc and Brown looked over at Packham's guard. He was another young kid, stocky, with a number one haircut.

"Excuse me, ma'am!" the soldier said with a Southern American accent, smirking and pushing her face first against the wall. He spread her arms out and continued to frisk her very liberally. As he made his way up her leg with both hands, he did his best to get another reaction out of her.

"Fuck off!" she spat, turning around and pushing him back.

"I saw that, corporal," Doc warned the guard.

He flashed Doc a sarcastic grin. "Saw what?" he said, holding his hands up in the air and shooting Lee a glance. "I was merely frisking her." Then he grabbed her and slammed her back against the wall and cuffed her roughly.

Harris looked back at Captain Lee, who was watching his guard with Packham carefully, before moving to lock eyes with Harris.

"That necessary, too, Captain Lee?" Harris asked, flatly.

Lee ignored him. "Move them," he ordered his men, then turned and headed off down the corridor. As Harris and the others followed, they saw a soldier up ahead walking Welles out of the hospital at gunpoint. She looked over at Harris's group, concerned, as the soldier grabbed her by the back of the neck and pushed her up against the wall. The soldier, a solid kid with his hair in a little ponytail and shaved sides, looked around and saw Lee's group approaching.

"Found this one walking around, captain," he called out in a European accent of some kind, then turned back to Welles. "Spread 'em!" He put his foot in between hers and kicked them apart. "Hands up," he ordered. He began to frisk her as the *Aurora* team watched closely, but he seemed a little more professional than Packham's guard. When he was done, he grabbed her arms and pulled them behind her back and cuffed her.

"Hey!" Doc called to him, then turned to Captain Lee. "She's a patient. She has a fractured skull and concussion."

Lee eyed him for a moment, then walked up to Welles. He grabbed her by the chin and lifted her head to view her neck, then studied the bandage over her swollen purple face.

"Put her with the other patients, Corporal Gusto," he ordered.

The soldier grabbed her by her arm and led her back into the hospital, but not before she managed to lock eyes with Harris and then Doc, who stood behind him.

Harris and his team lined up in the corridor outside the hospital, while Captain Lee entered to examine those inside. After a few moments, he reappeared and stood in front of Doc.

"You've got a full house in there, Lieutenant Walker."

"Yes, I have, sir. Can your medic handle that?" He eyed him squarely.

Lee gave a little smile. "We'll manage." He walked down the line and looked over the four of them. "You're confined to quarters until we reach Command. You will, of course, be provided with food and water, albeit in your rooms. These soldiers will take you there now. There will be armed guards outside your quarters for the remainder of the journey. Are we understood?"

None of Harris's team answered, but they all made eye contact with Lee acknowledging him.

"Good," he said, then turned to his own soldiers. "Take them."

The soldier that had frisked each of them seemed to assume the role of their assigned guard. Harris's guard stopped him in the corridor while the others were put into their quarters. They separated Doc and Brown, moving Brown onto McKinley and Hunter's room. They lined each of them up in front of their doors and began to uncuff them. Harris looked over at Packham and saw her guard lean over and whisper something to her, whilst undoing her cuffs.

"What was that, soldier?" Harris barked.

The soldier looked over at him with a smart grin on his face. Doc and Brown glanced around to see what was going on.

Harris turned to Lee. "He touches or taunts her again, you're going to have a serious problem. Do you understand me, Captain Lee?"

Lee hesitated a moment, then gave a quick nod. "Baker, go guard the hospital."

Baker finished uncuffing Packham, then grabbed her arm and leaned in to say something else to her, but Lee stopped him.

"BAKER!"

He smirked at Packham and walked off, and she quickly entered her room and shut the door. Harris turned back to make eye contact with Doc and Brown, before they were moved into their quarters and the doors locked.

Under Lee's escort, Harris was then marched to his own quarters and uncuffed.

"I'll check on you later, Captain," Lee told him. "I'll be sure to inform Command of your cooperation on our boarding."

"You make sure you keep Baker on a leash or I'll be informing Command of your *lack* of cooperation," Harris said.

"Don't worry about Baker. He knows his place with me."

"He'd better. My team has just been to hell and back and that shit is the last thing they need."

Lee's eyes narrowed in study of Harris. He could see a curiosity shining in the other captain's eyes, a curiosity which indicated that Lee was just following orders and knew nothing about what was going on here. Harris gave the captain a quick nod, then stepped inside his quarters. The door slid shut behind him and he let out a long sigh of release. He looked at his watch. 06:30.

Thirty hours, give or take, until they reached Command.

Carrie managed to doze through sheer exhaustion, but every little noise made her eyes dart open. She didn't trust the *Vortex* team and felt responsible for the others in Doc's absence. She especially didn't trust the new guard on the door, Baker. He was quick to offend, yelling at her to *"Shut the fuck up!"* for answering McKinley's inquiry as to where the others were, then made lewd comments as the *Vortex*'s medic examined her. The medic, Jackson, wasn't much better, his bedside manner leaving a lot to be desired. Chewing gum in a casual manner, he took care of only the bare necessities of the patients. McKinley didn't care for him much either, his hard stare making that clear. The medic retaliated by pretending to examine his leg, but instead he squeezed it and watched McKinley reel in pain. All the while, the guard, Baker, laughed.

She tossed and turned for the first few hours as best she could, given that her right hand was now cuffed, but eventually the tiredness got to her, and unable to resist, she finally fell into a deep sleep. Sometime later, however, she awoke with a start. She felt panicked, and as she was still half asleep, she freaked out at the sight of her hand cuffed to the bed until she suddenly realized where she was again. She looked around the room and both Baker and McKinley were staring at her.

Baker started laughing. "Who's *Chet?* Boyfriend?"

Carrie glanced back at McKinley, who eyed her quizzically for a moment before turning his head and closing his eyes again. She tried to roll over and face away from them both as best she could with her cuffed hand, wanting desperately to wipe the images from her mind of Chet, Logan and Sharley, and what they were about to do to her in her dream.

# 28

# Officer Dale

Harris looked at his watch. 12:04. *Not long now.* Showered and dressed in his uniform, he was ready and waiting. Ready to get away from the *Vortex* crew. Ready to see his own crew again. Ready to speak with Colonel Isaack. Ready for whatever was going to come his way.

Although he had to admit, he was very curious as to *what* exactly would come their way. He was convinced now that Lee knew nothing about what was going on. When he'd come to visit late yesterday with the medic in tow for a check-up, Lee's eyes had been filled with even more curiosity, and the words he spoken to Harris had stuck: *"It's best you have a good sleep tonight, Captain Harris, because before you know it you'll be back on Earth and knee-deep in debrief."* Lee's words had come across as though he were offering advice, not a warning. Like he was trying to help.

As Harris sat waiting on his bed, he'd heard the announcement over the PA of the arrival of the substitute pilots who would see their ship through re-entry into Earth's atmosphere, and land them safely at Fort Centralis. Since the *Vortex* had taken over they'd virtually been on autopilot, but now they needed real hands on deck to see the *Aurora* land safely.

He'd felt the ship shudder and shake violently as it re-entered the atmosphere, and felt the mild stomach flip as the ship evened out against the Earth's gravity, then he heard its loud humming dull to a minimum, and the clunking as it docked.

They were finally home.

Any minute now they would come to take him off the ship.

The knock came at his door, just as he'd been expecting. He got up as quickly as his ribs would allow. Captain Lee and another soldier, older than the rest and named *Coup*, according to his breast pocket, greeted him.

"Captain." Lee nodded, his eyes thoughtful. "It's time to disembark."

Harris nodded in return. They cuffed him and marched him down to the soldiers' quarters, where Doc, Brown, and Packham were waiting, also cuffed, with their guards. Harris eyed them carefully to make sure they were in the same condition he'd left them. Doc and Brown looked good. They'd caught up on some sleep, showered and shaved, and made good eye contact with him. He looked over at Packham.

"Y'alright, sergeant?" he asked her.

"No talking," her new guard yelled.

Harris gave him a look akin to an annoying little fly, dropping his eyes to the name sewn over his breast pocket: *Bryson*. He looked back at Packham. She gave him a slight nod and a smile, and he nodded back.

The soldiers marched them to the hospital where Jackson, the medic, was waiting. He held up his hand for them to stop.

"I got one more for you," he said, chewing gum, then motioned to someone in the hospital. "This one's fine to walk off the ship with this lot."

Baker walked out tugging a cuffed Welles along, and pushed her into the line between Doc and Packham. Harris noted he was a little rough with her. Lee disappeared into the hospital with Jackson.

Doc turned around and looked at Welles. "You alright? You okay?"

Baker stepped in, grabbed Doc and pushed him around to face the front. "Shut the fuck up! No talking!" He then looked over at Welles. "She's fine. She just stinks, don't you, sweetheart?" Then he leaned in a little closer to her, but spoke loud enough for everyone to hear. "You should've let me shower you when I offered."

Doc turned around again quickly and looked at Welles. "You're okay?"

Welles nodded, just as Baker stepped forward and landed a punch to Doc's jaw. "I SAID, NO TALKING," he yelled.

"HEY," Welles yelled back at him.

Doc stumbled sideways, but he didn't lose his footing.

Baker turned to Welles. "That goes for you too," he said, standing close in her face, pointing.

Harris looked over at Doc. He was angry but trying to control it. He stepped forward to Baker, as Brown stood watching closely.

"You want to take these cuffs off me, corporal?" Doc challenged him.

"Or how about you take *mine* off?" Brown glared at the soldier.

Baker smiled at them both. "But jewelry suits you girls so much."

Brown strode up to Baker and stood towering over him. "Take these cuffs off me and say that again!" Brown's guard followed him but clearly wanted to stay out of it. He was, after all, half Brown's size, and quite young, with thin wire-framed glasses. Harris read his name too; *Colberge*.

"Fall in, soldier," Lee ordered, reappearing from the hospital. He looked over at Harris. "This how you control your troops, captain?"

"Oh, I'm sorry, Captain Lee," he replied. "I was under the impression that you were in command here."

Lee gave him a stony look, then turned to his soldiers. "Get them off this ship!"

*

As soon as they were off the Fort Centralis Space Dock, the *Aurora* team were transported to Command and separated again. One by one they were taken to quarantine. They were stripped to their underwear, scanned and x-rayed in their departure physical, and "processed" in administration, all under armed guard. Afterwards, Harris was taken to the Command hospital to have his ribs looked at and taped up again. By the time he was done, it was late afternoon.

He was discharged from the hospital and escorted to where he would await the debrief. Doc, Brown and Packham were already there when he arrived, and he felt a slight relief to see some of his team again. He locked eyes with Doc, then let his sight fall to his jaw.

"I see a bruise coming up," he told him.

"Yeah, the jaw is a little sore," Doc said rubbing it. "Now, if I hadn't been cuffed..."

"It was a cheap shot, Doc. Don't sweat it."

"Quiet," a guard called, walking into the room and taking a seat at a table by the door.

Harris sat next to Doc and looked around. They hadn't been in this area before. It wasn't the normal debrief center, which was several floors above where they were now. They were in a small room with several chairs, and two doorways: the one they came in through, and one leading off to the side. He wondered where it led to and eventually figured that it was where they would be debriefing them.

He was feeling nervous by this new location, hidden and out of the way like it was. Then again this hadn't been a normal mission. He hoped it wasn't an ominous sign. Something didn't feel right to him, and the swirling in the pit of his stomach only seemed to confirm it.

Carrie sat on the edge of her bed, feeling so much better. She had finally had a shower and felt refreshed. Her neck bruises had faded to a brownish-yellow. They'd removed Doc's bandage over her stitches and replaced it with a couple of bits of tape. Her face wasn't as swollen anymore, but the bruises were still purple, and the stitched wound still looked a little nasty. She felt a constant headache, but it was much better than before. If anything, her neck and back actually felt worse.

She sat there waiting to be discharged. She'd seen them wheel Hunter, Colt and McKinley past her earlier and wondered how they were all doing. The medics here at Command seemed to have a much better bedside manner than Jackson from the Vortex, and McKinley, in particular, was in need of some "real" care. Toward the end of the journey home, he hadn't looked too good. Jackson had kept his pain relief to a minimum and, although it was showing on the lieutenant's face, he'd never once complained about it, suffering in silence. She had to admit, he was a lot stronger than she'd given him credit for. He'd spent hours stuck in that bed, handcuffed and in pain, forced to use a bedpan.

She was glad to finally be off the ship and away from them. Not just Jackson but Baker, too. As he'd announced to the *Aurora* crew, he had tried to offer his assistance to Carrie to shower, and he was right, she wouldn't have any of it. They'd argued, while McKinley watched on silently. Baker tried to get her out of the bed, laughing smugly as he did, but she kicked him away with all her might. She'd told him that she'd much prefer to stink, and he'd eventually stormed off when another more senior French guard, Jethro, ordered him to back off. When it came time to cuff her for the disembarkation, Baker did his best to do so as roughly as possible. He'd forced her off the bed, uncuffed her right hand, then spun her around and planted her face in the sheets while he pulled her arms around behind her back to cuff them, all the while resting his weight against her in a humiliating fashion. McKinley hadn't said a word. He knew it would've been futile and probably even fan the flames, so instead he just gave Baker his cold, hard stare.

So she sat there now, clean and refreshed, away from the *Vortex* crew and safely back on Earth. Her mind couldn't help but wander back to the Darwin, though, and picture Logan and Sharley in that bio cell. She heard Sharley's words again, *"I'll see you soon, Carrie Ann Welles,"* and felt a shiver run down her spine, as she tried to block out the dreams she'd been having of them since. Although "dreams" didn't seem like the right word to use. These "dreams" had been nasty. These "dreams" were more like nightmares...

Finally, a soldier came to discharge her and led her down into what seemed to be the bowels of the Command Center. It gave her an uneasy feeling. They eventually came to a room where a guard sat just inside the door at a desk. Doc, Brown and Packham were there, seated along an L-shaped row of chairs. She felt relieved to see them. *Finally, some friendly faces!*

"Where's Harris?" she asked, noticing he was missing.

"Sit down, soldier. Refrain from speaking," the guard at the desk ordered her.

She eyed the soldier as she took a seat, then looked back at Doc, who motioned over to a door leading off to the side. *He was already being debriefed.*

Out of the corner of her eye, she saw the lieutenant examining her facial wounds. She glanced back at him again. They locked eyes, and she noticed his held a mixture of relief and concern, as though he wanted to say something again. She felt as though she could've stared at those eyes for hours, but a wary glance from Packham made her look away.

Carrie sighed and wondered how long they would have to stay in that room. More importantly, she wondered just how long they'd keep Harris in there?

Harris stared back at Officer Dale, the man leading the questioning. He looked to be a few years younger than himself, pale-skinned, brown hair shaved close in a crew cut, and dark pondering eyes. He did not have a typical soldier's body, he was quite thin. *Definitely a paper-pushing JAGernaut...*

His colleague was much older, with a lined face and gray hair parted on the side. He sat in the corner, quietly observing, giving only a single nod when introduced as Senior Officer Edgely. He looked experienced, and his silence and watchful eyes made Harris a little nervous.

He'd been in the debrief for just over an hour and a half. He'd inquired as to Colonel Isaack's whereabouts but had been told he would not be joining them, which was of concern. He wondered whether maybe Isaack was being debriefed, too. But if he was, then who the hell was left to watch out for them?

So far he'd merely given his account of what happened from the day he got the call to come into Command, until now. At first he hadn't been sure just how much information to give, but he'd been told that for this debrief there was no classification. Dale and Edgely had been given clearance, so he was allowed to speak freely, and tell them everything. The younger officer had been poking and prodding at him but had not yet begun to grill him. Harris figured it wouldn't be much longer.

Dale leaned over the table taking an intimidating stance as he eyed Harris. It had little impact, though. Harris wasn't scared of him in the slightest. Not after the Jumbo soldiers he'd just faced.

"Well, Captain Harris?" he asked him impatiently.

"What would you like me to say, Officer Dale?"

"The truth would be a good start."

"I've told you the truth."

Dale smiled to himself and leaned away from the table. "You mean to tell me that you honestly believe that *all seven* deaths of the Darwin crew were warranted?"

Harris nodded. "Yes, sir, I do."

"All *seven*? Warranted?"

Harris gave a firm nod. "Like I said, Fairmont was attempting to kill First Sergeant Hunter, when he was shot and killed. May I remind you that Corporal Welles wounded him first, but he charged her, so she had no option. Grolsh had led two of my men into an ambush, to their deaths, and was running toward Second Lieutenant McKinley when he was shot and killed. The three men on the *Aurora* were either killed in self-defense or in defense of another crew member. Oxer was killed by Corporal Welles in defense of Lieutenant McKinley, and I killed Chet in defense of Welles."

"But in all cases, was a warning shot given? Did your soldiers attempt to wound the alleged attackers? Or did they shoot to kill?" he asked, walking up and down on the opposite side of the table.

"You mean, like Logan did with Smith and Louis? He went straight for their neck and they bled to death in minutes. Or do you mean like Chet did with Carter? Beating him viciously, then breaking his neck? Or perhaps you mean like the other guy did with Bolkov, hmm? Slicing him from armpit to hip."

"Right now, I'm talking about *your* soldiers, Captain Harris. From what you've told me, Lieutenant McKinley shot and killed Grolsh without any provocation. The man was unarmed, for god's sake!"

"These men did not need weapons to kil—"

"And Corporal Welles shoots Oxer in the head for simply breaking McKinley's leg. Same with Fairmont. Hunter suffered only a broken arm at that stage."

"Yes, and then Fairmont charged Welles, and then Grolsh shot Hunter twice."

"Yes, captain, in the *arm* and in the *leg*! Not the head or the chest, like your soldiers prefer," he said looking down at some notes he'd written. "And the list goes on. What about Lieutenant Walker? He shoots Ravearez three times in the head and neck region for merely tripping Welles. *Unarmed*, I might add. And what about yourself, Captain Harris? You shoot Chet for what? Hitting Corporal Welles."

"They had beaten her unconscious and had taken her hostage. When I entered the room, he was on top of her, attacking her and I had two other unfriendlies in the roo—"

"And Sergeant Packham shoots Carlisle through the chest for merely fighting with Bolkov," he said, ignoring Harris and looking back at his notes.

"Who had been stabbed by Carlisle's buddy and was slowly dying," Harris shot back.

Dale leaned over the table again. "Tell me, captain, did you order your soldiers to shoot to kill these scientists?"

Harris stared at Dale for a moment. He was doing his best to keep his anger under control, although he really wanted to step up and smack this guy in the mouth. What made it worse, was that he knew it would be very easy to do. *This guy probably wouldn't even see it coming.*

"My soldiers are trained to shoot to kill if their life or a fellow soldier's life is in danger. Standard UNF practice."

"And do you encourage them to shoot unarmed men?"

"Officer Dale, you have no idea what these men were capable of. They were not ordinary men."

"No," Dale answered, looking between his notes and the transcript spewing forth across the monitor in front of him. "According to your statement they had *extrasensory powers* and were *incredibly* strong. Do you mean kind of like 'the Hulk'? Or did you mean more like one of those old X-Men characters?"

Harris smiled, steely. "The UNF was undertaking a classified experiment to create advanced soldiers. We were sent there to test them, except we were not told that. The UNF advised me that we were going to check out a routine comms failure. The UNF also failed to advise the three female soldiers on board that they were being put forth as subjects for the next part of their experiment."

"Yes, Captain Harris, so you say. But did you really believe that you were going there just to check out a comms issue? I mean, I've read through the *Aurora*'s mission files. The *Aurora* is not sent to handle comms issues. The *Aurora* is sent to resolve issues with dangerous people: space pirates, thieves, smugglers, escaped cons. You don't do the technical things, captain. Your team is not built for that. You're built for handling human problems."

"Colonel Isaack advised me that we were being sent in case there was a human problem behind the comms failure."

"So, you *were* expecting it, then? This was not a surprise?"

"No to your first question, Officer Dale. And it most certainly was. A surprise is coming across a team of men who can hear you and smell you way before you're anywhere near them. Surprise is trying to fight off an attacker who is at least, *at least,* twice your strength. Thieves, pirates, smugglers? I can handle them. We deal with them regularly. They're human like us, except they don't have the training we do. *We* have the upper hand. But these Jumbos, they were like nothing I'd ever come across."

"I see—"

"No, I don't think you see at all, Officer Dale. Have you ever been in the field? Have you ever had a gun in your face or been attacked by a big soldier? Have you ever been separated from your team? Been on your own against an unknown number of unfriendlies?"

Officer Dale smiled. "I'm not the one on trial here, captain."

"No, you're not. Nor have you, I believe, ever been in a life or death situation. You've never been in a position where you've had to make *every* decision count in order to save you and your men."

"And do you think you made the right decisions, captain?"

"For the most part, yes."

"For the most part?" Dale raised his eyebrows.

"Well, if I'd followed my *gut* feeling, instead of UNF protocol, then I would never have released them from that bio cell in the first place. Grolsh never would have attacked Welles and we wouldn't be sitting here right now."

"Yes, Welles," Dale said as though he were thinking aloud. "How do you feel the female recruits went on the *Aurora*?"

"What, besides the whole Darwin incident?" Harris arched his eyebrow and shot Dale a derisive look.

"Yes, captain." Dale ignored the look and the sarcastic tone of his voice. "What's your honest opinion of their integration? How did your men react to the women? Did they accept them willingly? Or was there a little hostility?"

"They were treated like any new soldiers on a team."

"Like any other soldiers, huh? So, there were no issues within your team?"

Harris stared blankly at him.

"I just mean it's interesting that you say, and I quote," Dale pushed a button on the console in front of the monitor and played back a phrase Harris had said.

*"You've never been in that situation where you had to make every decision count in order to save you and your men."*

"It's interesting," Dale continued, "that you say 'you and your men'. You don't mention the women at all."

"It's a figure of speech, Officer Dale. It's not meant to be taken literally."

"Perhaps, captain, but you haven't answered my question. Were there any issues with the women?"

"No. My men did not attempt to strangle them, like Grolsh did Welles, nor did they attempt to kidnap them like the Darwin team did all three of the women at various times. *Nor*, Officer Dale, did they blatantly sexually assault them like Baker from the *Vortex* crew did with Sergeant Packham. Something he did right before my very eyes and those of First Lieutenant Walker and Staff Sergeant Brown." Harris gave him a satisfied look. Dale, for the first time, darted his eyes over at the older officer, then looked back to Harris.

"Well, we're not discussing the *Vortex* crew right now, captain."

"No? Well, I do hope I will be given the opportunity to air my grievance with the relevant CO."

"I'm sure you will, captain."

Harris saw the older officer look down at his watch. "Perhaps it's time we take a break," he said to Dale, although it came across more as an order, not a suggestion.

Dale nodded. "Very well. Care for some water, Captain Harris?"

Harris shook his head at Dale, fixing him with a flat, cold stare. "May I ask when I will get the chance to speak to *my* CO, Colonel Isaack? He was supposed to be taking part in these debriefs."

"The colonel is currently unavailable, captain." He smiled back.

Dale and Edgely left the room through a different door to the one he'd entered. Despite his concern for Isaack's absence, Harris kept his composure. He knew they'd be watching him from the other side of the wall.

Carrie was relieved when a soldier came into the room and dismissed her, Brown and Packham, advising them that they would be escorted to their rooms for the night and return at 0600 the next morning. Carrie gave Doc a sympathetic look as he leaned forward in his chair and rubbed his hands over his face. He was in for a long night. It only made her think of her father, then. *Where was he? What was he doing? Was he alright?*

They were each given a room at the UNF hotel located in the Command building. It was a simple room with a queen-sized bed and en suite. There was a TV, but no phone. She heard the guards close the door behind her, thankful she was finally alone. She moved over to the bed and fell onto it, feeling the muscles down the right side of her back pull and stretch as though they were dry, taut, old ropes. Her eyes were heavy. She couldn't seem to shake the tiredness she'd felt since they'd left the Darwin, although she knew it was to be expected with her head injury.

Exhausted, she removed her uniform, getting down to her singlet and underwear and climbed into the bed. She rolled over onto her side and stared at the empty pillow beside her. She couldn't help, then, but think of Doc, sitting in that room all alone, waiting for his turn to be grilled in the debrief.

*

At 0500 she awoke. Her head was sore, and her neck and back stiff like planks of wood. She looked over at the closed curtain of her room and the frame of light that crept in around it. She decided not to go back to sleep. She'd left some nasty dreams behind and did not wish to reconnect with them. Why hadn't they stopped now she was back on Earth? Maybe they would only go away once she'd made it through the debrief?

When it was time, her guard escorted her down to breakfast and then to the waiting room, where Brown and Packham were. Doc was gone. There was no sign of McKinley, Hunter and Colt, who, she assumed, were all still in the hospital, and still no sign of Harris. She eyed the door off to the side curiously, and wondered where Doc and Harris could be.

*

1300. An older gentleman with gray hair popped his head out of the door to the side.

"Corporal Welles. Please come through."

Brown looked over at Carrie. He seemed a little disappointed that it wasn't him going next, as he was the most senior of the three waiting. She

434

stepped inside the room and looked around. There was a sleek black table in the middle with e-files strewn across one side, around a monitor, and bright lights shining down from above. Around the edges, along the dark gray walls, the light was dim. A younger man stood in the corner pouring himself a glass of water. She heard the door close behind her, and the younger man looked over at her.

"Corporal Welles, would you care for a glass of water?"

Carrie nodded. "Thank you, sir."

He smiled and poured a second glass, while the older gentleman motioned for her to take a seat on the cleared side of the table. She did. The younger man placed the glass in front of her, while the older one took a seat in the dimly-lit corner.

"Corporal Welles, my name is Officer Dale," the younger man said, "and this is Senior Officer Edgely, who is here observing."

Carrie glanced over at Edgely then back at Dale.

"All classification has been put aside for these debriefs, so you may speak freely. Understand?"

"Yes, sir."

"Good. That's quite the black eye," he said motioning to where Logan had hit her. "Fractured, I believe?"

Carrie nodded.

"So," Dale said as he began looking through a file in front of him, "I've read your file and you have a good, clean record, Corporal Welles. You did well at school, have a fantastic marksman record and, of course, the commendation for the Santos mission. Six men!"

He looked up at her, eyebrows raised. She wasn't quite sure what the question was, but she nodded regardless.

"You basically single-handedly wrapped up the Santos Siege. That's quite a feat," he continued.

Carrie shrugged modestly. "I didn't do it alone. It was a team effort."

"But your bullets took out Gardos and five of his rebels. No?"

"Yes, sir."

"It's fair to say you're a very accurate shot, isn't it?"

Carrie shrugged again. "I guess."

"You guess? Only one of those rebels died in hospital after the siege ended. The rest you took out there and then."

Carrie nodded again. "My orders were to take out Gardos and anyone else who got in the way."

"So your orders were to shoot to kill?"

Carrie looked at Dale curiously, thinking that the question really answered itself. "Yes, sir. Gardos was holding two prominent politicians hostage, along with their staff. It was our job to ensure they were freed, given that negotiations had failed."

Dale nodded and looked back at his file. "Would you say that you always shoot to kill? I mean, you're a sharpshooter. It's what you're generally trained to do, isn't it?"

Carrie wasn't sure what he was getting at, but she decided to answer truthfully. "I do whatever I'm ordered to, sir. With the Santos mission I was ordered to shoot to kill. That's not always the case, though. Unless I have strict orders, I try to wound them first. Unless, of course, it's a life or death situation, then you do what you have to."

Dale jutted out his lower lip, pondering. "So, you believe they were life and death situations when you shot both Fairmont and Oxer."

Now she knew what he was getting at.

"Yes, I do, sir. We were under attack. Fairmont was assaulting First Sergeant Hunter. He had just snapped his arm and was about to finish him off when I shot him in the shoulder to stop him. He then charged me. Corporal Colt was also under attack at the time by Grolsh, so I did what I had to do."

"And Oxer?"

"That was a similar circumstance. Oxer was fighting with Lieutenant McKinley and he'd just broken his leg. If I hadn't shot him, he would've killed him."

Dale eyed her doubtfully. "But a bullet to the head, Corporal Welles. You couldn't shoot him in the kneecap or something. The UNF does believe in taking the enemy down, but not necessarily out."

"Sir, with all due respect, you have no idea what these men, if I can call them that, were capable of. We witnessed them killing our fellow soldiers with their bare hands, instantly. We didn't have time to try and wound them and hope that they'd stop and go away. It *was* a life and death situation and I did what I had to do, and both Hunter and McKinley are still alive today because of it."

"Corporal Welles, I wouldn't call Hunter's broken arm or McKinley's broken leg a life or death situation."

Carrie looked down at her hands resting on the table. She clasped them and took a subtle deep breath. *Stay calm,* she told herself, *keep your cool.* "Perhaps you would think otherwise if you had been there, sir," she said in a smooth, even voice.

"Perhaps. Perhaps I would've tried some restraint, though, Corporal Welles. Perhaps I would've tried wounding them first, and if they continued, then perhaps I would've tried wounding them again. But I guess *restraint* isn't one of your strongest points." He gave her a smile and there was a twinkle in his eye.

She wanted to know what that was for, but didn't ask in case he was baiting her. She was going to make him come to her, not the other way around.

"Tell me about your relationship with Captain Harris," he continued, changing tack with his questions.

Carrie eyed him. "What about it, sir?"

"Well, would you say your relationship was a good one?"

Carrie couldn't help but furrow her brow. "I would say it was the same as any other soldier on the *Aurora.*"

"Really?" He sounded surprised. "You never quarreled?"

She eyed him. "No, sir."

"That's funny. We've been through the footage from the security cameras on the *Aurora* and detected some hostility between the two of you."

Carrie's mind raced. *What footage? What footage?* She couldn't help but think of when she kissed Doc's hand in the hospital.

"Corporal Welles?" Dale asked again.

"There was no *hostility*, Officer Dale. I, er, I didn't understand why he wouldn't let us off the ship at first, but that became clear in the end."

"So, there was tension?"

Carrie looked him in the eye. "I don't believe so."

Dale swished his fingers down the screen of the e-file in front of him. "Okay, what about your relationships with the other men? Was there any tension there?"

"Sir, what does this have to do with what happened to the Darwin team?"

"I'm trying to establish your character, corporal. I'm trying to establish the frame of mind of the *Aurora* team was in, and therefore whether what occurred on the Darwin was warranted. So, tell me about Second Lieutenant McKinley."

"What about him? I saved his life, remember?"

"According to *you*, yes, you did. You…" he looked at the monitor in front of him, "and I quote, 'Did what you had to do'. But did you really?"

"I'm sorry?"

"Tell me about what happened in the gym. The surveillance footage seemed to capture some sort of, er, disagreement between the two of you. And our surveillance in the weapons store seemed to capture some more, er, disagreements."

"We had a difference of opinion, but we worked it out."

"And what was the difference of opinion about?"

Carrie glanced over at the older gentleman, then back at Dale.

"Well?" Dale asked impatiently.

She decided to go for honesty. "The place of females in the UNF."

"Oh, yes?" Dale seemed amused at this.

"Yes. He didn't believe women had a place being on a ship like the *Aurora*. I believe I convinced him otherwise."

"Did you?"

"Yes. I saved his life. I saved Hunter's life."

"Mm. But you needed rescuing several times yourself. Right?"

Carrie shrugged. "I guess you could say we came to an agreement that we needed each other. Teamwork got us through."

Dale took his glass of water off the table and sipped it, eyeing her all the while. He placed it back on the table and continued looking directly at her. "Tell me about First Lieutenant Walker?"

Carrie's heart thudded in her chest, but she kept a strong mask. "What would you like to know?"

"What was your relationship like with him?"

"Fine."

Dale stared at her.

"He's a good medic and he's a good soldier," she elaborated.

"And how do you feel you… interacted, with him?"

"Fine. Like all the other soldiers."

"You think your relationship with him was the same as with the other soldiers?"

"Yes, sir."

"You appeared to spend a lot more time with him than the other soldiers, corporal. At least that's what we picked up on the surveillance."

Her mind raced for a second. "What can I say? I was injured and he was the medic."

"Yes, but you were seen coming and going from his office quite a lot well before you were injured."

"Yes, sir. I wasn't allowed off the ship, so I tried to find other things to occupy my time, helping out where I could."

"Mm. Still, you spent an awful lot of time with him, don't you think?"

Carrie stared at Dale, "No, sir. I do not."

"Lieutenant Walker seemed to defend you quite a lot, didn't he? I mean we saw him go to your defense in the gym with Lieutenant McKinley, arguing with Captain Harris when you were in the hospital, and there seemed to be another altercation in the mess hall with Sergeant's Carter and Louis?"

Carrie felt a pang of regret when she heard the names of the dead soldiers, despite the grief they'd put her through on the *Aurora*. She looked at Dale as he waited for an answer. "That was just the guys messing around," she told him.

"Messing around? Lieutenant Walker didn't look like he was messing around."

Carrie shrugged and gave him a blank stare.

Dale stared back.

She shrugged again. "So, did your surveillance pick up the incident where Grolsh attacked me?"

A smile crept onto Dale's face. "Yes. We've got that on tape. Although, *technically*, you did assault him first."

"Pushing someone out of my face is assault? And worthy of him almost killing me?"

"Well, that's for us to decide, Corporal Welles. And nice try, turning the questions around onto me."

Carrie eyed him, then glanced back over at Edgely. He was watching her carefully, eyes slightly narrowed in thought, as Dale continued.

"Now, unfortunately, there seems to be some interference with the headcam footage from when you ventured onto the 'secret floor' of the Darwin. It's completely inadmissible. Even on the ground floor there seems to have been some sort of scrambling in place, so it's not altogether clear. All we really know is that Captain Harris and Mattieus Logan disappeared up there, then you followed, and then you and Captain Harris came back, looking somewhat worse for wear. Would you like to tell me what happened up there?"

# 29

# Waiting to Exhale

Harris sat in a small mess hall down the corridor from where they were debriefing the team. He'd just finished lunch and was staring off into space thinking about his eight-hour grilling. Dale had asked a lot of questions of his leadership and his methods of handling the team. Harris did well to control his emotion, remembering his own advice given to Doc. He was respectful, following UNF protocol like a good soldier, but he'd also made it clear to Dale that he stood by his actions, and that of his team.

He felt confident with all the answers he'd given, despite Dale trying to twist them around. He knew he'd done what was right at the time, but he was still unsure as to how the UNF would respond to all this. After all, seven UNF "scientists" were dead, and most had been unarmed at the time of their death. Thankfully they allowed "classified" information to be discussed, because it was the only way he could explain what had happened.

Still, in the back of his mind, he worried that the *Aurora* team could be used as scapegoats to cover up the mess. They could be used as the fall guys, blamed as a renegade unit out of control and incarcerated, while those in charge denied any knowledge and looked the other way. Or worse still, the *Aurora* team could have this held over their heads as a threat to buy their silence and make the truth go away, in exchange for any charges being dropped. But that could mean a potential life sentence of being a puppet on UNF strings.

What stuck in Harris's mind now, was the footage from the *Aurora*'s surveillance tapes that Dale had shown him. He'd watched the footage of Fairmont's attack on Hunter, and the footage of the standoff between Bolkov and the other Jumbos outside the flight deck. And as awful as it was to watch Bulk die, Harris was glad to have seen it. It was good for him to witness what had happened to his soldiers when he'd not been there to see it for himself. It gave him a sense of closure. Both Bulk and Hunter had put up a good fight, all things considered. Especially Bulk. Welles's shot at Fairmont was quick, clean and deadly accurate, and Doc's reflexes were second to none when the Jumbo, Ravearez, tripped and grabbed Welles on approach to the flight deck.

As there was surprisingly little footage available from the Darwin, due to some kind of interference, the *Aurora* tapes were what Dale focused on and what he chose to pick to pieces. So he'd shown Harris other footage, that mainly centered around Doc and Welles, and asked him a lot of questions about their relationship. Some of it Harris was aware of, like Doc standing up for her in the gym with McKinley, and their joking and laughing in Doc's office when he'd interrupted them the night they boarded. But there was also footage that he had not been aware of.

He saw footage of an awkward meeting in the door to the mess hall, another clip of an awkward moment in the hospital after they processed Smith's body, and another where Doc had blocked her exit from his office after a tense discussion, which Harris could only assume was when he'd "had a word" to her.

Dale had also shown footage of a few disagreements Harris had had with Welles, and others of Welles and McKinley at it. Harris knew what Dale was up to. He was trying to show the *Aurora* team as unstable and on edge, and therefore not in their right minds to handle the Darwin scenario. Harris found a way to explain most of it, although he had to stretch a little with some of the footage of Doc and Welles and the time they'd spent together, relating it to Welles being ordered to stay off the Darwin. It made him wonder now, exactly what questions Dale would be asking of them both and in particular how Welles would handle it. He knew Doc would be fine with his good poker face, but wondered whether Welles's fiery temper would betray her. If Dale could lock in on anything to discredit or use against the team, he'd do so.

Harris sighed and began to pack up his lunch tray when he saw Doc come walking into the mess hall. Their eyes met. Doc looked a little worn out, as he headed over to Harris.

"Doc," Harris greeted him.

"Captain."

"You just get out?" Harris asked, looking at his watch. 13:19.

Doc nodded. "They were going to take Welles in next."

"Welles? How do you know that?"

"They said it in front of me. They wanted me to hear it, I guess." He shrugged.

Harris eyed him a moment and nodded back. "Get some lunch," he motioned toward the counter.

Doc headed for the counter, while Harris pushed aside his tray and waited for him to return. He eyed their assigned UNF guards standing by the entrance, glad he was finally allowed to speak to a member of his team.

"Man, I'm hungry," Doc said, sitting down with his tray and shoving a stacked fork into his mouth.

Harris watched him chewing, focusing on the bruise that ran along his jawline. "How's the jaw?"

Doc looked up at him and shrugged. "Fine. What about you? How're the ribs? Your face looks better."

"They're getting there. It's easier to breathe now."

Doc nodded, eyeing him as he shoveled another forkful into his mouth.

"I wonder why they didn't take Brown in next?" Harris asked. "They normally go by seniority and seeing how McKinley and Hunter are still in the hospital, Brown should be next."

Again Doc shrugged, then swallowed. "Maybe it's because Welles had a lot more to do with the Jumbo's than Brown did?"

"Maybe."

Harris watched him eat for a little longer, then once his plate grew smaller, decided to start asking his own questions. "So, did they hammer you?"

Doc scoffed a short, sharp laugh. "Dale sure gave it a good shot!"

"They obviously questioned our practices?"

"Mm-hmm," he said taking another mouthful.

"They get personal?" Harris eyed him carefully.

Doc looked back at him and swallowed. "Of course."

Harris sat back in his chair, watching him.

Doc noticed. "What?"

"They showed me a lot of footage of you and Welles…"

Doc paused for a moment. "Yeah, they showed me some, too."

"There was a lot there that they could twist around if they wanted to, Doc."

"And Dale certainly tried to, but they're clutching at straws, captain. They tried to find anything they could to use against me. He even showed clips of me talking with McKinley and tried to make out that we were at each other's throats. They've got nothing. They questioned my relationship with Welles, with McKinley, with Carter and Louis, and even with you! They questioned my treatment of each patient. Dale even questioned whether I tried hard enough to save Bulk? Whether I had some beef with him and just let him go? They tried everything. It went on for hours, Saul, and they still got nothing."

Harris sighed as he watched Doc finish his plate angrily. "Yeah, they tried all of that on me, too. That's bullshit about Bulk, Doc. There was nothing you could've done."

Doc nodded and pushed his now empty plate away from him.

"Let's just hope Welles holds up," Harris said flatly.

"She will."

"She's got a head injury and she's been through a lot, Doc. I wouldn't be so sure," he said, picturing Sibbie and Etta in his mind.

"Are we talking about the same soldier that volunteered to go to the control room? The same soldier that went into the unknown, *on her own*, to retrieve your ass? She's got guts, Saul."

"Yeah, but she had a gun in her hands then. In that room she's got nothing but her stubbornness and her pride, and that can work against her if she loses control of it, or if Dale finds a way to hit the right buttons." Harris leaned over the table toward Doc and lowered his voice a little. "More to the point, Doc, if she breaks and lets Dale twist around what she has to say, then that can have repercussions for *all* of us." He stared Doc in the eye for a moment, hoping to drive home the seriousness of it, especially for him.

Doc sighed and ran his hands through his hair. "She'll be fine, captain. They've got nothing." He stood up from the table. "I'm going to go catch some z's. I'll talk to you later."

Carrie stared back into Dale's accusing eyes.

"Corporal Welles, are you expecting special favors because your father is a retired colonel? An Original?" he asked her. They were three hours in and Dale had dropped the Mr Nice Guy act, not that he had much of one to begin with.

"No, I do not," she answered with her voice tight.

"So why the transmission to him on your journey home?"

Carrie stared at Dale like an insolent child.

"I asked you a question, corporal."

"I nearly died up there, Officer Dale. I had a fractured skull. I needed to talk to my family."

"No-one else made a transmission. Then again no-one else has connections that high up in the UNF."

"As you said, Officer Dale, my father is a *retired* colonel. What possible strings could he have pulled? And for what? We've done nothing wrong. All we did was survive."

"You know what I think, Corporal Welles? I think you're a liar. I think you're lying about the call to your father, you're lying about your relationship with Captain Harris, you're lying about your relationship with Second Lieutenant McKinley and you are most definitely lying about your relationship with First Lieutenant Walker. I also think you're lying about whether or not it was necessary force that you used on Fairmont and Oxer. We're not in your little boarding school now, corporal. You can't call on daddy to save your ass this time."

Carrie tried to swallow subtly. "Well, I guess that's your opinion. I stand by the fact that I have told you the truth. If you choose not to believe it, then let that be on your head."

"Ah! The '*truth*' is a very powerful word, Corporal Welles, and one that can be bent to suit the speaker. So, I *will* let that be on my head. Now, let's go back to your relationship with Captain Harris, shall we?"

Carrie sighed loudly.

"Boring you am I, corporal? Do you think the deaths of seven men do not warrant a debrief?"

"I just hope the four murdered crew of the *Aurora* get the same treatment."

Dale ignored her. "When you killed Fairmont, do you think it would be fair to say that you were trying to win Harris's approval, so he would finally let you board the Darwin? Prove yourself so you could get to where the action was with the rest of the team. I mean, it was the first kill on your side. You won the prize over all the men. That would be a great way to get his attention, wouldn't it?"

"Fairmont was attacking First Sergeant Hunter. He charged at me. I had no choice. Captain Harris wasn't even on the dock at the time."

"Yes, but what a lovely trophy to show him when he returned. Do you think it's possible that you used excessive force to prove a point?"

"No, I do not."

"And what about Oxer? Second Lieutenant McKinley had been giving you a hard time about being on the team. What a *perfect* way to set him straight? Rescue him by blowing out Oxer's brains. Forget just wounding him. Cover that lieutenant in the enemy's blood. Take him out good and hard, and show that Lieutenant McKinley what you can do! Isn't that right, corporal?"

"No, it is not."

"And Lieutenant Walker seemed to be on your side. It made sense to keep him sweet, didn't it? That way you had someone looking out for you? Someone in authority. Tell me corporal," Dale placed his hands on the table and leaned across directly in front of her, "what did that cost you? For Lieutenant Walker's protection. I mean, he must've got something out of it, hmm? What was Walker's payment for looking out for you and keeping the other guys at bay? You did spend a lot of time alone with him off surveillance camera... I'm sure you did more for him than just stock his shelves?"

Carrie felt her face burn red with anger. She glared at Dale, her eyes flicking to Edgely to gauge his reaction. He seemed curious. For some reason, she suddenly thought of Harris, and could hear him ordering her to play it cool. She pictured Doc's face, too, and tried to let her cheeks simmer into her best poker face.

"Well?" Dale insisted.

"What exactly are you insinuating, Officer Dale?" Carrie asked with a calm voice.

"You tell me, corporal?"

"I really don't know, but making false allegations is against the UNF code, isn't it? Sullying a good soldier's name?"

"Corporal Welles, I merely asked what you did for Lieutenant Walker. If you've read more into it, then perhaps that's your guilty conscience talking?"

Senior Officer Edgely sat up in his chair then. "Perhaps it's time for a break, Officer Dale."

Dale looked over at Edgely, unhappy with the request. He seemed quite keen to continue clawing at Carrie. "Very well," he muttered, then turned and left the room.

Harris and Doc walked back into the mess hall for dinner at 1830. They saw Packham sitting at one of the tables with a guard close by. He locked eyes with hers and nodded and she gave a weak nod back. *No Brown*, he thought.

They filled up their trays and sat on the other side of the mess hall. They knew they would not be allowed near Packham until she had been debriefed.

"Brown must be in now, huh," Doc said, glancing around at Packham.

"Don't know. If he is, then where's Welles?" Harris asked.

They ate in silence for most of the meal, stealing glances at Packham every now and then. Harris's mind was racing. *Where's Brown? Where's Welles?* Various scenarios were playing out in his mind. He could see Doc trying to figure it out, too, but after about 25 minutes, Welles came walking in with her guard.

The corporal locked eyes with each of them. As she walked over to the counter, she glanced behind to see that her guard had dropped away and was waiting with the others by the door. She filled her tray then turned around to face them, as Packham was escorted out. Harris motioned for Welles to sit in the chair next to him, which she did.

"Captain," she nodded. "Lieutenant."

They nodded back at her, then sat in silence for a moment while she ate.

"So, how'd it go, corporal?" Harris eventually asked.

Welles eyed the guards in the corner, "Okay."

"Okay?" Harris studied her. "Did they hammer you?"

She looked back at Harris. "Are we bugged right now, sir?"

He paused and thought for a moment. "Possibly."

She nodded. "Officer Dale's a prick!" she said, making sure her voice was loud and clear.

Harris smirked. "You mean, he's good at his job."

Welles looked at Harris, but she didn't smile.

"Anything in particular I should know about?" He arched his eyebrow at her.

"Not really," she answered, "except apparently saving your own life or that of a fellow soldier does not warrant excessive force. Funny, I could've sworn that was UNF policy."

"Don't sweat it, Welles," he told her. "We all got the same treatment."

Harris glanced at Doc, wondering why he was being so quiet. Doc seemed to notice the look and turned to Welles.

"How's the head, corporal? Swelling's gone, I see."

Welles swallowed her mouthful, shot him a glance and nodded. "It's fine. I've been tired, and it has been aching a bit today."

"Yeah, a debrief can do that," Doc told her. "Get it checked out if you're worried, though."

She gave him a half-smile, then quickly looked back to her plate. Harris noticed she was being careful not to pay Doc too much attention. Almost too careful. They'd obviously shown her the footage and asked questions about their relationship. She quickly put her focus back on Harris.

"So what happens now, sir? Are we trapped here until we're all processed?"

"Pretty much," Harris answered. "I'd say it will take them a couple of days to finish the others."

"Have you seen the guys in the hospital yet?" Welles asked.

"No," Harris shook his head, "and I won't until they've been processed. There's no contact until the debrief is over."

"So, we just sit and wait?"

Harris nodded. "We just sit and wait."

Carrie sighed. She was tired, her head hurt and to be honest, she felt a little uncomfortable sitting there with Harris and Doc, not knowing what questions Dale had asked them. She was also paranoid as to whether there would be a camera on them now, watching their every move. She was worried about doing something that could be turned against her, whether it be looking at Harris the wrong way, or worse, looking at Doc the wrong way.

In fact, she wanted to avoid looking at Doc altogether. When she'd first entered the mess hall and her eyes had fallen on him, she'd felt a certain ache in her chest. She didn't know why this was happening to her, and now of all times. All this emotion, this weakness, was so unlike her. She'd never had feelings for any of her fellow soldiers before. In fact, she couldn't recall any man playing on her mind so persistently, the way Doc seemed to. Why him? Why now, right when she'd finally had her chance at Space Duty? Right in the midst of all this mess.

Despite this mess, however, she couldn't help but wonder what would happen between them if they made it through this debrief; back on Earth, off the ship, and away from prying eyes. This had only been a test case, right? So, technically, when this was over, they were no longer in the same unit. So how would things play out then? She had no idea if what happened on the *Aurora* would continue, or whether it was just a fleeting moment, a last desperate grasp for human contact in the face of death.

The three of them sat in silence for a while until Doc eventually ended it. Appearing a little edgy, he got up from the table.

"I'm going to head back to my room. I'll see you all in the morning." Then he turned and left.

Carrie didn't watch him leave, instead she looked at Harris, for distraction. "So, how do you think this will play out, captain?"

He looked down his shoulder at her, considering his answer. "I guess that depends on how everyone's debrief goes. Doc and I are satisfied with ours. Are you?"

Carrie nodded. She was confident they had nothing to use against them.

"Good," he said. "I have confidence in the others. But it's in the hands of the UNF now. It depends on who's making the decisions here, what their agenda is, and then who's behind them applying pressure. I think the debrief is just for show and they're using it to scare us into keeping quiet and cover up what really happened."

Carrie nodded, eyeing the guards in the corner carefully, recalling her father's warning not to trust anyone. It only made her wonder what had happened to her father to have made him so sure of that fact. It disheartened her a little to realize the mystery around her father had just grown tenfold, and the giant chasm of distance between them, even wider.

Harris locked eyes with her. "Maybe we should head back to our rooms, corporal. We've still got a lot of waiting to do," he said, as he stood. "And don't we know waiting is the hardest thing to do."

Harris was right, waiting was the hardest thing to do. Carrie sat on her bed, staring at the TV. The Moon elections were approaching and the news seemed to cover nothing else, switching between the five colonies for interviews and statistics. She decided to take a shower, wanting to wash away the day, but Dale's comments seemed to stick firmly to her. She worried about what questions Dale had asked of Doc, and worse, she worried about what he'd asked of the captain.

She'd been surprised when she'd seen the footage of Grolsh attacking her. It was almost like an out-of-body experience. After all, she'd been unconscious for some of it. It sent a shiver down her spine to think of how close to death she'd actually been. And more to the point, it sent a shiver down her spine to see Smith again, rushing to her rescue, not knowing that he, himself, only had hours to live.

Dale also showed her the hospital footage of her and Doc alone. The first, after they processed Smith's body, when she held his hand a little longer than necessary. She managed to pass that off as being upset over Smith, which she had been. Then there was the incident when Doc was treating her when it was all over. She hadn't known that there was a camera in the room, when she'd held his hand and kissed it. Luckily for her, the camera was behind and to the left, so it wasn't really clear what she had done. The footage showed her taking Doc's hand, but the kiss could not be seen. She passed that off to Dale as being in pain. Fortunately, the camera did pick up the side of her head that Logan had hit. It looked bad, and provided all the evidence she needed.

She stepped out of the shower and wrapped herself in a towel and headed back to sit on her bed in front of the TV. The Moon election coverage was over and they were onto the discovery of the last oil reserves on Earth, in the middle of the Indian Ocean. The reserves were on the border of Australian waters and international waters, but largely on the Australian side. Naturally the Australian government was claiming ownership, but other countries were begging to differ. *Here comes another war...*

Carrie's eyes were on the TV but she wasn't watching it anymore. She felt a wave of tiredness wash over her. She pulled the covers back on her bed, dropped her towel and slipped in. She rolled over onto her side and eyed the empty bed beside her. She started to think about Doc again. In her mind, she could see his brown eyes looking at her, trying to speak to her. She could see his hand, his arm, his neck, as he sat at his desk eyeing the monitor in his office. Then she started thinking about what it would be like to curl up into his side, to have that arm wrapped around her. And it was that thought that saw her safely to sleep.

*

She made her way to breakfast feeling quite unrested. She'd tossed and turned through the night, dreaming a thousand dreams. She'd been back on the Darwin, and back in the debrief room, and neither were pleasant places to be. Logan and Chet were there again, jumping out of their skin to get to her, hungry like vampires. She kept hearing Sharley's words echoing through her mind: *"I'll see you soon, Carrie Ann Welles,"* and Logan pointing viciously at her, telling her he'd make her pay. These dreams were choking her sleep every night like a thick plume of black smoke, and she prayed silently for them to end.

When she entered the mess hall, she saw Harris sitting on one side of the room, and Packham with her guard on the other. Carrie filled her tray and made her way over to Harris's table, shooting Packham a sympathetic glance on the way. She took the seat opposite Harris, who had his back toward Packham.

"Morning, corporal," he greeted her.

"Morning, captain." She started eating her breakfast, stealing glances over at Packham, who looked worn out. Carrie swore she could see the dark circles under her eyes from across the room.

Just then Brown entered. Harris saw this, too, and straightened in his seat. Brown grabbed a tray of food and made his way over, taking the seat next to Harris.

"Sergeant Brown," Harris greeted him, holding his hand out for a high-five slap. "Good to see you, soldier!"

"Captain," he said, slapping his hand. He looked over at Carrie and nodded. "Welles."

"Hey, Brown. How you going?"

He grunted. "I've been better. I gotta say, though, I'm glad the UNF has finally shit me out of its digestive system."

Harris gave a laugh and shook his head. "We're not out yet, Brown. Think of it more like moving into the lower intestine."

Doc entered and he joined them, grabbing a tray of food, and nodding at Packham as he passed. He placed his tray on the table beside Carrie.

"Sergeant Brown, good to see you!" he said, as Brown held out his hand. Doc clasped it, then swung into the seat beside Carrie, his knee knocking hers as he did. He quickly glanced at her, then looked at two men opposite.

"How'd it go?" he asked Brown.

"It went."

Carrie saw Harris look over his shoulder at Packham, then back at Brown, his mind ticking over.

"Who'd they call up after you?" he asked.

"I think they were going to hit up McKinley next," he said, in between chews.

Harris looked back at Packham and studied her for a moment. "They're trying to break her," he said as though thinking aloud, then turned back to the group.

Carrie, Doc and Brown all looked over at Packham. She saw them staring and shot them back a tired look. Carrie suddenly noticed that Harris was now staring at her.

"Well done, corporal," he said.

Doc and Brown glanced between them.

"For what, sir?" she asked.

"Dale obviously didn't get enough out of you, so he's trying hard to break Packham instead. She's his last resort. He's making her wait, trying to freak her out. Letting her sit in here, but over in the corner, away from us, watching us. He's trying to fuck her mind."

They looked back over at Packham, again. Carrie didn't exactly find it a comforting thought to know that Packham was paying the price for her success. Brown looked back at his food.

"She'll be alright. She tougher than she looks," he said.

"I sure hope so," Harris said.

Carrie noticed Doc eyeing Packham, analyzing her, mind ticking over.

"So, they kept you in a while, considering the fact that you didn't kill anybody," Harris said to Brown.

"No, but they were trying like hell to get me to give the dirt on you three and McKinley."

"Yeah? What dirt?" Harris arched his eyebrow curiously at him.

Brown hesitated, flashed Doc, then Harris, a look and said, "Just shit."

Carrie noted that neither Harris nor Doc pushed for more information, and they sat in silence for a while, finishing breakfast, sipping their coffees.

"So, McKinley's up next, huh," Harris said, looking off into the distance.

"Gee, I hope Dale got his rest last night," Doc said sarcastically.

Smiles seemed to sneak across their faces, before Harris suddenly dropped his.

"They've probably got him high as a kite on painkillers," he said. "Or worse, they haven't given him any and he's been in pain the past few days. If there's a way to cheat, they'll do it."

"McKinley can hold himself," Doc said. "He's got a high tolerance, believe me."

"Yeah," Carrie mused. "He's a lot stronger than I gave him credit for. On our way back, the *Vortex*'s medic, Jackson, refused to top up his painkillers, then he pretended to examine his leg, but all he did was squeeze it and watch McKinley's face."

Doc's face turned dark and serious as he looked at Carrie. Brown and Harris also stopped eating and stared at her.

"He was waiting for a reaction but McKinley didn't give it to him," she said. "He held it well. I don't know how he did it, though. I would've screamed like a baby."

"He's tough as an ox, McKinley," Brown nodded.

"I knew I shouldn't have left my patients with Jackson," Doc said through gritted teeth.

"We had no choice, Doc," Harris told him.

Doc stared at Harris. "Captain—"

"I know, Doc," Harris stopped him. "When this is over, I've got a few things to say about the *Vortex* crew, Jackson and Baker especially. It will be said, believe me!"

*

Once they'd eaten, Brown disappeared back to his room for more sleep, and soon after, Harris left as well. Doc and Carrie sat in the mess hall a little while longer, although there was a feeling of uneasiness between them. It seemed that they were both painfully aware that they were alone at the table, despite the two guards in the corner, and most probably some surveillance camera somewhere. Doc shuffled in his chair at one point and when he came to a rest, his leg fell against hers. He quickly changed position to remove it, sitting forward in his chair, and then eventually giving in and standing up.

"I'm going to head back up, corporal," he said, glancing at her briefly.

Carrie nodded and stood up too. "Yeah, me too."

*

The rest of the day came and went in much the same way. At lunch, Dale had Packham on display again at one end of the mess hall. The four "debriefed" soldiers sat around together for a while. Not much was said. The odd comment about how long it was taking. Predictions of what would happen next. Doc did his best to avoid contact with Carrie this time around, sitting diagonally opposite her. He gave her the odd glance, but for the most part, made no attempt to converse with her in particular.

By the time dinner came, Packham was absent. They decided that either she was finally being debriefed, or Dale was just holding her elsewhere to mess with *their* minds this time.

Harris and Brown eventually left for their rooms, leaving Carrie and Doc alone again. They eyed each other briefly, before the lieutenant fidgeted in his seat again, then stood up to leave as well.

454

"Is this how it's going to be from now on?" she asked. She couldn't help herself, and although it felt uncomfortable, she let herself look into his eyes again.

He held her gaze for a moment, his eyes trying to speak to hers again, then he nodded. "For the time being, corporal."

Harris felt the stiffness building in his body. He hadn't slept well, as his mind was crammed with far too many thoughts. It didn't help, either, that he'd dreamt *yet again* of Sibbie and Etta staring at him. It made him nervous. It made him edgy. It made him wonder whether Packham would hold up under the pressure. There was so much riding on the debriefs and it was going to come down to her, he was sure of it.

Packham had been absent at breakfast, and now again at lunch. He'd resigned himself to the fact that he wasn't going to see the rest of his team until the official UNF court-martial took place and a verdict was handed down. It bothered him some, as it had been a while since he'd seen McKinley, Hunter and Colt, and he wanted to know how they were doing. But he really wanted to see Packham and find out how she went. Brown said she was strong, but Harris remembered her wanting to hole up on the ship and wait until they were rescued. He wondered if she'd do the same with Dale and just give in? Welles had managed to get through Dale's debrief, but then again she'd been the one to volunteer to go onto the Darwin and do what needed to be done. She hadn't wanted to hole up like Packham had.

Although Welles looked a little worn down, as if she wasn't getting much sleep, she seemed to be healing nicely. Command had access to the best medicine, so at least that was something. Her neck was pretty much clear now, her left eye was almost white again, and the bruises down the left side of her face were beginning to fade. The corporal was a lot stronger than he'd given her credit for. Not only was she a fine shot, but she was brave, fit, smart and she had a lot better understanding of the workings of the UNF than most corporals. Having a colonel for a father had obviously paid dividends in her chosen career.

Thinking about his new recruits only led him to think about his dead soldiers, however. The ones he would never see again. The ones that left a hole in his team.

"Captain," Doc pulled Harris out of his thoughts, "have you heard anything about Carter and the guys? Do you know when they're going to release their bodies? Will they have an official service for them?"

"You reading my mind, Doc?" He arched an eyebrow. "I was just thinking about them. I put in a request during my debrief, but I've heard nothing yet. I'll follow it up this afternoon, but my guess is they'll be waiting to see how the debrief pans out before making any decisions."

"I'm done waiting," Welles muttered.

They all looked at her.

"We all are, corporal," Doc said firmly, then looked away again.

"C'mon, Welles," Harris said, trying to cheer her up, "you're a sniper. Waiting is what you do."

"Yeah, but that's different, captain. I wait around with a gun in my hand and eventually get to shoot a bad guy."

Harris dropped his smile. "Well, hopefully, we'll make it through this, and you'll get the chance again."

# 30

# The Verdict

Carrie opted to eat her meal in her room that evening. She didn't want to sit there in the mess hall again in silence, trying her best to avoid contact with Doc, worrying about what was going to happen to the team. She could do the same in her room; stare blankly at the TV and try not to think about it... or the dreams that haunted her.

She found that she only picked at her food, barely watched the TV and instead stared out the window. She watched as the lights of Fort Centralis twinkled in the darkness, traffic went by on the streets below and guards patrolled the pavements. She looked off into the distance catching the last glimpses of the ocean as the sun set behind the island's mini-skyline, and a ship took flight leaving its trail across the heavens.

She thought about everyone else out there on the various mainlands, working nine to five, sitting at home with their families, rubbing their bellies from their lovely evening meal, completely oblivious to Carrie locked inside this small hotel room. Oblivious to the Jumbo's the UNF had created. Oblivious to the far reaches of the galaxy the UNF was exploring. Ignorance was bliss, she thought. Unfortunately for her, she preferred knowledge. That was why she'd been drawn to the UNF; for the knowledge, the experience, and because her father had urged her not to. And that was why she couldn't be one of *them*, out there.

She heard a knock at the door and looked at her watch. 19:03. She opened it, and saw Harris standing there, alongside both their guards.

"Corporal," he gave her a nod, "we didn't see you in the mess hall this evening. Is everything alright?"

"Yes, sir."

"You feeling alright?" He studied her.

"Yes, sir."

Harris eyed her a while longer. "You get your orders for the next couple of days?"

"Yes, sir. Verdict tomorrow. Service the day after."

"Good… and you're sure everything's alright?"

She nodded. "I just felt like eating in my room tonight, captain."

He continued to study her face, then nodded back. "Well, if you need anything, these guards know where to find me."

"Thank you, sir."

He eyed her one last time then left. She could see the skepticism on his face, but she was too tired to care. She closed the door, went back to her window, and continued to watch the UNF world of Fort Centralis go by.

*

Carrie stood at the door to her room, ready to make her way to the court-martial proceedings. She ran her hand over her ponytail to smooth it, tucked her long fringe behind her ear, straightened her skirt and double-checked her heels were clean and shiny. This was the first opportunity she'd had to wear the "official" Space Duty uniform. It was smart, it was feminine and she felt it had class. If it were not for the bruises on her face, she could've almost been a poster girl for the UNF. An absurd thought, really, after all they'd put her through. But she'd heeded Harris's warning and was going to play the good little soldier until she knew where they stood with the UNF.

She opened the door, nodded at her guard, and headed toward the elevator. She had purposely cut it fine to avoid standing with the others. She wanted to just turn up and have it happen, whatever the outcome was to be. She didn't want time to be nervous. She didn't want to discuss possible scenarios or how she was feeling with anyone, and of course, she wanted to avoid Doc.

Unfortunately, when she opened the doors to the Command courtroom, he was the first person she saw. His eyes had been on the door. If she wasn't mistaken, he'd been watching for her. He was off to the side, talking to McKinley and Hunter, who along with Colt, were sitting in wheelchairs, although looking reasonably well. They were dressed in their service uniforms and they too looked smart. Especially Doc, who gave her a subtle smile and nodded her way. McKinley and Hunter looked over at her, and her eyes locked with McKinley's. She gave them a quick nod and immediately turned away. If it was painful to look at Doc in his combat uniform, then it was killing her to look at him now.

"I was about to come looking for you, corporal," Harris hissed quietly. "This is *not* a day to be late!"

"Sorry, captain."

Harris gave her a glare, then turned back around to face the front. Brown stood next to him and looked down at Carrie over his shoulder, very overtly running his eye over her.

"Well, well, well. Carrie the Kid in a skirt," he said quietly, seemingly amused. Clearly he was opting for humor to break the nerves in the room.

Carrie overtly looked him up and down too. "Brownie in official uniform."

"Look good, don't I?" He flicked his eyebrows up at her.

She flashed him a broad smile, but quickly controlled it, then looked around the room. Other than the *Aurora* team, there was only a sprinkling of other officers there, Dale included. It was clearly a "closed room" affair, which didn't surprise her. She saw Harris lock eyes with one of the uniformed men. He had gray hair and looked to be a colonel in rank. The man gave a slight nod to Harris, who eyed him back with a blank stare, then turned away from his gaze.

Carrie made her way over to join Colt and Packham.

"Corporal Colt," she said, with a half-smile, "how're you going?"

Colt smiled. "I'm alright. They're going to release me in a couple days."

"That's great. You look good," Carrie told her, then she looked up at Packham. "How're you holding up?"

Packham gave a weak smile. "Alright. I'm glad it's over."

Carrie gave her an empathetic smile.

"I hear you did good, girl?" Colt piped up.

Carrie shrugged. "I could've done better."

"Oh, Jesus! Who you kiddin'? I told you, didn't I? I told you there would be a time when you would get to do your shit and you did it, girl. Fairmont didn't know what hit him."

Carrie smiled. "Thanks, Colt... I missed you."

Colt nodded, her eyes glistening a little. "Ah, Welles, I missed me too," she said, shooting them a cheeky smile.

Packham smirked and Carrie couldn't help but break a smile. She looked up and caught Doc watching her. If she wasn't mistaken, he almost looked like he was in pain. At least, his eyes did. Did it hurt him to look at her, too? He quickly turned back to engross himself in McKinley's conversation.

Just then an officer stood and called everyone to attention. The room fell silent and he announced the arrival of military judge, Colonel Bates, who entered the room and took a seat in the middle of the elevated table, on one side of the room. As he sat, the rest of them gathered also took a seat.

Carrie eyed him closely. He looked to be a little older than her father, although his hair wasn't quite as gray. He had a hard, round face with flushed cheeks and dark beady eyes. He opened an e-file in front of him, placed some reading glasses on his nose and began flipping through the onscreen pages, skimming quietly. The room remained quiet, as the *Aurora* team waited patiently. Carrie noticed someone watching her out of the corner of her eye. She turned and saw it was Dale. She gave him a great poker face, then turned back to Bates. She was getting good at this, she thought.

She wondered what the judge was reading and what he would make of all this? The *Aurora* team sat before him scattered with their injured. She looked over at Colt and eyed the bandage showing across her neck. Her eyes then fell to Hunter, whose broken arm was in a special gel-sling, the bicep on his other arm bandaged and showing beneath the sleeve of his shirt. She looked down at his thigh and saw it looked thick with bandages too. She turned her head slightly and looked over at McKinley, whose leg was in some sort of brace that ran from toe to mid-thigh. She then glanced over at Harris, who was sitting, but holding himself very upright, as though his ribs were still bothering him. She thought about her own head, and her side. They didn't hurt so much anymore, but she could still feel the bruises sitting roughly on her skin.

Colonel Bates flipped back to the front of the file and tapped the microphone in front of him, to check it was turned on.

"Officers, soldiers," he nodded. "I have carefully read through the debrief report on the Darwin mission as prepared by Senior Officer Edgely."

Carrie felt a slap of shock, as the *Aurora* team all turned to eye Dale. They'd been led to believe that he was the one responsible for any findings on the debrief, and that Edgely was merely observing. It would appear that Dale was a decoy, and he seemed satisfied with his ruse.

"It would appear," the colonel continued, "that to thoroughly investigate the events that took place I would need to undertake a more comprehensive investigation of Darwin Station itself. However, as the intimate details of the Darwin's programs were classified, this could not be done. So, I am left with merely examining the events that took place from the time the *Aurora* docked to the time it disembarked. Although I have had to take into account the allegations of the *Aurora* team as to the nature of some of the programs being run on the station, I will not be referring to those allegations during this briefing, due to the classified nature of the said programs.

"Above all else, it is my job to decide whether any disciplinary action is to be taken with regards to the deaths of the seven UNF scientists and lab workers on Station Darwin, and whether there is any responsibility to be laid for the deaths of the four *Aurora* crew members. Today, I will pass only my judgment on the *Aurora* crew for the deaths of Darwin crew. It's been confirmed that one UNF team has already reached the Darwin to investigate the matter further. However, again, due to some of the allegations of the *Aurora* crew, a second *independent* team was dispatched to ensure all investigations are aboveboard. Judgement against the remaining Darwin crew for the deaths of the four *Aurora* crew will take place once they have been brought back to Earth."

Colonel Bates reached forward, picked up the glass of water in front of him and took a sip. He placed the glass back down and looked over the top of his glasses at those present.

"So, I will have the *Aurora* team standing in front of me as I hand down my findings. As I call your name, please step forward to this line," he said, pointing to a white line along the floor about four meters in front of his table.

"Captain Saul Harris."

Harris stood from his chair, walked up to the line, and stood straight, arms by his sides.

"First Lieutenant Daniel Walker."

Carrie watched as Doc stood at the line by Harris's side.

"Second Lieutenant James McKinley."

McKinley stood up from his wheelchair, and with the help of crutches handed to him by a nurse, made his way over to stand by Doc, who turned and watched him.

"First Sergeant Jacob Hunter. Sergeant James Jay Brown."

Hunter was pushed forward in his wheelchair by a UNF nurse. As he reached the line, she helped him to stand, resting his weight on his good leg, then wheeled the chair away slightly. Brown stood alongside him.

"Sergeant Sarah Packham. Corporal Sabrina Colt."

Colt, like Hunter was wheeled up to the line, and then helped out of her chair to stand on the white line beside Packham.

"And Corporal Carrie Welles."

Carrie stood and made her way over to stand by Colt in the line. Her heart was racing and her chest felt tight. She could sense the others felt the same way, as the tension hung in the air thickly like a stifling heat.

The colonel, still looking over the top of his glasses, ran his eye over the line, analyzing each and every one of them. "As I address you each individually, you will take another step forward, then fall back into line when done. Do you understand?"

"Yes, sir," they all replied.

"Captain Harris, if you would?" The judge motioned for Harris to step forward.

He did so.

"Captain Harris, according to the report, you were called to Command at 0600 on September 20th and issued with your orders for the Darwin mission. You were then informed that you would be taking on three new recruits. Is this correct?"

"Yes, sir," Harris answered, staring dead ahead, his face devoid of emotion.

"And you were advised the mission was a response to a loss of comms on the Darwin, and that your team, including your new recruits would be leaving that night. Is that correct?"

"Yes, sir."

"And when you arrived you found the station deserted, except for four survivors, whom you quarantined. First Lieutenant Walker, please step forward. Thank you, Captain Harris."

Doc stepped forward as Harris stepped back.

"Lieutenant Walker. You ran several tests on the 'survivors', finding no trace of a virus, despite them exhibiting symptoms indicating otherwise. You then held the survivors for some 12 hours to be sure there was no change in their symptoms. Is that correct?"

"Yes, sir."

"After waiting these 12 hours and running another series of tests, you recommended their release from quarantine to Captain Harris, as their results were clean and you had no reason to quarantine them any longer. Is that correct?"

"Yes, sir."

The judge looked down at his file again for a moment. "I've seen your medical files and I'm satisfied that your tests were thorough and you took the necessary precautions for the team. Step back, lieutenant. Captain Harris step forward again."

Harris did, as Doc stepped back.

"So, as per Lieutenant Walker's recommendations, captain, you approved the release of the four survivors into your custody and onto the *Aurora*. Is that correct?"

"Yes, sir."

"I'm satisfied, given the classified nature of the Darwin, that you exhausted all lines of investigation into the disappearance of the rest of the crew, had no reason to hold them further and therefore released the survivors under UNF law. *However*, it does appear that this is the moment the mission took a turn." The judge eyed Harris carefully over his glasses, then looked back at his file.

"Corporal Welles, would you please step forward," he called, looking over his glasses again.

Carrie's heart thumped against her ribcage so hard she thought it was going to burst right on through. She stepped forward and stared straight ahead.

"Corporal Welles, the incident between you and Tynek Grolsh set off a chain of events for your team that has ultimately led us all here today."

Carrie tried to hold it, but she couldn't help but swallow hard.

"I have watched the surveillance footage of the incident, and it is clear that Grolsh was the instigator, and that you were not at fault. In fact, corporal, I'd say you are very lucky to be standing here in front of me today." The colonel eyed her for a moment, then looked back down at his file, turning over a page. "Corporal, you are responsible for killing two members of the Darwin crew: Karl Fairmont and Eric Oxer. With regard to Fairmont's death, I've watched the footage from the *Aurora*'s external cameras and read the supporting testimonies of First Sergeant Hunter and Corporal Colt. It is clear that Sergeant Hunter was under attack from Fairmont and you did attempt to rescue him by first wounding Fairmont. Fairmont then charged you, and you shot and killed him. Is that correct?"

"Yes, sir."

"With regard to Oxer's death, I've read Second Lieutenant McKinley's supporting testimony of the incident and that of Walker, Brown and Packham who were watching from the *Aurora*'s flight deck. I have also seen the footage from the headcams, although they are, at best, hard to obtain any clarity from. There must have been some kind of interference with the relay during the recording process. However, it is quite clear that this time you made no attempt to wound the enemy, corporal. You fired a single shot to the head, killing Oxer instantly. Is that correct?"

"Yes, sir."

The judge eyed her again for a moment. "Corporal Welles, I have taken into account the fact that you are a sharpshooter. Hitting your targets accurately is what you do. Having said that, you are better placed than most soldiers to simply wound as opposed to killing your enemy. You have accuracy on your side to be able to make that decision. In Fairmont's case you did, *at first*. In Oxer's, you did not."

Carrie swallowed hard again.

"Corporal, I have also taken into account that this was your first mission as part of a team on the ground, in the firing line. Your previous experience has been as a sharpshooter, far away from hand-to-hand combat. You survived the attack by Grolsh, and I believe this was probably still on your mind, not to mention the deaths of your fellow team members, when you killed both Fairmont and Oxer.

"I believe the force was excessive. But I believe that you felt you were under attack and that you did what you are trained to do, and you did it to save a fellow team member, whom you also thought was at great risk. Therefore, I find no disciplinary action to be taken against you for the deaths of these two UNF lab workers. *However*, I will not be granting you the commendation that Captain Harris has recommended for your bravery, either. Corporal Welles, you showed elements of bravery, but I do not believe you showed more than your fellow soldiers. This has been a massive learning curve for you, corporal, and I hope you take what you've learned from this mission and keep it in mind on your future missions. You may step back."

"Thank you, sir." Carrie stepped back into line and took a deep breath. She felt a little numb, but like a weight had been lifted off her shoulders. More than that, she'd been taken by surprise and touched by Harris's commendation, despite it being refused.

"Corporal Colt, Sergeant Brown and First Sergeant Hunter, please step forward," the judge called.

Colt took a step forward, while Brown helped Hunter move forward.

"The three of you were not directly responsible for the deaths of any of the Darwin crew, and therefore you have no charges to answer. First Sergeant Hunter, Corporal Colt, you may step back."

They did.

"Sergeant Brown, Captain Harris has recommended that you receive commendation for stepping up as co-pilot on the *Aurora* to get your team home. I've looked at your file and note that although you're the chief engineer on the ship, it is in fact beyond the call of duty for you to be asked to co-pilot. But you did and your team made it home. The commendation has been noted in your file. You may step back."

"Thank you, sir." Brown stepped back into line.

"Sergeant Sarah Packham, would you please step forward."

Packham stepped forward, looking nervous.

"Sergeant, you are responsible for the death of Edgar Carlisle on board the *Aurora*. I have watched the footage from the *Aurora*'s onboard surveillance cameras and I have also read the testimonies of Lieutenant Walker and Corporal Welles. Sergeant Bolkov was injured and wrestling with Carlisle when you shot him in the back, killing him almost instantly. I note that your role as co-pilot generally means you are very rarely involved in hand-to-hand combat, and this was in fact your first experience of such. Is that correct?"

"Yes, sir."

"You shot an unarmed man in the back, sergeant, something I would not normally approve of. However, given the situation you were in and your lack of experience, I believe you did what you thought was right at the time. You shot Carlisle in an attempt to save your wounded teammate. I will not record disciplinary against you. *However*, I will not be granting you the commendation that Captain Harris recommended for your action in stepping up to pilot the ship when First Sergeant Hunter was wounded. As co-pilot, it *is* your duty to do this if required. You may step back."

"Thank you, sir."

The colonel took another sip of his water.

"Second Lieutenant McKinley step forward."

McKinley crutched forward a step.

"Lieutenant McKinley, you are charged with the death of Tynek Grolsh. I've watched your headcam footage of the incident, lieutenant, and as the third senior officer on board the *Aurora* and the resident sharpshooter, I'm a little unconvinced that your action was warranted. I understand that two of your team members were being attacked at the time and Grolsh had led them into that ambush, but Grolsh approached you unarmed. You came out from a hidden position and you shot him clean in the chest.

"You knew your shot would be fatal. You're a sharpshooter, that's what you do. More to the point you chose a rather painful way to take him out, rather than a good clean shot to the head, as I know you are capable of. No, I think you're smart, lieutenant. You shot him in the chest because you knew it would kill him, but there would be a few minutes of excruciating pain first, and that it could look like you didn't mean to kill him. Provided you weren't a sharpshooter, of course...

"I understand that on top of leading your teammates into that ambush, Grolsh was also wanted for the assault on Corporal Welles, and he had also assaulted you during the incident in which Private First Class Smith was killed. Therefore, I do believe that when you took out Grolsh, revenge was on your mind, lieutenant. On reading the testimonies of your fellow team members and of your captain, however, it seems they are all certain that your actions were warranted. I believe your team support you because they, too, wanted revenge. I will have it noted on your file that I believe your actions were excessive, lieutenant, but given the circumstances of this whole mess, you will not receive a formal strike... *this time*. But next time you have an unarmed man running toward you, lieutenant, I suggest you aim for his legs. Do you understand me?"

"Yes, sir."

"Step back, lieutenant." McKinley crutched back into place, his face a mask showing no emotion. Carrie felt sorry for him. As far as she was concerned, McKinley did the right thing.

"First Lieutenant Walker, would you please step forward again."

Doc stepped forward. She felt her heartbeat step up a notch.

"Lieutenant, you are charged with the death of Julian Ravearez. I have watched the surveillance footage and I have read the testimonies of Corporal Welles and Sergeant Packham, and I must say that I was a little undecided whether your action was warranted. You shot Ravearez three times in the face, neck and shoulder, killing him almost instantly. He was unarmed."

The judge took a good hard look at Doc over his glasses. "Ravearez had tripped Corporal Welles, who was to your left, as you made your way toward Bolkov and Carlisle who were wrestling. Lieutenant, you claim that Ravearez was trying to pull Corporal Welles toward him, and perhaps drag her away, when you shot him, *three times*, in the face, neck and shoulder. Is that correct?"

"Yes, sir."

"I've read your file, lieutenant. You have a good, solid record, cleaner than most, and Captain Harris rates you very highly. Your response to Ravearez attacking Welles does seem a little excessive, but given the situation of Bolkov under attack, not to mention the deaths of Carter and Louis that Corporal Welles had just informed you of, I believe you felt the team was being attacked and extreme measures were called for. You took control of the situation and did what you had to do to rescue your fellow team members and secure the ship. So there is no strike against you to be noted in your file. You may step back."

"Thank you, sir."

"And so this leaves me with you, Captain Harris." The colonel looked over his glasses again. "Please step forward."

Harris stepped forward, standing straight and tall.

"Captain Harris, you are charged with shooting Bradford Chet. I could not view the footage from your, or Corporal Welles's, headcam. Whilst the footage on the Darwin's main floor has interference, there appears to have been something blocking the signal altogether up there on this supposed second floor, but I have read Corporal Welles's supporting testimony of the incident. From what I can gather, Corporal Welles had been taken hostage, was suffering from a head injury and Chet was in the process of attacking her when you shot him. Chet had been wounded twice by Welles. A shot to the arm and she also stabbed him with the needle provided by Lieutenant Walker, yet he continued to attack. You went to her rescue, Captain Harris, and you did what you had to do to get both her and yourself out of there alive. I believe you have no charges to be answered."

"Thank you, sir."

Colonel Bates took off his glasses and looked back at Harris. "All in all, would I rate this mission as successful, Captain Harris? No, I would not. You left with a team of 12 and headed for a station of UNF scientists. You lost four men. A third of your team, captain. You also returned with five wounded soldiers, some seriously. Even *you* did not come out of this unscathed.

"This was not an ideal test case for the UNF. Although the three female soldiers returned alive and stand before me now, two of them were wounded badly and could have died. That would not have been a good result for the UNF, captain. I must say at this point, however, that Lieutenant Walker did a good job in keeping the wounded alive, and I do believe there was nothing he could have done to save the four men who did die.

"This mission was a mess, and many errors in judgment were made on all sides. And due to the classified nature of the Darwin and its programs, I believe this is a mission the UNF will not want known to any person outside of these four walls. Therefore, this debrief will now be classified, and all your personnel files will be elevated to a level 4 and locked. You will need to regroup, captain, and put this mess behind you. But I have faith that you will do so and continue to serve the UNF as you have done."

The colonel stared firmly at Harris for a moment, then scanned the row of soldiers before him again, making eye contact with each and every one. "You faced the unknown on this, soldiers. For the most part, you did well. You got out of there alive, and where possible you got your team out alive, too. Every mission, be it good or bad, is ultimately useful. You learn from failures. They make you stronger, better soldiers. So, learn from these events, but move on, and forget these events. Forget this mission… because it never happened. That is my order to you all."

The colonel closed the file in front of him. "Captain Harris, do you have any final words to say?"

A brief moment of silence passed before Harris firmly answered. "Yes, sir, I do."

"Very well."

"Sir, I would like to personally thank my team for pulling together and being the strong unit that I know them to be. It can be a difficult thing when you introduce new team members at the last minute, then throw them into a mission like this, but I believe the team integrated well and did what they had to when it counted. My experienced soldiers—Lieutenants Walker and McKinley and Sergeants Hunter and Brown—stayed solid as a rock and, as ever, I believe there are no better soldiers in the UNF with whom I would entrust my life. My new recruits, Sergeant Packham and Corporals Colt and Welles, stepped up to the level of my experienced soldiers and I was proud to have them in my team for this mission.

"I would like it to be noted, however, sir, that I am disappointed that more information was not readily available to me when my unit was sent in. My particular grievance being with Professor Martin, as he was in control of that station. It is hard to fight an enemy when you do not know their full capabilities, especially when their capabilities are beyond what is considered normal by UNF standards. Unfortunately, I had to lose four good soldiers to find that out. Four soldiers who, I believe, deserved better from the UNF they served. Four soldiers, whose deaths have left a gaping hole in my team.

"Having said that, I'm proud of my unit, sir. Providing the relevant disciplinary actions are taken against those responsible for this '*mess*', I can assure you we *will* re-group and continue to be as strong as we ever were. The *Aurora* will indeed set sail again, sir, and we will continue to serve the UNF as we have done."

The colonel sat quietly for a moment, seemingly mulling over Harris's words, then he finally nodded. "Is that all, captain?"

"I do have one more thing, sir."

"What is it?"

"I want to ensure that my complaints against the *Vortex* crew will be duly processed."

"What complaints are these? I'm not aware of this?"

Harris turned and shot Dale a glare. The judge noticed.

"Officer Dale, would you care to clarify?"

Dale stood. "Sir, the UNF *Vortex* was the ship that intercepted the *Aurora* and escorted it back to base. Captain Harris has made several complaints against certain members of the *Vortex* crew, concerning their treatment of the *Aurora* team. A report is being filed as we speak. However, it is being treated separately from this mission, therefore you have not been advised of it."

The colonel eyed him over his glasses. "Very well. I accept that it should be treated as a separate issue. However, I am *very* interested in seeing that report, Officer Dale."

"Yes, sir." Dale nodded.

"By 0800 tomorrow. Take your seat."

Dale sank back into his seat. Carrie felt a sense of satisfaction wash over her as he did.

"This court-martial is now adjourned," the colonel told them. "This mission is now classified, and as far as the UNF and you soldiers are concerned, it never took place. You are all dismissed."

Harris let out a quiet sigh and slumped his posture slightly. Part of him was relieved it was finally over, but part of him was surprised at just how well things had gone for them. Had Colonel Welles come through for them? Or did it mean something else? Was the UNF letting them walk away, because they now had good leverage against the team? Leverage that would pay for their silence and keep them in line? It left Harris uneasy.

He looked to his left, down his line of soldiers. They looked relieved, but also a little shocked, as though they were just as suspicious as Harris as to what would happen now. Hunter, Colt and McKinley reached for their wheelchairs, exhausted from the standing. He suddenly noticed Doc watching him.

"Good speech," his lieutenant said, eyes questioning.

Harris gave a slight nod then turned away. He wasn't really good with emotional intimacies, especially with his soldiers. Truth be told, he wasn't really sure how he felt about the last part of his speech, and he knew that was what Doc's questioning eyes were about. Harris had said what he had to for the sake of the team; playing the "good little soldier" and confirming that the *loyal Aurora* team would indeed set sail again for the UNF. But the question right now was: Could he?

As he walked off he called over his shoulder to Doc. "Get everyone to The Vicar by 1200."

"Yes, sir," Doc said.

He looked at no-one else, spoke to no-one else, and simply walked right out of there, glad he no longer required a guard to shadow him. He headed for administration to begin proceedings to discharge his team from the UNF debrief and lodge a claim for extended leave. After all, their previous leave had been cut short, and he knew it would take McKinley and Hunter several weeks to recover from their wounds, and Harris sure wasn't setting sail without them. Again, he was hit with that feeling; *could* he set sail for the UNF, after what they did? Did he even have a choice?

As he walked along the corridor the colonel's words resonated in his head. He thought about each of the findings against his team, what he agreed with and what he didn't. McKinley got the harshest treatment, he thought, but if he had the time again, he would have no problem sending McKinley in and ordering him to do exactly the same thing. Grolsh deserved to die. They all did.

His mind crept to thoughts of Logan and Sharley in the bio cell. He hoped Martin's team knew how to handle them, as Sharley's words rang in his ears: *"I may be submitting to you now, but the next time I see you, it will be you who submits to me."* Harris was very interested to see the outcome of their trial. He wondered, too, about Professor Martin and Colonel Isaack and what would happen with them. He'd seen Isaack there at the verdict. He'd been wanting to speak with him but had not yet had the chance. *Why did he show up now? Why wasn't he involved in the debrief?* He felt an overwhelming urge for the answers to the questions brewing inside him.

It took just over an hour in administration. While his body was on autopilot, lodging the forms, his mind couldn't help but constantly return to wondering about Colonel Isaack and where he stood in all of this. The more he thought matters through, the more questions he had. He decided that when he was done with Administration, he would find him and get those answers.

"I'm sorry, sir," the receptionist advised him. "Colonel Isaack has been reassigned and is no longer working from this office."

"Reassigned? I just saw him a couple of hours ago at a debrief hearing."

"That may be the case, sir, but as of three days ago he moved out of this office."

"Can you tell me where he's been transferred to?"

"I'm sorry, sir. That's classified."

"Do you know how I can get in contact with him? A number perhaps?"

"I'm sorry, sir. Classified."

Harris stared at her a moment. "Well, if you could please get a message to him. Tell him that Captain Harris of the *Aurora* would like to speak with him. It's quite important. He's got my number."

"Certainly, sir. I'll ensure he gets that message."

He turned and headed for his hotel room, his mind ticking over furiously. *Reassigned? Where? Why? Did he know too much?*

He closed the door to his room and moved over toward the window and looked out over Fort Centralis. He felt strange, not as relieved as he should. Although he felt a certain weight had been lifted, he still felt a pressing gloom hanging over him. He knew those alive had been taken care of, but he still had to deal with the dead...

He recalled his speech again, surprised at the words he'd spoken. After what the UNF had put him through, he was tempted to quit. But he knew that leaving wouldn't be such an easy thing to do now. Not with the Darwin hanging over him. Could he leave? What would he do? This was what he'd done his whole life. This was all he knew. This is what he was good at. He'd never thought of doing anything else.

He stared out over Fort Centralis and his mind continued to tick over, intrigued. There were so many questions unanswered. So many questions he *wanted* answered. As he rolled them around in his mind, Sibbie and Etta appeared like reflections in a window pane, staring at him like they did. And he felt a sudden strange sensation within. Despite all that had happened, he felt a pull to stay. A pull to Fort Centralis. It was like there was something that had to be done; like there was something he was needed for; like it was beyond his control to walk away...

It was only a small element within the UNF that had betrayed them, right? Just Martin. Maybe Isaack? And no charges were laid against the

*Aurora* crew in the end. So maybe someone, somewhere, *was* looking out for them. A serious fuckin' mistake had been made, but now it was being corrected, right? Too late for his dead soldiers, but he could still believe in the UNF and what it stood for.

Right?

He lay on his bed and stared at the ceiling. He pictured the faces of his four dead soldiers, and yet again, Sibbie and Etta, too. He sighed and closed his eyes.

*You're back on Earth, Saul. It's time to start again. Time to move forward.*

For the first time in days, he thought of the Jazz Club Woman, but sure enough, he very swiftly pushed her aside for thoughts of Taya and Ty.

*

He arrived at The Vicar at 1156. It was a small Irish pub, frequented by UNF soldiers, just down the road from the Command docks. At the end of a mission, he always met the team at The Vicar and bought them drinks. Today was only going to be a taste test, however; a quiet celebration of making it through the debrief. The real drinks would follow after the service tomorrow, although they would also double as a wake.

As he entered he saw the team gathered in one corner, wheelchairs and all.

"Gentlemen, ladies," he greeted them.

They all acknowledged him with quiet smiles, and nods.

Doc stepped forward and handed him a beer. "We took the liberty of ordering a round, captain."

Harris took a gulp, then stood near their tables and looked at them all. "So, the verdict's in. Most of us came out of it fairly unscathed. I knew we would. You all did a good job, given the circumstances we were thrown into. I meant what I said. You should be proud of yourselves." Harris raised his glass, the team joined him, and they took a drink in silence.

"Captain," Doc began, "I know I speak on behalf of everyone when I say that there's no-one else we trust more with our lives, either, than you."

Doc raised his glass to him, and the team followed suit. McKinley, Brown and Hunter called out in approval, drawing attention from the rest of the bar. Harris was touched, but somehow didn't feel worthy of it when four of his men were dead. He waved his hands at them to quieten down.

"Thank you, Doc, gentlemen… *and* ladies. I guess now is a good time to tell you that you are all officially released from UNF custody."

"Hallelujah!" Brown called out, then turned and slapped Hunter's hand which was already waiting for him.

"Now, I don't need to remind you that we need to play it cool for a while." He lowered his voice a little but kept it firm. "Whatever you think or feel, you cap that shit, alright? Keep your head down and play normal. I have requested extended leave for you. For the old team here, we're owed a few weeks, and I've requested a further five weeks on top of that. So, pending UNF approval, which I have requested be fast-tracked, you should all have a good eight weeks to get away, recharge, and for those of you injured, recover."

"Nice one, captain." McKinley raised his glass to him.

Harris gave him a nod. "After this drink, you will all go back and pack your things and leave Command. You *will*, however, stay in town, as we have a service tomorrow for the four soldiers who are not here right now, drinking with us." Harris eyed the team, as they drew quiet and still. "Carter. Bolkov. Louis. Smith. They should be here with us, but they are not. Now, you may be free men and women, but if any of you turn up hungover or drunk tomorrow, you will be visiting Captain Harris's world of pain."

"Yes, sir," they answered.

"Good. So shut up and let me drink this, would you," Harris said dryly, taking the spare seat next to Doc.

# 31

# The Visit

Carrie smiled to herself as she watched Harris take a seat. As each day passed, she became more intrigued by him, the respect for him growing. He was a strong, brave soldier, smart and intuitive; a leader who looked out for his team. He struck her as a man she could learn a lot from. She hadn't ever felt that way about anyone before. Other than her father, of course.

Harris noticed her watching him. He raised his glass to her, and she raised hers back.

"So, Welles, you took two of them out in the end, eh?" Hunter said, moving into the spare seat beside her.

Carrie looked at him and smiled modestly. "How's it all going?" she asked him, eyeing his wounds.

"It's good. My head's still a bit foggy from being in that pod, but they're releasing me tomorrow. I really will be a free man!"

She smiled.

Hunter took a mouthful of his beer, and his turquoise eyes looked back at her a little awkwardly. "Thanks… for taking out Fairmont," he said. "It was a good shot."

Carrie flashed another smile, a little shyly. "Next time I might shoot Grolsh first though, save you some bullet wounds."

"Ah, don't sweat it, Welles. I'm still here, aren't I? If you hadn't taken out Fairmont, then I might not be."

Hunter raised his glass to hers and they clinked them together. He flashed her a friendly smile, then stood up gingerly and limped over to Harris and Doc. Carrie locked eyes with Doc as he placed his glass on the table in front of him. He gave her a subtle smile, but held his eyes strong, and she did the same in return.

Out of the corner of her eye, she suddenly noticed McKinley watching her and turned to view him. They both held a poker face, staring each other out for a moment, before Carrie laughed to herself and shook her head. She lifted her hand, holding it as though it were a gun and pretended to shoot him. He cracked a smile, laughing quietly to himself, then turned back to Brown who was watching their exchange, amused.

When they had finished their drinks, Packham departed for some much needed sleep and Harris settled the bill at the bar.

"C'mon, you weak and wounded, I'll escort you back to the hospital," Harris announced as he returned to the tables.

"Oh, c'mon, captain! We were just getting started," McKinley said.

"Want me to break your other leg, McKinley?" Harris said dryly.

The team chuckled as McKinley smiled and placed his empty glass back on the table. Harris waved to the nurses who had been waiting by the door. They came and took their allotted patients and headed for the exit.

Harris turned to Brown, Doc and Carrie, who were still sitting at the tables. "I so much as smell anything resembling alcohol on any of you tomorrow..." he warned, pointing his finger at them.

"Yes, captain," Doc smiled.

"And don't forget you still need to sign those release papers," Harris told him.

Doc nodded, dropping his smile, as Harris turned and left with the others. Carrie, Brown and Doc looked at each other.

"Well, thank fuck that's over," Doc said, moving up a couple of seats, closer to them.

"I'll drink to that," Brown said, clinking his glass with Doc's. "You want another?"

Doc looked at his watch and smiled. "Alright, but only one more, sergeant!"

"Yes, sir," Brown replied, then turned to Carrie. "How about you, Welles? You up for another?"

Carrie glanced briefly at Doc, then smiled at Brown. "Sure. Why not?"

"Alright." Brown walked off to the bar.

Carrie watched him walk away, suddenly noticing the quiet surrounding her and Doc. She looked over at him, his eyes returning her glance.

"So, how you holding up?" he asked her, finishing the beer in front of him.

"I'm doing alright."

"Yeah? I was a little concerned when you didn't show up to the mess hall last night," he said eyeing the empty glass in front of him, twisting it back and forth.

"I thought I was supposed to avoid you?"

He looked up from the glass at her. "Don't confuse avoid with ignore," he said, returning his eyes to the glass.

She stared at him a moment, looking down at his tanned forearms as he twisted the glass back and forth. She glanced back up to his serious face, which looked tired and worn out, but still made her eyes want to linger. She hesitated, then spoke her thoughts.

"I don't think ignoring you is an option for me."

He stopped twisting the glass and looked up at her.

"So, how are you holding up?" she asked, quickly changing the topic of conversation, and watching Brown at the bar.

He eyed her carefully. "I'm alright. I'll be a lot better after the service tomorrow. Everything will be a lot better." He pushed his glass away and sat back in his chair. They stared at each other a moment, before he turned his gaze to Brown who was heading back their way.

"Carrie the Kid," Brown said, placing a beer in front of her, then placed one in front of Doc.

"Thanks, Brownie," she said.

The sergeant then held out his glass to them both. "For going to hell, and then getting the fuck back out of there!"

"Amen," said Doc, clinking his glass.

Carrie smiled and clinked them both, too, noticing that Doc was avoiding her eyes now.

They drank their drinks at a slow pace, while Brown recounted some rather large nights the *Aurora* crew had had at The Vicar before. Carrie sat quietly, observing them, her heart melting every time she saw Doc smile. Brown noticed that she was quiet and soon turned the conversation onto her.

"Say, Welles, you do know it's tradition to be initiated into the team? First drinks is usually when it happens, ain't that right, Doc?"

Carrie stopped Doc before he could answer. "I hate to disappoint you, Brown, but we were only a test case. I'm not an official 'new' member of the team."

Brown scoffed. "You were a member of our team for the Darwin mission, and that's the mission we'll be drinking to. So, don't think you're getting out of initiation, Welles."

Doc gave a half-smile. "Brown, as your senior officer I cannot condone initiation of any kind."

"Yes, you can, and yes, you *have*, sir!" Brown challenged him.

Doc pulled an innocent face and held out his hands as if to say, *Who, me?* "As the medic onboard the *Aurora*, I do not encourage irresponsible drinking, sergeant."

Brown gave him a challenging look. "I believe *you* bought the shots that Smith consumed that night."

"Hey, I had nothing to do with it," Doc said pointing at Brown. "I bought the *first* round of shots. Carter and Louis took care of the rest. It was their fault!"

There was a momentary pause, as they realized who they'd been speaking about. Doc sighed and leaned forward in his chair again and stared at Brown. Carrie watched as he returned the saddened stare, and she could almost feel the ghosts of their fallen comrades crowding around them.

Doc stirred the silence, glancing at his watch. "I'd better make a move. I've got some work to take care of."

Carrie and Brown looked at him curiously.

"The UNF release forms for their bodies," Doc answered, noticing their stares. He lifted his glass and downed the rest of his beer.

"Where you staying tonight, Doc?" Brown asked.

"Probably over at the Shackleton. You?"

"Yeah, the Shackleton sounds good. I'll see you over there later."

Doc stood and nodded at him, then he turned to Carrie. "Welles."
She gave him a sympathetic smile, but he quickly turned and left.
*Who's ignoring who now, Doc?*

Harris walked through the door of his apartment and felt a wave of relief wash over him. He was home, although it didn't quite feel the same knowing that a third of his team would not be getting to do this. His eyes fell automatically to the frame-screen on his wall, displaying a slide show of family photographs. The current picture was one of Ty from a few years back, shooting hoops. He walked up to it and studied it carefully, looking at the laughter on his son's face. *I nearly lost your old man on this one.*

He stared at his son for what seemed an age, then sighed, and walked through to his bedroom, where he dumped his bag on the floor. He sat on his bed and looked around the room, his eyes falling to a napkin on his bedside table. He reached out and grabbed it. The words scribbled upon it were written in lipstick. It was what she had given him:

*Jazz Club Woman*
*994 3000 451*

Harris eyed the phone but decided against it. He was tired and wasn't in the right frame of mind. He placed the napkin back on the bedside table and made his way into the bathroom.

Unbuttoning his shirt, he examined the bandage wrapped tightly around his ribs. He began to unwind it and put it aside. He eyed the bruises spread across his right side. They were healing, slowly. He looked up to the bruises on his face; they were almost gone, but still visible enough. He thought about the Jazz Club Woman again and figured he probably wouldn't be that appealing to her right now anyway. He was looking more like a losing boxer than the Jazz Club Man she'd met. He thought of his son and decided he didn't want him to see his father like this either, and he could just picture the worry on Taya's face if she saw him now.

He spent a good 20 minutes standing under his hot, powerful shower, thinking about his conversation with Colt earlier as he'd walked her back to the hospital. He'd offered to push her chair for the nurse and let the others walk on ahead slightly. He'd wanted a word alone with each new recruit. He needed to lock in his team for the *Aurora*, and stabilize it before too much time passed. For some reason, he felt an urge to hold onto his new recruits. They were in this thing together now, and he was sure they would be safer if they continued to stay together.

"So, Colt," he'd said, "what do you think you'll do during your break?"

"Go see my family, captain. I miss my mom's cooking," she smiled.

Harris laughed. "I bet. It's good to have something to look forward to when your leave comes around. You can use that as a focus when things get tough on the ship. I assume you will be returning to the *Aurora*, corporal?"

"Returning, sir?" She turned her head stiffly to look at him. "I thought this was a one-off?"

"Well, corporal, I've advised Command that I would like to offer you a permanent placement on the ship."

"Oh," she said softly, turning back around to look ahead.

He knew that wasn't a good sign.

"Corporal, this was not an ordinary mission. In fact, I can honestly say that I've never had one like it before. Don't let that turn you away."

"Captain, why would you want me back? I didn't really do anything, except get myself shot."

"That's not true, corporal. Besides, I think you have a lot of potential. We just didn't get the chance to explore it on this mission, but I've read your file and it's very promising."

"Thank you, captain. I... I just..."

"What is it, corporal?"

"I'm not sure, anymore..."

They continued on in silence for a moment.

"Has this got anything to do with your brother?" Harris eventually asked her. He remembered reading about her brother's death in her file.

Colt nodded, still looking ahead. "My mother's already lost one child to the UNF. After what happened to me, I'm lucky I didn't put her through that again. I just don't think I can do that to her, captain."

Harris nodded absently. "I understand, Colt. Any sort of trauma in the field can affect your confidence. Sometimes it takes a little time to spring back. I'll leave the offer open. You think it about, and when the *Aurora* is ready to sail again, I'll give you a call. How does that sound?"

Colt nodded. "Yes, sir."

He noticed there was a certain lack of conviction in her voice, and he couldn't help but feel as though he'd just lost her too.

Carrie stood in her kitchen and stared at the piece of paper in her hands. She'd found it on the floor when she'd entered her apartment. Someone had slid it beneath the door.

Ree,
Glad you made it back to Earth. I tried my best to keep the sun shining for your return—as good as I could from down here in Florida, anyway. Hope it was warm enough for you. Come and see me as soon as you can. I look forward to seeing you nice and tanned.
Dad

Carrie felt her eyes well up. She wasn't sure what he'd done, or who he'd spoken to, but whatever it was, she knew it had kept them all from being buried. Although she'd worried about his well-being, she should've known better. He was smarter than that, and his years in the UNF must've taught him how to navigate the channels safely. She wondered what he'd done and who he'd spoken to? Whatever, he'd come through for them, and she didn't know how she was ever going to repay him.

Suddenly PDP rang then. She answered it. "Hello?"

There was a hesitation before she heard Doc's voice. "Hey," he said quietly.

Carrie felt her body stop for a second; her breathing, her heartbeat, her brain. "H— hi," she managed, quickly wiping her eyes and sniffing, as though he could see her.

There was silence for a few moments. Carrie's mind began to race.

"Are you okay?" he finally asked, with a hint of concern in his voice.

"Yeah, I'm fine. What… can I do for you, lieutenant?" she asked formally.

He exhaled in thought. "I don't really… know… why I called."

"How'd you get my number?"

"I had all the files while I did the releases."

"I see." Carrie sat quietly, waiting for him to decide why he'd called.

"Look, I just want to make sure things are okay between us," he eventually said. "What you said today at The Vicar about... well, people aren't stupid. They're going to figure out something's up, and god knows what Dale showed them all in the debrief."

"I thought that was why we were avoiding each other. Or was that just a nice, easy '*out*' for you?" Her own directness took her by surprise.

Doc was quiet a moment. "It wasn't an 'out', Welles. I like my job. I'm good at my job and I'd like to stay on the *Aurora*. I'm also a private person. This isn't easy for me. It's not my style to mix business with pleasure..."

"Nor is it mine," she said quickly.

"Good! Then you understand where I'm coming from." His voice began to sound agitated.

This time Carrie was quiet a moment, as her mind ticked over. "So what happened on the *Aurora*?" she asked. "Was that just sympathy? Did you think I wasn't going to make it back? That it wouldn't be a problem?"

"Yeah, that's why I had McKinley arm the tracking device on your headset... to try and lose you," he said sarcastically.

Again, there was silence.

"Well, I don't know what to think, Doc. I'm not real good at reading minds, or eyes for that matter. You keep looking at me like you've got something to say, but you never say it. Is there something you want to say, or am I imagining it?"

"Look," Doc said eventually, sighing, "we can't have this conversation over the phone. I'll talk to you tomorrow."

"Will you?"

"Goodnight, Welles."

He hung up the phone, and Carrie stood there staring at the wall, listening to the silence.

*

Carrie's heart raced as she stood at the door to Doc's room. She was at the Shackleton, a middle of the road hotel, not far from the Command docks and just around the corner from The Vicar. She'd arrived in her civilian clothing, plain jeans and white singlet, so as not to draw attention, and kept eyeing her surrounds to make sure no-one saw her. She'd been to reception to check he was staying there, and sure enough he was: room

116. She stared hard at the shiny gold numbers on his door. She took a deep breath, pushed her long brown hair away from her face, then knocked gently, just in case Brown was in the next room.

After a few seconds the door opened and Doc stood there, surprised. He was still in his uniform, albeit barefoot, his shirt open and untucked. He looked at her, leaned out into the hallway to check it was clear, then quickly ushered her through into his room.

She stepped just inside, as he closed the door and walked slowly around her to stand a few feet away.

"Brown and Packham are staying here, too," he told her, eyeing her with a look of concentration. "What are you doing here?"

"You said we couldn't talk over the phone, so…"

Doc let out a sigh and headed over to a small table and chairs, where a large glass of scotch on the rocks was waiting. He picked it up, took a sip, then turned back and studied her.

"Drink?" he asked, holding up his glass.

Carrie's heart was racing. She nodded and walked up to him, locking eyes. She took the glass from his hand, had a sip, then handed it back to him. She tried hard not to wince as the liquor heated her throat. Doc glanced down at the glass, then back at her, giving her his best poker face. She wandered back toward the door casually, shoving her hands in her jeans pockets.

"So what can I do for you, corporal?" he said eventually, mimicking her from their phone conversation earlier.

She looked him in the eye and mimicked him back. "I don't know… why I came here really…"

He continued to look at her with his poker face, and she met his stare. She really did know why she came here, though. She wanted to put an end to the speculation. She wanted to know where she stood: good or bad, once and for all. She took a deep breath and let it out.

"I don't know what to do about something and I need you to help me decide," she told him.

He seemed to think this over for a second. "I'll try and help, Welles, but it's your life. Whatever it is, it'll have to be your decision."

She shook her head. "Not this. This is entirely your decision."

Doc's eyes betrayed his poker face with a look of confusion. "What is?"

Carrie swallowed hard, as her breathing became shallow. "You need to decide... whether or not you're going to kick me out. Right here, right now. Because if you don't... then I'm going to stay and spend the night with you."

Doc held her gaze for a moment, still as a statue, before breaking it and looking down at his glass. He knocked back the scotch inside, then slowly turned and placed the empty glass down on the table. The silence in the room would have been stifling were it not for the low sound of the TV in the corner. Carrie glanced over at it. A Moon election candidate rally was taking center stage in the colony of Meridian; there was clapping, cheering, banners waving.

Doc turned around to stare at her, but he still did not speak. She could see his mind wrestling with itself, his brow furrowed, his eyes looking around the room in thought. He eventually managed to get some words to his mouth.

"Welles," he began slowly, "I'm your senior officer. This shouldn't be happening."

She gave him a slight nod in acknowledgment "But it is... and it did. Look, you can end this right now if you want to, Doc. I'll walk out of here and I won't be a problem for you anymore. I promise. If that's what you want..." she said. "I just want to know either way."

He stood thinking again for a while. "And why is this *my* decision?" he eventually spoke up.

Carrie took her hands out of her pockets and clasped them in front of her stomach, rubbing her fingers as though she was playing with an imaginary ring. "Because I already know which option I choose... I'm here, aren't I?" she said quietly.

Doc's eyes wavered, and he lowered his head and ran his hand through his hair, exhaling loudly. He looked at her again, his face strong and serious, but his eyes weak.

"What about the *Aurora*?" he asked her.

"What about it?"

"What if Harris turns around and asks you to stay on? You think he'll let that happen if he finds out?"

Carrie glanced down at her feet for a moment, then back up at Doc. "Captain Harris has said nothing of me staying on. And to be honest, I don't know if that's what I want." She raised her hand to the stitches on the side of her face. "Maybe sitting on a rooftop away from it all isn't such a bad thing. Maybe McKinley's right and I shouldn't be on the front line. I don't know…" She shrugged. "I don't really know what I want beyond tonight… We almost died up there, Doc. And I don't know about you, but I'm glad we're still alive."

They stared at each other for another moment, before he took a couple of slow steps toward her, his mind still in turmoil. Her breathing suddenly became shallower, but she held his stare with an equally strong face.

"So, are you going to kick me out?" she asked, but her voice didn't have the volume she'd planned it to.

"Jesus, you're stubborn…" He shook his head, stopping a few feet from her.

She nodded back, *her* eyes wavering this time. Doc moved forward slowly another step, so that he was standing right in front of her now. He stared at her again, his mind still ticking over. He reached his hand up to the side of her face, gently examining her stitches and bruises.

She looked awkwardly down at her feet. "I know I don't exactly look the best right now… covered in bruises." She looked up as Doc reached out his left arm, past her, for the door handle. Her heart literally thumped against her ribcage now. He paused for a moment, then she heard the click of a button, startling her. Doc had locked the door.

He stood resting his arm against the door behind her, his eyes staring past her to the handle. His mind was still trying to fight itself, but if she wasn't mistaken, it was slowly admitting defeat. Carrie turned her face to his.

"Is that your decision?" she asked, her voice struggling to find the air to carry it.

He moved his eyes to hers. "I can't kick you out."

She swallowed hard. "Good…" she said breathlessly. "We never did finish that conversation we started."

She slowly ran her hand up his arm and over his shoulder.

"No, we didn't," Doc said quietly, sliding his hand onto to her waist, "but I warn you, I've got a lot to say."

She smiled nervously as she took her other hand and slid it through his open shirt, running her fingers down over his chest, his stomach, and then around his back, bringing herself closer to him, her lips right up to his cheek.

"I'm all ears," she whispered.

He turned his body to face hers straight on, cupped her face and kissed her, slow and firm. Leaning back on the door, she wrapped both arms around his neck and brought him with her, as he kissed her again, his mouth warm, inviting, and wanting.

She brought her hands down and slid them beneath his shirt, rolling it slowly off his shoulders, down his arms and to the floor. He pulled back slightly as it fell, and she ran her eyes and her hands over his naked torso, tanned and toned. She eyed the hair across his chest, and noticed two scars, one long, one short across his abdomen. She stepped forward, running her hands back up over his chest and kissed him firmly.

Reaching out, he turned off the room's lights, leaving only the TV and bedside lamp on to light the room. As they continued to kiss passionately, he slid his hands onto her waist, turned her around and started edging her backward toward the bed. She kicked off her shoes as he grabbed the bottom of her singlet and pulled it upwards. They separated long enough for him to remove her shirt and throw it on the ground.

As their mouths reconnected, they made their way onto the bed, slowly freeing each other from the rest of their clothes, eyes soaking up the sight of each other. His hands and mouth caressed the length of her body, and hers reciprocated, traveling over the undulating muscles of his arms, his chest, his back, enjoying the scent of his skin.

Unable to wait any longer, she pulled him forward and he gladly lay his naked weight upon hers, gazing down with those beautiful, heated, brown eyes. She gazed back with equal warmth as her body cradled his, knees curling up around his hips, skin sliding and caressing in the growing heat. Their mouths sought each other out again, eagerly, firmly, tongues connecting, as she slinked her fingers through his hair. He pulled his face away slowly, locking eyes in their simmering heat. Then they both watched the ecstasy ripple through the other, breathing heavily as their bodies became one.

*

Carrie lay in the afterglow, her body still cradling his, as their heartbeats thumped against the other's ribcage, and their panting faded. A few moments passed, then Doc's sated eyes washed over her, as he left her body, kissing each section as he went. He collapsed onto his back beside her, and she rolled over to face him, as they stared at each other. He threw his arm back over her head, inviting her into his side. She slid against it, as their heartbeats and breathing quietened.

After a few moments, Doc looked at her, his eyes holding a naughty look. "We're in a world of trouble now, Welles," he said softly.

She smiled back. "You've got a great poker face. I have faith in you."

He smiled. "And your poker face?"

She thought about it briefly. "It's only good when you're not around."

Doc dropped his smile a little. "Well, like I said. We're in a world of trouble now."

Harris stood in the Service Hall of the UNF Command building. It was 0920. He was alone and very glad about it. He'd purposely come early so that he could have this time alone. He walked up to the front of the hall and looked at the four coffins lining the elevated stage area. *Four men*, he thought. *Four men who trusted me to guide them on this mission. Four men who followed me into space to do their duty. Four men who didn't make it home because I did not know what we were up against. Four men who I will always be responsible for.*

He walked up to each coffin and looked at the framed photo adorning it. It was their official UNF enlistment photo, and each soldier looked proud to be wearing his uniform. Bolkov was not smiling in his, but he held a twinkle in his eye. Louis looked proud, sitting upright, chest out, a sly grin on his lips. Carter was cool, calm and collected, ready for business. Smith's young face looked proud and eager, as if looking forward to all the possibilities which lay ahead of him as a member of the UNF.

Harris sighed. He felt that tightness in his chest again that had nothing to do with his ribs. He was going to miss them. They'd each added a piece of themselves that had made life on the *Aurora* what it was. Even Carter and Louis, who tried him at times. He was going to miss their mischief. He was going to miss Smith's youthful curiosity, always watching carefully, wanting to soak up his experience. And he was going to miss Bulk's sturdy silence, graceful nodding and absent stares.

He slowly walked back and sat down in the front row of chairs. He continued to stare at their photos, trying to fight that crushing feeling in his chest.

*Our last quiet time together, gentlemen. But don't think this is the end. You will not be forgotten.*

Carrie looked in the mirror and tried to focus her mind on what she had to do that morning. From the moment she had woken, however, all she could think of was Doc, and last night.

She'd stayed with him for several hours. After their first encounter they lay there looking at each other, their minds thinking a thousand thoughts in the silence, until finally her stomach had rumbled, breaking the spell.

Doc had laughed, flashing his pearly white smile. "Worked up an appetite, Welles?" he said, running the backs of his fingers across her belly.

She'd blushed awkwardly. "I, er, forgot to eat dinner."

"You forgot?"

"I had other things on my mind," she said, settling him with a warm gaze.

"You want me to get something from room service?"

"But what if someone finds out?"

"I had a burger down the road with Brown earlier. One meal on room service we can get away with," he'd said, as he reached over for a menu.

He ordered and she ate, then afterwards lay back down, snuggling against him, feeling the safest and most content than she had in days, like the Darwin was a lifetime away. She ran her hand over his chest, sliding it slowly down to his belly and traced her fingers over the two scars that ran across it.

"How'd you manage these?" she asked curiously.

"That one," Doc said, pointing to the longer one that ran across the left side of his belly, over to his side, "I actually got on McKinley's first mission on the *Aurora*."

"McKinley cut you?"

"No. He saved me. Well, him and Harris both."

"What happened?" she asked, eyeing the scar curiously.

"It's a long story that ends with me being stuck on my own trying to take on two guys and failing miserably. McKinley took one of the guys out from down the corridor and Harris took care of the other one… er… *personally.*"

Carrie looked from the scar to Doc. "So, who looks after the medic when he's cut?"

"Carter stitched me up. Not bad, huh?"

"Carter?"

Doc nodded. "Yeah, he helped me out from time to time. He had good steady hands and he wasn't fazed by blood as much as the other guys. If it had been my leg or something I would've taken care of it myself, but this I couldn't. I was lucky though, it was mainly just a surface wound."

Carrie looked at the smaller scar. "And what about this one?"

"This one," he gave her a serious look, "is interesting. I got it when I was 24. I'm eating lunch one day and BOOM… my appendix burst." He broke into a cheeky grin, and she playfully hit him. He rolled over on his side to face her.

"You, on the other hand, are rather scar free," he said, running his hand up her thigh, over her hip and resting it on her waist.

"Almost…" she said, touching the side of her face where Logan had hit her.

He studied her face then looked back down at her body. "I like the fact that you don't have a soldier's body, Welles." He ran his eyes back up to her face then he leaned in and kissed her. It started soft and warm but it soon heated up, which led them to discover each other for the second time.

Afterwards they lay there again quietly, but this time they'd fallen asleep. Carrie awoke later to Doc shaking her shoulder gently.

"Welles, wake up."

She was lying on her side, and he was behind her. She turned her face toward him. "Hmm?" she said sleepily.

"It's 3 a.m. We fell asleep. I don't want to kick you out, but if Brown or Packham see you…"

Carrie nodded. "I know. I'll go," she said quietly, still half asleep.

"Sorry," he whispered, resting his hand on her waist.

She took his hand and pulled it to her chest, hugging it, moving him closer to her. He gently kissed her shoulder, and they lay there, cuddling, awaking. After a few moments, he began to nuzzle her neck and his hand began to caress her chest. She turned her face to his again and they kissed. Before too long, they were exploring each other yet again.

"I guess I really should go now," she eventually said, when they'd recovered. She leaned over and kissed him, then slid off the bed and started searching for her clothes on the floor. When she was dressed, she looked back at him. He had been watching her quietly.

"I'll see you tomorrow, I guess," she said softly.

"No... you'll see me in a few hours," he said, looking at his watch.

"Oh, right!"

He looked at her, and his eyes had a tinge of concern to them.

"I'll wear my best poker face. I promise," she told him.

He smiled.

"Okay," she said taking a deep breath and heading for the door.

"Wait," he said getting up off the bed and quickly throwing his trousers on. He walked over to the door, opened it, and leaned out to check out the hallway. It was clear. He came back in, cupped her face and kissed her quickly. Then he opened the door wider and she stepped out. She threw him a glance over her shoulder and quickly walked away.

And now she was about to see him again. She took one last look at her reflection in the mirror then shut her eyes tightly. She felt guilty for feeling so good.

She concentrated hard on where she was going this morning. She thought about the fact that she was about to pay her respects to the four soldiers she watched die. She heard Sharley's and Logan's last words ring through her ears again. And it made her shake to think just how easily she could've been one of them.

# 32

# The Vicar

Harris heard a noise behind him and turned to see a woman in uniform make her way down to the lectern and test the microphone. He looked at his watch. 09:40. He stood and headed out the door into the autumn sunshine of Fort Centralis to await his soldiers. Within minutes, Doc, Brown and Packham arrived. Harris greeted them with a nod.

"Morning, captain," Doc said.

He eyed Doc and Brown carefully. "How many drinks you have last night?"

"We left The Vicar after two, captain," Doc answered, looking him in the eye, then quickly averting his glance.

Harris arched his eyebrow, scanning his lieutenant's face. Doc looked back at him and held his stare. Harris was satisfied. He believed him. He looked over at Packham and studied her next. He considered speaking with her now about her future on the *Aurora*, but he suddenly noticed some of the relatives of his dead soldiers begin to arrive.

"Excuse me," he told his crew, as he made his way toward them.

Carrie entered the Service Hall and immediately saw the four coffins lined along an elevated platform, each draped with their country of origin's flag. She swiftly turned her eyes away from the stark stab of reality, and scanned the people in the room. Other than the *Aurora* crew and a few other UNF personnel, there was a sprinkling of civilians, who, she assumed, were the relatives of the dead. Seeing them sent another stab through her chest, as she thought of her father having to do this.

She glanced around for Doc and saw him talking with an attractive blond woman. His hand was on her shoulder, comforting her. Carrie wondered who she belonged to. *Smith? A sister maybe?*

Packham and Brown were already seated in one of the rows, so Carrie joined Colt in making their way down to them.

"Miss Colt," Brown said, standing up to help her in beside him.

"How you doing, Mr Brown?" she asked quietly.

"I been better," he said flatly.

Carrie joined Hunter in the row behind and looked around for the others. McKinley, on his crutches, made his way over to Doc and the blond woman, who turned and immediately hugged McKinley and began to quietly cry. McKinley looked awkwardly at Doc, not quite sure what to do, as he tried to stand on his crutches and hug the crying woman at the same time. Doc gently encouraged her to let McKinley go, taking her by the shoulders and sitting her down in one of the rows. As McKinley sat down beside her, Doc rested his crutches at the end of the row and glanced around the room. His eyes fell on Carrie's and he gave her a subtle nod. His face was soft, but his eyes intense. She gave him a subtle nod back, trying to fight off thoughts of their evening together.

They sat in silence while the remainder of those gathered took their seats. Carrie scoured the faces of those she did not know. There was a balding, stocky man with a serious face; a large dark-skinned woman with a look of anger in her eyes; the attractive blond, and a couple of other UNF soldiers in uniform. The she spotted Senior Officer Edgely's face in the crowd, staring at her. He gave a slight nod. She nodded in response, then suddenly looked down into her lap, as a thought occurred to her. *Was Edgely the friendly face her father had organized?* She looked back over at him, but he'd turned his eyes away.

Doc and Harris took a seat in the front row, and a UNF soldier she'd not seen before took to the lectern. He introduced himself as Major Babcock, and advised those gathered that it was his duty to preside over the brief ceremony today. He opened with a traditional spiel about how it was a sad day to have to farewell good soldiers who had perished in the line of duty. He went on to say how the UNF felt the loss deeply, how those gathered would feel it tenfold, and how soldiers put their life on the line for mankind every single day. He hit the right notes, talking about how they helped those in need, those in trouble, and that they helped to capture those who threatened everything we hold dear: our way of life, our freedom, our safety. Finally, he announced that the UNF was officially releasing the bodies of these four heroic soldiers back into the custody of their loved ones, so that they could go home and rest in peace. He then asked those gathered to take a moment to remember the fallen, after which one of the uniformed soldiers stood and began to play an emotional, soulful tune on a trumpet.

The song filled the silence in the hall with a loneliness and sadness that made Carrie's heart feel heavy. When the song came to a close, the major nodded to two of the other soldiers in the crowd, who stood and proceeded to march over to Bolkov's coffin, positioning themselves one each side.

Harris then stood and moved in front of the podium. Carrie listened as the major gave a brief speech about each of the fallen, and then she watched as the two unknown soldiers folded the relevant flag and marched it over to Harris. She felt sorry for the captain, who then had the unenviable task of handing the flag to the dead soldier's relative and saluting them.

The service didn't appear to be following seniority as Bolkov was the first "released". The flag of the Russian Federation was handed over to his brother Pieter. The stocky, balding man stood, face rigid, and walked over to Harris. He looked a little similar to Bolkov in the face, with his five o'clock shadow, but although he was stocky, he was a much shorter, smaller version of his brother. Harris handed him the flag and saluted. Bolkov's brother showed no emotion, much like Bolkov himself. He looked at Harris, then returned to his seat, avoiding eye contact with everyone else in the room.

Next, they released Louis. The two soldiers folded the French flag and marched it over to Harris, who awaited Louis's mother; Patrice-Marie. The dark skinned woman stood, holding herself straight and moved over to Harris. As he handed her the flag and saluted, she held her head high and defiant, staring Harris in the eye. She turned around and flashed the same defiant look at the *Aurora* team, then walked over to her son's coffin. She picked up Louis's framed picture and held it tightly against her chest, as she rested her free hand on the wood for a moment, then bent down, kissed it and returned to her seat, taking the photo with her.

Carter was the one they released next, and Carrie was shocked when the major announced that his fiancée had come to collect his body. She'd had no idea Carter was engaged to be married. He'd hidden it well with all his talk. She watched, stunned, as the attractive blond stood shakily with the help of McKinley's arm. She walked over to Harris and accepted the South African flag. As the captain saluted her, she began to cry again, shooting out her hand to hold onto Harris's shirt. The captain darted his eyes over her shoulder to Doc, who stood and gently ushered her back to her seat.

At that point Carrie felt a lump begin to grow in her throat. It was harder than she thought it was going to be. To see one brother say goodbye to another, a mother say goodbye to her son and a fiancée say goodbye to her future... she looked around the room and tried to see who was there for Smith.

Again, Carrie was shocked when the major announced that Captain Harris had been nominated at Smith's next of kin. She glanced around the room in disbelief, then back at the stage and saw the British flag presented to Harris. He saluted the soldier who gave it to him. No-one had come to claim Smith's body. He'd had no-one but his ship's captain. She felt her eyes well up with tears, as she looked at Smith's picture on his coffin. Her vision blurred, and she quickly blinked it clear, as the tears rolled down her cheeks. She quickly wiped them away, as Hunter glanced over at her, stony faced.

Major Babcock proceeded to launch into his closing speech, then. He talked of thoughts and prayers going out to the families of the deceased, as well as to those injured and recovering from their mission. He left the podium and walked to Harris and shook his hand, and people began to stir. Carrie watched as Doc stood and shook the major's hand as well. Her eyes drifted past them and onto the picture of Smith again, and then onto Carter's and Bolkov's, which caused another tear to roll down her cheek. She quickly wiped it away, locking eyes with Doc as she did.

Hunter glanced over at her again and motioned with his head for her to get up. "C'mon, let me out of here."

She walked out into the Centralis sunshine to wait for the others. It was a beautiful day with clear blue skies and a gentle breeze that brought with it the smell of the ocean. She thought of how it was the stark opposite to the cold, dark of space, and couldn't help but think how those four soldiers would never get to see this again. She suddenly thought of Edgely again and began to scan her eyes over the gathered crowd, seeking him, wanting to know more. But he was nowhere to be found.

Harris noted that the *Aurora* team waited outside until the families had left. It was respectful of them. It had been hard speaking to the relatives, looking them in the eye, knowing that this shouldn't have happened, and worse still being unable to give them any details about their loved one's death, but he knew it had to be done. He had to keep up appearances for the UNF's sake, and the *Aurora*'s.

He got very little out of Bolkov's brother. He was even more silent than Bulk himself, but he did get a nod and brief look in the eye. It was acknowledgment enough.

Louis's mother had been quite vocal. She was a proud woman, protective of her son, and she'd been very blunt, stating that this should not have happened to him, how Louis had deserved better. Harris could only agree with her. She made it clear that she did not blame him, but that she would never forgive the UNF for this. He understood her anger, he felt it himself.

Carter's fiancée was not angry. She hadn't reached that stage yet. She was still caught in the devastation. Harris had spoken with her briefly and passed on his condolences, and she managed to hold it together until Doc had approached them. Harris thought it best to leave her in the care of Doc and McKinley, who both knew her a little better. There had been times over the last year or so, when they'd caught up with Carter outside the ship on leave. So they were better placed to provide her with the support she needed to get through the service.

Although this was not something he ever looked forward to, speaking with relatives after their loved ones had been killed or injured, he had been saddened by the fact that there was no-one to represent Smith. When he'd been informed that morning that Smith had put him down as his N.O.K. (next of kin) nominee, he was surprised, but also touched. Smith deserved to have someone claim his body, and if that someone had to be Saul Harris, then he was more than prepared to step up and take care of him the way he deserved to be. He owed the kid at least that much, and silently vowed to see him right.

He rubbed his hand along his jaw and observed what was left of his team, as they stood scattered outside the Service Hall. They were bruised, they were battered, but they still had a whole lot of potential. He knew what he needed to do now, more than anything, was keep hold of the ones he had left.

*It was time to glue the pieces back together.*

*

Harris told the team to rendezvous at The Vicar by 1400, and it arrived quickly. By the time he'd left Command with Smith's ashes, made it across town to his apartment and grabbed a bite to eat, it was then time to get into his civilian clothes. He placed the ashes and British flag on the coffee table in his living room. He wasn't sure where else to put them for now. He sat there looking at them, holding the silver urn in his hands for a moment, staring at his own reflection. He sighed and put it back down. *I'll be back later, Smith.*

The first to arrive at The Vicar, he immediately set up a bar tab and took a seat in the back corner. While he waited for the others, his mind ran over the service, ran over the debrief, and ran over his conversation with Colt. He knew he had to find time alone with both Packham and Welles this evening, before they disappeared on leave. He was halfway through his first drink when, Doc, Brown and Packham arrived.

Harris held up his beer and pointed at the bar. Doc nodded and led them over to place their order, and as soon as their drinks came, Harris requested a private word with Packham. She looked a little nervous and surprised, but nodded and followed him around to the front bar, leaving Doc and Brown curious, as they watched them walk away.

Harris leaned against the bar, front on, placed his drink down and looked over at Packham. She stood quietly, sipping her beer, waiting for him to speak. *She's the opposite of Welles*, he thought.

"I wanted to have a word with you, sergeant, about your plans for the future. Have you had any thoughts about what you want to do?"

Packham looked a little surprised. "Er, no, sir. I've just been trying to get through these past few days."

Harris nodded, "I hear that!" He took a swig of his beer and placed it back down. "Well, as you know, the Darwin mission was only a test case, but there is opportunity for a permanent position, so I'd like to offer it to you, sergeant."

Packham again looked surprised. "Er, wow."

He gave a sad smile. "It's an unfortunate circumstance, but I need a new co-pilot. You're more than qualified. That would be the position you'd be taking. Are you up for it?"

She looked down at her beer, thinking, and he eyed her carefully.

"You don't have to answer me now, sergeant. You've got a few weeks to think about it if you need. I wouldn't blame you if you said no, given what happened. But just remember that we weren't charged with anything. Whatever reservations you might have, know that you can trust me. You can trust the *Aurora* team. It's a shame this was your first mission with us. But that said, it should be the worst you'll see, and I mean the worst." He watched as she kept looking down at her beer, avoiding eye contact. He turned his body to face her. "Is there anything you want to ask me, Sarah?" he asked. It was obvious something was on her mind. He used her first name as a means of leveling the field and trying to make himself more approachable.

She looked up at him. "I... I guess I'm just a little surprised, captain," she said.

"Why's that?"

She hesitated a moment, then looked him in the eye. "I was a coward... on the ship. You all wanted to go back on the Darwin and I wanted to stay on the *Aurora*. I freaked out. I... I just—"

"—wanted to make it home," he finished her sentence. He looked her in the eye. "There's nothing wrong with wanting that, Sarah. The word *coward* is a little harsh. You got spooked. It happens to all of us. But at the end of the day, you're the one that got us out of there, so don't sell yourself short. You came through for us in the debrief, too. They tried damn hard to break you, harder than any of us, but you held strong. That wouldn't have been easy. Sometimes we're strong in one field and weak in another. That's why we work in teams; to help each other out, to balance out those strengths and weaknesses. You were *unsure* on the Darwin. But what doesn't break you, makes you stronger, right?"

She nodded, giving him a small smile, and he noticed the delicate features on her face seemed to lighten up somewhat. He nodded back at her and grabbed his beer.

"I do understand if you'd prefer to go back to flying the cargo ships, though."

"I don't know, captain," she said, playing with the label on her beer.

He took another swig of his drink. "Well, I guess that's something you're going to have to figure out. What it is that you want." He studied her for a moment while she seemed to think about it. "C'mon, let's head back to the others. You think about it and I'll call you in a few weeks for your answer." With that, he pushed off the bar and began to head back to the others, worried how Colt and Packham would cope on their own without the *Aurora* looking out for them.

"Captain?" she called after him.

He turned around to her.

She looked him firmly in the eye. "I'm in."

He stared at her. "Yeah? You don't want to take a few weeks to think about this? You're sure?"

"Yes, sir. You didn't let them take us. You defended us. That's the kind of team I want to be in, sir. A team who has my back. I don't think I could trust any other now... so, if you'll have me, I'm in."

He smiled as he walked up to her and held out his hand for her to shake. "Welcome to the *Aurora*, sergeant."

She broke into a smile and shook his hand. "Thank you, captain."

Carrie entered The Vicar dead on 1400, but it appeared as though she was the last to arrive. Brown told her there was a tab at the bar, so she got herself a drink and made her way to the *Aurora* tables. She took a seat beside McKinley, who stared at her with his poker face. His piercing blue eyes seemed to twinkle back at hers, the blue of his shirt catching the color just right.

"Do you ever play nice, McKinley?" she asked directly, staring back at him.

He shrugged nonchalantly, caressing his jaw, the silver band around his wrist shining next to the woven leather one. "Sometimes."

"So, you *can* play nice, then?"

A smile broke his face, teeth and all. She noticed that he actually had a nice smile when he let one escape.

"You're just so easy to rile up, Welles," he told her, smile firmly in place. "Stop making it so much fun for me."

"Yeah, well, don't you forget who saved your ass. Next time I might miss," she said, with a satisfied look.

His face clouded a moment. "Yeah, you got me there."

Carrie almost felt bad for a moment as she looked at his somber face. He lifted his beer and held it out to clink with hers. She did so.

"I still want a rematch on the shooting range, though," he said, his eyes smiling at hers now.

Carrie grinned. "Bring it on, cowboy!"

He let out a short, sharp laugh, before going serious again. "How's the head?" he asked motioning to her bruises.

Carrie touched the side of her face. "It looks worse than it feels."

She suddenly looked across the table and saw Harris trying to get her attention.

"A word?" he mouthed, pointing over to the bar.

She suddenly felt a little nervous. *What does he want?* She nodded and stood, Doc and the others glancing at them, as she followed Harris to the front bar of The Vicar.

"How're you healing, corporal?" he asked, studying her face carefully, as they came to a stop.

"Okay. It doesn't really hurt that much anymore. It's just the tiredness."

"And how's everything else?" he said, leaning both elbows on the bar and taking a swig of his beer.

"Er… fine, sir," she stuttered, not quite sure what he was referring to.

"Yeah?" He glanced over at her and arched his eyebrow.

She looked back at him curiously, taking a mouthful of her beer, as he continued to stare.

"You went through quite a bit on this mission, Welles. I'm just wondering how you're going with it all. Sometimes, you know, people can benefit from some counseling if they need it."

"Oh, no, I'm fine, sir," she said quickly, waving it off.

"Are you sure? You survived a couple of nasty attacks. You nearly died. That's a lot to deal with. People have suffered after experiencing less." He turned his body to face hers and looked her in the eye.

She held his look for a moment but then turned her eyes away. "I'm doing, okay, sir."

Harris's eyes were skeptical. "You were having some… *interesting* dreams in the hospital on the *Aurora*. You still getting them?"

Carrie shook her head, lying, wondering what Harris must've heard while he was covering for Doc. "No more than anyone else, sir."

The captain, she noticed, stared at her a moment before suddenly averting his eyes, as though she'd hit a nerve. *Had he been having dreams too?* "Well," he said, putting his hand in his pocket and pulling out a card and handing it to her, "that's the number for the UNF counseling service. You need to talk to someone you give them a call. You don't want to talk to them, I've written my number on there, too. I'm always available."

Carrie stared at the card and at Harris's number scrawled across it. She looked back up at him, locking eyes. "Thank you, sir. I appreciate it."

"And don't be too stubborn or proud, Welles. This stuff can manifest if you don't take care of it."

She nodded. "Thank you, captain." She gave him a smile. "Was that all?"

"No," he said, eyeing her carefully.

She tried hard not to look nervous, but she noticed that Harris had a way of looking at her, studying her, as though he were reading her mind or something. She kept her face even.

"As you know, corporal, the Darwin mission was something of a test case for you new recruits."

She gave a short, sharp, sarcastic laugh. "Was it ever!"

Harris grinned. "As I was saying, it was a test case, but as with any stint in the UNF, there's always a view to a permanent placement should things work out."

"Yes, sir," she said, curious now.

"You impressed me, Welles. You exceeded my expectations. I know the Darwin mission was tough, *very* tough, but you stepped up. You got balls, corporal."

A smile crept onto Carrie's face, but she tried to keep it in check. Harris seemed to notice.

"I figure you can never have too many sharpshooters in your team. Besides, I like the fact that you're keeping McKinley on his toes," he said, flashing her a smile. "So, what I'm saying is that I would like to offer you a permanent place on the *Aurora*."

A smile lit up Carrie's face, but it quickly faded. She suddenly felt like she was caught between a rock and a hard place. She was thrilled with Harris's offer, which surprised her considering how tough the mission had been, and how tough the dreams were that had followed her since. But she felt vindicated. She'd won Harris's approval, against the odds, and yet, up until that moment, she thought that she was ready to give it all up if it meant being with Doc. But now the captain had given her his seal of approval. This intriguing man from the UNF was inviting her into his team, drawing her to follow him. Could she just turn away from that?

Harris seemed to detect her hesitation. "I don't need an answer now, Welles. Go on leave and think about it. I'll call you when I need an answer." He looked down at the card in her hands. "Take your time and use that card if you need to. And just remember that I'm always here... We made a good team, Welles. I think you'd have a bright future aboard the *Aurora* if you decide to join us again."

She nodded and took a gulp of her beer, trying to clear her throat of the lump threatening to build. Harris looked at her, then gave a sharp nod, "Okay. Let's get back to drinking, shall we?"

"Captain." She stopped him.

He looked back at her, and she locked eyes with him.

"Thank you for everything. I know I haven't exactly been the easiest soldier to deal with, but I *have* learned a lot from you. You, too, have exceeded my expectations, sir."

He glanced down at his beer then back to her again. "Thank you, corporal. It's not often the captain gets feedback from his soldiers. It means a lot. The colonel's done a good job with you. He should be proud."

"Oh!" Carrie reached into her pocket and pulled out her father's note. "I got this. I thought you might want to take a look."

Harris took the piece of paper from her, eyeing her curiously, opened it and read it in silence.

Ree,
Glad you made it back to Earth. I tried my best to keep the sun shining for your return—as good as I could from down here in Florida, anyway. Hope it was warm enough for you. Come and see me as soon as you can. I look forward to seeing you nice and tanned.
Dad

Harris closed it over and handed it back to her. "Burn it."

She looked at him surprised.

"Just in case, corporal. Burn it." Harris put his beer on the bar and asked the barman for a light and a bowl, assuring him it wasn't for cigarettes, which were considered illegal in Fort Centralis. He handed them to Harris, who turned and took the note back off Carrie and lit it. She watched the flame grow and swallow it whole. Harris threw it into the empty bowl, blew it out, and they both surveyed the ashes. The captain nodded to himself, then finished what was left of his drink, and put the empty bottle back on the bar.

"Come buy me a beer, Welles," he said, walking back over to the group.

Carrie followed him and saw Doc standing at the bar watching them both curiously. They both moved to flank the lieutenant: Harris on his right and Carrie on his left. Doc exchanged a look with Harris, but didn't mention anything about what he saw.

"Same again?" Doc looked over at Carrie.

She smiled and flashed a subtle, seductive glance. "Yes, please."

Doc cleared his throat, almost blushing, then turned back to Harris. "And you, sir?"

"I believe I will have *several*, lieutenant!"

They took their drinks and made their way over to the tables.

"So," Harris said, sitting down next to Hunter, "what are your plans, Hunter?"

The Kiwi pilot took a swig of his beer and smiled at Harris. "I'm going to go home, grab Leilani, jump into bed and not get out until you call me again."

"Leilani?" Colt asked.

"My beautiful, beautiful girlfriend!"

"She *is* beautiful!" McKinley offered with a grin.

Hunter threw his bottle cap across the table at him.

"You kept that one quiet, Hunter," Packham noted.

Hunter shrugged. "You never asked."

"Alright," Harris said looking over at Brown, "and you, Mr Brown?"

"Hell, I don't know. Probably go lie on a beach somewhere and drink some cocktails," he said, then looked over at Doc. "Doc tells me Hawaii is worth a visit. I hear the barmaids are pretty special." He flicked his eyebrows up and down.

Doc gave an embarrassed laugh and looked down at his beer bottle. "That's just what I hear, Brown!"

Carrie turned to Packham and started her own conversation. "What about you? What are you going to do?"

"Don't know. I haven't really thought about it yet. I'll probably just head down to Saint-Tropez."

"Saint-Tropez?"

"Yeah, my family have a beach house there."

Carrie stared at her for a moment, then looked her up and down. "You're rich, aren't you?"

Packham glanced at her, then at McKinley who had been listening in, then shrugged, nodded, and downed her beer.

Carrie glanced over at McKinley. "And you?"

"I'm not rich." He shook his head.

"No, I mean what are you going to do?" Carrie asked.

"Don't know," he said taking a swig of his beer. "I'll probably drink for the first week. Then when the hangover fades, I'll go visit my mother, play the good son, and try and make up for all the years of heartache I gave her." He looked her in the eye. "And you?"

"I don't know either. I'll go see my dad for bit. Just in case he… I'd better thank him for… you know."

McKinley nodded. "Yeah, you better do that."

"Alright," Harris said loudly, getting everyone's attention. "I think it's about time we raise a toast to the guys, before y'all can't even speak your own names!" He stood and raised his glass, looking around at his soldiers. "I'm going to keep this simple. I don't think you need me to tell you about your fellow soldiers, except to say that they were *great* soldiers, they were *good* people, and they will be sorely missed. So please raise your glasses to Carter, to Bolkov, to Louis and to Smith."

Everyone raised their glasses: "To Carter, to Bolkov, to Louis and to Smith!" then they all took a long drink.

"Quietest you bunch have ever been," Harris said, sitting back down.

Carrie eyed Harris as he took a seat again. "Captain?"

"Yeah."

"What are you going to do with Smith's ashes?"

Everyone looked at him. He seemed to ponder his answer for a moment.

"Smith once told me that he never really felt like he had a home until he came aboard the *Aurora*. So, I guess I'm going to take him back on board again, and when the time is right... I'll let him go."

The team remained silent for a moment, before Carrie broke it.

"I never knew Carter had a fiancée."

McKinley smiled sadly. "No, he liked to play that card close to his chest."

"Protecting her from you, huh?" Hunter grinned.

"No, he knew Leilani's my favorite!"

Hunter found another bottle top to ditch at McKinley, who tried to duck but it caught him on the shoulder.

"Hey, you nearly got me then, fool!" Brown warned Hunter, who laughed back at him.

"Gentlemen, gentlemen!" Colt gingerly raised her arms at them. "Calm down before you re-injure some of us!"

"Oh, he's only got a broken leg!" Hunter responded, waving McKinley off.

"Hey, my leg was practically snapped in half, buddy," McKinley shot back.

"So? One broken arm, and two bullet wounds; three, if you include the one that went right through my arm, entry and exit! That's *four* injuries, McKinley," Hunter said holding up four fingers. "I win!"

"Hello!" Colt joined in. "Bullet wound to the neck. *Narrowly* missing major arteries."

"What does a fractured skull count for," Carrie offered. "Or near strangulation?"

"Hell, Doc, you're best placed to judge this competition," Brown joined in.

"You forgot the captain's broken ribs!" Packham added.

Doc looked around the group and shook his head. "You're all as bad as each other!"

"Oh, c'mon, Doc!" Hunter called, then looked at Harris "Captain, as Doc abstains from the voting, judging is passed to you."

Harris eyed Hunter with an arched eyebrow, then ran his eyes over the group. "Alright," he said, "you all sustained some pretty good injuries and you all made it through, but only one of you survived more than one serious attack… and that's Welles."

"Oh, man!" Hunter exclaimed.

"What?" McKinley joined in.

"AND, I might add," Harris raised his voice over their protests, "she survived it without her gun, which *you*, Lieutenant McKinley, believed that she would not be able to do."

Carrie looked over at McKinley and gave him a big beaming smile. He looked back at her smile and scoffed.

"Yeah, but they weren't trying to kill her," he argued. "They wanted her alive. They were trying to *kill* us!"

"Yes, they were," Harris nodded, "and if I recall correctly, it was Welles who saved both *your* ass and Hunter's ass, and that is why you are now both sitting here today."

"Touché, captain!" Doc laughed, clapping his hands.

"Jesus," McKinley rolled his blue eyes. "I'm never going to hear the end of this, am I?"

"I tell you what, McKinley," Carrie said, leaning forward. "The time you beat me on the shooting range, is the time I'll stop rubbing your face in it."

This drew a lot of "oohs" from the group.

"Oh, game on, sister," McKinley smiled. "Find me a shooting range, *right* now!"

"Now, lieutenant, you know the UNF does not approve of drinking and shooting," Harris said, amused.

McKinley grinned, pointing at her. "We are *so* getting this game on. Mark my words!"

The group had a laugh at their competitive streaks but soon fractured into several different conversations again. Carrie smiled to herself as she looked down at her beer. It was half gone already. She took another mouthful and looked over at Doc, who was listening to an animated Colt. His brown eyes smiled at Carrie with a sexy edge to them. She looked back down at her beer. She was starting to feel relaxed, and figured she'd better be careful or she'd risk losing her poker face completely.

Regardless, before long she was ready for another round.

"Who's up?" she asked, standing up.

After taking several orders, Doc stood up also. "I'll give you a hand."

They headed over to the bar and stood facing it, their backs to the *Aurora* tables. The barman came straight over to them and they placed their order.

"So..." Doc said, staring straight ahead at the row of spirit bottles on display.

"So...?" Carrie said, doing the same.

"So, as your medic, I would advise you not to drink too much alcohol with that head injury, corporal," he told her.

"But it's making my head feel better, Doc," she teased.

He glanced over at her and saw her smile, then faced front again. "Yes, it will do that, but tomorrow..."

"Mm," Carrie nodded in agreement.

"Still, I could call on you later to check that you're alright, if you like?"

Carrie flashed him a glance, then returned her eyes to the bottles. "That's probably a good idea," she said softly.

"Yes, it is," he said nodding. "The only thing is, I'm not sure when I'm going to get out of here. Saul... the captain, is a *very* good drinker, and I can't see him letting me go easily. So we may have a problem."

"I see."

"However, I will certainly do my very best," he said throwing her another glance.

"That's all you can do."

"I'll call you."

Just then the barman came over with the drinks. Between them they took them back to the table and sat on opposite ends. Shortly after, the nurses from the UNF hospital walked back in the door.

"Are you kidding me?" McKinley said, looking at his watch.

"You're lucky we let you stay this long," his attractive brunette nurse said.

"C'mon," he smiled at her. "It's just my leg. There's nothing wrong with my mouth."

"You wanna bet?" she smiled back.

Brown cracked up laughing, while McKinley and Hunter looked glumly at each other.

Colt happily stood, and Carrie moved over to her to say goodbye.

"I don't know when I'll see you again?"

Colt smiled. "Well, if you're ever in Orlando, look me up."

"Well, my father just happens to live in Florida for six months of the year, so you never know."

"Yeah? Great! Come here." Colt leaned over and gave her a hug, patting her on the back. "You did good, girl. You should be proud."

"Thanks, Sabrina. You kept me sane!"

"Look me up." She nodded, then turned and walked over to Harris, as Carrie returned to her seat.

"Lieutenant, I won't tell you again!" McKinley's nurse smiled as she brought his crutches to him and walked off to get Hunter's wheelchair.

"I would be following that if I were you," Brown said, watching her walk away with a sly smile on his face.

McKinley stood, watching her too. "Mm-hmm," he said, then he turned back around to the guys. "Now, *she* makes me want to break my other leg!"

The guys burst out laughing and Brown held out his hand to McKinley for a high-five, which he did.

McKinley looked over at Packham.

"Sergeant," he nodded.

Packham nodded back and smiled, then McKinley turned to Carrie.

"I look forward to seeing you on the range, corporal," he said with a straight face.

"As do I *you*, lieutenant," she smiled.

He shook his head, fighting the smile threatening to break out on his face, then crutched his way over to Harris.

They watched McKinley, Hunter and Colt leave with their nurses, then Harris glanced around at those left: Doc, Brown, Packham and Carrie.

"I believe the night has just begun, people," he said.

Doc looked at his watch. "Make that afternoon! It's only 1600."

Harris scoffed.

"Now, I must say, captain, you need to take it easy," Doc warned. "One false drunken move and those ribs are gone again. I advise you not to drink much more."

Harris looked at Doc, then glanced over at Brown, then back to Doc. "You can TRY, doctor!"

They all chuckled.

"Now, Packham," Brown began, "I was telling Welles earlier about initiation. We've already lost Colt, so I think we'd better get started before anyone else leaves."

"Initiation?" she asked, looking between Carrie and Brown.

"Brown, don't be using the 'I' word in front of me," Harris said, shaking his head.

"Or me," Doc joined in, smiling.

"Oh, man!" Brown said slumping in his chair. "Where's McKinley when you need him?"

"About to get a bed bath from a hot nurse, I suspect," Packham offered.

"I know where I'd rather be," Harris smiled.

"Well, the night is young, ladies," Brown winked. "You're not safe yet!"

Carrie looked over at Packham and they exchanged an amused look before Carrie turned back to him. "You know, Brown, with Captain Harris and Doc sitting on the sidelines, you're the one outnumbered here. Perhaps *we* should initiate *you*?"

Packham grinned cheekily, as Brown gave Carrie an incredulous look.

"What the hell are two little white girls going to do to me?"

Carrie smirked and gave an evil laugh. "You have no idea!"

"Hell, I'd be afraid of that Brown," Harris said, drinking his beer. Doc started laughing and Harris shook his head. "Another night at The Vicar!"

# 33

# Forward Motion

Harris watched as Welles left the bar. It was just after 1800. She'd said her goodbyes to them all, although he noted she seemed a little more formal with Doc. Almost too formal considering they'd been pretty close on the ship. *Hopefully, that's a good thing.* He was keen on having her return to the ship, even more so than the other women. He didn't know why exactly, but there was just something about her that intrigued him. He wanted her back aboard the *Aurora* to see if she was as good as he thought she was. So, if things were formal between her and Doc, that could only be a good thing.

"I hereby dub these 'The Aurorans'!" Brown said clunking a tray of shots on the table, interrupting Harris's thoughts.

"What the hell?" Harris said, looking down at the murky green liquid that filled the test tube glasses.

"Oh, Jesus!" Doc said, running his hand through his hair.

The four of them grabbed a shot and downed it. Harris looked over at Packham, who winced, but then shook it off. She noticed him looking at her.

"Boarding school," she said. "We did a lot of training!"

The three men laughed at her.

"Looks like you're initiating yourself, Packham!" Brown said, with a sly smile.

She looked over his shoulder at the pool table in the corner. "Pool table, now!" she ordered. "That will determine who gets to initiate who, sergeant!"

Brown looked over at the table and back to her. "Hell, you're on, sister!" The two of them got up and walked off toward the table.

"My money's on the boarding school, Brown!" Doc called after them.

Harris gave a throaty laugh.

Doc picked up his glass and moved closer to Harris. "It is good to be back at The Vicar, isn't it?"

Harris nodded. "Yes, it is. Although it's not the same…"

Doc sighed, looking down at his beer. "No."

They sat in silence for a moment, then Harris glanced at his lieutenant. "So how're things with Welles?" he asked.

Doc looked up at him a little surprised. "What do you mean?"

"I don't know. Things were a bit weird on the ship for a bit, weren't they? If you ask me things still seem weird."

Doc shrugged and ran his hand over his mouth, looking back at his beer. "I don't know. I've been avoiding the situation."

"I know you have."

Doc looked at him but didn't say anything. Harris watched him for a moment.

"I asked her back onto the *Aurora*. I've offered her a permanent position. That going to be a problem?" he asked carefully.

Doc shook his head but averted his eyes. "No."

"Good. I'd like to have her on the team."

"So, she said yes?" he asked, looking at his beer and twisting it back and forth slightly in his hand.

Harris watched him again for a moment. Doc looked up at him and took another swig of his beer, waiting for his answer.

"No. She's going to think about it."

Doc nodded, looking back at the beer, considering what he said. After a moment, he looked back at Harris, noticing that he was still watching him.

"So, is that what your conversation was about with Packham earlier? You ask her, too?"

Harris nodded. "And Colt."

"Yeah? What'd they say?"

"Packham's in. She's our new co-pilot. Colt, like Welles, is going to think about it. Welles, with some encouragement, will come back a yes, I think. But I'm not too sure about Colt. I think it's in their best interest if they come back aboard. Given what's happened, we should stick together for a while until we're sure things are okay."

Doc nodded again, seemingly thinking something over.

Harris took another sip of his beer. "Regardless, I'd like to have Welles back aboard either way. She did good on the Darwin, and despite the rough start, I think she'll work well with McKinley. And I like the fact that she has that element of surprise. No-one will expect much from her on first look, but we know now that she can deliver." He sighed. "I'm still going to have to find more soldiers, though."

"You will, Saul. And you've always found the right ones before."

"Finding them's easy. Letting them go is another…"

Doc nodded sympathetically. "What do you think will happen with the Jumbo program?"

Harris looked him in the eye. "They'll have spent too much money on it to let it go."

"Yeah," Doc nodded.

"I was hoping to have heard something about Sharley and Logan. They should've made it back to Earth by now. Probably going through the debrief as we speak. I'll give it a couple of days, then I'll follow it up. I'm keen to know what they're going to do with them both. Especially Logan."

Doc nodded again in thought, then finished his beer. "Have you spoken with Colonel Isaack since you've been back?"

"I tried to get a hold of him, but he's been reassigned to a classified posting."

"Is that right?" Doc stared at him, intrigued.

"Mm-hmm."

"Should we be worried about something here?"

Harris noted the seriousness of his lieutenant's voice and face as he locked eyes with him again. "They didn't charge us, Doc. Whether Colonel Welles had something to do with that, I don't know. But don't think for a second that means we're off the hook. We just need to keep our heads down and our nose clean, and hopefully we'll be fine."

Doc's face showed real concern.

"Anyway," Harris said loudly, "I do not want to spend my first night of leave talking about the Darwin, or Sharley or the UNF for that matter. I am going to get shit-faced drunk, pass out and then sleep until my back gets sore!"

Doc laughed. "Or your ribs as the case may be!"

"I can handle the ribs, Doc."

"Well, in that case, captain, allow me to fetch you a scotch," he said getting up.

"Thought you'd never ask," Harris saluted him.

Professor Martin stared nervously at Quint, who moved to stand right in front of him.

"You made sure to find my body in one of the *Belgo*'s barrels, didn't you?" Quint asked with threatening eyes, his gray hair doing nothing to fool the professor into thinking he was weak.

Martin nodded nervously. Quint had this effect on him, and he knew it. As much as the other Jumbos made Martin uncomfortable, there was just something about Quint that he feared. He knew the only thing stopping the man from killing him on the spot was Sharley. Thankfully, Sharley had Quint on a respected leash. Although, that said, Martin was a little unsure exactly, as to where he stood with Professor Sharley right now, after all that had gone down.

"If someone goes digging, it's certainly implied," Martin assured Quint, "and as I told Sharley, the remains were slush. There was no way anyone could tell who or what is in there without running forensics. And unfortunately, the so-called barrels of waste were given to your fisherman friend as discussed. I have no doubt they are now sitting comfortably in the belly of a shark somewhere."

"Good," Quint eyed him with his pale green eyes, "'cause I do my best work as a ghost."

Martin nodded. "I have no doubt."

Quint continued to stare at him, and Martin tried hard not to be impressed by his Jumbo physique; tall and broad. Fearless. Deadly.

"Well, as I have done this favor for Sharley and ensured your safety, Quint, perhaps now you could ensure mine?" Martin asked firmly, but calmly. "The UNF was starting to ask a lot of questions when I left. The shit has well and truly hit the fan, and heads are going to roll."

Quint didn't answer, he simply gave a casual, uncaring shrug.

Martin exhaled impatiently. "*I* should have your allegiance too, goddamnit! You should obey *my* instruction! You forget, I'm in charge of this program," he hissed.

"No, you're not," Quint said, placing his face in Martin's, staring at him with those pale, threatening, green eyes. "Sharley's in charge. Always has been. And I think it's about time you learned that."

Martin stepped backwards, unable to contain his fear. "W—what are you going to do?"

Quint gave a small, terrifying smile. "Finish what we started."

Carrie lay on her bed and yawned. She looked at her watch. 20:17. She flicked the TV over, even though she wasn't really in the mood for watching anything. She contemplated turning everything off and going to sleep. There was no guarantee that Doc was going to call, and she could just imagine how much Harris could drink, not to mention Brown, who were both still in the bar when she'd left.

She got up and double-checked the locks, then brushed her teeth. She went back into her bedroom and laid back down, but didn't have the heart to turn off the TV... just in case. After flicking through the channels for a few more minutes, she heard the beeping of her PDP. She reached over and looked at the screen.

*You still awake?*

She smiled like a teenage schoolgirl and typed in her reply: *Maybe. Who is this?*

*Your doctor. Should I make a house call?*

She smiled again, as a wave of excitement raced through her body, waking it up instantly. *I think you'd better. Just in case.*

*Very well. I'll be there in...*

Just then, she heard her front door buzz. Startled, she got up and made her way to it. *It couldn't be, could it?* She flicked on the monitor beside the door and smiled. It was Doc. She opened the door and stuck her head around.

"That was quick," she smiled.

"I was in the neighborhood," he smiled back.

She pulled the door back and he stepped inside and looked around.

"Welcome," she said closing the door.

He glanced around the room then turned back to her, stopping when he saw what she was wearing. "You always answer the door like that?"

Carrie looked down at the flimsy white singlet and cotton underwear she was wearing and looked back at him. "Only when I'm expecting my doctor."

A smile spread across his face. "I see…"

He took a step toward her and slid one hand over her hip, while the other brushed her hair behind her ear. She slid her hands up along his arms and he leaned in and kissed her. Carrie brought her arms up around his neck and pressed her body against his.

"Shall I give you the tour?" she asked, when they came up for air.

"Mm-hmm," he nodded, heading back in for another kiss.

She led him, kissing all the while, through her apartment to her bedroom. "That's… the rest of my apartment…" she managed in between kisses, "and this… is my bedroom."

"Mm-hmm," he replied, his mouth never leaving hers.

She pulled him over to her bed and they climbed on. She could taste both beer and scotch on his tongue, yet he didn't seem to be drunk.

"How come you're still sober?" Her curiosity gave way.

"Well, I'm a little happy… but for the most part I cheated," he smiled as he slid his hand underneath her singlet.

"Cheated? How?" she asked, curling her leg over his.

"I offered to buy the drinks," he said, in between kisses as he found her breast with his wandering hand. "So I ordered Harris doubles while I had straight coke."

"Oh," she breathed, partly because of his stroking hand, "you're sneaky, lieutenant. I hope the captain doesn't find out!"

Doc laughed quietly. "So do I!"

Carrie slid her hand up the back of his shirt, pressing her body even more tightly against him.

"So, do I get to kick *you* out tonight?" she purred in his ear.

"Mm-hmm," he agreed as he ran his mouth along her neck, "but we've got plenty of time to kill first."

They were done with talking then, as Doc swiftly removed his shirt and she curled her legs around him.

*

Afterwards, Doc and Carrie lay there staring at each other again. She curled one hand around his upper arm, while the other interlocked her fingers with his. She kissed his shoulder, and he reached over with his other hand and caressed the bruised side of her face.

"Here we are again, lieutenant," she said softly.

He nodded in reply, and they lay in silence for a few minutes more, before Doc broke it.

"I hear Harris has offered you a permanent spot on the *Aurora*?"

Carrie felt a guilty look shoot across her face, then nodded. "He just asked me today."

Doc nodded slowly then dropped his hand to his chest. "So, what are you thinking?"

"I don't know." Carrie rolled onto her back, continuing to hold his hand. "But you know what? I've got eight weeks to think about it." She looked back at him, and saw that he was turning something around within his mind's confines. She moved onto her side and slid her free hand along his torso. "Penny for your thoughts, lieutenant?" she asked quietly.

He looked down at her. "Have you been having more of those dreams you were having in the hospital on the ship?"

Carrie was a little taken aback by the change in conversation. "Er... I've been okay," she lied.

"Yeah?"

"Yeah, why?" She propped herself up on her elbow.

"Harris just mentioned something in his drunken state about giving you his number and the counseling number. Did you ask for it?"

"No," Carrie gave him a reassuring smile, "that was Harris doing his job."

Doc nodded, his thoughts drifting him off into space again.

"What?" she asked.

"It's just, you were having some pretty decent nightmares in the hospital. If you're still getting them... those numbers can help."

She laughed and rolled onto her back and let go of his hands. "Jesus, what are you trying to say? This mission's sent me crazy? If I'm crazy, then what does that say about you being with me?"

He rolled over on his side and put a reassuring arm over her. "I'm not saying you're crazy... although Harris may call you crazy if he ever finds out about us."

"How's he ever going to find out?"

"I don't know, but if you decide to come back onto the *Aurora*, it will certainly be interesting."

Carrie sighed. "I don't want to think about that right now. I just want to think about this..." She ran her hand along his arm and they looked at each other for a moment, before he leaned in and kissed her again. She traced her hand along his cheek, losing herself in those brown eyes and that beautiful smile.

"Let's talk about something else," she smiled. "Why don't you tell me all about Colorado, Snowflake?"

*

Harris lay down on his bed and stared at the ceiling. He was drunk, but not nearly as drunk as most nights at The Vicar left him. He thought that Brown and Packham looked pretty happy, but that Doc hadn't been his usual self. *He made out like he was with us, but his mind was somewhere else. There was something about him that was reserved tonight, holding back. Why?* Had Harris spooked him with talk of the UNF's potential leverage over them?

He yawned and stretched his body out. A pain shot across his ribs, and he paused for a second, but it slowly dissipated. He glanced over at the napkin on his bedside table and grabbed it and read it again:

*Jazz Club Woman*

*994 3000 451*

He smiled to himself, holding it against his chest. He glanced over at the clock: 22:01, then stared back at the ceiling. He'd never felt so glad to be back on Earth. He focused on the softness of his bed, the stillness of the room, the calmness of the Earth. *Time to heal, Saul,* he told himself. *Time to fix that brain of yours. No more crazy dreams, alright?* He promised himself he was going to sleep for as long as his body would allow. He was so tired he was confident he wouldn't even be able to dream.

"Lights!" he called, and his room slowly plunged into complete blackness. Blackness, stillness, calmness. The Jazz Club Woman appeared in his mind, smiling and dancing, but only briefly. She soon morphed into visions of Taya: smiling, dancing and laughing. It sent a warm smile across his face, and he promised himself he would call her first thing in the morning. His shoulders and ribs eased off as he continued to watch Taya in his mind, slowly making his way toward her, as the sleep began to envelop him.

But suddenly he noticed something that made him pause…

Standing in the background of his mind were Sibbie and Etta, holding that phone, eyes fixed on him with desperate, haunting stares like they did.

His eyes flashed open. His heart was thumping.

And suddenly, he was wide awake again.

# Epilogue

Captain Saul Harris sat in an empty room at the UNF Command Center on Fort Centralis. He looked at his watch. 15:23. He'd been waiting there since 1500. His mind was ticking over at a fast pace, his curiosity mounting. Finally, he heard someone punching the keypad on the other side of the door. It opened, and he recognized the broad, ash-blond man who entered. He quickly stood and saluted him.

"Colonel Marchant," he greeted him.

"Captain Harris," he nodded, holding out his hand to shake, which Harris did. They both took a seat and Marchant placed an e-file pane on the table in front of them.

Harris eyed him carefully. "So, is the UNF getting some kick out of pulling me off my leave, colonel? Or are we experiencing a shortage of soldiers in the UNF?"

Marchant looked back at him. "Well, you got six and a half of your eight weeks, captain. Unfortunately, we had to call you up because you're the only one qualified to do this mission."

Harris's interest was definitely piqued, but he stayed silent, waiting.

Marchant watched him and then looked down at his e-file, chose one of the pre-loaded folders, and opened it. He turned it around and pushed it in front of Harris. He looked at the photo displayed in front of him and recognized the man in it instantly. It did not leave him with a good feeling. He knew the white-gray hair, the dark eyes, the long face, and angular nose, very well. It was Professor Ray Sharley, the man behind the chaos that was the Darwin mission. The man ultimately responsible for the loss of four of Harris's soldiers.

"Why are you showing me this?" His face turned steely.

Marchant pulled the e-file back and closed the folder. He took a second, staring back at Harris. "There's no easy way to say this, captain, so I'm just going to say it. Sharley is not in the custody of the UNF. The fact is, he hasn't been for some time now."

"What?" Harris's face turned to stone, and his eyes froze on Marchant's. "I kept calling Command for updates. They kept telling me that he was in custody and that I would be advised of any outcomes once they were cleared to do so."

"Command instructed the relevant parties that that was the case until we sorted out this mess. We were in damage control. It turns out there was an unsavory element within the UNF who were on Sharley's payroll. It appears a back door was left open on the Darwin and he walked right out of there."

Harris's eyebrows jumped to the top of his forehead. "He walked right out of there? Just like that? And Logan?"

"He walked right out of there with him. We have no idea where they are."

"Fuck," Harris said, sitting back in his chair, as though winded. "Professor Martin, right?"

"Possibly. Both he and Officer Dale, who ran the Darwin debriefs, have gone AWOL."

"Officer Dale? You're kidding?"

Marchant shook his head somewhat embarrassed. "Professor Martin had us initially convinced that Sharley had begun to stray from the UNF, that he was doing his own thing and that he, Martin, had been unable to control him. He assured his CO that he was going to the Darwin to rein him in. Now both Sharley and Martin are missing. I've been handling the case ever since. We've been investigating the whole scenario, trying to trace everyone involved, and more importantly, trying to track down Sharley and Logan themselves. We've uncovered minimal information. They've hidden themselves very well. I guess this is where you come in, and why we need you."

"Why *do* you need me?" Harris folded his arms defensively.

"We need you, because you and your team are the only ones who, a) have seen and dealt with Sharley recently, and b) know what his Jumbos are capable of."

"Jumbos? Logan's the only one left, isn't he? Or are there more out there?"

Marchant looked down at the e-file and scratched the back of his head in thought. "We don't know for sure, but it's always a possibility he's created more. We think it would be foolish to assume otherwise. We are certain of one thing, however," he looked back up at Harris, "and that is, that Chet's body was never recovered."

Harris felt a strange feeling crawl down his spine. "I shot Chet. He went down."

"Yes, you did, but I read the transcripts from the Darwin debriefs. Neither you nor Corporal Welles could confirm unequivocally that he was, in fact, killed. You said you shot him, he went down, and then you left him on the second floor."

Harris felt the blood slowly running down his body to his feet.

"After this whole thing went down," Marchant continued, "I went and personally inspected the bodies of the other Jumbos. *All* their bodies were accounted for, except Chet's. Why would they take his and leave the others? If he was dead, why would they take him?"

Harris took a moment, trying to block out the feeling crawling up his spine, and subtly catch his breath. "So, you think he's still alive?"

"We don't know, captain. All we know is that his body is missing."

Harris exhaled regretfully and rubbed the back of his neck.

"So, this means, captain," Marchant continued, "that Sharley and at least one Jumbo, if not two, or maybe even more, are out there somewhere on the loose. We need to stop them. We need to contain them. We need to bring them in."

"You need to destroy them!" Harris said firmly, shooting the colonel a hard look.

"That order has not been given as yet, captain. My orders are strict. They are to be captured and brought in *alive*. That is what I want you and your men to do."

Harris took a moment, then stood from the table and walked over to the coffee station in the corner of the room. He poured himself a straight black, then sipped it, keeping his back to Marchant while his mind ticked over. He suddenly remembered Sharley's last words to him: *"I may be submitting to you now, but the next time I see you, it will be you who submits to me."*

"I believe you've been searching the database for soldiers to replace the crew you lost?" Marchant asked, pulling him from his thoughts.

Harris turned back around and nodded. He knew the UNF tracked all searches in the UNF Portal, especially those involving personnel.

Marchant gave him a nod back and continued. "I see Second Lieutenant McKinley has made excellent progress recovering from his broken leg. I hear he's been working very hard and is back to full fitness. And First Sergeant Hunter's almost there as well."

"I believe so," Harris nodded.

"And Brown and Walker were uninjured, so they're ready to go?"

"Yes, sir."

"I also see that one of the women has already signed on for a permanent placement on the *Aurora*?" He pulled up another folder on the e-file. "Sergeant Packham. She's going to be your co-pilot?"

"Yes, sir."

"And the other women?"

"Corporal Colt contacted me last week to decline my offer. She wanted to get in first before I called her."

"And Corporal Welles?"

"I've not spoken with her yet."

Marchant nodded. "You should do that asap, Harris. We need to get the *Aurora* out there looking for them. And we want you to persuade Welles to join up. It would be very useful to have her back on board."

"Why's that?"

"We've had some of our best UNF psychologists go over Sharley's profile. They tell me that he's a control freak, which means he does not like to lose. *Technically*, he lost against the *Aurora* team. Our psychologists think that Sharley may just take up the chance for revenge, should it be offered to him... or should I say, should *she* be offered to him."

"She?" Harris arched his eyebrow, as that crawling feeling moved down his spine again.

"Yes. Corporal Welles. Packham's your co-pilot, we can't offer her up. Besides, Sharley almost had Welles and wanted you to leave her behind. There's a greater connection that we can play on." Marchant pushed the e-file pane over to Harris's side of the desk. "All the info is in here. Take a read of this tonight and we'll meet back here at 0600 tomorrow."

Harris eyed the pane and then Marchant, as the colonel stood and stepped closer to him.

"You're the only one with the experience and the inside knowledge to do this Harris. The UNF is counting on you. *I'm* counting on you to get these fuckers before they kill anyone else." Marchant shook his hand, grasping it tightly and eyeing him firmly. "You left them unattended on that station,

Harris. You have to right this wrong." The colonel dropped his hand, then turned and left the room.

Harris's eyes fell back to the e-file, lying like a quiet little bomb on the table before him. He stared at it for a moment, feeling his heartbeat banging within his throat. He moved over to the table and sat down, placing his coffee cup next to him, and flicked his fingers across the pane, to open it.

*Jesus fuckin' Christ.* He thought. *This shit cannot be happening. Can it?*

Join the next action-packed adventure of the Aurora crew:

**Aurora: Pegasus (Aurora 2)**

If you enjoyed reading *Aurora: Darwin* (Aurora 1), let people know! Leave a simple rating or write a brief review wherever you can. It means a lot to the author, and really helps with making this book visible to others.

Keep up to date with new releases here:
www.amandabridgeman.com.au

# Acknowledgements

This book emerged from the secret shadows and saw the light of day because of those who encouraged me to believe in myself. To them I owe many thanks for setting me on this course and making me the happiest I have ever been.

To my first 'Sounding Boards': Tia, Todd, Shannon and Mel, for liking what they read and encouraging me to continue.

To the 'Grammar Queen', Joan: For telling me my grammar was shit, but that my action scenes and dialogue were very good. My harshest critic (and non sci-fi fan to boot) was won over – a real achievement!

To the rest of my family (Dad, Ross & Emma, Glenn & Vinka), and my friends for all their support and excitability. I feel lucky to have so many great people surrounding me.

To 'Nurse Claire': For helping me treat those I tried to kill.

To the Momentum (Pan Macmillan Australia) team, who initially signed this book for publication (and the next several books to boot!): Joel, for spotting this rough diamond and giving me my chance. Mark, for all his help and advice (and patience with my questions!). Stephanie, my editor, for her expertise and encouraging words.

To the many wonderful writers I have met since stepping onto this path, for being so helpful and for welcoming me into their tribe.

And to all the readers who have fallen in love with the Aurora series and wait patiently for each new book – I couldn't have done it without you.